ON DARK WINGS

The dragon folded its wings against its sleek body; the stones of the keep shuddered under its weight. Four years ago, when they had first encountered Sfithrisir in a high valley in the Fal Erenn, Grace thought the dragon looked like an enormous sooty swan. Now it seemed more like a vulture. Its featherless hide absorbed the starlight, and its eyes glowed like coals. The small saurian head wove slowly at the end of a ropelike neck, and a constant hiss of steam escaped the bony hook of its beak.

Fear and smoke choked her, and Grace fought for breath and to keep her wits. She had to have both if she was going to survive.

"Answer . . . answer me this, and an answer you shall have," she said in a trembling voice, speaking the ancient greeting which she had learned from Falken. "One secret for one secret in trade. Why have you—"

"Mist and misery!" the dragon snorted, the words emanating from deep in its gullet. "There is no time for foolish rituals concocted by mortals whose bones have long since turned to dust. I did not come here to barter with you for secrets, Blademender. The end of all things comes. Have you not seen the rift in the sky? Surely it has grown large enough that even your mortal eyes can see it now. And it will keep growing. Now it conceals the stars, but soon it will swallow them, and worlds as well. It will not cease until it has consumed everything there is to consume, until all that remains is nothing. . . ."

THE
FIRST
STONE

BOOK SIX OF
THE LAST RUNE

MARK ANTHONY

BANTAM BOOKS

NEW YORK   TORONTO   LONDON   SYDNEY   AUCKLAND

THE FIRST STONE
A Bantam Spectra Book / August 2004

Published by
Bantam Dell
A Division of Random House, Inc.
New York, New York

ISBN 0-553-58334-4

Manufactured in the United States of America
Published simultaneously in Canada

OPM 10 9 8 7 6 5 4 3 2 1

And again,
For Chris

PART ONE

RIFT

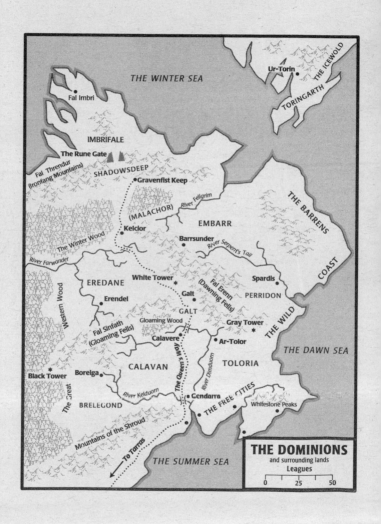

THE WINTER SEA

Fal Imbri

IMBRIFALE

The Rune Gate

Fal Threndur
(Irontang Mountains)

SHADOWSDEEP

Gravenfist Keep

(MALACHOR)

Kelcior

River Fellgrim

EMBARR

Barrsunder

River Serpent's Tail

THE BARRENS

Ur-Torin

TORINGARTH

THE ICEWOLD

The Winter Wood

River Farwander

Western Wood

EREDANE

Erendel

Fal Sinfath
(Gloaming Fells)

White Tower

Gloaming Wood

Calavere

CALAVAN

Borelga

Black Tower

The Great

River Kelduorn

BRELEGOND

Galt

GALT

Fal Erenn
(Dawning Fells)

Gray Tower

Ar-Tolor

TOLORIA

River Dimduorn

Gendarra

THE FREE CITIES

Spardis

PERRIDON

THE WILD
COAST

THE DAWN SEA

Whitestone Peaks

The Queen's Way

Mountains of the Shroud

To Tarras

THE SUMMER SEA

THE DOMINIONS
and surrounding lands
Leagues

0   25   50

We live our lives a circle,
And wander where we can.
Then after fire and wonder,
We end where we began.

*"Forget not the Sleeping Ones.
In their blood lies the key."*

THE
FIRST STONE

1.

The dervish stepped from a swirl of sand, appearing on the edge of the village like a mirage taking form.

A boy herding goats was the first to see him. The boy clucked his tongue, using a switch to prod the animals back to their pens. All at once the animals began to bleat, their eyes rolling as if they had caught the scent of a lion. Usually a lion would not prowl so near the dwellings of men, but the springs that scattered the desert—which had never gone dry in living memory—were failing, and creatures of all kinds came in search of water and food. It was said that, in one village, a lion had crept into a hut and stolen a baby from the arms of its sleeping mother.

The boy turned around, and the switch fell from his fingers. It was not a lion before him, but a man covered from head to toe in a black *serafi*. Only his eyes were visible through a slit in the garment, dark and smoldering like coals. The man raised a hand; its palm was tattooed with red lines. Tales told by the village's elders came back to the boy—tales about men who ventured into the deepest desert in search of forbidden magics.

Obey your father and your mother, the old ones used to tell him when he was small, *else a dervish will fly into your house on a night zephyr and steal you away. For they require the blood of wicked children to work their darkest spells.*

"I need . . ." the dervish said, his voice harsh with a strange accent.

The boy let out a cry, then turned and ran toward a cluster of hovels, leaving the goats behind.

". . . water," the dervish croaked, but the boy was already gone.

The dervish staggered, then caught himself. How long had he been in the Morgolthi? He did not know. Day after day the sun of the Hungering Land had beaten down on him, burning away thought and memory, leaving him as dry as a scattering of bones. He should be dead. However, something had drawn him on through that forsaken land. What was it? There was no use trying to remember. He needed water. Of the last two oases he had gone to, one had been dry, and the waters of the other had been poisoned, the bloated corpses of antelope floating in its stagnant pool.

He moved through the herd of goats. The animals bleated until the dervish touched them, then fell silent. He ran his hands over their hides and could feel the blood surging beneath, quickened by fear. One swift flash of a knife, and hot blood would flow, thicker and sweeter than water. He could slake his thirst, and when he was finished he would let the blood spill on the ground as an offering, and with it he would call them to him. They would be only lesser spirits, enticed by the blood of an animal—no more than enough to work petty magics. All the same, he was tempted. . . .

No—that was not why he was here. He remembered now; he needed water, then to send word, to tell them he was here. He staggered toward the circle of huts. Behind him, the goats began bleating again, lost without the boy to herd them.

This place was called Hadassa, and though the people who dwelled here now had forgotten, it had once been a prosperous trading center built around a verdant oasis. Over the decades the flow of Hadassa's spring had dwindled to a trickle. The merchants and traders had left long ago and had not returned; the city's grand buildings were swallowed by the encroaching sand. Now all that remained was this mean collection of huts.

When he reached the center of the village, the dervish stopped. The oasis, once a place of sparkling pools and shaded grottos, was now a salt flat crazed with cracks. Dead trees, scoured of leaf and branch, pointed at the sky like burnt fingers. In their midst was a patch of mud, churned into a mire by men and goats. Oily water oozed up through the sludge, gathering in the hoofprints. The dervish knelt, his throat aching.

"You are not welcome here," spoke a coarse voice.

The dervish looked up. The water he had cupped dribbled through his fingers. A sigh escaped his blistered lips, and with effort he rose again.

A man stood on the other edge of the mud patch. His yellowed beard spilled down his chest, and he wore the white robe of a village elder. Behind him stood a pair of younger men. They were stunted from a poor diet, but their eyes were hard, and they gripped curved swords. Next to the man was a woman who wore the red *serafi* of a seeress. In youth she had been beautiful, but the dry air had parched her cheeks, cracking them like the soil of the oasis. She gazed forward with milky eyes.

"The cards spoke truly, Sai'el Yarish," the woman said in a hissing voice. "Evil flies into Hadassa on dark wings."

"I cannot fly," the dervish said.

"Then you must walk from this place," the bearded man said. "And you must not come back."

"I come only in search of water."

One of the young men brandished his sword. "We have no water to spare for the likes of you."

"It is so," the old man said. "A change has come over the land. All that is good dwindles and fades. One by one, the springs of the desert have gone dry. Now ours is failing as well. You will not find what you seek here."

The dervish laughed, and the queer sound of it made the others take a step back. "You are wrong. There is yet water to be found in this place." From the folds of his *serafi*, he drew out a curved knife. It flashed in the sun.

"Do not let him draw blood!" the blind woman shrieked.

The young men started forward, but the mud sucked at their sandals, slowing them. The dervish held out his left arm. The knife flicked, quick as a serpent. Red blood welled from a gash just above his wrist.

"Drink," he whispered, shutting his eyes, sending out the call. "Drink, and do my bidding."

He felt them come a moment later; distance meant nothing to them. They buzzed through the village like a swarm of hornets, accompanied by a sound just beyond hearing. The men looked around with fearful eyes, and the blind woman swatted at the air. The dervish lowered his arm, letting blood drip from his wound.

The fluid vanished before it struck the ground, as if the hot air gobbled it.

"Water," the dervish murmured. "Bring me water."

A moment ago they had been furious in their desire. Now they were sated by blood, their will easy to bend. He sensed them plunge downward, deep into the ground. Soil, rock—these were as air to them. He felt it seconds later: a tremor beneath his boots. There was a gurgling noise, then a jet of water shot up from the center of the mud patch. The fountain glittered, spinning off drops as clear and precious as diamonds.

The village elder gaped while the young men dashed forward, letting the water spill into their hands, drinking greedily.

"It is cool and sweet," one of them said, laughing.

"It is a trick!" the blind woman cried. "You must not drink, lest it bring you under his spell."

The young men ignored her. They continued to drink, and the man in the white robe joined them. Others appeared, stealing from the huts, the fear on their sun-darkened faces giving way to wonder.

The seeress stamped her feet. "It is a deception, I tell you! If you drink, he will poison us all!"

The village folk pushed past her, and she fell into the mud, her robe tangling around her so that she could not get up. The people held out their hands toward the splashing water.

The dervish bound his wound with a rag, staunching the flow of blood, lest the bodiless ones come to partake of more. *Morndari*, the spirits were called. *Those Who Thirst.* They had no form, no substance, but their craving for blood was unquenchable. Once, he had come upon a young sorcerer who had thought too highly of his own power, and who had called many of the *morndari* to him. His body had been no more than a dry husk, a look of horror on his mummified face.

Water pooled at the dervish's feet. He bent to drink, but he was weak from hunger and thirst, and from loss of blood. The sky reeled above him, and he fell. Strong hands caught him.

"Take him into my hut," said a voice he recognized as the village elder's.

Were they going to murder him? He should call the *morndari* again, only he could not reach his knife, and he was too weak. The spirits would drain his body of blood, just like the young sorcerer he had once found.

The hands bore him to a dim, cool space, protected from the

sun by thick mud walls. He was laid upon cushions, and a wooden cup was pressed to his lips. Water spilled into his mouth, clean and wholesome. He coughed, then drank deeply, draining the cup. Leaning back, he opened his eyes and saw the bearded man above him.

"One such as yourself came here not long ago," the old man said. "We feared him, but he worked no spells. He babbled that his power was all dried up like the springs, that magic was dead."

"Did you kill him?" the dervish said.

The other shook his head. "He was mad. He ran into the desert without a flask of water. The ground shook when you worked your spells. We have felt many such tremors of late. Some have been strong enough to knock down all of the huts in a village. Do the spirits cause the trembling?"

The dervish licked blistered lips. "No—perhaps. I don't know."

The *morndari* were attracted by the tremors, that he did know. That was how he had followed them. How he had found it.

The old man set down the cup. "All the tales I know tell that a dervish brings only evil and suffering. Yet you renewed our spring. You have saved us all."

The dervish laughed, a chilling sound. "Would that what you say were so. But I fear your seeress was right. Evil does come, on dark wings. To Hadassa, and to all of Moringarth."

The other made a warding sign with his hand. "Gods help us. What must we do?"

"You must send word that I am here. You must send a message to the Mournish. Do you know where they can be found?"

The old man stroked his beard. "I know some who know. But surely you cannot mean what you say. Your kind is abomination to them. If they find you, your life is forfeit. The working of blood sorcery is forbidden."

"No it isn't," the dervish said. He looked down at his hands, marked by fine white scars and lines tattooed in red. "Not anymore."

2.

It was the quiet that woke Sareth.

Over the last three years he had grown used to the sound of Lirith's heartbeat and the rhythm of her breathing. Together they made a music that lulled him to sleep each night and bestowed blissful dreams. Then, six months ago, another heart—tiny and swift—had added its own cadence to that song. Only now all was silent.

Sareth sat up. Gray light crept through a moon-shaped window, into the cramped interior of the wagon. She had not been able to make the wagon any larger, but by her touch it had become cozier. Bunches of dried herbs hung in the corners, giving off a sweet, dusty scent. Beaded curtains dangled before the windows, and cushions embroidered with leaves and flowers covered the benches against either wall. The tops of the benches could be lifted to reveal bins beneath, or lowered—along with a table—to turn the wagon into a place where eight could sit and dine or play *An'hot*. Now the table was folded up against the wall, making room for the pallet they unrolled each night.

The pallet was empty, save for himself. He pulled on a pair of loose-fitting trousers, then opened the door of the wagon. Moist air, fragrant with the scent of night-blooming flowers, rushed in, cool against his naked chest. He breathed, clearing the fog of sleep from his mind, then climbed down the wagon's wooden steps. The grass was damp with dew beneath his bare feet—his two bare feet.

Though it had been three years, he marveled daily at the magic that had restored the leg he had lost to the demon beneath Tarras. He would never really understand how Lady Aryn's spell had healed him, but it didn't matter. Since he met Lirith, he had grown accustomed to wonders.

He found her beneath a slender *ithaya* tree on the edge of the grove where the Mournish had made camp. A tincture of coral colored the horizon; dawn was coming, but not yet. She turned when she heard him approach, her smile glowing in the dimness.

"*Beshala*," he said softly. "What are you doing out here so early?"

"Taneth was fussing. I didn't want him to wake you." She cradled the baby in her arms. He was sound asleep, wrapped snugly in a blanket sewn with moons and stars.

Sareth laid a hand on the baby's head. His hair was thick and dark, and when they were open, his eyes were the same dark copper as Sareth's. However, everything else about him—his fine features, his rich ebon skin—was Lirith's.

The baby sighed in his sleep, and Sareth smiled. Here was another wonder before him. For so long, Lirith had believed herself incapable of bearing a child. Years ago, after her adoptive parents were murdered by thieves in the Free City of Corantha, she had been sold into servitude in the house of Gulthas. There she had been forced to dance for the men who paid their gold—and to do more than dance. Countless times a spark of life had kindled in her womb, only to go dark when she consumed the potions Gulthas forced all the women in his house to drink. Finally, no more sparks kindled.

Lirith had wept the night she finally told Sareth these things, thinking that once he knew what she had been in the past he would turn away from her. She was wrong; her revelations only made him love her more fiercely. That she could endure such torture, yet remain so good, so beautiful inside and out, showed there was no one in all the world more deserving of love than Lirith.

Besides, even if she could have conceived a child, he could not have given her one. Or so he had believed. When the demon below Tarras took his leg, it had taken something else—something intangible, but no less a part of him. He could love Lirith with all his heart, but he could not *make* love to her.

Worse, both of them had dreaded the day when the laws of his people would sunder them, for Sareth could only marry one of his clan. Then, not a month after Queen Grace destroyed the Pale King, they feared that day had come when the Mournish arrived at Gravenfist Keep. Though they were great wanderers, never to Sareth's knowledge had the Mournish traveled so far north. What brought them there could only be of the greatest importance.

It was.

"She is of our clan," his al-Mama said, touching Lirith's cheek with a gnarled hand.

"How?" Sareth had finally managed to say.

The old woman let out a cackle. "I am old, but I am not blind. I saw the look in your eyes when you gazed at her. But the laws of our people are clear, and you are of the highest blood of ancient Morindu. You above all must not marry outside our clan." Her gaze softened. "Yet I would not see you be in pain. I studied the cards for long hours—more precious time than these old bones should spare—and at last I saw the truth."

They listened, amazed, as al-Mama told the tale she had pieced together by gazing at the *T'hot* cards and speaking to elders among the various bands of Mournish. Twenty-seven years ago, a band of Mournish from the farthest south were run out of the Free City of Gendarra by an angry guildmaster. He had purchased a love potion from one of the Mournish women, and it had worked as she said it would, granting him the love he deserved. However, this had not been the love of the beautiful lady he admired, but rather that of a sow who merrily trotted after him everywhere in the city. For as a selfish man he deserved no better.

Enraged, the guildmaster sent his mercenaries after the Mournish, and they were waylaid. Most escaped, but not all. One wagon was caught and burned, and the young Mournish couple within died. They had had a baby, an infant girl, and it was believed she perished with her parents. Only it was not so, and al-Mama's cards had revealed the rest of the tale, which no one had known until then: how the infant had been thrown into a thicket of bushes when the wagon toppled, and how a day later she was found by a tradesman on his way home to southern Toloria. He took the baby with him, for his wife had always wanted a child.

Thus Fate had taken Lirith away from the Mournish, and Fate had brought her back—to her people, and to Sareth.

When the Mournish departed Gravenfist Keep, Lirith had traveled south with her people and her husband, and life had seemed joyous beyond imagining. Then, one night a little over a year ago, as the two of them lay together, they had discovered one more wonder wrought by Lady Aryn's spell. Their bodies had become one, and they had laughed and wept with a pleasure neither had thought themselves capable of. Over the moons that followed Lirith's belly had swelled, and here now in her arms was the greatest wonder of all: little Taneth, dark and sweet and perfect.

Lirith sighed, turning her gaze toward the east.

Sareth touched her shoulder. "Are you sure it was because of Taneth you came out here, *beshala*? Is there not another reason?"

She gazed at him, her eyes bright with tears. "I don't want you to go."

So that was what this was about. Last night, a young man from another Mournish band had ridden hard into the circle of their wagons, bearing ill news.

"I do not wish to leave," Sareth said. "But you heard the message just as I did. A dervish has come out of the desert, or at least one who claims he is a dervish. He must be seen."

"Yes, someone must go see him. But why must it be you?"

"I am descended of the royal line of Morindu."

Lirith's dark eyes flashed. "So is your sister, Vani. She is the one who was trained at Golgoru. She is the *T'gol*. It is she who should be doing this thing, not you."

Sareth pressed his lips together; he could not argue that point. Three thousand years ago, the sorcerers of Morindu the Dark had destroyed their own city lest its secrets fall into the hands of their foe, the city of Scirath. The Morindai became wanderers and vagabonds, known in the north as the Mournish.

After their exile, the Morindai forbade the practice of blood sorcery until Morindu was found again. However, there were those who defied that law. Dervishes, they were called. They were renegades, anathema. The silent fortress of Golgoru had been founded to train assassins who could hunt down the dervishes and destroy them with means other than magic.

Sareth moved to the edge of the grove. "My sister is gone, and the cards reveal not where, though al-Mama has gazed at them time after time. I know of no way to find her—unless you think Queen Grace may have heard some news."

Lirith shook her head. "You know I have not Aryn's strength in the Touch. I cannot reach her over the Weirding, let alone

Grace. They are too far away." She frowned. "Indeed, it seems my ability to reach out over the leagues grows less these days, not more. I can hardly weave the simplest spell of late. The Weirding feels . . . it feels tired, somehow."

"Perhaps it's you that's a little tired, *beshala*," Sareth said, touching Taneth's tiny hand.

She smiled. "Perhaps so. Still, it is strange. I will have to ask Aryn about it the next time she contacts me."

While Sareth did not doubt Lirith was happy living among the Mournish, he knew she missed her friends. The Mournish had journeyed to Calavere—where Aryn and Teravian ruled as king and queen over both Calavan and Toloria—only once in the last three years, and they had not returned at all to Gravenfist Keep, where Queen Grace dwelled. Still, the three witches could speak from time to time, using magic, and that was a comfort.

An idea occurred to Sareth. "Why don't you and Taneth go to Calavere, *beshala*? It will not take you long to journey there, and the roads are safe. Aryn is to have her own child soon, is she not? I am certain she will enjoy seeing our little one. And when I am finished with my work in the south, I will send word."

"I believe you are trying to distract me," Lirith said, giving him a stern look. However, she could not keep it up, and she laughed as she hugged Taneth to her. "I confess, I long to see Aryn with my eyes, not just hear her voice over the Weirding. And if I stayed here, I imagine I would do nothing but fret and worry about you."

"Then it's settled," Sareth said. "You will go to Calavere at once. I will ask Damari to accompany you." He scratched his chin. "Or maybe I'd better make that Jahiel. He's much less handsome."

"Damari will do just fine," Lirith said. Then her mirth ceased, and she leaned her head against his bare chest, Taneth between them. He circled his arms around them both.

"Promise me you won't worry, *beshala*."

"I will be waiting," was all she said, and they stayed that way, the three of them together, as dawn turned the sky to gold.

3.

Sareth left that day, taking only one other—a broad-shouldered young man named Fahir—with him. Word had been sent to the fastness of Golgoru, in the Mountains of the Shroud, but there were few *T'gol* these days. Nor was it likely one would reach Al-Amún sooner than Sareth; from here it was only a half day's ride to the port city of Kalos, on the southern tip of Falengarth, at the point where the Summer Sea was narrowest. Sareth hoped to reach the city by nightfall and book passage on a ship tomorrow.

Before he left, his al-Mama called him into her dragon-shaped wagon and made him draw a card from her *T'hot* deck. His fingertips tingled as they brushed one of the well-worn cards, and he drew it out. As he turned it over, a hiss escaped her.

"The Void," she rasped.

There was no picture on the card. It was painted solid black.

"What does it mean? Do I have no fate, then?"

"Only a dead man has no fate."

He swallowed the lump in his throat. "What of the *A'narai*, the Fateless Ones who tended the god-king Orú long ago?"

She snatched the card from his hand. "As I said, only a dead man has no fate."

His al-Mama said no more, but as Sareth left the wagon he glanced over his shoulder. The old woman huddled beneath her blankets, muttering as she turned the card over and over. Whatever it portended, it troubled her. However, he put it out of his mind. Perhaps the dead had no fate, but he was very much alive, and his destiny was to return to Lirith and Taneth as soon as possible.

They reached Kalos that evening as planned and set sail the next morning on the swiftest ship they could find—a small spice trader. Fahir, who had never been at sea before, was violently ill during the entire two-day passage, and even Sareth found himself getting queasy, for the Summer Sea was rough, tossing the little ship on the waves. The ship's captain remarked that he had never seen such ill winds this time of year.

Fortunately, the voyage was soon over, and they disembarked in the port city of Qaradas, on the north coast of the continent of Moringarth, in the land of city-states known as Al-Amún. Sareth had traveled to Al-Amún several times in his youth; it was a custom among the Mournish of the north that young men and women should visit the southern continent, where most of the Morindai dwelled. Qaradas was just as he remembered it: a city of white-domed buildings and crowded, dusty streets shaded by date palms.

"I thought the cities of the south were made of gold," Fahir said, a look of disappointment on his face.

Sareth grinned. "In the light of sunset, the white buildings do look gold. But it is only illusion—as is much in Al-Amún. So beware. And if a beautiful woman in red scarves claims she wishes to marry you, don't follow her! You'll lose your gold as well as your innocence."

"Of the first I have little enough," Fahir said with a laugh. "And the second I would be happy to dispense with. This is my first trip to the south, after all."

They headed to the traders' quarter, and Sareth examined the front door of every inn and hostel until he found what he was looking for.

"We will be welcome here."

In answer to Fahir's puzzled look, Sareth pointed to a small symbol scratched in the upper corner of the door: a crescent moon inscribed in a triangle. This place was run by Morindai.

Inside, Sareth and Fahir were welcomed as family. After they shared drink and food, the hostel's proprietor suggested a place where camels and supplies for a journey could be bought at a good price. Sareth went to investigate, leaving Fahir with orders to rest, and to not even think about approaching the innkeeper's black-haired daughter.

"By her looks, I think she favors me," Fahir said. "Why shouldn't I approach her?"

"Because by her al-Mama's looks, if you do, the old woman will put a *va'ksha* on you that will give you the private parts of a mouse."

The young man's face blanched. "I'll get some rest. Come back soon."

They set out before dawn the next day, riding on the swaying backs of two camels as the domes of Qaradas faded like a mirage behind them. At first the air was cool, but once the sun rose heat radiated from the ground in dusty waves. All the same, they drank sparingly; it was a journey of six days to the village of Hadassa, where the rumors of the dervish had originated.

During the middle part of each day, when the sun grew too fierce to keep riding, they crouched in whatever shade they could find beneath a rock or cliff. They were always vigilant, and one would keep watch while the other dozed. Thieves were common on the roads of Al-Amún.

Nor was it only thieves they kept watch for. While the sorcerers of Scirath had suffered a great blow in the destruction of the Etherion over three years ago, recently the Mournish had heard whispers that their old enemy had been gathering again. Even after three thousand years, the Scirathi still sought the secrets lost when Morindu the Dark was buried beneath the sands of the Morgolthi. Because the dervishes sought those same secrets, where one was found the other could not be far off.

The days wore on, and water became a hardship. The first two springs they came to had offered some to drink, though less than Sareth had been led to believe. However, after that, every spring they reached was dry. They found no water, only white bones and withered trees. Doing their best to swallow the sand in their throats, they continued on.

Fahir and he never spoke of it, but by the fifth day of their journey Sareth knew they were in grave danger. There were but two swallows for each of them left in their flasks. It was said that Hadassa was built around an oasis. However, if its spring had gone dry like the others, they would not make it back to Qaradas alive.

You could cast a spell, Sareth thought that night as he huddled beneath a blanket next to Fahir. Once the sun went down the desert air grew chill, and both men shuddered as with a fever. *You could call the spirits and bid them to lead you to water.*

Could he really? The working of blood sorcery was forbidden among the Morindai; only the dervishes broke that law. True, the elders of the clan had allowed Sareth to use the gate artifact to communicate with Vani when she journeyed across the Void, to Earth. However, that had been a time of great need, and it was not a true act of blood sorcery. Sareth had spilled his blood to power the artifact, but he had not called the bodiless spirits, the *morndari*, to him as a true sorcerer would.

Besides, Sareth asked himself, *what makes you believe you could control the spirits if they did answer your call? They would likely consume all your blood and unleash havoc.*

Yet if he and Fahir did not find water tomorrow, what choice did he have but to try?

The next day dawned hotter than any that came before. The white sun beat down on them, and the wind scoured any bit of exposed flesh with hard sand. They were on the very edge of habitable lands now. To the south stretched the endless wastes of the Morgolthi, the Hungering Land, where no man had dwelled in eons—not since the land was broken and poisoned in the War of the Sorcerers.

The horizon wavered before Sareth. Shapes materialized amid the shimmering air. He fancied he could almost see the high towers of the first great cities of ancient Amún: Usyr, Scirath, and the onyx spires of Morindu the Dark. . . .

Sareth jolted from his waking dream. He lay sprawled on the sand as his camel plodded away from him. Fahir slumped over the neck of his own camel as the beast followed its partner toward a cluster of square shapes. That was no mirage; it was a village.

Sareth tried to call out, but his throat was too dry. A moment later shadows appeared above him, blocking the sun. Voices jabbered in a dialect he couldn't understand, though he made out one word, repeated over and over: *Morindai, Morindai.* Hands lifted him from the ground.

He drifted in a void—as dark and featureless as the card drawn from his al-Mama's deck—then came to himself as something cool touched his lips. Water poured into his mouth. He choked, then gulped it down.

"More," he croaked.

"No, that's enough for now," said a low, strangely accented voice. "You have to drink slowly or you'll become sick."

Sareth's eyes adjusted to the dim light. He was inside a hut, lying on a rug, propped up against filthy cushions. A man knelt beside him, holding a cup. He was swathed from head to foot in black; only his dark eyes were visible.

Fear sliced away the dullness in Sareth's mind. Was this one of the Scirathi? They always wore black. He remembered how he had been tortured by the sorcerer who had followed them through the gate to Castle City. That one had enjoyed causing Sareth pain.

No, they always wear masks of gold. The masks are the key to their power. This is no Scirathi.

Fresh dread replaced the old. Sareth pushed himself up against the cushions, knowing he was too weak to flee.

"What have you done with Fahir?"

"Your friend is being cared for in another hut," the dervish said. "You need not fear for him."

Sareth licked his cracked lips. This was not how he had intended for things to unfold. He had planned to come upon the dervish unaware, so the other could not cast a spell, only it had been the opposite, and now he was in the other's power. He tried to think what to say.

The dervish spoke first. "You're her brother, aren't you? Vani, the assassin. We knew she was in communication with her brother through the gate artifact, and the resemblance is clear enough."

Confusion replaced fear. How could the dervish know these things? And why did his accent, strange as it was, seem familiar?

"Who are you?"

The dervish laughed. "That's a good question. Who am I indeed? Not who I was before, that much is certain." The dervish pushed back his hood. His pale skin had been burnt and blistered, and was now beginning to heal. "However, I used to be a man called Hadrian Farr."

Sareth clutched at the cushions. "I know who you are. Vani told me of you. You're from the world across the Void. How can you be here?"

The other made a dismissive gesture. "That's not important now. All that matters is that you take word back to your people."

"Word of what?" Sareth did not care for the other's proud manner of speech. "Why don't you tell them yourself?"

The dervish moved to a window; a thin beam of sunlight slipped through a crack in the shutters, illuminating his sun-ravaged face. "Because, once I am done here, I must go back. Back into the Morgolthi. After all these ages, it has finally been found."

"What are you talking about?" Sareth said, rising up, angry at not understanding, angry at his fear. "What has been found?"

The dervish—the Earth man named Hadrian Farr—turned and gazed at him with eyes as sharp and gray as knives.

"The lost city of Morindu the Dark," he said.

Outside the hut, the wind rose like a jackal's howl.

4.

Beltan knew there was no way out of a fight this time.

Not that he minded, he had to admit, baring his teeth in a grin. After all, during the course of his five-and-thirty years, he had been a knight of Calavan, a commander in Queen Grace's army, a master swordsman, and a disciple of the war god Vathris Bullslayer. It went without saying that he enjoyed a good battle.

The monster hulked before him: gleaming red, belching heat and smoke, blaring a shrill cry to signal its aggression. Beltan's fingers tightened around a shaft of cold steel, green eyes narrowing to slits, nostrils flaring. He sized up his enemy, and each of them tensed, waiting for the other to make the first move. Both of them knew there could only be one victor in a duel like this. And by Vathris, Beltan vowed it was going to be he.

The traffic light changed. Beltan floored the gas pedal, double-shifted into third, and spun the steering wheel. The black taxicab roared in front of a red sports car, cutting it off, and whipped around the traffic circle.

"Hey there!" came an annoyed voice from the backseat of the cab. "I told you to be careful. I've got a tart on my lap."

It was one of the magics of the fairy blood that ran in Beltan's veins that it helped him to understand the language of this world. Even without it, he probably could have made do, for he had learned much about the world Earth in the last three years. All the same, some words—like *tart*—still had the ability to confound him. He glanced in the rearview mirror, not certain if he would see a pie on the man's lap, or a saucy-smiled wench like one might find in King Kel's hall.

It was pie. Though it wasn't just on his lap. It was on his shirt and tie as well.

"Sorry about that," Beltan said cheerfully.

The man dabbed with a handkerchief at the crimson goop on his shirt. "I wouldn't be expecting a tip if I were you."

Beltan wasn't. He didn't drive the taxi because they needed the gold; he did it for fun. Behind him, the driver of the red sports car honked his horn and made a rude gesture. Beltan stuck a hand out the window and waved, then turned down Shaftesbury Avenue.

He dropped his fare in Piccadilly Circus—the man paid with a sticky wad of cherry-covered pound notes—then maneuvered the cab through the frenzy of cars, buses, and tourists that filled the traffic circle. A group of men and women wearing white bedsheets like they were some sort of ceremonial robes clustered beneath the winged statue that dominated the center of the Circus. They held up cardboard signs bearing hand-scrawled messages. The Mouth is Hungry, read one of the signs. Another proclaimed, Are You Ready To Be Eaten?

The people in white sheets were almost always in Piccadilly Circus these days. More could be found haunting other busy intersections around London. The tourists gave the sign-holders a wide berth, edging past them to snap furtive pictures of the statue before retreating. Above, gigantic neon signs blazed against the dusky June sky, glimmering as if made of a thousand magic jewels.

After several quick offensive maneuvers—and a few more offensive gestures from other drivers—Beltan was out of the Circus and heading down Piccadilly Street, toward the Mayfair neighborhood and home. Driving a taxi in London was definitely a warrior's job. All the same, it had not been Beltan's first choice of occupation.

After arriving there, he had assumed he would join the army.

Peace was simply the time a warrior spent sharpening his sword before his next battle, the old saying went, and Beltan wanted to make sure his sword—and his mind—stayed sharp.

He knew this country had a queen. No doubt she was good and just, for this land was free and prosperous. So he decided to go to her, kneel, and pledge his sword. However, when he went to her palace, the guards at the gate had given him dark looks when he spoke of presenting his sword to the queen, and he had been forced into a hasty retreat.

After that, he asked some questions and learned one could join the army simply by speaking to one of its commanders and signing a paper. He went to see one of these commanders—*sergeant* was his title. He was a doughy man, and didn't look like he had swung a sword in a while, but Beltan treated him with deference. He bowed, then informed the sergeant that he had served in the military all his adult life, that he was a disciple of Vathris, and had heard the Call of the Bull.

The sergeant didn't seem to know what to make of all this, which seemed odd, but Beltan explained, and the man's face turned red.

"We have quite enough of a problem with that sort of thing already," he said, shaking his head. "Good day!"

Later, when Beltan stopped for an ale at a pub where other men who had heard the Call of the Bull often gathered, he had told this story, and the bartender said he wasn't surprised, that in most places in the world men like themselves weren't welcome in the military.

That seemed nonsense to Beltan. The generals of this land could not think it was better to send into battle men who would leave families behind, rather than men who were comfortable in one another's company and who would leave no children fatherless should they never return from war.

And do you not have a child, Beltan?

He turned the cab onto a narrow lane and had to concentrate as he wedged it into a parking spot that was no more than four hands longer than the car itself. There was no doubt that having fairy-enhanced senses was an advantage when parallel parking.

Beltan paused a moment to clean out the cab, using a discarded newspaper to wipe the pie off the backseat. As he did, a headline caught his eye: CELESTIAL ANOMALY EXPANDING.

The article below discussed the dark spot in the heavens that had been detected some months ago. Beltan had never been able to see this dark spot himself—the night sky was obscured by London's bright lights—but he had watched a program on the Wonder Channel about it. Men of learning called astronomers had discovered the spot by using giant spyglasses that let them see far into the heavens. They did not understand what caused the darkness—some suggested it was a great cloud of dust—but according to the article in the paper, it had just blotted out Earth's view of two more stars, and the pace of its growth seemed to be increasing. Soon now it would be visible to the naked eye, even in London.

While the astronomers in the article claimed the anomaly was too far away to affect Earth—out beyond the farthest planet—a few people claimed the blot was going to grow until it consumed the sun, the moon, and everything. People like the sign-holders in Piccadilly Circus. So far, no one took those people seriously.

Beltan stuffed the trash in a nearby bin, locked the cab, and headed toward the narrow building of gray stone where they lived on the third floor. It was a good location, as there were a small, friendly pub and several eating establishments in the alley next to the building, and all sorts of markets lined the street before it. With the tall buildings soaring around like parapets, it made Beltan think of living in a modest tower on the edge of a bustling castle courtyard.

In other words, it felt like home.

He stretched his long legs, bounding up the timeworn steps, and started to fit his key into the front door. As he did, a tingling coursed up his neck, and he turned. Just on the edge of vision a shadow flitted into the alley, its form merging with the deepening air. Compelled by old instincts, Beltan leaped over the rail and peered into the alley. Four people sat at a table in front of the pub, and a waiter was setting up chairs outside one of the restaurants. There was no sign of the shadow.

All the same, Beltan knew his senses hadn't lied to him. Something had been there. Or some*things*, for it had seemed more like two shadows than one. Only what were they? He had felt a prickling, which meant *danger*. Perhaps they had been criminals, off to do some wicked deed. Sometimes the fairy blood allowed him to sense such things.

Whatever it had been, the shadow was gone now, and his stomach was growling. He headed back to the front door, let himself in, and bounded up two flights of steps to their flat.

"I'm home," he called, shutting the door behind him.

There was no answer. He shrugged off his leather coat and headed from the front hall into the kitchen. Something bubbled in a pot on the stove. Beltan's stomach rumbled again. It smelled good.

He headed from the kitchen into the main room. It was dark, so he turned on a floor lamp—even after three years, being able to bring forth such brilliant light by flicking a switch amazed Beltan—then moved down the hall. Their bedroom was dark and empty, as was the bathroom (a whole chamber full of marvels), but light spilled from the door of the spare room at the end of the hallway. Beltan crossed his arms and leaned against the doorframe.

"So here's where you're hiding."

Travis looked up, setting something down on the desk by the window, and smiled. Beltan grinned in return. A feeling of love struck him, every bit as powerful as that first day he saw Travis in the ruins of Kelcior.

"What are you smiling about?" Travis said.

Beltan crossed the room, hugged him tight, and kissed him.

"Oh," Travis said, laughing. He returned the embrace warmly, but only for a moment before his gaze turned to the darkened window.

Beltan let him go, watching him. Travis's gray eyes were thoughtful. He looked older than when Beltan first met him; more than a little gray flecked his red-brown hair and beard. However, the years had done his countenance good rather than ill, and—while sharper—it was more handsome than ever. Beltan's own face had been badly rearranged in more than one brawl over the years. How Travis could love someone as homely as he, Beltan didn't know, but Travis *did* love him, and these last three years had been ones of quiet joy and peace.

Only they had been years of waiting as well. The Pale King was dead, and Mohg was no more, but Earth and Eldh were still drawing near. What that meant, or how soon the two worlds would meet (if they would even meet at all) Beltan didn't know. But somehow—maybe through some prescience granted him by the fairy's blood—he knew Travis's part in all this was not over. And neither was his own. Sometimes, in the dark of night, he found himself hoping he was right—hoping that one day the waiting would be over, and his sword would be needed again.

You're a warrior, Beltan. You aren't built for peace.

He dismissed that thought with a soft snort. This wasn't about him and his warrior's pride. Something was troubling Travis; Beltan didn't need magical senses to know that.

"What is it?" he said, laying a hand on Travis's shoulder. Then he glanced at the desk and saw the frayed piece of paper lying there.

Beltan sighed. "I miss her, too. But wherever she is, she is well. She knows how to take care of herself."

Travis nodded. "Only it's not just her, is it?" He kissed Beltan's scruffy cheek. "It'll take me a few more minutes to finish burning dinner if you want to take a shower." Then he was gone.

Beltan hesitated, then picked up the piece of parchment. It was as soft as tissue. How many times had Travis read the letter?

Probably as many times as you have, Beltan.

One cloud had dimmed their happiness these last three years, and that was thinking of all those they had left behind. Grace, Melia and Falken, Aryn and Lirith, and so many others. But of them all, none were in their thoughts more than one.

"Where are you, Vani?" he whispered.

He had asked himself that question a thousand times since the day they found the letter in her empty chamber at Gravenfist Keep. It had been early spring, just a month after Queen Grace slew the Pale King and Travis broke the Last Rune. A caravan of Mournish wagons had arrived at the fortress, bearing the happy news that Lirith was one of their own, that she and Sareth could wed. Yet the Mournish must have brought other news, for the next morning Vani was gone.

Without thinking, his eyes scanned the letter. However, he needn't have bothered to read, for he had the words committed to heart. The letter was addressed to him, and to Travis.

> *I hope you both can forgive me, but even if you cannot, I know what I do is right. I think, in time, you will agree. It does not matter. By the time you read this, I will be gone. There is no point in trying to search for me. I am T'gol. You will not be able to follow my trail, for I will leave none.*
>
> *For many years I have known it was my fate to bear a child by the one who will raise Morindu the Dark from the sands that bury it. As so often happens, my fate has come to pass, but not in the way I imagined. I will indeed bear a child by you, Travis Wilder, but not to you. And nor to you, Beltan of Calavan, though you are the one who made her with me. Instead, I choose to be selfish and take her for my own.*
>
> *Why? I am not certain. The cards are not yet clear. But I have spoken to my al-Mama, and one thing is certain: Fate moves in a spiral about my daughter. She is at the center of something important. Or perhaps something terrible. What it is, I cannot say, but I intend to find out. And if it is dangerous, I will protect her from it. Even if it means keeping her from her father. From both her fathers.*
>
> *Again, I beg your forgiveness. I have taken our child away from you both. In return, I give to you something I hope you will find equally precious: I give you one another. Do not squander this gift, for what I have taken from you cannot be replaced. You must love one another. For me. For us. Just as I must do this thing for our daughter.*
>
> *May Fate guide us all.*
>
> *—Vani*

That was it. There was no more explanation, no chance of stopping her. She was simply gone.

What she meant when she said lines of fate swirled around her—around *their*—daughter, they didn't know, and nor had Vani and Sareth's al-Mama offered more explanation. The old woman simply cackled and said that each had their own fate to worry about. "Except for you, *A'narai*," she had added, pointing a withered finger at Travis.

A'narai. The word meant *Fateless.* Which made no sense to Beltan, because the Mournish seemed to think Travis was the one destined to find the lost city of their ancestors one day.

"I think fate is nothing more than what you make it," Grace had told Travis and Beltan that night, after a celebratory feast in the keep's hall—one of a dozen such feasts King Kel had arranged since their victory over the Pale King. "The only way to have no fate is to never really make a choice."

Maybe she hadn't been trying to tell them what to do. Or maybe she had, for she had left something in Travis's hand when she went: half of a silver coin. Either way, that night they made a choice.

"I don't think Eldh needs me anymore," Travis had said as they stood atop the keep's battlements.

Beltan wasn't so certain that was true, but there was one thing he did know. "*I* need you, Travis Wilder."

Travis gazed at the silver coin on his palm. It was whole now, a rune marking each side. One for Eldh, and one for Earth. He looked up, his gray eyes the same color as the coin in the starlight. "Come with me."

So much had happened in the time they had known each other—so much pain, sorrow, and confusion. All of that vanished in an instant, like ashes tossed on the wind.

"Haven't you figured it out by now?" Beltan said, laughing. "I'm always with you."

Travis gripped the coin, and they embraced as a blue nimbus of light surrounded them. And that was how they came to Earth.

Beltan opened a desk drawer and placed the letter gently inside. Then he headed to the bathroom, leaving a trail of clothes behind him. Hot showers were a luxury he did not know how he had ever survived without. How could he ever go back to bathing in a tub of lukewarm water or, worse yet, diving into a cold stream?

I knew this world would make you soft, he thought as he stepped under the water and grabbed the bar of soap. The sharp, clean scent of lavender rose on the steam. Ah, good—Travis had finally gone to The Body Shop as Beltan had been pestering him to.

He washed away the day's layer of car exhaust and sweat, then stepped out of the shower. Living on Earth hadn't made him quite as soft as he had feared. Once it was clear he would not join the army, he had worried he would go all to flab like many warriors who traded their swords for cups. Then he had discovered a place down the street called a *gym*.

At first he had taken the various mechanical contraptions inside for torture devices. Then a young man with large muscles had shown Beltan how to use them. He went to the gym often now, and he was happy to note that his ale belly was a bare wisp of its former self.

He toweled off, then scraped his cheeks with a straight razor, preferring the blade to the buzzing device Travis had bought him one Midwinter's Eve, leaving a patch of gold on his chin and a line above his mouth. His white-blond hair seemed determined to keep falling out, but a woman at a shop next to the gym had cut it short, and had given him a bottle of something called *mousse*. (That was another one of those confusing words.) The mousse made his hair stick up as if he had just gotten out of bed, but that seemed to be the fashion of this world. Besides, Travis said he liked it, and that was all that counted.

He picked up his discarded clothes on the way to the bedroom, traded them for fresh jeans and a T-shirt, and appeared in the kitchen just in time to see Travis set dinner on the table.

"It smells good," Beltan said. "What is it?"

"What do you think it is?" Travis asked with a pointed look.

Beltan eyed the full bowls. "It looks like stew."

"Then let's call it that."

Travis said he was a poor cook, but Beltan thought everything he made was excellent. Then again, Beltan thought any food that didn't bite back was good, so maybe Travis had a point. Beltan ate three helpings, but he noticed Travis hardly touched his own food. He never seemed to eat much these days, but Beltan tried not to worry about it.

"I don't think I need food like I used to," Travis had said once, and maybe it was true. Even without going to the gym, he looked healthy. He was leaner than when they first met, but well-knit and strong.

All the same, sometimes Beltan did worry. A few times, after they had made love, Travis's skin had been so hot Beltan could hardly touch him, and he had seemed to shine in the dark with a gold radiance. While Beltan didn't like to admit it, those times made him think of the Necromancer Dakarreth, whose naked body in the baths beneath Spardis had been sleek and beautiful, gold and steaming.

The blood of the south runs in his veins now, Beltan, just as it did in the Necromancer's.

Beltan didn't know what it meant—only that both he and Travis had been changed by blood. And maybe that was all right. Because, no matter what had been taken from them, if they could still love one another, then they had everything.

"I'll get the dishes," Beltan said.

"No," Travis said with mock sternness, "you're going to go watch TV while I clean up. Remember, I'm unemployed at the moment, and you're the hard worker who's bringing home the bacon."

Beltan frowned. "Was I supposed to stop at the butcher and get salt pork on the way home?"

Travis laughed, and it was a good sight to see. The bookstore where he had worked for the last year had closed, and he hadn't found a new job yet. That was probably why he had been reading Vani's letter. He had been home by himself all day, and sadness usually waited until people were alone to creep in and touch them. However, the mirth in his eyes seemed genuine.

"Go," he said, pushing Beltan into the living room.

Beltan did as commanded. He sat on the couch, listening to the cheerful clatter coming from the kitchen. Maybe they should call Mitchell and Davis Burke-Favor. It had been over a year since the two ranchers had last journeyed from Colorado to London for a visit. It would be good to see them. Then again, their ranch kept them busy, and it was hard for them to get away. Beltan hoped Travis would find a job soon. Not that they needed the money; the Seekers had taken care of that.

It had been Travis's idea to go to the Seekers as soon as they reached Earth. He reasoned the organization would find them sooner or later. Besides, it had been good to see Deirdre Falling Hawk, though there had been no sign of Hadrian Farr—nor had the last three years brought any news of him, at least as far as Beltan knew.

Travis and Beltan had cooperated with the Seekers, submitting to interviews and writing lengthy reports about Eldh—its geography, peoples, languages, cultures, history, politics, and magic. In exchange, the Seekers had given them new identities, along with the papers to make them legal. They were now, officially, Travis Redstone and Arthur Beltan. The Seekers also granted them an amount of money that had no meaning for Beltan, but which according to Travis meant they would never want for anything for the rest of their lives.

All the same, they had to do something. Beltan had wondered if Travis wanted to return to his hometown, to Castle City, to rebuild the tavern he had once owned there. However, when he mentioned this, Travis had asked how Beltan liked London.

Beltan liked it very much. London was like nothing on Eldh. The ancient city of Tarras seemed a simple village in comparison. They had bought the flat in Mayfair, and had found jobs. Since then, they had spoken little with the Seekers, and it had been over a year since they had last seen Deirdre. Evidently, as far as the Seekers were concerned, Travis and Beltan's case was closed, and that suited both of them just fine.

Beltan picked up the remote and switched on the television: another one of those marvels he had begun to take for granted. There was an astonishing array of choices called *channels* on TV (many displaying sights as vulgar as they were fascinating), but of them all Beltan's favorite was the Wonder Channel. He enjoyed learning about this world that was now his home. Over the last three years, he had read voraciously—now that he *could* read, thanks to Grace's tutelage in the Library of Tarras— though one day, after noticing the way he squinted at a page, Travis had taken him to a doctor to get him a pair of reading spectacles. The spectacles helped, but sometimes, like tonight, Beltan's eyes were too tired for a book.

Television wasn't as good as reading, but Beltan still liked it, and he pressed a button on the remote, changing to the Wonder Channel. A show called *Archaeology Now!* was just starting. He had seen this program before. It showed live footage of archaeologists working at various sites across the world, hoping to catch them at the very moment of a great discovery.

Archaeologists, Beltan knew, were learned men and women who dug up and studied the remains of ancient cultures and civilizations. It intrigued him to know that, in its past, Earth had been more like Eldh, but the problem with this show was that archaeology was, by any estimation, tedious work, and usually involved scraping away at dirt with tiny little picks and brushes. The pert young woman who hosted the show did her best to make every chipped bead or broken piece of pottery that came out of the ground seem like a breakthrough discovery, but often her smile seemed more than a little strained.

"Today, we'll take you to the jungles of Belize," her excited voice blared through the TV's speakers, "where archaeologists are about to open the tomb of a Mayan princess that has remained hidden for over a thousand years. After that, we're off to Australia, to uncover what could be the first signs of human habitation on that continent. And finally, we'll venture into a cave to discover what incredible artifacts were revealed by a recent earthquake on the island of—"

A knock sounded at the door of the flat. Beltan muted the sound on the television and stood. The knock came again, hard and impatient.

"Coming," Beltan grumbled, determined that this time he was not going to buy anything from whoever was on the other side of the door. He undid the lock and threw the door open.

So his instincts had been right after all. Their peaceful time in London—the waiting—was over.

She looked older than he remembered, her face honed by care, but she was still lithe and beautiful, wearing an aura of danger as well as sleek black leathers. In her arms she held a small girl with gray-gold eyes. The girl laughed and reached a chubby hand toward Beltan.

"Please," Vani said, her voice low and urgent. "Let us in."

5.

Travis had always liked the simplest things best.

After the Second War of the Stones—much to his horror—Grace had wanted to make him a baron of Malachor. There was a ruined castle in the west of the Winter Wood, she said, only three days' ride from Gravenfist Keep. He could take five hundred men and twenty Embarran engineers with him. In a year, the castle would be in good working order. His men could bring their families from the south; they could hunt the forests and clear land for farming, and Travis could be their lord.

"I'll need smart and trustworthy barons if I'm going to have a chance of making this kingdom work again," Grace had said with such characteristic matter-of-factness it made him laugh.

However, to be a baron—to have a great hall and vassal lords and servants—was the last thing Travis wanted. A two-bedroom flat in London was more than enough castle for him, and he was content to share the duties of ruling it with Beltan. The sorts of things he had done today—watching ships pass beneath Tower Bridge, walking home through the energetic streets of the West End, cooking a dinner that Beltan wolfed down no matter how awful it was—those were all he desired. Maybe it was because of everything he had witnessed in his time on Eldh, but these days Travis didn't need much to be happy.

Only if that was so, why had he felt so gloomy today? Yes, he had lost his job at the bookstore and hadn't found another to replace it. But money wasn't a worry, and another job would come along. That wasn't what was troubling him, and that wasn't what had made him read her letter.

The dishes were done. Travis pulled the sink plug, leaned on the counter, and stared as the dishwater swirled down the drain. It circled around and around before vanishing.

Spirals are symbols of great power, spoke the echo of Jack Graystone's voice in his mind. *They attract magic, and trap it within them.*

There had been a vast spiral inside the White Tower of the Runebinders, Travis remembered. It had drawn them into its center, and there he had first come face-to-face with wraithlings. The pale beings had come to take the Stone of Twilight from him; they had reached out spindly hands, and in their touch was death. Only then, without even knowing how, Travis had bound the tower's broken foundation stone. The tower's magic had awakened; the wraithlings were destroyed.

Looking back, Travis supposed that was the moment he became a wizard. However, that life was over. He wasn't a wizard anymore. The Great Stones were a world away, on Eldh; he had given them to Master Larad for safekeeping. True, there was magic here on Earth, but it was a faint shadow of what it was on Eldh. Travis hadn't even attempted a spell since the day he and Beltan came to Earth.

Yet if he wasn't a wizard anymore, why did it feel like he was the thing trapped in the spiral?

Until it happened, Travis had never believed he could be so happy as he had been these last three years in London. For the first time in his life, he wasn't someplace just because that was where he had ended up, but rather because he had chosen to be there. To be *here*, with Beltan. Yet he couldn't leave the past behind, not completely. Jack's voice still spoke in his mind from time to time, along with the voices of all the Runelords who had gone before him. Travis would never truly escape the spiral of power that had drawn him in, that had taken him to Eldh.

Nor were the voices the only reminders of what he had been, for sometimes his right hand ached to hold the Great Stones again, and if he looked in those moments, he would see a silvery symbol glimmer on his palm: three crossed lines. It would vanish after a few seconds, but it was always there, just beneath the surface. Waiting.

Once a thing is made, it cannot be unmade without breaking it. That was what Olrig—the Old God who was also the Worldsmith and Sia and the hag Grisla—had said to Master Larad, when Larad asked to be a Runelord no longer. The same was true for Travis. He could not change what he was.

Only what was he, exactly?

First Jack had made him into a Runelord. Then the fires of the Great Stone Krondisar had burned him to nothing before making him anew. And there was one more transformation that had changed him. . . .

A compulsion came over Travis, so swift and strong that a small paring knife was in his hand before he realized what he was doing. He longed to see blood, to see if here on Earth *they* would come if he called. He pressed the knife against the skin of his left forearm . . .

A noise broke the spell; he jerked the knife away. It had left a white mark in his flesh, but it had not drawn blood. He swallowed the sickness in his throat, then forced himself to set down the knife.

Out in the living room, the blare of the television ceased. A moment later came the sound of the door opening. He thought he heard a low voice saying something. Then the door shut. Beltan must have told whoever it was to go away.

Travis picked up a damp plate and a dish towel to give his trembling hands something to do, then headed into the living room. "Who was at the door, Beltan? I didn't hear you—"

The plate slipped from his wet fingers. It seemed to make no sound as it struck the floor, shattering into a dozen white shards.

"You look well, Travis," Vani said. Beltan stood just behind her, but Travis couldn't look at him. He stared at the *T'gol*.

She wore supple leathers as she always had, and her gold eyes were just as piercing. However, her black hair was longer than he remembered, frosted by a streak of white that started at the peak of her brow. Though her bearing was as proud as always, there was a weight to her shoulders and a shadow on her expression he had never seen before.

"You look tired," he said.

She nodded. "We have journeyed far to get here."

It wasn't until she spoke those words that he realized she held a child in her arms: a girl with dark hair, clad in an ash gray dress. She seemed too large to be three years old—Travis would have guessed her to be five—but there was no doubting who she was. The resemblance to each of them was plain to see: her sharp cheekbones, his high forehead. Travis looked at Beltan. The blond man's eyes were locked on the girl.

"Please set me down, Mother," the girl said in a voice that was precise and articulate despite a marked lisp.

She slipped from Vani's arms, padded across the floor, and crouched beside the broken plate. She arranged the pieces, fitting them together with motions that seemed too skilled for such tiny hands.

The girl looked up at Travis. "Make it whole."

He was too startled to do anything but kneel beside her and place a hand on the broken plate.

"*Eru*," he said, trying to gather all the force of his will into the word.

He heard a chorus of voices echo the word in his mind. Only the chorus became a dissonant chord. The familiar *whoosh* of magic in his ears ceased, and he felt a wrenching sensation deep inside. He lifted his hand. The shards of the plate had fused together into a melted gray blob.

The girl frowned. "It didn't work right."

"No, it didn't." Travis held a hand to his throbbing head. Both Vani and Beltan glanced at him, her expression curious, his concerned.

The girl moved to Beltan, took one of his big hands, and curled her own hand inside it. "Hello, Father."

Beltan's expression transformed into one of wonder, and his hand closed reflexively—gently—around the girl's. She turned, her eyes on Travis now. They were gray, like her dress, but flecked with gold.

"Hello, Father," she said again.

Travis couldn't speak. For so long he had wondered if she was fair-haired or dark, if she had all her fingers and toes; he had tried to picture what she would look like, the image in his mind changing a little with each passing month. Now she was here, so much like he had imagined, and utterly different, and he had no idea what to say to her.

Beltan knelt, laid a hand on her shoulder, and gave her a solemn look. "What is your name, child?"

Her look was as serious as his. "My name is Nim."

Again the voices spoke in Travis's mind, echoing the name. Only it wasn't just a name, it was a rune.

"*Nim*," Travis murmured. "Hope." He moved toward Vani. "Did you name her that?"

The girl—Nim—laughed, all traces of seriousness gone. "Don't be silly, Father," she said. "You did."

"I told her she was my greatest hope," the *T'gol* said to

Travis, "and that it was you who told me the ancient word for hope was *Nim*."

Travis tried to clear the lump from his throat. "You spoke about me—about us—often?"

Vani nodded. "As soon as she could speak—which was quite early—she always wanted to know everything I could tell her about you both. She can be quite . . . persistent."

"You're very brave, and your father was a king," Nim said, pointing at Beltan, then she pointed at Travis. "And you're a great wizard."

Travis glanced down at the melted plate, and his stomach churned.

"Nim," Vani said, kneeling beside the girl, touching her arms, "why don't you go play in the bedroom for a while?"

The girl heaved a dramatic sigh for the obvious benefit of Travis and Beltan. "That means she wants to say things to you that I'm not supposed to hear."

"Yes," Vani said, gold eyes flashing, "it does." She turned Nim around and gave her a gentle but firm push toward the hallway. Nim made a show of dragging her small black shoes on the floor, then vanished into the bedroom. The door shut behind her.

"So now what?" Travis said, his voice going hard.

Both Vani and Beltan stared at him.

Travis had always imagined that, if this moment somehow ever came, he would feel immeasurable joy. And for a moment he had. It was good to know Nim's name, to know she was whole and healthy and beautiful. Only that moment was over, and now anger oozed from Travis, hot and thick, like blood from a reopened wound.

"You can't do this, Vani."

"Do what?"

"What you're doing." He clenched his hands into fists and advanced on the *T'gol*. "Don't you understand? We've been happy here. For three years, we've been just fine without you."

"Travis . . ." Beltan started to say, laying a hand on his shoulder, but Travis shook it off.

"We didn't have a choice," he said, moving in until his face was inches from hers. "And you know why? Because you left us."

"I had my reasons," she said, her voice cool. "Did you not read the letter I left for you at Gravenfist Keep?"

Travis let out a bitter laugh. He had read it all right, over and over, and each time it made less sense than the last. "It doesn't matter why you did it. You went, and you took something away that we can never get back, not even now that you've brought Nim here. That was the choice you made, and I don't know what you're doing in London, or how you even got to Earth, but you can't just walk through that door like nothing ever happened. You don't have that right. You gave it away the night you left us without even bothering to say good-bye."

As he spoke, his voice had risen, and her body had grown rigid, her eyes sparking. She was *T'gol*; she could reach up and snap his neck with her bare hands before he could blink. In fact, she looked as if she wanted to do it right then. Beltan started to reach for her, but she shut her eyes and turned away, crossing her arms over her stomach.

"I know," she said. And again, the words soft and broken, "I know."

Travis wanted to harden his heart, to refuse to hear the sorrow, the regret, the anguish in her voice. Only wasn't that what he had given up so much to fight against? Those whose hearts were made of cold iron rather than weak, mortal flesh?

The anger drained from him like the dishwater in the sink, leaving him empty and shaking. He felt Beltan's strong arms wrap around him, and he leaned his head on the blond man's shoulder.

"Maybe you'd better tell us why you've come," Beltan said, the words gruff, and Vani nodded.

6.

Ten minutes later, they sat around the kitchen table, drinking mugs of coffee Beltan had brewed. Nim was in the living room now, lying on her stomach on the floor, drawing with a pencil and some paper Beltan had found in the desk. Before heading into the kitchen, Travis had paused for a moment, watching her. The pencil seemed far too large for her fingers, but she moved it across the paper with deliberate motions, sticking out her tongue as she concentrated.

"She seems older than three winters," Beltan said. "She looks like five, and speaks as if she is older than that."

Vani wrapped her hands around her mug. "She's always been that way. She was born after only seven moons, as if she was anxious to be out and learning about the world." She smiled, and the expression smoothed away some of the lines from her face. "She was only six moons old when she first spoke, and then not simply a single world. I will never forget it. I was cradling her in my arms, and she said, 'Set me down, Mother.' I did, and she walked over to a pebble and picked it up. I've never seen a child speak or walk so early."

"I heard her," Travis said. "When she was still in your womb, Vani. It was in Imbrifale, after you and Beltan had passed through the Void, when I spoke the rune of fire to warm you. To warm her. I heard her voice in my mind. It was so small, I thought I was just imagining it, but . . ."

"You weren't imagining. What did she say to you?"

Wonder filled Travis, just as it had then. "She said, 'Hello, Father.'"

Beltan's eyes shone, and he gripped Travis's hand.

There was so much Travis wanted to know, so many questions to ask—where they had been, what they had done—but before he could speak, Vani reached inside her leathers, drew out a small object, and set it on the table. It was a tetrahedron fashioned of perfect black stone.

"The gate artifact," Beltan said, leaning over but not touching the onyx tetrahedron. "So that's how you reached Earth."

"My people have had it in their keeping these last three years," Vani said. "I gave it to them when they came to Gravenfist Keep."

"Before you left," Travis said. The words sounded harsher than he intended, but he didn't care.

"Yes," Vani said, turning her gold eyes on him. "Before I left. Then, a few weeks ago, I went to my people, to ask if I might have the artifact back. I found them in the far south of Falengarth."

Beltan picked up the coffeepot and refilled their mugs. "Were Sareth and Lirith with the Mournish?"

"I fear I missed them. My brother had taken a ship across the Summer Sea, to Moringarth, a week before I arrived, and Lirith had gone north with their son, Taneth, to visit Aryn at Calavere."

Despite everything, Travis couldn't help smiling. So Lirith and Sareth were parents now. A sudden desire to see them, to see everyone they had left on Eldh, came over him. Only that was impossible, wasn't it? Even as he thought this, his fingers crept toward the fragment of the gate artifact on the table; he jerked his hand back.

"Why did you go to your people to get the gate?" Beltan said.

"For the same reason I left you three years ago and could not return."

Travis took a breath. "And what reason is that?"

"I am fleeing the Scirathi."

They listened, too stunned for speech, as Vani described in brief but vivid words why she had left Gravenfist that day three years ago, and where she had been in the time since.

She hadn't known the sorcerers of Scirath were pursuing her, at least not at first. After leaving Gravenfist Keep she had journeyed south, sailing across the Summer Sea to Al-Amún, seeking out oracles and seers, trying to understand the fate her al-Mama had seen in the cards.

Your daughter is not yet born, the old woman had told Vani, *yet already powerful lines of fate weave themselves around her. You dare not stay, lest you be trapped in the net.*

It was there, in Moringarth, where the Scirathi first attacked her. Several of the gold-masked sorcerers had surrounded the hostel where she was staying. She was heavy with child then, and she could not have fought them, except that they seemed unwilling to harm her. They only wanted to capture her, to keep her from escaping. One cut himself and began a spell of binding. However, Vani managed to take his knife and cut him deeper, so that more blood flowed than he had intended. Many spirits came in answer to his spell, and they consumed his blood, draining him dry. The other sorcerers were forced to weave their own spells to keep the ravenous *morndari* under control. In the confusion, Vani fled.

After that, she was vigilant, and they did not catch her unawares again. However, she was forced always to keep moving. By the time she gave birth to Nim she was on a ship sailing north. For the next three years she kept traveling from place to place, never staying in one spot for more than a month or two, and never daring to return to a location where she had been before, for fear they would be waiting for her.

When she finished, Travis and Beltan could only stare at her. Through the door they heard Nim humming as she drew. At last Travis forced himself to speak.

"So have you learned what the Scirathi want with you?"

"They don't want me."

"Nim," Beltan said, his voice hoarse. He stood, pacing around the table. "It's Nim the sorcerers want, isn't it?"

Vani nodded, her expression haunted.

Beltan slammed a fist on the countertop. "The filthy Scirathi—I will kill them all with my bare hands."

Sparks shone in his green eyes. Alarmed, Travis rose and moved to him, touching his arm. For a moment Beltan was rigid, then he sighed and his shoulders slumped. "I'm sorry, Travis. It's only . . . we've just met her, and now they want to take her away."

Travis looked at Vani. "What do they want with her?"

"I would that I knew," Vani said, gazing at her hands splayed on the table. "But whatever the reason, the Scirathi have grown more relentless in their pursuit these last weeks. I could not stay anywhere more than a few days before I was forced to flee. That was why I sought out my people and asked for the gate. I knew it was the only way to escape."

Travis gazed at the piece of the artifact. "How did you open it, Vani? The gate."

Beltan gave him a startled look.

Travis sat again. He slid his hands across the table toward her own but did not touch them. "The blood I filled it with beneath the Steel Cathedral would have been consumed when you and Beltan returned to Eldh. So what blood did you use to open the gate?"

Vani opened her mouth, but no words came out.

"It's all right, Mother," said a small voice behind them. "You can tell them. I don't mind."

Nim stood in the kitchen door, holding a piece of paper.

"Tell us what, sweetheart?" Travis said, keeping his tone light, unsure how much she had heard.

The girl pranced to the table and set the paper down. "How we came here. Look, I drew you a picture. It explains everything."

Travis turned the paper around. The drawing was made up of simple but expressive lines. At the bottom of the paper was a small black triangle. Above the triangle was a large circle with wavy edges. On either side of the circle stood a stick figure, one tall, the other short. The shorter figure held a hand toward the triangle. Small black shapes like teardrops fell from the little figure's hand onto the triangle.

Only the drops weren't tears, Travis knew. A sweat sprang out on his skin.

Vani picked up the paper, folded it in half, and gave it back to Nim. "It's time for you to go to sleep."

"I know," the girl said. "I can put myself to bed. I just wanted my fathers to kiss me good night first."

They did. Beltan picked her up and hugged her, and Travis gave her a solemn kiss on her forehead. She ran to the door, then stopped and looked at Vani.

"I'm lucky, Mother," she said.

Vani's gaze was thoughtful. "How so, daughter?"

"Most children have just one father. But I have two."

With that, Nim was gone. Travis and Beltan sat again at the table. Vani stared at the door where the girl had vanished.

"How?" Travis said simply.

Vani didn't look at him. "She told me to do it. I refused at first—older though she seems, she is only three—but the sorcerers were close behind us, and I knew my people would not be able to delay them for long. I had little choice. And I learned early on that she knows things. Things she shouldn't know, yet does all the same."

Beltan pressed his hand to the inside of his right arm.

"So her blood activated the gate," Travis said, feeling ill.

"She didn't even cry as I pricked her finger with a needle." Vani hesitated, then touched his hand. "Somehow, through some magic of the Little People, she truly is your child, Travis. Even as she is my child, and Beltan's. She is what she is because of all of us."

Travis struggled to comprehend. How could Nim really be his child? The Little People had tricked Vani and Beltan, making each think the other was Travis. The two had lain together, and Nim was conceived. But it was only illusion; he hadn't really been there. Or was it some enchantment of the Little People? Some magic that had taken something from all three of them and imparted it to Nim?

"There's something else I have not told you." Vani circled her hands around the onyx tetrahedron—the topmost portion of the gate artifact. "It has been three weeks since I came to Earth. It took me that long to find you, for I began my search in Colorado."

"Sorry," Travis said. "We didn't know we needed to leave a forwarding address."

Vani did not smile. "I kept the lid of the gate artifact so that I might remain in contact with my people. While a Mournish man or woman's blood is not enough to open the gate—"

"It's enough to send a message," Travis said. "Yes, I know. Are you saying you've heard something?"

"Hold out your hand."

Travis did so, and she set the onyx tetrahedron on his palm. It was warm, and he felt a hum of magic. Blood flowed beneath his skin. Blood of power. Just the proximity to it was enough to awaken the artifact. A tiny, transparent image of a man appeared above the tetrahedron.

It was Sareth. He held a knife, and there was a dark line on his forearm.

"Sister," the image spoke in a reedy but clear facsimile of Sareth's voice, "I returned from the south, from Moringarth, only today, and our al-Mama tells me that you are already two weeks gone. I wish that I could speak with you in person. But I fear, whatever dark wonders you might tell me, the news I bear would be darker yet."

A grimace crossed the image of his face. "I must be brief.

Let me say this: I think it is fate you chose to journey to Earth. In Moringarth, I spoke to a dervish, and though what he told me seems impossible, I am certain it is true. The burial place of Morindu the Dark has been discovered. Already the Scirathi seek it out, and our people move to hinder them and reach the city first. And, sister, this news is even stranger than you imagine, for the dervish who brought it to me is a man from Travis Wilder's world, a man named Hadrian Farr. He says word must be sent to Travis, that the time draws near when he must return to Eldh and—"

The image of Sareth flickered, then vanished. The tetrahedron grew cool and heavy in Travis's hand. He could feel both Vani's and Beltan's eyes on him as he set it on the table. His mind buzzed, and his hands itched. What had Sareth been about to say before the spell of blood sorcery ceased? What was Travis supposed to return to Eldh and do?

They want you to raise it, Travis. To raise it from the sands that swallowed it long ago. Morindu the Dark, lost city of sorcerers.

He shoved his chair back from the table and stood.

Beltan's green eyes were worried. "What are you doing?"

"I'm calling for help," Travis said as he picked up the phone and dialed.

7.

"Come on," Deirdre Falling Hawk muttered as the train rattled to a stop at the Green Park station.

The doors lurched open, and she squeezed through the moment the opening was wide enough. "Mind the gap," droned a recorded voice, but she had already leaped onto the platform, breaking into a run as her boots hit the tiles. Travis hadn't said why he wanted her to come over, but there had been something in his voice—a sharpness—that made her heart quicken. Besides, Travis and Beltan hadn't invited her or any other Seeker to their flat in the three years since they had come to London.

Something told her this wasn't an invitation for a drink and casual conversation.

She gripped the yellowed bear claw that hung at her throat as she pounded up the steps and into the balmy night. A man wearing a grimy white sheet stood next to the entrance of the Tube station, holding a cardboard sign, a blank look on his face. The sign read, in neatly printed letters, You Will Be Eaten.

"Are you ready for the Mouth?" he said as she passed him, the words accompanied by a puff of sour breath.

Deirdre ignored him—the Mouthers were everywhere in the city these days—and darted across Piccadilly Street. She had never been to Travis and Beltan's flat, but she knew exactly where it was. The Seekers had a penchant for keeping tabs on otherworldly travelers. Even those whose cases were closed.

Except the case would never really be closed, whether the Seekers were actively investigating it or not. And it wasn't just because of the phone call from Travis that Deirdre ran headlong down the sidewalk, daring other pedestrians to get in her way.

Just before the phone rang, she had been sitting at the dining table in her flat, working on her laptop computer, doing some cross-indexing between two databases. It was tedious work, but necessary as well. The kind of work she'd been doing a lot of lately.

Not that she wouldn't rather have been investigating rumors of unexplainable energy signatures or artifacts of unknown origin, journeying to exotic locations, poring over lost manuscripts, or decoding hieroglyphics. However, if there were any otherworldly forces lurking out there, waiting to be discovered, then they were studiously avoiding her, because she hadn't worked on an interesting case in over a year, and the last several leads of any promise she had found had all run into dead ends.

Eyes aching from staring at the computer, Deirdre had just decided to call it a night when the machine chimed. On screen, a message appeared.

Do be sure to take this call.

That was all. There was no indication of the sender, no box in which she could type a reply. She was still staring at the message when the phone rang, causing her to jump out of her seat.

If the call had come a minute before, she would have been

tempted to let the answering machine get it, to soak in a bath before going to bed. After all, what could be so important she couldn't deal with it tomorrow? Deirdre didn't know, but the message on the computer screen changed everything. She lunged for the phone, unsure who it would be on the other end, though somehow not surprised when it was Travis Wilder.

"Deirdre, I'm so glad you're home," he had said, his words clipped. "Can you . . . can you come over right away?"

"Of course," she had said. "I'll be there in half an hour." She hung up and glanced at the computer. The message was gone, but she knew now who had sent it.

It was *he*. There was no other possibility, even though he hadn't contacted her in over three years. The last time had been just a few weeks after the events in Denver, when the Steel Cathedral was destroyed, and the truth about Duratek's involvement in the illegal trade of the drug Electria was revealed. After that, for a time, she had hoped. Every phone call, every e-mail message, had caused a jolt of excitement.

Only they were never from him. Whoever the mysterious Philosopher was who had helped her in the past, he had fallen silent. But hadn't he said it would be like that? *It may be some time until we speak again*, he had told her at the end of their first and only telephone conversation. *But when the time comes, I'll be in touch.*

That time was now. Yet what did it mean? Something had happened—something had changed—but what?

You know what it is, Deirdre. Perihelion is coming. Earth and Eldh are drawing near. That's what he told you three years ago. Maybe it's close now. Maybe that's why everything is changing. . . .

She turned down a deserted side street, half jogged the last block to their building, and started up the steps. Just as she reached the door, the short hairs on the back of her neck stood up. Again she gripped her bear claw necklace—a gift from her shaman grandfather—and turned around.

The black silhouette of a figure stood on the edge of a circle of light cast by a streetlamp. A thrill of dread and wonder sizzled through Deirdre. Was it him? Surely he was keeping watch on Beltan and Travis. How else would he have known Travis was about to call her?

The figure reached out a beckoning hand. As if compelled by a will not her own, she started back down the steps.

"Deirdre!" a voice called from above. "Up here."

She turned and looked up. Beltan leaned out of a window two floors above her.

"I'll let you in," the blond man said, then his head ducked inside. A second later the building's front door buzzed, and the lock clicked.

Deirdre glanced over her shoulder, but the circle of light across the street was empty. She pulled on the door before the buzzing stopped, then bounded up two flights of stairs. The door of their flat opened before she could knock on it, and she was hauled inside by strong hands.

"It's been too long since we've seen you," Beltan said as he lifted her off the floor in an embrace.

"So you're going to crush me as punishment?" she managed to squeak.

Beltan set her down and straightened her leather jacket. "Sorry. For me, hugs only come in one strength."

"That would be maximum," she said, returning his grin. However, her smile vanished as she caught Travis's troubled gray eyes. He moved forward and laid a hand on her shoulder.

"Thank you for coming."

"I'll always come when you call, no matter how long it's been or how far away you are. But what's going on? And why couldn't you tell me over the phone?"

He stepped aside. The first thing she noticed was the broadsword hanging above the sofa; that had to be Beltan's. Then her gaze moved down, and she saw the woman sitting there. The woman stood, stretching limbs clad in supple black leather.

"Oh," Deirdre said, and would have fallen to the floor if not for Beltan's strong hands.

They set her on the sofa, propped her up with a pillow, and pressed a glass of porter into her hand. A few sips of beer revived her enough that she was able to tell them she was fine, though she wasn't certain that was really the case.

For the last three years, Deirdre had done her best not to think about them. The Seekers had officially closed the Wilder-Beckett case. The gate to the world AU-3—to Eldh—had been destroyed, and Duratek Corporation had been destroyed as well. The company had been dismantled by the governments of Earth; its executives were in jail or, in many cases, dead. There would be other investigations, maybe even other worlds. But the door to this one had been shut. It was over.

At least, that was what she had told herself. But deep within, Deirdre had known it wasn't over, not truly. They had all of them been waiting, that was all. Waiting for a day when two worlds would draw closer. Waiting for a time they would be called again.

"All right," Deirdre said, setting the empty glass on the coffee table. "Who's going to tell me why I'm here?"

Vani and Beltan both cast glances at Travis. He sat down on the sofa next to her and took her hand in his.

"I supposed I always let myself believe it was just a story, that there was nothing behind it." His gray eyes were solemn. "I thought it would never come. Only now it finally has."

Deirdre shook her head. "I don't understand. What's come?"

"Fate," Travis said.

Before Deirdre could ask what he was talking about, Vani spoke, and for the next several minutes Deirdre listened as the *T'gol* explained how and why she had come to Earth, and of her last three years fleeing from the Scirathi. Vani's words were terrible and fascinating, but Deirdre found it hard to focus on them. A droning noise filled her skull; there was something she needed to tell them, but what was it?

She stared at the *T'gol*. Vani's face was sharper than before, but still lovely, even delicate. Tattoos like vines accentuated the exquisite lines of her neck; thirteen gold rings glittered in her left ear. However, Deirdre knew it would be a mistake to let that beauty lull her. Vani was an assassin, trained since girlhood in the arts of stealth, infiltration, and killing in swift silence.

There was much Vani alluded to that Deirdre already knew, things she had learned when she first met the *T'gol* and which Deirdre had included in her reports to the Seekers. How Vani's people believed Travis Wilder was the one destined to raise

Morindu the Dark from the sands that had swallowed it long ago, and how the gold-masked sorcerers, the Scirathi, hoped to reach it first, to steal the magics entombed within for their own purposes.

"Only what exactly is buried in Morindu?" Deirdre said as she rubbed her temples, voicing her thought without meaning to.

"Good question," Beltan rumbled. The big man sat on the floor, making steady progress through an enormous bowl of popcorn.

"My people cannot say for certain," the *T'gol* said, prowling back and forth before the curtained window. "No records survive from the last days of the War of the Sorcerers. We have only what our storytellers have passed down. Nor were any of the Morindai there at the very end, for the people of Morindu were ordered to flee the city as the army of Scirath approached. Only the Seven *A'narai*, the Fateless Ones who ruled in the name of the god-king Orú, remained behind. They and the Shackled God, Orú, himself."

The War of the Sorcerers. Deirdre had heard Vani speak those words before. In Denver, the *T'gol* had told them of the great conflagration that, three thousand years ago, had engulfed the ancient city-states of Amún on Eldh's southern continent. The sorcerers, powerful and angry, had risen up against the arrogant god-kings of the city-states, seeking to cast them down and take their place. However, Morindu was unique, for it was a city of sorcerers, ruled by the most potent among them. In fear and mistrust, the other city-states named it Morindu the Dark.

Near the end of the War of the Sorcerers, a great army led by the sorcerers of Scirath had marched toward the city. Rather than fall to its foes and let its secrets be plundered, Morindu had chosen to destroy itself. When the army arrived, they found only empty desert.

Soon after that, the War of the Sorcerers ended in a violent cataclysm that destroyed the city-states and blasted all of Amún, transforming it into a wasteland. What few people survived fled north to the shores of the Summer Sea, to begin civilization anew in Al-Amún. Eventually, some of the Morindai found their way across the sea, to the northern continent of Falengarth, and there became a wandering folk known as the Mournish. These were Vani's people. However, Vani was no mere gypsy. Deirdre knew the *T'gol* could trace her lineage all the way back to the royal line of Morindu the Dark.

"All right," Beltan said around a mouthful of popcorn. "If the Mournish don't know what's buried in Morindu, then tell me this: What do the Scirathi *think* is buried there? What are they so eager to get their paws on?"

Vani rested her hands on her hips. "Many things, I imagine. Books of spells. Artifacts of power. Treasures of gold and gems. Or perhaps—"

"Blood," Travis said. "They want blood."

Deirdre shivered. At one time Travis had possessed an artifact shaped like a gold spider, a living jewel called a scarab. The scarab had contained three drops of blood taken from the god-king Orú. With it, Travis had been able to activate the gate artifact, opening a crackling doorway to Eldh.

"You think they want blood of power," Deirdre said. "Blood from the god-king Orú."

Travis shook his head. "No. I think they want Orú himself." He turned his gaze on Vani. "He's still there, isn't he? The Seven stayed with him to the end, and they buried him with the city."

Vani knelt on the floor. Beltan gave her a suspicious look and edged the bowl of popcorn out of her reach.

"We suppose he is still there," the *T'gol* said. "But we do not know."

"You mean his body," Deirdre said. "It's been three thousand years. It's not like Orú can still be alive."

Vani shrugged. "Who is to say what can and cannot be? It is said Orú was five hundred years old at the time Morindu was destroyed. He was the most powerful sorcerer ever known. So powerful that Fate itself tangled around him, its strands unraveling, so that only the Seven *A'narai* could stand in his presence. Yet in time that power consumed him. He fell into a deep slumber, and so it was that the Fateless Ones drank of his blood, becoming sorcerers of dreadful might themselves, and ruled in his name."

"Okay," Deirdre said, hoping logic might make all of this seem less terrifying. "Let's pretend for a moment Orú is somehow still alive, buried beneath the desert. What would happen if the Scirathi found him?"

"That must not be allowed to happen!" Vani said, her eyes flashing. "With Orú's blood, there is no limit to the evils the Scirathi might work. I have no doubt that they would first hunt my people, slaying the Morindai down to the last man, woman, and child." Vani stood, pacing again. "But that would only be the beginning. With Orú's blood at their command, they might enslave all of Moringarth—all of Eldh. They would dominate its people with all the hatred, all the cruelty, they have fostered in their hearts all these ages. Nothing could stand before them. That is what the Seven understood. That was why they destroyed their own city."

Travis cleared his throat. "The way you describe them, the Scirathi make the Pale King sound like a chap who just wanted to come out of his kingdom and play."

Vani raised an eyebrow. "Compared to what the Scirathi might become, he was."

"Wait just a minute," Beltan said, a handful of popcorn halfway to his mouth. "Weren't all of the Scirathi killed when the demon destroyed the Etherion in Tarras?"

"All of the Scirathi in Falengarth, yes," Vani said. "But far more yet dwell on Moringarth. If each of them was to drink of the blood of Orú, they would become an army such as you cannot imagine."

"She's right," Travis said, slipping from the sofa to the floor and sitting across the coffee table from Beltan. "Remember what happened to Xemeth after he drank from the scarab? He would have destroyed us if it hadn't been for the demon. And he was only one man, and not even a sorcerer at that. The blood made him . . ."

Travis gripped his right hand inside the left, and Beltan gave him a look of concern. Deirdre wondered what he had been about to say.

"All right," she said, trying to get all of this straight in her mind. "I understand that Orú's blood is powerful, and that the Scirathi would do anything to get their hands on it. But Morindu has been lost for ages. Why is this so important now? And what does any of this have to do with me?"

"I believe this will answer both of your questions," Vani said, setting a tetrahedron of black stone on the coffee table. "Travis?"

Travis hesitated, then reached out and touched the stone. Deirdre sucked in a breath as the image of a man appeared above the tetrahedron. She had never seen him before, but their kinship was clear in his striking, angular features, and she knew he was Vani's brother. This was a message from Eldh.

The message was brief, and it changed everything. By the time the image of Vani's brother vanished, Deirdre's heart was racing.

"You bastard, Hadrian," she murmured. "You fabulous bastard. You actually did it."

"Did what?" Beltan said, brow furrowing.

She hugged a throw pillow to her chest. "He had a Class Zero Encounter. Translocation to another world. Something every Seeker has worked for, and something none of them has ever achieved."

Until now.

"Maybe I should be a Seeker," Beltan said brightly. "I've been to another world. This one."

Despite the buzzing in her head, Deirdre grinned at the blond man. "Don't be such a show-off."

She reminded herself that she was having multiple Class One Encounters herself at this very moment—something rare enough in the history of the Seekers. Resting her chin on a hand, she gazed at the onyx tetrahedron. What did it all mean? How had Farr gotten to Eldh? And why was he the one who had told the Mournish that Morindu had been found?

You always were a fast learner, Hadrian. They said you're a dervish, which I gather is some sort of sorcerer. I wish I could talk to you now. I know I should do something, but I have no idea what.

The only thing she knew for certain was that this case wasn't over. In fact, she had the feeling that—despite everything that had happened—it had only just begun.

"So now what?" Deirdre said.

"Now Travis must fulfill his fate," Vani said as if everything had already been decided.

Beltan's eyes narrowed. "What are you talking about?"

"Travis must return to Eldh," Vani said, standing. "He must journey into the Morgolthi and reach Morindu before the Scirathi."

Beltan jumped to his feet. "Why don't you go find it yourself, you and the Mournish? It's your bloody city."

Vani kept her eyes on Travis. "It is his fate to do it."

"Why?" Beltan said, cheeks ruddy. "Because you want it to be?"

Vani's face was hard. "No, because it is. Our oracles saw it long ago: The wizard who came to Eldh to defeat a great evil in the north would also be the one to raise Morindu. This task is his."

"Don't you think he's done enough already? He gave up everything to fight the Necromancer, and the Pale King, and Mohg. He's done enough for the world. For both worlds. This is his time now. Our time. And you can't just walk in here and take it from him. By all the gods, I won't let you!"

Deirdre felt she should turn her head, that she shouldn't be seeing this, only she couldn't look away. She had never seen Beltan cry before, but he was weeping now, tears running down his cheeks, and the big man's anguish made her own heart ache. Even Vani did not appear unmoved. The *T'gol* cast her eyes downward, but again she said, her voice low this time, "It is his fate."

Travis laughed, and all of them stared. It was a bitter sound. He was gazing down at his hands. "I still can't figure out how it can be my fate to find Morindu if I'm supposed to be one of the Fateless."

"What you say is true," Vani said, kneeling beside him. "But it is the fate of my people to find Morindu through you."

Beltan wiped the tears from his face with a rough gesture. "Then you have no idea what his fate really is. For all you know, you're telling him the wrong thing. Maybe it's because he refuses to go to Eldh that you find the city yourselves."

Vani started a hot reply, but Travis held up a hand.

"It doesn't matter. Even if I wanted to try to find Morindu—" he gave Vani a sharp look "—and I'm not saying I do, but even if I did, I couldn't. There's no way for me to get back to Eldh."

Deirdre ran a hand through her close-cropped hair. "What about the artifact?" However, even as she spoke, she remembered what she had learned before about the way the gate artifacts functioned.

"This is only part of the artifact," Vani said. "With it, I can receive messages from my brother. But he has the greater part, and without it we cannot open a gate." She gave Travis a piercing look. "But do you not have other means to travel between the worlds?"

Beltan let out a loud guffaw. "You mean you just assumed he could go back to Eldh?"

Vani gave him a dark look but said nothing, and it was clear this was exactly what she had believed.

"It's not like he can just snap his fingers," Beltan said, grinning, though it was a fierce expression. "By Vathris, even I know that much. True, he could use the Great Stones to travel between worlds, but he left them in Master Larad's care. And the silver coin he has only works in one direction, to bring him to his home—and that's here."

Vani gave Travis a stricken look. "Is this true?"

"You doubt Beltan?" he said simply.

She hunched her shoulders and looked away.

"What about Brother Cy?" Deirdre said.

She was as surprised as the others that she had spoken—after all, they were the otherworldly travelers, not she—but now that their eyes were on her, she felt braver. In his reports, Travis had spoken of the mysterious preacher Brother Cy, and Deirdre had encountered one of his cohort, the purple-eyed Child Samanda. According to Travis, Cy, Mirrim, and Samanda were Old Gods. A thousand years ago, they had helped to banish Mohg beyond the circle of Eldh, only in the process they were exiled with him. Then, when Travis inadvertently created a crack between the worlds by journeying back in time, Mohg was able to slip through the gap into Earth—and so were Cy and the others.

"Brother Cy helped you get to Eldh more than once," Deirdre said. "Couldn't he help you again?"

Travis's face was thoughtful. "I don't think Brother Cy is here anymore. When Larad broke the rune of Sky, Mohg was able to return to Eldh. I think Cy and Mirrim and Samanda went as well. It's their home, after all. I don't think we'll be getting any help from them this time around."

"There must be another way," Vani said, her words imploring.

Travis laid a hand on the *T'gol*'s shoulder. "I'm sorry, Vani. But even if I wanted to help, I can't. You have to face the fact that there's no way for any of us to get back to—"

The telephone rang.

They all gazed blankly at one another for a moment, as if the sound had jarred them out of a spell, then Beltan picked up the cordless phone and held it to his ear.

He cocked his head, then held the phone out toward Deirdre. "It's for you."

Deirdre fumbled as she took the phone. Who could be calling her here? She hadn't told anyone where she was going—not the Seekers, not even her partner Anders. However, as soon as she heard the rich, accentless voice emanating from the phone, she knew who it was.

"Turn on the television," the nameless Philosopher said. "I think you'll be interested in what you see."

There was a click, and a dial tone replaced his voice. Deirdre set down the phone, her heart pounding.

"Who was it?" Travis said.

She licked her lips. "Where's the remote control?"

A minute later, they gathered around the television. In quick words, Deirdre had described the message she had received on her computer just before Travis called and what he had said just now on the phone.

"You say this Philosopher friend of yours hasn't contacted you in over three years." Travis said. "I wonder why now?"

"Let's find out," Beltan said, and clicked a button on the remote.

The television glowed to life, displaying a scene of a blue ocean breaking against white rocks. The camera panned, focusing on weathered columns—what looked like the remains of an ancient Greek temple—rising toward an azure sky. A small graphic image in the corner of the screen advertised the name of the program: Archaeology Now!

"Wait a minute," Beltan said. "I was watching this show hours ago. How can it still be on?"

He punched the remote, trying to change the channel, but it no longer seemed to function. The volume came up.

"I didn't do that. What's wrong with this thing?" Beltan banged the remote against the table.

Travis grabbed his arm, stopping him. "Listen," he said.

Now the television showed a man dressed in khakis standing next to one of the columns. "—and which were opened by a recent earthquake here on the Mediterranean island of Crete," he was saying. "Tonight, we're taking our cameras and you into one of those caves, not far from the ancient palace of Knossos, to an excavation where Dr. Niko Karali is hoping to uncover evidence that could further our understanding of ancient Minoan culture, and perhaps provide new clues to an age-old mystery: why the thriving Minoan civilization vanished almost overnight three thousand years ago. As always on our program, we have no idea what we'll find, because everything you see is live. So let's head—"

The sound cut out, and the video began to move rapidly.

"Don't look at me," Beltan said, pointing to the remote control, which sat on the coffee table.

Despite the announcer's statement, Deirdre was certain this show was anything but live. It had been recorded earlier that night, and now it was being played back for their benefit. The video became a blur of images too fast for the eye to decipher. Then the video froze, and a single image filled the screen.

It was a stone arch, or part of one at least, set against rougher rock. A hand held a brush, clearing away dust and debris from one of the stones of the arch. Beneath the brush, Deirdre could just make out a series of angular marks.

She clapped a hand to her mouth at the same moment Travis swore.

"By the Blood," Vani whispered, her gold eyes wide.

Beltan cast them an annoyed look. "Great. Am I the only one who doesn't know what that writing says?" His expression grew thoughtful, and he rubbed his arm. "Although I feel like I should know."

Deirdre gripped the silver ring on her right hand. The ring

Glinda had given her. She didn't need to look to know that the angular characters etched inside it were shaped just like those on the television screen.

Travis drew closer to the TV. "I've seen writing like that before."

"It is the ancient writing of Amún," Vani said. "Few know it now. Even I cannot read what it says, though there are some among my clan who could. And there are others . . ."

"You mean sorcerers," Travis said. "There was writing sort of like that on the stone box that one Scirathi created to hold the gate artifact."

"Not sort of," Vani said. "The writing is identical."

All of them seemed to understand at once, as if a jolt of electricity had passed between them, carrying the knowledge.

"A gate," Deirdre said. "That arch is a gate, isn't it?"

Or part of one, anyway. She didn't need to wait for the archaeologists to uncover the entire thing to know that they wouldn't find the arch's keystone—that it was missing.

Only it wasn't missing. Deirdre knew exactly where it was: in the vaults of the Seekers. The Seekers had discovered it in the tavern that sat on the same spot that centuries later would house Surrender Dorothy. It was in researching Glinda's ring that Deirdre had discovered the existence of the keystone, for the writing on the ring and the keystone were identical.

Travis pressed his hand against the television screen. "Maybe there is a way back," he murmured.

Vani's eyes shone, and Beltan gave her a dark look. However, before the blond man could speak, the sound of small feet broke the silence. Deirdre tore her gaze from the TV. A girl stood at the end of the sofa. Her hair was dark, but her skin was moon-pale.

"You must be Deirdre," the girl said, her words articulate, though *must* came out as *muth*.

"Nim," Vani said, kneeling beside the girl. "What are you doing out here? You're supposed to be in bed."

Nim. Deirdre didn't recognize the name. However, she knew who this girl was. It was Vani and Beltan's daughter.

"I can't sleep," Nim said.

Vani brushed her hair from her face. "And why is that, *be-shala*?"

"Because there's a gold face outside my window," the girl said yawning. "It keeps watching me."

Vani held the girl tight. "It was a bad dream, dearest one. That was all."

However, there was doubt in the *T'gol*'s eyes, and a terrible certainty that the girl hadn't been dreaming came over Deirdre. Fear cleared her mind, and at last she understood what it was that had been troubling her all evening, what it was she had forgotten.

"Vani," Deirdre said, her mouth dry. "You came to Earth to escape the Scirathi, right?"

"Yes," the *T'gol* said, clutching Nim to her. "Why do you ask?"

Sickness rose in Deirdre's throat as she recalled the picture *he* had sent her during their final conversation three years ago: an image of two figures in black robes slinking down an alley in a modern Earth city, their faces concealed behind masks. Gold masks.

Deirdre drew in a breath. "Because I think they're already—"

Her voice was drowned out by the sudden sound of shattering glass.

8.

The bones would always be there.

Over the last three years, the grass of the vale had grown up around them, lush and dense, and had crept up the sides of the larger mounds, shrouding them in green. Just that spring, on the sides of those mounds, a tiny flower of the palest blue had begun to bloom in profusion. No one—not even the eldest of the witches, and the wisest in herb lore—had ever seen a flower like it before. And while no one was certain who had first used the name, soon everyone called the little flower *arynesseth*.

In the old language, the name meant Aryn's Tears. Almost as soon as the name came into use, a story sprang up around it, growing as quickly as the grass in the vale. It was said, in the days after the Second War of the Stones, brave Queen Aryn of Calavan stood upon the wall of Gravenfist Keep, and there she let fly the ashes of the knight Sir Durge, who had been noble and true above all other men. The wind carried the ashes out into the vale of Shadowsdeep, and one could always know where they came to rest, for in those places the *arynesseth* bloomed the thickest.

In places like this.

Grace Beckett—Queen of Malachor, Lady of the Winter Wood, and Mistress of the Seven Dominions—stood at the foot of the mound she had ridden to that morning. It was one of the highest in the vale, rising up no more than a furlong from the Rune Gate, whose gigantic iron doors hung open, steadily rusting away.

As her honey-colored mare Shandis grazed nearby, Grace knelt and parted the grass with her hands, revealing a skull bleached white by sun and rain and snow. The skull was elongated, the eye sockets large and jewel-shaped. There was no mouth. She let the grass fall back and stood, holding her right arm against her chest. The wraithlings had perished. So had the *feydrim*, and their master the Pale King. All the same, the pain in her right arm lingered on, just like the bones beneath the grass. Just like the memories.

Grace started up the side of the mound. It was Lirdath, and even this far north in the world the morning was already growing fine and hot. Soon she was mopping the sweat from her brow with a hand and wishing she had chosen something lighter than a riding gown of green wool.

After several minutes of steady work, she reached the top of the mound. She panted for breath and pushed her blond hair from her face; it was getting too long again. Others might have thought it beautiful, a gilded frame to her regal visage, but to Grace it was simply a nuisance. She would take a knife to it as soon as she got back to the keep.

Hands on hips, she gazed around. She could see the whole vale from up there. Sharp mountains soared against blue sky, and in the distance Gravenfist Keep rose like a mountain of gray stone itself. Summer had come, and the vale was a verdant emerald. Still, here and there white patches gleamed like snow.

She half closed her eyes, and through the veil of her lashes she could see it again, pouring out of the mouth of the Rune Gate like a foul exhalation of hatred: the army of the Pale King. Its ranks of *feydrim* and wraithlings and trolls, heartless wizards and witches, was without number, and they had come for one purpose—to cast the world into shadow forever.

Only they had failed, thanks to the bravery and sacrifice of countless men and women. And of one man more than any other. Grace knelt, letting her fingers brush across the *arynesseth* that bloomed atop the grass-covered mound. She plucked one of the small white-blue flowers. Its scent was faint and clean, like snow.

"I miss you, Durge," she murmured. "I could use your help. There's still so much more to do."

She stayed that way for a time, content to listen to the wind and the far-off cries of a hawk. At last she stood, and as she looked back toward the keep she saw a horseman coming. His need must have been great for him to make no effort to conceal himself.

By the time the horseman reached the foot of the mound, she had descended to meet him.

"I thought I might find you out here, Your Majesty," Aldeth said as he climbed down from a horse as gray as his mistcloak.

Grace raised an eyebrow. "All I told Sir Tarus was that I was going for a ride in the vale. How did you know to find me here?"

"I serve you with all my heart, Your Majesty," the Spider said with a rotten-toothed grin. "But that doesn't mean I have to tell you the secrets of my craft."

She folded her arms and waited patiently.

Aldeth threw his hands in the air. "Well, fine, if you're going to torture me like that. He can't blame me for not being able to resist your spells."

"I'm not casting a spell, Aldeth," she said, but the spy seemed not to hear, and he rattled on for several minutes about how it wasn't *his* idea to go to Master Larad, how he had been dead set against it, knowing how offended she would be, but how Sir Tarus had insisted that they ask the Runelord to speak the rune of vision, and how he—Aldeth—would never have dreamed of compromising his queen's privacy in such a manner.

"No, you'd simply sneak after me."

"Exactly!" the Spider said, snapping his fingers. "That way, you'd never even know I was—"

He bit his tongue, and he looked as if he was going to be sick. Grace couldn't help a smile. He really was getting better; a year ago he would have dug himself a far deeper hole before having the sense to shut up.

"Oh, Aldeth," she said, patting his cheek. Then she climbed into Shandis's saddle and whirled the mare around. As she did, she cast one last glance at the Rune Gate.

Last summer, at Sir Tarus's urging, Grace had finally ordered an exploratory mission into Imbrifale. Tarus himself had led the small company of knights through the gate, with the Spiders Aldeth and Samatha serving as scouts. Master Larad and the young witch Lursa had gone as well, for there was no telling what fell magics might remain in the Pale King's Dominion.

For an entire month, Grace had paced the outer wall of Gravenfist Keep, gazing out across the vale, waiting for them to return. She had hoped to be able to speak across the Weirding to Lursa. However, the moment the troop passed through the Rune Gate, all contact with them ceased, as if their threads had been cut by a knife. The Ironfang Mountains, woven with enchantments to imprison the Pale King, proved a barrier that could not be pierced by thought or magic.

At last, on the first day of Revendath, they returned to Gravenfist Keep. The company had not lost a single member on the journey; however, all of them suffered in spirit. None seemed able to speak of what they had found except for Master Larad, and even he spoke in halting words, so that it took many days before Grace finally learned all they had discovered.

Imbrifale was dead. Nothing lived in that Dominion—not men or monsters or animals, or even trees or plants. Every living thing that had dwelled there had been infused with and twisted by the Pale King's magic over the centuries. Nothing had not been bound to him, and when he and his master Mohg had perished, so did all else.

What had happened in the thousand years the Rune Gate was

shut would never truly be known, for no written records had been found, but some things could be gleaned from what the company saw. They came upon terrible cities, built like the hives of some insect species. There the *feydrim* and other inhuman slaves of the Pale King were bred and born, fed through holes in tiny chambers, where they either perished or grew strong enough to break their way out.

Other cities were more like the castles and keeps of the Dominions, though sharper, harsher, made only for function, with no consideration for beauty or comfort. There the human subjects of the Pale King had dwelled, and beneath one such keep they had found a labyrinth of chambers that contained stone tables large and small, and racks filled with knives and curved hooks. In one such chamber they discovered a cabinet containing iron lumps, some the size of a man's fist, some tiny, no larger than a robin's egg. In the next chamber was a pit filled with bones, many of grown men and women, but others the birdlike bones of infants—the remains of those who had not withstood the transformation.

Elsewhere the company came upon mines: immense wounds gouged in the land, oozing fetid liquids and emitting noxious fumes. Near each mine stood a foundry, many of them still filled with half-finished machines of war. At last they had reached Fal Imbri, the Pale King's palace, and they had looked upon his throne: a chair of iron forged for a giant, carved with runes of dread, its edges sharp as razors.

The throne was empty. The company had turned around to begin the long journey home.

"Do you want us to go back there, Your Majesty?"

Grace turned in the saddle. Aldeth was gazing at the open Rune Gate, his expression grim, his gray eyes distant. He seemed not to notice the way his hand crept up his chest.

"No," Grace said softly. "There's nothing for us there." She forced her voice to brighten. "Now come, let's go see what Sir Tarus wants with me."

9.

Half an hour later, they rode through an arch into the courtyard between the main tower of the keep and Gravenfist's outer wall. Once this place had thronged with warriors, runespeakers, and witches desperately battling to hold back the army of the Pale King. It was crowded today as well, though there were far more farmers, weavers, tanners, potters, merchants, and blacksmiths than there were men-at-arms.

Over the last three years, Gravenfist Keep had become less of a military fortress and more of a working castle. Most of the men who had marched here with Grace had stayed, and their families had come north to join them. There were now a number of villages in the valley, and farms were springing up in the fertile lands between the mountains and the Winter Wood—lands that had lain fallow for centuries.

There had been a brief time when Grace had considered relocating her court to the old capital of Tir-Anon, some thirty leagues to the south; that was where the kings and queen of Malachor had dwelled of old. She had journeyed there the autumn after the war, along with Falken and Melia, but they had found little. Tir-Anon had been utterly destroyed in the fall of Malachor seven hundred years ago. There was nothing save heaps of rubble overgrown with groves of *valsindar* and *sintaren*. They had returned to Gravenfist sober, and determined to make it their home.

"There you are, Your Majesty," Sir Tarus said, rushing up as Grace brought Shandis to a halt before the main keep. His face was nearly as red as his beard.

"So it appears," she said. "Thanks to a little help from Master Larad, Aldeth here was able to ferret me out."

She glanced to her left, but where the spy had ridden a moment ago there was now only empty air. A sigh escaped her. "I wish I could disappear like that."

Tarus clucked his tongue. "Queens don't get to disappear, Your Majesty."

"And why is that?"

"Because they must be ever available to their counselors, vassals, and subjects, of course."

She allowed him to help her down from her horse. "That's exactly why I wish I could vanish sometimes."

"None of that now, Your Majesty," Tarus said, giving her a stern look. "There's work to be done."

Grace sighed. This was part of an ongoing battle with Sir Tarus. She had made him her seneschal three years ago (after Melia gently pointed out that Grace didn't have to try to run the kingdom all by herself), and in the time since Tarus had taken the job seriously. Too seriously, she sometimes thought. He worked at all hours of the day and night, and he hardly seemed to smile anymore. Where was the dashing young knight with the ready grin she had first met in the forests of western Calavan?

He's still in there, Grace. Just older, like each of us.

A groom came to take Shandis to the stables, and Tarus walked with Grace to the main keep.

"Well," she said as they approached the doors of the great hall, "were you going to tell me what was so urgent it couldn't wait? Or are you simply going to spring it on me and see if I faint from shock?"

"Now that you mention it, I was sort of favoring the latter option," Tarus said. "Only then I reconsidered," the seneschal hastily added when she gave him a piercing glance.

However, even after he told her what had transpired, Grace still felt a keen jolt of surprise as she stepped into the great hall and saw the two men standing before the dais. One she did not recognize at all. He was a younger man, short but well built, dark-haired, and clad in a gray tunic. His face was squarely handsome, but softened by a sensuous mouth. He held a staff carved with runes.

The other man she did recognize, but only after careful consideration. When she first met him, at the Council of Kings in Calavere, he had been a corpulent man dressed in ostentatious clothes, his gaze haughty, his thick fingers laden with rings.

The years had aged him greatly. He was rail-thin now, and wore a simple black tunic and no jewelry. His bulbous nose was still ruddy—a testament to a past penchant for too much wine—

but his close-set eyes were clear and sober. He and his companion knelt as she entered.

"Rise, Lord Olstin of Brelegond, please," she said when she managed to find the breath to speak. "You are welcome in Malachor."

A sardonic smile played across his lip, though the expression was self-deprecating now rather than arrogant as it once had been. "You are kind, Your Majesty. Kinder than you have either right or reason to be. Though it has been nearly five years, I have not forgotten how uncivilly I treated you at the Council of Kings, and I warrant you have not forgotten either."

Grace winced, for it was true. She remembered well how Olstin had wheedled and cajoled, attempting to play her against King Boreas, and then—after she ordered him to step away from a serving maid he had slapped—had threatened her.

"You didn't know at the time I was a queen, Lord Olstin." She couldn't help a small laugh. "Of course, I didn't know I was a queen, either. So let's call it even, shall we?"

"I don't think so, Your Majesty," Olstin said, approaching her. "You see, we are not even at all."

Tarus cast Grace a sharp look, but she gave her head a small shake. "And why is that, Lord Olstin?"

"Because Brelegond owes you something, Your Majesty. It owes you its gratitude, and its allegiance."

Grace was too astonished by these words to reply, but Sir Tarus took her arm, led her to the chair atop the dais (she refused to call it a throne), and sat her down. Additional chairs were placed for the guests on the step below Grace, and Tarus found a servant to bring them all wine, though Olstin chose water instead. Gradually, Grace's shock was replaced by fascination as she listened to Olstin speak. Little news had come from the Dominion of Brelegond these last three years. It was farthest of all the seven Dominions from Malachor, and during the war it had been sorely damaged by the Onyx Knights.

The rebuilding had been slow, according to Olstin, but over time much had been accomplished. King Lysandir, who had been chained in the dungeon beneath Borelga after Brelegond fell to the Onyx Knights, had never truly recovered from his ordeal, and had passed away last winter. His niece, Eselde, had been crowned queen, and under her rule Brelegond had regained its former strength; indeed, it was stronger than it had been before the war.

"The gods know we were a foolish people, ruled by a foolish, if not unkind, man," Olstin said. "We were the youngest of the Dominions, and so became caught up in fostering the appearance of prosperity and importance, rather than doing anything to truly *be* prosperous or important. However, young as she is, Eselde is quite practical. Even before her uncle died she was ruling in all but name, and she has accomplished much in a short time."

"I'm glad," Grace said, and she meant it. "But now, Lord Olstin, you must tell me what you need."

Olstin laughed, wagging a finger at her. "No, Your Majesty, this rudeness I will once again do you: You must not dare to offer Brelegond help, at least not now. Much news has come to us these last years, and we are quite aware of all you have done. You have helped Brelegond, and all the Dominions, quite enough. Now it is our turn. My queen knows Brelegond is the last of the Dominions to offer allegiance to you as High Queen. We hope we shall not be the least."

Again Grace found herself speechless as Olstin described Queen Eselde's offer of gold, resources, and men to help in the restoration of Malachor. Grace's first instinct was to decline; Brelegond needed these things for its own rebuilding. However, a meaningful look from Tarus reminded her that Malachor's coffers were rather empty at the moment, and there was much work yet to be done. So she accepted, with no qualms at expressing the humbleness she felt.

"I have one other thing to offer you," Olstin said when the business had been concluded. He gestured to the young man who had listened silently and intently throughout their conversation. "This is my nephew Alfin. For many years, out of ignorance, we forbade our young people who displayed a talent for runes or witchcraft to pursue such arts. Perhaps, if we had chosen differently, we might have stood against the Onyx Knights. Regardless, we are changing that now. Alfin has learned much on his own, but he would join your new order of Runelords, Your Majesty, if you would accept him." He glanced at the young man fondly. "I am partial, of course, but he has talent I think."

"I believe that remains to be seen, uncle," the young man said, blushing. The combination of humility, fine looks, and obvious intelligence made for a fetching combination that was not lost on Grace. Or on Sir Tarus by the way the knight gazed at the other man.

"I think he looks very promising, Your Majesty," Sir Tarus said and, for the first time in a long time, smiled.

"Indeed," Grace said. She was still no expert on the subject of human feelings—she never would be—but she had learned enough to see that Alfin returned Tarus's smile with far more than polite interest.

"Come," Tarus said to the would-be Runelord. "I'll take you to meet Master Larad."

After the two men left, Olstin confessed his weariness from traveling, and as he pushed himself up from his chair Grace noticed the scars on his wrists; King Lysandir was not the only one who had been hung in a dungeon by the Onyx Knights. She had a servant show Olstin to a chamber upstairs, then found herself alone in the great hall.

Grace was often by herself these days. Being a queen was a lonelier job than she had imagined. But that was all right. She hadn't become a doctor on Earth to make friends, and she hadn't become a queen to make them, either. Although her job now wasn't putting broken people back together, but broken kingdoms.

She glanced up. Hanging above her chair, near Durge's Embarran greatsword and the shards of Fellring, was a banner emblazoned with a silver tower. When she first saw such an emblem, on the shield of the Onyx Knights, the tower had been set against a black background, and above it had been a red crown. However, this banner was as blue as the sea, and above the tower flew the white shapes of three gulls.

The banner had been a gift from Ulrieth, the Lord of Eversea. Two years ago, in this very hall, Grace and Ulrieth had signed a treaty, forging a peace between the lands of Malachor and Eversea. The treaty proclaimed that both kingdoms were equal and independent, that one should never seek to rule over the other, and also that should one face a threat, then the other would come to its ally's aid.

It had been a triumphant day. Talking with Ulrieth, Grace knew that the dark spell the Runelord Kelephon had cast over Eversea was finally broken. The order of the Onyx Knights—who had slain Grace's parents and caused so much strife in Eredane, Embarr, and Brelegond—had been disbanded.

"We are a people of peace now," Ulrieth had said. He was a white-bearded man who carried much sorrow—and much wisdom—on his brow. "We have no more taste for war. And we remember from whence we came."

He had shaken Grace's hand and, after seven hundred years, Malachor was finally whole again. For after Malachor fell, some of its people had fled to the far west of Falengarth, founding the kingdom of Eversea. Many others went south, forging the seven Dominions. Grace was Mistress of the Dominions, and so with this treaty all the descendants of Malachor were united once again.

The signing of the treaty almost hadn't happened, though, because Grace had had a difficult time coming up with twelve nobles to be her witnesses. Her kingdom was so new it didn't have nobles. Before the signing, she had hastily made earls and countesses, barons and baronesses, of those she relied on most: Tarus, the Spiders Aldeth and Samatha, the witch Lursa, Master Graedin (much to his delight), Master Larad (much to his chagrin), and of course Falken and Melia. Both the bard and lady had protested, of course—until Grace lamented she wouldn't have enough nobles to sign the treaty, at which point the two had relented to becoming the count and countess of Arsinda, a fiefdom between Gravenfist and Tir-Anon that these days was thickly overgrown with forest.

In addition to her own homegrown nobles, King Vedarr of Embarr had attended the ceremony; it had been good to see the grizzled old knight—now the ruler of Embarr—who had helped to defend Gravenfist so staunchly. King Kylar of Galt had also come. The king no longer looked so young, and while he still stuttered, people had stopped calling him Kylar the Unlucky. Rather, he was called Kylar the Rock, for during the war, and against overwhelming odds, he had held back the Onyx Knights who had tried to press into Galt from Eredane.

The new king of Eredane was also at the signing. His name was Evren, and he was a distant cousin of former Queen Eminda, who had perished at the Council of Kings. It had been hard for Eredane to find an heir to its throne, for the Onyx Knights had murdered virtually all in the royal line. However, the people of Eredane seemed to have done well in rallying behind Evren, for he was a thoughtful, well-spoken man.

Grace had believed all was in order, but two days before the signing she found she was still one noble short. She had counted herself among the twelve needed to witness the document, only to discover Ulrieth had twelve in addition to himself. Luckily, at the last moment, she realized there was one more noble she could call upon. A messenger was sent with the fastest horse in Malachor down the Queen's Way to the petty kingdom of Kelcior. Two days later, just minutes before the treaty signing, he arrived in all his bluster and swagger. He had burst through the doors of the great hall, and the first words out of his mouth were—

"Hello there, Queenie!"

Grace gasped as the booming voice shocked her out of her reverie, though for a dazed moment she wondered if he wasn't a figment of her memory. But no, his burly figure couldn't be anything but real. After three years of growth—and with the help of a witch's potion, some rumored—his red beard was bushier than ever. And, if it was possible, he seemed even larger than the last time she had seen him.

His laughter rang off the stones as he strode through the doors of the hall to the dais. Something limp was slung over his massive shoulders, and only as he tossed it on the floor did she realize it was a stag.

"You look sad, Queenie," King Kel thundered, "but I know something that will cheer you up." He gave her a wink and rested his boot on the dead stag. "Let's have a feast!"

10.

A visit from King Kel always raised her spirits, and by the time Grace stepped into the great hall that night, she found both the hall and her mood much transformed. Trestle tables had been pulled out to offer plenty of places to sit, and the high table now commanded the dais. Torches infused the air with smoky light, and the music of drone, lute, and pipe drifted down from the gallery, played by unseen minstrels.

"Let's dance, Queenie!" Kel said, pouncing on her the moment she passed through the doors.

Grace's first instinct was to curl up and play dead, as dancing with King Kel was much like getting mauled by a bear. However, she was too slow, and he grabbed her hands, proceeding to toss her about in a series of wild motions that could be termed *dancing* only by a person of uncommonly generous spirit.

Fortunately, before the centrifugal force gave her an aneurysm, servants entered bearing goblets of wine. Kel liked drinking better than dancing, and the only thing he liked better than drinking was eating, and the servants had brought in trays laden with food as well. The gigantic man let Grace go in the middle of a spin and stalked toward the servants; they backed away like small, frightened animals.

Once she came to a halt, Grace found herself near the dais. Gentle hands helped her up the steps and sat her down in her chair at the center of the table.

"Thank you, Falken," she said, giving the bard a grateful smile.

"Here, dear," Melia said, handing her a glass of wine. "This should help you forget the ordeal."

Grace drank, and after a few sips the room's spinning slowed to a leisurely roll.

"So did he ask you to marry him again?" Falken inquired.

Grace sighed and nodded. Kel asked her to marry him every time he visited.

"I'm big, you're pretty, and we're both royalty," he would say. "What match could be better?"

Melia patted her hand. "Don't worry, dear. I'm sure Sir Tarus will keep him away from you."

"Actually," Falken said, "I think Kel could stuff Sir Tarus in his pocket and use him as a handkerchief."

Grace laughed. "It's all right. I can handle King Kel." After all, she had faced far greater perils. Besides, Kel was an important ally now that the seven Dominions had all agreed Kelcior was to be recognized as a sovereign kingdom. And while she had no intention of ever accepting them, she thought Kel's proposals were sweet. After all, it wasn't as if other men were beating a path to her door.

You know that's not true, Grace, she chided herself. *King Evren of Eredane would marry you in a heartbeat to gain a favorable alliance.*

But that wasn't what Grace had meant.

"Is something wrong, dear?" Melia said, concern in her golden eyes.

"I'm fine," Grace said, and she tried to produce a smile, but it came out more as a grimace, so she took a sip of wine to conceal the expression. What was wrong with her lately? Ever since spring a gloom had kept stealing over her, even though she had every reason to be happy.

Two of those reasons were sitting next to her now. Grace didn't know what she would have done without Falken's and Melia's advice these last years, or their company. She had never known her parents, but she often let herself imagine they had been like the bard and the lady.

Falken's hair was more silver than black these days. In the time after the war it had become clear to all of them that the bard—who had lived for over seven hundred years—was aging. Though they hadn't realized it at first that summer in Perridon, the curse of eternal life Dakarreth had cast on Falken was broken when the Necromancer perished. Falken was mortal again.

However, he was still the same Falken, and if he looked more wolfish than ever, he still had the same ringing laugh, and the same magical silver hand. Their work done at last—Malachor avenged, and the Necromancers destroyed—he and Melia had finally been able to acknowledge the love they had borne one another for centuries. They had wed two years ago, and they intended to live out the rest of their days here in Malachor.

The rest of *his* days, at least. For Melia was the last of the nine New Gods who descended to Eldh to work against the Necromancers, and though a goddess no longer, she was still immortal. What would happen to her once he was gone—once all of them were gone?

"Are you certain you're well, dear?" Melia said. Falken had gone to fetch them more wine.

Grace hesitated, then decided to tell the truth. "I was just thinking about you and Falken, about how you're . . . and one day he'll . . ." She couldn't bring herself to speak the words.

Melia did. "How one day he'll die, you mean?" She let her gaze follow after the bard, her expression full of love. "But that's no reason to be sad, dear. That time is long off yet. Besides, we all must die one day."

She brushed a hand through her hair, and Grace saw it for the first time: a streak of white marked Melia's blue-black hair. All at once the lady's words struck Grace. *We all must die one day. . . .*

She clutched a hand to her mouth, unable to stifle a gasp.

Melia studied her, then nodded.

"How?" Grace finally managed to speak.

"I chose mortality when we were married," Melia said.

"You . . . you can do that?"

"I can, and I did. It was the one power left to me. And nor can the decision be reversed."

"Does he know?"

"Not yet. But he will in time." She touched Grace's arm. "Please, Ralena. Let me be the one to tell him."

"To tell who what?" Falken said, setting down three goblets and sitting next to the two women.

Grace drew in a deep breath. "To tell you how much we love you," she said, and kissed his cheek.

The feast continued with much cheer. Falken and Melia danced until Kel cut in and began tossing the small, amber-eyed lady about as if he were intent on juggling her, much to both her and Falken's mirth. Lord Olstin made a brief appearance and paid his respects to Grace, though he ate little and drank nothing, and soon retired. His nephew, Alfin, stayed a good deal longer, though Grace had little opportunity to speak with him, as Tarus kept the young Runelord largely to himself throughout the evening. Grace wondered if they had made it to see Larad yet.

Speaking of Master Larad, where was the Runelord? Of all her advisors, he had in many ways become her most valuable. Ever since they first met him, Larad had done what he believed was right regardless of what others wished, and regardless of the consequences to himself. While that trait—and his acerbic nature—made him difficult to endure at times, she always considered his point of view seriously.

At last she gave up searching the hall for Larad. However, she did come upon Lursa. The Embarran witch was married now; her handsome warrior had finally won that battle—or perhaps it was the other way around, for he had traded his sword for a plowshare. After her wedding, Lursa had become Matron of the witch's coven at Gravenfist Keep. Grace wove with the coven when time allowed, but since that was almost never these days, she always enjoyed hearing from Lursa what patterns they had been fashioning.

Lately the witches had been working on spells to encourage crops to grow faster and bear more fruit. However, they had been having considerable trouble completing the enchantment. There was a gap in their weaving that would not be soon mended, for last winter the spry old witch Senrael had passed from the pattern of life into the warp and weave of memory. While another witch deemed old and wise enough had donned the shawl of Crone, Senrael was sorely missed.

"May I take my leave, Your Majesty?" Lursa said, her intelligent gaze straying across the hall. "I see Master Graedin, and I want to speak to him. Earlier this year, it seemed I was making progress in rune magic. Once I spoke the rune of fire, and I swear I made a candle flicker. But now I only seem to be getting worse. Lately nothing happens at all when I try to speak a rune." She sighed. "I suppose it's hopeless to think I ever could."

Grace felt a note of concern. Lursa was usually brisk and cheerful, but her expression seemed dull now, even despondent.

"I'm sure Master Graedin will help you sort things out," Grace said, and granted the witch leave to go.

Lursa crossed the hall to where Graedin stood against the far wall. The young Runelord was as tall and gangly as ever, and a grin crossed his face as Lursa approached, though his smile soon faded as they spoke. No doubt Graedin would help Lursa with her problem. He had suspected there was a connection between rune magic and the magic of the Weirding well before it was revealed that Olrig, patron god of runes, and the witch's goddess Sia were one and the same—and were in fact simply two guises of the being known as the Worldsmith.

Except Olrig and Sia weren't the Worldsmith anymore. The world had been broken, and the fact that it had been remade exactly as it was before didn't change the fact that someone else was the Worldsmith now.

I miss you, Travis, Grace thought. *And Beltan, too.*

Sometimes when she thought of them her heart ached, just as her right arm did when she remembered standing before the Pale King. She missed them even more than she did Lirith or Aryn, for at least she could speak to the two witches from time to time, even if it was only across the threads of the Weirding.

Not that she had spoken to them often of late. Lirith was too far to the south for Grace to contact on her own; she could only do it with Aryn's help. And Aryn had been too busy in recent times for idle conversation. She was a queen now, not of one Dominion but two. Teravian was not only King Boreas's son, but Queen Ivalaine's as well. As Ivalaine had had no other heir, Teravian was now king of Toloria as well as of Calavan, and Aryn was queen of both realms.

They spent their time traveling between the two courts, and by all accounts had done much to earn the admiration and loyalty of their subjects in both Dominions. But their labors had prevented them from journeying to Gravenfist save once, and Grace doubted future visits were in the cards, given that Aryn was now expecting her first child. Still, it was enough to get occasional reports, and to know that despite their labors both Aryn and Teravian were happy, and these days very much in love.

However, as much as she cared for all her friends, it was to Travis her thoughts most often turned.

I want so badly to talk to you, Travis, Grace thought, gazing into her goblet of wine and wishing she had the power to see a vision in it as Lirith sometimes could, wishing she could get a glimpse of him. *I think you'd understand what I'm feeling better than I do.*

Only what was she feeling? It was so strange. There was a sorrow, yes. But there was something else: a tinge of nervous expectation. But what exactly was she expecting to happen?

For them to not need you anymore.

It was the dry doctor's voice that spoke in her mind, making its diagnosis. The thought startled her, but not so much for its suddenness as for how true it felt.

You did your part, Grace, you gave Malachor a second chance to be. But its people don't need a queen, not anymore. They've built this kingdom themselves. Why can't they rule it themselves?

Yes, it made sense. If Travis could create a world, then depart from it, why couldn't she do the same with a kingdom? She pressed a hand to her chest, feeling the rapid beating of her heart.

"Are you all right, Your Majesty?" spoke a sharp-edged voice.

Grace looked up from her wine to see Master Larad standing above her. He was clad in a twilight blue robe. His eyes glittered in a face that was made a fractured mosaic by a webwork of fine white scars.

She sighed. "Why does everyone keep asking me that tonight?"

He shrugged but said nothing. Larad never offered an answer unless he had a strong opinion.

"Did you speak to Alfin, the young man from Brelegond?" she said in hopes of changing the subject.

"Yes, for a few moments." Larad's expression soured. "Before Sir Tarus whisked him away. More confirmation will be needed, but I believe Alfin has significant talent."

Grace smiled. "So, is everything well in your new tower?"

She had ordered a tower to be raised on the south side of the keep for the use of Larad and the Runelords, and construction had just recently been completed. The tower included a chamber on its highest floor built to house the three Imsari, for it was the mission of the new Runelords to guard the Great Stones.

The tower also housed a runestone: a relic covered with writings of the Runelords of old, and which the new Runelords were actively studying. The runestone had been discovered beneath the keep last year, when the Embarran engineers performed an excavation in order to make some repairs to the foundations.

"It's not my tower, Your Majesty," Larad said, glowering. "It is yours. The Runelords dwell here at your pleasure."

"No," Grace said softly, tightening her right hand into a fist. "No, it's not up to me. This is your home."

Larad gave her a speculative look, but he did not respond to this statement. Instead he said, "I am sorry to disturb you during a time of merriment, Your Majesty, but I have made a discovery that I did not believe could wait."

Actually, Grace suspected Larad was not sorry at all to disturb her with important news, and that was one reason she appreciated him. "What is it?"

"There's something wrong with the runes."

"You mean there's something wrong with a specific rune you're trying to understand?"

He sat at the high table beside her, his dark eyes intent. "No, Your Majesty, I mean with all runes. I began to suspect something was amiss about a month ago. Some of my fellow Runelords were beginning to have difficulty speaking runes they had previously mastered. They would speak a runespell just as they had before, but only a feeble energy would result, or no energy at all. I sent a missive to the Gray Tower, hoping for advice from All-master Oragien, and last week I received his reply. It seems the same troubles have been plaguing the runespeakers there. Since then, I have performed many experiments, but only today were my misgivings proven beyond doubt."

"How?" Grace said, her throat tight.

Larad held out his hand. On it was a triangular lump of black stone. One side was rough, the other three smooth and incised with runes. "This is a piece of the runestone, the one that was discovered beneath the keep."

Shock coursed through Grace. "Why did you do it? Why did you speak the rune of breaking on the runestone?"

"I didn't, Your Majesty," Larad said with a rueful look. "This morning, one of the apprentices discovered this piece lying next to the runestone. It broke off on its own. And once I examined the runestone carefully, I saw many fine cracks that had not been there before."

"But you can bind it again," Grace said, glad the music drifting down from the gallery masked the rising pitch of her voice. "You can speak the rune of binding and fix it."

"So I thought, until I tried." Larad tightened his hand around the broken stone. "Despite all my efforts, I could not bind this piece back to the runestone."

That was impossible. Larad was a Runelord—a real Runelord, like Travis Wilder. Speaking the rune of binding should not have been beyond him. Only it was.

Grace recalled her earlier conversation with Lursa. "You should talk to the witches. They've been having difficulty weaving a new spell. Maybe it's not just rune magic that's being affected."

Larad raised an eyebrow. "If so, that is dark news indeed. I will speak to the witches. Perhaps they have sensed something I have not."

And I'll speak to some witches as well, Grace added to herself, resolved to ask Aryn and Lirith about it the next time they contacted her.

Larad begged his leave, and once the Runelord was gone Grace was no longer in the mood for revelry. She bid Melia and Falken and Kel good night, putting on a cheerful face. Even if Master Larad was right—and Grace had no doubt he was—there was no use spoiling the revel for everyone else until they knew more.

She left the great hall, ascended a spiral staircase, and started down the corridor that led to her chamber. The passage was dim, illuminated by only a scant collection of oil lamps, and as she rounded a corner she did not see the servingwoman until she collided with her. The old woman let out a grunt, and something fell to the floor.

"I'm sorry," Grace said, stumbling back. "I didn't see you there."

The other wore a shapeless gray dress and oversized bonnet.

She bowed low and muttered fervently, no doubt making an apology, though Grace couldn't understand a word of it.

"It's all right," Grace said. "Really, it was my fault."

However, the old woman kept ducking her head.

So much for the whole not terrifying the servants thing, Grace thought with a sigh. She glanced down and saw that the object the old woman had dropped had rolled to a stop next to her feet. It was a ball of yarn. Grace bent to pick it up.

"Oh!" she said.

Carefully, she pulled the needle from the tip of her finger. It had been sticking out of the ball of yarn, but she hadn't seen it in the dim light.

"Well, I suppose that evens the score," she said with a wry smile.

Grace stuck the needle back into the ball of yarn, then held the ball out. The old woman accepted it in a wrinkled hand. She muttered something unintelligible—still not looking up—then shuffled away down the corridor, her ashen dress blending with the gloom. Grace shrugged, sucked on her bleeding finger, and headed to her chamber.

Two men-at-arms stood outside the door. Though it irked her they were always stationed there, they were one of the concessions she had made to Sir Tarus. The men-at-arms saluted as she approached. Grace gave them a self-conscious nod in return—she still had no idea how she was supposed to greet them, if at all—then slipped into her room and pressed the door shut behind her, sighing at the blissful silence. Maybe the men-at-arms weren't such a bad idea after all. They could keep King Kel from barging in at odd hours and asking her to dance.

Bone-tired, she shucked off her woolen dress and shrugged on a nightgown, wincing as she did. Though the pain in her right arm never entirely went away, most of the time it was a dull, bearable ache. Tonight, however, despite all the wine she had drunk, it throbbed fiercely.

She held her arm to her chest, gazing at the lone candle burning on the sideboard. Its flame blazed hotly, just like his eyes had, burning into her as he raised his scepter, ready to smite her down. Only at the last moment the sky had broken, and as he looked up she had thrust the sword Fellring through a chink in his armor, up into his chest, cleaving the Pale King's enchanted iron heart in two.

Fellring had shattered in the act, and Grace's sword arm had been numb and lifeless for days afterward. Only slowly, over the course of many months, had she regained the use of it, and she knew it would never be the same again. But none of them were; the battles they had fought had changed them forever, and maybe it was all right to have some scars. That way they would never forget what they had done.

Grace blew out the candle and climbed into bed.

It wasn't long before a dream took her, and an hour later she sat up, staring into the dark, her hair tangled with sweat. She clutched the bedclothes, willing her breathing to slow.

It was only a dream, Grace, she told herself, but it was hard to hear her own thoughts over the pounding in her ears.

It had been a wedding. The dream was so vivid, she could almost see them still: a king dressed all in white, and a queen clad in black. A radiance emanated from him, and he was handsome beyond all other men; a halo of light adorned his tawny head like a crown. She was like night to his day: dark of hair and eye and skin, a mysterious beauty wearing a gown woven of the stuff of shadows. They gazed at one another with a look of love. He took her dusky fingers in his pale hand as the priest—a commanding figure all in gray—spoke the rites of marriage.

Only before the priest could finish the words, a figure strode forward, a gigantic warrior. The people who had gathered to witness the marriage fled screaming, and the priest ran after them. The couple turned to face their foe. The warrior was neither light nor dark, solid nor transparent. He could be seen only by his jagged outlines, for where he was there was nothing at all, and he held a sword forged of nothingness in his hand.

You are the end of everything, the white king said.

The black queen shook her head. *No*, she said, her dark eyes full of sorrow. *He is the beginning of nothing.*

The warrior swung his empty sword, and both their heads, light and dark, fell to the ground, their bodies tumbling after.

That was when Grace woke. She climbed from the bed, lit the candle with a coal from the fire, and threw a shawl about her; despite the balmy night she was shivering.

Grace didn't usually place much stock in dreams, but once she had had dreams about Travis Wilder that had come true, and this dream had been unusually vivid, like those had been. Only what did it mean? She didn't recognize the light king or the dark queen, though in a way they made her think of Durge's alchemical books. She had paged through some of them when she packed up the knight's possessions a few months after he died. The books had been written in a kind of code and were rife with metaphorical tales about fiery men marrying watery ladies, resulting in the birth of new child elements with fantastical properties, such as the power to turn lead to gold, or to cause a man to live forever.

However, the king and queen in her dream hadn't created something new. They had been slain. Slain by . . . nothing. Grace had no idea what it meant, if it meant anything at all. Which it almost certainly didn't, she reminded herself. Dreams were simply the brain's janitors, cleaning out the day's synaptic garbage.

All the same, she knew rest would be impossible for the remainder of the night, and she felt trapped in the stuffy chamber. She needed to get out, to breathe some fresh air.

She padded to the door, weaving a quick spell about herself, so that the men-at-arms outside would detect her passing as no more than a fleeting shadow. It was a simple spell, but at first the threads of the Weirding seemed to slip through her fingers and tangle themselves in knots.

You're just half-asleep, Grace, that's all.

She concentrated, and after some effort the spell was complete. It unraveled after less than a minute, but by then she was already ascending a spiral staircase and was well out of sight of the men-at-arms. Getting back into the chamber was going to be tricky, but she could worry about that later.

Pushing through a door, Grace stepped onto the battlements atop the keep. The night was clear and moonless. A zephyr caught her hair, brushing it back from her face, and she breathed deeply, feeling the sweat and fear of her dream evaporate.

Grace approached the south side of the battlement and cast her gaze upward. The stars were brighter and far closer-seeming than those of Earth, as if Eldh's heavens were not so very distant. She searched for a single point of crimson among the thousands of cool silver, hoping to glimpse Tira's star. It wasn't the same as hugging the small, silent, flame-haired girl who had become a goddess, but seeing her star always made Grace feel a little closer to her.

However, there was no sign of Tira's star near the peaks of the mountains. Maybe the hour was later than Grace thought. She craned her neck, raising her gaze higher into the sky.

It felt as if an invisible anesthesia mask had been pressed to her face, filling her lungs with cold, paralyzing her. The wind snatched her shawl from her shoulders, and it fluttered away like a wraith in the gloom. In the center of the sky was a dark hole where no stars shone. The hole was larger than Eldh's large moon, its edges jagged like the warrior in her dream.

Only that was impossible. A circle of stars couldn't simply vanish. Something was simply covering them up—a cloud perhaps. She blinked; and then she did see something in the dark rift: a fiery spark. Was it Tira's star?

No. The spark grew brighter, closer, descending toward Grace. A new wind struck her face, hot and acrid, knocking her back a step. Vast, membranous wings unfurled like shadows, and the one spark resolved into two: a pair of blazing eyes. Even as Grace realized what it was, the dragon swooped down, alighting atop the battlement, its talons digging into solid stone as the keep groaned beneath its weight.

Grace knew she had to flee. She should run down the stairs and sound an alarm. Only then the dragon moved its sinuous neck, turning its wedge-shaped head toward her, and she could not move. So close was the thing that she could feel its dusty breath on her face as it spoke, and in that moment she realized she had met this creature once before.

"The end of all things draws nigh, Grace Beckett," the dragon Sfithrisir hissed. "And you and Travis Wilder must stop it."

11.

The dragon folded its wings against its sleek body; the stones of the keep shuddered under its weight. Four years ago, when they first encountered Sfithrisir in a high valley in the Fal Erenn, Grace had thought the dragon looked like an enormous, sooty swan. Now it seemed more like a vulture to her. Its featherless hide absorbed the starlight, and its eyes glowed like coals. The small, saurian head wove slowly at the end of a ropelike neck, and a constant hiss of steam escaped the bony hook of its beak.

Fear and smoke choked her. For some reason the reek made her think of the smell of burning books. Grace fought for breath and to keep her wits. She had to have both if she was going to survive.

"Answer . . . answer me this, and an answer you shall have," she said in a trembling voice, speaking the ancient greeting she had learned from Falken, and the proper way to address a dragon. "One secret for one secret in trade. Why have you—?"

"Mist and misery!" the dragon snorted, the words emanating from deep in its gullet. "There is no time for foolish rituals concocted by mortals whose bones have long ago turned to dust. I did not come here to barter with you for secrets, Blademender. The age for such petty games is over. Did you not hear what I spoke? The end of all things comes. Have you not seen the rift in the sky? Surely it has grown large enough that even your mortal eyes can see it now. And it will keep growing. Now it conceals the stars, but soon it will swallow them, and worlds as well. It will not cease until it has consumed everything there is to consume, until all that remains is nothing."

Grace gritted her teeth and did her best to look the dragon in the eyes, though matching the weaving of its head made her queasy. Sfithrisir wasn't lying about the rift; dragons could only speak truth—though that truth was always twisted to their own ends.

"I don't understand, Sfithrisir," she said, sticking to the truth as closely as she could, but formulating it carefully, like a dragon herself. "I thought the destruction of the world was what your kind craved." The dragons had existed long before the Worldsmith created Eldh, dwelling in the gray mists before time.

"The end of the world, yes! How I loathe this wretched creation." His talons raked the stones, cracking them. "It is a prison, binding us and everything in it. Blast the Worldsmith for making it."

Despite her fear, Grace managed a grim laugh. "Travis Wilder is the Worldsmith now."

"Do you think I do not know that, mortal?" The dragon ruffled its wings. "I am Sfithrisir, He Who Is Seen And Not Seen. In all of time, no one's hoard of secrets has been greater than mine. I know what Travis Wilder has done. Runebreaker he was. He destroyed the world just as I knew he would. Only then he betrayed us by making it anew. That I had not foreseen, and if I could, I would burn him to ashes for it."

Grace held a hand to her forehead. "If you're so mad at Travis for forging the world again, shouldn't you be happy about the rift in the sky?"

"You know nothing, mortal. Do you think this material thing you see before you is all that I am?"

The dragon sidled closer and the air about it rippled, distorting everything around it like images seen through crystal. It felt as if Grace's own body was stretching and contracting in impossible dimensions. The sensation was not painful, but wrenching and deeply *wrong*.

"You believe order gives power and purpose," the dragon said. "But you are mistaken. Order only limits, confines. In the chaos before this world existed, there was such freedom as you cannot possibly imagine. There were no limitations, no arbitrary rules to be obeyed. I would destroy this world, yes. I would return to the mayhem of before."

"Then why fight against the rift?"

Sfithrisir's wings spread out like smoky sails. "Because the rift discerns not between a world of stone and air and water and fire, or a world of formless mists! At the rift's borders, all of being ends—order and chaos alike. It is the annihilation of all existence, not only for this world, but for all those worlds that draw near to it."

A shard of understanding pierced Grace, freezing her heart and shattering her soul. She could comprehend destruction. A rock could be crushed to dust, a piece of wood burned to ash, a living organism sent back to the soil that gave it life. But in each case something—dust, ash, soil—remained. Travis had destroyed the world Eldh when he broke the First Rune, but even before he forged the world anew *something* had existed. He had told her about it: the gray, swirling mists of possibility.

But the rift was not like that. Inside it was neither light nor dark. It was a place without potential, without possibility. It was a vacuum, a field in which nothing existed, or could ever exist. In that moment, in the presence of Sfithrisir, Grace truly understood what the rift was. It was Pandora's box emptied of everything it had contained.

It was the end of hope.

Grace clutched her stomach. She was going to be ill. No human mind should try to comprehend what hers just had. But already the crystalline moment of understanding was passing, her mortal faculties too feeble to hold on to it.

"It's . . . it's like the demon below Tarras, isn't it?" she gasped. "The sorcerers had bound one of the *morndari*, and it wanted to consume everything in the city. It almost did."

"Wrong again, mortal. The spirits, the beings which the sorcerers call Those Who Thirst, come from a place which is like this world reflected in a mirror. It is the opposite of this creation in all ways, a place not of *being*, but of *unbeing*. Yet all the same, it is something; it exists. The rift will eradicate the *morndari* just like everything else."

Despair weighed upon Grace, pressing her down like a hundred blankets. The dragon's words rang in her mind. The world would cease to be. And those worlds which drew near it.

Earth, she said to herself. *He means Earth*. But the name hardly felt real, as if the world it signified was already gone, its lands, its cities, its people swallowed by the rift and replaced by nothing at all.

"How?" Grace said. "How can Travis and I do anything to stop it?"

"I am wise beyond all," Sfithrisir said, letting out a soft hiss of steam. "Yet even I do not know the answer to that question."

Sudden anger filled Grace. She clenched a fist and shook it at the dragon. "I don't believe you. You're supposed to know everything. Even Olrig had to steal the secret of the runes from you."

Sfithrisir's head bobbed in what seemed a shrug. "And can you truly steal knowledge, mortal? Is not the knowledge retained by the one it is stolen from even as the thief makes off with it?"

Grace's anger faded. Somehow the dragon's words made sense to her. Olrig stole the runes from the dragons, who had heard them spoken by the Worldsmith. But Olrig *was* the Worldsmith.

There have been countless Worldsmiths, Grace. Olrig or Sia or whoever the last Worldsmith is wasn't the first. The world before this one was destroyed, and afterward only the dragons remained. They've always been there, watching, listening, hoarding knowledge. Then Olrig learned the runes of creation from them, just like all the other Worldsmiths before him must have, and used the runes to make Eldh.

Which meant, much as the dragons loathed creation, they were part of its cycle. And that was why Sfithrisir had come to her. If the rift continued to grow, Eldh would never be created again. Or destroyed again.

"You don't know we can stop it," Grace said, looking up at the dragon, meeting its smoldering eyes. "If there's nothing in the rift, then your knowledge ends at its borders. There's no way you could possibly know that Travis and I have the power to stop it."

The dragon's wedge-shaped head ceased its constant movement. "Perhaps your mind is not so limited after all. No, I cannot see into the rift, and so I know not how it can be defeated. All the same, much as I loathe this creation, I know it must be saved, and that you and Travis Wilder have the power to do so. The knowledge of it is woven into the very fabric of this world, and I have read it there. I do not know how to close the rift. But this one thing I do know: Only the Last Rune can save this world."

"You mean the rune Eldh?"

"No," the dragon hissed, eyes sparking. "Eldh was the first

rune spoken at the forging of this world, and it was the last rune at the end of this world. But what will be spoken at the end of all being, of all worlds? Even I do not know the rune for that."

The dragon uncoiled its long neck, stretching its head toward the sky, spreading its wings. Red light tinged the horizon. Dawn was coming. The dragon beat its wings. Its talons left the stones of the battlement.

"Wait!" Grace shouted over the roar of the wind, reaching a hand upward. "How can I find out what the Last Rune is?"

"Seek the one who destroyed this world." Sfithrisir rose upward in a cloud of smoke. "He will come in search of it."

The creature beat its gigantic wings, and Grace was knocked back by the blast. By the time she looked up, the dragon was a red spark in the gray sky. The spark winked out and was gone.

Footsteps sounded behind her, and Grace turned to see Sir Tarus along with the Spiders Aldeth and Samatha running toward her across the battlement.

"Your Majesty!" Tarus said breathlessly as they reached her. "Are you injured? By all the Seven, that was a sight I never dreamed I would see in my life. Are you well? Did it harm you?"

She was so dazed she could only shake her head.

Samatha gripped a bow, aiming an arrow at the sky, then swore. "It's gone. I can't see it anymore."

"It's not as if an arrow would have done you any good against a dragon," Aldeth said with a snort.

Samatha lowered the bow and glared at him, the expression making her face even more weasel-like. "And how would you know? Have you ever met a dragon before?"

"No," Aldeth said. He looked at Grace, his gray eyes solemn. "But Her Majesty has."

Grace gazed up at the sky. It was getting lighter. The stars had faded, and she could no longer see the rift. Only it was still there. And it was growing.

"What is it, Your Majesty?" Tarus said, touching her arm. "Are you certain you are not harmed?"

"I'm fine, Sir Tarus. Let's go downstairs. I need to talk to Melia and Falken at once."

However, it was Aryn and Lirith she spoke to first.

Their voices came to her across the Weirding just as the sun crested the summits of the southern mountains. She was in her chamber, hastily donning a gown so she could go downstairs, when Aryn's voice spoke to her as clearly as if the blue-eyed witch had been in the chamber.

Grace, can you hear me?

She gripped the back of a chair, gasping in surprise and delight.

Aryn, yes, it's me. I can hear you just fine.

Happiness hummed across the threads of the Weirding, and love. But there was more. A sense of urgency, and something else. Before Grace could ask about it, another voice spoke—deeper, smokier.

Sister, it is so good to be with you again, even if only over the web of the Weirding.

Despite all that had happened, Grace couldn't help smiling. "Lirith," she murmured aloud. Then, in her mind, *How is Sareth? And little Taneth? And your al-Mama?*

Very well, though given to fussing a bit.

Which one do you mean?

All three of them, I confess, Lirith said, her laughter like chimes in Grace's mind. *But I departed the south several weeks ago. Taneth and I are in Calavere now, with Aryn and Teravian. They're both doing well, and Aryn looks beautiful.*

No, I look large, came Aryn's reply. *I don't think I'm ever going to have this baby. I'm just going to keep getting more enormous. Soon I won't be able to fit in the castle at all, and Teravian will have no choice but to erect a gigantic tent for me in a field.*

Grace could imagine Lirith pressing dark, slender hands against Aryn's belly. *Do not believe her, Grace. The baby is healthy and will come very soon. And I can see in Teravian's eyes every time he looks at her that he has never found his queen more lovely.*

Grace didn't doubt it. She sighed, wishing she could be there with the two witches and spend all day laughing and talking about such simple joys. Only . . .

What is it, Grace? Aryn said. *Something is wrong, isn't it? Lirith was certain of it when she woke this morning.*

Grace gripped the chair. *Have you had a vision, Lirith?*

No, I haven't. And that's what's so strange. I haven't had a vision in months. Or at least . . .

At least what?

She could sense Lirith struggling for words. *I suppose I have had visions. Or what feels like a vision of the Sight to me. The same queer feeling comes over me, and my gaze goes distant, or so Sareth tells me, and I have the usual headache when the spell passes. Only it's as if the magic is broken somehow. I never see anything with the Sight anymore. Instead, I see nothing. Nothing at all.*

A coldness came over Grace, and she sank into the chair. *Your magic isn't broken, Lirith.*

She told them everything, sending words, thoughts, and feelings over the Weirding, so that in moments they knew all that had happened. *I think you did have a vision, Lirith. If Sfithrisir is right, if the rift keeps growing, then that's all there will be in the future: nothing. Just as you saw.*

She could feel both Aryn and Lirith recoil in horror. However, neither had seen the rift, nor had they heard of anyone who had. That gave Grace a small amount of hope. The rift must only be visible in the far north. That meant it was still small. And that meant there was still time to do something. At least, she had to believe that.

Do you think the rift has something to do with what's happening to rune magic? Lirith said.

Grace curled up in the chair, hugging her legs to her chest. *I suppose it's too much to believe it's a coincidence. And it's not just the Runelords. Lately, the witches here have been struggling with weaving spells.*

That is troubling news, came Aryn's reply. *I confess, it was more difficult than usual to reach you over the Weirding. Were it not for Lirith's aid, I'm not sure I would have succeeded.*

So magic was being affected in the south, not just the north. That was troubling news.

I have to go, Grace said reluctantly. *I have to talk to Melia and Falken about what we're going to do.*

Wait, Grace, Lirith said, and something in her voice made Grace sit up straight in the chair. *We have news ourselves. Such strange news . . .*

Grace stared, her body going numb, as she listened to Lirith speak of the letter she had received from Sareth just last night, brought to Calavere by a rider from the south. After three thousand years, Morindu the Dark, lost city of sorcerers, had been found. But it was not so much the news that stunned Grace as the name of the dervish who had brought this knowledge to the Mournish.

Grace, I'm getting tired, Aryn said when Lirith finished. *I know there's so much to talk about, but I can't hold on to this thread any longer. It keeps slipping through my fingers. We'll have to talk again later.*

"No, wait!" Grace cried out, standing. "Please don't go!" But their threads had already slipped away.

She moved to the window, gazing outside, letting the morning sun fall on her face. A hawk wheeled against the flawless blue sky.

"How?" she murmured, her hand creeping up her chest, pressing against her heart. "How did you get here, Hadrian?"

That was a question that would have to wait. However, this news changed everything. Grace no longer needed Melia and Falken to help her decide what to do. She already knew.

Seek the one who destroyed this world, the dragon had said. *He will come in search of it. . . .*

Travis would help her find the Last Rune—the rune that had the power to stop the rift.

And now she knew where she would find Travis.

Grace turned from the window, opened the door, and went downstairs to tell Melia and Falken that she was leaving Malachor.

12.

Vani and Beltan were already moving toward the back of the flat before the sound of falling glass ceased. The blond man paused to grab his sword from the wall above the sofa. Its broad blade gleamed, a decoration no longer.

"Travis," he said gruffly, "you and Deirdre stay in here."

Travis gave a wordless nod, then the knight and the *T'gol* vanished into the darkened hallway. His heart raced, but all it would take was a single spell cast by a sorcerer and its beating would stop forever.

He bent down on one knee. "Come here, Nim."

The girl walked to him, her gold-flecked eyes solemn, and pressed a small hand against his cheek. "You shouldn't be afraid. Mother always sends the gold men away, and this time she has my father Beltan to help her. He's very strong, you know."

Despite his fear, Travis couldn't help smiling. "Yes, he is." He scooped the girl into his arms, amazed at how light she was, and stood. Deirdre was frantically dialing a number on her cell phone.

"What are you doing?" Travis whispered.

She held the phone to her ear and ran a hand through her shaggy red-black hair. "Calling for backup."

Holding Nim, Travis took a step toward the hallway. He couldn't see Beltan and Vani anymore; they must have slipped into the bedroom. There was no sound now. What was happening in there?

By the hand of Olrig, why don't you go find out for yourself? Jack Graystone's voice spoke in his mind. *You're a Runelord, Travis. You can take out a mere sorcerer. You've done it before.*

Yes, he had slain a sorcerer before, but not with rune magic. It had been in Castle City, in the year 1883, when he had finally come face-to-face with the Scirathi who had followed them through the gate. A drop of blood from the scarab had entered Travis's veins, and that blood of power had allowed him to turn the death spell back on the Scirathi, slaying him.

That's right, I quite forgot, Jack's voice spoke excitedly in his mind. *Runes won't be much help on this world without the Great Stones to lend them some punch. But you're a sorcerer now yourself, and a fine one at that. You have nothing to fear from them, my boy.*

Travis was quite certain Jack was wrong about that. All the same, he started toward the kitchen to get a knife.

Behind him, Deirdre swore softly. Travis halted and turned around. "What's the matter?"

She lowered the cell phone. "My partner, Anders, wasn't home. I was leaving a message on his machine, only then there was a burst of static and the phone went dead."

Nim tightened her arms around Travis's neck. "The air feels funny," she said. "It's all tickly."

Travis tilted his head back and shut his eyes. He didn't know how she had sensed it, but Nim was right. Power crackled on the air.

His eyes snapped open. "Deirdre, get away from the—"

The front door of the flat burst open in a spray of wood.

Deirdre stumbled to her knees under the force of the blast, the cell phone flying out of her hands. Travis hugged Nim to him. In the doorway stood a figure clad in black, a serene gold face nestled into the cowl of its robe. Before Travis could think, the sorcerer raised a hand, stretching its fingers toward him.

Nim screamed, and Travis felt his heart lurch in his chest.

"*Meleq!*" he shouted.

The rune was weak—weaker than he would have expected even here on Earth—but it was enough to lift a chunk of wood from the floor and fling it at the sorcerer. The blow was far too feeble to cause damage, but on instinct the sorcerer moved his hand to bat the chunk of wood aside. Travis felt his heart resume its rapid cadence.

"*Sinfath!*"

A sick feeling came over him, just as when he had tried to bind the broken plate and failed. The sorcerer stepped through the door. Travis swallowed the bile in his throat.

"*Sinfath!*" he shouted again.

This time it worked, though again the rune was pitifully weak. All the same, a foggy patch of gloom precipitated out of thin air around the sorcerer. It would obscure his vision, but only for a moment.

"Come on," he croaked, grabbing Deirdre's hand and hauling her to her feet. Clutching Nim to his chest, Travis ran toward the hallway, Deirdre stumbling on his heels.

They were only halfway across the living room when the windows shattered, knives of glass slicing the curtains to shreds. Black gloves parted the tatters of cloth, and a second figure hopped down from the windowsill, robe fluttering like shadowy wings as it alighted on the floor.

Travis stopped short, and Deirdre crashed into him. He shot a glance over his shoulder in time to see the last effects of his runespell dissipate. The first sorcerer stalked toward them, while the second positioned himself in front of the entrance to the hallway, blocking their egress.

"What do we do?" Deirdre hissed, grabbing his arm.

"Nothing," he said.

Behind the second sorcerer, the air in the hallway rippled, like the surface of a pool disturbed by a falling stone. Travis's lips pulled back from his teeth in a feral grin, and the Scirathi tilted his gold mask to one side in what seemed a quizzical expression.

"You forgot something," Travis said.

The dim air of the hallway condensed in on itself, solidifying into a thing of sleek fury. The Scirathi started to turn, but he was too slow. A fist lashed out, striking him in the face. There was a bright flash of gold, and the sorcerer screamed. He groped with trembling fingers, touching the scarred ruin of what had once been his face. His gold mask clattered to the floor across the room.

For eons, the Scirathi had poured all their will and energy into the forging of the golden masks. The masks channeled their magic, focused it, granting a sorcerer abilities that otherwise would lay beyond his skill. Yet there was a price. Over time, the Scirathi had become dependent on the masks, and so without the devices they were powerless.

The sorcerer started to stumble toward the mask, but Vani landed soundlessly next to him. She laid her hands on either side of his head and made a motion so gentle it seemed a caress. There was a popping sound, and the sorcerer slumped to the floor.

Beltan jumped over the corpse, sword before him.

"Travis," he growled. "Duck."

Travis knew not to question. He grabbed Deirdre, pulling her to the floor along with Nim, and rolled to one side. He looked up in time to see the remaining sorcerer reach a hand toward Beltan's chest to cast a death spell. However, the blond man's sword was already moving. The Scirathi's hand flew off, hitting the floor with a thud. A hiss escaped the mouth slit of the sorcerer's mask, and he clutched the stump of his wrist to his chest. Beltan pulled his sword back, preparing a killing blow.

"No, Beltan," Travis said, the words sharp. "Wait."

Beltan gave him a puzzled look, but he did as Travis asked. Travis set Nim on the floor next to Deirdre and stood. The sorcerer let out another venomous hiss, reaching toward Travis's chest. Only his hand was gone. Blood rained from the stump.

The red fluid vanished before it touched the floor.

Travis could hear it now: a buzzing noise, growing louder. The sorcerer jerked his gold face upward. Yes, he heard, too.

"You called them to you with your spell," Travis said softly. "Now they're coming."

The sorcerer frantically clutched the wounded stump of his wrist, trying to staunch the flow of blood with his robe.

It was no use. They howled in through the window like a swarm of angry insects. Travis knew they would be invisible to the eyes of the others, but he could see them as tiny motes whirling on the air: sparks of blackness rather than light. Travis knelt and shielded Nim's eyes with a hand.

A part of him watched with disinterested fascination. He had always wondered if the *morndari* existed on this world. But of course they had to; otherwise the magic of the sorcerers would not work here. The spirits had passed through the crack Travis had opened between the worlds in 1883, just like the power of rune magic.

Only just like rune magic, the *morndari* were far weaker here on Earth. They should have consumed the sorcerer's blood swiftly, granting him a quick, if not painless, end.

Instead it was slow. Horribly slow. He waved his remaining hand in frantic motions, as if he could beat them away, though that was impossible, for they had no substance, no form. They swarmed around the stump of his hand like bees around a flower dripping nectar, consuming the blood that poured from it. Then, hungry for more, they passed through the wound into his veins. He fell to the floor, back arching, crimson froth bubbling through the mouth slit of his mask.

At last the sorcerer went still. His body was an empty husk;

there was no more blood to drink. The *morndari* buzzed away and were gone. They had been sated, for now at least.

Deirdre wiped her mouth with the back of her hand. "What the hell just happened?"

"A sorcerer must control the flow of his blood," Vani said. "He did not, and so the *morndari* he summoned turned on him." She moved forward and picked up Nim. "Are you well, daughter?"

The girl gave a somber nod. "My father Travis is a powerful sorcerer."

Travis felt Vani's gold eyes on him.

"Yes," the *T'gol* said. "He is."

"What was in the bedroom?" Deirdre said, looking as if she was trying hard not to vomit.

"A stone through the window," Beltan said. "It was a distraction, meant to separate us. It nearly worked. I should have known the Scirathi would try a trick like that. They're sly dogs." He looked at Vani. "I wonder how they knew you and Nim were here."

Travis crossed his arms over his chest, trying not to think of the way his own blood surged through his veins. "I have a better question: How are the sorcerers here on Earth at all? Sareth has the one gate artifact, and the other was lost when the Etherion collapsed."

"Perhaps it was found," Vani said.

Beltan pulled the robes of the sorcerers over their faces. "And maybe they still had some of the fairy's blood. I mean Sindar's blood. He gave himself up to the Scirathi so he could get to Earth and find you, Travis, to give you the Stone of Twilight. The sorcerers might have preserved some of his blood."

Travis couldn't help a grim smile. As usual Beltan saw the simple solution the rest of them had overlooked. "That explains how the Scirathi got here, but how did they know you were here, Vani?"

"I would give much to know the answer to that," the *T'gol* said. "I cannot believe they followed me."

Nor could Travis. The *T'gol* could make herself virtually invisible when she wanted. No one could have followed her, not even a sorcerer. All the same, somehow they had known she and Nim were there.

Beltan picked up the gold mask, which had fallen to the floor. "Vani, do the Scirathi usually attack in twos?"

The *T'gol* shook her head. "There will be more. We must go."

"Go where?" the blond knight said.

"The Seeker Charterhouse," Deirdre said, gripping Travis's arm. "There's no place in the city with tighter security. Not even Buckingham Palace."

Beltan tossed down the mask. "We'll take my cab."

Vani moved down the hallway. "We will take the fire escape and go through the alley. The front of the building might be watched."

However, by the time they peered around the corner of the alley, the street beyond was dark and silent.

"Can you see anything?" Beltan whispered to Travis.

Travis could see in the dark better than even Vani; it was one of the ways he had been changed by the Stone of Fire. But there was nothing there. In fact, he had never seen the street so utterly devoid of signs of life. Every window was dark; even the streetlamps seemed dim, their circles of light contracted.

Beltan motioned for the others to follow and led the way to his cab. They climbed in—Beltan and Vani up front, Travis, Nim, and Deirdre in the back. Beltan cranked the key in the ignition.

Nothing happened. Beltan made a growling sound low in his throat. "By the Holy Bull's Big Bloody B—"

Vani slapped the blond man's cheek. Hard.

He shot her a wounded look. "What was that for?"

"I think it was for swearing when children are present," Deirdre said, hugging Nim on her lap.

"No," Vani said, then reconsidered. "Well, yes, now that you mention it. But it was mostly for this."

She opened her hand. On her palm was what looked at first like a crumpled piece of gold foil.

"Get out of the car," Travis said. "Now!"

They scrambled out of the taxi. Travis grabbed Deirdre, spinning her around, searching for any signs of them on her or on Nim.

"Are you trying to make me throw up?" the Seeker said, staggering.

"Gold spiders," Travis said. "Do you see any gold spiders on you or Nim? The Scirathi create them. They move like they're alive, only they're not. They're more like little machines, filled with venom. One bite and you're—" He clamped his mouth shut, aware of Nim's wide eyes locked on him.

"I don't like spiders," the girl said, pronouncing the word *thpiderth*. "They have too many legs."

"I'm with you on that one," Deirdre said in a cheerful voice. "But look—they're all gone now."

They were, as far as Travis could tell, though there could be more of them in the taxi, hiding in niches and recesses, waiting to crawl out when a hand passed nearby. It didn't matter. The car was dead.

"We must go," Vani said, giving him a sharp look.

Travis started to reply, then froze. He saw them before the others possibly could have, making out the hump-backed shapes against the gloom. They loped down the street, moving swiftly on both feet and knuckles. A moment later Beltan swore, and Vani went rigid. So they had seen the things as well.

"Run," Travis said. "Now."

They turned and careened down the street. Travis muttered the runes of twilight and shadow through clenched teeth. They only seemed to work half the time, and when they did they were pitifully frail, but he had to hope their magic would conceal the five of them. Because there was no way they could outrun the things that were after them.

Beltan took Nim from Deirdre, holding the girl easily under one arm as he ran.

"Are those things back there what I think they are?" Deirdre said between ragged breaths.

"They are if you think they are *gorleths*," Vani answered. "I am not certain how many are following us."

Travis tried to count the shadows he had seen. "Too many," he said, and ran faster. The *gorleths* were abominations spawned by the Scirathi, creatures pieced together from the blood and flesh of multiple beasts. Their strength, hunger, and desire to kill knew no limits.

"Where are we going?" Beltan asked as they rounded a corner.

Travis pointed. "There. The Tube station. We can catch a train to the Charterhouse."

They pounded the last hundred yards to the entrance of the station, and Travis uttered a constant litany of runes as they dashed down a flight of steps. It was late, and there was no attendant on duty in the booth next to a bank of turnstiles. Deirdre stopped, searching in her pockets.

Travis stared at her. "What are you doing?"

"Looking for a ticket. Ah." She pulled a small cardboard rectangle from her pocket, put it in the slot, and passed through the turnstile.

Vani jumped over the turnstile after her. Beltan handed Nim to the *T'gol* and followed suit, as did Travis.

Deirdre grimaced. "Well, if I had known we were going to be a gang of hoodlums, I would have saved the fare."

"Come on," Travis said, grabbing her hand.

They dashed down the steps that led to the southbound platform of the Jubilee line. They could take the train to Westminster, then catch either the District or Circle line to the Blackfriars station. From there it was only a few blocks to the Seeker Charterhouse.

And what if the Scirathi know where the Charterhouse is? What if they're staking it out?

Travis set aside the question. They could worry about that on the train ride there. They halted at the edge of the platform. Travis leaned out, peering down the lightless tunnel, hoping to feel the puff of air that would indicate an arriving train.

"How long until a vehicle comes?" Vani said, cradling Nim. The girl seemed unable or unwilling to blink.

Travis peered at the electronic sign over the platform. It was blank. There were no other passengers in sight; the platform was deserted.

"I don't see a schedule anywhere," Deirdre said, gazing around. "The trains don't run as often this late at night."

"Or maybe not at all," Beltan said. He knelt to pick up a

length of yellow plastic tape from the tile floor—the kind of tape often used for police or construction barricades. The blond man held out the tape. Words were printed on it: DO NOT ENTER. CLOSED FOR MAINT—

"Great Spirit protect us," Deirdre murmured, gripping her bear claw necklace, but Travis knew it was too late for that, that there was nothing to protect them now.

Vani turned, arms locked around Nim. "We were herded here. This is where they wanted us to come all along."

Even as the *T'gol* spoke, the first hungry, guttural sounds skittered along the curved tile walls of the station.

13.

There was a stairway at either end of the platform; the growling noises emanated from both.

"Get ready, Vani." Beltan said as he raised his sword. Travis hadn't realized the knight had carried it all this way.

"Deirdre, take Nim," Vani said, handing the girl to the Seeker. "I must be free to fight."

"I don't want you to fight the *'leths*," Nim said, then began to cry.

Vani caressed her damp cheek. "You must be brave, daughter."

Nim nodded, her sobs ceasing if not her tears, and Deirdre hugged the girl tight, looking as if she was trying to be brave herself.

"Travis," Beltan said, alternating his gaze between both stairways, "can you speak any runes that might help us?"

Travis was so tired. Speaking runes on Earth was like running through water: great effort for little effect. "I'll try."

The first dark forms appeared at the foot of both stairways. They were the size of apes. But then, the *gorleths* had been apes once—or at least part of them had. Chimpanzees were one of the animals the Scirathi used in fashioning the *gorleths* here on Earth. What other animals they had used, Travis could only imagine. Muscles writhed under the skin of their humped backs, their digits ended in curved talons, and knifelike teeth jutted from their maws.

Beltan and Vani each faced one of the stairwells, with Travis, Deirdre, and Nim between them. The first *gorleths* had already covered half the distance across the platform, their talons scraping against the tiles, making a sound like fingernails being dragged across a blackboard. Their pale eyes shone with hungry intelligence.

"Not to rush you, Travis," Beltan said, holding his sword ready, "but now would be a good time for those runes."

Travis drew in a breath, but he felt so weak—just like rune magic did here on Earth.

By the Lost Hand of Olrig, that's no way for a Runelord to think! Jack Graystone's voice thundered in his mind. *You're a wizard, Travis, on this or any world. Now speak a rune.* Gelth *should do nicely, I think.*

This time Jack was right. Travis clenched his right fist, knowing without looking that the silvery symbol—three crossed lines, the rune of runes—had blazed to life on his palm.

"*Gelth,*" he intoned.

Again he felt the deep wrenching sensation inside, as if someone had just punched him in the gut. The rune had no effect.

Beltan tightened his hands around the hilt of the sword. "Travis . . ."

There was love in the blond man's voice, and urgency. The *gorleths* were so close Travis could hear their whuffling, could smell the putrid reek of their breath.

"*Gelth!*" Travis shouted, straining with all his being.

This time a thousand voices chanted the rune in his mind, and he felt a hum resonate through him like a tone through a pitchfork. Instantly, tiny, glittering crystals precipitated out of thin air, frosting the *gorleths'* dark fur, and sheeting the tiles of the platform with a glaze of ice.

On Eldh, Travis would have been able to conjure an ice storm; he could have frozen the *gorleths* solid. However, in some ways, the coating of ice was equally effective. The curved talons of the *gorleths* could find no purchase. The nearest creatures let out shrieks of fury as they fell, skidding across the platform.

One slid close to Beltan, and the blond knight took the opportunity to swing his sword, lopping the beast's head off. Another *gorleth* flew over the edge of the platform. There was a sizzling sound as the creature struck one of the electrified rails on which the trains ran.

Vani gazed at the smoking *gorleth*, then glanced at Beltan. "Are you thinking what I'm thinking?"

The blond man snorted. "I think everyone is thinking what you're thinking."

Three more *gorleths* remained close by and were starting to slowly crawl toward them, while five or six of the beasts clustered at the foot of each stairwell, testing the ice with their talons; it was already beginning to melt. They could fight four of the creatures, maybe five. But not a dozen of them, not even with Beltan and Vani.

The *T'gol* prowled toward one of the nearby *gorleths*, moving across the ice as surefooted as if it were rough cement. Beltan started to do the same, but he swore as he nearly lost his footing, only catching himself by digging the point of his sword into the ice.

Travis knelt and touched Beltan's boots. "*Krond*," he murmured.

"What are you doing?" Beltan yowled stamping his feet. "That's hot!"

The ice melted through to the tiles where his boots touched.

"Oh," he said, then started toward one of the struggling *gorleths*, able to move across the ice now, if not as quickly as Vani. The creature reached for him, trying to rake open his stomach, but Beltan swiped with his sword, sending the beast's arm spinning across the ice. He kicked, and the *gorleth* flew over the edge of the platform, striking the rails. Again came the sizzle of electricity, a sound that continued as Vani heaved first one, then another *gorleth* over the edge. However, one of them raked its claws across her leg, and she limped as she came back toward them, trailing a line of blood.

"It is a scratch," she said in answer to their looks, but her words were more for Nim's benefit than theirs. The ice was growing slushy beneath her feet, not just Beltan's.

"*Gelth*," Travis said, pressing his hand against the floor, murmuring the rune over and over. The tiles froze again, but they began to melt almost immediately. Despite the chill that radiated from them, Travis was sweating, and he couldn't stop shaking. He kept speaking runes.

A group of *gorleths* edged away from one of the stairwells. They crept across the ice, pressing themselves against the wall at the end of the platform for support, moving toward the edge.

"What are they doing?" Beltan said.

Vani's gold eyes narrowed. "They're learning."

When they reached the edge of the platform, the beasts lowered themselves into the trench where the trains ran, careful to avoid the electrified rails. Slowly, the *gorleths* began making their way parallel to the rails. Creatures from the other end of the platform were following suit. Travis knew what would happen when they reached the center of the platform. They would climb back up; and then there would be no escaping them.

Deirdre eyed the advancing monsters. "Travis, stop it with the ice runes. I think we need to run for the stairs."

However, even as she said this, several more *gorleths* appeared at the foot of each stairwell. Vani and Beltan stood at the edge of the platform, ready to try to fend off the creatures when they started to climb up, though there were far too many of them. The snarls of the *gorleths* echoed off the curved walls of the tunnel, a cacophony that drowned out the voices of the Runelords in Travis's mind. He stopped speaking the rune of ice and knelt on the tiles, bowing his head, exhausted.

A puff of air caressed his cheeks—warm rather than cold, smelling of steel and soot.

In Castle City, Travis had often stood on the boardwalk in front of the Mine Shaft Saloon, facing toward the mountains. He would feel an ache of possibility in his chest as he waited for the wind, wondering what it might blow his way. Only he knew what this wind was bringing. Already he could feel the tiles vibrating beneath his knees.

"Vani, Beltan! Get back!"

The two hesitated, then stepped away from the edge. Travis

stood and grabbed Deirdre, pulling her and Nim back. The first *gorleths*, three of them, started to scramble up onto the platform, their eyes glowing with malice. They opened their fanged maws and roared.

The roar grew louder, deeper, filling the tunnel like thunder. The *gorleths* shut their maws, but the roar continued. Their pale eyes flickered with confusion, and they turned to look down the tunnel—

—just as the oncoming train struck them.

Two of the *gorleths* went flying through the air, their bodies limp and broken before they crashed onto the tiles. The third was caught between the train and the platform, its body smearing into a stripe of black jelly. The *gorleths* in the trench shrieked, then their cries were cut short.

Beltan, Vani, and Deirdre all stared, motionless with shock, but Travis knew they only had a moment. The ice had melted. Already the *gorleths* from the stairwells were loping toward them across the platform. The train slowed, wheels screeching in protest.

"Everyone!" Travis shouted. "Get into the train!"

His words shattered their paralysis; they started moving. The train rattled to a stop, and a set of doors whooshed open before them.

Anders stood on the other side.

"Hello there, mates," he said in his cheery, gravelly voice. As usual, the Seeker wore a sleek designer suit that could barely contain the bulk of his shoulders. His close-cropped hair looked freshly bleached—an unnatural contrast to his dark beard and eyebrows.

"Anders," Deirdre breathed. "How—?"

Travis shoved Deirdre, pushing her through the doors.

"Mind the gap," intoned a voice over the loudspeakers. The *gorleths* snarled as they drew close. Vani and Beltan jumped into the train, Travis on their heels.

"Close the doors!" Anders shouted into a black walkie-talkie.

The doors whooshed shut just as the *gorleths* struck them. The train rocked under the blow. Vani and Beltan stumbled back, and talons slipped through the crack between the doors, wrenching them open. A snarling head shot through the gap, and before Travis could scream, the thing's maw clamped around his upper arm.

The *gorleth's* teeth sank easily into his flesh. He could see the creature's gullet moving. It was suckling, pulling blood out of the wound with terrible force, swallowing it. A buzzing noise filled Travis's ears. The world began to go white, and he no longer felt pain.

He watched through a veil as Vani and Beltan shoved on the doors, closing them, catching the creature's neck as in a vise. It opened its maw to let out a hiss, releasing Travis's arm. Travis stumbled back, and Beltan's sword flashed. The *gorleth's* head rolled to the floor, and the doors clamped shut. Outside the windows of the train the creature's decapitated body slumped backward onto the tiles.

Vani took Nim from Deirdre. The girl was not crying. Her face was ashen and her eyes were circles of fear as she stared at Travis.

"Anders," Deirdre said, grabbing her partner's arm, "get this train running again."

"You got it, mate." Anders raised the walkie-talkie and pressed a button. "Eustace, take us out of the station. Now."

The train lurched into motion, pulling away from the platform. Travis caught one last glimpse of the remaining *gorleths* on the edge of the platform, swarming around the headless body of their kin. Then the train passed into the darkness of a tunnel, and he felt strong hands lowering him into a seat.

"Travis, are you all right?" It was Beltan, his green eyes worried.

"He has lost much blood," Vani said.

Before Anders could react, she tore one of the sleeves from his suit coat and bound it around Travis's arm.

"Hey, now!" Anders said, annoyance on his pitted face. "You don't just go making bandages out of Armani."

Travis shook his head. The fog was beginning to lift. "I'm fine, really. I just got dizzy for a moment."

But was it the loss of blood that had made him dizzy, or the smell of it? It filled his nostrils now: the rich, coppery scent.

Were the *morndari* still sated? Could he not call them to him with blood such as his?

"Travis?" Beltan touched his cheek.

He focused on the blond man's face, letting the desire to work blood sorcery fade away. Only it didn't, not completely.

Deirdre slumped back against one of the seats. "How did you find us?" she said to Anders. "Not that I'm complaining, mind you."

"I got your message, mate," Anders said, gripping a pole as the train rattled around a corner. "I must have just missed you, only when I called back you didn't answer. It sounded like you'd gotten yourself into a bit of a scrape, so I decided to investigate. I went to the Bond Street station to hop on the Tube to Travis and Beltan's neighborhood, and I knew something was definitely wrong when I ran into this chap."

The Seeker picked up something resting on one of the seats: a gold mask. There was a small hole between the mask's eyes.

"Needless to say, I was a bit surprised," Anders continued, clearly enjoying telling the story. "This fellow here wiggled his fingers at me, and I suppose my heart should have exploded. Only I think something made his magic go all wonky. He got flustered, and I took the chance to get a shot off. Turns out their masks don't stop bullets so well. Eustace showed up then. You remember him, Deirdre—the new apprentice you met the other day, scrappy lad. He had caught some chatter on the police radio scanners, something about a commotion at the Green Park station, and right away we had a pretty good notion what was up. So Eustace headed to the front of the train. There was no sign of the driver, but he got the train running, and here we are."

Deirdre stood and gave Anders a fierce hug.

Surprise registered in his vivid blue eyes and—for a moment, Travis thought—a note of wistfulness. "Now there, mate, that's enough of that. You would have done the same for me. Besides, I don't think partners are supposed to fraternize quite like this." He gently pushed her away.

"Are we heading to the Charterhouse?" she asked.

"On the double. I'd say it's the only safe place in the city for these folks right now."

"I do not understand this," Vani said, sitting next to Travis.

Nim was curled up on her lap. The girl's eyes were closed now, but Travis was certain she was listening to every word. "There is no way the Scirathi could know I brought Nim to Earth," Vani went on, her face hard with anger. She looked at Travis. "How could they have followed me across the Void, let alone to your home?"

Anders cleared his throat. "Actually, miss, I don't think they did. I found something on the body of that sorcerer fellow— something that tells me it wasn't your daughter they were after." He reached into his coat pocket and pulled out a sheet of stiff paper. It was a photograph of a man.

"By the Blade of Vathris," Beltan growled. "I swear I'll kill them all!"

Another wave of dizziness swept over Travis, and not just from loss of blood. The man in the photo was him.

14.

It was far after midnight by the time they gathered in a mahogany-paneled parlor in the Seekers' London Charter-house.

Deirdre sank down into one of the parlor's comfortably shabby chairs. For the first time since they heard the sound of glass breaking in Travis's and Beltan's flat her heart rate slowed to a normal cadence, and a feeling of safety encapsulated her, as familiar and reassuring as the embrace of the wing-backed chair.

It had taken over two hours to get through all of the Charter-house's security checkpoints. While it hadn't been difficult to gain entry for Travis and Beltan—their files were on record with the Seekers—new dossiers had to be created for Vani and Nim. Fingers were printed, retinas scanned, and Deirdre's authoriza-tion codes processed. She had thought the security guards would call Director Nakamura for confirmation, but to her sur-prise they hadn't. It seemed Echelon 7 clearance was good for more than just access to Seeker databases.

"How long can we stay in this place?" Vani said, prowling

around a Chippendale sofa where Nim lay curled up. The *T'gol* limped slightly, favoring her injured leg. The nurse—there was always one on duty at the Charterhouse—had cleaned and bandaged the wound.

"You can stay as long as you need to," Deirdre said.

Vani gripped the laminated ID badge that hung from a lanyard around her neck. "And we can leave at any time?"

"Of course you can leave," Anders said, hanging his torn suit coat on the back of a chair. "Not that I'd recommend it. In case you hadn't noticed, it's not exactly safe out there."

Vani spun around, advancing on him. "You Seekers are arrogant fools. I have watched you. You believe you know everything, yet there is so much you cannot understand. Is it truly so safe here?"

"Not if you keep talking like that, it isn't," Anders growled, cracking his knuckles.

Vani treated the Seeker to a scornful look. "If you think simply because you have large muscles that you have any chance against me, then you deceive yourself."

"It sounds to me like you're the cocky one," Anders said. "Just because you're some superspooky assassin type doesn't mean you know every trick in the book. I worked security long before I became a Seeker, and I don't need muscles to take out the likes of you. Go on, Deirdre. Tell her how I aced all those logic tests the Seekers gave me."

Beltan interposed himself between the Seeker and the *T'gol.* He faced Anders. "I doubt I'd do very good on those tests, but my logic tells me you'd better back off if you want to keep your brain inside your skull." He glared at Vani. "You, too. Do you think this is a good example for Nim?"

Vani's scowl became a worried expression. "She is asleep."

"Not anymore," Travis said.

Nim was sitting up on the sofa, her gray eyes wide. "Are you going to hurt the bad man, Mother?"

Deirdre pushed herself from the chair, then knelt on the carpet next to the sofa. "Don't be afraid, Nim. Anders isn't a bad man."

"Yes he is. That's why Mother wants to hurt him."

"No, he's my partner, and he helped us get away from the monsters. Don't you remember?"

Nim hesitated, then nodded.

"Anders and your mother are just a little tired, that's all. We're all tired." Deirdre smiled, touching the girl's chin. "You, too, I bet. Why don't you go to sleep?"

Nim held her hands out before her. "No, I don't want to sleep. I won't see the gold men if my eyes are closed. They want to take me away from my mother because I'm a key. That's what they tell me, only their mouths don't move."

"Hush, daughter," Vani said, sitting on the arm of the sofa and stroking Nim's dark hair. "There is no need to fear. You are safe here."

"That's right," Deirdre said, doing her best to sound convincing. But they *were* safe there. Underneath all the rich wood paneling, every door in the Charterhouse was made of tempered steel fitted with electronic locks. This parlor was like a bank vault. Nothing could pass the doors. Or the windows. "Show her, Anders."

The Seeker moved to one of the windows. "See that little beam of green light here? That's a laser. Look what happens if something gets in the way of that beam." Anders stuck a finger in the path of the laser beam—then snatched his hand back just in time to keep it from getting smashed as a row of gleaming metal bars whooshed into place, covering the window.

Nim clapped her hands. "Again!"

After several more demonstrations of the automatic safety features of the windows and doors, Nim was finally content to lie down on the sofa. She yawned and stuck a finger in her mouth, and her breathing grew slow as her eyes drooped shut.

Deirdre would have liked to curl up herself, but there was too much to try to understand. They moved to the other side of the parlor and spoke in low voices so as not to disturb Nim. A sleepy-eyed butler brought coffee, and Deirdre helped Anders pour cups for all of them.

"It's not fair," he grumbled in a low voice as they stood at a sideboard, backs to the others. "I get the train rolling along, smash all the baddies, and somehow I'm still the bad man."

"Don't worry about Nim. She just doesn't know you like I do. Remember, I didn't exactly trust you at first, either."

However, in the time since, Deirdre had learned that she could rely on Anders in any situation. In fact, she trusted Anders more than she had ever trusted Hadrian Farr. With Farr, she had always felt there was some deeper agenda she didn't know about, that if he ever thought he needed to, he would abandon her in an instant. Then he had, and now she knew why. Somehow he had found a doorway to Eldh, and he had taken it, leaving her behind. She supposed she couldn't blame him for that.

Only she did. Farr had found what they had always sought together, and he had gone on without her. Something told her Anders wouldn't do the same—that if he found a portal to another world, he would hold the door open like a gentleman and let her go first.

"You trust me now, don't you, mate?" he said, pouring cream.

She laid a hand on his broad shoulder, drawing closer. Anders wasn't handsome, but damn if he didn't always smell good. . . .

Stop it right now, Deirdre.

Her hand pulled back. She wasn't certain when she realized she could fall in love with Anders if she let herself. It wasn't at all like what she had felt for Farr when she first met him. Back then, she had been as infatuated with the idea of the Seekers as with Farr's film noir good looks. It was hard to say which of them had seduced her.

With Anders, it was different. There had been so much to get through: her mistrust, the fact that he had worked security, and the realization that underneath that heavy Cro-Magnon brow lurked a sharp mind. Even then she probably wouldn't have realized the truth if it hadn't been for Sasha.

"Quit glowing," Sasha had said to her one day.

"What?" Deirdre had said, utterly confused.

"I said quit glowing. You're like a night-light."

Deirdre was scandalized. "I don't glow."

"You do when you look at Anders," Sasha had said with a wicked grin. "Grant you, we've all gotten rather attached to the big lug, and not simply because he makes heavenly coffee. But it's best to keep one's professional relationships from becoming unprofessional. And by that I mean personal. I know you agree, darling."

Just to confuse things, which Sasha had a great fondness for, she gave Deirdre a warm kiss on the lips before sauntering away on her lanky supermodel legs.

Ever since then, Deirdre had been careful, and as far as she knew Anders didn't suspect anything. Which was good. Deirdre valued him too much as a partner and a friend to ever do anything to jeopardize their relationship.

"Come on," she said, leading the way as he carried a tray of coffee cups to a table in the corner. While Nim slept, the adults gathered around the table, trying to make sense of everything that had happened.

"So it was me they came looking for," Travis said, looking at Vani, "not you and Nim." He touched the bandage on his arm and winced.

Vani circled her hands around her cup. "Yes, but it does not matter, for they have learned I brought Nim to Earth. There is nowhere I can take her now that will be safe from them."

"But why do they want us?" Travis said, his gray eyes serious. For the first time Deirdre noticed that they were flecked with gold, just like Nim's.

"You're the one fated to raise Morindu," Beltan said. "They must know that."

"That is impossible," Vani said, her visage darkening. "Besides the people in this room, and Grace Beckett and her closest companions on Eldh, only a few among the Mournish know this fact. I do not believe our closest friends have betrayed us to the Scirathi."

"All the same," Beltan said, using a cloth to wipe the edge of his sword, "they must know. And that means the Scirathi will come again."

Deirdre cast a glance at the sofa where Nim lay. Something the girl had said echoed in her mind. "What did she mean?" She turned her gaze on Vani. "Nim said something about how the Scirathi wanted her because they think she's a key. A key to what?"

Vani sighed, brushing her sleek hair from her brow. "I do not know what she means. A few times she has told me that the Scirathi have spoken to her. However, her story keeps changing. First she said they told her she was a precious jewel, then it was a little spider, and now it's this—a key, she says. But I can only imagine she was dreaming. They have never gotten close enough to speak to her."

"Haven't they?" Travis said. "They were right outside her bedroom window tonight. Besides, you've forgotten how . . ." He cast a furtive glance at Beltan. "She's not like other children, Vani. You know she's not."

Deirdre had heard the story: how the fairies had tricked Beltan and Vani, making each believe the other was Travis. While under the fairy spell, they had conceived Nim between them. Only it was more than that. Duratek had performed experiments on Beltan, infusing him with fairy blood. In a way, Nim was a fairy child. What that meant, Deirdre wasn't sure, but the girl was certainly not a typical three-year-old.

Talk turned then to the matter of the stone arch—the gate—that had been discovered on the island of Crete. Vani was convinced it was a sign of Fate that the arch had been uncovered just when Travis needed to return to Eldh in order to fulfill his destiny.

"I don't know if it's Fate," Travis said, gazing down at his hands. "But I'm willing to bet it's not a coincidence that gate came to light on this world just when Morindu has been found on Eldh. There has to be a connection. Only what is it?"

Vani reached across the table, gripping his hands. "You are the connection, Travis Wilder. Don't you see? The gate has come to light *because* Morindu has been found. It wants to take you there."

He snatched his hands back. "What it if I don't want to go?"

"You will go, because it is Fate."

"I don't have a fate," Travis snapped, and Beltan cast him a worried look.

Vani seemed undisturbed. "Perhaps not. But my people do, and that fate is bound up with you. You will go to Morindu. We must go to this gate at once. Your blood will awaken it."

"Blood," Deirdre murmured, her mind humming. She

glanced at the sofa and Nim's sleeping form. "It's what you and Nim have in common, Travis. That's what connects you. Blood of power."

Beltan cast a startled look at Nim. "A jewel, a spider, a key. Those things she said—all those words could be used to describe a scarab."

"And the scarabs contain Orú's blood." Deirdre felt hot, a sheen of sweat breaking out on her skin. "That's why the Scirathi want both of you. Either one of you could be used to open a gate."

"Or perhaps open something else," Vani said, her coppery face turning ashen. "Why did I not see it before?"

Anders refilled her empty coffee cup. "Sometimes it's hard to see the truth when you're too close to it."

Deirdre had to agree with that. And there was one truth the others couldn't see yet. "The gate on Crete won't do you any good. You won't be able to open it."

Vani scowled at her. "Why is that?"

"Because the arch isn't complete. The archaeologists won't find the center keystone with it."

"This is madness," Vani said, clenching her hands into fists. "You only say this to keep Travis here. How can you know the keystone will not be found?"

"Because it's in the vaults of the Philosophers."

Deirdre couldn't help feeling a little satisfied as they all stared at her. It was good to be the one with the astonishing revelation for a change.

"You remember the Philosopher who was helping me?"

Anders cocked his head. "He hasn't contacted you again, has he, partner?"

Deirdre thought of the message on her computer screen, just before Travis had called. "Actually, I think maybe he has. But he first helped me to learn about the keystone over three years ago."

It had been almost that long since she had gone over her notes on the case, but it didn't matter; she remembered every detail of the mystery as if she had just uncovered it. Anders knew all of this already—she had vowed not to keep any secrets from him, and she had kept that promise—but to the others it would all be new.

She began by explaining how her shadowy helper—the one who she was convinced was a Philosopher—had first contacted her, just after she had stumbled upon a computer file with her new Echelon 7 clearance. A file that was deleted from the system the moment she found it.

Deirdre had never learned what was in that file, but soon after she made another breakthrough with the help of the unknown Philosopher. She explained how she had stumbled across a reference to the keystone in the archives of the Seekers while researching an old case, one concerning a Seeker named Thomas Atwater. In the early seventeenth century, Atwater was forbidden to return to a tavern where he had worked prior to joining the Seekers. The tavern had stood on the same spot where the Seekers would later discover the keystone, and which, three centuries after that, would house the nightclub Surrender Dorothy.

Talking about Glinda was still difficult, even after this long. Deirdre gripped the silver ring Glinda had given her as she described the nightclub and its half-fairy denizens. Duratek had been using them, hoping to learn from the experiments they performed on the folk of the nightclub, then had destroyed the tavern once they gained access to a true fairy.

"Are you all right, Deirdre?" Anders asked, his voice husky. As always, he pronounced her name *DEER-dree*, but she no longer found it quite so annoying as she used to.

She did her best to smile. "I'll be fine. Really."

"You said there was writing on the keystone," Travis said, his gray eyes curious. "Were you ever able to read it?"

Deirdre nodded. "My mysterious helper gave me a photograph of a clay tablet that bore the inscription on the keystone, as well as the same passage written in Linear A. Back then, I wondered at the connection, but now it's fairly obvious."

"To you, maybe," Beltan said with a grunt.

She grinned at the blond man. "Linear A is the writing system used by the Minoan civilization on ancient Crete."

Vani's expression was guarded. "So what does the inscription on the keystone say?"

"It says, 'Forget not the Sleeping Ones. In their blood lies the key.'"

"The key," Travis murmured, looking at Nim. However, whatever he was thinking, he kept it to himself.

There was one last thing she had to tell them. Deirdre took off the silver ring Glinda had given her and showed them how the same inscription as on the keystone was written inside it. However, there was one thing she did not tell them, and it was the one secret she had allowed herself to keep even from Anders: how, in the moment they had kissed, Deirdre had loved Glinda with all her being.

"'The Sleeping Ones,'" Beltan said, scratching the tuft of blond hair on his chin. "That doesn't really sound familiar. What does it mean?"

No one, not even Vani, offered an answer.

Deirdre slipped the ring back on her finger. "The inscription talks about blood, and traces of blood were found on the keystone—blood with DNA similar to Glinda's. Whoever they were, these Sleeping Ones were important to the folk at Surrender Dorothy for some reason." Though why that was, they would never know, thanks to Duratek.

"This all seems a small complication," Vani said, standing and stalking around the table. "True, the gate will not be complete without this keystone. However, it could be in a vault in this very building. Cannot this Philosopher ally of yours deliver the keystone to us?"

Deirdre opened her mouth, not certain how she was going to answer that. Would the unknown Philosopher really respond to a direct request for help? Before she could speak, there was a knock at the door, and the butler entered. On the silver tray he carried was not another pot of coffee but a manila envelope.

"A message just arrived for you, Miss Falling Hawk," he said, holding the tray toward Deirdre.

She stared at the envelope. "Who's it from?"

"I have no idea, miss." The butler looked slightly ruffled, as if she were accusing him of snooping.

She took the envelope off the tray. "Thank you, Lewis."

The butler retreated from the parlor; the door shut.

"It's from him, isn't it?" Travis said. "Your Philosopher friend."

Anders thumped the table. "Well, that was right on cue. He's an eerie fellow, but you can't fault his timing, now can you?"

Deirdre was beyond words. She forced her trembling fingers to open the envelope. Inside was a folded up sheet of newsprint. Trying not to tear it, she unfolded the sheet and spread it on the table. It was a page taken from the *Times*—the coming day's edition, according to the date. It must have come right off the presses.

They all leaned over the page. At the top was a large article about Variance X, the growing stellar anomaly that astronomers had observed beyond the boundaries of the solar system. However, the article didn't hold Deirdre's attention. Nor did the headlines about devastating typhoons in India, or the jittery United States stock markets. Instead, her eyes were drawn to the small headline at the bottom of the page: DARING ARCHAEOLOGICAL THEFT ON CRETE.

Numb, she scanned the article. It described how a stone archway was stolen mere hours after it had been revealed live on the program *Archaeology Now!* There was no clue as to the perpetrators, but one worker at the site reported seeing men dressed in black and wearing masks.

Gold masks.

Vani looked up, her own face becoming a mask: one of fury. "Sacred Mahonadra, they have taken it!"

Beltan and Travis exchanged a grave look, and Deirdre understood what it meant. Somehow, the Scirathi had taken the gate, and without it there was no way to open a doorway to Eldh. But the gate wouldn't do the Scirathi any good either, not without—

A sound like the crackle of electricity permeated the air, along with the metallic scent of ozone. Deirdre turned, and her heart became stone. On the other side of the parlor, a circle of darkness hung in midair, rimmed by blue fire. Nim was no longer on the sofa. Instead the girl padded across the carpet on bare feet, approaching the mouth of the portal.

Vani sprang forward. "Nim, get away from that!"

Fast as she was, Beltan was ahead of her, leaping over the back of the sofa. Travis scrambled after them.

Nim stopped before the dark circle and gazed into it. After a moment she nodded, the way a child might when obeying an adult's instructions. She held her chubby arms out.

"No!" Beltan shouted.

A pair of black-gloved hands reached out of the circle of blue sparks, snatching up Nim. The girl screamed.

"Mother!" she cried, twisting in the gloved hands that gripped her, looking back, her eyes large with fear.

Beltan dived forward, lunging for the girl. His arms closed around empty air, and he crashed against an end table. The hands pulled Nim into the blazing iris of the portal, and both they and the girl vanished. At once the gate began to shrink in on itself, a blue eye winking shut.

Travis thrust a hand into the rapidly dwindling circle. Azure magic crackled around his wrist, biting his hand like a hungry maw.

"You must not let the gate close," Vani said, her voice hard as steel. "There is no other way we can follow her."

Travis nodded, his face lined with pain. However, the blue circle constricted more tightly about his wrist. Beltan lay on the floor. He wasn't moving.

"Anders, help me," Deirdre said as she knelt beside the blond man. Anders helped her roll him over. He was breathing, but his eyes were shut, and there was a bruise forming on his forehead. Anders helped her haul his limp body onto the sofa.

"Vani," Travis gritted between clenched teeth. "My bandage. Take it off. I think it was my blood they used to open this gate. They must have gotten it from the stomach of the dead *gorleth*."

Her eyes blazed. "What fools we are! We should have known they would do this."

Travis flinched as she jerked the bandage off his wound. Blood began to ooze forth.

"More," he said.

She dug her fingers into the wound, and a moan escaped him. Blood flowed freely from the *gorleth's* bite marks, running down his arm. When it reached his wrist, the circle of blue sparks flared, then began to expand outward. Travis stuck his other hand into the opening, gripping its blazing edges, straining as he forced it wider. More blood flowed down his arm, and it vanished as it reached his wrist. The gate was consuming it.

Travis staggered. His face was white, and alarm coursed through Deirdre. *He's lost too much blood. He's going to pass out.*

"Do not stop!" Vani said, her voice a cruel slap.

Again Travis strained. The gate expanded a fraction; it was as wide as his shoulders now.

"Hello there, mate," Anders said as Beltan drew in a shuddering breath and sat up on the sofa.

"What's going—?" The blond man's eyes went wide. "Travis!"

Travis cast a look of pain, sorrow, and love over his shoulder, his eyes locking on Beltan's.

"Now, Vani. Help me."

In a single motion, the *T'gol* gripped his shoulders and pushed him forward, into the mouth of the gate. However, she did not loosen her grasp on him, and his momentum carried her forward as she dived into the circle after him. Travis's feet vanished, then Vani's, as the ring of azure magic rapidly contracted.

"No!" Beltan shouted, pushing himself free of Deirdre and Anders, throwing himself forward. However, before he could reach it, the blue circle collapsed into a single point, then disappeared.

The gate had closed.

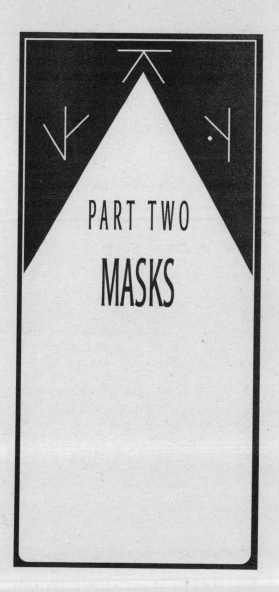

PART TWO
MASKS

15.

"So, dear," Melia said, regarding Grace over the rim of a steaming cup of *maddok*, "I hear you had a chat with a dragon."

The amber-eyed lady sat beside the window in the chamber she and Falken shared. The chamber was small, but it was the sunniest in the keep, and that was why Melia had chosen it over grander rooms. She had been born long ago in a land far warmer than this, and her bronze skin seemed to absorb the morning light that streamed through the window.

Daylight had diminished Grace's dread a fraction—the rift was invisible against the flawless blue sky—and she gave Melia a crooked smile. "News travels fast."

"No, dragons travel fast," Falken said, his hair disheveled from sleep. He poured a cup of *maddok* and handed it to her.

Grace sighed as she breathed in the rich, slightly bitter aroma, then sat in a chair opposite Melia while Falken perched on the windowsill.

"You're blocking my sunshine, dear one," Melia said in the kind of pleasant tone that demanded immediate attention.

"I thought I was your sunshine," Falken said dryly, though he hastily hopped off the windowsill and retired to another chair.

A black cat sprawled on the carpet, licking a paw as it regarded Grace with moon-gold eyes. It had finally outgrown its seemingly eternal kittenhood over two years ago. Grace should have realized then that Melia was no longer immortal.

"So what did the dragon speak to you about?" Melia said, her amber eyes as curious as the cat's.

Grace gripped the hot cup. "Nothing."

A frown shadowed the lady's brow. "If you'd rather not tell us, that's your prerogative, but please don't speak a falsehood, Ralena. Sfithrisir is not one for idle conversation. I doubt the dragon flew all the way here from the Fal Erenn simply to tell you about nothing."

"But that's it," Grace said, struggling to find a place she could begin. "That's exactly what the problem is. It's nothing at all."

Falken raised an eyebrow, glancing at Melia. "I think the dragon addled her wits."

"They've been known to have that effect," the lady agreed.

Grace set down her cup and stood. "It's the rift in the sky," she said, shaking with frustration and fear. "It's growing. It's going to annihilate this world, and Earth, and any other world that lies close to them, and when it's done, there won't be anything left. There'll be nothing. Nothing at all."

Melia and Falken were no longer smiling. As precisely as she could, Grace recounted her conversation with Sfithrisir. When she was done, both the bard and the lady stared, their faces ashen.

"This cannot be true," Melia said, shivering. The sun had gone behind a cloud. "Things cannot simply . . . cease to be."

Grace looked at Falken. "You're the one who told me dragons can only speak the truth."

"That's so," Falken said, doubt in his faded blue eyes. "But you have to be wary of what a dragon says. They speak the truth, but they also twist that truth to their own ends."

Grace thought about this, then shook her head. "He was afraid, Falken. I know that seems impossible, that a creature that existed before the world was even created could feel fear, but he did, I'm sure of it. Whatever the rift really is, Sfithrisir is terrified of it, and he can't stop it."

"And you believe Travis can?" Melia said.

"I have to."

Falken rose from his chair. "What will you do, Ralena?"

She gripped the bard's hand. "I am making you regents of Malachor, you and Melia both. I want you to keep things running. It won't be hard—Sir Tarus pretty much does everything. All you have to do is put my stamp on things once in a while."

Sorrow shone in Falken's faded blue eyes. "So you're leaving us."

She nodded, unable to speak for the tightness in her throat. Melia stood, her blue gown fluttering as she drew close.

Tears streamed from her amber eyes, but she smiled. "Do tell Travis hello for us when you find him, dear."

Then Grace was weeping, too, as she hugged them both.

Preparations for her departure began at once. Horses were readied, supplies packed, and a proclamation granting regent power to Falken and Melia penned, though Sir Tarus handled the majority of this, and mostly what Grace did was tell people they couldn't come with her.

Aldeth and Samatha were the first, though the two Spiders were squabbling so intently over which of them should be the one to go south with Grace that they hardly heard her say that both of them were staying there, and she finally had to shout.

"But you'll need a spy with you, Your Majesty," Aldeth said, looking as if he had been slapped.

"The idea is to find Travis, not hide from him. Besides, Malachor needs you both. I won't be able to focus on my task if I have to worry about what's going on here." Grace lowered her voice to a conspiratorial whisper. "I'll sleep much better if I know you two are keeping an eye on . . . well, I dare not say, but you know exactly who I mean."

By the look in their eyes, they didn't have the foggiest idea who she meant, which was precisely Grace's intention. Trying to figure out who she was referring to ought to keep them occupied while she was gone. Although, as the two Spiders vanished, she supposed she had just doomed everyone in the keep to weeks of constant spying.

Master Graedin came next, then King Kel, and even the witch Lursa. Grace thanked them but told each that they could not come on the journey, that this was something she had to do alone. She was taking a small retinue of knights with her for security on the road, but that was all. Both Graedin and Lursa were disappointed but wished her well, and while Grace feared King Kel would maul her after she refused his offer of company, instead he caught her in a bear hug.

"My little Queenie is all grown-up now." He released her, then sniffed, wiping a tear from the corner of his eye. "Go on, then, fly from the nest. Have your adventure out in the world. But don't you forget me, lass."

Grace winced, probing her aching ribs. "I honestly don't think that's possible, Your Majesty."

By late morning everything was ready for her departure, and the good thing about having to tell everyone they couldn't come with her was that she had already taken care of all her good-byes. Or make that almost all, for there was one person who hadn't come to her. She found him in the highest chamber of his tower, his face close to the runestone; both face and stone were covered with a webwork of thin lines.

"Your Majesty," Master Larad said, looking up. "Forgive me—I did not see you there."

She approached the runestone. "It's getting worse, isn't it?"

"I found another piece sundered from it this morning."

So the power of magic was continuing to deteriorate. "I think maybe I know what's happening," Grace said. "What's affecting magic."

"You mean the rift in the heavens."

She stared at him. "You know about it?"

It almost seemed a smile touched his lips. "You were not the only one looking at the sky last night, Your Majesty."

"I suppose this means," she said, moderately perturbed, "that you're not going to be at all surprised when I tell you I spoke to a dragon?"

He shook his head.

Giving up all hope of ever astonishing Master Larad, Grace told him everything Sfithrisir had said, and what she had decided to do. When she was done, his scarred face was expressionless. However, a light shone in his eyes, though it seemed more curious than alarmed.

"I am not certain how this knowledge helps me, Your Majesty. However, it cannot be chance that the rift has appeared just as the power of magic is faltering. I will focus my studies on it."

She touched his arm. "If anyone can find a way to keep magic from getting any weaker, it's you, Master Larad."

He pulled away. "Dragons cannot lie, Your Majesty. You must find Travis Wilder. Is it not time for you to depart?"

She moved to a narrow window. From there she could see the

keep, blue banners bearing the white star of Malachor snapping above. "Yes," she murmured. "It *is* time."

"You sound as if you've decided something, Your Majesty."

Grace hadn't meant to speak aloud, but she longed to tell someone what she had been thinking. She looked down at the people moving in the bailey below. They were her subjects, yet at that moment she felt so distant from them. They were like patients who had been discharged from Denver Memorial Hospital; they didn't need her anymore.

"Melia and Falken will be good regents," she said, "but in time I think the people of Malachor should elect a leader."

"Elect?" Larad said, a note of scorn in his voice. "You mean let the people choose who their ruler will be?"

"Yes." She turned to face him.

His eyes narrowed. "And whom do you think they would choose?"

"You, perhaps."

Almost never had she seen Larad laugh, but he did now, a sound at once ironic and genuinely mirthful. "I think not, Your Majesty. Yours is a keen mind, but I think in this matter reason has eluded you. I have heard what you speak of before—the absurd notion that common people are capable of choosing their own ruler wisely."

"It isn't absurd," Grace said, a little angry now. "People *can* make wise choices for themselves, if they're given the chance."

"Perhaps," Larad said, though he did not sound convinced. "But even if the people of Malachor did choose their leader, whom do you think they would select? A man who spends all day studying runes in a tower? The people do not follow you because they have to, Your Majesty, but because they wish to. They have already made their choice. There is no need for them to elect a—"

The Runelord staggered back, gripping the window ledge for support. "You're not coming back. You're leaving, and you don't intend to return to Malachor, do you?"

So he had seen the truth—the truth which, like a dragon, she had concealed in a fog even from herself. She crossed her arms over her chest, her heart beating with anguish. Or was it excitement?

"I don't know if I'll come back, Larad," she said softly. "I honestly don't know."

He said nothing. She had finally managed to astonish Larad, but already his shock was gone, or at least concealed, and his eyes were hard and unreadable once again.

"Farewell then, Your Majesty," he said.

Grace found she had no words to reply. She nodded, then descended the stairs, leaving the tower of the Runelords.

A short while later she mounted Shandis beside the gates of the keep. Four stern-faced knights sat ready on their chargers. There was no wagon for supplies, only a packhorse that carried the absolute minimum, for Grace intended to ride fast. She arranged her riding gown over the saddle, then sighed. Now came the hardest good-bye of all.

"No, Sir Tarus," she said as the red-haired knight placed his foot in a stirrup, ready to mount his charger.

He turned around. "Your Majesty?"

She could not bring herself to speak the words, but by his stricken look he understood her. He drew close, clutching the hem of her gown, and shook his head.

"No, Your Majesty." His voice was ragged with despair. "Please do not do this thing to me. Do not command me to stay."

She had to keep her voice hard, or she would not be able to speak at all. "You must, Sir Tarus. Melia and Falken cannot run this kingdom without your help."

His face grew red, but from grief this time, not frustration. "I am your seneschal. I serve you, Your Majesty."

"And so you must do what I bid," she said, hating how cruel the words sounded.

"Have I served you so ill, then, that you must leave me behind?" He was weeping now, and Grace nearly lost her resolve, for in that moment she finally understood why he had been so stern these last three years, so grim and determined.

He had been trying to be Durge.

"No, Tarus," she said, on the verge of weeping herself. "You have served me better than any other. And that's why I must ask you to do this. For me. And for Malachor."

"But I have every reason to go with you."

She thought of the young Runelord Alfin, and despite her

sorrow she smiled. "I believe you have a better reason to stay, Sir Tarus."

She bent over and kissed the top of his head. Then she urged Shandis toward the gates, the four knights behind her, and without fanfare or further farewells, Grace, Queen of Malachor, left her kingdom.

16.

She spoke little with the knights who accompanied her as they rode south from Gravenfist Keep along the Queen's Way. When she gave Tarus the names of the warriors she wished for her retinue, she had deliberately chosen the most reticent and taciturn in the keep; she had no desire for idle conversation on this journey.

Her only purpose now was to ride as swiftly as possible, to reach Sareth, and have him lead her to Hadrian Farr. Not because she wished to see the Seeker—though, she was forced to confess, the thought of seeing him again did give her a strange thrill she couldn't quite analyze. For a reason she couldn't name, she kept trying to picture him, though all she could seem to see were his eyes: dark, mysterious, compelling. Not that it mattered. All that mattered was that Farr could lead her to Morindu the Dark. And if she found Morindu, then she would find Travis—she was certain of it.

The weather was fine and clear, and they made good time that first day. Over the last few years, the Embarran engineers had labored on the Queen's Way, clearing away fallen trees, replacing cracked paving stones, and shoring up bridges. By nightfall they had covered nearly all the ten leagues of the Queen's Way the Embarrans had repaired. They were deep in the Winter Wood now, and they made camp in a grove of *valsindar* trees as the last sunlight filtered between silver-barked trunks.

They ate a supper of the foodstuffs that would not keep— bread, a clay pot of butter, fruit, and some roasted chicken, which was already a little questionable after a full day riding in their saddlebags—then readied for sleep as purple dusk crept among the trees. The summer night was balmy, and the four men spread blankets on beds of old leaves, while Grace slipped into a small tent they had set up for her. She wouldn't have minded sleeping out in the open like the men, but maybe it was better not to. This way she wouldn't try to peer through the leafy branches of the *valsindar* to see if the dark hole in the sky had grown.

Grace had just shut her eyes when she heard the ringing of steel. She threw back the flap and scrambled out of the tent. All four of the knights stood with their swords drawn. As Grace's eyes adjusted to the gloom, fear stabbed at her heart. A figure stood on the edge of the clearing where they had made camp, hooded and robed in black.

"Move, and you will be slain," said one of the knights—a stout, gray-bearded man named Brael.

"How about if I simply speak?" the figure said in a sardonic voice, and before the knights could move, the one cloaked in black uttered a word in a commanding tone. "*Lir!*"

There was a flash of blue light, and the knights staggered back. However, the light quickly shrank to a ball hovering above the man's palm, and in its soft glow Grace saw that the man's garb was not black, but rather deep blue. There was a look of satisfaction on his scarred face.

The knights recovered, and looked more ready than ever to use their swords. However, Grace hurried forward.

"That wasn't particularly wise, Master Larad," she said in a sharp whisper. "These men might have killed you."

The Runelord simply shrugged, as if to say he was less certain of that outcome than she.

Brael regarded Larad with suspicion. "This one must have been skulking after us all day, Your Majesty. I'd like to find out why. I've always thought he had a crafty look about him."

"You can put that sword away," Grace said to Brael. She gave the other knights what she hoped was a commanding glance. "All of you. I've been expecting Master Larad. Though he's a little late."

Brael gave her a startled look. He began to speak, but she turned her back on him, and she knew the knight would not dare to question her. Being a queen did have certain advantages. She heard the men grumble as they sheathed their swords. Taking Larad's arm, she steered him to the other side of the grove. The ball of blue light bobbed after them.

"You can thank me later for saving you from getting your head lopped off," she said quietly. "Right now, I want you to tell me what you think you're doing. And I had better be mightily entertained by the story, or I'm handing you back over to Brael."

"I'm coming with you," Master Larad said.

It was a statement, not a request. Grace knew it was neither useful nor queenly, but she could only gape at him.

"I must speak with Master Wilder," the Runelord went on. "After you left my tower, I considered all that you told me. I can only believe the rift and the weakening of magic are linked somehow. Perhaps both arise from the same cause. In which case, my recent studies regarding magic may prove useful to Master Wilder in his search for the Last Rune."

Grace finally found her tongue. "And it didn't occur to you this morning to ask if you could come with me?"

"It did, and I rejected that idea, for I knew you were refusing all who asked."

"So you decided to follow me without my permission." She placed her hands on her hips and glared at him. "What's to stop me from sending you back to Gravenfist?"

"You won't, Your Majesty."

"And why not?"

"Because yours is a logical mind, and you've already realized that I must come with you on this journey." He nodded to the ball of light. "Even this simple runespell is proving a challenge to maintain. Something must be done before all magic ceases to be, and our chances of finding a solution are greater if Master Wilder and I can work together."

Grace was angry enough to disagree out of spite, but before she could, the dry doctor's voice spoke in her mind.

He's right. You didn't refuse the offers of the others because you didn't want their company, but because you knew that this time they couldn't help you. However, Larad is a Runelord. There's a significant probability he can help Travis discover what the Last Rune is.

Even so, she had the feeling Larad was not telling her all his reasons for following her. The Runelord had a history of keeping his true motivations secret. However, he also had a history of doing what he believed was for the greater good, without regard to the cost to himself.

She looked him in the eye. "No more tricks, Master Larad. From now on, if you want something, then you ask me for it. Do you understand?"

His scarred face was as unreadable as ever. "Yes, Your Majesty." He closed his hand around the ball of blue light, snuffing it out, and night closed back in over the forest.

Dawn found them already riding down the Queen's Way. Larad had ridden after them on one of the trusty mules the Runelords favored. With a rider, the mule would not be able to travel as fast as the horses, so they had transferred the foodstuffs and gear to it, and now Larad bounced in the saddle of the former packhorse. The Runelord was every bit as poor a horseman as Travis. Grace was beginning to think a talent for wizardry precluded any ability whatsoever for riding. Luckily, the horse was a placid beast, and it bore Larad with a resigned look on its long face.

They moved at a steady pace over those next days, though their progress seemed maddeningly slow to Grace. On the second day they left behind the section of the Queen's Way the Embarran engineers had repaired. While the road continued to cut unswervingly over the landscape, its stones were cracked and weathered, or in some places gone altogether, replaced by grass or trees, so that the way could be discerned only as a flat space between two sloping banks. However, all of the bridges they came to still stood, arching over stream or gorge, a testament to the skill of the ancient builders who had erected them.

On their fourth day they left the silvery trees of the Winter Wood behind and found themselves riding over plains that had been baked gold by the summer sun. To their left rose the Fal Erenn, the Dawning Fells: a purple-gray range of mountains, their tumbled brows crowned by circlets of white clouds. For the first time in a long time, Grace found herself thinking of Colorado. The Beckett-Strange Home for Children—the orphanage where she had spent most of her childhood—had been built on a high plain not so different from this. Except its windows had all been boarded up, shutting out the beauty of the mountains.

"What is it, Your Majesty?" Master Larad said as his horse veered close to Shandis. "Is something amiss?"

She smiled, not taking her gaze from the mountains. "No, I was just looking out the window."

The next afternoon they came to a crossroads. A timeworn statue stood watch over the meeting of ways, a nameless goddess who gazed with moss-filled eyes. The main road continued on straight, while a smaller path led off to the left, winding up a steep embankment. Grace had never been that way—despite many invitations over the last three years—but she knew that if she followed the path she would come to a valley and a half-ruined keep on the shores of a lake.

She had long wanted to visit Kelcior, though she was always afraid doing so would convince King Kel she had at last acquiesced to his proposals of marriage. Now it was but an hour's ride away. However, Kel was not at his keep; he had remained in Malachor to give Melia and Falken advice on ruling in her absence.

"The bard has more experience at wrecking kingdoms than running them, in case you didn't know," Kel had told Grace in a gruff attempt at a whisper that half the keep could hear.

Besides, she didn't have even an hour to spare. Now that they had left the forest behind, Grace had been able to see the rift again at night. It was still there, and she was certain it was larger than when she first saw it—a dark hole twice the size of Eldh's enormous moon.

They left the silent goddess at the crossroads and rode on.

Three days later they came to the town of Glennen's Stand. The town stood on the banks of a stream a few furlongs from the Queen's Way: a hundred or so slate-roofed houses clustered beneath a hill with a modest stone keep. As they drew near, Grace noticed that here and there a section of a pale stone wall still stood on the perimeter of the town, though in most places it had been knocked down and its stones hauled away. A lot of walls had been torn down since the war, Grace thought as they rode closer. And not just those around towns.

They found Glennen's Stand crowded, dirty, and thronging with life. There were at least as many animals as people, and all of them were talking, laughing, or braying loudly. The Dominion of Eredane had suffered longest under the oppression of the Onyx Knights, and its people were perhaps the most grateful to be freed from it. As they rode through a market in the heart of the city, Grace saw folk selling mysteries—small figures carved of wood, representing the gods of the seven Mystery Cults—and hedgewives hawking potions. Such acts would have been punishable by death under the rule of the Onyx Knights. Now they were practiced in broad daylight.

They reached the edge of the market. There, an old woman was taking small bottles of green glass from a table where they had been displayed and, one by one, opening them and pouring their contents into the gutter.

Grace pulled her horse away from the others and rode close. "What are you doing, sister?"

The woman did not look up. "Wrong," she muttered. "All wrong."

"What's wrong?" Grace said, shaking her head.

"My simples, that's what. All the good has gone out of them. There's no use in selling them anymore. This morning I tried to weave a spell of plenty over my hens. Only they pecked at each other, and broke one another's eggs. Sia is angry. She has placed a curse on the world."

The crone took another bottle and poured out its contents. The emerald fluid blended with the sludge in the gutter. Grace opened her mouth, but then she saw Brael motioning for her to follow. The old woman kept muttering as she emptied out her potions. Grace turned Shandis around and followed after the others.

They rode on, to an inn near the town's center. After a discussion with the proprietor, who was as jovial and red-faced as an innkeeper should be, they were led to rooms on the upper floor. Now that they were in Eredane, Grace should have presented herself to King Evren to request permission to ride through his Dominion. However, there wasn't time for such formalities; the king's castle of Erendel lay fifty leagues to the west. She told the innkeeper she was the daughter of a Calavaner merchant traveling on business for her father. No one would question her story. There were many travelers on the roads these days—another benefit of freedom.

They took their supper in a private dining chamber and retired early to their rooms. As night fell, music and laughter rose from the common room below, but Grace felt no temptation to go down and join in the merriment.

It was after midnight when she woke. The inn was silent, and starlight filtered through a crack in the shutters, slicing across the chamber like a silver knife. Grace tried to will herself back to sleep, but it was no use; her bladder would not be denied. She rose and used the chamber pot, then started back to bed.

Halfway there, she halted and moved to the window. She hesitated, then opened one of the shutters. The window faced north, and she wondered if she might be able to see it: the rift.

No. A haze of smoke hung over Glennen's Stand. She doubted if the folk in this town even knew it existed. How could they, if they had been so willing to sing and clap and laugh in the common room below? Only perhaps some did know. Grace thought of the old woman in the market, pouring out her potions. Sighing, she reached to close the shutter.

And froze. A shadow moved in the narrow street below. It slunk toward the inn, keeping low to the ground, avoiding any stray beams of light that spilled from nearby windows.

It's just a dog looking for scraps, Grace told herself, even though she knew it was too large to be one, that it moved nothing like a dog.

A night breeze wafted down the street, and the shadow's outlines appeared to ripple. The thing's motions were slow and purposeful, almost languid; it seemed to ooze rather than creep as it drew closer to the inn, heading straight for the wall below her window.

A door opened across the lane, and a beam of firelight fell onto the street. In an eyeblink the shadow slipped into the alley between the inn and the stable, vanishing as if absorbed by the darkness. Grace snatched the shutter back and locked it with an iron bar, her heart thudding.

She considered waking Brael. However, that was absurd. What would she tell him? That she had looked out her window and had seen a drunken man crawling home? For that was surely all it had been. She climbed back into bed, and at last she fell asleep.

By daylight, the memory of the shadow was less sinister, and she nearly forgot about it until Larad asked her as they rode from the town how she had slept, and she mentioned it to him.

"You should have come to me at once, Your Majesty," the Runelord said, his expression stern. "I could have spoken the rune of vision. We might have gotten a glimpse of it."

These words startled her. "It was only a shadow, Master Larad."

"If you wish, Your Majesty."

However, rather than reassuring her, the Runelord's words ate at her like acid all that day, and she resolved that if she saw something out of the ordinary again, she would alert Larad at once.

Only she didn't, and as they continued their journey south, it became harder to maintain the same keen sense of urgency she had felt on setting out from Gravenfist Keep. Instead, the monotony of the journey dulled the edge of her fear as well as her mind. Every day was the same: The mountains rose up to their left, the plains swept away to their right, and the road stretched on before them: straight, predictable, and—as far as the eye could see—endless.

Her urgency might have been renewed each night if she could see the rift, only she couldn't. The air in southern Eredane was moist, and at night all the stars were lost in haze. By day the weather was unseasonably hot and muggy, and she found the woolen riding gowns she had packed heavy and oppressive.

At last, on their twelfth day out from Gravenfist, the Queen's Way veered sharply in its course, turning to zigzag its way up a steep ridge in a series of switchbacks. They had reached the juncture of the Fal Erenn and the Fal Sinfath, the Gloaming Fells.

All that day they climbed upward, and in some places the road was so steep they were forced to dismount and walk in front of the horses so as not to exhaust the beasts—though Larad's mule plodded along as placidly as it had when the road was level.

They reached the top of the pass just as night began to fall. Before them lay the rock-strewn highlands of Galt, while behind and far below lay the rolling fields of Eredane. Grace panted for breath, for they had gone the last half mile on foot. Then she turned around, and her breath ceased. They had ascended far above the hazy air of the lowlands, and there was nothing to block her view.

"It has grown," Larad said beside her.

A hard wind scoured across the highlands, evaporating the sweat from Grace's skin. Though the stars were only just beginning to come out, there could be no doubting it: The rift had indeed grown, eating a dark hole in the northern sky. The dullness of boredom vanished; fear once again sliced into Grace's chest with a sharp blade. She welcomed the pain, for it cleared her mind and reminded her of her purpose.

Larad touched her arm. "Look, Your Majesty. Down there."

It took Grace a moment to see it in the failing light. Below them—far, but not so far as she might have liked—a dark blot moved along the road. It progressed rapidly, smoothly, ascending toward the highlands like a drop of dark liquid flowing up rather than down.

"It seems your shadow has followed us," the Runelord said softly.

Grace knew it was anatomically impossible, but it felt as if her heart was lodged in her esophagus. "Can you see what it is?"

Larad held out his right hand. "*Halas,*" he whispered. In the gloaming, the silver rune shone clearly on his palm: three crossed lines. At the same time his eyes glowed crimson, like those of an animal caught in the beam of a flashlight.

The night was deepening. Grace couldn't be sure, but it seemed the shadow halted, then flowed toward a crevice in the rocks, vanishing.

She clutched the sleeve of Larad's robe. "Did you see what it was?"

"No," he said, the red light fading from his eyes. "Whatever our stalker might be, I think it realized we had detected it. Even as I gazed at the thing, it seemed to melt away into the rocks. I doubt we will see it again tonight. Or at all, after this. It is likely to be even stealthier."

Grace wrapped her arms around herself, shivering. "But why would someone be following us?"

Larad did not answer. The sound of boots against gravel approached. They turned to see Sir Brael walking toward them.

"The men have found a flat space just off the road," he said. "A stone shelf affords some protection from the wind. Shall we set up your tent there, Your Majesty?"

Grace thought of the way the shadow had moved with liquid stealth along the road. "No," she said, shuddering. "The moon will rise soon, and it's close to full. We ride on to Castle Galt. We can be there by midnight if we hurry."

17.

They reached Castle Galt just before midnight, as Grace had hoped. It was not a vast, walled complex like Calavere, but rather a blocky tower keep perched on a windswept spur of rock. They pounded on the gate, and though the guards answered, they were suspicious of any travelers who arrived so late, and would have turned them away. However, at that moment the king himself came downstairs, clad in a nightshirt and carrying a candle, drawn by the commotion. He recognized Grace at once, scolded his guards—though not too harshly, at Grace's urging, for they were only doing their duty—and ushered the travelers inside.

Grace pleaded with the king to return to his bed, and not to let them be a trouble, but he would not hear of it, and called for a late supper to be set on the board in the hall. His twin sister, Kalyn, appeared—looking fresh-faced as ever, despite being disturbed from her rest—and served them bread, meat, and ale with her own hand. Grace was careful to take only a polite sip from the tankard of dark, foamy brew that was set before her. She had heard stories about Galtish ale, and most of them ended with falling down and taking a long time to get up again.

"C-c-can you tell us the reason for your j-j-journey south,

Your Majesty?" Kylar said when they had finished eating. "I c-c-confess, I am surprised to see you here. Since the shadow appeared in the northern sky, most people k-k-keep close to their homes and do not stray far. These are strange t-t-times, to be sure. Goats go lost, and their owners don't b-b-other to look for them. Old women stare at their looms as if they have never woven cloth in their lives. And it seems every other c-c-cask of ale my steward taps has spoiled."

"I'm sure Queen Grace's reasons for traveling are her own," Kalyn said crisply. She glanced at Grace, concern in her gentle brown eyes.

"Of c-c-course," King Kylar sputtered, looking mortified. The tassel at the end of his nightcap bobbed up and down. "P-p-please forgive me for b-b-being so rude, Your Majesty."

Grace pushed away her tankard. "No, I won't forgive you, because you have every right to ask, Your Highness. You've been so kind to take us in at this late hour. I want very much to tell you, and—"

Larad gave her a sharp look.

"And it's best if you don't," Kalyn said, touching Grace's hand. "Don't worry, Your Majesty. We know that whatever you're doing, it's for the greater good. We needn't hear the particulars."

Grace sighed. "Thank you."

"Now," Kalyn said, "there is one thing you must tell us, and that is how we can help you."

After an abbreviated but welcome night's rest, they set out again an hour after dawn. Grace considered telling Kylar to keep watch for their shadowy pursuer, then decided against it. Whatever the shadow was, it would not be lingering in Galt. The only thing Grace knew for certain was that it was following her.

"Is something wrong, Master Larad?" she asked as they mounted the horses. The Runelord's face was gray and pinched, and he seemed unable to stand up straight.

She couldn't understand his muttered reply, though she caught the words "hammer" and "skull." Apparently he hadn't heard the stories about Galtish ale.

They made good time that day—despite Larad's indisposition, for King Kylar kept the section of the Queen's Way that passed through Galt in good repair. The pack mule was now laden down with supplies from Kylar's larder and wore something of a betrayed expression on its long face. The beast really hadn't signed on for all this, Grace supposed. She had taken to calling the mule Glumly, for that was he how did everything, though he never balked and always kept pace with the horses.

They spent that night at a small, cheerful inn, though Larad hastily retreated to his room, hand to his mouth, when the innkeeper set a foaming tankard before him. The next day the road descended a rocky valley, following the course of a noisy stream, and by evening they made camp on the edge of greener, gentler lands. As they set out the next morning, Grace found herself leaning forward in the saddle, and it was afternoon of the day after that—their fourth out from Galt—when they crested a rise and she finally caught sight of what she had been straining to glimpse: a castle with seven towers rising on a distant hill.

"Calavere," she murmured, her heart quickening. Shandis let out a snort, and even Glumly pricked up his long ears. They cantered the last league to the castle, not afraid of tiring their mounts, for despite their haste Grace intended to stay there for a day. It would be good to rest—if only for a short while—in the company of friends.

When they arrived at Calavere's gates, they found Aryn, Teravian, and Lirith waiting for them.

"How did you sense we were near the castle?" Grace asked as she gripped Aryn's hands. "I can hardly reach more than a hundred paces with the Touch these days."

I don't need magic to sense when you're coming, sister, came Aryn's warm reply over the Weirding. *My heart knows.*

Grace laughed, holding the other witch tight, and for the first time in days she thought nothing of dragons or rifts or shadows. Teravian and Lirith pressed forward then, and there was a good deal of embracing all around—so much so that even Master Larad could not escape a hug or two, despite the Runelord's best efforts.

However, that evening found them all in a grimmer mood as they gathered in Teravian's chamber for a private supper. Though the fare set on the table by the servants—roasted goose, golden loaves of bread, berries and fresh cream—was far more sumptuous than anything they had gotten on the road south, Grace found she had little appetite as she listened to Aryn and Teravian speak of affairs in Calavan and Toloria.

There had been a good deal of unrest already that summer. The weather had been unusually hot; it had seldom rained, and when it did the storms were violent, pounding the crops in the fields to pulp. A two-headed calf had been born at a farm not far from the castle—an event considered an ill omen by most folk. Stranger still, stories told that the old witch who had gone to dispel the curse that hung over the farm had dropped dead when she tried to weave the spell.

"But can that be, sister?" Lirith said, looking at Aryn.

The young queen hesitated, then nodded. "It could, if the threads of the Weirding tangled around her tightly enough. Her own thread might have been strangled."

Lirith clasped a hand to her mouth.

"A week ago, my castle runespeaker tried to speak the rune of purity at dinner," Teravian said. "Only he couldn't. 'My tongue sticks to the roof of my mouth every time I try to speak a rune,' he told me. The poor man was nearly in tears. He returned to the Gray Tower the next day, saying that he would have a replacement sent to Calavere right away." He looked at Grace. "But I don't suppose one will come?"

"Not if the rift keeps growing," Grace said, trying not to think of the witch who had been strangled by her own spell. "Have you seen it here? I don't know if it's visible this far south yet—the last few nights have been cloudy."

Teravian picked up a glass of wine but did not drink. "Yes, we've seen it. Ten nights ago, it appeared in the north—a dark hole in the sky, just like you described."

"Are people afraid?" Grace said.

Teravian frowned. "That's the peculiar thing. I thought they would be. I thought there would be fire and panic, and I was ready to send my guards out to stop it. Only there was no need. The people go about their daily lives as before. They tend to their fields, their shops, their children. Only there is no joy to it, no meaning. They're going through the motions, that's all. Folk have stopped leaving offerings at the shrines of the Mystery

Cults. They say the gods have abandoned them, only they do nothing to bring the gods back. It's as if they've run out of—"

"Hope," Aryn said softly. She sat in a chair near the window, her left hand resting on her full belly. "They've run out of hope."

Teravian set down his goblet and knelt before her. "There *is* hope, Aryn." He laid his hand over hers. "It's right here."

Despite the dread that seemed to be a permanent fixture in her chest, Grace found herself smiling. Aryn and Teravian hadn't chosen one another. If fact, given a choice, surely either would have selected almost anyone else. All the same, in the three years since their marriage, love had grown between them, and it was all the more precious because it had been so unlooked for, like a flower blooming in the midst of winter.

Aryn had bloomed herself. The lovely but tentative young woman Grace had first met in this castle was gone, replaced by a beautiful and regal queen. Her blue eyes were still vivid, but tempered with wisdom now, and her raven hair framed a porcelain face that was sharper than before, but no less kind. She seemed complete: a woman, queen, and witch in the full of her power. Even her withered right arm, so small and delicately twisted, was a part of the whole.

Teravian had changed as well. Although he would never be brawny like his father, King Boreas, his lean frame had filled out, and he no longer hunched his broad shoulders. He wore a black beard now, like his father had, and when he bared his teeth in a grin, he reminded Grace of bullish King Boreas indeed—so much so that she felt a pang of grief in her chest. However, when he grew serious and thoughtful, which was far more often, it was his mother, Queen Ivalaine, who was reflected in the young king's visage.

"What I hope," Aryn said, shifting in the chair and grimacing, "is that this baby comes soon."

"It will," Teravian said.

She glared at him. "You can't know that."

"Actually, I can," he said, his voice growing testy. "I have the Sight, remember?"

"No, you don't. I could be ready to explode, and you

wouldn't know it, because the Sight isn't working anymore. Is it, Lirith?"

The dark-haired witch took a step back. "I believe I'll stay out of this one, sister."

Grace didn't dare demonstrate her mirth, but inwardly she laughed. Although Aryn and Teravian had found true love, that didn't mean they had entirely forgotten how to argue. In fact, they seemed to remember quite well. Fortunately, their quarrel was interrupted as Taneth began to cry.

Master Larad held the baby out at arm's length, a distasteful expression on his face. "I think it wants something."

"Perhaps to be held like a child rather than a sack of grain," Lirith said, hurrying over to the Runelord.

"I do not believe giving it to me was a wise idea," Larad said. "I have no talent for comforting children."

"It doesn't take talent, Master Larad," Lirith said. "Only knowledge. Surely a scholar such as you is not afraid to learn something new."

The Runelord glowered at her, but he did not disagree.

"Here, place your arm under him for support, and let his head rest in the crook of your elbow. And keep him close against you. Babies want to feel they are safe and loved. There now."

Taneth had stopped fussing, and his eyes drifted shut. The corners of Larad's mouth twitched in the hint of a smile, then he looked up and glared at the others. They all studiously turned their attention elsewhere. However, when Grace stole a glance a few minutes later, she saw Larad in the corner rocking Taneth with awkward but gentle motions.

All the next day, they spoke not of the rift and the weakening of magic, but of mundane things—babies, and weaving blankets, and the day-to-day drudgery of running a kingdom—which, with the help of much wine come evening, soon led to mirth.

However, they were all sober the next morning when Grace and Larad set out from Calavere—along with Lirith and Taneth. Aryn's cheeks were dry, but by the redness of her eyes Grace knew she had been weeping.

I want to go with you, sisters, Aryn's voice quavered across the threads of the Weirding.

And we want you to come, Lirith spun back, *but you know you must stay. They both need you.*

Aryn sighed, touching her belly with her left hand, and leaned her head against Teravian's shoulder.

"Do you have everything you need for the journey?" the young king asked.

"We do," Grace said. Glumly was once again laden with supplies, and looking forlorn as usual. "Thank you."

Master Larad and the knights already sat astride their mounts. Lirith climbed into the saddle of her horse, and Grace handed Taneth up to her. She nestled the baby in a linen sling, so that he was held securely against her breast. It was time for Lirith and Taneth to return to their people; Sareth was waiting.

Grace embraced Aryn and Teravian, kissing them both and climbing onto Shandis before she could begin weeping herself.

Teravian's face was grave, and tears shone in Aryn's blue eyes. But all she said was, "Give Travis our love."

The journey south was strangely pleasant. Grace was glad to no longer be the only woman in the party; Lirith's company was a rare gift, and it was wonderful to finally meet little Taneth. The weather was fine and sunny, and as they rode through familiar lands they eschewed inns, instead camping in copses or dells, or more than once in the shaded enclosure of a *talathrin,* an old Tarrasian Way Circle.

The Way Circles were always built around a spring next to which grew *alasai,* or green scepter—an herb good for removing the taint from meat, and whose clean, sharp scent was a balm to the lungs. When she drank from the spring in a *talathrin,* Grace always remembered to sprinkle a few drops for Naimi, goddess of travelers, as Melia had taught her to do. Nor did she worry about the shadow that had been following them when she laid down to sleep. There was no magic in the Way Circles, but a goodness abided in them; nothing would harm them there.

Although they traveled from sunrise until late afternoon each day, it took a fortnight to reach Tarras. Grace let out a breath of wonder when she glimpsed the ancient city rising up from the azure waters of the Summer Sea in seven circles of white stone. People went about their business as they had for a thousand years. But why shouldn't they? Magic was practiced by northern barbarians, not the civilized people of Tarras. And the rift was not visible there, so far south in the world. It had been many days since Grace had seen it last, low in the northern sky.

As they rode close to Tarras, Grace thought it would be good to go into the city, to ascend to the First Circle, and pay a visit to Emperor Ephesian—her cousin many times removed. However, there was no time for catching up with old acquaintances. They rode past without stopping.

Now, each day they journeyed, the air grew a little warmer, becoming gold and honey-sweet with the perfume of unfamiliar flowers. They followed the coastline, riding along a road lined with a green-gold colonnade of *ithaya*, or sunleaf, trees. Below, the ocean crashed against white cliffs while gulls wheeled above.

At last they could go no farther; they had reached the southernmost tip of Falengarth. As twilight fell—nearly a full month since they had set out from Gravenfist Keep—they ascended a bluff above the sea, passed through a grove of *ithaya* trees, and rode into a circle of painted wagons shaped like animals both ordinary and fantastic.

Before they even dismounted, Sareth was there. He caught Lirith and Taneth in his arms, pulling them down to him, and embracing them with ferocious strength. Nor was Grace forgotten, for after he finally released Lirith, Grace found herself hugging the Mournish man. She breathed in his spicy, familiar scent, and only then realized how much she had missed him and his deep, bell-like laugh.

The Mournish gathered around the travelers, leading them into the circle of light while music and the rich scents of cooking wafted on the air. Women in colorful garb approached Brael and the other knights, placing circlets of flowers around their necks, and even Master Larad was treated to a warm welcome. Perhaps warmer than the Runelord might have cared for. He was obviously flustered as three young women slipped necklaces of flowers over his head, and he looked as if he was about to speak stern words of reproach, only then a fit of sneezing took him, and he sat down hard on a stump. The women laughed and clapped their hands.

For a time, Grace let herself forget why she had journeyed there. She sat on a log on the edge of the firelight, eating nuts and drinking smoky wine, and swaying in time to wild music as many of the Mournish men and women whirled about the bonfire in a dance, scarves, jewelry, and smiles all flashing. Sparks rose up to the sky, and as Grace followed them upward she saw a point of crimson light. Tira's star was not low to the southern horizon as it was in the north, but instead high in the sky.

"I love you," Grace murmured like a prayer. Maybe it was at that, for the little red-haired girl was a goddess now, and the center of the world's newest Mystery Cult.

And perhaps its last as well. Grace's gaze moved northward. She could not see it, but she knew the rift was still there, and still growing.

The wind rustled through the leaves of the *ithaya* trees, and only then did Grace realize that the music had stopped. She lowered her gaze and was startled to see that the bonfire had burned low, and that the Mournish were gone. How long had she been gazing at the sky?

"Come, Grace," Sareth said, kneeling before her. "My al-Mama is waiting for you."

She looked around. There was no one in view save Sareth and Larad. "Where did everyone go?"

"Lirith has taken Taneth to his bed, and your knights have been shown to theirs. Come."

Grace and Larad followed Sareth to a wagon on the edge of the circle. It was shaped like a dragon, its sinuous outline blending with the night. Sareth opened the door and indicated they should climb the steps and enter.

The cramped interior of the wagon was lit by a single candle. In the dim light it took a moment to pick the woman out from the various bundles of cloth and dried herbs. She look like a bundle of rags and sticks herself. Sareth's al-Mama was far thinner than the last time they had met; her bones were prominent beneath skin as translucent and yellow as parchment. Grace didn't need to probe along the Weirding to make her diagnosis. Jaundice. Liver failure.

"Yes, yes," the old woman said testily. "I'm dying. And it's about time. These old bones are long overdue for a rest. But that does not matter now. Come closer so these old eyes can see you."

The old woman leaned forward as they approached. Though clouded with cataracts, her gold eyes were still bright. At last she nodded and sighed, leaning back on her pallet.

"So you have come, as has been fated. I am satisfied. You will find him, and you will help him reach it."

Grace swallowed. "You mean Morindu."

"Of course I mean Morindu!" the old woman snapped. "But who is this with you? I see a cloak of power about him, though its cloth is unraveling. A great wizard of the north, he is. Yet he is not the one. What role is his to play?"

"Can you not see in your cards?" Larad said, gesturing to a deck of worn *T'hot* cards scattered on a table.

"Bah!" the old woman spat. "The cards are useless now. The threads of Fate are all tangled. Nothing is clear. A darkness looms before us, and I know not what lies on the other side, if anything lies there at all. But this I do know." She pointed a thin finger at Grace. "You will find him, and you will lead him to his destiny. I have summoned ones to help you on the journey. That is all I can do. As for the rest . . ." She lowered her hand and heaved a rattling sigh. "It is up to Sai'el Travis."

Grace wanted to ask her more—how she was supposed to find Travis, what she should tell him when she did, and what they needed to do.

"Go," the old woman said, her voice a sullen croak. "I wished only to look upon you, and now it is done. I will not see the end of this, but now I know that an end indeed draws nigh. Go, and leave me to my own end."

Grace met Larad's eyes, and the two of them stepped from the wagon. They found Sareth standing near the remains of the bonfire.

"She's dying," Grace said.

Sareth nodded, his coppery eyes reflecting the glow of the embers. "So she has told us many times. Only this time it is true."

Grace touched his shoulder, "I'm sorry."

"No, don't be." Despite the sadness in his voice, he smiled.

"Hers has been a long and wondrous life. And perhaps it is better this way. Perhaps it is better if she does not see . . ."

Grace tightened her grip on his shoulder. "We'll find him, Sareth. We'll find Travis."

"I know you will. But there is one thing you do not know. At this time, my sister Vani is on Travis Wilder's world, on Earth. Even now she searches for him."

Hope surged in Grace's chest. She started to ask Sareth how this could be, but Larad sucked in a breath.

"We are not alone."

Even as he spoke, three dark forms parted from the darkness beneath the *ithaya* trees. Grace went cold. Had the shadow followed them there, bringing others like it?

No, these shadows moved not with strange fluidity, but rather with feline stealth. Even as they stepped into the starlight, Grace knew what they were. Two of them were men, one a woman. Intricate tattoos coiled up their necks, and each one's left ear bore thirteen gold rings. All wore sleek black leather.

"*T'gol*," Grace whispered.

Larad gave her a startled look. "You mean assassins?"

"No that's not what the word means," Sareth said. "In our tongue, *T'gol* means *to protect*. My al-Mama summoned them from the Silent Fortress of Golgoru. They will accompany you on your journey."

"Why?" Grace said.

One of the *T'gol* moved forward. He was tall and slender, his eyes the color of aged bronze. "It is for this that our kind has trained for a thousand years, Sai'ana Grace. Three of us were chosen for this highest honor. We will accompany you on your journey to the dervish, as well as to the ancient city of our people. We are yours to command."

Three *T'gol*—three warriors all trained like Vani—following her orders? The thought stunned Grace, even as it renewed her will.

"We leave at dawn," she said.

"We will be ready." The *T'gol* made a sharp gesture with his hand, then he and the others melted away into the shadows.

18

Grace, Master Larad, and the three *T'gol* left the circle of the Mournish caravan before dawn. Only Sareth and Lirith rose in the gray light to see them off; the other wagons were dark, their doors and windows shut.

The Mournish man was clearly torn. Last night, he had started to speak as if he was going to accompany Grace on the journey. However, a stern look from Lirith had silenced those words.

"You have already done the work of the *T'gol* once, when you sought out the dervish," Lirith murmured, bending over Taneth's head. "This time the *T'gol* have come to do what is their rightful task. It is their duty to seek out Morindu the Dark."

"And what of my duty?" Sareth had said in a low voice, his face bathed in the glow of the fire's last coals. "I am descended of the royal line of Morindu. Should I not be there when the city comes to light once more?"

Her voice was hard. "If the royal line is truly so precious as you say it is, then it is your duty to protect it and stay with your son."

Sareth had pressed his lips into a tight line, holding back any other words he might have said. And though his eyes were troubled, they were full of love as well. The Mournish man had won this argument once; now it was Lirith's turn.

Sareth was not the only one who was upset at not continuing south with Grace. Earlier that morning, after they rose in the dark before first light, she had commanded Bracl to ride back to Gravenfist Keep with the other knights. The gray-bearded man was clearly upset.

"The southern continent is a queer and dangerous place, Your Majesty," he had said, sputtering. "You cannot possibly think to go there alone. We are coming with you."

"I won't be alone. And you're not coming with us. That's an order, Sir Knight. I need you to tell Melia and Falken that we made it this far safely. And tell them we've learned Vani has already gone to find what we seek, to bring it back to us. They'll know what the message means."

The anger faded from Brael's eyes, replaced by anguish. However, a knight could not disobey a direct order from his queen, and he gave a stiff nod. "May Vathris walk with you, Your Majesty."

Grace hoped he did; she was going to need all the help she could get.

"It is nearly dawn," spoke one of the *T'gol*—the tall man who moved like a dancer. His name was Avhir, Grace had learned. "We must leave now, Sai'ana Grace, if we are to reach the city of Kalos before nightfall."

Already the eastern horizon was brightening, and below the cliffs the Summer Sea shone like a mirror of beaten copper.

Sareth touched Grace's cheek with a warm, rough hand. "May Fasus, God of Winds, speed you on your journey, and back to us."

Lirith handed Taneth to him, then moved forward to throw her arms around Grace. *I cannot see the future, sister*, she said, her voice humming along the threads of the Weirding. *I cannot see if you will return to us.*

Grace embraced the witch, concentrating on this moment so she would never forget it. *Good-bye, sister.*

Lirith turned away, brushing her cheeks with her fingers, and took Taneth back, holding the baby tight against her.

Grace mounted Shandis, and as the knights were to take all of the horses with them back to Gravenfist, Larad awkwardly climbed into Glumly's saddle. The *T'gol* would go on foot; they did not need mounts to move swiftly.

"Do not trust the dervish," Sareth said. "You believe you know him, but you do not. The desert changes a man, as do the secrets one might discover there. He has called the *morndari* to him, he has worked blood sorcery, and he cannot possibly be the same as you knew him."

Avhir gave Shandis a slap on the rump, and the mare started into a trot down the path that led from the Mournish circle, Larad's mule following. Grace gazed back over her shoulder, and she thought she saw two dim figures beneath the *ithaya* trees waving farewell. Then the path began to descend the side of the bluff, and the figures were lost to sight.

"I want to thank you," she said to Avhir, who walked beside Shandis. "For coming with me."

He did not look at her. "There is no point in thanking me, Sai'ana Grace. We come because it is our fate."

Grace smiled. "That doesn't mean I don't appreciate it all the same."

Either these words annoyed Avhir, or he did not know what to make of them, for he stalked away without replying and approached the other two *T'gol*. With some effort Grace had been able to learn their names. Kylees was a fine-boned woman whose lovely face was marred by a persistent scowl, while Rafid was a compact man, as short and muscular as Avhir was tall and lithe.

Avhir spoke something in a low voice to the other *T'gol*. All three wore grim expressions. Grace sighed. Something told her she was going to have to rely on Master Larad for lively conversation on this trip.

All that day they traveled along the road that followed the sinuous line of the cliffs above the sea. Once the sun rose into the sky, the outlines of the *T'gol* blurred, and they seemed to vanish. However, Grace knew they were still there. From time to time she could see a shimmering on the air, like that of a heat mirage, and if she looked at the ground, she would detect a faint shadow.

Despite her hope for a little conversation to pass the time, she spoke little to Master Larad as they rode. The Runelord seemed intent on studying the landscape, the trees, and the plants. All would be exotic to a man born and raised in the far north, and were no doubt intriguing to his inquisitive mind. Grace decided not to lament the silence. After all, she had other matters to mull over.

Do not trust the dervish . . . the desert changes a man . . .

What had Sareth meant by those words? Did he believe Hadrian Farr to be dangerous in some way?

All dervishes are dangerous, Grace. By definition. They're people who've shunned the laws and ethics of their society in order to learn ancient secrets of sorcery. There's no way you can trust someone like that. They've already shown they're not beholden to anything. Anything except the quest for knowledge, for power.

Only Farr hadn't given up the laws of his society. He wasn't one of the Mournish; he was from Earth. And while she supposed it was possible Farr did crave power, she thought it more likely his thirst for knowledge had compelled him to become a dervish. Farr was a Seeker through and through; more than anything he wanted to learn, to comprehend mysteries no other person before him had. That wouldn't change just because he somehow found a way to Eldh.

Or would it? *He has worked blood sorcery, and he cannot possibly be the same as you knew him. . . .*

Perhaps. But had she ever really known Hadrian Farr anyway? He had helped her, yes. First on that October night when all of this began, when he aided her escape from the ironheart detective at the police department, and again when she and Travis returned to Denver in a desperate attempt to save Beltan's life. But while he had had files and photos and documents about her, she had nothing to tell her about Farr. Other than his eyes, she still could not picture him in her mind. He was like a vague silhouette, wreathed in cigarette smoke and lit from behind. What would she say to him when she saw him? She didn't know. All the same, a thrill ran through her when she thought of seeing him again, of being close to him. Unconsciously, she urged Shandis into a swifter pace.

Late that afternoon, as they neared the port city of Kalos, one of the *T'gol* reappeared; it was the woman, Kylees.

"Avhir has gone ahead to arrange passage on a ship," the assassin said. She resembled Vani only in that she was lean in her black leathers, and her dark hair was closely cropped. She was smaller than Vani, even petite. Clad in one of the colorful dresses favored by young Mournish women, she would appear pretty and vulnerable. Grace had no doubt many large, strong, foolish men had thought the same thing. Just before their necks snapped.

"Is Rafid with Avhir?" Grace asked.

The *T'gol* scowled. "Do you think I am not strong enough to protect you as well as Rafid or Avhir if your pursuer appears?"

That wasn't what Grace had meant. She had only been trying to be polite.

"Keep close," Kylees said, and moved swiftly down the road.

Grace did as instructed. She had told Avhir about the shadow that had followed them, and though they had seen no signs of pursuit, it was a good idea to stay vigilant.

They reached the city just as the sun melted into the sea. Kalos was situated on a narrow peninsula that formed the southern tip of the continent of Falengarth, and so was surrounded by water on three sides. On the east, tall cliffs formed a deep harbor, and this—along with the fact that the Summer Sea was narrower here than anywhere else—made Kalos a bustling city of traders, merchants, pilgrims, and other travelers. It was a good place to begin a journey. And to lose pursuit.

Avhir appeared as they rode through the city's gates. "I have found a ship to bear us across the sea," he said to Grace. "Tonight we will stay at a hostel in the Merchant's Quarter. Try not to speak to anyone, but if you must, tell them you are the daughter of a northern spice trader and that you are here on an errand of business for him."

That wasn't going to be a problem. Grace didn't plan on engaging in any idle chitchat with the locals. When they reached the hostel, they retired at once to their rooms and did not leave again until first light, when they set out for the shipyards. Though the sun had not yet risen, Kalos was already awake and bustling with activity. Grace bought dates from a smiling, toothless man, and she and Master Larad made a breakfast of them as they rode through the city.

They were nearly to the docks when Grace saw a man in a white robe surrounded by a crowd of people. She supposed he was a priest of one of the Mystery Cults, preaching to a group of followers. However, as she and Larad drew nearer, she saw that the man's white robe was dirty and ragged, and that it did not bear a holy symbol of any of the New Gods. Instead, a blotch as black as old blood was painted on the center of robe, over his heart. The man was speaking, his voice chantlike, but the people gathered around him seemed not to listen; instead, they stared at the ground or into thin air with slack expressions. They were filthy, their faces darkened by flies.

"You!" the man said, his voice rising into a shout. He was pointing at Grace and Larad. "Do not think you can flee it on a ship! It does not matter where you go. The Mouth will eat you."

Grace pulled on the reins, bringing Shandis to a halt. He was right. What did she think she was doing? There was no point in going south across the sea. Nothing she could do would change anything. She started to nudge Shandis toward the man in the dirty white robe.

"Come, Sai'ana Grace." The air rippled, and Avhir was there, gripping Shandis's bridle. "The ship is ready to sail."

Grace blinked, and the torpor fell away from her, replaced by urgency. Yes, they had to go at once. She and Larad rode after Avhir as the *T'gol* led the way into the dockyards.

The ship Avhir had arranged for their passage was a sleek two-masted spice trader. It reminded her of the *Fate Runner*, the ship on which she had first journeyed to Tarras and which had carried her back north, only to founder and sink off the coast of Embarr after they were attacked by Onyx Knights. She thought about Captain Magard, and his rough, kindly humor. And the way he had died in the keep of Seawatch—the same keep where Lord Elwarrd had died rather than let his ironheart mother deliver Grace to the Pale King.

For a short while, Grace had almost believed she could love Elwarrd—if that was even something she was capable of. It was only now, as she thought of him for the first time in years, that she realized how much the handsome, dark-eyed lord had reminded her of Hadrian Far. . . .

"Is something wrong, Your Majesty?" Larad asked as they dismounted at the end of the pier.

Yes, Grace suddenly realized, there was. "I forgot about Shandis and Glumly. What are we going to do with them? We can't just leave them here."

Larad looked as if he would be perfectly content to leave the mule behind, but Grace sighed, stroking both Glumly's and Shandis's muzzles. Fortunately, she had worried for nothing.

"I have hired a courier to return your mounts to the Mournish," Avhir said, appearing out of thin air, and Grace was too grateful for his words to be annoyed at the way the *T'gol* had startled her.

"That was kind of you," she said.

He waved the words aside with a long hand. "It was not done out of kindness. You must focus on your fate. Your mind must not be distracted by petty concerns such as the welfare of an animal."

Grace didn't care what he said. It *felt* like kindness. She kissed Shandis's flat face and tried not to cry. "Lirith will take good care of you," she said, then she stepped back as a young man led the honey-colored mare and the mule away.

They boarded the ship, and apparently they were the last cargo to be loaded, for almost at once the plank was pulled back, the lines thrown down, and the sails unfurled. The ship pulled away from the dock, speeding out into the harbor and toward open sea. Grace gripped the rail and faced into the wind, letting the spray moisten her face.

"Something is wrong with this ship," Master Larad said behind her. "Terribly wrong."

Grace turned around. The Runelord clutched one of the masts. His face was an unnatural and vivid shade of green.

"The floor is heaving as if it's about to rend apart," the Runelord gasped. "This cannot be right. We must abandon ship!"

Grace couldn't help a laugh. "Not just yet, Master Larad. The rolling is perfectly normal. And it's called a deck, not a floor."

"Normal? You mean this is how it's going to be for the entire passage?"

"No," Grace said cheerfully. "Once we're out of the harbor, the rolling will be much more pronounced."

Larad stared at her, an expression of horror on his scarred face. Then he ran to one side of the deck and leaned over the rail. Grace didn't know the rune for nausea, but it seemed Larad was quite familiar with it. Fortunately, she had packed some herbs in her luggage.

You'd better go brew him a simple, Grace.

She went in search of Avhir, to find out where her things had been stowed. The *T'gol* found her first.

"We have conducted a search of the entire ship, Sai'ana Grace," the *T'gol* said. Even in the bright morning light, it was hard to look at him, as if his body was a projection that was slightly out of focus. "There is no one on board save for ourselves and the crew."

Grace nodded. It was impossible that someone could be on the ship and the *T'gol* would not find them. Even so, she had made her own inventory as they boarded the ship. She had used the Touch to seek out and locate the life thread of every living organism on the ship, down to the last rat. It had been exhausting work—the web of the Weirding had kept knotting and tangling in her fingers—but she had done it, and she knew Avhir was right. Whoever or whatever had been pursuing them, it was not on this ship.

"The passage to Al-Amún will take two days, Sai'ana Grace. I suggest you use that time to rest. I will show you to your quarters."

She took Avhir up on his offer, but she did not stay in her tiny cabin belowdecks. Instead she fashioned a quick simple and went in search of Master Larad. On deck, the crewmen were lashing down ropes; they had given the ship full sail now that they had left the harbor behind.

"Excuse me," she said to one of the sailors—a man with blond hair and a boyish face. "You haven't seen a sick wizard around, have you?"

"No," the sailor said.

He was tying a rope to a metal hook. As he worked, Grace noticed a rather nasty-looking gash on his arm. It was fresh and had barely begun to scab over. He had probably gotten it while working the ropes; a loose line could crack like a whip.

She started to reach for him. "Would you like me to take a look at that cut? I'm a healer."

"You'd best leave me be and go to your cabin," he growled. "A woman has no business on a ship. It's bad luck."

Then he turned his back on her, grabbed a rope, and scrambled up into the rigging. So much for that sweet, boyish face. She started along the deck, continuing her search for Master Larad, and hoping her sea legs decided to show up soon.

She found the Runelord still leaning over the rail. With effort, she managed to get some of the simple down him, and then with the help of Kylees transferred him to his hammock in the main hold belowdecks. Grace had asked Rafid for help first, but he had scowled and stalked away. A moment later Kylees appeared.

"What's wrong with Rafid?" Grace asked.

"He will not touch a sorcerer except to slay one," Kylees said.

"Larad's not a sorcerer. He's a wizard."

Kylees did not answer. Despite her small size, she looped Larad's arm around her shoulder and hauled him to his feet.

Grace spent most of the voyage at Larad's side, bathing his brow with a cool cloth and getting what herbs into him she could. Blessedly, the passage was short and the winds fairer than usual of late, and it was just after dawn two days later when they sailed into the harbor at Qaradas.

Master Larad's condition improved almost immediately upon disembarking, though he remained pale and weak. Grace knew that speed was of the essence, but she wondered if it wouldn't be better to wait a day in the city to let Larad recover his strength.

"With all due respect, Your Majesty," the Runelord said, "I would rather ride at once. At the moment, I wish to get as far away from water as possible."

"Then you shall get your wish," Avhir said, appearing out of a swirl of dust. "The others have arranged camels and supplies for our journey. We will set out for Hadassa at once."

Grace bit her tongue to keep from thanking the *T'gol*. She cast a glance at the ship—her last connection with the lands of the north—then followed Avhir and Larad through the gritty streets of Qaradas.

19.

The blond-haired sailor walked along the pier, away from the docked ship.

"Where are you going, Madeth?" a rough voice called out. A group of his crew mates gathered near the end of the pier. "We're off to find ourselves some wine and dancing women. I've heard that in Qaradas they wear nothing under all those fluttering scarves."

The sailor called Madeth did not stop walking.

"Ah, forget him," said another man. "He's still a boy. He'd only get in our way."

The sailors moved away down the dock. That was good. He could not allow himself to be seen.

Why? a part of him started to question. *Why can't I be seen? Where am I going?*

However, those tremulous thoughts were quickly drowned out by a surge of hot blood in his brain. His legs pumped with mechanical efficiency, carrying him into the city. His eyes scanned back and forth until they found what they sought: the mouth of an alley between two white buildings. He moved into the alley, away from the hot eye of the sun, letting the dim coolness envelop him.

The alley was empty save for a dog that snarled at him. Its ribs were showing. He ignored the beast as he had the men. It was time.

He pulled away the rag he had bound around his arm two days ago. The wound beneath was puckered like an angry mouth. Pus oozed from beneath a crusted scab, and red lines spread out from the gash, snaking up his arm. He had gotten the cut while loading the ship, gouging his arm on an exposed nail while he hoisted crates on the dock at Kalos.

And then what happened? He tried to remember. He had cut himself, and then all at once everything went dark, as if a shadow had fallen over him. There was pain—far more pain than a simple cut on his arm should cause, coursing through his body. And then . . .

Oh, by all the gods, then—

Again blood sizzled in his brain, erasing the thoughts. With his free hand he dug under the scab, prying it loose, and pressed his fingers into the wound, opening it up and tearing it wider.

Blood gushed out, and Madeth screamed.

He staggered back against the wall. Dark red fluid poured down his arm, raining onto the ground and pooling there. The puddle grew larger, then the blood began to flow—not down the gutter—but upward, into the air. It gathered in on itself, rising up before Madeth, twisting and writhing like one of the waterspouts he glimpsed from time to time on the open ocean. And which he would never glimpse again.

His heart ceased its work; there was nothing left for it to pump. The column of dark fluid undulated and took on a new shape: that of a man. Two hot sparks appeared in its face, glowing like eyes. They watched as the empty husk of the young sailor slumped to the ground. The dog's snarling became a piteous whine as it backed deeper into the alley.

A glistening arm lashed out, reaching much farther than a normal man's might, and the whining was cut short. The arm retracted, drawing the body of the dog closer, and in a moment its empty body lay crumpled next to that of the sailor.

The creature's body rippled with pleasure. It re-formed itself into a tight ball and rolled to the back of the alley, then let itself sink back into a puddle on the ground. This form took the least energy to maintain, and it was best to conserve; soon, it would need all its strength. It would rest while the hot eye glared down from the sky. Then, when darkness covered the world, the hunt would begin again. She was close. It could taste the nearness of her blood. It would pursue.

And when this over, when it had brought its creators to what they sought, it would drink her dry.

20.

Deirdre winced as a crash emanated from the other side of the paneled mahogany door. This was not going well. They had left Beltan alone in the parlor, hoping some rest might calm him. Instead, it seemed to have had the opposite effect. Another crash sounded. She tried to picture the parlor's decor. There weren't any Roman busts, Ming vases, or priceless medieval artifacts in there, were there?

Not anymore, she thought.

She looked up to see Anders hurrying down the corridor, a satchel in hand. Thank the Great Spirit, he was back.

"How is he?" Anders said in his gravelly voice. He had donned a fresh suit—one with two sleeves.

"Fabulous," Deirdre said, "In a screaming, thrashing about, throwing things against the wall sort of way."

"I figured as much," the Seeker said. "Big warrior types never have tidy little emotional outbursts. He's got to be pretty broken up."

Something thudded against he wall, rattling it.

"Him and the parlor," Deirdre said. But that wasn't fair. Beltan was just displaying what all of them were feeling inside. The Scirathi had taken Nim. Travis and Vani had followed through the gate, but there was no way to know if they had succeeded, if they had managed to pursue the sorcerers to Eldh, or if they had been lost in the Void between the worlds. Beltan had just met his daughter. Now he might well have lost her forever, and his life mate as well. Given similar circumstances, Deirdre doubted her outburst would have been very tidy either.

"I brought some of his clothes from their flat," Anders said, hefting the satchel. "Maybe a shower will help settle him down and clear his head. Let's talk to him."

Deirdre was doubtful, but it was worth a try. "You go first."

Anders opened the door, then ducked as a coffee cup whizzed over his head, past Deirdre, and shattered against the wall of the corridor.

"Hey, now," Anders muttered under his breath. "I hope that wasn't aimed at me."

"You're the one who wanted to go in," Deirdre said, and shoved him in the back, urging him forward.

No more projectiles hurtled their way as they entered the parlor and shut the door behind them. The destruction was not as bad as Deirdre had feared, and was largely limited to their coffee cups and saucers from the night before. She made a quick survey of the room. There was a large Grecian urn on a pedestal next to the fireplace, looking both priceless and fragile, but it was untouched.

The same could not be said for Beltan. He stood in the center of the room, hands empty and twitching, staring blankly. An ugly bruise darkened his right temple. She had never known what a proud warrior defeated looked like; she did now.

"Good morning, mate," Anders said, his voice a touch too far on the cheery side. "I brought you some fresh clothes. I thought you might like to get cleaned up."

Beltan said nothing. He did not look at them.

Deirdre gathered her courage, then moved to him, touching his arm. He was shaking.

"Beltan, please," she said, trying to meet his eyes. "Talk to us."

"Why?" the blond man said, his voice hoarse. "What can you say that will change anything? Travis is gone. He has left me."

Anders set down the satchel. "He didn't leave you, mate. He went after Nim. I'd say there's a pretty big difference between the two."

"And yet either way I am still here, without him," Beltan said. "I am alone. It is hopeless." He turned away from Deirdre, scrubbing his face with a hand, but not before she saw the tears that ran down his cheeks.

"Well, now," Anders said, "that doesn't sound very warrior-like to me. I don't think Vathris would approve of that kind of talk."

"And what would you know of Vathris?" Beltan snarled over his shoulder.

Anders shrugged thick shoulders. "Not much, I confess. Just what you wrote in your reports for the Seekers."

Beltan flinched. "It doesn't matter what Vathris would think. There is nothing I can do."

"You sound pretty sure. But maybe for a moment stop thinking about what you can and can't do. Why don't you tell me what you *want* to do?"

"What do you think I want to do?" Beltan clenched his hands into fists, advancing on the Seeker. "I want to go after them. I want to find them and help them!"

Anders was grinning. "Now that sounds like a man of Vathris."

Beltan blinked, and for a moment shock replaced anguish, then shame. "You are right. As long as I am alive, I must try to find a way to reach them." He gave Anders a grudging look of respect. "You would make a good warrior, you know."

Anders winked at him. "Been there, done that, mate. I'm the brains now, not the brawn."

"Warriors can have brains."

"I suppose they can at that," Anders said wistfully.

They sat down at the same table where they had gathered last night. Deirdre called for Lewis, and the butler brought a plate of sandwiches as well as coffee and new cups. He cleared away the broken shards of china without batting an eye, then silently slipped from the parlor. To be a butler for the Seekers was to quickly learn not to ask questions.

"I feel strange," Beltan said. "It's like I'm made of water inside, not muscle and bone. I want to swing my sword, but there's nothing to swing it at, and my hands are shaking so much I don't even think I could hold it. What's wrong with me?"

Despite feeling watery herself, Deirdre smiled. "Nothing's wrong with you, Beltan. You're afraid, that's all. Welcome to the club. It's how a lot of us feel a lot of the time."

His jaw dropped. "And yet you still keep on going? You must be very brave. I don't know if I am strong enough to do this."

"Maybe a sandwich will help," Anders said, taking one and pushing the plate toward Beltan.

"I doubt it," the big man said, then took three sandwiches at once.

The food did seem to help. Beltan's color grew better, and as they spoke a fierce light ignited in his eyes.

"You're right," he said around mouthfuls of food. "I know I have to do something, and I will. Only I don't know what it is, or even how to find out. All I know is that somehow I've got to get to Eldh."

"There might be a way," Deirdre murmured.

Only when she saw both Beltan and Anders staring at her did she realize she had spoken the words aloud.

Anders leaned over the table. "All right, out with it. What's going on in that crafty little noggin of yours?"

"There's only one way to get to Eldh," Deirdre said, "and that's to use a gate."

"Only there aren't any gates," Anders said. "You can bet those sorcerer baddies took their gate artifact with them when they went."

"You're forgetting about this." Deirdre picked up the newspaper the mysterious Philosopher had sent last night.

"All right, so there's another gate," the Seeker said, confusion on his pitted face. "But the sorcerers have the arch, too."

"No they don't. Not all of it." Deirdre couldn't believe she was saying this. "The arch isn't complete without the keystone, and right now it's still in the vaults below this Charterhouse. If we could somehow get the arch . . ."

She couldn't finish the sentence. They had gone to a great deal of trouble to steal it; surely they wouldn't leave it unguarded. However, she had said enough. Beltan leaped to his feet.

"We must take the arch from the Scirathi!"

Anders raised an eyebrow. "Now that's a bit of a bold plan, don't you think?"

"It's not a plan," Deirdre said, doing her best to backpedal. "It's just one possibility, that's all. One very ridiculous, stupid, unlikely possibility." However, it was too late; the damage had been done.

"It can work," Beltan said. "It has to—it's the only way." He locked gazes with Deirdre. "Promise you'll help me."

Deirdre swallowed hard. "I don't know . . ."

Beltan made a growling sound low in his throat. "You have to help me get that gate. I will not lose Travis. I will not!" His hands twitched, and he started for the Grecian urn.

Deirdre jumped up and stepped in front of the big man. For a moment she wasn't so certain that was a good idea. No doubt, when tossed against a wall, she would make every bit as satisfying a smashing sound as the urn. He reached for her.

She grabbed his hand, holding it. "I promise, Beltan. On the Book, I swear it. Anders and I will help you find a way to get to Travis if it's the last thing we do."

And it very well might be. However, the words seemed to calm him. He returned to the table, and Deirdre let out a breath. Had she really just offered up her life to save an old vase? But she hadn't promised they would try to take the arch back from the Scirathi, only that they would help Beltan find Travis.

Is there really a difference between the two, Deirdre? You know there's no other way to Eldh besides the archway.

"I don't want to be the cloud that rains on the parade," Anders said, taking a sip of his coffee, "but even assuming the Scirathi hand over the arch when we politely ask for it, and even assuming that keystone fits, how are we supposed to activate the gate? In case you've forgotten, that takes some extra special blood, which we just happen to be fresh out of."

"Oh, that's not a problem," Beltan said. "I kept this."

He pulled a dark, wadded-up piece of cloth from his pocket. It was the sleeve of Anders's suit coat, which Vani had used last night as a makeshift bandage. It was crusted with dried blood— Travis's blood.

Anders let out a low whistle. "Warriors can have brains indeed."

"Is anyone going to eat that last sandwich?" Beltan said, and reached for the plate before either of them could answer.

21.

An hour later, Deirdre sat at her desk in the basement office she shared with Anders. Beltan was all for making a raid on the Scirathi right away, but Anders had managed to convince the blond man to get some rest first. Besides, they had no idea where the Scirathi had taken the arch after they stole it from the site on Crete. It could be anywhere in the world.

Deirdre supposed she should rest, too. She hadn't gotten a wink in twenty-four hours, and sleep deprivation wasn't generally part of the formula for successful research. However, she felt jittery and strangely alert. As foolish as her promise to Beltan was, she didn't regret it; she wanted to help him find Travis. After all, Hadrian Farr had managed to find a way to Eldh. Why couldn't she?

Is that what this is, Deirdre? asked a detached aspect of herself—the wise voice she didn't always listen to but should, the shaman in her. *Is it all just some competition with Hadrian Farr? He got to Eldh, so now you have to as well?*

Before she could answer that, Anders set a steaming mug of coffee amid the stacks of papers on her desk.

"Nice way to include me in that little vow of yours, mate. How did it go?" He raised his husky voice into a falsetto. "'Anders and I will help you find a way to get to Travis if it's the last thing we do.'"

Deirdre winced. "Sorry about that. I didn't have much time to think. I was protecting a very important urn."

"It's all right," he said, sitting on the corner of her desk. "I want to help. Bloody hell, what red-blooded Seeker wouldn't want to? Opening up doors to other worlds . . . that's what we're all about. It's what I signed on for. So let me know what I can do."

Deirdre felt her dread recede. Even when things looked hopeless, Anders was incessantly cheery. Only it wasn't annoying, now that she thought about it. Instead, it was heartening. . . .

"What is it, mate?"

She shook her head. "What is what?"

"Do I have a bit of sandwich on my face or something? You were looking at me funny just now."

Horror flooded Deirdre. She must have been doing it again. Glowing. Quickly, she grabbed a random folder, opened it, and bent her head over the papers inside.

"There's one thing that would be a big help," she said. "See if you can get any images of the arch from newspaper and television sources. Our first step is to learn everything we can about the arch. If we do, we may find a clue that will tell us where the Scirathi have taken it."

"Now that's thinking like a Seeker, partner. I'll get right on it."

After Anders left, Deirdre cleared everything off her desk, then spent the next several hours welded to her notebook computer, typing and clicking as she called up every document related to the keystone, the Thomas Atwater case, Greenfellow's Tavern, Surrender Dorothy, and Glinda. Once she had gathered all the printouts and photos, she shuffled them on her desk, moving them around like the pieces of a puzzle, trying to see if they fit together in a way she hadn't seen before.

The DNA sequence of Glinda's blood had been the clue that first led Deirdre to the keystone. A sample of dried blood had been collected from the keystone centuries ago, and it had just recently been sequenced in part of an ongoing effort to analyze all organic samples in the Seeker vaults before they deteriorated. The sequence from the blood on the keystone had been incomplete, but it had been enough to know it was statistically similar to the sequence of Glinda's blood.

Knowing what Deirdre did now, that made sense. The keystone had been collected at a location that in modern times corresponded to the nightclub Surrender Dorothy with its half-fairy denizens, like Glinda. And which, in the seventeenth century, had housed Greenfellow's Tavern.

Only what was the link between Glinda and Thomas Atwater? That was a question Deirdre still couldn't answer.

Atwater joined the Seekers as a young man in the year 1619, shortly after the order was founded. As a condition for acceptance to the Seekers, the Philosophers forbade him ever to return to Greenfellow's Tavern, where he had worked before joining the Seekers. However, some years later, it was discovered that Atwater had returned to the tavern, though the Philosophers had never punished him for this clear violation of the Seventh Desideratum. Not long after that, Atwater died at the age of twenty-nine, no doubt of one of the many diseases prevalent in that era. But what did he, and Greenfellow's Tavern, have to do with the keystone?

Forget not the Sleeping Ones. In their blood lies the key. The words were inscribed on Glinda's ring as well as on the keystone—although the keystone was so worn no one had ever been able to decipher the symbols. Deirdre only recognized them because she had studied the ring so closely. And even if the symbols hadn't been worn with time, they still wouldn't have been decipherable, because they weren't written in any language known on Earth. After what they had seen on the television last night, she knew now that the symbols were written in an ancient language indigenous to the southern continent of the world Eldh.

The language of sorcerers.

Except the language is *known here, Deirdre. At least by one person.*

She picked up the photograph the mysterious Philosopher had sent her: the photo of the clay tablet, which showed the inscription written in the same language as on the keystone as well as in Linear A. All of her searches for the tablet in the archives of the Seekers had come up empty. That meant this tablet had to be in *his* private collection. Three years ago, Deirdre had given a copy of the photo to Paul Jacoby over in linguistics, and he had been able to translate the portion written in Linear A.

The linguistic connection between the keystone and Eldh was a new piece of the puzzle. Only it didn't make the picture any clearer. The arch was a gate—a gate created by sorcerers. But why had they fashioned it? How had it ended up buried on Crete while the keystone came to rest at the site of Greenfellow's Tavern? And who were the Sleeping Ones, and what was their blood the key to?

Deirdre stared at the documents and photos until her head ached, but all she came up with were more questions. By the time Anders returned that afternoon, she was staring at the wall like a zombie.

"Afternoon, partner," Anders said, shrugging off his suit coat.

She didn't answer.

"What's the matter, mate? Cat got your tongue?"

"More like my brain," she croaked. She took a deep breath, trying to clear her mind. Coffee. She needed coffee. Her eyes strayed toward the percolator.

"I'm on it," Anders said before she could speak the word, grabbing the empty coffeepot.

Twenty minutes later she sat at the timeworn mahogany table that dominated the center of their office. Deirdre gripped her second mug of coffee and enjoyed the pleasant tingle as caffeine permeated her brain.

"So did you get them?" she asked Anders.

"Did he get what?" Beltan said from the doorway.

Deirdre glanced up and smiled. By his much improved appearance, the blond man had gotten a shower as well as some rest. His green eyes were clear, though his face was still grim.

Anders set another mug on the table, as well as a plate of shortbread cookies. Beltan took several of the cookies, crammed them in his mouth, and chased them down with a long swig of the scalding coffee.

"So what were you supposed to get?" he said, eyeing Anders.

"Photographs of the arch." Anders had rolled up his

shirtsleeves and had loosened his tie, which was as close to casual as Deirdre had ever seen him. "It turned out it wasn't too hard. I've got a source at one of the satellite television companies. He dubbed a copy of the archaeology program to tape for me. I saved some stills from the tape, but they were a bit on the grainy side, so I took them down to the lab for computer enhancement. The techs said they'd have them done by—wait a minute. Here's Eustace now."

A speck of a man appeared in the doorway. Even sitting, Deirdre was nearly as tall as he. His thick shock of brown hair stood straight up—an effort to win him another inch, perhaps—and he wore wire-rimmed glasses as well as an eager expression.

Eustace bounded into the office, holding a large manila envelope, and his blue eyes went wide behind his glasses. "Is that really him? The otherworldly traveler?" The apprentice didn't wait for an answer. Instead, he approached Beltan, who towered above him. "I can't believe this is happening. I'm having my first Class One Encounter, and I've only been a Seeker for six months." He thrust out a hand. "I'm terribly honored to meet you, sir. Is there something you can tell me—some bit of knowledge from another world you can impart?"

Beltan squinted down at the young Seeker. "The cookies are not for you."

Deirdre could see Eustace silently repeating the words to himself, as if trying to fathom the wisdom they contained. And there *was* wisdom in them, because if given cause, Beltan might scoop the small Seeker up and crumple him into a ball like so much aluminum foil.

Luckily, Eustace appeared uninterested in the cookies. He kept gaping at Beltan with a look of awe.

Anders cleared his throat. "So what do you have for us, Eustace?"

The young man snapped back to his senses. "The techs in the lab told me to bring this to you right away." He handed the envelope to Anders. "So what's in it?"

Anders grinned. "None of your business. At least not until you've got Echelon 3 clearance. Which you'll never get if you don't keep at that research Nakamura assigned you. So scurry along now."

Eustace cast one last glance at Beltan, then hurried from the room, shutting the door behind him.

"Let's see those photos," Deirdre said.

The lab had done a good job. Though still a bit grainy, most of the symbols were clear, incised into the stones of the arch with sharp, angular lines. When she was finished examining the photographs, she slipped them back into the envelope.

"So what are you going to do with those?" Anders asked.

She sealed the envelope with wax. "I'm going to send them to Paul Jacoby over in linguistics. He was able to translate the passage in Linear A on the clay tablet, and I know he's been comparing it to the passage written in the language of the Scirathi. I'm going to see if he has enough information to decipher any of these symbols."

Anders cleared his throat. "And you think we can trust him?"

"I don't think we have a choice. We have to learn everything we can about the arch if we're going to have any chance of using it." She sighed. "That's assuming, of course, that we ever find it. I don't know how we're going to manage that one."

Beltan frowned at her. "Isn't it obvious?"

"Not particularly." She glanced at Anders.

"Don't look at me, mate. I'm beginning to think I'm not the one with the brains here, after all."

"You don't have to be smart to think like a thief," Beltan said, pacing lionlike alongside the table. "The Scirathi must want the arch for something important. Why else would they go to all the trouble of stealing it? However, it's worthless to them if they don't have the keystone. That means at some point they will have to come for it."

"But the Scirathi can't know the keystone is here," Deirdre said, trying to follow his logic.

"They could be made to know."

Anders let out a low whistle. "So you want to set a trap for them, to lure them with the keystone and nab them."

"No," Beltan said, his voice hard, "I want to let them capture the keystone. Once they have it, they will surely go to where the arch is located. All we have to do is follow them."

"You make it sound easy."

"I did not say it would be easy," Beltan growled. "I imagine it will be anything but. Yet it is our only chance of getting to the arch."

Anders looked queasy. "I suppose it is. All the same, I can't imagine the Philosophers will let us take a priceless artifact from their collection and dangle it out there like a piece of bait."

"They will, if you convince them to."

"I don't know, mate. . . ."

Beltan leaned on the table, green light flickering in his eyes. "You promised to help me."

Deirdre knew she had to intervene before this came to blows. "It's a good plan," she said, standing up and touching Beltan's shoulder. She felt the big man relax. "But we still need to learn what we can about the arch before we do this. If we're going to follow the sorcerers back to where they've hidden the arch, then we have to be ready to act when we get there. We won't get a second chance."

Beltan grunted; he couldn't disagree with that.

Anders gave her a grateful look. "There's one thing about all this that doesn't make sense. The Scirathi already had a gate, and they used it to kidnap Nim. So what do they need the arch for?"

Deirdre chewed her lip. She couldn't answer that one. "The only ones who know the answer to that question are the Scirathi themselves."

"Then why not ask one?" Beltan said.

Anders scowled at him. "This is no time for jokes, mate."

"I'm not joking."

By the look on his face, Deirdre knew he wasn't. Anders stared at him, then suddenly grinned.

"I'm starting to like the way you think. Better to do something, however bonkers, than to sit around on your bum. Mind if I join you on your little hunt?"

Beltan nodded. "Your help would be welcome indeed."

An alarm sounded in Deirdre's skull. She gripped Beltan's arm. "We don't know how many Scirathi are still on Earth. Are you sure you want to do this?"

"I can't just wait here, Deirdre. I need something to do. And this can help us, you know it can." His expression softened a fraction. "Don't worry. We won't take unnecessary risks."

"Come on, mate," Anders said, putting on his suit coat. "Let's go see if we can nab ourselves a sorcerer."

Once they had gone, Deirdre spent the remainder of the afternoon combing through the documents on her desk—ostensibly trying to find any clues she might have missed, but mostly trying not to think about Anders and Beltan, or what might be happening to them.

They're big boys, Deirdre. They can take care of themselves.

Then why did she feel like she needed to run after them and protect them? Especially Anders. He was strong. He had a gun, and he was trained to use it. But he didn't have experience facing enemies with magical powers, not like Beltan did. Except that wasn't true; Anders had taken out the one sorcerer at the Tube station.

Deirdre rose and moved across the office. He had left the sorcerer's gold mask on his desk. She picked it up, touching the bullet hole between the mask's eye slits. What if that had been a lucky shot? Anders might not be so fortunate the next time he came face-to-face with a sorcerer. Or make that sorcerers. She went back to her desk, propped up the mask against a stack of papers so that its serene gold face seemed to gaze at her, and kept working as the wall clock ticked away the silent seconds.

The back of her neck tingled, and she looked up.

Sasha stood in the doorway, slender arms folded, leaning against the doorjamb.

Deirdre gasped. "How long have you been there?"

"Just a minute or two," Sasha said, her red lips parting in a smile. "I was watching you."

Deirdre scowled, now more annoyed than startled. "You shouldn't do that."

"I know. I'm a naughty girl. But you look so adorable when you're working manically, I couldn't resist."

"I was probably picking my nose," Deirdre said.

"If only. I would have snapped a picture." Sasha gestured to the tiny digital camera that dangled from a silver chain around her neck. She wore it all the time these days, like a piece of jewelry, and was constantly catching people in compromising positions and displaying the resulting snapshots on her computer. "Do you mind if I come in?"

Before Deirdre could answer, Sasha sauntered languidly—
she never merely walked—into the office. Today's fashion included saffron slacks and a fluttery chartreuse top that made her
look like an exotic bird. Her coffee-with-cream skin gave off a
healthy glow despite the office's fluorescent lights, which made
Deirdre—who wasn't exactly well acquainted with the sun
these days—look like she had consumption.

After all their years working together, Deirdre still wasn't
entirely certain what Sasha did for the Seekers. She was an at-
taché to the Director of Operations, which meant these days she
spent most of her time with Richard Nakamura. Although precisely what she did for Nakamura, Deirdre couldn't say. All she
knew was that, more than any other Seeker, Sasha seemed to
have her finger on the pulse of the organization. Nothing
seemed to happen that she didn't know about first, or know
more juicy details about than anybody else.

*Probably because she's always spying on people. And who
knows? Maybe that's her real job.*

Deirdre wasn't worried. Nothing she was doing here was
clandestine. In fact, she had already begun to draft a prelimi-
nary report on the events of the last thirty-six hours for Nakamura. Deirdre might as well give Sasha a copy since she was
there. She opened the document on her computer and clicked
PRINT.

"So what have we here?" Sasha said when Deirdre handed
her the copy, still warm from the printer.

"A draft of a report I'm writing for Nakamura, to keep him
apprised of what we're doing." Deirdre sat on the edge of her
desk.

Sasha folded the papers without reading them. "That's good
of you, but it's not necessary. You're Echelon 7, Deirdre. You've
got free rein on this mission—it's under your complete control.
There's no need for you to submit a report until you deem the
case is closed."

Deirdre wasn't sure whether those words were reassuring or
not. It was good to know she wasn't going to be second-guessed
all the time. On the other hand, she wasn't entirely certain she
knew what she was doing here. How did the Desiderata apply
when the otherworldly being you had vowed not to interfere

with also happened to be a dear friend you had vowed to help? It was hard to rely solely on one's own judgment.

"Take the report to Nakamura anyway," Deirdre said. "I don't want there to be any secrets here."

"Funny you should mention secrets," Sasha purred. "That's just what I came to talk to you about."

Deirdre gripped her bear claw necklace. "What do you mean?"

Sasha glanced at the door, then drew in close, her expression no longer one of sly amusement, but rather solemn. "Do you remember how I once told you to keep your curiosity outside the Seekers, that it was better not to turn up stones left untouched?"

Deirdre felt a chill pass through her. She could only nod.

"Well, maybe it's time to start turning up a few of those stones after all."

"What are you talking about? What stones?"

Sasha picked up the gold mask and ran a long finger over it. "So this is one of the masks they wear. Those sorcerers you've written about in your reports. It's so much more beautiful than I ever would have thought. Only it covers ugliness, doesn't it? Ugliness and hate."

None of this made any sense. Deirdre ran a hand through her close-cropped hair. "Sasha, what is this really about?"

The other woman was silent for a time. Finally she spoke in a low voice. "The sorcerers aren't the only organization that requires its members to wear masks, Deirdre. Sometimes the Seekers do, too. And you can't always know what's behind those masks. Sometimes it's good. Sometimes they're keeping secrets to protect you. And sometimes . . ."

Deirdre was sweating, but she felt cold. "What do you know, Sasha? If you know something, you have to tell me."

Sasha shook her head. "All I know is that there are secrets. Things that most of us don't know, that others don't want us to know."

"Secrets like what?"

Sasha set down the mask. "This was a mistake. I've told more than I should have. But I just wanted you to . . . you need to keep your eyes open, that's all." She started toward the door.

Deirdre stood up, her heart thudding in her chest. "Sasha, please. You've got to tell me what you're talking about."

Sasha hesitated, then glanced over her shoulder, her dark eyes unreadable. "Has Anders ever told you why he can carry a gun when no other Seeker is allowed to?"

Deirdre could only stare.

"Take care of yourself, honey," Sasha said, then headed out the door, leaving Deirdre alone.

22.

It was late. Deirdre gazed out the window of her flat, watching as rain snaked in rivulets down the panes. She held a glass of scotch in her hand; she hadn't taken a sip since she poured it two hours ago.

Has Anders ever told you why he can carry a gun when no other Seeker is allowed to?

Like uninvited guests, Sasha's words from earlier that day slipped into her mind. Deirdre tried to ignore them. She didn't know what Sasha was trying to do, but she wasn't going to suspect Anders of wrongdoing. Not after he had saved her life—and the lives of others—multiple times. Not after she had vowed she was going to trust him.

But what if you're being blind, Deirdre?

Was that her Wise Self speaking, the shaman in her who often saw things in a clearer light? Or was it her Shadow Self—her darker and more destructive side—that was speaking?

You've developed feelings for Anders —you can't deny that you have. And what if that's what he's been counting on? The coffee, the flowers, the designer suits and expensive cologne—what if it's all been part of a precise operation, one designed to charm you, and to distract you from things you would otherwise see. Great Spirit, no one can be that cheerful all the time. It has to be an act.

No, she wouldn't believe that. Anders was a good man. A true heart beat in that barrel chest of his, she was sure of it. Besides, if someone had wanted her to be seduced, surely they would have sent an agent more suave, more good-looking than Anders to do the deed.

Or would they? Not if they were clever—not if they knew Deirdre well. She had fallen for a striking, mysterious man once—for Hadrian Farr—and she wouldn't make that same mistake again. If Anders had been too slick or handsome, her guard would have gone up at once. Instead, Anders had infiltrated the barriers of her affections like a stealth jet, flying low and under the radar.

This is ridiculous, Deirdre. Now it was neither her Wise Self nor Shadow Self talking. It was just her plain old Angry and Afraid Self. *Anders isn't an airplane, he's a person, and he hasn't been keeping secrets from you. You know it.*

Really? Or had her judgment been impaired by broad shoulders, a gravelly voice, and crinkly blue eyes? Because, much as she had done her best to ignore it these last three years, Sasha was right—there was one secret Anders kept from her. He still had never told her why he was allowed to carry a gun when no other Seeker had that privilege.

Not that she was entirely sorry that was the case. More than once he had used that gun to protect her and others. All the same, the fact that he did carry it nagged at her, now more than ever. He had told her his story—how he had worked security for the Seekers before becoming an agent, and how, since he had the proper training to use it, Nakamura was letting him keep the gun temporarily, until a final decision about it came down from the Philosophers.

But such a decision had never been made, at least not as far as Deirdre knew. So why did Anders carry a gun? Did he have special connections in the Seekers? That seemed absurd; Anders was still only a journeyman. However, the fact that a former security guard had been admitted to the organization at all was unusual. It could be there was more to Anders's becoming a Seeker than was visible on the surface.

Deirdre sighed. Her head throbbed, and it was long past her bedtime. She could think about all of this tomorrow. She started to push herself up from the chair—then froze.

Something moved in the darkness outside the window.

She leaned forward, until her breath fogged on the glass

panes. She had only glimpsed it for a second, but it had been a vaguely manlike shape, she was sure of it. Only it hadn't been down below on the street. Instead, it had seemed to float in the night, directly outside the window.

There was a soft *click* as the door of her flat closed shut. The glass of scotch tumbled to the floor. Heart pounding, Deirdre sprang out of the chair and whirled around.

There was no one there.

"Anders?" she called out. "Is that you?"

He had a key to her flat; he always took care of her houseplants when she was away. But there was no answer. Not that she expected any. Whatever Sasha thought of him, Anders was a gentleman; he always knocked before entering. Besides, he had said he was going to stay at the Charterhouse that night to keep an eye on Beltan.

Earlier that evening, the two men had returned: wet, hungry, and more than a little grouchy from their mad hunt for a sorcerer. They had found no signs of the Scirathi in the city. Not that Deirdre had expected any different; it wasn't as if sorcerers tended to hang out at the local coffee shop. Though maybe the blood bank would have been a more likely place to find them.

Despite their failure, Beltan's resolve to find one of the Scirathi had not lessened, and Anders wanted to keep close to the blond man in case he decided to try continuing the search on his own. Deirdre had agreed; in his current frame of mind, it was best if Beltan wasn't left alone.

And what about you, Deirdre? Are you alone right now?

She didn't know what she had glimpsed in the window, but there was one thing she was certain of: Whatever it was, it hadn't been outside her flat.

It was a reflection in the glass. A reflection from behind you. Someone was in here.

Whoever it had been was gone now. A thorough exploration of all the rooms of her flat—as well as the closets—confirmed her instincts. The intruder had fled. She headed back to the kitchen, thinking maybe she had better give another glass of scotch a try. Her hands shook as she tilted the bottle, and she slopped half the liquid onto the counter. She reached for the roll of paper towels.

A manila envelope lay on the countertop. She had not put it there.

Deirdre gulped down what scotch she had managed to get into the glass, then picked up the envelope. There was a lump inside it. She undid the string, opened the flap, and tilted the envelope. A small black cell phone slipped out. She drew in a deep breath, then picked up the phone and switched it on.

It rang.

She was so startled she nearly dropped it. She fumbled with the buttons, then held the phone to her ear.

"Hello?"

"Good evening, Deirdre."

She had known it would be he. Once before he had made contact with her in this fashion. All the same, a thrill ran through her at the sound of his rich, accentless voice.

"Who was just in my flat?" she said. "You or one of your minions?"

Laughter emanated from the phone. "Minions? What a marvelous word. It makes me feel like a villain just to say it. I really must try to have more minions."

"So it was you." Fear rippled through her, and excitement. He had been here, in her flat—her Philosopher. She moved to the window and peered out into the darkness and the rain. "Where are you?"

"Close, Deirdre." His words were a murmur in her ear. "I am always close now. The worlds draw near. And so does the end."

"The end of what?"

"Why, of everything."

Deirdre sank down into the chair. She had to be smart, she had to think of the most important questions and ask them first. He wouldn't stay on the phone long; he never did.

"Where is the arch?"

Again he laughed. "That's why I like you, Deirdre. You always get right to the point."

She bit her tongue. If she was silent, he would have to keep speaking. There was a dreadful pause in which she feared he had hung up. Then, once more, his rich voice emanated from the phone.

"It's nearer than you might think. However, I'm not going to tell you where it is. Now is not the time to seek it out."

"Why?" she said, unable to stop herself.

"Because if you do, you will die. So will the man from the otherworld, the knight Beltan. I cannot let that happen."

This time it was he who paused. Deirdre had no choice but to say something or risk the conversation ending. "Beltan is determined to find the arch, and I can't control him. Today he and Anders went looking for a sorcerer to question."

"That's an excellent idea. Do go have a chat with a sorcerer. That will help you see your next step is not to seek the gate. There are other mysteries that must be attended to first."

Deirdre clutched the phone, as if that could keep him from hanging up. "But how can we find a sorcerer? We don't even know if there are any left in London."

"There are. Their work here is not done. Finding the girl, Nim, was simply a happy accident. An act of Fate, as they might say. It was not the reason they came to our world."

"But where can we find one of the Scirathi?" she said, unable to keep the words from sounding as desperate as they were.

"That's simple enough. The man Beltan possesses something the Scirathi crave, something that is sure to tempt them into the open. As for where to go—I think you already sense the answer to that. They know now what flows in Travis Wilder's veins. They are keeping watch, just in case he returns."

Deirdre thought maybe she understood, but she had to be certain. However, he spoke again before she could.

"By the way, your friend Sasha was right in what she said to you earlier today."

"What?" It was the only word she could manage.

"You do not know what you think you know, Deirdre. That is the one thing—the only thing—of which you can be certain. Do not let yourself believe you can trust anyone other than yourself. Even within the Seekers, there are those who would work against you."

"I don't understand," she said, her pulse thudding in her ears.

"Why do you think I always make contact with you in such a secretive manner? Contrary to what you might believe, it's not for my amusement. I do it because there are those who, if they

knew I had told you the things I have, would not hesitate to—"
He paused; she could hear his breathing. "No, that's not important now. All that matters is that you understand one thing:
There is much you do not know, much you cannot even guess at.
And there are those who will do anything to keep it that way."

The phone was slick in Deirdre's hand. "What should I do?"

"I can't tell you that, Deirdre. But I will give you something
to think about. The sorcerers used Travis Wilder's blood, taken
from the belly of the *gorleth* that attacked him, to power the gate
artifact in their possession and abduct the girl."

"We already know that."

"Good. Now ask yourself this: How did the sorcerers know
they could do that? How did they know that blood of power,
blood that could fuel their gate, ran in Travis Wilder's veins?"

Deirdre hardly heard his words. She could feel him starting
to slip away. "Please, don't go. There are so many questions,
and I don't have any idea how to get the answers."

"That's not true, Deirdre. You're a resourceful woman. I have
every faith you'll find a way to get those answers of yours." His
voice dropped to a whisper. "And I think a time is coming when
all questions will be answered. Perihelion approaches. This
world and the otherworld draw nearer every day. It is not chance
that the earthquake on Crete revealed the arch. Things long
buried are now coming to light because they *need* to be found."

"What do you mean?" Deirdre said, clutching the phone.
"What things need to be found?"

But the only reply was the drone of a dial tone in her ear.

23.

It was well after ten o'clock by the time Deirdre straggled into
the Charterhouse the next morning. She stopped at the front
desk, picked up a pen fastened to a chain, and signed in on the
clipboard. The receptionist, Madeleine, looked up from her
computer, though her fingers continued to flay the keyboard.

"How good of you to join us today, Miss Falling Hawk," she
said, peering over moon-shaped reading glasses.

Deirdre was not in the mood for irony. "You misspelled 'Sincerely,' " she said, pointing at Madeleine's computer screen.

The receptionist gave her a sour look, which Deirdre could at least appreciate for its honesty, then pushed her glasses up her nose and studied the screen. Deirdre made her way down the hall and descended a flight of stairs to her office.

Anders wasn't there. She didn't know whether to be disappointed or relieved. With regard to the lack of coffee, it was certainly the former, but otherwise it could only be the latter. Surely he would have seen it on her face the moment she looked at him. Doubt.

She tossed the newspaper she had bought on her desk and slumped into the chair. There was a note neatly tucked under the blotter. She pulled it out. It was written in Anders's cramped, precise hand.

> *Good morning, partner!*
> *Beltan and I decided to get an early start. We're off to nose about the city. Back by noon. Shall we lunch at the M.E.?*
> *Cheers!*
>
> *—Anders*

Deirdre winced. Gods, even when he wrote he sounded insanely chipper. She started to toss the note in the trash can, then stopped, folded it carefully, and tucked it back beneath the blotter.

She hated this. She hated the way she felt, and she hated what she was going to do. However, she had no choice. Once again she asked herself the question that had been eating at her.

How did the sorcerers here on Earth know about the blood of power that runs in Travis's veins?

The only people who could possibly know that information were Travis's closest companions. And any Seeker who had read the Wilder-Beckett case files. Deirdre could not believe Beltan or Vani had informed the sorcerers. That meant there was only one other possibility.

There's a traitor in the Seekers, and Sasha must know it—or at least suspect it. That's why she was trying to warn you yester-

day. Someone with access to the reports about Travis is in league with the sorcerers.

And, much as it turned her heart to ash to admit it, all the signs pointed to one person. He had read all the reports about Travis. He was capable of keeping secrets; the gun he carried proved that. And the night they were attacked by the Scirathi, he had shown up at the Tube station almost too miraculously.

Only that doesn't make sense, Deirdre. If Anders was really working for the Scirathi, why did he save all of you that night?

For the same reason he brewed fabulous coffee and brought flowers to the office. To win their trust, their affection.

Think about it, Deirdre. No one actually saw him shoot that sorcerer he claimed he killed. You read his report. Even Eustace didn't see it happen. A Scirathi could simply have given Anders one of their gold masks to use as a prop, to help back up his story.

The thought made her sick, but she couldn't dismiss it. Her grandfather had always told her to trust her instincts. And all those instincts told her that Anders was concealing something.

So what was she going to do?

Keep him close, Deirdre. And don't act as if anything's changed. Whatever his work is, it isn't done; otherwise, he wouldn't still be playing this game. The longer you can make him believe you know nothing, the better your chances of figuring out what it is he's up to.

Deirdre massaged her throbbing temples. She had spent all night going over these thoughts again and again. Right now she wanted to think about something—anything—else. She unfolded the copy of the *Times* she had bought and bent her head over it.

However, she found little solace in reading the paper. On the front page there was an article about the worldwide increase in violent natural phenomena over the last few months. Earthquakes, volcanic eruptions, hurricanes—all were happening with greater frequency than normal. The article discounted the common belief that the change in the Earth's climate was a result of the celestial anomaly, and instead offered various theories about possible geologic and meteorological causes. However, Deirdre knew the article was wrong.

It's perihelion. That's what the Philosopher said. Eldh is drawing close, and somehow it's affecting Earth. It's like the pull of gravity.

Only it wasn't gravity, it was something else. But what then? Magic? All Deirdre knew was that it wasn't chance that an earthquake had shaken Crete, revealing the stone arch.

And what about the dark spot in space? It can't be chance that it's appeared now as perihelion approaches.

According to a report she had seen on a morning TV news show, the anomaly was now visible to the naked eye in the northern hemisphere—at least to those who didn't live in major cities. However, even if it hadn't been cloudy the last several days, Deirdre doubted she would have been able to see it through the glare of London's streetlights.

And maybe that explained why people in the city continued to go about their lives as if nothing had changed. That morning, Deirdre had taken the Tube with countless people trudging to their jobs, the expressions on their faces as dull as the leaden sky. On the streets, double-decker buses ferried tired, trapped-looking tourists to Buckingham Palace, Westminster Abbey, and St. Paul's. Ships oozed up and down the sluggish Thames. Yet surely, if people could see the dark spot in the sky, they would be panicking.

Or would they? Because even if they couldn't see it through the London fog, people had to know it was there. Just as it had expanded in the sky, stories about Variance X had grown more prominent on television and in the newspaper. Reports about it were everywhere. Only no one seemed to be paying attention.

Except for the Mouthers. Deirdre had passed several of them that morning, standing on a corner outside the Blackfriars Tube station in their white sheets. Each member of the group had carried a sign that bore, not words, but instead a black circle scrawled on white cardboard. They did not accost passersby, but simply stared, their eyes as vacant as the circles on their signs.

Deirdre had ignored the Mouthers, as had everyone else passing by. No one ever looked at the people in white, or up at the sky. Or, it seemed, at the articles in the newspaper.

Maybe people are tired of hearing about disasters, Deirdre. Fires. Floods. Wars. Famines. Maybe there are too many troubles here on Earth to worry about something in the sky.

Maybe. But while others might be disinterested, Deirdre was anything but. Like the storms and earthquakes, Variance X had to be related to perihelion somehow. She leaned over the paper, scanning the article in the *Times*.

It began with a summary of what was known about the anomaly: how it had first been detected a few months ago, at a distance of about 10 billion miles from Earth—or fifteen hours as the light beam flies. At the time, the anomaly was dubbed Variance X by skeptical astronomers. The name was a joke. Over the years, various astronomers had put forth the theory that the solar system contained a dark, distant tenth planet—Planet X. Such a planet had never been found, and those who theorized it existed were generally regarded as pseudoscientists and crackpots.

However, no one was laughing now, for the joke soon ended as countless observatories around the world confirmed the existence of Variance X, as well as the fact that it was growing.

Some researchers speculated that the anomaly was indeed a tenth planet, surrounded by a cloud of black, icy comets, approaching the solar system on the short end of its elliptical orbit. Others suggested it was a disk of dark matter that until recently had been angled with respect to Earth so that it was invisible, like a dinner plate turned on edge. Now, as the disk rotated on its axis, it was coming into view, and blotting out Earth's view of the stars beyond it. Others suggested Variance X was a cloud of light absorbing gas trailing a small, wandering black hole.

However, one researcher—an American astronomer who had recently accepted a position as a visiting professor at Oxford—had proposed a very different theory: that the dark blot was in fact an instability in the fabric of space-time. So far, according to the newspaper article, most leading astronomers had rejected that theory.

Yet perhaps such an explanation is unthinkable, the article went on, *not because it is impossible, but instead because the consequences are so dire. If Variance X is a rip in space-time—*

the cloth from which our universe is cut—what's to stop it from unraveling? Nothing, says American astronomer Sara Voorhees. According to Voorhees, unless the instability that gave rise to it somehow corrects itself, the anomaly will keep expanding until the universe is torn apart in one final, violent blending of matter and antimatter that will leave nothing at all. It's not difficult to see why that prospect has proven unpopular.

Feeling ill, Deirdre folded the paper and tossed it in the waste bin. What did it all mean? Maybe two different worlds were on a collision course. Maybe that was what perihelion meant. If so, then there was no hope for anyone on Earth or Eldh.

Except, the problem was, Deirdre *did* have hope. She couldn't wait quietly for the end of the world like the Mouthers; she had to do something. And she was going to. With a deep breath she rolled up her sleeves, turned on her computer, and got to work.

By the time Beltan and Anders showed up, she had a plan.

"What's going on, mate?" Anders said, setting a tall paper cup on her desk. "You've got an extradetermined look about you today."

She picked up the cup and took a sip. It was coffee: rich, bitter, and with just the perfect hint of cream. "Have you found a sorcerer yet?"

"No," Beltan said, slumping into a chair next to her desk. "It's like looking for something very small lost in an enormous pile of things that are also very small. Only not the same as the first thing."

"You mean it's like looking for a needle in a haystack," Anders said.

Beltan frowned at him. "By Vathris, why would anyone look for a needle in a stack of hay?"

"It's an expression. It means just what you said."

"I'm talking about people, not needles. And how did it get in the hay? Did some mad seamstress put the needle there?"

"Never mind," Anders growled. He shrugged off his suit coat and glanced at Deirdre. "As you can see, we haven't exactly made a lot of progress in our hunt for a sorcerer."

Muscles played beneath the skin of his forearms as he loosened his tie. Deirdre gulped the scalding-hot coffee.

"Don't worry," she said, her throat burning. "I think I've got it figured out."

"You've got what figured out?" Beltan said.

"How we're going to catch a sorcerer."

24.

They waited until nightfall. The Scirathi were more comfortable working under cover of darkness; that was one of the few things they had learned in their dealings with the sorcerers.

And what about Anders? Deirdre thought as they drove in a black sedan along Shaftesbury Avenue. *What's he learned about them?*

She glanced at him as he drove. Would he betray her tonight? After all, if he was really working for the sorcerers, he couldn't allow her to catch one of them. Except he had to, if he was going to keep up his act; he would have to go along with her plan.

As the lights of the city came on against the gathering dusk, Anders turned the wheel, guiding the car onto a narrow lane. Beltan's and Travis's flat was just ahead.

"We already checked out the flat," Anders had said earlier that day, when she told him where they would go that evening. "Beltan and I sniffed all around his old neighborhood and didn't see a thing. It wouldn't surprise me if there's a sorcerer lurking about there—returning to the scene of the crime and all that. But if so, he won't come out to play."

"He will if you make him want to," Deirdre had said.

It was time. Anders brought the car to a halt two blocks away from the flat. Deirdre climbed out. Beltan unfolded his long frame from the backseat.

"I'm ready," he said, one hand in the pocket of his jeans.

Deirdre touched his arm. "Make sure you're seen."

He nodded, then turned and took long strides down the sidewalk, vanishing into the gloom.

Anders leaned out the window of the car. "Is your radio working, mate?"

Deirdre held the device to her mouth to test it. She heard her voice emanate from inside the car. She gave him a thumbs-up, then tucked the radio into her jacket pocket, alongside something else.

"Good luck," Anders said, winking at her.

The car sped away down the lane. Deirdre didn't like letting him go by himself, but she had no choice, not if this plan was going to work. Besides, it was too late for him to warn them. If one was keeping watch, then at that moment he was already observing Beltan open the door of the flat. Deirdre looked at her wristwatch, letting thirty more seconds pass. Then she started moving.

She walked quickly down the sidewalk and up the front steps of the building. If the Philosopher was right, it wouldn't take long. She waited a few seconds in the lobby of the building, eyes on her watch. The plan called for Beltan to be alone in the flat for three minutes, not one second more. With thirty seconds to go, she started up the stairs.

Five seconds still remained when she reached the door of the flat. It was closed; no sounds emanated from the other side. She drew in a breath to steady herself. Was Anders in position? What if he wasn't?

There was no more time to worry about it. The watch ticked the last seconds away. Deirdre slipped a hand into her jacket pocket, then pushed through the door of the flat.

The sorcerer was killing Beltan.

It was hard to see. The flat was darkened, and only a few scraps of light filtered around Deirdre into the living room, but her imagination filled in what her eyes could not discern.

The window was open, and the night air billowed the white curtains like the garb of a ghost. Beltan was on his knees, his head thrown back, the cords of his neck standing out. One hand clutched at his chest. The other gripped a small glass vial filled with dark fluid. The sorcerer stood above him, clad all in black, a smile frozen on the serene gold face. One hand reached toward Beltan. The sorcerer's fingers curled together, and Beltan jerked as a spasm passed through him.

Fear stabbed into Deirdre's chest, as if it was her heart the sorcerer was stopping with a spell. And if she didn't act quickly, in a moment it would be. She pulled two objects from her pocket—and fumbled them in sweaty hands. They fell to the floor: the radio, as well as something sleek and silvery.

A squawk emanated from the radio. Before Deirdre could move, Anders's voice crackled out of it. "Is that you, Deirdre? Are you in position yet? I can't see anything in the flat; it's too dark in there."

The sorcerer hissed, and the gold mask swung in Deirdre's direction. Beltan drew in a gasping breath, but he still couldn't move; the sorcerer had not lowered its hand. And it had another. It stretched its left hand toward Deirdre's chest.

There was no time to think. Deirdre dived to the floor, grabbing the things lying there. She punched a button on the radio.

"Now, Anders!" she shouted. And with her free hand she gripped the other object and flicked a switch.

A beam of white-blue light pierced the darkness of the flat, slicing crazily through the shadows. Deirdre threw down the radio and gripped the flashlight in both hands, angling the beam upward. It struck the sorcerer's gold mask, and the Scirathi staggered back, dazzled by the sudden light. Beltan started to struggle to his feet.

Again the sorcerer thrust a hand toward the blond man, and Beltan grunted, falling back to his knees. The other hand pointed at Deirdre, and she gasped as pain crackled through her. She couldn't breathe; the flashlight started to slip from her hands.

Something hissed through the open window, and there was a soft *thunk*. The sorcerer took a step back, and a soft exhalation of air passed through the mouth slit of its mask. Then the Scirathi slumped to the floor.

Although he had been under the spell of the sorcerer longer, Beltan was the first to recover. As he knelt above her, Deirdre could see his green eyes glowing faintly in the dark. He helped her sit up, and a ragged breath rushed into her lungs.

"Are you all right?" he said, his voice hoarse.

She nodded. Her heart had resumed something like a normal

cadence in her chest. The sorcerer's spell had not done as much harm as she would have thought. "How is he?"

Beltan moved to a dark lump that sprawled on the floor. "He's not moving, but I think he's still conscious."

Good. The drug was working exactly as it was supposed to. She had feared Scirathi physiology might be different, but it wasn't. For all their powers, they were still men.

Deirdre groped for the flashlight, then crawled on hands and knees to Beltan. She trained the light down, onto the crumpled form of the sorcerer. Its body twitched, and gurgling sounds emanated from behind the mask. A silver dart protruded from the center of its chest.

"The mask," Beltan said. "Take it off. He's powerless without it."

Deirdre hesitated, then with trembling hands gripped the edge of the gold mask, pulled it off, and handed it to Beltan.

The sorcerer was not a man after all. The face was a blasted landscape of scar tissue, crudely stitched wounds, and oozing scabs. The ears were gone, and the nose reduced to two pits above the featureless slit of the mouth. However, the bone structure—plain to see—was fine, even delicate. This sorcerer was a woman.

Or had been once. Now her face was a ruin from which all traces of humanity had been cut away with the blade of a knife. Only the sorcerer's eyes were recognizable as something human. They gazed at Deirdre with hatred. And with fear.

"It looks like everything went off without a hitch," said a cheerful, if breathless, voice behind them.

Both Deirdre and Beltan glared at Anders as he stepped into the flat.

"Or not," he said, grin fading as he shut the door.

It hadn't taken him long to get here from his position in the hotel across the street. He had been stationed on the third floor with the dart gun, waiting for Deirdre to shine the light on their target. Once he got off his shot, he must have run here to the flat. Good. That meant he wouldn't have had time to communicate with anyone else.

Anders knelt beside them. "Gads, that's a nasty sight." He looked up from the sorcerer. "Are you both all right?"

"We're alive, if that's what you mean," Beltan said, his voice still ragged.

"Let's talk to her," Deirdre said.

Anders reached into his breast pocket and pulled out a syringe. He handed it to Deirdre. She took off the cap, flicked the syringe to remove the bubbles, then inserted the needle into the sorcerer's throat.

"This will relax the muscles around your larynx. You'll be able to talk, but that's all."

Anders started to reach for the dart embedded in the Scirathi's chest, but Beltan grabbed his hand.

"No, leave the dart in place. We do not want her to bleed."

Anders swallowed. "Good point, mate."

"Blood," hissed a voice like a serpent's. It was the sorcerer. The slit of her mouth twitched. "Give me the blood. . . ."

"Never," Beltan growled. He made sure the glass vial was stopped tightly, then slipped it into his pocket.

The mysterious Philosopher had been right; Beltan had indeed possessed something that would tempt a sorcerer. That morning, they had used alcohol to wash the blood from the bandage Beltan had kept from Travis's arm. Most of the alcohol had evaporated, leaving only the residual fluid in the vial. It amounted to only a few drops of blood, no more, but it was enough. The moment Beltan had opened the vial in the flat, the sorcerer had appeared, drawn out of hiding by the scent of such power.

"I think it's time you answered a few questions, friend," Anders said.

Deirdre gave him a sharp look. Was he trying to take over the questioning, to keep them from learning everything they might?

"I'll do this," she said. Anders gave her a surprised look, but before he could protest she bent over the sorcerer.

"Where is the arch you stole from Crete?"

The sorcerer made a gurgling sound low in her throat.

"I know you can understand me. You just spoke English a moment ago. Now answer me."

The gurgling became words. "I will tell you nothing."

She was wrong about that. The drug on the dart had been a

potent mixture, one intended not only to paralyze the body but soften the mind, to make it pliant and cooperative.

"Where is the arch you stole from Crete?" Deirdre repeated. "If you tell us, we'll give you a drop of the blood. His blood."

Beltan gave her a sharp look, but she shook her head.

"I do not know," the sorcerer hissed. "Now give me the blood of power! It will heal me."

Deirdre made her voice hard. "You're lying."

The Scirathi muttered in a language she did not understand, then spoke again in English. "I do not know, I tell you. We gave it to them, and they took it. That is all."

Anders raised an eyebrow, and Beltan let out a low grunt.

"They were working for someone else," Deirdre said.

Beltan leaned over the sorcerer, gripping her shoulders. "Who did you give the arch to? Tell us!"

The drug had taken full effect by then. The sorcerer spoke rapidly, almost babbling, spittle trickling from her lipless mouth. "I do not know who they are. I do not care who they are. The arch means nothing to us now. We need a gate no longer. The worlds draw near. Soon the walls between them will come tumbling down, and we shall return. We shall take what should have been ours long ago. And both the worlds will tremble before the might of the Scirathi."

Anders let out a low whistle. "That doesn't exactly sound like cause for celebration."

It didn't. The sorcerer's words sent a chill through Deirdre, even though she didn't fully understand them. She decided to try a different tactic. "If you're so powerful, why steal the arch for these others? Why do someone else's bidding?"

"Knowledge." The sorcerer writhed in Beltan's grip. "They gave us knowledge we did not possess. We did not know she was here—we did not guess it. But they told us where to find him, and of the blood of the scarab that flows in him. We sought him out, to slay him so that he cannot stand in our way. But instead we found her. Like a perfect jewel she is, one beyond worth. We were dazzled, and so we took her. . . ."

"Nim!" Beltan roared. "Where is she? Where have you taken her?"

He shook the sorcerer—violently, so that her head flopped—

and Deirdre gripped his arms, forcing him to stop. If he killed her, they would learn nothing.

The sorcerer let out a high, keening sound. At first Deirdre thought it was a sound of grief. Then she realized it was laughter.

"They have taken the child unto the Dark," the sorcerer croaked. "After so long, all its secrets will be ours. She is the key that will open the way. . . ."

Deirdre bent over the sorcerer. "Nim is the key that will open the way to what?"

"Him . . ." The sorcerer's head lolled back and forth, eyes fluttering shut. Her voice was nearly drowned in a wet gurgle. "The arch . . . blood so near . . . the seven cannot . . . be far."

They were losing her. "The seven what?" Deirdre said, shaking the sorcerer herself in desperation.

"Sleep," the sorcerer breathed in a faint exhalation. "Sleep . . ."

Her body shuddered once, then went still.

25.

The sun beat down on them like a molten fist. They had been in this place only minutes, and already Travis could feel his skin beginning to crisp. He used a hand to shade his eyes against the glare as he gazed up at the top of the sand dune.

"Can you see anything from up there?" The air parched his throat and lungs.

A dark form glided down the lee side of the dune toward him. "We are in Moringarth," Vani said. "Of that much I am certain. We are not in the wasteland of the Morgolthi, so our circumstance is not as bad as it might be. But we are near its edge, I would guess, so it is not good either."

The Morgolthi. Travis had heard tales of it among the Mournish. They called it the Hungering Land. Eons ago, it had been a land of prosperous city-states, strung like glistening pearls along the River Emyr. The river was the lifeblood of ancient Amún, carrying traders between the cities and bringing water to the fertile farmlands along its banks.

Then came the War of the Sorcerers, when the wielders of magic rose up against the god-kings who ruled the city-states and sought to usurp their place. War consumed city after city, and the river ran red with the blood of ten thousand sorcerers.

In the final conflagration, the land was shattered, and the course of the River Emyr was changed, so that its life-giving waters flowed west to the sea, not east across Amún, and the once lush land of city-states became a sun-blasted desert, a place of thirst and death.

Dead though it was, the Morgolthi had given birth in an unexpected way. Over time, the blood of sorcerers that had drenched the sand dried, became dust, blew into the air, and was carried by the wind to the lands of Al-Amún, where civilization had sprung up anew, and across the sea to Tarras and the other cities of southern Falengarth.

The dust was breathed in by thousands upon thousands of people, and power yet lingered in it, for when enough people had taken the dust into them, their collective hopes, and desires, and fears became manifest. So the gods of the Mystery Cults were born. . . .

There was a sharp but distant sound, like a far-off gunshot.

"Travis!"

Only when pain crackled through his jaw did he realize Vani had slapped him.

He staggered back. "What was that for?"

"You did not respond to my words. You must guard yourself in this place. It is said the air of the Morgolthi is strangely sweet to a sorcerer, that it can intoxicate him like wine."

"But I'm not a—"

Travis clenched his jaw shut as she gave him a piercing look. He tried to breathe more shallowly and not to think of the powdery traces of blood that must still swirl on the air in this place. "The sorcerer must have brought Nim here. Once it's been opened, a gate has only one exit. That means we can't be more than a few minutes behind them. Did you see their footprints from up there?"

"A few minutes is all the wind needs to scour the sand clear. We will not be able to track them that way."

"So what do we do?"

"The sorcerer will go north, toward human habitation and water. It is his only choice to survive, and ours. We must do the same."

"Great," Travis said. "And which way exactly is north?" He turned around. Sand dunes undulated away from them in every direction.

Vani looked up at the sky. Sweat slicked her coppery skin, and she had unbuttoned the top of her leather jerkin. "The sun has risen in the time since we came through the gate. East lies in that direction, so this way is north. We must hope we are not far from a settlement. Come."

She started along the trough between two dunes, keeping close to the lee side of the dune on their left, out of the worst of the wind. However, they were soon forced to abandon the path when it veered east, and instead they struggled up the windward side of a dune. Sand hissed through the air and made Travis think of the bodiless spirits of the *morndari*. They could pass through solid matter, and the sand seemed able to do the same. It dug into any bit of exposed skin, stung their eyes, filtered through their clothing, and worked its way deep into their ears and noses.

The sun ascended to the zenith, and heat radiated from the sand in waves. Travis sweated in his jeans and sweater—chosen for a misty London evening, not a blazing desert day—but he did not even think of shedding them, as they were his only protection from the wind and sun.

He and Vani did not speak. They kept their mouths clamped shut, breathing through their noses, trying to keep out the sand and conserve the moisture in their breath. Each time they crested a dune, Vani scanned the horizon, and Travis knew what she was looking for: the green smudge of an oasis and the white shapes of human habitations. All they saw were more dunes.

You really are an idiot, Travis told himself as he trudged after Vani. *We don't have food or water. We're completely unprepared for this. You should have thought about what you were doing.*

Only there hadn't been time to think. He had leaped for the gate, not knowing what he was going to do on the other side, only knowing that jumping through that portal was his only chance to save Nim. He hadn't expected Vani to follow, but he was grateful she had. He doubted he would survive five minutes in this desert without her.

Wouldn't you, Travis? a dry voice spoke in his mind. It wasn't Jack's voice; it was his own. Only it was more sibilant, a coaxing hiss, like that of a serpent. *Vani is right. You're a sorcerer. And this land is their home. All you have to do is spill your blood—just a few drops—and they will come to you and do your bidding. The spirits. Those Who Thirst . . .*

Only when he felt pain did he realize his fingernails were pressing into the skin of his forearm. He willed his hand away and instead thought about Beltan. It was possible he would never see the blond man again. But Beltan would have done the same in Travis's place. He would have gone through the gate after Nim. How could he not? She was his daughter. Their daughter.

All the same, sorrow scoured at Travis's heart. What was Beltan doing right now?

He's trying to find a way to follow you, Travis. You know he is. He won't let you go.

Three years ago, everything had seemed so muddled and confusing. His emotions had been a labyrinth, and he had stumbled through the maze, not knowing who—if anyone—waited for him at its end. Even during these last years in London, as happy as he had been, he had sometimes wondered if things might not have been different had she not left them. Then she stepped through the door of his and Beltan's flat, and in that moment his wondering ceased.

Vani did not love him.

She *had* loved him once, that much Travis did not doubt. He had held her in his arms, he had felt her body trembling, he had kissed her. And in those moments he had loved her back. However, he knew now their love had been a trick—one every bit as cruel as the ruse the Little People had played on Vani and Beltan. Only this was not a trick of fairies.

It was a trick of Fate.

Vani had loved Travis because she believed it was her destiny to love him; she had willed her love into being in an act of sheer faith. And he had loved her back because, confronted with such a ferocity of emotion, his only choice was either to drive her away or bring her close. He couldn't cast her away, not when she needed love—real love—so badly and didn't even know it.

However, while the *T'hot* cards spoke the truth, as so often happened when trying to interpret Fate, that truth misled her. The cards had said she was destined to bear a child *by* Travis, but not *to* him, and that destiny had come to pass when she gave birth to Nim. Yet perhaps Fate was not so cruel after all, because in the end Vani had indeed found love—a love that was true, not based on any trick or deceit.

Her love for Nim.

Travis had seen it shining in Vani's eyes when she held her daughter. And he saw it now in the hard set of her jaw as she marched up and down the endless dunes. He quickened his pace—

—and nearly ran into Vani, who had come to a halt atop a dune.

"I see something." She was looking, not ahead, but off to their left.

"What is it?" He tried to follow her gaze, but the sand made his eyes water. "Is it a settlement?"

Vani squinted. "I'm not certain. It is difficult to see. Perhaps it is—blessed Mother of Orú!"

Travis screened his eyes with his fingers. There, on the horizon, a red-brown wall rose into the sky. Was it the mud wall of a city?

No. The wall rose higher into the sky, sending out swirling tendrils toward the sun.

"This is ill fate," Vani said. "It is a blood tempest."

"What's a blood tempest?" Travis said, raising his voice over the howl of the wind.

"A storm that blows out of the heart of the Morgolthi. To be caught in one is certain death. We must run. Now!"

Vani grabbed his arm, pulling him down the lee side of the dune. He lost his footing on the slick sand and went tumbling down the slope. At the bottom he rolled to a stop, then pushed himself up to his knees, spitting out a mouthful of sand.

A strong hand jerked him to his feet. "Keep running!" Vani shouted.

The wall of the tempest loomed above them, its rusty surface roiling like a violent sea. Even as Travis watched, it blotted out the sun, casting the world into ruddy twilight.

Vani pulled his arm so hard he heard his shoulder pop. He stumbled after her in a headlong run.

"It's coming too fast!" His throat was raw; he tasted metal. "We can't outrun it!"

"We do not have to," Vani shouted back. "A blood tempest is long and narrow in shape. Think of it as a serpent striking. We have only to flee to the side, to get out of its path, and we will be safe."

As the wall of the storm advanced from the south, they ran east. At first the wind seemed to lessen in its ferocity, and Travis began to think they had a chance. Then they reached the top of a slope, and he turned and watched as dune after dune was enveloped by clouds of boiling red dust. A gritty blast struck him, and sand hissed all around.

The hissing phased into whispering words.

Lie down. Let the sand cover you as a blanket. You are weary—so weary of your burdens. Lie down. . . .

The voices were soothing. The howl of the wind faded, and all he heard were the gentle whispers.

Lie down and go to sleep. . . .

Travis sighed. He felt warm and safe, like a child in his bed. It was time to shut his eyes.

"Get up!" This voice was different than the voices in the wind: harsher, and full of anger. "Do not give up on me, Travis Wilder. Not now!"

Something grabbed him, jerking him up, and only then did he realize he had been laying face-first in the sand. He rolled over with a groan. Vani knelt over him. Above, the sky churned, and sick yellow lightning flickered between the red clouds.

"Voices," he croaked. It was hard to speak; his mouth was full of dust. "I heard voices."

Vani pulled him to his feet. "They are sand spirits—the

voices of dead sorcerers from long ago. They want you to die, for your blood to soak into the sand, then dry to dust and be drawn up into the storm, feeding it. You must not listen to them!"

He nodded. It was too hard to speak.

"Come. We are still on the edge of the blood tempest, or we would already be dead. We can make it."

They careened down the side of the slope, then ran through the gap between a pair of high dunes. Wind buffeted them from all sides, and it was so dark it was impossible to tell which way they were going. Fear gripped Travis. Perhaps they were running into the path of the storm, not out of it. The voices began to whisper again in his ears.

There—up ahead. It was hard to be sure, but for a moment he thought he glimpsed a faint patch of light, as if the clouds of sand were thinner. He staggered toward it, but his feet caught on something, tripping him, and he fell down on top of a soft lump.

It was Vani. She wasn't moving. Her nose and mouth were caked with dust. He tried to clear it away, to help her breathe. Only he couldn't breathe himself. There was no air left, only sand and dust. Only the dried blood of sorcerers, more than three thousand years dead, whose power and malice had given birth to the tempest when chance winds in the desert brought enough of the red-brown powder together. The voices hissed again in his ears.

Travis! Can you hear me? I know you're out there....

This voice seemed different than the others. There was no hate in it, and it was ... familiar to him. He tried to call out in answer, but dust choked his throat. It was no use. He slumped over Vani, letting the sand cover them both.

A sound roused him from his stupor. Was it a shout? Somehow he lifted his head and looked up. He could just make it out amid the swirling sand: a figure shrouded in a black robe. Was this one of the sorcerers, then, come to take his blood?

The dark figure reached out a hand.

"Be dead!" intoned a commanding voice.

Then there was only silence.

26

After a long time, Travis heard voices again. The voices fluttered about him in the dark, as soft as the murmur of moth wings.

Travis . . .

A light shone in the darkness, a light as green and gold as sun through leaves.

You can wake up now. You're safe. I'm here with you. . . .

Travis opened his eyes. A face hovered over him. A beautiful, dusty, worried face he knew and loved.

"Grace," he croaked.

She smiled and brushed his hair from his brow. "Welcome back, Travis." She lifted his head and helped him drink water from a clay cup. It was cool and sweet. He tried to gulp it. "Slow, now. We need to get fluids back into you gradually."

Grace set down the cup, and with her help Travis managed to sit up in the cot. They were in some kind of low dwelling. Its walls were made of whitewashed mud, their corners rounded. The door was covered with a heavy cloth; the sound of sand hissed outside.

"Where's Vani?" His voice was still raspy, but better after the water.

"I am here," the *T'gol* said, drawing close to the bed. Her hair was white with dust, and it made her look old and weary.

He leaned his head back against the wall. "What happened to us? I remember the sand tempest, and I remember finding you on the ground. Then I heard the voices. They told me to sleep."

"They were sand spirits," a man's voice said.

Travis looked up. He had not seen the other standing in the corner of the hut; his black garb blended with the shadows. But now the man stepped forward, into the gold circle of light cast by an oil lamp. His dark hair was long and shaggy, as was his beard, which grew high up his cheeks. The skin of his forehead was deeply tanned. Only his dark eyes looked familiar. They still glinted with sharp intelligence. But there was something else in them now—a hot light, like that of a fever.

"Hello, Hadrian," Travis said.

Farr brushed the words aside as if they were beyond introductions. Or as if the name no longer applied. Red tattoos coiled across the palm of his hand. "The sand spirits were trying to take you, and had Grace not sensed your presence, they would have succeeded. As it was, I feared I had found you too late. I commanded the spirits to be what they were—to be dead— only when the storm cleared and I saw you lying on the ground, I assumed you were both dead as well."

Grace pressed a moist cloth to his brow. "But you're not. You're here, Travis. You're really here. I found you."

There was much to understand. Had Farr really been able to command the spirits in the sand tempest? If so, he was a powerful dervish indeed. Travis felt a pang of jealousy.

What an impudent upstart, Jack Graystone's voice sounded in his mind. *He's done nothing but ride along on your coattails. Surely you're a more powerful sorcerer than he is, Travis. And you're quite a good wizard as well. Why, you should wave your hand and—*

No, this wasn't a competition. Besides, Farr had had three years to learn secrets and delve into magics Travis had never even wanted to know about.

"Thank you for finding us," he said to Farr, then he looked at Grace. "And you, too. I'm glad you were able to sense our life threads. But what are you doing here in the first place? Why were you looking for me? And how did you know I'd be here?" He frowned. "Come to think of it, where exactly is *here*, anyway?"

Grace smiled. "You're in the village of Hadassa, on the southern edges of Al-Amún, on the continent of Moringarth." She touched his cheek. "You're on Eldh, Travis."

"Nim," he croaked. That was why he had come to Eldh—to save Nim. Fear renewed his strength in a way the water had not. He swung his feet over the edge of the bed to stand.

And immediately sat back down.

"Careful, Travis," Grace said, hands on his shoulders, steadying him. "You're still very weak."

"Vani is standing up," he said, feeling more than a little ashamed of himself. The room spun in a lazy circle around him.

"And before everything went black, I found her lying on the ground."

Farr looked at Vani. "After I dismissed the sand spirits, she was able to help me carry you back here. I believe the *T'gol* have training that can help them resist mind-altering effects, such as those of a sand tempest."

"I was deep in meditation when you came upon me, Travis, forging a wall around my mind so that I could shut out the voices of the spirits. I believed our only chance of survival was for me to retain my own will." She cast a look at Farr. "It was fortunate I was wrong."

"Being caught on the edge of a sand tempest is dangerous for anyone," Farr said. "But it's especially perilous for a sorcerer. The spirits were focused, not on Vani, but on you and your blood, Travis."

Travis clenched his right hand. "So you know about that."

Grace sat on the cot next to him and covered his hand with her own. "I told him everything."

"Then I'd say it's his turn."

"I will tell you anything you wish to know," Farr said.

Travis nodded, but he doubted that was possible. Even Farr couldn't know everything. Like where Nim was, and how they were going to get her back.

A silence settled over the hut, and only then did Travis realize that the wind was no longer hissing outside.

"The storm has passed," Farr said, pulling back the cloth covering the door to let a shaft of hot light into the hut.

Grace took a step toward him. "Does the village look all right?"

"You need not fear for these people. They have weathered far more sand tempests than I have. They know how to set the proper wards, and to keep their doors and windows shut. Besides, I believe the worst of the storm passed to the west of the village."

"And was that your doing?" Grace said.

Farr did not answer. He moved away from the door, and a man stepped through. Travis laughed in surprise and delight.

Master Larad glared at him, a sour expression on his scarred face. "Does something amuse you, Master Wilder?"

"Yes, very much," he said, far more glad that he might have guessed at the unexpected sight of the Runelord. Maybe it was just that it was good to know that the wizards in this hut now outnumbered the sorcerers two to one.

No, they don't, Travis. You're a sorcerer as well as a wizard. Besides, Master Larad has never exactly been on your side.

However, even when it appeared otherwise, the sardonic Runelord had always been on the side of good, and that was more than enough for Travis. This time, when he stood up, he managed to stay standing, and he moved to Larad, gripping his hand. He was grinning, and even Larad—never one for sentiment—could not conceal the hint of a smile.

"Why didn't you tell me Larad had come with you?" Travis said, glancing at Grace.

"I thought it would be a fun surprise."

Larad gave her a sharp look. No doubt the Runelord was not used to being considered in any way *fun*. "The storm has ceased. And Master Wilder has been successfully retrieved. It is time we talked."

Travis felt stronger in both body and spirit as they gathered around a table, drank *maddok*, ate dried figs, and spoke of their respective journeys to this place. Travis couldn't help but think this was probably one of the oddest parties this—or any village—had ever seen: a witch, an assassin, a dervish, and two wizards.

They listened first as Grace described her and Larad's journey south. Over the last month they had traveled to the southern tip of Falengarth, then had sailed across the Summer Sea, to Al-Amún, and with three *T'gol* as guards had taken camels into the desert, to this village.

When she was done, Travis shivered. "It's on Earth, too—the rift in the sky. Scientists are calling it Variance X. They know it lies just outside the solar system, but they have no idea what it is or why it's growing."

"It's the end of everything," Grace said. "That's what Sfithrisir said. The end of all possibility."

"It's only just now visible to the naked eye on Earth," Travis said. "It sounds like it's bigger here."

Grace nodded. "Just like the moon is bigger than on Earth,

and the stars brighter. I think the heavens are closer here on Eldh. The rift must be closer, too." She reached across the table, touching his hand. "Only the Last Rune can stop it. That's what the dragon said."

Travis didn't understand that part. "You mean the rune Eldh?"

She shook her head. "That was the last rune spoken at the end of the world. Sfithrisir said that only the last rune spoken at the end of everything can heal the rift."

"And did he maybe happen to mention what it was?"

"The dragon said you'd know what the Last Rune was. That's why I came here to find you." She squeezed his hand, her expression troubled. "Only you have no idea what the Last Rune is, do you?"

He sighed, then shook his head.

"It does not matter," Larad said. "Dragons can only speak the truth. You *will* find the Last Rune." However, the Runelord's eyes were not as certain as his words.

Farr turned his dark gaze on Travis. "If you didn't come here to look for the Last Rune, then why have you come to Eldh?"

"To find my daughter, Nim," Vani said before Travis could reply.

Travis took a sip of *maddok*, gathering his thoughts, then did his best to recount everything that had happened during their last hours on Earth. When he spoke of Deirdre and their conversation at the Charterhouse, Farr got up and paced, as if excited or agitated. Finally, Travis described how the gate crackled open and hands reached through, snatching Nim. He and Vani had managed to follow, but not Beltan. His throat grew tight, and he could no longer speak. Vani was gazing at her hands.

Oh, Travis. . . .

Grace's voice spoke in his mind. He felt her love, and her sorrow, enfold him like an embrace.

"It's all right," he said aloud. "We're going to get Nim back. That's why we came here."

And I will return to Beltan, he added silently.

He felt Grace's resolve flowing into him. *Yes, you will.*

Farr stopped his pacing. "Do you know why the Scirathi captured your daughter?" he said to Vani.

"I was not certain before. All I knew was that powerful lines of fate gather around her. But now we suspect it is her blood they want. They seek to use it as a key. Nor do we believe it was a coincidence that the sorcerers have pursued her even as Morindu the Dark has been found."

"I imagine you're right," Farr said. "The Scirathi are remarkably single-minded. At any given time, they will pursue only one goal, so that all their powers are focused on it. Right now that goal is Morindu. Somehow your daughter must be a part of their plans."

"I think we figured that much out," Travis said dryly.

Vani turned her gold eyes toward Farr. "I believe it is time we heard your tale, Seeker."

"Seeker," he said with a husky laugh. "I haven't been called that in a long time."

He fell silent, and Travis began to think that was all Farr was going to tell them. At last he spoke in a low voice.

"It began with the man in black."

Travis shivered despite the stifling air.

"I found him in Istanbul," Farr said. "Or rather, he found me, for I doubt I would have come upon him had he not wished it. He wore the black robe of an imam, and his skin was dark rather than pale, but all the same I knew at once who he was. I had read your descriptions of him many times over, Travis."

"Brother Cy."

"Yes."

Travis should have known that was how Farr had gotten to Eldh. But why had the Old God—who seemed to favor the garb of a holy man no matter what land he was in—transported Farr here?

"I wasn't even certain why I had gone to Istanbul," Farr went on. "I had investigated rumors of an otherworldly portal there once. I had never found any evidence of a door, but I always felt there were a few leads that I had not followed as fully as I might have, so I took the Orient Express from Paris. However, I never had the chance to perform any research, for he found me almost the moment I stepped off the train.

"He told me to meet him the following evening beneath the dome of the Hagia Sophia, then vanished. I went to my hotel, phoned Deirdre and left her a message, spent a sleepless night, then went to the museum to meet him, hardly expecting him to be there. Only he was, along with the other two—the girl and the blind woman. I knew it was them, though they were robed and veiled."

"Samanda and Mirrim," Grace murmured. "What happened then?"

The dervish shook his head. "The imam—Brother Cy—said he could show me the way to what I searched for. I said I didn't know what that was, but the girl said that was a lie. And she was right, because I *had* gone to Istanbul looking for something. I was looking for a door to Eldh. I wanted to stop searching for those who had traveled to other worlds and instead go there myself.

"The blind woman whispered something in my ear, something that made no sense to me, then suddenly they were gone. I thought that was it, that nothing else was going to happen. In despair, I left the Hagia Sophia. Only when I stepped out of the door, I found myself not on a street in Istanbul, but rather standing among ruined stone columns in the middle of a desert. The sun was blazing, and I had no water. There was no sign of a doorway behind me. Vultures circled above, and I laughed bitterly, because I had finally gotten what I wanted—I had traveled to another world. And I was going to die there." Farr sighed. "Only then . . ."

"Then what?" Travis said, fascinated, even envious. He remembered what it was like to first come to Eldh.

"Then I was found," Farr said.

For the next hour, they listened as Farr told them what had befallen him during his last three years on Eldh—although Travis was certain the former Seeker was not telling them everything. In the ruins he was found by a dervish, much as Travis had been found by Falken in the Winter Wood the first time he journeyed to Eldh. In both cases, Brother Cy had chosen their destinations with care.

The ruins where the dervish discovered him turned out to be all that was left of Usyr, once the greatest city of ancient Amún, and now little more than a few heaps of stone that jutted out of the desert like the bones of giants. The old dervish had come to

Usyr to find secrets of sorcery. Instead he had found death. While opening a box of scrolls, he had sprung an ancient trap, releasing a cloud of poisonous dust, and even as he stumbled upon Farr he was dying.

You must take them, the dervish had said, giving the scrolls to Farr. *All my life I have searched for them. I have sacrificed everything to seek them out: my home, my people, my blood.*

The scrolls had been filled with writing Farr could not understand. *What are they?*

They are a story, the dervish said. *The story of the birthing of all the worlds. Those that are, and those that are not.*

All night Farr huddled in the ruins with the dervish, listening to the old man speak. He told Farr everything that had happened to him in his years as a dervish, everything he had forsaken and everything he had learned. Then, as the horizon turned from gray to white, the old man fell silent; he was dead.

As the sun rose, Farr took the dervish's bag of food, his waterskins, and the scrolls, then donned the old man's black *serafi*. He set out on foot, in the direction from which the dervish said he had come.

For three days Farr walked through the desert, beneath the blazing sun, avoiding scorpions, vipers, and sandstorms, until his water was gone. Another day he walked, but still there was no sign of a village. The vultures began to circle again; death drew near. At last Farr fell to his knees, ready to die. Only then he remembered there was one other thing he had taken from the dervish: his knife.

Farr cut his arm, let his blood spill upon the sand, and called the *morndari* to him, just as the dervish had described.

"I didn't really think they would come," Farr said, the words quiet. "Even after all that had happened, after all I had seen, I don't think I truly believed in magic. Only then they did come, just as the old man had said." His eyes went distant, and he touched his left arm. "At first I was nearly intoxicated, and they drank deeply of my blood, drawing it from me with terrible force. Then fear sharpened my mind, and I commanded the spirits to lead me to water. To my amazement, they did.

"They carved a line in the sand, and I stumbled along it before the winds could blow it away. It turned out I was very close to a village. It was just on the other side of a ridge. However, if I had kept on in the direction I had been walking, I would have passed it and never known. I managed to stumble into the village, and I fell down next to the oasis and drank as the spirits buzzed away."

Vani studied Farr with a look of grudging respect. "Only one in a hundred has any talent for sorcery. And only one in a thousand might call the *morndari* and command them successfully on the first try. It is fate you came here, for you were born to this. And yet . . ." A knife appeared in her hands.

"Are you going to kill me?" Farr said. He made no attempt to move away from her.

The *T'gol* ran a finger along the edge of the knife. "To be a dervish is anathema. The working of blood sorcery is forbidden by my people."

"I am not one of the Mournish."

Vani sheathed the knife. Only then did Travis realize he had been holding his breath. He glanced at Grace; her eyes were locked on Farr. Larad watched with cool interest.

"You are right about one thing," Farr said, sitting down at the table again. "To be a dervish is to be an outcast. I learned that at the village I first came to. The people came for me, throwing stones at me, driving me from the village. Luckily, I had had time to refill my waterskins, and this time there was a road to follow, leading to a larger city. Once there, I made sure to hide my black *serafi* and dress in the garb of common folk."

"You're not hiding your robe now," Travis said.

"One can only hide what one truly is for so long. I believe you understand that well, Travis Wilder."

"So you really are a dervish," Grace said softly.

Now the expression on his face became one of wonder. "I didn't mean for it to happen. At first I thought I was still being a Seeker. And what Seeker wouldn't want to understand the origin of all the worlds? I began to study the scrolls I had taken from the old dervish, and to research how I might read them. But the course of my studies kept leading me back to ancient Amún. And to sorcery."

"Was it only that?" Vani said. "Was it only research, as you say? Or was it not that you enjoyed summoning the spirits and wished to do it again?" Her gaze moved down to his arms.

Farr pulled down the sleeves of his *serafi*, but not before they all saw the fine scars that crisscrossed his skin.

"So have you ever learned what was in the scrolls?" Grace said after a long moment.

Farr shook his head. "I have learned some of the ancient tongue of Amún, but not enough to translate the scrolls fully. They are written in a peculiar script—used only, I believe, by a secret cabal of sorcerers long ago. It is possible that some among the Mournish might be able to read more of the scrolls than I have, but I wouldn't exactly expect a friendly reception if I were to go to them."

He cast a glance at Vani. The *T'gol* said nothing.

"What I have been able to read is intriguing," Farr went on, and he seemed more like a scholar or researcher now, speaking with growing excitement. "Of course, it's all heavily coded in metaphor. It reads like a myth—though like all myths, I think there is truth at its heart. The scrolls describe how in the beginning there was nothing. Then the nothing, quite spontaneously, spawned two twins. The twins were opposites in every way: one light and giving, the other dark and consuming. From the moment they were born, the twins were separated and kept apart, and each built many cities beholden to him. However, the scrolls speak of a time when the twins will come together again. When they do, they will war, and all that both of them created will be destroyed. Even the very nothingness that spawned them will be annihilated. All of existence will be like an empty cup, only with no chance of ever being filled again."

The story made Travis sick. "It's just like what you said about the rift, Grace. It's the end of everything."

Larad leaned on his elbows, his fingertips pressed together. "Do the scrolls speak of how the twins might be prevented from warring?"

"Not in any passages that I have been able to decipher."

Travis stood up. He had heard enough. "We can worry about what's in the scrolls later. Right now we have to find Nim. The sorcerers will be taking her to Morindu, won't they?" Vani nodded. He turned his gaze on Farr. "And you know the way, don't you?"

Farr hesitated. "I believe I do. There has been an increasing number of tremors in Moringarth in recent months. Many ruins, previously buried and lost, have been uncovered. Not long ago, while investigating the rumors of just such a ruin, I came upon a Scirathi. He had crawled out of the deep desert and was nearly dead. I think he was hallucinating and thought I was one of his kind, for he clutched at my robe and babbled that he had seen a spire of black stone jutting up out of the sand. He told me where he had seen it, but before he could tell me more, a band of his ilk attacked, and I was forced to flee."

"A black spire," Vani breathed, her gold eyes gleaming. "Of all the cities of ancient Amún, only Morindu was built of black stone."

"That is why I believe what the sorcerer said was true: that after all these eons, Morindu has at last been found."

"What happened to this sorcerer?" Larad asked.

"I can only believe the Scirathi retrieved him, and that they learned what I did from him, and perhaps more."

Vani clenched a fist. "You should have slain him."

Farr glared at her, and Travis stepped between the two. They didn't have time for arguments. "You can fight about this later. The Scirathi know where Morindu is, and that means right now they're taking Nim to it. The storm is over—there's no more reason to wait here. We have to go."

Grace stood beside him. "I'm going with you."

He gave her a grateful look. She took his hand and gripped it tightly.

Vani turned away from Farr, a look of shame on her face. "Travis is right. Nothing matters now save for finding my daughter."

"What of the rift?" Master Larad said, rising from his chair. "I journeyed here with Queen Grace because I wished to speak to you about the weakening of rune magic, Master Wilder. I believe it might be related to the rift, as well as to the Last Rune. If we answer one mystery, we may answer the other as well."

Seldom in his life had Travis felt certain about what to do. At that moment, he did. Nim was more important than everything else. Even the world. All the worlds.

"We can talk about it on the way," he said.

27.

They made ready to leave the village of Hadassa as evening drew near.

"It's best if we journey into the desert by night," Farr said as they let the camels drink their fill from the village's oasis. "The moon is almost full. We will have more than enough light, and it will be far cooler than traveling by day."

The *T'gol* Avhir crossed lean arms, his bronze eyes on the former Seeker. "The heat is not the only danger in the Morgolthi."

"No, but it's the only danger we can hope to easily avoid," Farr said. He turned his back on the assassin. "I will be on the south edge of the village. I want to see if I can spot any storms while there is still light. Meet me there when you are ready." He walked away among the white huts, his dark *serafi* gusting behind him.

"Well, it's nice to see he's as cuddly as ever," Travis said.

Grace followed Farr with her gaze. "He's only doing his job. He's promised to take us to Morindu."

"And the brooding helps with that how?"

"I'm going to go get my things," Grace said, and headed toward one of the huts.

Travis sighed and turned his attention back to the four camels, amazed at how much the animals could drink. A thought occurred to him. He approached Avhir. Of the three *T'gol* who had accompanied Grace south, the tall man seemed the most talkative—which wasn't saying much.

"We've packed water for ourselves," he said to Avhir, "but where will the camels get water?"

"Nowhere. I do not imagine the beasts will survive this journey. I can only hope they will bear us close to our destination before they perish."

His words shocked Travis. "This isn't right. We can't kill them for nothing."

"So you believe this journey is for nothing?"

Travis clenched his jaw. They both knew the answer to that question. "Maybe we could go on foot."

Avhir shook his head. "You cannot travel as fast on foot as *T'gol*, and time is against us. The sorcerers are already on the move."

Travis couldn't disagree. However, he doubted that saving Nim was the assassin's sole reason for hurrying.

They want to find Morindu the Dark. They've been searching for it for three thousand years. Now it's been found, and they think I'm going to raise it from the sands that bury it.

And was he? Travis didn't know. If that was what it took to save Nim, he would find a way to do it. Otherwise, Morindu the Dark could stay buried for countless eons more for all he cared.

"Do not pity the beasts, Sai'el Travis." Avhir stroked the neck of one of the camels as it used its long tongue to draw water into its mouth. "After all, you do not pity the animal whose flesh you eat. Instead, be grateful for their sacrifice and accept it."

These words were scant comfort. Travis started to move away, then paused. "So how are we going to get back? If the camels don't survive, how will we leave Morindu?"

"You and the dervish are great sorcerers. Once the power of Morindu is at your disposal, there will be little either of you cannot do."

Travis stared at him; the assassin's eyes shone in the gloom.

"Come," Avhir said. "The camels are ready. It is time to go."

They set out as the enormous Eldhish moon rose above the horizon, flooding the desert with white light so that the dunes seemed made of snow rather than sand. Of the four *T'gol*, only Vani and Avhir were in view, and even they were difficult to see, skimming over the sand like shadows. Travis could only assume the other two were up ahead, scouting.

The camels moved at a languid but unceasing pace, keeping to the troughs between the dunes, and the huts of the village quickly vanished from sight. Just as when she rode a horse, Grace looked assured and regal atop her camel, clad in a flowing white *serafi*, as if she had done this all her life. Even Farr did not seem so at ease as she though he was clearly a practiced rider.

Travis, in contrast, bounced in the hard, square saddle that perched on the hump of his mount, his black *serafi* flapping around him. The camel paced with an odd gait that rolled from side to side, and he felt like an egg sitting on a tray balancing on the top of a mountain. In an earthquake. The sand was shockingly far below him, but at least it would provide a soft landing if—or more likely, when—he took a tumble.

Besides, Travis could take consolation in the fact that he wasn't having nearly as hard a time as Master Larad. The Runelord's scarred face was pasty in the moonlight, and evinced a greenish cast.

"Up and down, back and forth," he hissed between clenched teeth. "Cannot this wretched beast stop rocking? By Olrig, this is worse than being on the sea. Steady, now. Steady!"

Travis made a poor attempt to stifle his laughter. He had planned to speak to Larad once they set out; the Runelord had wanted to talk about the rift. However, Travis decided it could wait. Besides, he had other matters on his mind.

Once the power of Morindu is at your disposal, there will be little either of you cannot do. . . .

Travis's laughter died. What had Avhir meant by those words?

You know what he meant. Morindu was an entire city of sorcerers—the most powerful sorcerers that ever lived. Who knows what knowledge is buried in there, what secrets, what artifacts?

He found himself gazing to his left. Did Farr know what was buried in Morindu? Is that why he was helping them? Not to get Nim back, or to stop the Scirathi in their quest for power, but rather to claim those secrets, that power, for himself?

Travis studied the former Seeker, as if the moonlight might reveal secrets that daylight had not. Before they had set out, Farr had cleaned himself up. He had shaved his beard and trimmed his hair, and except for the black *serafi* he looked like the man Travis remembered: darkly handsome, compelling, but dangerous as well, like the haunted protagonist of a noir film. Then

Travis looked past Farr and saw that his was not the only gaze locked on the former Seeker.

He waited until they began to wind around the base of a curving ridge of sand, then—with far more tugs on the reins than he would have thought necessary—brought his camel close to Grace's.

"Can we trust him?" he said in a low voice.

Grace gave him a startled glance, then her gaze moved ahead, to where Farr rode.

He seems different, Travis said in his mind. He knew she—and only she—could hear him.

He is different, Grace's voice—her presence—spoke in his mind. *Sareth said that working blood sorcery changes a man, and that's why we shouldn't trust him. But I don't think we have a choice.*

Travis licked his lips; they already felt dry and cracked. "He fell in love with you, Grace, when he was watching you as a Seeker. Deirdre told me about it."

"I know," Grace said. "At least, I think I did."

"And do you love him?"

She smiled: a sorrowful expression. *In Malachor, I would think about him sometimes. I would wonder what I might say if I saw him again, what it might be like if he was near. But I didn't believe it would ever happen. That made it safe to think about him. Only this feels . . .*

Dangerous, he said in his mind.

She shook her head. *Whatever I feel for him isn't important. The only thing that's important is finding Nim. I'm no expert when it comes to feelings, but there's one thing I am certain of: I love you, Travis, and I love Beltan. And we will find your daughter.*

"Thank you," he managed to croak.

"Don't worry about him, Travis," Grace said, speaking aloud now. "If Hadrian tries to do something, she'll know about it." She nodded toward a shadow that flitted just behind Farr's camel.

Travis sighed. *We don't love each other anymore, Vani and I. I know.*

He felt Grace's reply as much as heard it, and it was enough;

she understood. And even though he didn't love Vani, he knew he could trust her. Vani had spent the last three years doing everything she could to protect Nim. She was not going to stop.

They rode in silence after that. Travis concentrated on breathing through his nostrils, to preserve the moisture in his breath. And to keep himself from breathing too deeply. He had not forgotten Vani's warning; the air of the Morgolthi was intoxicating to sorcerers. This place was dangerous because it could make *him* dangerous.

The moon soared to its zenith, then began to descend. The dunes rose and fell like ghostly waves, and the rocking of the camel caused Travis to drift into a kind of waking sleep. From time to time he saw a shadow slink down the lee side of one of the dunes, or flit by on the edge of vision, and he knew one of the *T'gol* was close. They were keeping watch, and if there were any perils in the desert, the assassins skillfully led the party around them.

Travis jerked in the saddle. They had come to a stop. He looked up and saw the last sliver of the moon just vanishing behind a ridge.

"We will stop here," Avhir said.

They made camp in a hollow beneath the lee side of a dune. Travis clambered down from his camel, limbs stiff and aching. He noticed Grace shivering, fetched a blanket from one of the packs, and wrapped it around her shoulders. The desert night had grown cold, though Travis didn't really feel it. These days, his blood was always hot.

Once the sun crested the horizon, the need for blankets evaporated, and in minutes the air began to shimmer with heat. The *T'gol* erected a simple shelter by tying the blankets to wood staves pounded into the sand. The tent offered a small patch of shade, and as the blankets were woven with desert colors, it offered concealment as well.

Not that Travis could imagine there was anyone who might detect them. As far as he could see, there was only desert. No trace of any living thing—plant, animal, or person—broke the monotony of sand and sky.

They spent the day doing as best they could beneath the cover of the shelter, though even in the shade the heat was oppressive, and any sleep led to fitful dreams from which they woke sweating, with heads throbbing. Travis considered speaking to Master Larad as a way to pass the time, but his mouth was too dry for conversation, and he had already drunk his ration of water for the morning. Besides, the Runelord was curled up on a small carpet and lay so still that Travis began to worry about him.

He's fine, Grace spoke in Travis's mind, touching his arm. *At least mostly. He's still feeling seasick from last night's camel ride. Or sandsick, I suppose. I gave him a simple that's helping him keep down some food and water. He just needs to rest.*

Travis nodded, glad Grace was keeping an eye on Larad, then tried to rest himself. He could speak to the Runelord later.

Throughout the day, the *T'gol* moved in and out of the shelter, appearing and vanishing like the shadows in Travis's half dreams. He saw more of them than he had at night; even the assassins needed rest. In addition to Avhir, there was Rafid—a compact man with a harsh, brooding face—and Kylees, a dark-skinned woman who would have been lovely if she smiled. She didn't.

Travis did not speak to the *T'gol*, though he often felt their eyes—bronze, copper, and gold—upon him. Also, Rafid seemed often to glower at Farr, though the dervish appeared not to notice.

At last the sun sank toward the western dunes. The *T'gol* dismantled the shelter and lashed the packs to the camels.

"You've got a cut on your hand," Grace said to one of the assassins. It was the woman Kylees.

"It is nothing," the *T'gol* said, starting to pull away, but Grace caught her hand with surprising speed and turned it over.

"The wound is small," Grace said in her brisk doctor's voice. "However, there's some swelling. It could be infected."

"I said it is nothing. There was a sand scorpion in my hut in the village yesterday. I was foolish enough to be slow in smashing it with my hand, giving it time to sting me. However, their poison is weak, and I bled it out with my knife."

"Good. Then it should heal well. But let me give you an ointment—"

"I do not need your petty northern magics," Kylees said, pulling her hand back and stalking from the camp.

"Proud much?" Travis said, watching the assassin walk away.

Grace sighed. "I think I embarrassed her. She shouldn't have let that scorpion sting her. *T'gol* don't like to make mistakes."

"Only sometimes they do," Travis said, his gaze moving to Vani.

Grace took his arm. "Come on. I think your rear end has a date with a camel."

They set out again as dusk stole over the desert. As before, the night zephyrs soon died down, and the silence of the desert was broken only by the groan of sand settling: an eerie sound that made Travis think of distant voices moaning in pain.

Master Larad appeared to have grown somewhat accustomed to the gait of his camel. He looked only moderately nauseous, and Travis decided to see if talking might take his mind off his discomfort. With some effort, he managed to get his camel close to the Runelord's.

"So what was so important that you traveled hundreds of leagues, crossed the ocean, and rode a camel just to tell me?"

Larad grimaced. "If I had known what the journey would be like, perhaps I would have rethought undertaking it." His grimace became a bitter smile. "But is that not always the way, Master Wilder? The foolish blithely go where the wise dare not venture. So here I am."

"And?"

"And magic is failing, Master Wilder," Larad said, his eyes glinting in the light of the full moon. "Both runic magic and the magic of the Weirding, which is spun by witches."

Travis let out a breath. "Grace told me. But I think I knew it before I even came to Eldh. Magic is always weak on Earth, but the last few runes I spoke there seemed to keep going awry, even though they should have been simple."

"The runestones are crumbling," Larad went on. "As are all bound runes. Do you understand what that means?"

Of course he did. How could he not? He was the one who had broken it, then bound it again.

"Eldh," Travis said softly. "It's a bound rune."

"Yes, it is. And if the power of runes continues to weaken, soon there will be nothing to hold that rune together."

Travis clutched the reins in numb hands. "Did you tell Grace this?"

"Her Majesty's thoughts have been focused on the rift in the sky, and on finding you. I saw no need to add to the knowledge that already weighs upon her."

"She believes I can stop the rift," Travis said, sighing.

The scars that crisscrossed Larad's face were silver in the moonlight. "So the dragon said, and dragons can only speak truth. You have the ability to discover the Last Rune, Master Wilder, and to wield it. But there is one thing Queen Grace does not realize."

To Travis it was as clear as the moon. "The end of magic. If runes no longer work properly, how can I speak the Last Rune? Or bind it?" He was sweating despite the chill air. "But maybe there's still time. Magic hasn't stopped working, not completely."

"Yet it grows weaker each day, and you tell me that for you even simple spells go awry. What of greater magics? Have you tried any powerful runespells of late? Perhaps they cannot be worked anymore. Perhaps time has already run out. I journeyed here to tell you that. And to bring you these."

He reached inside his robe and drew out an object: a small iron box, carved with runes.

Travis gave him a startled look. "You brought the Imsari with you?"

"Magic is weakening, but the Great Stones can amplify the power of a runespell many times over. I thought you might need them in order to speak the Last Rune."

Larad held out the box. Travis started to reach for it; his hand ached to hold the Imsari, to feel them pulse against his palm.

By force of will, he pulled his hand back. There was already too much temptation to use power in this place. "You keep them for now," he said, the words hoarse.

Larad gave him a quizzical look, then shrugged and tucked the box back inside his robe.

They rode in silence after that. As the camel paced, Travis rubbed his right hand, feeling the tingle of the rune of runes on his palm. It was quiescent now, but if he spoke a rune it would flare to life.

Or would it? Magic was growing weaker, and Travis hadn't tried speaking a rune of significant power in over three years. What if he tried and couldn't?

Why not find out, Travis? Jack's voice spoke in his mind. *How about Lir? The rune of light can be used to work wondrous magics. It's always been one of my favorites. We shall all speak it with you in chorus, and create a midnight sun blazing in the sky!*

A thousand voices murmured in Travis's mind; he moistened his lips, preparing to speak the rune.

"By Olrig!" Larad swore, gazing upward, his camel coming to a halt.

The camel Farr rode halted as well. "So it is true, then."

Travis pulled on the reins, managing to bring his camel to a stop beside Grace's. He followed her gaze toward the sky. The moon had set, and the stars were brilliant against the heavens—

—except for a jagged gash in the south where there were no stars. Only darkness, grinning like a black mouth.

"It's another rift," Grace said, her voice quavering.

So the rift wasn't a single tear in the fabric of the heavens. Instead, that fabric was full of holes. How long did they have before it unraveled completely?

Before Travis could speak his thoughts, the night coalesced into a lithe shape: Vani.

"We must seek shelter," she said. "A blood tempest comes."

28.

A keening rose on the air as they guided their camels after the shadowy shapes of the *T'gol*. Dust whirled on the air, and Travis fastened a cloth tight over his nose and mouth. Farr did the same.

One of the *T'gol* glided down the slope of a dune. It was hard to see in the murk, but Travis recognized the short, compact shape of Rafid.

"The blood tempest comes quickly!" Rafid shouted above the growl of the wind. "We will not be able to outrun it. It is almost as if it is drawn to us." He cast a dark glance at Farr.

Farr ignored the look. "We have to find shelter now."

Only there was none. The surrounding dunes were low with wide, wind-scoured flats between them. Already the air was thick with blowing sand. The stars winked out in the sky.

Kylees stepped out of a swirl of sand. "Quickly, this way— there is a high dune ahead. It may offer some shelter. We must take the *A'narai*. Leave behind the weak if we must."

Vani moved past her. "We leave no one."

Kylees glared at Vani, then turned away.

The wind had risen to a howl, and sand buffeted them from all sides. The *T'gol* used cloths to cover the faces of the camels, then each assassin took the reins of one of the beasts, leading them on. Travis huddled close to his camel's neck, holding on with all his strength. He could not see three feet ahead of him; if the wind knocked him down, he would be lost.

They had not gone far when the voices began.

Lie down, hissed the wind. *Let the sand cover you. . . .*

Before he realized what was happening, Travis was slipping out of the saddle; his fingers had let go of the camel's neck. He groped but could not regain his grip.

Strong hands caught him, pushing him back.

"Do not listen to the voices!"

His eyes stung and watered; he could not make her out, but he knew her touch. Vani. He thought he saw a shadow circle around to the front of the camel, then the beast began moving again.

Travis wrapped his arms around the camel's neck and shut his eyes. The voices continued to hiss in his ears; he clenched his teeth, trying to shut them out. However, that only seemed to make the storm angrier. The wind clawed at him from all sides, shrieking in his ears.

Let go! Lie down! Your blood will join ours!

He was so weary; his arms ached to let go. The wind scoured at his being, wearing it away like a stone. It was no use. He could not resist. . . .

Just as Travis let go of the camel's neck, the force of the wind lessened, and the shrill voices receded, growing fainter. He tumbled to the ground, then sat up and coughed sand out of his lungs. In the faint light he saw Vani crouching before him.

"Are you—?"

He gripped her hand. "The voices are more distant now."

She nodded, then vanished. A moment later Grace appeared out of a swirl of sand, collapsing next to Travis, followed by Master Larad. Farr stumbled into view and crouched beside them. His face was a mask of dust, and his eyes were hazed with pain. So even Farr had not been able to resist the power of the voices with ease. For some reason Travis felt a grim note of satisfaction.

They were out of the worst of the wind now. In the gloom Travis made out steep slopes rising around them on three sides.

"Where are we?" he called over the wind.

"I don't know," Farr shouted. "I have never seen a dune shaped like this. But the high slopes are protecting us."

"We are still in danger," Vani said, reappearing from a cloud of sand, along with the other *T'gol*. "We are in the center of the blood tempest now. If the winds shift and blow from the north, we will die. And even if the winds do not shift, we may not yet survive. Cover yourselves!"

They huddled beneath blankets at the base of one of the slopes as the storm raged around them. Time no longer had meaning. There was only the keening of the wind, and the hiss of sand, and the murmur of voices. Travis curled up next to Grace beneath the blanket as a weight slowly pressed down on him. . . .

The quiet was so sudden and complete it was deafening, making Travis's ears ring. He tried to sit up, but he couldn't move. It was as if strong arms held him, pinning his body in place. His lungs could barely expand to draw in a scant breath. Next to him, Grace made a small sound of pain. He tried to reach for her but could not.

"They're here!" called out a voice, though it was muffled, distant.

There was a scrabbling sound, then all at once the crushing weight vanished. With a rasp of sand the blanket that had covered him and Grace was torn aside.

Air rushed into Travis's lungs. He blinked against the white light, then made out two dark silhouettes above him: Larad and Farr. Larad took Travis's hand, pulling him out of the drift of sand, while Farr helped Grace to stand. She was coughing violently, but she waved her hand, indicating she was all right.

"We could see no trace of you," Larad said. "It was as if the sand had swallowed you. But Kylees told us to dig here, that we would find you. I don't know how she knew."

Travis looked back. Part of the dune had collapsed, covering the place where he and Grace had huddled beneath the blanket with a mound of sand. Above, a row of tall, slender shapes jutted out of the top of the dune, exposed by the winds of the storm. At first Travis wondered if they were trees. Then he realized what they were: stone columns, their tops broken off so that they looked like a row of teeth.

"What is this place?" he croaked.

Farr gazed around them, his dark eyes narrowing. "Somewhere we should not be."

It was not a natural dune that had sheltered them from the storm. Sand had covered it, but the tempest had scoured much of that sand away, revealing the columns and walls of pitted, buff-colored stone. In one place the remains of a broad stairway plunged down into the sand.

Grace turned around. "It looks like a temple."

"Or perhaps a palace," Farr said, shaking sand from his black robe. "This might be the ruins of Golbrora, or perhaps one of the royal villas near Xalas. It is difficult to say. Those cities have been lost for eons, and their precise locations can only be guessed at."

Travis moved toward a rectangular block of stone that was half-exposed by the sand. The stone was large, its narrowest edge as wide as the span of his arms, and there were carvings on it, though they were too worn to be made out. Perhaps if he brushed away some of the remaining dust . . .

Fingers closed around his wrist, halting him.

"Do not touch anything," Farr said, his eyes locked on Travis. "We are deep in the Morgolthi now. There's no telling what ancient magics yet remain."

Travis pulled his hand back. "Isn't that why you're a dervish now? To look for things like this? For ancient magics?"

Farr turned his back. "It's time to make camp. Let's find the *T'gol.*"

The *T'gol* found them first. The assassins had explored the ruins, but they had not discovered anything that warned of immediate danger, and so had decided it was safe to stay in the ruins for the day. Not that they had much choice. Although it was still morning, the day was already blistering, and there was no sign of any other shelter.

Rafid drew close to Farr. "Do not go exploring among the ruins, dervish. I will be watching you."

The former Seeker's expression was unreadable. "And who will be watching you?"

The *T'gol* spat on the sand, then turned and stalked away, vanishing like a mirage.

"He fears magic," Farr said. "It will be his death."

Vani gave him a sharp look. "Let's set up a shelter."

They used blankets to create a makeshift canopy in the corner of a half-crumbled wall and huddled in the scant shade. As the hours passed, they sipped a little water from their skins and ate some dried fruit, though Travis could hardly gag it down. He did not feel hungry.

He must have fallen into a fitful daze, for he woke with a start and sat up. His mouth was parched, and dried sweat crusted his skin. The sun was sinking toward the horizon, and the shadows of the stone columns stretched across the sand. In another hour, it would be time to start traveling again.

Grace was curled up on a rug next to him, asleep. Larad lay nearby, and beyond him was Farr. Their eyes were closed, their breathing shallow but steady. Travis gazed around. The camels huddled in the scant shade of the wall, heads drooping. There was no sign of the *T'gol.* No doubt they were keeping watch.

Travis picked up the waterskin, took a sip, then sealed it, careful not to spill a drop. He started to lie back down, then halted.

His eyes focused on the block of stone he had drawn close to earlier. It was canted at an angle in the sand, so that one end was completely buried. How big was it? There was no way to know how far it went into the sand. The block was a different color than the rest of the ruins, a nearly pure white. The low angle of the evening light cast shadows in the carvings on the stone so that he could almost make them out, only he was too far away. . . .

Before he thought about what he was doing, Travis was walking toward the stone.

I'm just going to look at the carvings, he told himself. *I'm not going to touch it, so I'm not doing anything wrong.*

All the same, he moved quietly, and he cast several glances back over his shoulder to be sure the others were still asleep.

He halted beside the stone. Its top was smooth, though here and there dark flecks, like the remains of black paint, were embedded in its porous surface. The carvings on the sides were easier to discern in the angled light of the sun, though they meant nothing to Travis. They were long and sinuous, forming interlocking patterns. It occurred to him that if Grace was right, if this really had been a temple once, then the stone must be some kind of altar.

Travis licked his cracked and blistered lips, and the metallic taste of blood spread over his tongue. He was sweating, and a rushing noise sounded in his ears, along with a low susurration like a whispering voice, though it did not speak in words. At least not human words. All the same, Travis understood. The voice wanted him to touch the stone. His fingers stretched toward the stone's surface. . . .

A shout broke the spell.

Travis snatched his hand back. Beneath the shelter, Grace and Larad sat up, eyes wide. Farr sprang to his feet, glaring at Travis.

The shout came again, from the other side of the mound of sand from which the columns jutted. Travis started running. The others followed, but he was closer. He ran around the edge of the mound, to the other side of the row of columns.

The storm had exhumed a section of a stone wall from the mound. Set into the wall, beneath a massive lintel, was a stone door, shut. One of the *T'gol* stood in front of the door: Rafid. His face, always before stern and hard, was now pale with fear. He struggled as if trying to get away from the door, the muscles of his compact body straining beneath black leather, only something was holding him in place. Then Travis saw what it was. There was a hole in the center of the door, about as large as a splayed hand. Rafid's arm was stuck in the hole, up to the elbow.

The *T'gol*'s body jerked, and his arm was drawn several more inches into the hole. He shouted again.

"What's going on?" Grace said, panting as she halted next to Travis. Farr and Larad were right behind her.

"Idiot!" Farr said, clenching a fist. "He should have known. I thought *T'gol* were trained better than that."

Rafid opened his mouth, making a dry, weak sound. By then his arm was completely consumed by the hole, his shoulder against the stone door. His skin, once bronze, was ash gray.

Larad started forward. "We must help him."

Farr grabbed the Runelord's shoulder. "You can't help him. Not now. Not unless you know the rune of death."

Travis didn't care what Farr said. They had to do something. He started moving; Grace was with him. However, before they could go three steps, the air blurred, and Vani was there before them.

"Do not go near him!"

They stumbled backward, colliding with one another. Ahead, a patch of air shimmered like a mirage, then Avhir appeared, gripping a curved scimitar. The tall assassin swung the blade, lopping off Rafid's arm at the shoulder. Vani pulled the man back, away from the door; no blood pumped from the stump of his arm. Rafid stared at the other *T'gol*, opening his mouth as if to speak something. He shuddered once.

Then his body crumbled into dust.

The wind snatched the dust, blowing it away in gritty swirls. Avhir threw Rafid's empty black leathers to the sand, his bronze eyes hard. Vani stalked toward them. Travis and Grace ran after, Larad behind.

"Stay away from the door!" Farr shouted, but they ignored him.

Just as they reached the assassins, Kylees appeared. "What has happened?" she said, staring at Rafid's crumpled leathers.

Avhir uncoiled long legs, standing. "I am not certain. I had posted Rafid at this wall to keep watch to the east. I came when I heard his shout. He was—"

Something black and sinuous shot from the hole in the door, wrapping itself around Avhir's neck, hissing. With a quick motion the *T'gol* dived into a roll, disentangling himself and flinging the thing to the ground as he stood back up.

It was a serpent, pure black except for its eyes and flicking tongue, which were bloodred. The viper bared curved fangs, its neck flaring. Moving so fast it was a shadowy blur, it struck again at Avhir.

The *T'gol* was faster. He swung his scimitar, cleaving the viper in two. It vanished in a puff of black smoke.

"Beware!" Kylees called out.

Another viper writhed out of the hole, and another. They kept coming faster than Travis could count, pouring down the surface of the wall like dark water until the sand was black with them. The vipers slithered forward, hissing, puffing out their necks, baring fangs that dripped venom.

Avhir lashed out with his scimitar, and two more vipers vanished in puffs of acrid smoke. However, more replaced them. Travis grabbed Grace's hand and started to back away, but the serpents had already wriggled across the sand, circling around them. The *T'gol* kicked at the vipers, flung them away, and hacked at them with weapons until black smoke choked the air, all the while dodging their hissing strikes. But there were too many of them. Sooner or later, one of the *T'gol* would move too slowly, and fangs would sink into flesh, injecting venom. The assassins formed a circle around Grace and Travis; the vipers closed in.

"Dust!" a voice shouted.

Farr stood a dozen paces away, holding up his left hand. Blood rained down from his palm, but it vanished before it hit the sand. The air buzzed and shimmered, as if filled with insects too small to be seen save for the glint of sunlight on wings.

As if drawn to him, the vipers slithered toward Farr; sweat poured down his brow. He thrust his hand forward.

"Dust!" he shouted again.

Each of the vipers exploded in a black puff. For a moment sight and breath were impossible. Then a gust of wind snatched the foul smoke, carrying it away and clearing the air.

Travis rubbed his stinging eyes. There was no trace left of

the serpents. Farr was hastily binding a cloth around his hand, staunching the flow of blood. The buzzing faded to silence; the *morndari* were gone.

Farr gave the three *T'gol* a disgusted look, then approached the stone door, careful not to touch it.

"What is it?" Travis said, his throat burning from the smoke.

"It is a blood trap." Farr looked at Grace. "You're right. This was a temple, and I know now these are the ruins of Golbrora, whose sorcerer-priests held the black viper sacred. Blood traps were set to keep thieves from stealing the temple's treasure. A thief who reached into the hole to try to unlock the door found himself trapped, held in place while his blood was drained."

"And the vipers?" Larad said, raising an eyebrow.

"They were meant to take care of any companions the thief might have had. It was difficult—my spell was weak—but I destroyed them."

Travis felt the blood surging in his veins, and his hands twitched into fists. Despite his claim that his spell was weak, Farr seemed smug, even arrogant. But Travis could have dispelled the vipers, and by spilling less blood than Farr. He was sure of it.

Stop it, Travis. This isn't a contest. Hadrian has studied these things, and you haven't. And be grateful he has, or all of you would have ended up like Rafid.

Grace knelt, touching Rafid's leathers. "I don't understand. Why did he try to open the door?"

"Voices," Travis said, remembering the whispers he had heard as he approached the altar. "He heard voices."

Farr nodded. "It is as I said. He feared magic, and so was compelled by it."

"He was weak not to resist," Kylees said, her words harsh. She turned her back and walked away. Avhir cast his bronze gaze on the empty leathers, then followed after her.

"Come," Vani said, touching Grace's shoulder. "The day is nearly done."

Travis cast one last glance at the door, not even daring to wonder what lay on the other side. Had Rafid really been weak? Travis doubted it. One did not survive for thirteen years in the Silent Fortress by being weak.

It could just as easily have been you who stuck a hand in that hole, Travis, not Rafid.

Only it hadn't been; that fate wasn't his. Travis clamped his hands under his arms and trudged after the others just as the sun touched the western horizon, staining the ruins of Golbrora crimson.

29.

The camels paced over the silver dunes, silent as wraiths in the moonlight.

Grace huddled inside a blanket as the camel's hump rose and fell beneath her. The day's sweat had dried to a crust on her skin, and now she was shivering. Once night fell, the desert had quickly surrendered its heat to the cloudless sky. Stars glittered like cold gems above—but not in the rift, which was as dark as the vipers that had slithered from the stone door in the ruins of Golbrora. Only the rift wasn't something that could be fought with blood sorcery, not like the serpents. It wasn't anything at all.

How can you fight nothing, Grace?

It seemed impossible, but she wouldn't let herself believe that. Their only hope was for Travis to find the Last Rune, wherever—whatever—it was. But first they had to find Nim.

And maybe this is how it's meant to be, Grace. Sfithrisir said Travis would lead you to the Last Rune, and dragons can't lie. Well, this could be how he does it—by going after Nim.

It didn't make much sense, but maybe Fate didn't have to. Or maybe it was something else altogether that had drawn them to this place. Something simpler—and far stronger—than mere Fate. Maybe it was love.

And what do you know about love, Grace?

A lot more than she used to. She had learned so much since coming to Eldh: how to be a witch, a warrior, and a queen. But more amazing than any of those things, she had learned that her heart, however damaged, could still hold love.

Her gaze drifted to a dark form riding just ahead of her.

Hadrian Farr. As often happened when she gazed at him, her pulse quickened, though she didn't quite understand what it meant. She could catalog all of the symptoms—shortness of breath, elevated blood pressure, a ringing in the ears—but she couldn't diagnose the disease. What was it that looking at him did to her?

Grace didn't know. Only that it made her feel frightened, and excited, and strangely free. It was like what she had felt at the last feast in Gravenfist Keep, when she had realized that Malachor didn't really need her anymore.

It was like letting go.

"Is something the matter, Grace?"

Her pulse spiked in alarm. Hadrian had slowed his camel, and now he rode close to her. His dark eyes glittered in the moonlight, studying her; he must have noticed her staring.

"I was just wondering," she said and cleared her throat, trying to think of something she could possibly say to him. Then, to her surprise, she did. "I was just wondering what Sister Mirrim told you in the Hagia Sophia, in Istanbul. You said she whispered something to you there, something important, but you never said what it was."

Farr turned his gaze forward, into the night. "She said she knew the answer to the mystery."

"What mystery?"

"That's exactly what I asked her. What mystery did she mean? And she said. . . ." His voice trailed off. Grace wondered if was going to answer at all. Then he drew in a breath. "She said the mystery was for me to determine, but the answer was 'the catalyst does not change.'"

Grace couldn't help a wry smile. "That sounds like something one of them would say, all right. Suitably cryptic."

He gave her a sharp look. "Do you know what it means?"

"I haven't the foggiest idea. Maybe you should ask Travis about it. He's spoken with the three of them a lot more than I have—Cy, Mirrim, and Samanda."

Farr's gaze moved past Grace, toward where Travis and Larad rode. "I don't know if that's a good idea."

"Why?" Grace said, her heart rate quickening again, only for a different reason this time.

"He doesn't trust me."

Grace licked her cracked lips, but this time her attempt to find something to say failed.

"What about you, Grace Beckett?" He was looking at her again, his dark eyes unreadable. "Do you trust me?"

"I want to."

Farr nodded. "You might regret that in the end."

He flicked the reins of his camel, and the beast quickened its stride, distancing itself from Grace's mount. She stared after him. Her pulse was no longer rapid; instead, it seemed her heart did not beat at all.

They rode all that night, hid from the sun during the heat of the day, then pressed on again as darkness fell. Nothing assailed them, yet Grace felt her fear growing with each passing league. Was the Morgolthi drawing them on, waiting until they were deep within it to swallow them?

Just before dawn they halted at a dead oasis. It must have been beautiful once. No more. What had once been a sizable pool fed by a spring was only a shallow depression caked with salt and littered with the bleached bones of antelope and jackals. Trees circled the oasis, reaching out of the sun-baked ground like skeletal hands from a grave. Their branches bore no leaves, only thorns.

Grace's camel lowered itself to its knees, and she half climbed, half fell from the saddle, her legs and back aching. The beast bowed its head, eyelids drooping; a yellow crust of dried spittle framed its mouth. Travis, Larad, and Farr dismounted as the air shimmered and the *T'gol* appeared.

"The camels grow weak," Avhir said, stroking the neck of one of the animals. He turned his bronze eyes toward Farr. "They cannot go on much longer. One more journey is all they have left in them."

"It will be enough," Farr said. He sat with his back against one of the trees, covered his face with the hood of his robe, and did not move.

Travis drew close to Grace. "I wouldn't have thought it possible," he said under his breath, "but Farr is starting to make Master Larad look like Mr. Congeniality."

"He's just tired," Grace said. "Like all of us."

Travis gave her a questioning look, but she moved away, to the scant shade beneath a clump of dead trees, and sat down. She had been avoiding talking to Travis. Because if she did, she would have to tell him what Farr said to her two nights before.

You might regret that in the end. . . .

Were Travis's suspicions right? Was Farr taking them to Morindu for his own ends—out of his own desire for power? Maybe. But it didn't matter. All that mattered was that he was taking them there, that he was helping them find Nim. And, once they were there, if he did anything that put Nim in danger, Grace would . . .

She didn't finish that thought. Instead, she took out her leather flask and drank a little water. It was hot, and tasted sour, but all the same she had to will herself not to guzzle it. The flask was already less than half-full, and there was no hope of finding water there.

Grace lay down on a blanket, shut her eyes, and soon fell asleep. However, it was a fitful repose, haunted by dreams in which the dead trees began to move, their wood creaking with a dry sound like laughter. She tried to run, but the trees grabbed her, holding her tight in their branches, as thorns drove deep into her flesh. . . .

She sat up. Master Larad knelt beside her.

"What's happening?"

"It's time to eat something, Your Majesty."

Grace pushed sweat-tangled hair from her face. She had slept longer than she intended; the sun was already halfway to the western horizon.

"I was having a nightmare," she said.

"I know. We were all having nightmares, Your Majesty. This is an evil place. Death lingers here." Larad tilted his head. "And something else."

Grace looked up at the dead trees arching over her. "It's hatred. This place hates life. I can feel it."

"Come." Larad held out a hand, helping her to her feet.

They joined Travis and Farr beneath a larger clump of dead trees. Grace wished they could get away from the trees, but they offered the only shade, and the day was still hot. Vani and Avhir were there, but Rylees was nowhere in view.

"She is scouting," Vani said. "To the south of here, the land is riddled with pockets of slipsand. To step in one is certain death. We must find a way around."

"I already told you," Farr said, his face dark with anger, "there is no way around. We have to go through."

Avhir let out a snort. "If you try it, you will be swallowed before you walk five steps. The slipsand will fill your lungs and suffocate you, if it does not first crush your body as you are dragged down into its depths. We must go around."

"We don't have time for that," Farr growled. "I spoke with the dying sorcerer, and he told me about this place. The region of slipsand stretches on for leagues to both the east and west. The camels are nearly dead, and it would take us days to go around on foot, even weeks. We'll die, too, before we can do that. We have to go through."

"How?" Travis said.

"The sorcerer told me the region of slipsand is no more than half a league across from north to south. If we continue south, we can pass over it quickly. The burial site of Morindu lies not far beyond."

Avhir's eyes narrowed. "I will repeat Sai'el Travis's question. How can we go through even half a league of slipsand without perishing?"

Farr licked blistered lips. "The spirits can guide us through. As you said, the slipsand lies in pockets, with stable areas between. All we have to do is make our way around the pockets without stepping in them."

"You cannot tell slipsand from normal sand by looking at it," Vani said. Her words were not combative, not like Avhir's; they were merely a statement of fact.

"That's where the *morndari* can help us. The sorcerer told me the spirits guided him through the slipsand. I can summon them and bid them to do the same for us."

"Can you?" Master Larad said, his scarred face turned toward Farr. "I confess, I know little of blood sorcery, but I watched you in the ruins of Golbrora. You had to command the *morndari* twice before they would obey you and destroy the vipers. The powers of sorcery are weakening, just like rune magic, and the magic Queen Grace wields."

The former Seeker said nothing; his silence was answer enough.

Avhir stood. "It is still two hours until sunset. We will think about what has been said, then decide."

Farr opened his mouth to protest, but before he could speak the air shimmered and Avhir was gone. Those who remained beneath the trees made a frugal meal of dried figs and a little water. Grace chewed without relish. Everything tasted like sand, even the water.

"Maybe it's good," Travis said, drawing spirals in the sand with a stick. "Maybe it's good that magic is weakening."

"How so?" Larad said, raising a jagged eyebrow.

"Because if the sorcerers get to Morindu before us, maybe there won't be anything left for them to find."

Grace hugged her knees to her chest. Despite the heat, she felt chilled, as if with fever. "What *will* we find if we get there?"

She glanced at Vani and Farr. However, before either could speak, the air rippled, unfolded, and Avhir was there.

Vani leaped to her feet. "What is it?"

"I cannot find Kylees," Avhir said, his voice sharper than usual.

"Where did you last see her?"

"Just south of here, near the edge of the slipsand. She was attempting to see if a route could be found through the area, as the dervish suggested." He shot Farr an accusatory look; Farr said nothing.

"She has not returned here," Vani said. "We must continue to look for her."

She started to move, but Travis gripped her arm, halting her. "Wait. Maybe there's a better way." He turned his gray eyes toward Grace. "Can you sense her nearby?"

"I'll try."

Grace shut her eyes and reached out with the Touch. It should have been simple; she had done it a thousand times. Instead, the threads of the Weirding tangled in her imagined hands. She tried to tease them apart, only they were so thin— like wisps of gossamer. If she pulled too hard they would tear. Carefully, she cast her net wider . . . .

"I sensed something," she gasped, eyes opening.

Vani moved close. "Was it Kylees?"

She held a hand to her forehead. What had she glimpsed? It was life, it had to be; the threads of the Weirding had coiled around it. Only something about it hadn't seemed right.

"I'm not sure. I think so, but—"

"Where?" Avhir said. "Where did you sense her?"

Grace pointed south and west. "That way."

Vani and Avhir were already moving. Grace, Travis, Larad, and Farr hurried after them, but they could not keep up with the assassins. The *T'gol* vanished over a low rise.

"What was it, Grace?" Travis said, panting as they ran. "What did you see?"

"Hurry," was all she said.

To their right, the sun sank toward the horizon, spilling bloodred light over the sand. Sweating, their breath ragged, the four reached the top of the rise. They saw a lone, dark figure below, standing on the edge of a vast plain of sand. Vani and Avhir bounded down the slope like black leopards. Grace and the others followed. As they drew near, Grace saw that the lone figure was indeed Kylees, and that Vani and Avhir had halted a half dozen paces from her.

"Stop!" Vani said, holding out a hand. "There is a pocket of slipsand just ahead."

Grace stumbled to a halt alongside Travis, Larad, and Farr. Strangely, Kylees's back was turned to them, her shoulders hunched. She was shaking. What was wrong?

Avhir edged forward a step. "Kylees, what has happened?"

She did not answer.

"If you come directly toward me, you will avoid the slipsand." Avhir held out a hand. "Come!"

A spasm passed through Kylees's body, then she turned around. The *T'gol*'s eyes were dull as stones, and her pretty face was puffy and bloated. Her right hand twitched at her side. Grace saw that the small cut on her hand was red and crusted, oozing fluid. Was Kylees sick, suffering from an infection? She could have blood poisoning.

Vani moved forward, probing the sand carefully with her boots. "What has happened to you, Kylees? Tell us."

For a moment a light of recognition flickered in Kylees's

gold eyes. "Flee," she croaked. Another spasm, more violent than the last, passed through her.

Then her skin split open.

It happened swiftly. Kylees's skin slipped away from her body, falling to the sand along with her black leathers, as if both had been mere garments. Left in her place was a thing that was human in shape, but only vaguely. It had no nose, mouth, or hair; twin points of light burned where its eyes should have been. It was dark, its surface glossy and smooth, but not hard like onyx. Instead, its skin moved and rippled like dark water.

Only it wasn't water. As the thing moved, it left crimson footprints behind it on the sand, as well as a jumbled pile of bones.

"A blood golem!" Vani hissed, leaping back, pulling Avhir with her. "Do not let it near you!"

Grace stared, at once horrified and fascinated. Blood. The thing was made of blood. And not only Kylees's.

Its volume is too large to be made up of the blood of only a single person, she thought, her scientific curiosity operating despite her terror. *It has to contain the blood of several people.*

"Do not come closer!" Avhir shouted, brandishing his scimitar, but the blood golem continued to advance, moving with a silky fluidity that was familiar to Grace. So this was the shadow that had followed her on her journey south. She had thought they had left it behind when they crossed the sea, but she had been wrong. Only how had it followed them?

The cut on Kylees's hand, her doctor's voice spoke in her mind. *There was a sailor on the ship who also had a cut. The blood golem must enter its victims through an open wound and travel inside them.*

These rational thoughts vanished, replaced by primal fear, as the blood golem lashed out with an arm. Vani sprang back, but the golem's arm extended, stretching into a long pseudopod. It snaked through the air, reaching for the *T'gol*.

Avhir swung his scimitar, cutting the pseudopod in two. One end snapped back toward the blood golem, causing the surface of its body to ripple. The other end rained to the sand, wetting it with crimson.

So the thing could be harmed. They could destroy it—as long as it was not able to draw more blood into itself. They couldn't let it touch them. Even as Grace realized that, the blood golem's arm re-formed and lashed out toward her. At the same moment its other arm shot toward Travis.

Avhir spun, slashing through one of the tentacles with his scimitar. However, the other snapped out of reach, then struck like a whip, coiling around him. Avhir cried out, falling to his knees, but the sound was muffled as the pseudopod forced itself into his mouth, his nose. The *T'gol* went rigid, back arching, the scimitar slipping from his hands.

Vani materialized out of thin air, kicking at the tentacle with a boot. The pseudopod burst apart in a spray of scarlet. Avhir gripped his scimitar and lurched back to his feet.

"Keep striking at it!" he called out, his face stained with red. "If it loses enough blood, it will not be able to hold its form."

He was right. Each time the golem shot out another pseudopod, he and Vani hacked at it, and more blood soaked into the sand. The thing began to move more slowly, and its surface rippled constantly.

"We must help them," Farr said, drawing a dagger from his *serafi*.

However, there was no need. Vani and Avhir had continued to kick and hack at the blood golem, and now blood oozed from it, drunk greedily by the sand. Pseudopods reached out from its body but were just as quickly reabsorbed. Vani aimed a kick at the center of its form, while Avhir slashed with his scimitar, separating its head from its body.

Like a water balloon pricked with a pin, the blood golem burst apart in a crimson spray, covering the two *T'gol*. The dark fluid pooled on the ground for a moment, then the sand gobbled it.

30.

"I don't like this," Farr said, kneeling beside the crimson stain on the sand. "That was too easy."

"Not for Kylees," Vani said, using a cloth to wipe blood from her face, her hands, her leathers. It was black and smelled foul.

Larad moved closer to Grace. "Surely this was what was following us on our journey south, Your Majesty."

Grace only nodded; she could find no words.

Travis circled around the remains of the golem, careful not to get too close. "How was this thing created?"

Farr stood; his fingers were wet and dark. "Only the Scirathi have such skill. A blood golem is created using the blood of a sorcerer. One must give his life in order for the golem to come into being. His blood is animated by sorcery while it still flows in his veins, and the golem bursts forth. From then on, the golem must periodically take more blood into itself in order to maintain its form and strength."

"You know much about the forbidden craft of the Scirathi," Avhir said, wiping blood from his face.

Farr did not look at the *T'gol*.

At last Grace found her voice. "How was it able to follow me all the way here? And why?"

"Why it was following you, I'm not certain," Farr said, regarding Grace. "As for how, there is only one way a blood golem could track you all this way. A drop of your blood must have been incorporated into its being. Once that was done, it could follow you by the scent of your blood."

Bile rose in Grace's throat; she forced herself to swallow. "That doesn't make sense. How could one of the Scirathi have gotten a drop of my—oh!"

So much had happened the night of the feast, and it was such a small thing. She had completely forgotten it. However, now the memory came back to her with perfect clarity. Quickly, in trembling words, she described the old servingwoman she had collided with in a corridor of Gravenfist Keep—how the other had dropped a ball of yarn, and how Grace had bent to pick it up, and was pricked by a needle. Grace never saw the other's face. All she had seen was a hand, reaching out to accept the ball of yarn. At the time she had thought it wrinkled with age. However, the light was dim. The hand could just have easily been covered with scars.

Larad stroked the dark stubble on his chin. "That explains how the Scirathi gained a drop of your blood, Your Majesty. Yet it still does not tell us why the Scirathi wished to follow you."

"It was me."

They turned to look at Travis. His gray eyes were haunted.

"They knew you would come in search of me, Grace." He reached out and took her hands; his own hands were so hot she could hardly bear their touch, but she didn't pull back. "The Scirathi were hunting me on Earth. They want me for something. Or maybe they just want me dead. Either way, the Scirathi were using you to find me."

Grace shook her head. She wanted to weep, but her eyes could produce no tears.

"He's right," Farr said, wiping his hands on his black robe. "It is the only answer that makes sense."

Travis let go of her hands. "You've got to go, Grace. All of you. You have to get out of—"

A scream rose on the air, coming from the other side of the low ridge. It was a terrible sound, shrill and wet: a sound of animal pain. More screams joined it, then all were cut short.

Grace turned around, heart thudding. "What was that?"

"It was the camels," Avhir said, unsheathing his scimitar again.

Larad caught the sleeve of Grace's *serafi*. "Master Wilder is right, Your Majesty. We must go."

"It is too late," Vani said. "They are here."

A half dozen figures appeared at the top of the ridge, their black robes stark against the coppery sky. Sorcerers.

Vani and Avhir stalked forward, hands and weapons ready, as the Scirathi descended the slope. Grace, Travis, and Larad pressed close to one another, but Farr stood a short distance away. A dagger appeared in his right hand, poised over his arm, ready to draw blood.

"Why are they coming so slowly?" Larad said, his words hoarse. "Would they not rather make quick work of us?"

The sorcerers seemed almost to shuffle down the slope, making no effort to guard themselves. Grace shut her eyes, spinning out a thread. The Weirding was growing weaker, but maybe she could still use the Touch to probe them, to learn something of what they intended to do. She cast her strand out across the desert. . . .

Her eyes flew open. "They're not alive!"

There was no time for the *T'gol* to respond to her words; the sorcerers had shambled within striking range, tattered robes fluttering, stretching withered arms toward the assassins. Their gold masks gleamed in the light of the setting sun, expressionless, serene. Avhir struck first, his scimitar glittering as it hewed off the hand of one of the sorcerers.

Sand poured from the stump of the sorcerer's wrist instead of blood.

For a moment the *T'gol* stopped, staring, but the sorcerers continued to close in. Vani launched a kick. There was a crunching sound of bones shattering, and one of the Scirathi flew back a dozen feet. The sorcerer fell to the ground—then got up and began to shuffle forward again. At the same moment Avhir slit the throat of another Scirathi. As with the first, no blood spilled from the wound. Instead, copper-colored sand rained to the ground.

"Stop!" Farr called out. "You must not wound them!"

Grace wondered what he meant. The Scirathi were corpses—animated husks, nothing more. Wounding them would not kill them because they were already dead, but surely it could not cause harm either.

She was wrong. Avhir either did not hear or did not heed Farr's words. He made a flicking motion with his wrists, and the scimitar flashed, lopping off the head of one of the Scirathi. The sorcerer's body toppled, and ruddy sand poured from the stump of the neck, falling onto the desert floor.

The ground began to churn. Red sand swirled with gold. Then, like a waterspout on the sea, a pillar rose up from the ground, building upon itself until it was as tall as Avhir. The sand coalesced, forming a solid shape with thick arms, column-like legs, and a featureless head set upon bulky shoulders.

Avhir swore in the tongue of the Mournish, then swung his scimitar again. The blade passed through the sand creature's body, but without apparent effect. Sand gave way around the blade, then coalesced again. The thing struck out with a heavy arm. Avhir grunted, flying through the air, then hit the ground and rolled a dozen feet.

The thing started to shamble forward, toward Grace, Travis, and Larad, but Vani interposed herself. She leaped into the air, hanging there so long she seemed to defy gravity, launching a flurry of punches and kicks at the sand creature. The thing stumbled back as its head exploded in a spray of grit—

—then started forward again as more sand rose up from the ground, becoming part of its form. A new, bulbous head thrust up from between its shoulders.

Another creature was already forming from the patch of sand where the headless Scirathi had died, and red powder continued to pour from the neck of the sorcerer that was wounded. Its body slumped to the ground, an empty shell, and the desert sand roiled beneath it as yet another sand creature started to coalesce.

"How do we fight these things?" Vani called out to Farr, leaping aside as the first sand creature struck at her.

"You can't," Farr shouted back. "You cannot wound them, or strike off a limb. They have only to draw more sand into themselves."

"What about the slipsand?" Avhir called, springing back to his feet. "Might we lure them into it?"

"Sand is sand. It cannot harm them—not when they are made of it. Whatever you do, do not slay another sorcerer!"

That was easier said than done. The four remaining sorcerers threw themselves at the *T'gol*, withered limbs flailing. Avhir cast aside his scimitar, and Vani ceased striking at them. However, the shriveled bodies of the sorcerers were fragile. Vani tried only to brush one aside and its skin tore beneath her hands like old parchment as red-brown dust spilled out. The dust fell to the ground, and the desert sand began to swirl.

There were three of the sand creatures now, and unlike the sorcerers they seemed uninterested in the *T'gol*, only striking if the assassins got in their way. Instead, they kept moving toward Grace, Travis, and Larad. The three backed away, trying to keep the *T'gol* between them and the sand creatures.

"Grace, can you do anything?" Travis said, gripping her arm.

She fought for breath. "They're not alive—the sorcerers or the sand creatures. No threads spin around them. Even if there wasn't something the matter with the Weirding, I would have no power over them."

"What about conjuring a wind? You've done that before."

"I can't," she said, hating how worthless the words were, but the Weirding was too weak, and there was so little life here in the desert.

Travis nodded, his eyes sad but not accusing; he didn't blame her. He glanced at Larad. "Do you know the rune for sand?"

"In case you hadn't noticed, there aren't many deserts in the north," the Runelord said, his words sardonic as ever despite the fear in his eyes. "I do not know the rune for sand, but the rune for dirt is *Khath*."

"Speak it with me," Travis said.

Together the two Runelords chanted the rune. Grace felt magic shimmer on the air, but it abruptly faded. Larad pulled something from his robe: a small iron box. He opened it, and three orbs shimmered in his hand, one white, one gray-green, and the other blazing crimson. The Imsari—Larad had brought them with him.

Travis and Larad chanted the rune again, and the Stones flared. However, it was no use. Either it was the wrong rune they spoke, or rune magic had no power over these things born of blood sorcery. The sand creatures kept coming.

Avhir tried to dodge one of the sorcerers, but as he sprang aside it dived at him, and his boot caught its jaw. The sorcerer's mandible flew away from its skull, and red powder poured from its gaping mouth. The others had also managed to harm themselves by flailing at the *T'gol*. Their wounds were small, but dust flowed from them. Now there were five of the sand creatures, and in several spots the sand was pushing itself up into pillars, forming more.

"What do these fiends want?" Larad said, staggering back. He thrust the box with the Imsari back inside his robe.

The sand creatures kept advancing. Vani and Avhir combined their attacks on one of the creatures. They rained blows and kicks upon it, pummeling the creature down into the sand. Grace felt a spark of hope, but it was extinguished as the ground churned, and the sand creature began to re-form. Grace, Travis, and Larad were forced to back up another step.

Grace's foot sank deep into the sand. A hundred invisible hands seemed to pull at her, dragging her foot down. There was a moaning sound deep in the ground. She would have gone under in a second if Travis and Larad hadn't grabbed her arms, pulling her back.

"Slipsand," Larad said, glancing over his shoulder at the flat expanse behind them. "We can't go any farther."

Nor could they go forward. The *T'gol* stood between them and the sand creatures, battling furiously, their arms and legs blurring. Sand filled the air as heads and torsos exploded under the fury of the assassins. However, the sand creatures continually re-formed themselves, and already the *T'gol* were beginning to slow down. Sweat poured down Vani's brow; Avhir's breath came in ragged gasps. They could not keep this up.

A low chant sounded, and Grace looked up to see Farr's dagger flash in the light of the dying sun. Blood spilled from a gash in his arm, and a buzzing filled the air like a swarm of unseen insects. The buzzing swarmed around one of the sand creatures. The thing stood still for a moment, as if frozen, then ruptured in a cascade of sand. This time it did not coalesce again. Farr had destroyed it.

Grace glanced at the former Seeker. He had fallen to his knees, and his face was gray. She reached out with the Touch and at once saw that he had lost a large amount of blood. If he lost any more, he could go into shock. All the same Farr gripped the dagger and, moving weakly, began to lengthen the gash in his arm.

No! Grace spun the words over the Weirding. *You can't afford to lose more blood.*

She felt his surprise, and he looked at her. Then, faint but clear, she heard his reply. *There is no other way. . . .*

Grace wouldn't believe that. "Travis, you're a sorcerer. Can you do what Hadrian just did?"

Travis didn't answer. He gazed at the sand creatures, less than ten paces away. The *T'gol* were losing ground. There were seven of the creatures by then—no, eight. Avhir fell to his knees. Vani jerked him back up. Only it didn't matter. Even the *T'gol* could not win this fight. They would fall, and Farr would die from loss of blood. In moments it would be over.

Larad gripped Travis's shoulders, shaking him. "Rune magic is no use against them. But you are a sorcerer, Master Wilder. You can do something!"

"Yes," Travis murmured. "It's the only way. It's me these things want. Once I'm gone, they'll go, too."

Grace stared at him. "What are you talking about?"

There was a fey light in his eyes; he touched her cheek. "Don't worry, Grace. You'll bring me back. I know you will."

Vani let out a cry of pain. Two of the sand creatures had flanked her, and they were crushing her between them. Avhir staggered, trying to defend himself and failing as three of the creatures pummeled him with fists of sand. Beyond, Farr sprawled on the ground, motionless, a dark stain spreading out from his arm. Three of the sand creatures broke through the line of the assassins. They shambled forward, arms out before them.

Travis drew in a breath. "I believe in you, Grace."

Then he took a step backward.

Instantly, the slipsand gave way beneath his boots. One moment he was there, gazing at her with his gray eyes, and the next he was gone. There was a low moan as the sand shifted. It poured back into the hole where he had vanished, filling it, and in the space of a heartbeat all traces of it, and of Travis, were gone.

The sand creatures hesitated, as if uncertain what to do, and the *T'gol* took the chance to free themselves.

"No!" Grace screamed, flinging herself to the ground. She would have been sucked into the slipsand herself but for Larad's hands pulling her back. She reached out with the Touch, probing deep into the sand, willing the magic to work. All was dark. She groped, searching blindly, flinging her spirit after him. There—she felt a glimmer of life. It was him, it had to be. . . .

The glimmer of light went dark.

"No!" Grace shouted again, but it was no use.

Master Larad pulled her away from the edge of the slipsand. Through her tears she barely saw the sand creatures collapse into heaps of motionless dust; she hardly noticed as the *T'gol* approached, or as Farr slowly pulled himself up from the ground. It didn't matter. Nothing mattered anymore.

Travis was dead.

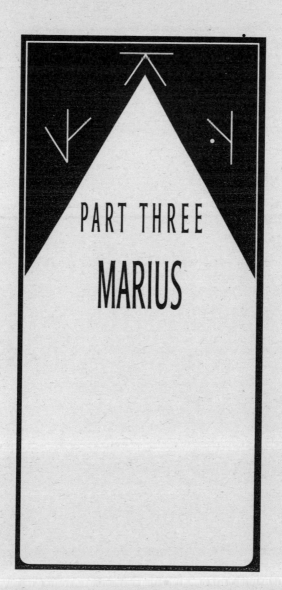

PART THREE

MARIUS

31

It was early when Deirdre reached the Charterhouse. Behind the reception counter, Madeleine's chair was empty, the computer screen blank. Only a single fluorescent light flickered overhead.

Eschewing the elevator, Deirdre headed down a shadowed corridor, descended a flight of stairs to the basement, and made her way to the door of her office. It was locked; he wasn't there yet. That had been her hope, and the reason she had left her flat before dawn. She needed time to think before he showed up, time to decide what to do.

Time to figure out whose side Anders was really on.

The office was dim—only a faint gray illumination oozed through the office's one small window—but she left the overhead lights off. Her head hurt, and her stomach churned, and like a sick animal she wanted nothing except to curl up in a safe, dark spot.

But you're not safe here, Deirdre. Not if you're right.

She switched on the desk lamp, squinting against even that modest glare. The throbbing in her head rose a notch in magnitude, and belatedly she realized she should have picked up some coffee on the way. Now she would have to wait until Anders showed up.

That's nice, Deirdre. You can't convince yourself he's not a traitor, but you're still willing to let him fix you a cup of coffee. If he was smart, he'd put rat poison in it and get you out of the way.

Like he got the sorcerer out of the way?

She reached into the pocket of her leather jacket and pulled out an empty syringe. It was the syringe Anders had used the previous night on the sorcerer. The drug had been intended to both allow and compel the sorcerer to speak; instead it had killed her.

Deirdre rolled the syringe back and forth on the desk. She

shouldn't jump to conclusions. Maybe Scirathi physiology was dissimilar to human physiology after all. Maybe the woman sorcerer had suffered an allergic reaction, going into anaphylactic shock.

Or maybe Anders had given her the wrong dose on purpose.

One way or another, Deirdre would find out. Last night, a special Seeker task team had been dispatched to Beltan's and Travis's flat, and at that moment the sorcerer's body rested in a refrigerated drawer in a laboratory beneath the Charterhouse. An autopsy would be done, and tests performed. The cause of death would be determined, along with the levels of the drugs in the sorcerer's blood. Once the report came back, she would know whether Anders had deliberately killed the Scirathi. But that would take a few days. What should she do in the meantime?

Keep working, Deirdre. It'll get your mind off things. Besides, Beltan isn't about to rest. He's going to continue looking for the arch.

Only where was it? The Scirathi had stolen the arch from Crete, but not for themselves. Instead, they had given it to someone else—someone who, in exchange, had led them to Travis Wilder. But who was it? Who had hired the sorcerers to steal the arch, and why?

Maybe going over everything that had happened would help her understand. Deirdre opened her computer and started to type, writing a report of their operation last night while the details were still fresh in her mind. When that was done, she pulled a digital voice recorder from her pocket. She had carried it on her last night to record their conversation with the sorcerer. At the touch of a button words emanated from the recorder, spoken in a dry, hissing voice. Deirdre's fingers trembled on the keyboard as she transcribed the conversation.

There wasn't much. She typed the final words. *The arch . . . blood so near . . . the seven cannot . . . be far.*

Her own voice came then: louder, desperate. *The seven what?*

A long pause, then one last sibilant whisper. *Sleep . . . sleep . . .*

That was all. Deirdre stopped typing and switched off the

recorder. She clicked the SAVE button on her computer, then leaned back, rubbing her temples. There were so many questions she had wanted to ask the sorcerer. Only the sorcerer had died, and Deirdre doubted they would capture another. The Scirathi would be more wary than ever now. And if Anders was working for them, he was bound to warn them of another ambush. Or was Anders allied not with the Scirathi, but with the same people for whom the sorcerers had stolen the arch?

Stop it, Deirdre. You don't know Anders is working for anyone except the Seekers. You need a lot more evidence before you can say for sure he's a traitor.

Or before she could say for sure that he wasn't. Sighing, she picked up the copy of the *Times* she had bought out of habit from a newsstand outside the Tube station. She needed to give her mind a break.

In which case she shouldn't have read the paper. The news was more troubling than ever. Variance X continued to expand; it was now over twice the diameter of the moon as seen from Earth. And it was no longer the only blot in the sky. Another anomaly had appeared, visible from the southern hemisphere and growing at a rapid rate. Like the first, astronomers had determined it to be outside the solar system, a bit more than twice as distant from the sun as Pluto.

There was bad news here on Earth as well. Violent earthquakes had struck Turkey again, dormant volcanoes in South America were erupting, typhoons were flooding much of India, and another hurricane was battering the east coast of the United States. With all that was going on, it was no surprise the world stock markets were crashing.

All the same, people kept going on with their lives. That morning, the Tube station had been filled with the usual throng of weekday commuters and tourists dragging crying children. It was the same as any day—at least if one didn't look closely.

But Deirdre *had* looked closely, and what she had seen disturbed her. The commuters had stared with blank faces, not bothering to read the newspapers they held in their hands. The tourists had seemed deaf to the shrieks of their children, trudging as if on a death march rather than a vacation. There was no joy, no urgency in their expressions or actions. Not even annoyance or anger as people jostled into one another, or a train's doors shut before someone could climb aboard.

Deirdre had watched a man standing, staring, his briefcase hanging open and papers swirling about the platform. She picked up some of the papers, but before she could give them back to him he dropped the briefcase and walked over to a group of Mouthers in the center of the platform. One of them put a white sheet around his shoulders, draping it over his business suit. Another gave him a sign to hold. I Have Been Eaten, it read.

Maybe people weren't going about their normal lives. Maybe, instead, they had already given up. For what was there to fear from the dark blots in the sky when one was already defeated—already consumed?

Deirdre sighed. She had read enough of the news. She folded the paper to toss it in the trash bin.

A small white envelope fell from between two sections of the paper, landing on her desk.

She stared for several seconds, then set down the newspaper and picked up the envelope. Her name was written on the front in elegant script. Hands shaking, she opened the envelope and unfolded the single crisp sheet of notepaper within. It bore a message written in the same elegant hand as on the front of the envelope.

> *You are closer than you think to the answers you seek.*
> *However, you have forgotten something—a mystery*
> *from before this mystery began. It is time to*
> *remember it now. And to find an answer, don't forget*
> *that it is always best to go directly to the source.*

That was all. Deirdre turned the notepaper over, but there was no more writing, and no signature. What did it mean? What mystery had she forgotten about? She had no idea. However, there was one thing she did know: The note was from her mysterious Philosopher. Only how had he gotten it inside the newspaper?

Deirdre thought back. It had been dark still, and she had hardly looked at the attendant at the newsstand when she handed him a pound coin and took the newspaper. She remembered he had been tall, wrapped in an overcoat, a hat shadowing his face . . .

A chill coursed up her spine. It had been *he*. It had to be. Her hand had brushed his, and she hadn't even known it. She bent her head over the note to read it again.

The overhead lights switched on, and another gasp escaped her.

"You shouldn't read in the dark, mate," said a cheery, gravelly voice. "You'll ruin your eyes."

"Anders," she said, breathless.

As usual, he was dressed in a sleek designer suit. His hair looked freshly bleached, and as he set a paper cup on her desk she noticed that his fingernails were perfectly buffed and trimmed.

How can he be a spy, Deirdre? Clearly he spends all of his free time grooming.

Despite her dread, the thought actually made her laugh, but she swallowed it, and it came out more as a gagging sound.

"Are you all right, mate?"

Deirdre answered with the truth. There was no reason not to. "Not exactly. I just got this in my morning paper." She handed him the note, then took a deep, restorative swig of the coffee.

When he finished reading the note, Anders let out a low whistle. "Crikey, you were right next to him this time. He's been taking bigger and bigger risks to communicate with you. Seems to me like he's getting a little edgy. Things must be desperate for him."

Deirdre hadn't thought of that, but Anders was probably right. As usual, he had seen things in a way she hadn't. And that was why she hated being suspicious of him. She needed Anders—she needed his sharp wit and his absurd good cheer and his coffee.

Only you can't have them, Deirdre. Not if you can't trust him.

But maybe she could; maybe there was still a chance. If he would answer one question for her, then she would know for certain that he was still on her side.

"Anders," she said, and cleared her throat. "Anders, there's something I've been wondering. And it's important to me. Very important. I need you to answer a question."

He shrugged his big shoulders. "You got it, partner. Anything."

She met his vivid blue eyes. "Why do you still carry a handgun? I've never received any orders regarding it, but I know Nakamura is aware you still have it and hasn't done anything about it. Why?"

For a moment he didn't move. His eyes stayed locked on hers. Hope surged in her chest.

Then he winked at her and grinned. "Not that old chestnut again," he said, his voice big and affectionately mocking. "I swear, you're like a dog with a bone, mate. Only there's no meat left on this one. Like you said, Nakamura knows all about it. Now, how's your coffee?"

The hope burned to ash in her chest. She clutched the paper cup. "Great," she said, and she took a sip, though she didn't taste it.

Beltan showed up at the door then, and Deirdre was grateful for his interruption. Deirdre offered the blond man a sip of her coffee, and he slugged it down in one long gulp, returning the cup and the last dregs to her with a sheepish look.

"You seem raring to go this morning," Anders observed.

"We spoke to one of the Scirathi like you said we should," Beltan answered, looking at Deirdre. "Now it's time to get the keystone and use it to lure the thieves who stole the arch."

Deirdre wished Beltan hadn't drunk all the coffee. She could have used a sip to gather herself. "You heard what the sorcerer said. The Scirathi don't have the arch."

"That doesn't matter." Beltan's green eyes were overly bright. "Whoever it is the Scirathi were working for, surely they will be lured out of hiding when we dangle the keystone before them. Else they might send more Scirathi to fetch it for them. Either way, the thieves will lead us to their hiding place."

Deirdre wanted to tell him that it was too risky, that they didn't know enough yet about those whom the Scirathi were allied with. However, she knew by the set of his jaw that Beltan was going to get the keystone if he had to tear up the Charterhouse with his bare hands. She opened her mouth, unsure what she was going to say.

"Good morning!" said a voice every bit as cheerful as Anders's, only higher-pitched and far more grating.

"Hello, Eustace," Anders said with a wave.

The diminutive apprentice bounded into the office. He grinned at Deirdre, then looked up at Beltan with an expression of awe. "Do you think . . . do you think maybe I could touch him?"

"Only if you want to lose a hand," Deirdre said, noticing the look of annoyance on the big warrior's face. She stepped in front of Eustace just in case the young man tried to make a dash for it. "So what's going on?"

The apprentice managed to tear his gaze away from Beltan. "Sasha told me to give you this." He handed a manila envelope to Deirdre.

She took it, wondering what it might be, but set it on her desk. Now was not the time to open it.

"So how do you like Earth?" Eustace said to Beltan once Deirdre stepped out of the way.

Beltan didn't answer.

"Can you understand me?" Eustace spoke the words slowly and loudly, with exaggerated enunciation.

Beltan snorted, then looked at Deirdre. "Is he simple?"

Before Deirdre could reply to that, a knock sounded at the door. They all looked up to see a middle-aged man standing in the open doorway. He was balding, and his mustache was as crooked as his bow tie. A threadbare cardigan sweater and thick glasses lent him a professorial air.

"Paul," Deirdre said with a sigh of relief. "What can I help you with?"

Paul Jacoby hurried into the room, his small eyes excited behind his glasses. He held a folder in his hands. "I have something for you, Deirdre. It's not much, but I was able to—"

"Sorry, mate," Anders said, laying a hand on Eustace's shoulder. "This is where you step out."

Eustace let out a groan. "I'm never going to be a higher Echelon."

"Not with that attitude," Anders said. "Now off you go."

Anders gave him a firm push, and Eustace scooted out the door. Deirdre shut it behind him.

"So, is everyone in the room cleared to see this?" Jacoby said to Deirdre, patting the folder.

"Yes," Deirdre said, forcing herself not to glance at Anders. "What have you got?"

Jacoby headed to the table in the center of the office. He opened the folder and spread out several photographs and diagrams. "As I said, it isn't much. However, a few of the symbols on the stone arch are identical to those on the clay tablet you gave me a photo of several years ago. In addition, I ran several diachronic analyses on the computer, and the results suggest that some characters in Linear A could possibly be derived from characters in the language on the arch. On the assumption these derivations are accurate, I can tentatively make some attributions for symbols in the sample you gave me."

Deirdre's head buzzed. "Meaning?"

"Meaning I was able to translate a few of the words on the arch."

They gathered close around the table.

"Here we go," Jacoby said, holding up one of the photos of the arch. "These characters signify *sun*. This means *distance*, or *journey*." He picked up another photo. "I can't make out most of these, but this word appears on the clay tablet—*blood*—and this group of characters almost certainly signifies *death*. Although what the symbol placed in front of it means, I don't know. It might alter the meaning of the word."

"Is that all?" Anders said.

"No, there's more." Jacoby picked up another photo, clearly quite excited. A sequence of symbols was circled in red marker. "I was able to translate an entire phrase here—assuming the results of my diachronic analysis were accurate, of course. It reads, *the flame and the awe*."

That was it; Jacoby had been able to translate nothing more, though he intended to keep working.

"Absolutely fascinating, isn't it?" Jacoby said, gathering his papers. "We always thought Linear A was one of the oldest writing systems known. However, it appears the language on the arch is even earlier." He pushed his glasses up his nose. "You'll let me know if you discover any more samples of this earlier writing, won't you?"

"Of course, Paul," Deirdre said. "Thank you so much for all your work on this." She tried to sound sincere, but after Jacoby left she couldn't help letting out a sigh.

"Not quite what you hoped for, was it, mate?"

She sat at her desk, gazing at the copies Jacoby had left for her. "I'm not sure what I was hoping for."

"I'm hoping for some breakfast," Beltan said. "Then it's time to get the keystone."

"Come on, mate," Anders said, taking Beltan's elbow. "I'll help you with that first one at least. You coming, Deirdre?"

She gave them a wan smile. "You eat something for me."

Once the two men had left, she bent her head over the photos of the stone arch. However, the symbols were meaningless to her. She shuffled the photos around, looking at the words Jacoby had written in red marker.

Sun. Journey. Blood. Death. Those were easy enough to interpret. The builders of the arch had come from the deserts of Eldh's southern continent, and they had been sorcerers, workers in blood and death. But they knew all this already. Deirdre looked at the other photo and the words Jacoby had written on it. For a moment she simply stared.

Then she leaped up from the chair. *Flame and awe.* Jacoby had chosen those words for his translation. But he could just as easily have chosen synonyms, couldn't he? Words that meant the same thing . . .

"Fire and wonder," she murmured.

She sifted through the papers, then found it: the note from the Philosopher. He said she had forgotten something, a mystery from before this mystery.

"Think, Deirdre," she said through clenched teeth. "Think."

What had she been researching before she learned about Thomas Atwater, and the tavern, and the keystone? What had she been searching for before he first contacted her? The last pieces of the puzzle rearranged themselves in her mind. Slowly, she sank into the chair.

Fire and wonder. That was the first search phrase she had entered into the computer after receiving Echelon 7 clearance. The strange god-child Samanda had spoken those words to her once. The search had brought up a single file, one that was deleted from the system at the exact moment her search had discovered it.

In the strange days that followed, leading up to the assault on the Steel Cathedral in Denver, she had forgotten all about the mystery of the missing computer file. But he had told her to remember, and now she had. Only what did it mean? It couldn't be a coincidence that those same two words were inscribed on the arch. Whatever was in that missing file, it was related to the stone gate.

Deirdre opened a file drawer and pawed through her notes. It took her a minute, then she found it: a computer printout from that night's session, three years earlier. Her eyes scanned down the page. And there it was.

> *Search completed.*
> *1 match(es) located:*
> */albion/archive/case999-1/mla1684a.arch*

She had performed searches on that case number three years ago, and nothing had come up. What about the file name itself? Did it hint at what the file contained? Maybe. What the letters *mla* stood for, Deirdre couldn't guess. However, the *.arch* suffix suggested this was an archive file, and *1684* had to refer to a year.

Deirdre opened her computer and brought up a search window. "Display a summary of all major cases and events recorded in the annals of the Seekers for the year 1684," she muttered the query as she typed it.

She hit the ENTER key, and seconds later a glowing green list appeared on her screen. It only took a moment before she saw the entry that mattered.

> *7 August 1684. Seeker agent Marius Lucius Albrecht dies, aged 29.*

Deirdre leaned back, staring at the screen. The initials—*mla*—could only refer to him, to Marius Lucius Albrecht: the legendary Seeker who was expelled from the order for falling in love with Alis Faraday, the woman he had been ordered to observe. In the years that followed, Albrecht redeemed himself and was admitted again to the order, becoming perhaps the greatest Seeker ever before his untimely death at the age of twenty-nine.

The file, *mla1684a.arch*, had to be an archive of his final papers or reports. Whatever the file contained, clearly someone didn't want her to read it, as they had deleted the file before she could access it. Or perhaps an automatic guard had been set up around the file: a program designed to delete the file the moment anyone tried to open it.

Either way, there was one thing she did know: He had first made contact with her just after her search located the file. The Philosopher who had been helping her. Now the note he had given her had reminded her of this old mystery. For some reason, her mysterious helper wanted to point her in the direction of Marius Lucius Albrecht.

But why was Marius Lucius Albrecht important? She was still missing that piece of the puzzle. Like every Seeker, she had studied the history of all the cases he had worked on. They were fascinating—the result of a brilliant mind and a superb researcher—but none of them had anything to do with the keystone or the tavern or the arch on Crete.

None of the ones you read at least, Deirdre. But maybe you haven't read everything of Albrecht's. I'll bet you no Seeker has seen what's in that file that was deleted, at least not in recent history.

She wished Farr were there. He had studied Albrecht's career in greater depth than any Seeker she knew. Indeed, many in the order had considered him to be a modern-day Albrecht. He was as dazzling an investigator, and his rise in the order as meteoric. And, like Albrecht, Farr had even fallen in love with the woman he had been ordered to watch: Dr. Grace Beckett. However, Farr hadn't been cast out of the order; he had quit of his own accord. And something told Deirdre he was never coming back. She was on her own in this one.

So what do you do, Deirdre? You can't get at that deleted file, not even with Echelon 7 clearance.

She gripped her yellowed bear claw necklace, centering herself. She needed to treat it like any other investigation—which meant starting by gathering all the information she could concerning Marius Lucius Albrecht. She pulled her computer toward her and began typing.

The wall clock ticked away the hours as she worked. Anders and Beltan didn't return from their quest for breakfast, but Deirdre only noted that in passing. She called up every file in the system that concerned Marius Lucius Albrecht. Searching the documents for the terms *keystone* and *tavern* revealed nothing of import, as she had guessed, and soon she found herself focusing on a summary of Albrecht's life.

By the time she finished, she knew what she had to do. She leaned back from her computer, rubbing her aching neck, as Anders stepped into the office.

"Looks like you've been hard at work, mate."

She shut her computer. "I've just been doing some cross-referencing on the terms Paul Jacoby translated on the arch." She hated how easily the lie slipped off her tongue.

"Sounds good. Any luck?"

"Zero," she said with a sigh. "So where's Sir Give-Me-the-Keystone-Now-Or-Else?"

"Beltan? He's in the parlor taking a lie-down. I actually convinced him to leave the keystone scheme alone for today."

Deirdre sat up straight. "How did you manage that?"

"I used my preternatural powers of persuasion," he said, then winked. "All right, the truth is I managed to get a large number of bloody Marys into him at breakfast. He's conked out at the moment."

Anders got Beltan drunk? Maybe it wasn't the subtlest way to derail Beltan's enthusiasm for tracking down those who possessed the arch, but Deirdre had to admit it was effective. And she was glad Anders had managed the feat. The nameless Philosopher had said it wasn't time to go after the arch, that if they did they would perish. Besides, there was somewhere else she needed to go.

"He's going to be angry when he wakes up," she said.

"And he's going to have one bugger of a hangover to boot. I had the bartender double the vodka in each of his drinks."

Deirdre gave her partner a sharp look. Why exactly had he gotten Beltan drunk? Was he trying to prevent them from going after the arch?

"I'm going to put on a pot of coffee," he said, taking off his coat. "Want some, mate?" He turned his broad back as he worked at the counter.

"Sure," she said. She couldn't stand doubting him. She couldn't stand believing he was a traitor. But did she really know for certain he was? He wasn't telling her the truth about the gun, yes. But she had no hard proof that he—

Her gaze locked on the corner of a manila envelope sticking out from underneath her computer. It was the envelope Eustace had brought earlier, the one from Sasha. Deirdre pulled it free, opened the flap, and slid the contents into her hand.

It was a photograph. The photo was pixilated, and slightly blurred, but clear enough to make out the scene. It had been shot through a door that was cracked open an inch. The room beyond was this one, her office. Half of Deirdre's desk was in view. A figure bent over it, going through the papers on her desk.

It was Anders.

"Here we go," Anders said.

Deirdre wadded up the photo and tucked it into the pocket of her jacket, which hung on the back of her chair. Anders turned around, smiling, two cups in hand. She took one. It was blistering hot, but she squeezed her hands around it, letting the pain clear her head.

"So, now that our good sir knight is sleeping it off," Anders said, "what are you going to do with the rest of the day?"

Deirdre gave him her cheeriest grin. "I'm going to go home and take the afternoon off."

32.

Two hours later Deirdre sat on a train, watching as the English countryside blurred past the window. She glanced down at the note in her hands. *To find an answer, don't forget that it is always best to go directly to the source. . . .*

She had taken that advice. To learn about Marius Lucius Albrecht, she was going to the source—to Scotland, where he had spent his first nineteen years before joining the Seekers. There was a manor house in Midlothian, not far from Edinburgh, where—according to the history she had read—he had spent many formative years as the adopted ward of a nobleman. The manor was now some sort of private museum.

This is ridiculous, Deirdre. You can't believe you're actually going to find something at the manor. And what will Anders and Beltan do when they discover you're not really relaxing at your flat like you said?

Only she did expect to find something. The nameless Philosopher's clues had never led her astray before.

Well, there's a first time for everything. Why has he been helping you, Deirdre? What if he's just using you for some purpose of his own?

She was certain he was. Surely he had not been helping her out of charity, or to advance her career. He wanted her to find something, only he couldn't tell her directly what it was; for some reason it wasn't safe, or he wasn't able to do so. And as for Anders and Beltan—well, she could worry about what to tell them when she got back to London. If she ever spoke to Anders again, that was.

She stuffed the note into her jacket pocket and pulled out the photograph. Sasha had said not to trust Anders, and she was right. She must have snapped the photo with her digital camera, catching Anders in the act of riffling through Deirdre's desk. What had he been hoping to find among her papers?

It didn't matter. All that mattered was that he had been spying on her. Later, she would thank Sasha for sending her the photo. At the moment she had to get to Scotland before Anders discovered she was gone. Because whatever it was the mysterious Philosopher wanted her to discover, she was certain the people Anders worked for wanted just as much to keep it secret.

It was still light out when she exited the train station in Edinburgh. In the summer, so far north in the world, the sun lingered late. The castle loomed on its crag above her, stark against the silver sky. Carrying her satchel, she walked down Princes Street to her hotel.

She checked in, leaving orders for an early wake-up call and a taxi. If she could have, she would have gone to the manor directly, but according to the scant information she had found about it, it was unlikely anyone would be there at such a late hour.

The night passed slowly. Deirdre didn't sleep, and she kept expecting to hear a knock at the door and Anders's angry voice. She heard nothing until the phone rang, causing her to leap out of bed. Trembling, she picked up the phone. A computerized voice wished her a pleasant morning. It was time to go.

Deirdre dressed, choked down half a pastry from the tray that had been left outside her door, then went downstairs to find the taxi waiting for her. She gave directions to the manor, and agreed to the exorbitant fee the driver promised to charge her for taking her so far outside the city. As the taxi sped down Princes Street, she leaned back against the seat and willed herself not to glance out the rear window, to see if anyone was following.

It took less than an hour of winding along narrow roads to reach the manor. After traveling half a mile down a single-track lane, the taxi stopped in front of a set of iron gates. Deirdre got out. The gray sky hung low, and it was misting; moisture beaded on her leather jacket.

"Are you sure you don't want me to wait for you, miss?" the taxi driver said, leaning out the window.

"No, thank you. You can go."

"Suit yourself."

The taxi turned around, then rolled away down the lane and out of sight. Deirdre approached the gate. Beyond, two stately rows of elms bordered a driveway that curved away into the mist. The manor was not in view. Nor were any other people.

Deirdre looked around and saw a sign on the gate, as well as a black box that bore a speaker and a red button with the word CALL stenciled above it. The sign read: MADSTONE HALL. And below that, in smaller type: PRIVATE MUSEUM—VIEWINGS BY APPOINTMENT ONLY.

Maybe she shouldn't have sent the taxi away after all. She hesitated, then pushed the button on the box.

"Hello?" she said, leaning forward.

Silence. Then, just when she was about to push the button again, a woman's voice crackled out of the speaker. "Yes?"

Deirdre pressed the button again. "I'm sorry to bother you. My name is Deirdre Falling Hawk, and I—"

"Oh, yes," the tinny voice came from the speaker. "We've been expecting you. Please come up to the manor directly. You can use the front door."

There was a buzzing noise, then with a metallic grating one of the gates swung open. Deirdre gazed around, then slipped through the gate and walked up the driveway.

Once she rounded the corner she saw the manor. It was beautiful: a long, three-story structure of gray stone, with tall windows, and handsome columns framing the entryway. Gardens surrounded the manor on all sides, wild and vivid green against the gray air.

There was a single car next to the carriage house. Deirdre passed it and walked up stone steps, to the front door of the manor. It opened before she could knock. On the other side was an older woman, past sixty, and quite small. Her white hair was short and neatly coiffed, and she wore a well-tailored skirt suit of gray wool.

"You must be Miss Falling Hawk," she said with a warm smile. Her eyes were bright blue behind moon-shaped spectacles.

Deirdre was too dumbfounded to do anything but nod.

"Well, then, come out of the mist," the woman said, gesturing for Deirdre to enter. "I'm Eleanor Tate. I'm one of the docents here at Madstone Hall. Would you like a cup of tea? It's a chilly day out there."

Deirdre followed her into the front hall. It was grand and dim, obviously well kept but shabby from age. A sweeping staircase rose up to the second floor, while halls led off to either side.

"Thank you," Deirdre said. "Tea would be wonderful."

"I thought you might like some," Eleanor said, taking Deirdre's jacket and hanging it on a rack, "So I brought a thermos with me. I can't brew it here, as Madstone Hall itself isn't wired for electricity, though we do have power in the carriage house."

No electricity. That explained why it was so dim.

"I'm surprised you've come today," Eleanor went on, apparently content to carry on the conversation without any help from Deirdre. "Usually historians stay away on dreary days like this, as it's hard to see anything. But then, we haven't had many researchers at all lately. I don't think the consortium likes having them poking about. You're quite lucky to be allowed in. And they tell me you're to have the run of the place, which is quite unheard of. You must stand very high in their regard."

Deirdre shook her head. "In whose regard?"

"Why the consortium, of course. They own Madstone Hall, and they've kept it private all these years, rather than turning it into a public museum. Their goal is to preserve it just as it was in the late seventeenth century. As you'll see, very little has been changed since then. There's no plumbing, so if you need to use the loo, you'll have to go out back to the portable. All the furniture is original, and the paintings on the walls, and everything else you'll see. The only work we've done over the years is what we must: repairing the roof, and replacing broken windows, and airing the place out, of course, so everything doesn't mold. It's marvelous to see something as it was so long ago. I'm the third in my family to be a docent here, and so it is for the other caretakers. It's as though Madstone Hall belongs to our families. Or rather, I should say, as if our families belong to it."

As she spoke, Eleanor had opened a stainless-steel thermos, filled a chipped teacup, and handed it to Deirdre. The tea was sweet and fragrant with lemon.

"Thank you," Deirdre said, trying to take all of this in.

"You're quite welcome." Eleanor took an overcoat from the coatrack and pulled it on. "Now, I'm sure you have a great deal of research to do, so I'll leave you alone. Do try not to disturb anything as you work. But of course, the consortium told you all about that, so you know what to do. I live just a half mile away, in the white house at the start of the lane—you would have passed it on your way in. If you need anything, my telephone number is by the phone in the carriage house. You'll find tin lanterns and matches on the table by the stairs. Do be careful with them. And please be sure to shut the door If you leave. And watch the fifth step —it's loose. Good day, Miss Falling Hawk."

Eleanor whisked herself out the door, shutting it behind her. Deirdre stood, staring, as she heard a car door open and shut. The sound of an engine roared to life, then faded. She was alone. Alone in the manor where Marius Lucius Albrecht had lived before he joined the Seekers, and where nothing had been altered since.

How was it she had never heard of this place? The history of Albrecht she had read had mentioned Madstone Hall only in passing. Yet surely this manor was a treasure trove of information about the famous Seeker. And clearly the Philosophers knew about it. It had to be *his* doing that she had been granted entrance. All of this had the mark of her unnamed helper on it.

"So what is it you want me to find here?" she said, looking around.

Dim faces gazed at her out of the shadows: portraits adorning the walls. She moved to the table by the stairs and, with some effort, lit one of the lanterns. Gold light seeped out, not so much pushing back the dimness as making it deeper, more mysterious.

She ascended the stairs—careful to avoid the fifth step— holding the lantern up to each of the portraits. Nameless men, women, and children—all dressed in the finery of lords and ladies—gazed back at her.

At the top of the stairs was a full-length portrait. It showed a man dressed in black. His dark hair tumbled over his shoulders, framing a bearded face that was grim rather than handsome, yet compelling. She raised the lantern higher. The figure's eyes seemed to reflect the gold light; they had been painted with gilt rather than pigment of blue or brown.

Deirdre explored the upper levels, though she did little besides peek into each room. They were mostly bedchambers and sitting rooms, places where the manor's noble residents and guests would have spent their private time. The top floor contained more austere accommodations—for the manor's servants, no doubt.

She headed back downstairs and one by one explored the grand front hall, the dining room, the cavernous kitchen, and a large parlor that offered spectacular views of a distant ridge, now mantled in clouds. Everywhere she went she saw tarnished candelabras, Louis XIV chairs, and Chinese porcelain.

This place is remarkable, Deirdre. Museums or collectors would pay a fortune for some of these pieces.

Only they had rested there for centuries, just where they had been left. According to the history she had read, Marius Lucius Albrecht had lived in Madstone Hall until about 1674, and Eleanor had said nothing had been altered here since the late seventeenth century.

Which means everything is as it was about the time Albrecht left. Deirdre felt a spark of growing excitement. *In fact, it's possible that no one else lived in this manor after he left it.*

Again she wondered why the Seekers seemed not to know about this place. Surely this manor held vast amounts of information that could shed light on Albrecht, the greatest Seeker in the history of the order. Why wouldn't the Philosophers want the Seekers to know about it?

Maybe for the same reason someone deleted that file when you found it, Deirdre.

She opened a door at the end of the front hall, then stared in wonder at the room beyond. Shelves lined the walls, filled with leather-bound books. A sword hung above the fireplace, gleaming dully in the lanternlight. There was a large globe in one corner, and a claw-footed desk dominated the center of the room.

Deirdre moved to the desk, then drew in a breath. Ink stained the felt blotter—the ghosts of letters written long ago. Something near one corner of the blotter attracted her eye: a symbol drawn in dark lines.

It was a hand holding three flames.

Gripping the lantern to keep from dropping it, Deirdre circled around the desk. Unlike the faded ink stains, the symbol was crisp and black; it had been made recently. But by whom? By Eleanor? She didn't seem the type to go about the manor idly doodling on furniture. And what would she know about the Seekers?

Deirdre bent down. On the right side of the desk, just beneath the sigil, was a drawer. She reached out, then hesitated. She wasn't supposed to disturb anything. Or was she? Maybe it was precisely to disturb things that she had been brought there. She opened the drawer.

It was empty. At least she thought so. She couldn't see the back of it; there wasn't enough light. She stuck a hand in the drawer, groping toward the back.

Her fingers closed around something hard and cool. She pulled her hand out. On her palm was a silver key, blackened by tarnish.

Deirdre's neck tingled. She walked around the library, searching. It didn't take long. Tucked in a corner near the globe was a small cabinet of dark wood. The cabinet had two doors. One bore a keyhole. Deirdre set down the lantern. Her hand was trembling so hard it took her several tries to fit the key in the lock. She turned it, expecting it not to work. But there was a click, and the cabinet door swung open.

She crouched. In the cabinet were two shelves. One was lined with books. Deirdre ran a finger over their well-worn spines, certain it would be fascinating to read them, but also certain that was not why she was there. On the other shelf was a wooden box. She took it, carried it to the desk, and set it down. Dust swirled up. She held her breath a moment, letting the dust settle, then opened the lid.

There were three things in the box. One was a glass vial, empty. Its stopper was made of gold wrought into the delicate shape of a spider. The other two objects were books. One was small, its leather cover battered, its pages so dry they started to crumble when she tried to open the book. Hastily, she set it down.

The other book was larger. Its cover was smooth and new, and its pages white, cut into a clean, mass-manufactured edge. This was no antique book. It was a journal such as could be bought in any present-day stationery shop. Deirdre opened it to the first page.

A wave of dizziness came over her, forcing her to sit in the desk chair. In the dim light of the lantern, her eyes scanned the first lines.

You should not read this. Because if you do—if you learn the secrets contained within this journal,

*if you come to see the Philosophers for what they
truly are—then I will have doomed you just as surely
as I doomed her over three hundred years ago. They
will condemn you, they will hunt you with all their
powers, and they will destroy you.*

*Yet I beg of you, in the name of Hermes, keep
reading.*

"Great Spirit," Deirdre murmured, her hands shaking so
badly she had to set the journal down.

It was not just the words themselves that stunned her. It was
the smooth, elegant hand they were written in. She didn't need
to reach into her pocket, to pull out the handwritten note she had
received from him yesterday, to know that the handwriting was
identical. He had written this journal—and just recently, by the
look of it—this nameless Philosopher who had been helping
her.

Only he wasn't nameless, not anymore. Because the moment
she read those first lines, she had known at last who he was, who
it was who had been guiding her all this time, advising her, leading her to this very place.

"You're Marius," she murmured to the shadows, as if he was
listening. "You're Marius Lucius Albrecht. Somehow you're
still alive. You didn't die in 1684. You became a Philosopher.
That was what was in that file; that was why the Philosophers
deleted it. They didn't want me to learn the truth."

Only he did. But why?

Deirdre held the answer to that question here in her hands.
The daylight was failing outside the high windows; a storm
must be coming. She moved the lantern closer, adjusted the
wick to brighten the gold light, then opened the journal and bent
over it.

You should not read this. Because if you do—if you learn the
secrets contained within this journal, if you come to see the
Philosophers for what they truly are—then I will have doomed
you just as surely as I doomed her over three hundred years ago.

They will condemn you, they will hunt you with all their powers, and they will destroy you.

Yet I beg of you, in the name of Hermes, keep reading.

Forgive me the recklessness of these words, for I must write them in haste. It is ironic, for a being who is immortal, that I should have so little time in which to fill these pages, but they will soon turn their eyes in my direction. Unlike the ones they seek to understand, they do not sleep and have always kept watch on me. From the very beginning they have doubted my intentions, even as they transformed me into one of their own and brought me into their order.

But then, is it not safer to keep the wolf where you can see him? Except I know now it is the lamb I am to play in this bit of mummery, and for good or ill it is nearly at an end. Would that I could use a computer to set down these words more quickly, but they monitor all such devices, and perhaps it is just as well that I compose this on paper with an old-fashioned quill pen. It reminds me of a time long past. Of my time.

I did not seek to become immortal—that is the first thing you should know. On the contrary, when he first found me, life had no worth to me whatsoever, and at the ripe old age of fourteen I was doing everything I could to throw mine away. It was spring, in the year 1668, and Edinburgh was just beginning to stink.

In that era, Edinburgh was one of the most densely populated cities in all of Europe, for the entire citizenry—compelled by fear of the English—had crammed itself within the confines of the city's stone walls. They had come seeking protection. What they found instead were filth and poverty, disease and death.

In Greyfriars graveyard, along the Cowgate below St. Giles, layers of corpses were stacked with barely a layer of soil between them, so that after a hard Scottish rain limbs would jut out of the ground like tree roots. The living fared little better. With no room to build out because of the constricting embrace of the city's walls, the people of Edinburgh built up instead. Wooden tenements sprouted from the tops of stone buildings like fungi encouraged by the damp air. They were wretched structures, drafty in winter, stifling in summer, and rat-infested at all times, with narrow windows that opened only to allow the

foul contents of a chamber pot to be thrown onto the street—
and any unwary passersby—below.

The tenements were always catching fire, or falling down entirely, taking their unlucky occupants with them, and thereby
contributing to the population of Greyfriars. However, un-
wholesome and unsafe as they were, the folk who dwelled in
those structures were not the city's poorest by any means. For
there was one other direction in this crowded city in which to
build—and that was down.

There is no telling when the excavations beneath Edinburgh
began. Perhaps, in the gray time before the dawn of history,
primitive men used crude tools to hew at the volcanic crag
where the city would be built in a later age, carving out chambers in which to practice secret, blood-drenched rites. By the
time I came to know them, the delvings were ancient and vast,
and they were filled with a darkness that was far more than a
mere absence of light. If fair maidens like Hope and Joy had
ever stumbled into that place by mistake, then they had been
ravaged and left for dead.

While the warrens beneath Edinburgh were the only home I
knew as a child, I was not born in them. Nor would my mother
ever tell me how she had come to that place.

"That's a dark tale, James, and it's already dark as Hell down
here," she would mutter. "Do not ask me of it again."

However, even as a small boy, I had a way of getting others to
tell me their secrets. Over the years I prodded and probed, and
when she was tired or ill or drunk—all of which happened often
enough—my mother would let things slip, so that in time I
pieced together the story myself.

It was a simple enough tale. Throughout her youth she lived
with her father: a former sailor who owned a shop on Candlemaker Row. Who her own mother was, she did not know. People
along the Row claimed that, when her father returned from his
last voyage at sea, he had carried a baby in his arms, swaddled
in a fine silver cloth. He said the girl's name was Rose, and that
was all he ever said when anyone asked where the child had
come from.

When Rose was seventeen, her father perished of the fever
that had swept Edinburgh that winter. One of his cousins inher-

ited the shop, and as the man was not inclined to charity, Rose was forced to manage for herself. Thinking herself fortunate, she took a position as maid in the house of a well-respected judge. However, neither her status as maid nor the judge's respectability lasted long. Though I can recall her only as a hunched and withered thing, others told me that my mother was beautiful in her youth, with raven hair and sea-green eyes. Barely a year after her arrival at the judge's household, she gave birth to a son with striking gold hair—a match to the master's own glided locks.

His adultery revealed, the judge promptly repented his sins and proclaimed he had been placed under a spell by the lovely young maid. No one doubted him. Rather than find herself on Grassmarket Street hanging by her neck for witchcraft, Rose fled into the sewers with her infant son and found her way into the labyrinth beneath the city.

The warrens were populated by beggars, whores, thieves, and murderers who preyed as often upon those dwelling below as those living above. What Rose did to ensure the survival of her and her baby, I will never know. That knowledge even I could never pry from my mother. She would cackle with laughter when I asked her about her first days in the dark, then weep and pull at her snarled hair. I grew weary of her muttering and moaning, and as I grew older I ceased asking.

One morning—I was about ten, I suppose, though I did not know it at the time—I nudged her shoulder to wake her, and she did not move. This was in the cramped niche where we made our home: a hollow barely large enough for us both to curl up in, carved into the wall of a tunnel that, if you followed it upward, led all the way to a drain in Covenant Close.

I gave her a hard shove and yelled at her, but still she did not move, and I knew by her coldness that she was not simply in one of her drunken stupors. For a time I stared at her, listening to distant, wicked laughter echoing down the passage. Finally I rummaged in our niche and found the last bit of bread we possessed. I sat cross-legged and ate both my share and hers, and after that I looted the body.

There wasn't much on her. A single halfpence, a small knife with a worn bone handle, and—tucked inside her filthy dress—

a carefully folded piece of cloth. It was the size of a kerchief, and exceedingly fine, shimmering like silver in the gloom. The cloth was unsoiled, and even my dirty fingers left no mark on it.

The laughter drew closer. The sound was crude—a man's laughter. Others joined in.

I wadded up the cloth and shoved it inside my shirt, then tucked the knife and halfpence into the pocket of my breeches. Often men would poke their heads into our little niche while we were there, looking to steal from us, or worse. My mother would brandish the knife, driving them back. Except it was the light in her eyes that kept them at bay more than the blade. They would spark green in the blackness, and even I would be afraid of her. The men would snarl and curse. *Witch*, they'd call her, and *Jezebel*. But they would leave us alone.

A woman's scream echoed up the tunnel, drowned out by the sound of rude jeers. That would keep them occupied, at least for a short while. I crawled through the niche's opening and lowered myself down to the floor of the tunnel, making no noise. Red light flickered from down the passage, and shadows writhed there. I turned and ran up the tunnel as fast as my short legs would take me.

"Hey, there!" a rough voice shouted behind me. "I see you, little rat. Come back here!"

The heavy sound of boots thumped behind me, and I heard the grunting of breath, but I didn't look back. I kept my head down, pumping my arms, and rounded a bend in the tunnel. Just ahead was a crack in the wall. It was barely more than two hands wide, but I was such a skinny little thing that I slithered through, quick as a snake.

A hand shot in after me, clamping around my ankle.

"Now I got you," said a man's voice, thick and slurred from whiskey. "No need to wait my turn. There's nothing they can do with a lady I can't do with you. Now come back here, little rat."

Another hand pawed up my leg. I kicked back with my bare foot, contacting something soft and fleshy, mashing it beneath my heel. By the wet cry of pain I guessed it was his nose. The hands let go.

Free of his grasp, I wrigglod up the passage, which had been carved into the stone not by human hands but by the action of flowing water long ago. There were many such ways, connecting with the crypts and passages that had been hewn beneath the foundations of the city, and like all the children who dwelled down there—the ones who survived, at any rate—I had explored many of them. I knew that crack connected to a drain that spilled out on Grassmarket Street, in the shadow of the castle.

However, it had been at least a year since I had last used that particular passage, and I had grown. Bony as I was, I came to a bend where my chest became wedged. Panic gripped me, and I feared I would have to shimmy back down. Or worse yet, that I was stuck, and that some smaller child in years to come would find my bones and take the knife and coin and silver cloth even as I had taken them from the corpse of my mother.

I strained with all the might in my skinny limbs, bracing my feet against either side of the crack. Stone sliced though my shirt and bit into my chest, drawing blood, and the fluid acted as a lubricant. My body popped through the narrows and tumbled down the crack into a larger way—a clay pipe slicked with water and mold. Out of control, I slid down the pipe toward a circle of gray light that rapidly dilated before me. I shot through the hole, landing on hard stones, wet with slime like a newborn baby. Air rushed into my lungs, hard and shuddering, as if they had never drawn a breath before.

I looked up, squinting against the sullen daylight, which seemed inordinately bright to my dark-adjusted eyes. When was the last time my mother had brought me up to the surface? I could not remember. People walked by, but no one paid me more heed than they would a rat that had just crawled from the sewer. I touched my chest, wincing, and my hand came away red with blood. It hurt, but I had suffered worse. I was alive, and indeed I was like an infant again, wet with ichor, birthed from the canal of the drain, with an entire new life before me.

It was not, as I would come to learn, the last time in my existence I would be reborn.

I spent that first morning on the surface lurking in the stairs and walled closes along the Grassmarket. Horses trotted down the muddy street, pulling glossy carriages; trinkets of gold and silver shone behind shop windows. Though tempted to venture closer, I kept to the shadows, watching as folk in fine clothes passed by, conscious of the soiled rags that clad my own rawboned form. This world was strange to me, and though it seemed fair compared to the labyrinth below, I sensed it was every bit as perilous.

As the day wore on I grew bolder and crept up the steep curve of Candlemaker Row, passing—unbeknownst to me at the time—the shop where my mother had spent her childhood. It was the rich smells of roasted meat and tobacco, drifting from the pubs that lined High Street, which lured me upwards.

The afternoon was drawing on toward evening, but it was June and still light. I skulked along alleys like the numerous stray dogs, obeying the instinct to keep out of sight. Finally, as dusk stole through the city, I ducked into a courtyard tucked among tall buildings—a place I would later come to know as Advocate's Close, and a good bet for picking a rich man's pocket.

Stairs led down to a door in which a small window glowed with the warmest yellow light I had ever seen. It was the back entrance to one of the pubs that faced High Street. The door opened, and more light spilled out, along with raucous laughter. A woman with frowsy hair and an ample bosom emptied the contents of a bucket on the cobbles.

"Here 'tis, ye whelps," she called. "Coom an' take it away fer me." She stepped inside and shut the door.

Several dogs slunk from the shadows toward the heap of slop. I was faster. I leaped forward, snarling as I brandished the knife I had stolen from my mother, and to my surprise the dogs slunk back, tails between their legs. I grabbed as many of the choicest bones as I could, then ran across the close, leaving the rest for the curs.

I climbed atop a wall, then ate. The bones were legs of lambs pulled from a soup pot, and there was little meat left on them, meant as they were for the dogs, but to me they comprised a succulent feast. I ate, smacking my lips, enjoying the feel of gristle against my teeth and gums. I cracked the bones against the wall and sucked the marrow out.

Finally I was done. The dogs were fled. Above, the last gray light was fading from the sky. It was time to find a place to curl up and hide for the night—time to go back below the city. I wiped my greasy hands on my shirt, and as I did I felt a lump within.

I pulled it out. It was the silver cloth I had taken from my mother. My shirt was stained with blood, yet the silver cloth remained as clean as before. I held it up, marveling at the silken feel. It seemed to catch the twilight, shimmering in the gloom.

"Hey, you up there!"

I knew at once there was nowhere to run. The back entrance by which I had entered the close was now barred with an iron gate. Someone must have locked it as dusk fell, and in the rapture of gnawing on the bones I had failed to notice. There were several other doors lining the close, but I was certain all would be locked, save perhaps the back door to the pub. However, I dared not try that way. One big hand on my scrawny neck, and my flight would be in vain.

The only other way out of the close was by the main archway that led out onto High Street. Two men stood in that archway.

"Where did you get that?" one of the men said, pointing at the silver cloth.

He was corpulent, his jowls spilling out of a lace-collared shirt. His velvet coat was just as rich, sewn with brass buttons, and at first I supposed him some sort of lord. When I did not answer him, he turned to his companion. "This will take just a moment."

The other remained silent. He was tall, a dark cloak draping his broad shoulders and his face shadowed by the wide brim of a hat.

The gentleman marched forward. "I daresay that kerchief is too fine for the likes of you, boy," he said, his breath wheezing, as if he had walked up a long flight of steps rather than just across the close. "Where did you steal it?"

"It's mine," I said. "My mother gave it to me." It was not exactly the truth, but close enough to it.

"Liar," the man spat, and before I could move he snatched the cloth from my hands. A new emotion cut through my fear: anger.

He pawed at the cloth with thick fingers. "This is fine indeed.

I'd warrant you pilfered it from some noble lady. It's malefactors like you that are ruining this city. I'm a barrister for the king's court. I'll have you hauled up to the castle and thrown in the dungeon."

I started to push myself off the wall, but then the other—the tall, shadowy one—stepped closer. He raised a gloved hand.

"Let him go, Brody," he said, and I froze. His voice was deep and resonant, and for some reason it sent a shiver up my spine. "Let us go inside." He gestured to the back door of the pub. "I would see to our business."

Although the other spoke to the barrister, Brody, I felt certain it was me he was watching, even though I could not see his face.

Brody glanced back at his companion, and I knew this was my chance. I leaped down from the wall and snatched the cloth from the barrister's hand. He moved faster than I would have guessed for one so large, whirling around and grabbing for me. I let out a snarl and glared at him. He stumbled back, his face pale in the gloom, and I knew at that moment my eyes flashed green just like my mother's.

Clutching the cloth to my chest, I ran for the archway. I was forced to pass so close to the barrister's companion that I brushed against his black cloak—the fabric was heavy and soft—but he did not stop me.

I pounded barefoot over the stones of High Street, dodging horses, coaches, and people, expecting a hue and cry to rise up behind me at any moment, but it did not. I careened around a corner onto Candlemaker Row, then ran on, down toward the Cowgate and the fringes of the old city. I had left the throngs behind; there were no people to observe me as I scrambled up a stone wall, then dropped down the other side.

The noises of the city receded. A hush closed around me. Pale stones shone in the dimness.

This was Greyfriars cemetery—though at the time I did not know its name, only that it was a graveyard and that it suited me. The living would not bother me there, and I feared them far more than I did the dead. I moved deeper into the cemetery, shivering as the sweat brought on by my flight evaporated. Even in summer, nights in Edinburgh were cool.

I suppose I surprised the grave robber as much as he surprised me. I came from around a large headstone topped with a Celtic cross, and there he was, hunched over his work, muttering to himself as he pried at the door of a mausoleum with a pickaxe. He had already broken away a corner of the stone door.

Startled, I let out a gasp. The grave robber dropped the pick and turned around, his eyes like saucers in the gloom.

"Mother Mary, save me!" he said, clutching a marble column, his face a mask of dirt and fear.

I reached out a hand and tried to tell him it was all right, that I wouldn't hurt him, but he let out a strangled cry and turned around to flee. As he did, his cloak caught on a hawthorn bush. He jerked free of the garment, then ran away through the graveyard.

I suppose he thought I was a ghost, pale as I was, scabbed with blood and dressed in rags, and that I had risen from the grave to punish him. Quite the opposite, I was grateful for his actions, as now I had discovered where I could spend the night.

I retrieved the cloak from the bush, then squeezed through the gap the grave robber had made—too small for a man, but perfect for a thin boy. Only the faintest light followed me into the mausoleum. There was a musty smell, from the rats that had long ago built a nest in a corner, but the odor was faint and old. Crypts lined the marble walls; one of them was open and empty, awaiting a body.

I gave it mine. Bruised, aching, and tired beyond imagining—yet strangely pleased for a reason I couldn't quite name—I wrapped myself in the robber's cloak and lay down inside the cold crypt. The stone seemed to me the softest feather bed, and there I slept like a corpse, born and dead in the very same day.

Perhaps it was from dwelling among the dead for so long that I came to care so little for the worth of my own life.

Over the course of those next few years, I slept many nights inside the mausoleum, and in time I came to think of its denizens as my family. I could read a little; my mother had taught me, writing with bits of charcoal on the walls of our niche in rare, peaceful times. Thus I was able to make out some of the inscriptions on the marble crypts.

There was Lord John Gilroy, surely a fatherly figure, stern of face, and demanding of obedience, but kindly in quiet moments. Old Lady Gilroy had lived a generation earlier, to the ripe age of ninety-two, and so she became my imagined grandmother, comforting me when all seemed cold and bleak. Then there was little Jennie Gilroy—deceased at the tender age of nine, according to the writing on her crypt—a little sister whom I would fiercely protect, and in whom I could confide when I was lonely and afraid. Sometimes when I lay down inside the crypt to sleep, I would drape the robber's cloak over me like a burial shroud, then fold my hands together on my breast and pretend I was dead as they were, and at peace.

Only I was neither. And like some restless and unholy spirit, I would rise from the crypt each day and slip out of the mausoleum to prey upon the world of living men.

I had no name besides that which my mother had given to me—James—for my bastard-making father the judge had not deigned to lend me his appellation. Nor did it matter. One made one's own name on the streets of Edinburgh, and I came to be known among the people who dwelled there, in the gutters and in the shadows, as Jimmie Golden—for my fair locks, which were the only inheritance my father had granted me.

Early on I learned that my hair—thick, yellow as wheat, and curling about my thin shoulders—was my greatest asset. Though my clothes were invariably grimy, I kept my golden locks as clean as I could, dunking my head in one of the city's fountains even on the coldest days and using my fingers to comb through the ringlets. I knew they fancied it—the gentle ladies who fretted over me.

I would stand along High Street, positioning myself in a shaft of sun so that the light would shine upon my hair. As a fine carriage passed by, perhaps on its way from the castle down through Canongate to the palace of Holyrood, I would affect a look at once placid and forlorn—a beatific expression I had copied from cherubs painted inside St. Giles cathedral, which I had seen once when I sneaked in through the doors.

Most of the coaches would clatter on by, but eventually, if I waited long enough, a carriage would stop and a lady would emerge. Sometimes she was young and fresh-faced, dressed in a gown sewn with ribbons, at other times older and motherly. Either way, while I gazed up with plaintive eyes, the lady would cluck her tongue and fuss over me. She would murmur that she had never seen hair so gold, and how I had the face of an angel, and that surely God had touched this poor, wretched orphan.

Quickly enough, a man—sometimes her husband, sometimes her attendant—would leap from the carriage and race after the lady, gently but forcibly pulling her away from me. The lady would protest, the man would give me an angry look, then he'd pull several coins from his purse, toss them at my feet, and tell me in gruff tones to be off. Not needing to be told twice, I'd snatch up the coins and run.

The men were red-faced and hard-eyed—I felt no qualms taking their money—but I liked the ladies, especially the younger ones. They smelled like flowers, their voices as gentle as the calling of doves. I liked that they could imagine God had touched me, even though I knew it wasn't true.

"It's the devil in ye, Jimmie, not our Lord, that's for certain," Deacon Moody said to me as often as the pretty ladies spoke otherwise, and with greater conviction in his voice.

I could find Deacon Moody almost any day, fair or foul, along the Grassmarket, the hem of his black robe dragging in the muck, speaking the gospel to all who would listen to him, and taking any alms—coin, food, or preferably ale—where it was given. No one seemed to know for sure if Moody had been a real deacon once, but a few times I heard it whispered he indeed had been one, only that he had committed some heinous act, and was ejected from the Church years ago.

Whatever the truth, the folk who lived on Edinburgh's streets—and in the dark ways below—often came to Deacon Moody, asking him to speak a rite of marriage, or to baptize a newborn babe, or to grant forgiveness when the supplicant feared death drew nigh, for the doors of the city's churches were closed to folk such as they. Nor did Moody ask for any recompense for these acts, much as he sought handouts at other times, and that was what made me think the stories about him were true.

"Where are you off to, lad?" Deacon Moody said to me one autumn evening as he caught me dashing through the Grassmarket. For nearly four years I had been living on the streets of the city by day and dying by night in Greyfriars cemetery.

"Nowhere," I said.

It was true enough. It wasn't where I was running to that concerned me, but rather where I was running *from*: a stair that linked the Grassmarket to High Street, where I had just lifted a man's purse. I didn't usually resort to such brazen thievery, but the purse had been full and heavy, dangling from the man's belt like a ripe fruit ready to be plucked.

"If it's nowhere you're going, then you've time to indulge me in a bit of conversation," Moody said, his voice and breath thick with drink. A falling mist beaded on his black robe and dampened his gray hair. "Now tell me, lad, have you given any further thought to your salvation?"

I gave him a pert grin. "I sleep in a crypt, Deacon, you know that. So you can't save me, seeing as I'm already dead."

The deacon's expression, previously jovial, became grim. "No, you're not, lad," he said, laying a rough hand on my shoulder. He gazed around the Grassmarket. "There are many on these streets who are dead indeed. They keep on walking and eating and breathing, but they've forgotten what it's like to be alive, and their hearts have gone cold as iron. All they care for are hard things, like the weight of gold in their pockets, or the feel of a gun in their hands. Beyond grace, they are. But not you, Jimmie Golden. Not yet. Do you hear me, lad?"

I reached into my own pocket, feeling the heavy purse. Perhaps the man I had stolen it from had planned to use the money to settle an account. Perhaps now he would be thrown in debtor's prison to rot.

Dread grew in me, and my own heart felt cold, but I quickly traded the feeling for anger and directed the full force of it at Moody. They had cast him out of the Church for his sins. What did he know? I was a thief, that was all. Grace was not for the likes of me.

I glared at him, and I know not what he saw upon my face, but he jerked his hand from my shoulder, and a soft word escaped his lips. It might have been, *Mercy*.

Moody stumbled back against a wall, and I pushed past him, racing down the Grassmarket. I reached the square where witches and criminals were hanged, then veered right, heading down toward Greyfriars.

Dusk was thickening to dark, and the mist clung to my eyelashes; I suppose that was how I did not see him standing before the iron gates of the graveyard. I rounded a corner of the wall and ran into him headlong. He was tall, and solidly built. I glanced off him like a bird striking a window and fell dazed to the cobblestones.

Strong hands picked me up and shook me out, standing me back on my feet.

"Sorry, my lord," I said, keeping my eyes down, then started to move past him.

His hand touched my shoulder, stopping me. "Perhaps you can help me," he said, his voice deep and thrumming. "I'm looking for someone."

I kept my eyes on his black boots, but a shiver coursed through me, for I recognized that voice, though it had been almost four years since I had heard it last, in the confines of Advocate's Close.

"I've been looking for this person for some time," the man said. "I recently heard that he lives here, in Greyfriars."

"No one lives here, my lord," I said. " 'Tis a graveyard."

"Is that so?"

A strong finger touched my chin, tilting my head up. He was even taller than I remembered. As before, a wide-brimmed hat shadowed his face, but I caught two glints of gold light in the darkness. His eyes were locked on me, and they were yellow like a wolf's.

"Who are you?" I said in a hoarse rasp.

"Someone who can help you."

My fear receded a fraction, and I felt a spark of anger flicker up in me again. First Deacon Moody, now this stranger in black. Why did they want to help me? Couldn't they see it was no use?

"Leave me be," I said, jerking away from him.

"As you wish, James."

These words stunned me so much that I stopped in the act of turning away. I looked over my shoulder. A stray shaft of light fell from a window above, illuminating a strong mouth framed by a dark beard.

"If you change your mind, come to Advocate's Close at twilight on the first day of any month. You'll find me then, just as you did before."

I clenched my hands into fists. "I won't come."

The man said nothing. He turned and walked down the street. When I could no longer see him, I gazed up at the gates of the cemetery. I was weary and longed to lie down in the crypt to sleep. Only I did not dare—not now, not ever again. Somehow he had learned that I made my home there. Someone on the street had told him, and that meant I could never sleep in Greyfriars again. No more would I know the peace of the Gilroy mausoleum, or the comfort of my imagined family. A pang of sadness pierced my heart.

I crumpled the feeling and tossed it away, like refuse in the gutter. Deacon Moody was an old, drunken fool, but he had been right about one thing. Sorrow was not for the dead. I straightened my bony shoulders and passed into the night.

After that, I put all thoughts of Greyfriars and the stranger in black out of my head. A change had come over me, as sudden as a storm sweeps out of the Highlands. While before I had been quick to laugh or make a jest with other folk on the street, now I was grim and silent, and I spoke to no person except out of need. I no longer slept in a crypt, but all the same I had died, just like the people Deacon Moody had spoken of.

It was not simply temptation that had caused me to steal that man's purse on the stair below High Street. Desperation had factored in as well. As the years passed, despite the wretchedness of my diet, I had sprouted. My breeches had become knickers of their own accord, and my shirtsleeves reached barely past my elbows.

The taller I grew, the harder it became to compel the ladies to charity. Fewer carriages stopped, and when they did I received smaller coins for my troubles. Then, for a long time, no carriage stopped at all.

I had all but given up on winning alms by the time I robbed

that fellow. However, the day after I fled the dark stranger at Greyfriars, I tried one more time, cleaning myself up as best I could and standing beside the road. To my surprise, it was not long before a glossy coach stopped in front of me. To my further surprise, it was not a woman who opened the coach's door, but a man: a barrister or other well-to-do gentleman, edging on toward middle years, but still handsome in his fine attire.

Looking back, I should not have been so astonished. With the change that had come over me, I had not bothered to affect the cherub's forlorn and beatific expression. Instead, I looked exactly like what I was—a young man with yellow hair, thin and pretty and dangerous. I should have known they would stop for me.

The piercing light in the fellow's eyes told me he did not seek to do charity unto me, but the coins in his hand, gold as my hair, removed any qualms I might have felt. I climbed into the carriage, and the door shut behind me.

After that day, I realized it did not matter if the fair ladies would no longer make a fuss over me. There were men who would give me far more money, and for far different reasons. One thing, though, remained the same: they all favored my golden locks. I let my hair grow long and luxuriant, and always kept it clean.

Sometimes, as on that first day, I stood beside High Street, waiting for a carriage to stop, but I soon found only the boldest favored that method. More often I could be found as dusk fell, lingering in the square just below the Tron kirk, whose wooden steeple beckoned like a finger against the sky. That's where I'd find them waiting in shadows, eyes hungry and furtive. I'd give them a look, then lead them away down a side street, toward a crib in a wooden tenement I had rented with my first earnings.

Usually I'd let them pay their coin and do things to me before I robbed them while they slept on the dirty straw mattress in the crib. If they were fat or smelled bad, I'd just rob them right away, pulling my mother's knife on them once we were alone in an alley. Either way, I didn't worry about getting caught. The men would be far too ashamed to go to the constable to report a robbery. After all, there was a special place in Hell for men with appetites such as theirs; that's what the ministers inside the Tron said—a place where tongues of fire licked at your nether regions and devils dug at your entrails with hot pokers for all eternity.

As for me, I was not concerned with devils. After all, if I was dead, then I was already in Hell. Or perhaps I was one of Lucifer's devils myself, sent here to torture the wicked.

Autumn edged into chill winter, and I used my newfound money to buy clothes, including a gray cloak that was in truth quite plain, but still fine by the standards of those who lived on the street. Those who had greeted me with friendly words when I was younger now gazed at me with suspicious or jealous looks. More than once I saw Deacon Moody at a distance, gazing at me from across the Grassmarket. I paid no heed to any of them.

One of the men who came to me introduced me to the fiery taste of whiskey, and I found I quite liked it, though more than once I became too besotted to remember to rob my clients, and once one of them rolled me while I slept in a stupor. However, that did not inspire me to caution, and soon the majority of what I earned went to buy bottles of the stuff, for I favored it over food. I grew taller yet, but remained thin as a whip, and pale from haunting the night and sleeping in the crib by day.

I did not know it at the time, but as winter released its grip on Edinburgh and the warmth of spring seeped onto the air, in the year of our Lord 1668, I was near to death. A cough had afflicted me, and often in the morning I would bring up gobs of yellow phlegm flecked with blood. Even on chill days sweat sheened my pallid skin, for it seemed I always had a fever. I could keep little food down, and only the whiskey seemed to dull the pounding in my head, though it made the gnawing in my stomach worse.

To compound matters, I found my money running short. Rarely now could I keep my wits about me long enough to rob the men who followed me from the square below the Tron. Too often I would fall unconscious, leaving them to paw at me as they wished without making payment. I would wake to find them gone and my body so sore I could scarcely walk. All the same I would shrug on my clothes, untangle my hair, drink a little whiskey, then head out to find another I could offer myself to.

I began to grow reckless, not bothering to wait for the shadows of night, and approaching men directly rather than waiting for them to slink after me. When a constable would ask me what I was doing, lurking about, I would try to bribe him by offering my services for free. The first two or three accepted, but then one—a big fellow with ruddy cheeks and red hair—struck me with the back of his hand, so hard that blood burst out from my lip and I had to run through twisting streets to escape him.

For some reason I could not name, after that happened, I thought to go see Deacon Moody. Not for help—I was beyond that—but perhaps simply so I could remember something of my younger days. It is said that, as death approaches, one often relives the events of one's life.

When I reached the Grassmarket, however, I found no sign of Moody. I inquired here and there and soon learned that the Deacon had been found a few months ago, dead.

"How did it happen?" I asked the grog seller who told me the news.

"By his own deed," the woman said, wiping hands against her dirty smock to no effect. "'Tis whispered both his wrists were laid open, and that into each he had carved the figure of a cross."

She pressed her thin lips together and made the sign of the cross herself. I turned and left without a word, feeling neither sad nor stunned, simply empty. The dead cannot feel, the Deacon had said. I pressed a hand to my heart, yet it seemed forged of iron. Not even my swollen lip hurt. I walked back toward my crib, and I did not think of Deacon Moody again.

I might have died that day, curled up like a dog on my matted bed, but something roused me from my torpor. Only what was it? It had sounded like the bells of the Tron kirk, only clearer, more distant. Purer.

Pulling myself up with weak arms, I peered out the narrow slit in the wall that passed for a window. Outside the day was ending, and twilight filtered down between the tenements like soot. A shadow moved on the street below. It vanished around a corner, heading up toward High Street, but I had caught a glimpse of a black robe, its hem stained with mud, and of lank gray hair.

Was this sight a hallucination brought on by fever, a regurgitation of what I had learned in the Grassmarket that day? Or was it something more? It is sometimes said that ghosts appear to those who are near to death themselves.

Even now, after more than three centuries, I still believe it is the latter of these two explanations that was true. Regardless, I knew I must follow the man in the black robe.

New strength flooded my body. I felt bright and powerful of a sudden, as a candle flaring just before it burns out. I flung myself through the door of my crib and down the rickety stairs of the tenement, then out onto the street. Though evening fell, the spring air was balmy, and already tainted with the rich scent of rot that would ripen into a stifling miasma as summer drew close. A black cat slunk away from me, crossing my path as I lurched up the lane toward High Street.

I saw the shadow once more as I reached the Tron, just vanishing around the corner of the church, then again drifting past St. Giles cathedral. Why I followed the wraith, I do not know. I had no words for Deacon Moody, except perhaps to ask if he was glad he was dead, if he felt nothing now. The thought occurred to me that I was dead myself—truly dead—and even at that moment my corpse lay stiffening in the crib as the first rats discovered me, squealing their delight.

The world darkened around me, torches and lanterns burning like distant stars. I saw the shadow just ahead, beckoning to me, and I followed through an archway. Muted laughter drifted on the air. I rubbed my eyes and saw that I was no longer on the High Street, but rather in a courtyard. It seemed familiar to me, and then I saw the moldy stone plaque on the wall. ADVOCATE'S CLOSE, it read. There was no trace of the shadow I had followed.

"Well, what have we here?" said a rough voice.

I turned and saw a man in the archway, illuminated by dirty light spilling out of windows above. He was big, clad all in blue. A grin parted the thatch of his red beard, and I recognized him as the constable I had fled from earlier that day.

"What is it, MacKenzie?" A second shadow appeared in the archway. He was short and heavy-shouldered, his voice slurred with drink.

"It's the devil's own, that's who," the constable said, stalking forward at a leisurely pace. The iron gate behind me was locked. "Tell me, boy, given anyone Lucifer's Kiss today?"

His companion laughed. "So he's one of those, is he? How about you bend yerself over, MacKenzie, and let him plant a kiss on you."

"Shut your trap, Ralph," the constable said, glaring. "I'm no lover of Satan or his ilk. Not like this whelp. A scourge on this city, you are." He edged closer, big hands flexing.

I didn't move. "You can't hurt me," I said quietly.

"Think so?" he said with a hard laugh. "Your face looks bad enough from where I got you this morning. Did I ruin your pretty looks? Well, there's plenty more where that came from. You may serve Satan now, but I can beat the fear of God into you."

I didn't flinch as his fist descended toward my cheek. He could not harm me. I was beyond that now. Although I had not thought of her in many months, I called out to her now.

I'm coming, Mother!

"Stay your hand," spoke a deep voice.

It seemed impossible, given the force and speed behind it, but the constable's fist froze not an inch from my cheek.

"What's wrong with you, MacKenzie?" the short man said. "Come on, give the whelp a good one."

"I can't," the constable said through clenched teeth. Sweat glittered his brow. His arm shook, as if all his muscles strained, but his fist moved no closer.

"Bloody Hell, if you've gone all soft, then I'll do it." The one named Ralph marched forward and reached for me with both hands.

"I said stay," the voice intoned.

Ralph went stiff as a corpse, arms before him, and his eyes bulged. A gurgle sounded low in his throat, but he made no other sound. A figure clad all in black parted from the shadows and drifted into view. It was not the ghost of Deacon Moody.

"Are you well, James?" he said, gazing down at me.

I tried to speak, but I seemed as paralyzed as the two men. I had grown since our last meeting, but the stranger still towered over me, and his voice—full of danger a moment ago—had been as resonant with kindness as I remembered. A stray shaft of light illuminated his face, and I thought it stern and wise and handsome.

"Who are you?" I finally found the breath to ask.

"That is a long tale, and there is no time to tell it now, James. I would that you come with me tonight."

I glanced at the two motionless men. Spittle dribbled from their mouths.

"You can do with me as you would," I said. "I can't stop you."

He bent down and, as he had long ago, laid a hand on my shoulder. "No, James. I'm not like them. I will not make you do something you would not. I want you to come with me because you choose it, because you want something better for yourself than what you have been given. Because you want to live."

A moan escaped me. For so long I had believed I was dead, capable of feeling nothing. Only I had been terribly wrong, for at that moment a pain pierced my heart, and a longing came over me—though for what I could not name, except that I thought of the calling of the bells that had awakened me, and how clear the sound had been. I thought as well of Deacon Moody, and how he had wished to save me. Perhaps he had after all.

"I will come with you," I said.

"I am glad, James." Keeping his strong hand on my shoulder, he guided me from the close, past the two men who stood still as statues, and like ghosts ourselves we passed into the night.

While it was years before I would finally learn the secret of the Sleeping Ones, before my own eyes would become gold as his, the moment I walked from Advocate's Close with the stranger was the moment I left death behind and first embarked upon the path to immortality.

While the days that followed are a blur to me now—events seen through a gray fog—I remember that night with perfect clarity: how he led me to a coach waiting on High Street and spoke quiet words to a man clad in a servant's coat.

"Lay him down in the back. Be gentle with him. And after

you arrive at Madstone Hall, you must send for the doctor at once."

"What of yourself, sir?"

The servant's voice was rich with an accent I could not name, unlike the stranger's speech, which seemed to bear no accent at all.

"I must finish my business here in Edinburgh. I'll take a horse to the manor later tonight."

"We'll keep a fire burning in the library for your arrival, sir."

I could not see—yet I felt—his smile. "Thank you, Pietro. Even after all these years, I haven't grown used to the chill of this land. To think, they call this springtime. Here—use this to keep him warm."

He removed the dark cloak and wrapped it over me. It was soft, and laced with the sweet, masculine smell of tobacco. Though his hair was white, and his angled face weathered with age, the servant picked me up with little strain, for I was light as a bird. The tall buildings tilted; stars wheeled in the sky above, then vanished as the coach door opened and I was set on the leather seat inside.

"Go quickly, Pietro. A fever burns in him. I fear he is near to death."

No, I tried to call out. *I am well now.* But my lips could not form the words, and it didn't matter, for the door was shut, and moments later the coach was clattering down the High Street.

I lay on the seat, wrapped in his cloak, weary in every bone of my young body, but strangely awake and alert. I had the sense that the coach was heading downward, and in my mind I could see it moving through the Canongate, past the spires of Holyrood Palace, and into the night-shrouded world beyond, like a tiny craft on a wide, dark sea.

It occurred to me that I should perhaps be afraid. Maybe the stranger had not saved me after all. Maybe he merely wanted me, and sought to use me just as all the others had before him. But no, he was not like other men; that was the one thing I was certain of.

After that my mind drifted, and soon it seemed I was floating on the dark sea. From time to time I heard voices, and I think they were what kept me from sinking into the water. The voices were difficult to make out; they blended with the murmur of the waves. One was the strangely accented voice, while another spoke in the lilting tongue of a well-to-do lowlander. Then, sometimes, there was the other voice, as deep as the ocean I drifted on.

"Come back to us, James," I heard it say once, and I tried to call out in answer, only black water filled my mouth.

"The fever burns hotter in him than ever," said the Scottish voice. "It must break soon, or it will burn him to death."

"It will break," the deep voice said.

I felt something cool touch my brow. A peace came over me, and I smiled as at last the water pulled me down.

When I woke, it was quite to my surprise.

By the light streaming in through the window, it was late morning. I propped myself up and found I was naked beneath clean white sheets in a large bed. The chamber around me was large as well, with a fireplace, a pair of chairs, and three tall windows, one of which stood open to let in a sweet breath of spring air. Beyond gauze curtains I saw green hills rolling away to a misty horizon. I stared, for I had not been beyond the walls of the city in all my fourteen years, and I had never seen a sight so beautiful.

I was still staring when the door opened and a man stepped through. I recognized him at once by his servant's coat and his gray hair, which was pulled into a knot at the nape of his neck. His nose was hooked like a hawk's, and his wrinkled skin was a deep olive color I had never seen before. He regarded me with black eyes and nodded.

"The doctor said you would likely wake today." The servant, Pietro, seemed more to sing than talk, for all words were musical and trilling upon his tongue. "The master will wish to speak with you, but first we must see to your appearance."

I felt strong and ready to talk to the master at once. I started to tell Pietro this, but as I slipped from the bed I found I was anything but strong. My limbs shook with an uncontrollable spasm, and I would have fallen but for the older man's tight grip.

Such was my state that I felt no shame at my nakedness as Pietro bathed me before the fire in a wooden tub and dressed me as if I were an infant. He dusted my shoulders and turned me to face a mirror. The figure of a young nobleman gazed back. His coat and breeches were a soft dove gray trimmed with silver, and his shirt was as crisp as snow. A dark ribbon held back long gold hair from a face that was pale and delicately wrought. His eyes glittered like twin emeralds. The only thing that spoiled the image was the bruise that marred his left cheek.

Pietro nodded. "I believe the master will approve. You look a fine young lord, sir."

I ran my fingers over the cool silver buttons. "Tell me, Pietro, who is he? The master."

"A kind man," the servant said. "Though a private one. He shall tell you in good time, I believe."

"But what is his name?" I said, turning from the mirror. "I must know what I am to call him."

"His name is Albrecht. He is lord of this manor, and so you may address him as Master."

"But what does he want with me?"

"Your fingernails need paring," Pietro said, clucking his tongue, and went to fetch a knife.

To my great disappointment, I did not see the master that day.

"He has been called to Edinburgh on sudden business," Pietro informed me as I ate breakfast in the manor's kitchen. It was a great, rambling stone room with fireplaces as large as the niche in the tunnels where I had slept with my mother as a child. Pietro waited on me himself, and I might have found that unnerving save I was ravenous, and my thoughts were wholly occupied by the dishes prepared by the kitchen staff that Pietro set before me.

In all my life, I had never eaten such marvelous food. There was crusty bread and butter, eggs and fat sausages fried crisp, and dried fruits drowned in the thickest cream. I ate until my belly visibly protruded from my thin body.

After that I thought no more of the master, but only of sleep. Docile as a lamb I let Pietro lead me back to my room, remove my fine new clothes, and lay the bedcovers over me.

When I woke it was evening, and the doctor was there, a corpulent, red-cheeked man with a jovial air about him. He examined me, used a silver knife to let a small amount of blood from my arm, and pronounced me firmly on the mend, much to his amazement.

"Favored by God, this lad is," he said to Pietro as he gathered his things. "The Lord must have some purpose on this Earth for him."

At his words I shivered, but perhaps it was only some last remnant of the chill that had afflicted me.

"Master Albrecht thanks you for your service," Pietro said, then saw the doctor to the door. When the man was gone, Pietro brought me a cup of water.

"Does God really have a purpose for me, Pietro?" I touched my bandaged arm. It hurt where the doctor had cut me.

"Such things are beyond me, Master James."

My gaze went to the window and the deepening twilight outside. "He has a purpose for me. Doesn't he?"

"Go to sleep," Pietro said, and I did.

When I woke again, the sky was still gray outside my window, but I knew that many hours had passed, and that it was no longer dusk. Rather, dawn grew near. I heard a faint ringing noise, and I thought perhaps it was the sound of bells. Then I knew it for what it was: the music of a horse's bridle jingling.

I leaped from the bed, feeling shockingly strong for the food and rest, and ran to the window. My chamber looked over the manor's courtyard, and below I saw a figure wrapped in a cloak—Pietro, by his stoop—shuffle forward as another, clad all in black, rode into the courtyard on a massive stallion. He swung down from the horse in an easy motion and handed the reins to Pietro. The rider started across the courtyard, then paused and looked up. Two sparks of amber flashed, their gleam directed at the window through which I peered. I stumbled back from the sill. Then I moved to the wardrobe and—fingers fumbling with the unfamiliar buttons and clasps—donned my new clothes.

By the time Pietro entered my chamber, I was ready. He led me downstairs to a room carpeted with Oriental rugs and walled with books, bound in leather and writ upon their spines in gold ink. A fire roared in the fireplace, making the room warm. Objects decorated the mantelpiece: porcelain figurines, a golden mask, and metallic devices that seemed to have scientific purposes I could not fathom. Fascinating as these items were, I gave them barely a glance.

He sat in a chair by the fire, and his hat and cloak were gone, so for the first time I truly got a look at him. Even sitting back in his chair he was tall, his long legs stretched out toward the fire, one large hand resting upon his thigh. He was still clad in riding attire—a form-fitting coat, breeches, and boots all in black—and as I drew near him I caught the rich scents of leather and horses. His dark hair was held back by a ribbon, and the firelight played across a bearded face that was too strong and sharply hewn to be handsome, but which was nonetheless striking.

As I approached, he turned his eyes—gold as old coins—upon me. I froze, and it was then I noticed there was something in one of his hands. It was a cloth of silver.

"I believe this is yours, James," he said, holding out the cloth.

I hesitated, then stepped forward and took the cloth from him. Relief flooded through me at its cool touch. I had feared that, in my fever, I had left it behind in the crib.

"Pietro found it tucked inside your shirt when we brought you here three nights ago. I fear we had to burn your other clothes. But not this." His amber eyes locked on me. "It was without stain or rent."

"My mother gave it to me."

He nodded, then turned his gaze to the fire, as if this were all he had required of me. I stood silently, until I could bear it no longer.

"Why have your brought me here, Master?" I blurted out.

"Can you read?" He did not take his gaze from the fire.

I frowned, puzzled by this question. "A little. My mother taught me some words when I was very young."

"Good. Then you shall read, James. You shall begin on the morrow. Pietro will help you."

There was so much more I wished to ask him, but he seemed lost in thought, staring at the fire, then Pietro was there. Gently but firmly he led me from the library. He took me to the kitchen for supper, and eating temporarily quelled my curiosity, but it flared again as soon as Pietro guided me back to my chamber.

"Why does he want me to read, Pietro?" I asked as he helped me off with my coat.

"In this modern time, all fine young lords are expected to be well-read," the gray-haired servant said.

However, that only raised new questions—I was no young lord—and after Pietro left, as I lay in the bed, I was certain there was something more to the master's command. There had to be.

"If he wishes me to read," I said aloud to the darkness, "then I shall read every book in the library."

That was easier said than done. My mother's teachings did not carry me so far as I had thought they would. I knew my letters, and while I could read simple sentences, the books in the manor's library were filled with long and arcane words that were beyond my ability to pronounce, let alone comprehend. What was more, I could not write at all, not even my own name.

Pietro became my teacher. In the mornings, we sat in the drawing room off the manor's vast main hall, or on fine days outside at a stone table in the garden. We drank tea, brought to us by one of the other household servants. I had never had tea before, and I liked it so much I soon forgot my cravings for whiskey.

My reading began with an English translation of Virgil, a poet who lived in the great city of Rome a long time ago. Pietro admired him, being from Italy himself, as he informed me.

"What of the master?" I asked. "Is he also from Italy?"

"Let us begin at the beginning," Pietro said, and opened the book.

It was slow going at first, but Pietro was a patient teacher, and I soon found myself drawn in by the tale of the hero Aeneas, and how he fought bravely at Troy, then fled after King Hector told him to found a new city that would later become Rome. I was fascinated by how the ghost of Aeneas's wife appeared to him, and I liked especially the section in which Aeneas went to Africa and fell in love with Queen Dido, only to abandon her when the gods reminded him of his duty to found Rome. After that, Dido threw herself upon a funeral pyre, which I found horrible and compelling.

I practiced writing, and though clumsy at first, I improved so rapidly that Pietro declared I was gifted by God. I soon took to drawing as well, and playing music on a harpsichord, and I excelled at both, for my fingers were long and dexterous, and if I imagined something in my mind it seemed no effort to make my hands bring it into being.

I saw the master regularly, if not often. Usually several days would pass, and I would see him little if at all about the manor. Then, on the third or fourth evening since I had last spoken with him, he would call me to his library and ask what I had learned since our last meeting.

"I learned it is better to die than lose what one loves most," I said one evening. This was while I was in the midst of reading *The Aeneid*.

He raised a dark eyebrow. "And what taught you that?"

"Queen Dido," I said excitedly, for I was obsessed with her story and liked nothing better than to speak of it. "The warrior Aeneas left her, called away by the gods, and rather than go on without him she threw herself on a fire and stabbed herself with a knife while her people watched. There was a great amount of blood, then she burned up." I never spared the gory details, and indeed tended to embellish them in the retelling.

His golden eyes were thoughtful. "I see. And do you not think Queen Dido was foolish in her actions? Might she not have done good to live on and continue to lead her people?"

I chewed my lip, thinking of how to answer that. His words seemed wise. Why shouldn't Dido have gone on? She was a queen. "It just seemed right what she did," I said finally, unsure how else to explain it. "It was sadder that way. And more beautiful."

To my astonishment, he laughed—a deep, ringing sound. "Continue with your studies, James," he said, and our meeting was ended.

As spring passed into summer, I grew determined to learn where the master went and what he did in the days between our meetings. Most often he went to Edinburgh, I knew, always late in the day and returning the next morning. From what scant crumbs Pietro dropped, I learned it was business that took the master to the city—though what sort of business it might be, my young mind could not guess.

At other times he took his horse and rode out across the lands of his manor, and we would not see him all the rest of the day, no matter if the weather was fair or foul. Then, past midnight, I would wake to the clatter of hooves in the courtyard, and I would look out my window to see Pietro limp forward and take the reins of his horse. He would stride into the manor, black cape fluttering, and sometimes it seemed to me he held something in his arms. One time he glanced up, his golden eyes fixed on the window through which I peered, and I quickly jumped back into bed, my heart pounding.

On the days he did not leave the manor, the master most often remained locked in his library. Usually he was alone, though some days horsemen arrived, coats spattered with mud, bearing papers sealed with wax, and Pietro would rush them into the library. Soon after they would depart with new papers, imprinted with the master's own seal. What was written upon those papers, I didn't know, but I would have given anything to try out my reading skills upon them.

It was Midsummer's Day—when the simple folk of village and croft venture out onto the hills, to the old standing stones, and leave offerings of the season's first fruit to forgotten gods—when the visitors came to Madstone Hall. They arrived just as the sun touched the western horizon, in a glossy black carriage drawn by fine horses. Three figures climbed from the carriage, all wreathed and hooded in rich black. One was slighter than the others, and wore a veil rather than hood, so I guessed it to be a woman beneath the shrouding attire.

I imagined a feast would be prepared for such obviously important guests, only then Pietro told me the servants had been commanded to their quarters, and that I, too, was to remain in my room. However, he seemed too preoccupied to lead me all the way to my chamber himself, and so—left to my own devices—I crept back downstairs and concealed myself in the manor's hall, in a corner behind a chair. Since I was a child, I had always found it simple to spirit myself into shadows and remain unseen, and my skill had not diminished in my time at the manor, for Pietro walked right past me as he opened the door of the master's library.

"They are here," he spoke through the open door.

"Send them in, Pietro," came the master's deep voice. "There is no use in delaying, I suppose."

A moment later three dark figures entered the hall. I shrank into the shadows behind the chair as they drew near, and a certainty grew in me that I did not want to be seen by them. There was something about the three—not a wickedness or malice, but all the same a kind of peril—that caused me to shudder. I bit my lip, lest a sound escape me.

As they drew even with the chair behind which I had concealed myself, one of the three—the slender one—paused. She turned her veiled head back and forth, and I felt the hair on my arms stand on end. Beneath the black veil, I caught two sharp glints of gold. Her gaze passed over the chair . . .

. . . then moved on. The three stepped into the library. Pietro shut the door. He pressed a trembling hand to his brow, then shuffled across the hall and was gone. Once he was out of sight, I bolted away like a rabbit who had just seen a fox—three foxes—and dashed up the stairs. I spent the rest of the evening in my chamber, and when I heard the sound of horses and the rattle of a carriage's wheels, I did not look out my window.

Although curiosity burned in me, neither Pietro nor the master spoke of the visitors the next day, and I did not dare to ask about them. I tried to occupy myself with my studies, but as the hours passed it grew harder and harder to concentrate on books and ink and quill pens. Would the master never tell me anything at all?

Because of my petulant sighs and inability to perform any meaningful work, Pietro dismissed me early from my studies. He gave me a sharp look, but I ignored him and went to my room. I felt bitter and lonely in a way I had not since the master plucked me from the streets of Edinburgh and brought me here. Why had he not revealed his purpose for me?

But perhaps there was no great purpose in his actions. As I paced before the window, I became more and more certain this was the case. I was simply a thing to him: a pretty object like those he had collected for the mantelpiece in his library.

I glanced at my reflection in the mirror. All traces of the scabs and bruises from my days on the street were gone. My golden hair framed my face, pale and delicate almost as a woman's, but with the first hints of a man's hard, square lines, and I knew with calm detachment that I was beautiful.

"If I am a thing to him," I murmured to the mirror, "then it is past time that he used me."

I would not have minded. While the master was not handsome—his face was too grim, too rough and angular—he was tall and strong, and I had sold myself to far worse on the street. I crept into his room and slipped naked into his bed, letting his rich smell encapsulate me. A warmth kindled inside my body, and I drifted into sleep.

"No, James, this is not what I wish from you," a voice, deep and soft said, awakening me.

I felt a weight beside me. Half in a dream, I reached for him, slipping my hand inside his robe. Gently, but firmly, he took my hand and pushed it away. I was too weary, too full of sadness, to resist. I wanted to lie on a fire, like Queen Dido, and let the beautiful flames burn away my sorrow. For the first time I could remember in my life, I wept.

I did not resist as he clothed me in a robe and carried me like a small child—lanky though I was getting—to my own bed. He pulled the covers over me, then laid a hand on my brow.

"You have more worth than this, James. More worth than you can possibly know."

I didn't know what to say. His words made me feel strange inside, as if a fish wriggled in me, lovely and silvery and sparkling, but much too slippery to grasp.

"Who were they?" I said instead. "The ones who came to the manor yesterday?" I thought of the golden eyes I had glimpsed beneath her veil. "They are the same as you."

He was silent for a long moment. "Yes," he said. "In the beginning at least. But now? I think we are no longer the same. Just as you are no longer the same as you were." He smoothed my hair back from my brow. "I think it is time we said farewell to James. He served you well on the streets of the city. He was strong and clever and brave, but you need him no longer."

My weeping ceased, and wonder crept into my chest. "If he is gone, who shall I be, then?"

"I believe you shall be Marius." He smiled. "Yes, that's a fine name. Marius Lucius Albrecht."

Sorrow faded away into the dark. A peace came over me. I was so tired, but it was a good feeling.

"Marius," I murmured, and fell asleep.

Though there is little I need tell of them now, those next five years were the richest and happiest of my life, both since and ever.

The majority of my time each day was spent in the comfortable confines of the manor's drawing room, learning of the marvels of language and mathematics, history, music, poetry, and philosophy, and the study of the heavens. At first Pietro was my constant and patient teacher, but after that first year I worked with other teachers as well: learned men and professors whom the master invited to Madstone Hall. They came from Edinburgh and Glasgow, or sometimes even from York or London.

Then, one spring morning, I entered the drawing room to discover neither Pietro nor some black-robed scholar waiting for me, but rather the master himself, his right hand—laden with rings—resting upon a book. The tome was thick, covered in worn leather decorated with tarnished symbols whose meanings I could not fathom, but which filled me all the same with anticipation.

The hint of a smile touched the master's usually stern mouth. My excitement had not gone unnoticed. "Pietro tells me you have made excellent progress in your studies, Marius. I am pleased. And I believe you are ready to begin a new subject— one I think you shall find of great interest."

Bees swarmed in my stomach. I did not know what was going to happen next, only that I was sure it would be wonderful. He gestured to an empty chair at the table, and I hurried to it and sat. As I held my breath the master opened the cover of the book, and that was when my education in the arcane arts began.

The book—which had no name other than the mysterious gold symbols on its cover—contained many chapters. We began that morning with the first, which concerned the art of astrology, then in time moved on to divination, runic lore, numerology, and other occult sciences. Fascinated as I was with each of these topics, always my eyes seemed to skip ahead, gauging the thickness of the book, and wondering what lore was contained in the yellowed pages of its final chapter.

It was some time before I found out. Far more often than not, when I entered the drawing room in the morning, I found Pietro or one of the black-robed scholars sitting at the table rather than the master. Doing my best to hide my disappointment, I would force myself to focus on the lesson at hand, and would try, though often without great success, not to wonder about the big leather-bound book with the gold symbols.

"Where is the master today?" I would ask if it was Pietro who was my teacher.

Always the answer was the same. Business had called the master out to one of the villages on his lands, or to Edinburgh, or sometimes even all the way to London. That last news always filled me with melancholy, for I knew it would be many days before the master returned, and that when he did he would be weary. Always he seemed pallid when he came back from London, and grimmer than usual, and he would have neither time nor energy for our studies together for many days.

Eventually, I learned the master kept the book of the occult in his library, for I saw it on the shelf one evening when he called me in to speak with him. However, even if I might have been tempted, I knew it would be folly to attempt to steal a glance at its pages. Certainly the master would know if I entered his library unbidden, and while his wrath had never been directed at me, I remembered the way he had, with a look, frozen the two men who had tried to harm me in Advocate's Close.

Fortunately, I had other activities to occupy me. On my sixteenth birthday—an anniversary that we had come to celebrate on the summer solstice, for we could only guess at my true age—the master gifted me with a horse. It was a handsome roan gelding, full of spirit, but gentle and forgiving with its young and inexperienced rider. I named the horse Hermes, for I imagined he would run very swiftly.

At the master's bidding, his stableman, Gerald, gave me

lessons in riding, and while he was neither as patient nor gentle as Hermes, before the summer was out I had skill enough that he left me to my own devices. Once released from my studies for the day, if the weather was even remotely fair, I would go out riding.

Sometimes I visited one of the villages that were beholden to the manor, but most often I kept to the bridle paths that led past field and croft, through copse and heather, over bridges and near standing stones, out to the open spaces. There Hermes and I would race across the moors, the wild wind whipping our manes—his of rusty red, mine of bright gold—and my blood would rush with a sensation I could not name. All I knew was that it made me feel strong, and bold, and pure.

One day Gerald saw me riding Hermes from a distance, and that night he swore to the master he had never seen a horse run so fast. I felt a childish pleasure, thinking simply that my horse was special, and that I was lucky to have him, and perhaps even deserving. The master gave me a sharp look, but I thought nothing of it—though I might have, if I could have seen the way my eyes sparked with green fire when I leaned over Hermes' neck, urging him swiftly over heath and down.

Winter was the hardest season for me to bear, for more days than not, once my morning studies were done, I could do no more than visit Hermes in the stable and watch the gray rain sheet down outside. Also, it seemed the master was gone more often in the winter, and when he was about Madstone Hall he was more likely than ever to be grim and silent.

As time passed, his trips away from the manor grew longer and more frequent, and I knew he was often gone to London. I did not ask Pietro what he did there, I knew he would not tell me, but I thought of the visitors with the golden eyes, and I was certain his trips had something to do with the three who had once come to the manor.

"Can I travel with you, Master?" I would ask each time I learned he was leaving for London.

"In time, Marius," he would say. "When the time is right, I will take you with me." Then he would open the book of occult lore to a new chapter, somewhere in the middle now, though as always my eyes strayed toward the end of the tome.

Seasons passed, and though I was happy and content, as I grew taller and broader, and the down on my chin and cheeks became a short beard as thick, gold, and curling as my hair, a shadow stole into Madstone Hall.

The shadow was faint at first, like a fleeting cloud that dimmed the light of a long June day, hinting at the cool purple of twilight to come. Sometimes I would round a corner and see the master leaning against a chair or balustrade, a hand pressed to his chest, his face gaunt. Then he would see me and smile, and at that rare gift all dark thoughts were dismissed.

On my eighteenth birthday, we walked together to one of the standing stones on the moor and, like the common folk, laid down our own offering of bread and wine. He gripped my arm as we made our way up the hill, and I was surprised at how thin his fingers felt against my arm, and how hot, but again it was easy to forget these things when he leaned against the stone and spoke in his deep voice of old gods now lost and forgotten.

"Where did the gods go?" I asked, pressing my palm against the weathered stone.

"Even I cannot say, Marius. Perhaps they returned to the world from whence they came."

His words caused me to shiver despite the warm midsummer evening. "What world do mean?"

He sighed. "Or perhaps they are no more."

"But a god cannot die," I said.

He gazed at his hands. "Even gods die, Marius, when they are old enough, and weary from the weight of long ages."

That was the first time I remember noticing the way the shadows gathered in the hollows of his cheeks. But it was only the failing light, I told myself, and we walked back down the hill, speaking of brighter things.

However, if in summer the shadow had been easy to dismiss, in the pale blue light of winter its effect was far harder to ignore. The master was always cold, and Pietro commanded the servants to keep great fires roaring in every fireplace in the manor, so that all of us shed our coats and vests and still sweated in our shirts. Yet the master would sit in a chair, clutching a blanket around him with thin fingers. Sometimes, as I passed the closed door of the library, I would hear Pietro speaking in urgent tones.

Never could I hear what he was saying, but it was clear that the old servant was pleading with the master, and that the master was refusing.

Then, one night when sleep eluded me, I ventured downstairs to fetch a glass of wine, and again I heard voices as I passed through the main hall. Only this time a wedge of yellow light fell through the door of the library; it stood ajar. I knew I should hurry on, but like some insect compelled by the light, I approached, moving silently over the carpeted floor.

"Do you have it, Pietro?" I heard the master speak as I drew close to the door. "I am sorry to make you do this thing, but I have not the strength to ride out myself."

"Yes, I have it. But it will do you little enough good, Master."

"Bring it here, Pietro."

I heard a whuffling noise, and a muffled squeal, almost like the cry of an infant. All at once the squeal ceased, replaced by the gurgling sound of liquid falling into a metal bowl.

"Give it to me," the master said, and his voice shook with an eager, hungry tone. There was a long pause, then the master sighed, a soft sound, at once satisfied and full of revulsion. "There, Pietro. You see? I am much better now."

I could envision Pietro's worried expression. "You should return to Crete, Master Albrecht. It has been long years since you have been to Knossos. You should leave this very night. You will be healed there."

"My good Pietro, all your life you have been loyal to me, since you were a boy, and you have received little in return. Always you have cared for me, and for that I thank you. But you know not what you speak. Life I might find if I were to return there, but not healing. This must be brought to an end, what we started long ago."

"But he is not ready, Master," Pietro said, his voice shaking. "There is so much more for him to learn."

At these words, a thrill ran through me. I drew closer to the door, daring to bend my head so that I could see through the gap with one eye, into the room beyond.

On the desk, still half-covered by the dark cloth that had wrapped it, was a suckling pig. The thing was dead, its neck slit open. A knife lay next to it, stained dark. The master still held the silver bowl that had caught its blood. His lips were tinged red.

"He knows more than you think, Pietro," the master said, and his golden eyes shifted, gazing toward the door.

I stumbled back, clamping my jaw shut to stifle a cry. It was impossible that he had seen me. The library was bright with fire and candle, and the hall outside where I had crouched was dark. While I had grown, I had not lost my boyhood ability to melt into shadows. All the same, as I stole back to my chamber, I knew I had been seen.

The next morning I found the master waiting for me when I entered the drawing room. I thought he wished to scold me for eavesdropping the night before, or perhaps to cast me out of the manor. Instead, he passed a hand over the worn cover of the book of the occult, then he opened it to the final chapter.

"Everything you have learned until now has been a prelude, Marius. Prelude for this—the most secret and profound of all arts."

"What is it?" I said, hardly daring to whisper.

"It has many names, in many different tongues. Some call it the Great Work, a name I prefer."

I bent over the book and read the word written in ornate script at the head of the chapter. It said, simply, Alchemy.

Our lesson lasted all that day, but the hours seemed to fly by as the master and I read together from the book. When that was done, I asked him question after question, listening to his deep voice as he answered, trying to drink in every word he spoke.

Grand and wonderful visions filled my head. I had always thought alchemists were rogues and charlatans who tricked people into thinking they could make gold out of lead. And most of them were. But there was a deeper art, more secret and precious. The transmutation of base metals was not the true goal of alchemy. Rather, transmutation was a symbol for something else—something greater and altogether more subtle than the making of gold. However, as people so often did, they found it more comfortable to think in literal rather than metaphoric terms.

"People would prefer to simply believe something blindly, rather than think about what it means, Marius. Yet in believing without question, they lose sight of the thing's deeper meaning, its true beauty and purpose."

I rested my chin on a hand, thinking about these words. "Sometimes, when I was young, I would creep through the doors of St. Giles and listen to the priests speak. They said the world was made in six days, but that's mad. What would days mean to God? It's just a story, that's all."

"No, Marius, not just a story. Stories can have great meaning, and thus great power as well. And the story of alchemy is one of the greatest stories of all."

A strange feeling filled me: excitement, wonder, and an ache of longing. "But what does it mean, Master?"

He shut the book. "That is enough for today, Marius. We will continue this lesson tomorrow."

However, the next morning Pietro told me the master was ill, and that I should go riding if I wished, for the late-winter day was fine and bright. I did go, but I hardly noticed the landscape as it blurred past, or the feeling of Hermes' strong back rising and falling beneath me.

I did not see the master the next day, or the next, but on the fourth day Pietro brought him from his chamber to a chair in the hall, where he might sit and receive some sun. He looked gray and brittle, like a tall tree withered by blight. All the same I went to him gladly, kneeling and laying my head on his lap, and though I craved to ask him more questions about the art of alchemy, a stern look from Pietro silenced me.

Nor were my questions answered as the weeks passed. Spring brought life back to the land, but not to the master of Madstone Hall. He spent more and more time in his chamber, allowing only Pietro to see to him, and when he did emerge his tall form was stooped. His dark hair had gone silver, and it occurred to me that perhaps the master was not ill, but rather was simply growing old. Yet how could age have come upon him so suddenly? When he took me in, he had been a man in his prime. Now he looked older than Pietro. His eyes, though, remained brilliant gold.

Then, one fine day in June, Pietro came to me in the drawing room. I was gazing at the book of the occult, which the master had left there after our last session together. I flipped through the pages, but my mind was dull, and mysteries that had seemed so clear when he explained them now confounded me as if I were the simplest child.

I looked up at the sound of Pietro's limping gait. An anguished light shone in his brown eyes. I shut the book and stood.

"You must go to him, Master Marius. He is waiting for you."

When I entered his chamber, I did not see him at once. So small he had become, so shrunken, that it took my eyes a moment to pick him out amid the tangled bedclothes. I sat beside the bed, taking his hand in mine. It felt as if I held a bundle of sticks.

"Master," I murmured, not knowing what else to say.

"It is your birthday, Marius," he said, and his voice was still deep and clear. "Yet I fear I will not be able to walk to the standing stone with you today."

My birthday? I had forgotten. I was nineteen. A man, I suppose, though at that moment I felt like a boy again, lost and frightened, crawling through the tunnels beneath Edinburgh.

"Why did you not go to Crete, Master?"

His gold eyes pierced me. "Why do you say such a thing, Marius?"

"I listened to you and Pietro speaking." The words poured out of me in guilt and misery. "He said you would be healed if you went to Knossos. I read about it in a book. It was the palace of King Minos, where the minotaur was imprisoned in the labyrinth."

His thin chest heaved in a sigh. "No, I cannot go there, Marius. Never again. It is ending for me at last. That is my choice."

Tears streamed down my cheeks; I felt no shame. "But why, Master? What lies there? Could I not go and fetch it for you?"

"No, Marius, do not seek it!" His voice was sharp, and his eyes flashed. "I thought, when I first found you in the city, that perhaps . . ." He shook his head. "But I was wrong. I want you to live your life, Marius. I've adopted you—the papers are complete. Madstone Hall is yours now. You must marry, and have children, and live your days to their fullest." A spasm passed through him. "And you must beware, Marius. Once I am gone, they will come. You must not trust them. I am sorry. There is so much I should have told you, and now there is no time."

"No, Master," I said, clutching his hand to me, kissing it, too full of despair to truly hear what he was saying. "No, you must not leave me. I still need you."

He smiled, and it was like sunlight upon my face. "My dear Marius. Everything you need is right here."

His hand touched my chest, lightly, then fell to the bed-covers. A soft breath escaped him, and I watched as his eyes changed from gold to lead gray, as if the alchemy of life had been worked in reverse. I sat with him for a time, my hand upon his brow. Then, as the evening sky caught fire outside the window, I went to tell Pietro he was dead.

The weeks that followed remain dim to me. Pietro brought me food, but I do not remember eating it. I rose before dawn each morning, but I do not recall sleeping. Every day I walked to the grave on the hill behind the manor, but I have no recollection of when it was dug. There was no marker, save for the ancient standing stone we used to visit together, its pitted surface without writing, worn of memory long ago by wind and rain.

I spent much of my time wandering the manor, as if I were the ghost. It seemed I was searching for something. However, what it was I could not name, and I did not find it, though I looked everywhere for it. Everywhere, that was, except for one room. I would drift toward the library, as if compelled by an unseen force, but at the last moment I would pull my hand from the knob and turn away.

Somewhere in the mists I remember men coming to the manor, dressed in the black frock coats of lawyers. They brought me papers and told me to sign them, which I did without reading, and when I was done they said I was now the lord of Madstone Hall. I asked Pietro what that meant, and he said not to worry, that the master had hired men in Edinburgh who would see to the legal and business affairs of the manor.

"Your only goal is to continue your studies, Master."

"You should not call me that," I said, and went to saddle Hermes.

But riding my horse could not calm my mind, and I would go

back to wandering the manor. However, as time honed the moon of October to a thin sickle, I realized I was not searching after all. Rather, I was waiting. Waiting for something to come. For someone.

Then, on All Hallows Eve, which the folk of the villages still called the Feast of the Slaughter, they came. I stood at the window in the master's chamber—I had taken to sleeping there, at Pietro's request, though in my mind it was still his room— watching as the village folk set torches to great wooden wheels and rolled them down the sides of hills. The common folk believed that the borders between the world of the living and the world of the spirits grew thin on this night, and that demons and ghosts might slip through cracks from one realm to the next. Thus they lit great blazes to scare the spirits away.

"Master," Pietro said behind me. I had not heard him enter. "Master, they have . . . you have visitors. Shall I send them away?"

I did not need to look at him to know he was trembling. Outside, the fiery wheels blazed down the hills. They looked like golden eyes, gazing at me from the night.

"No, Pietro. I will meet them in the drawing room."

The old servant started to protest, but I turned and gave him a sharp look, and I could see the sparks of green reflected in his own startled eyes. He bobbed his head and hurried from the chamber.

Standing before a mirror, I donned a coat of brown velvet, then bound my hair with a ribbon. My gold beard, thick and full, lent me years beyond the nineteen I possessed, as did the grim expression I wore, which to my amazement reminded me of his own. I looked lordly enough, and only hoped I could feel the same, that I might hold my own against them.

When I stepped into the drawing room, a man and a woman rose from two chairs by the fire. They were not dressed in black, and the pair gazed at me with curious eyes of blue and brown, not gold. Such was my shock that I staggered, gripping the newel post at the foot of the stairs for support.

"Hello, Marius," the woman said. She was not young—near

forty perhaps—and fine lines marked her face, but she was still handsome and lithe in her green gown.

"You may address me as Lord Albrecht."

She winced, perhaps mistaking the sharpness in my voice for a note of authority rather than fear.

"We are gladdened to finally have the opportunity to meet you, my lord," the man said. He was much younger than the woman, though less handsome. He was tall but spindly, like a plant grown in a dark closet. All the same, his blue eyes were bright with humor, and his broad grin was genuine and infectious, putting me somewhat at ease.

"And what was preventing our meeting before?" I said.

They exchanged uneasy glances, and I felt my dread recede further. I was at the advantage here, not they. They wanted something—something the master had not granted them. And, now that he was gone, they thought they could get it from me.

For some reason a boldness came over me, and I began a dangerous game. "I know why you've come." I gestured for them to sit. They did, and I took a chair opposite them. Pietro had left glasses of sherry for each of us, and I picked one up. "In fact, I'm surprised it took you so long."

The man grinned at the woman. "It's just as I said, Rebecca. He's heard of us. I told you he would already know all about the Seekers." He picked up his own sherry glass and took a drink.

Seekers. I had never heard the word before, at least not in the sense that the man seemed to use it.

"Hush, Byron," the woman said, not touching her own glass. She turned her brown eyes on me. "So you know of us."

I shrugged, as if this required no reply, when in fact I was burning to ask questions. All the same, I was certain I'd learn more if I did not ask them. The man, Byron, seemed talkative enough, but I sensed the woman, Rebecca, would not be so easy to maneuver around.

"I know Master Albrecht often went to London on business with the Seekers," I said. This was a calculated guess; their accents were English, not Scottish.

Byron laughed. "Well, his business was not so much with us as with the Philosophers, of course. They always keep to themselves. I've never even met one in person." He winked at me.

"We Seekers are just their lackeys, you see, and they don't associate much with us mere mortals."

"Byron!" the woman said sternly, and his grin vanished as he sank back into his chair.

The man's words fascinated me. Who were these Philosophers he spoke of? By Rebecca's tone, they were not people to be trifled with. However, I forced my expression to remain neutral.

"Is there something I can do for you?" I said.

Rebecca smoothed the green fabric of her gown. "I hope instead it is the opposite, my lord. I will be plain with you, for I can see there is no need for pretense here. We have never met, but we know a good deal about you. We know you have proven adept at the occult arts, and that you have certain other talents as well—skills our organization is in need of. Thus we have come to extend you an invitation."

This startled me so greatly I forgot to appear disinterested. "An invitation?"

"Yes, my lord," Byron said, and while Rebecca frowned at him, this time she did not preempt his words. "We'd like you to come to London with us, to join our order."

Realization came to me. "To join the Seekers," I murmured.

"Indeed, my lord," Rebecca said, meeting my eyes.

Speech fled me. I was right. These two had come to Madstone Hall seeking something of the master's. Only it wasn't a book or an arcane object. It was I they were seeking. But why? I was clever, I knew, but surely any talents such as I possessed could readily be found in London. I doubted they were forced to trek all the way up to the northlands for fresh recruits.

They gazed at me expectantly now, but what could I say? Despite my little charade, I knew nothing of the Seekers, yet I dared not ask them about their organization now for fear I would be revealed. I knew I should tell them to be on their way, that I had no interest in their invitation.

Only, little as I knew at that moment, I *did* have interest.

You must beware, Marius. Once I am gone, they will come. You must not trust them. . . .

But surely the master had meant the gold-eyed ones, not those two people. They were curious, to be sure, but not strange and forbidding as the three strangers had been. They were, as Byron had said, merely mortals. What harm could they bring to me?

Yet surely, from all they've said, the ones with the golden eyes are their masters—these Philosophers they spoke of, the ones the master so often went to London to see, and who came once to visit him here.

Which meant Master Albrecht himself had been one of them. Only what did it mean? He had said not to trust them, yet he was one of their kind. I needed more time—time to decide what to do.

"It grows late," I said. "You must be weary from your journey. I will have Pietro ready rooms for you. We can discuss this on the morrow."

Byron quaffed the rest of his sherry, his expression affable, but Rebecca gave me a cool look. "As you wish, Lord Albrecht."

I shivered, wishing I had not told them to call me that, and without another word rose and left the drawing room.

"You must send them away in the morning," Pietro said as he turned down the bedcovers in my chamber. His hands shook. "Please Mast . . . please, Marius. For him, you must do it."

"Good night, Pietro," I said, and I did not look at him as he shuffled from the chamber.

I did not undress and lie down in the bed. Instead I sat in a chair, watching as a beam of moonlight crept across the darkened room. Then, when I was sure midnight had come and gone, I slipped through the door and passed, silent as a wraith, down the stairs and through the manor's main hall, toward a door at the far end.

The library. Not since he died had I entered that room, but now I opened the door without sound, stepped inside, and shut the portal behind me. With my dark-adjusted eyes I could see all was exactly as he had left it. A thick shroud of dust covered the desk and mantelpiece. Even Pietro had not been in there.

I dared to light a single candle, then sat at the desk. It felt strange to sit in his chair, yet not altogether wrong. I hesitated, then one by one opened the drawers of the desk. I knew not what I sought, only that it was there, and that I would recognize it once I found it. There were sheaves of parchment, feathered quills, a small knife for trimming pen tips, bottles of ink, and sealing wax. Mundane things. Then, in the last drawer I found it, just as I had been sure I would—a silver key.

Standing, I gazed around the library. There—in all my visits to that room I had never seen it before. I suppose my attention had always been on him, but for the first time my eyes seemed to seek it out: a small cabinet lurking in a corner behind a globe of the Earth. I moved to it.

The cabinet was plain, save for a single keyhole. The key fit, and I opened the doors. Inside were two shelves. One held a row of books. The other contained stacks of papers, as well as a small wooden box.

The writing on the spines of the books made little sense to me, though it was clear from flipping through them that all pertained to various magical arts—with the exception of the art of alchemy. Interesting, perhaps, but they could tell me nothing that might help me just then. The loose papers were no more illuminating. From what I could tell they referred to various business dealings—deeds and notes and the like, that was all.

My eyes fell again upon the box. It was small and quite plain, without latch or lock. All the same, for some reason I trembled as I lifted it, and I opened the lid with fumbling fingers.

There were two things in the box, resting on a silk cushion. The first thing was a book. It was very small, like a personal prayer or chapbook, its brittle pages sewn together with gold thread. The second thing was a small glass vial. The vial's stopper was made of gold as well, and had been wrought with great skill into the shape of a spider, its abdomen inlaid with a single ruby. I lifted the vial. It was filled with a dark, viscous fluid that I knew at once to be blood.

I sat at the desk with the box and removed the little book. Clearly it was more ancient than anything else in the library. Its cover was made of a thin piece of yellowed wood, incised with strange symbols arranged in a circle; its pages crackled as I turned them, flecks of dust swirling up to glow like sparks in the light of the candle.

As the hours of the night stole by, I pored over the little book. Its pages were filled with archaic words composed in a spidery hand, and my head ached as I tried to decipher what they meant. Unlike the others, this book was about alchemy, that much was clear. It seemed to be some sort of diary, written by a man early in the fifth decade of his life, telling the tale of his quest for the Philosopher's Stone: an object that could transmute metals into their perfect state—gold.

Only it was more than that. It was as my master had said; the Great Work was a story, a metaphor. From what I could make out, it was not simply base metals this alchemist sought to transmute. It was himself. The Philosopher's Stone could bring anything to perfection— even human flesh.

"Immortality," I murmured. "He was seeking immortality."

But who was it who had written this journal so long ago? I turned to the last page, and there at the bottom was inscribed his signature. Breath escaped me as I stared at the words.

Martin Adalbrecht, Anno Domini MDCVII

No, it couldn't be. This diary had been penned in 1607. Which would mean he was over one hundred years old when I met him five years earlier, though he had looked no older than forty. Only that couldn't be so.

My brain worked feverishly as I flipped back through the crumbling pages as quickly as I dared. There had to be answers within the book. The two Seekers had spoken of the Philosophers, and the master had been one of their order, of that there could be no doubt. The name the Philosophers gave themselves could not be a coincidence; surely there was some connection between them and the Philosopher's Stone. But what was it? And what did it have to do with the island of Crete and the ancient palace of Knossos?

A soft sound reached my ears. At once I blew out the candle. Silence, then came another noise: a soft thump, followed by a hiss of breath. Though it was dark, my eyes had adjusted, and I could see easily. I shut the book, placed it with the vial in the box, and closed the lid. Tucking the box in the breast pocket of my coat, I moved to the cabinet, locked it, then returned the key to the desk. I paused by the door of the library, listening, then opened it a crack and peered through.

Two dark figures moved in the dimness of the hall, one petite, the other tall and gangly. So perhaps I was not the only thing they had come searching for after all. The two groped their way across the hall, moving toward the library door. I wondered if I should sneak past—I would be no more than a silent shadow to their senses—or if I should confront them.

Before I could decide, a light appeared in the arched doorway at the far end of the hall, accompanied by the sound of shuffling steps. The two figures tensed, then darted through a side door and were gone. A moment later Pietro entered the hall, carrying an oil lamp. He gazed about, his dark eyes glittering with suspicion, then turned and headed back the way he had come. I took the chance to slip from the library and return to my chamber. It mattered not to me if the two returned to their late-night searching, for I was confident that I now carried in my pocket the very thing they had been sent to find.

The next morning I met the Seekers at breakfast and inquired after the quality of their rest. The dark circles under their eyes belied their polite replies; they had not slept. Nor had I, but I felt strangely fresh and awake. I knew what I had to do. He had said not to trust them, and nor would I. But there was so much I had to learn, things he should have taught me himself. I savored the look of shock on their faces when I told Rebecca and Byron that I would accept their invitation.

"I will journey with you to London at once," I said. "We shall depart this very day."

The surprise and satisfaction on Rebecca's face gave way to a look of perturbation. She knew her late-night wanderings had been detected, and she would have no chance to repeat them. All the same, a moment later she managed a smile that seemed not altogether counterfeit.

"We are fortunate indeed, my lord."

"Call me Marius," I said.

Two hours later, I stood before the manor beneath a leaden sky, watching as Rebecca and Byron climbed into the waiting coach. The luggage was already strapped atop, and the driver was ready.

"We shall await your return, Master Marius," Pietro said. A chill wind howled from the north, and the old servant shook.

I rested a palm against his withered cheek. "Dear Pietro," I said, then climbed into the coach.

The driver cracked the reins, and the coach lurched into motion. I turned in the seat and watched until the manor was lost from view. It would be many long years before I would return to Madstone Hall, and I never saw Pietro again.

"This is all terribly exciting, Marius," Byron said. The two Seekers sat on the bench opposite me. "You won't regret joining us. There's so much for you to discover."

"Yes," I said, noticing Rebecca's eyes were on me. "Yes, there is."

I am afraid I must now leap ahead in my tale, for it has taken me much longer to set down this account of my first two decades than I had imagined. However, I believe it was vital for you to see how I was made in my early years—for otherwise, when at last you reach the end, you might not understand why I chose as I did. Why I chose differently than Master Albrecht. And while I have had more time to pen this journal than at first I dared hope—it seems even eyes of gold do not always see clearly—the hour now grows late. Thus I will fly over those next years of my life, to a gray autumn day in London when once again my world was changed forever.

The year was now 1679, and at five-and-twenty years of age I was a man grown into his full power, yet still filled with vigor and optimism that the harshness of the world had not yet had time to wear away. As an order, the Seekers were much the same. Founded in A.D. 1615, the Seekers—like myself at the time—were just coming into their own.

The fractious early years, in which the order was little more than a motley collection of wild-eyed alchemists scrabbling for the secret of making gold in filthy, smoke-hazed dungeons, had been left behind, and already the organization would have been recognizable to a modern-day Seeker. The Age of Discovery and the Renaissance were giving way to an Age of Reason, and thus we chose a scientific approach.

The ideas of transmutation and the Philosopher's Stone—a mystical catalyst that could bring about the instantaneous achievement of perfection in anything it touched—were thrown in the dustbin along with the ashes of myth and superstition. The Seekers had undergone their own Reformation, and while the order was founded on a belief in the existence of magic—a core conviction we had not rescinded—it was agreed we would approach the subject not with flights of fancy, but rather with logic and cold rationalism. Evidence that pointed to an other-worldly origin of magical forces on Earth was already mounting, and by the time I entered the Seekers the order's focus was steadily being directed toward a single goal: the discovery of worlds other than this Earth.

It was an intoxicating notion, and at the time not so out-landish as it might seem today. Before the discovery of the Americas, people had believed a ship that sailed too far west would fall off the edge of the world. However, Columbus, da Gama, and Magellan had proven otherwise. So who was to say there were not other New Worlds waiting to be discovered? Ex-cept to find them, one would indeed have to sail over the edge of the Earth. And we thought we were the ones to do it.

Master Albrecht had warned me not to trust the ones who would come after he died, and while I did not entirely forget his words, I kept them at the fringes of thought. Surely his concern was with the Philosophers—the result of some old argument or misunderstanding with his peers—and while they were purport-edly the leaders of the Seekers, it quickly became clear they were a distant authority at best. Rebecca and Byron had never seen the Philosophers themselves; in fact, I soon realized that none of the Seekers had. The Philosophers communicated with them only through letters sealed by wax and imprinted with their sigil—a hand holding three flames—and never appeared in person.

I considered telling Rebecca and Byron of the time the three with golden eyes had come to Madstone Hall, but decided against it. The last thing I wished was for something that would mark me as different. I had never had a family. My mother, the Gilroys in their silent mausoleum, Master Albrecht and Pietro—all had offered comfort in some way. However, none had been able to provide that all-encompassing sense of inclusion I now felt. The Seekers were my first true family, and I embraced them with all my might.

Those first months were filled with constant wonder and delight. The Seekers worked to discover new worlds, but I felt as if I already had, as if Rebecca and Byron had pulled aside a curtain woven in the dull grays and greens of Scotland and shown me the gilded door to a fantastical land I had never dreamed existed. London was grand and glorious, so full of life and beauty and grand squalor that it made Edinburgh look like one of the backward villages huddled around Madstone Hall.

Once my initial astonishment at my new life was complete, I threw myself into my work as a journeyman Seeker. Rebecca had not lied; my talents were indeed perfectly suited to the organization. I had a zeal for both ancient and modern knowledge, and a keen curiosity; but then, so did many of the Seekers. What caused me to excel was my ability to combine these skills with the instincts I had acquired on the streets of Edinburgh. Just as I had been able to sense which passages beneath the old city led upward to light and which plunged into darkness, I was often able to discern the avenues of investigation that would bear fruit from those that were dead ends before concrete evidence favored one over the other.

"You rise more quickly in the order than even I believed you would," Rebecca said one evening as we lay entwined together on her bed.

We had become lovers not long after our arrival in London. It was not a serious affair. Both of us were far too interested in our work to devote our hearts to another. All the same, our match was a good one. I was tall and handsome, and she had made it clear during the long journey to London that she favored my look. In turn, I found her mature flavor of beauty alluring.

For all my work as a youth in Edinburgh, I had never lain with a woman, but that suited Rebecca well enough. We spent many hours in her chamber, on the upper floor of a small but comfortable house near Covent Garden, in which she taught me the art of making love. And when our bodies were pleasantly spent, we would engage our minds instead, drinking wine as we sat half-naked on the bed, speaking long into the night about modern science, and philosophy, and the nature of our vocation as Seekers.

I learned much from Rebecca, and perhaps more than she knew—though I suppose she might have said the same of me, for it is hard not to become at least a little vulnerable in the arms of a lover. Still, I think each of us guarded our inner hearts from the other.

I thought little about the life I had left behind in Scotland. Letters came from Madstone Hall—many at first, but fewer as time went on. I paid them little heed, and so I did not notice when they stopped coming altogether. I had no time for such cares. I threw myself into my work by day, while at night, if I was not in Rebecca's bed, I could be found in one of London's more raucous pubs with Byron—whose jovial company I had come to greatly enjoy—along with a band of the Seekers' best and brightest young men.

Once I made the mistake of letting Byron take me to the Cup and Leaf on a night that Rebecca was expecting me. When I tried to beg my leave, the boys grabbed my coat and hauled me back down to the bench.

"Where did you think you're going, Marius?" Richard Mayburn said. "You've had but a single ale." Richard was a short, stout, red-haired young man who won every drinking bout he entered.

"I have somewhere to go," I said, glancing at the window in hopes of a glimpse of the moon, knowing I was already late.

Byron gave me a sharp look. "By Zeus, you've got a woman waiting for you, don't you, Marius? You sly cur."

My blush was all the answer he needed and elicited whoops of laughter all around.

"So who is this tasty little trollop?" Richard said with an exaggerated leer. "And better yet, are you going to share her?"

"Not with the likes of you, Richard Mayburn," said a cool voice.

We turned as one to see Rebecca stride across the pub. All eyes were on her, for she was out of place, but wonderfully so, like a dove in the midst of a flock of grackles. The smoky light softened the lines of her face, and her wine colored gown accentuated the curves of her body.

"What on Earth are you doing here, Rebecca?" Byron hissed. "This is no place for a lady."

"I've only come to fetch what's mine," she said, laying a hand on my shoulder.

Byron's eyes bulged, and Richard let out a loud guffaw.

"Good show, Marius," the red-haired man said, grinning. "Every man in the Seekers has tried to woo Rebecca and failed miserably, and now you've succeeded. What's next? I suppose you'll be telling us you've seen the Philosophers themselves."

In the humor of the moment, caution fled me. "I won't keep it a secret from you any longer, gentlemen. The man I dwelled with in Scotland—"

"Was purported to have seen the Philosophers once," Rebecca smoothly cut me off. Her grip on my shoulder tightened, her fingers digging in. "Yes, so we learned before we came to see you, Marius. Though it's just a tale, that's all."

I looked up. Rebecca's brown eyes glinted in the lamplight. Did she know that Master Albrecht had once been one of them? Byron and the others clearly did not, for their eyes went wide at her words, and they plied me with many questions about my former master. However, I kept my answers short, for I could feel Rebecca's gaze upon me, and told them only that he had been an enigmatic gentleman who had taken me in as an orphan and about whom I learned little before he died. It was true enough.

Not long after that night, my affair with Rebecca cooled. I went to her house with diminishing frequency, and we seldom shared her bed when I did. All the same, our partnership within the Seekers seemed stronger than ever, and we often worked together in our investigations. So often, in fact, that I fear Byron grew a bit jealous.

Byron was a good lad, but he was woefully unskilled with women. Somehow, when he tried to speak with them, he always ended up with ale in his face. While the Seekers have had female members from the start, in that time Rebecca was something of a rarity, for I had met no other lady Seekers. Thus it was only natural that Byron should be somewhat fixated upon her; she was the one woman he could speak with and not end up all wet. I feared he would grow angry upon learning of my affair with Rebecca. However, such was his good nature that he said nothing of it, and he remained as jovial a companion as always at pub.

I continued to rise in my career as a Seeker, and in only my fourth year as a journeyman I achieved a significant breakthrough. It was chance, really, that I came upon it at all, but my instincts alerted me that something was not as it seemed, and further investigation proved my hunch.

Near the house where I rented a room, little more than a stone's throw from the Tower of London, was a bookshop I often haunted for its unusual and varied collection of volumes, especially relating to history. I often engaged in cordial conversation with the proprietor of the shop, a fine, white-bearded gentleman who went by the name of Sarsin. When he learned of my love for Virgil's *Aeneid*, he clucked his tongue.

"The Roman poets were little more than thieves of the Greeks," he said, then rummaged through his shelves and came up with many classic works of ancient Greece. After that, much of the wage the Seekers paid me went directly into Sarsin's coffers, and I spent many hours sitting by the Thames, poring over the poetry of Homer and the tragedies of Aeschylus, Sophocles, and Euripides.

It was when I moved on to the works of Shakespeare that I began to grow suspicious. Sarsin claimed that his uncle, who had owned the shop before him, had known the Bard, for he had often come into the shop. I did not doubt that. However, more than once, when recounting these stories, Sarsin spoke as if he were the one who had met Shakespeare, rather than his uncle.

The shop owner was likely daft, I told myself. Yet I didn't quite believe that, and my investigations soon proved I was right. Sarsin claimed that, like Shakespeare, his uncle had been something of a poet, and I convinced him to show me some of his uncle's work, and to even lend me a yellowed piece of parchment with one particular song.

That night, I compared the handwriting of the song to that on the receipts Sarsin had written for me when I purchased books. There was no doubting it; both documents had been written by the same hand. Certain I was onto something, I began to question the oldest folk I could find on the lanes around the bookshop, and I soon found an old woman, quite blind now but still sharp of wit, who recalled the former proprietor of the shop. She described him as a handsome, elderly man with a white beard, thinning hair, and bright blue eyes.

It was Sarsin, of course. Not the fantastical uncle, but the one and only. Research into the city's legal records confirmed what by then I already knew. Every fifty years or so, the owner of the Queen's Shelf "died" and left the shop to his heir. However, though the names changed, the handwriting of the signatures on the deeds was always the same. There was only one answer: The man Sarsin had owned this shop for over a century and a half, and in that time he had not aged a day.

Excited, I reported my findings to Rebecca and Quincy Farris, our superior in the order, and that was when I entered into my first argument with the Seekers, for Farris foolishly decided to approach Sarsin. This was strictly against the First Desideratum, of course; the Nine Desiderata were set down in the Book by the Philosophers, and every Seeker, upon joining the order, swore a Vow to uphold them. However, Farris was an ambitious man—overly so—and no doubt he thought by winning over Sarsin he could seize this finding from me and claim it for his own, thus furthering his rise in the Seekers.

His action had the opposite effect; Farris was stripped of his rank as master and banished from the order. He hanged himself by the neck in a filthy shack in Cheapside a week later. Unfortunately, his death could not undo the damage he had caused, for now Sarsin was alerted to the Seekers, and he would have no conversations with any of us, myself included. The Sarsin case was closed, and all associated documents sealed in the vaults of the Seekers. There they were forgotten—though I did retain a copy of Sarsin's song for my personal collection. It captured my fancy for a reason I couldn't quite name, particularly the final verse:

> *We live our lives a circle,*
> *And wander where we can.*
> *Then after fire and wonder,*
> *We end where we began.*

Though Farris's meddling bungled the case beyond repair, my work in discovering the Sarsin matter did not go unnoticed, and in the summer I was elevated to the rank of master— the same rank as Rebccca, and ahead of Byron, who was still a journeyman, though the good-natured fellow seemed to hold nothing but genuine satisfaction for me. We celebrated with much ale, and everything in my world was good beyond my dreams. Then, on that dull autumn day in 1679, though I had no way of knowing at the time, the seeds for my undoing were sown.

"I believe you'll enjoy this particular assignment," Rebecca said as she tossed me a folded square of parchment. It was the first of October, a thick layer of mist cloaked London, and we had retreated into the warm, crowded interior of a coffeehouse in Covent Garden to escape the chill.

"What is it?" I asked, catching the paper and turning it over. It was sealed with a circle of red wax. Imprinted in the wax was a picture of a hand holding three flames.

"How should I know?" she said, arching an eyebrow. "It's from the Philosophers themselves."

Byron leaned over the table, his blue eyes bright. "Go on, Marius. Open it."

Although I was every bit as eager as Byron, I forced myself to break the seal slowly. I unfolded the letter, then scanned the contents. They were written in a thin, elegant hand.

"What a dreadful burden," Rebecca crooned in a tragic voice. "You're to follow a noble lady about town and keep an eye on her. I've heard she's quite lovely. Poor Marius."

I glared at her over the letter. "Prevaricator. You knew all along what my new assignment was to be."

Rebecca smirked and sipped her chocolate.

"Following a lovely lady?" Byron said in a wounded voice, reaching for the letter. "Why did I not get this assignment?"

"Because I'm the master," I said with a laugh and tucked the letter inside my velvet waistcoat before he could snatch it away. I rose. "Now, if you'll both excuse me, it seems I have work to do."

Despite my nonchalant air, my heart pounded as I walked

from the coffeehouse and turned down a narrow lane. This was my first assignment since being elevated to the level of master in the Seekers, and my first to come directly from the Philosophers themselves. I had expected something interesting, even remarkable, but this surpassed anything I had imagined. And despite her arch manner, I doubted Rebecca knew everything that was contained in the letter.

I was to keep watch on a fairy.

Or a half-fairy, at least. I ducked into a green, quiet space protected by stone walls: the courtyard of St. Paul's Church. This was not Christopher Wren's grand cathedral, which was still under construction. Rather, it was a small church built by Inigo Jones, and to me looked more like a forgotten Greek temple than a Christian holy house. I sat on a bench beneath a drooping wisteria tree to read the letter again.

According to the information the Philosophers had given me, fairies were not mystical creatures that inhabited children's stories and Shakespearean comedies; instead, they were unearthly beings, born of another world. And while the Philosophers knew of no true fairies on this Earth, they had encountered a few individuals who bore some fraction of fairy blood in their veins.

Who these otherworldly people were and where they could be found, the letter did not say. If the Philosophers knew, they had not deemed it necessary to relate this information. What the letter did say was that there was a young noble lady—one Alis Faraday—who, unbeknownst to herself or her parents, was descended from one of these half fairies. How it could be that the young lady and her parents were unaware of her fantastical heritage was also not explained. All the letter told me was to observe this lady, keeping notes on everything I saw and heard, while adhering to the Desiderata, especially the first: *A Seeker shall not interfere with the actions of those of otherwordly nature.*

At all costs, the letter closed, *this young lady must never learn from you or any Seeker her true nature. For it is the purpose of this study to determine if one of otherwordly nature, who is unaware of this fact about herself, will—through her own volition, intuition, and power—come to learn of her unique her-*

*itage, or if she can be content to live as any other denizen of this
Earth, with no knowledge of her inherent strangeness.*

I drew a breath to steady myself, then tucked the letter into
my coat and stood up from the bench.

"Be careful, Marius."

I turned as Rebecca descended several stone steps, into the
courtyard. Her gown was a gray so dark it was nearly black; she
looked like a mourner, headed to church to weep for one lost.

"Rebecca," I said, and left it there, for I could think of nothing to say to her. The words of the letter burned in my brain, as
if writ there with fire.

She moved under the canopy of the wisteria; the mist had
turned to rain. "An assignment from the Philosophers should
not be taken lightly. You are no journeyman now. A master may
be placed at far more risk. There is peril before you."

"What risk is there in watching a young lady, Rebecca?"

"I'm not certain." Her lips formed a sharp smile. "No, Marius, I don't know all that is contained in that letter—only what
the Philosophers relayed to me themselves, and that is little. I
have no particular reason to worry for your safety. But guard
yourself all the same."

There was genuine concern in her eyes. However, I was too
excited to listen to her words. There was a person in this city
with true otherworldly connections, and I was going to observe
her. Perhaps, as she discovered her own heritage, I would learn
as well—learn things that would help me find a way to another
world. For by then I had already determined that I was going to
be the first to accomplish what the Seekers had set out to do: to
journey to a world other than this Earth. Master Albrecht had
warned me not to trust these people, but I knew how I could be
certain they would never rule me; I would rule them instead. I
was going to be the greatest Seeker the order had ever known.

"Good-bye, Rebecca," I said, and hurried from the courtyard.

I began my work that afternoon, examining public records
and making inquires about the city—though I was never too direct in my questioning, so as not to draw attention. With little effort I learned that the Faradays were an old, wealthy, and
respectable family, if not particularly remarkable in London

society. They dwelled in a fine but not opulent house a half mile beyond Nottingham Hall, and less than two miles from the Houses of Parliament. There the current Lord Faraday, William, sat in the House of Lords, the third in his line to do so.

Lady Beatrice Faraday had been born to a less wealthy, but still well-regarded, family from York. Young Lady Alis, who was in her twenty-third year, was their only daughter, and was rumored to be quite beautiful, as Rebecca had said, though it seemed she was seldom seen outside the family's home.

That was going to make things difficult. How was I to observe her if she never left her home? As I sat in a tavern that night, letting the ale I had ordered languish, I unfolded the letter from the Philosophers. However, despite much rereading, the letter contained no more clues, and I was not going to go to the Philosophers to beg for help on my first assignment as a master.

With nothing else I could do, I rose the next morning and put on my finest clothes, gathering my blond hair into a ribbon in the current fashion so that I might pass for one of London's many fine young lords. Of course, that would not be a complete fraud, for I *was* a lord. Madstone Hall was mine, though I thought of it seldom, and while I had not been born a noble, by Master Albrecht's dying hand I had been made one, and in truth the look suited me.

I hired the finest stallion I could find, though the beast was nothing compared to my old horse Hermes, and rode out past Whitehall, trading the gray air of the city for sun and blue sky.

After asking directions of a band of workmen, I found my way to the Faraday estate, which lay down a lane bordered by tall hedgerows. It was not so grand as Madstone Hall, being rather squat and square in the Tudor style, but it looked comfortable, nestled between a grove of ash and beech on one side and a pond on the other.

I dismounted and approached the iron gate, which was closed, refining my story in my head: how I was a young lord from Scotland visiting family in London, and while out riding I had lost my way, and so required directions for the way back to Whitehall. I hoped the steward of the house would be polite enough to invite me in for a refreshment, and I would gain a glimpse, perhaps in a portrait, of young Lady Alis. I reached up to ring the bell hanging on the gate.

"Good day, my lord."

I nearly leaped out of my boots. Seldom could a person come upon me unawares, but so intent had I been on my plan that I had not heard as someone approached me from behind. I turned on a heel, and at once my apprehension vanished. It was simply an old woman, clad in a servant's frock. There was nothing remarkable about her, save that her green eyes were bright and her wrinkled cheeks as red as apples.

"Is there something I can do for you, my lord?" She drew closer, holding a covered basket.

I gave her a simplified version of my story; there was no need to explain myself to a servant. She nodded, listening to my tale, then smiled.

"I can give you directions back to Whitehall easily enough, my lord."

A coldness descended in my chest. This would not do. I needed to gain entrance to the manor, in hopes of seeing a painting of Alis Faraday. I had to know what she looked like. Before I could speak, she went on.

"But are you certain it is not directions to Westminster Abbey you would rather have, my lord?"

"Westminster Abbey?" I said. "Why should I ride there?"

"Why, to gain a look at young Lady Alis, of course."

I felt my face blanch, and a sickness filled me. How could this old woman know of my true purpose there? It seemed impossible, but if she did, then I was already ruined.

She clucked her tongue. "Now there, my lord, no need to fear. You're hardly the first young man who's ridden to the gate hoping for a glimpse of Lord Faraday's daughter. Surely you didn't dress so finely simply for a ride in the country! But you'll not find Lady Alis here this morning."

What a fool I was. Of course this old woman knew nothing of my purpose there. She had simply assumed, and not so far from the truth. However, I saw no reason to correct her.

"And where might one find Lady Alis on a morning such as this?"

"I've already told you, my lord, and more than I should have.

But I daresay you have a different look about you than the other young men who come to call." Her green eyes grew sharp. "Quite different indeed."

I had no notion what her words meant, but I realized the woman had indeed told me where to go.

"How shall I know her?"

The old servingwoman laughed. "A beautiful young noblewoman should not be difficult to pick out from the crowd, my lord. Then again, one cannot always trust one's eyes." She opened the gate a fraction, slipped through, and shut it behind her.

"Please," I said, gripping the bars, not knowing what else to say.

Again the old woman's gaze grew sharp, and after a moment she nodded. "She favors the sun in the Cloisters."

It was midday when I reached Westminster Abbey.

I straightened my coat as I passed through the western doors, into the long hall of the nave. Columns soared to the arched ceiling high above, and despite the urgency of my quest I was forced to pause and gaze upward. It is the purpose of grand churches to inspire awe, to make one believe there is something beyond the world of men.

Indeed there was something beyond it, and that was why I was here. I lowered my gaze and moved on. Although a hush was on the air, the nave was a busy place, filled with clergymen, sightseers just in from the country, and city folk who lingered in niches and alcoves, beneath some marble saint or king, to light a candle and speak a silent prayer.

There were many ladies about the nave; so many, in fact, that the swish of their gowns murmured off the stone walls like the whispered chants of monks. I watched them surreptitiously as I moved past, paying attention to those ladies whose gowns and refined air indicated a noble heritage. Some of them were pretty enough, but none seemed out of the ordinary, and all were more interested in showing off their clothes and flirting with their male companions than in paying reverence at the shrine of any ancient ruler or goodly martyr.

I moved through the sanctuary, and the Henry VII Chapel, and the quiet solitude of the Chapter House, where rays of light—infused with color by stained glass—scattered the floor like a ransom of jewels. It was only when I caught a glimpse of green through a doorway that I recalled the old servingwoman's words. I hurried out the door, into the open courtyard in the midst of the Cloisters.

The Cloisters were neither so grand nor so crowded as the nave. I prowled along the covered walkways that surrounded the square lawn, but the only women I saw whose mode of dress marked them as noble were a group of gray-haired ladies who appeared to be on a tour of the crypts, and I wondered if they were perhaps shopping for a future abode. Weary of walking, I halted and leaned against a column.

"Excuse me, but you're standing on Sir Talbot."

It took me a moment to see her, for she was quite plain. Her gray dress blended with the stone wall against which she sat, and I could barely see her face for the shadow of a serviceable—but far from fashionable—bonnet. Several sheaves of parchment rested on her lap, and her hands were smudged with charcoal. I took her for one of the abbey's servants, though why she was resting there, and why she would so boldly speak to one who was clearly her better, astonished me.

"I said you're standing on Sir Talbot. He doesn't like that at all. It would be kind if you moved at once."

I glanced down. Beneath my boots was a slab of marble covering a crypt. The floor of the abbey was so thick with gravestones that one thought nothing of walking over them. Like many, this stone was worn by the passage of countless feet, and I could not make out the name carved upon it. However, in deference to the peculiar request, I moved a step to the next crypt over.

"Very well." The young woman in gray nodded. "Lady Ackroyd believes you have a decent look about you. She does not mind if you linger a while on her stone."

"I'm glad to hear it," I said. On second consideration, she was not a servant. Her manner of speech was anything but coarse, and her clothes, though plain, were finely made. Perhaps she was the daughter of a successful tradesman, I thought. My innocence then astounds me now. "So tell me, do you often speak with those who have departed this world?"

"I don't speak with them." Her tone was scandalized. "Our Lord would never allow such an unholy mingling of realms. Rather, it's just that . . ."

"Just what?" I said, curious despite myself.

"It's just that I know what they would have wished in life," she finished. "It's a dreadful fancy, I know. I'm sorry. I shouldn't have told you. Good day."

She bowed her head, and I knew I should return to the nave. The day had turned gray and cold, and the old woman at the Faraday estate had said Alis enjoyed sun. I would not find her out here. All the same, I found myself hesitating.

"I find I'm actually rather weary," I said. "Do you think Lady Ackroyd would mind if I departed her stone and instead took a place on the bench next to you?"

The young woman tilted her head, then nodded. "She does not mind at all."

I sat down beside her. At once I regretted it, for I had no idea what to say. "What are those?" I blurted the first thing that came to mind, pointing to the sheaves on her lap.

She flipped through the papers. Names and dates were outlined on them in charcoal. "They're rubbings. I make them from the tombs inside the abbey. Did you know Chaucer is buried here at Westminster?" She pulled out one of the papers. "Here is the rubbing of his crypt."

Her face was alight with excitement, and I saw that her clothes had misled me, for she was not nearly so plain as I had thought. Her features were finely wrought, her complexion moon-pale, and her blue eyes bright and absent of guile.

"Charming," I said, not looking at the rubbing.

"You're too polite," she said, folding the paper, bowing her head.

I laughed. "I don't believe I've ever been accused of that before."

She did not look up, but I saw a smile flit across her pink lips. "My father says it is a foolish pastime. He says if I applied as much effort to gaining the society of the living as the deceased, I should be well married by now."

I felt my smile fading. "And what do you say?"

"I say nothing, of course. He is my father. But in my heart I feel it is only right that I make my society here. After all, I shall—" She bit her lower lip, silencing herself.

A breath of understanding escaped me. Her pale skin, her bright eyes, her slender fingers—these things were not due simply to youthful beauty.

"Are you very ill then?" I said.

She tucked a stray lock of hair, dark as shadows, into her bonnet. "The doctors cannot say. I have been frail ever since I was a child, and they feared I should never reach sixteen. But now I am twenty-three. So you see? There is cause for hope, and perhaps my father is right after all." She set the papers on the ground. "Now you must tell me, sir, what has brought you to the abbey today?"

I looked out across the Cloisters. "I came looking for someone who is said to often be here, but I haven't found her."

"I am often here myself. Perhaps you can tell me what this individual looks like, and I can say if I have ever seen her."

"I'm afraid I don't know what she looks like."

"Well, that makes it more of a feat, doesn't it?"

"Indeed it does. But I was given to understand she liked sitting here in the sun."

"Well, then I fear I shall never have seen her. For I prefer days such as this." She drew in a breath. "The fog is so soft. It's the gentlest thing."

I smiled. "I've always liked fog myself, but for different reasons. I favor the way fog conceals one. It's secret, private."

"I see. So you're a man of secrets. And here I thought you might favor me with your name."

"But that's no secret," I said, and I told her my full name, for there was no cause not to do so.

"That is a most auspicious appellation."

I raised an eyebrow. "How so?"

"Albrecht—it comes from Adalbrecht, I am sure, which means 'Brightly Noble.' And Marius Lucius means 'Warrior of Light.'"

A shiver passed through me. "You know much."

"No, I cannot claim so. But I read a good deal when I was

young, on days when I could not go out, of which there were a great number. One picks up many odd facts and notions reading books."

"I daresay."

The bells of the abbey began to toll, and pigeons rose up, vanishing into the gray sky.

"I must go," she said, rising and gathering her things.

I rose as well. "May I offer you any assistance?"

She shook her head, holding an armful of papers. "You are too kind, Mr. Albrecht. But I am well. My father's man will be waiting for me out front with the coach."

A coach? Clearly her father was quite well-to-do. I bowed to her, and only as she started away did I realize I had not gotten her name. I called this fact out to her, and she halted in a doorway, glancing back.

"My name is Alis," she said with a smile. "Good day, Mr. Albrecht."

And as I stared, jaw agape, she vanished into the church.

A mistake—I had made a terrible mistake. But how could I have known? Her manner had been refined, if peculiar, but her dress had been completely at odds with her status. Besides, the old woman had said she favored sun. Had that wretched beldam tricked me deliberately?

It didn't matter; none of it did. This was only the first day of my investigation, and already I had broken the First and the Third Desiderata. Surely, once the Philosophers found out what I had done, I was to be expelled from the Seekers.

That night I encountered Byron at the pub, and he inquired after my evident misery. I knew there was no point dissembling, though I didn't dare tell him all the facts contained in the letter from the Philosophers. As I hunched over a cup, I related what I could—how I had inadvertently made my presence known to the young woman I was to watch.

"Well, it does sound like you've made quite a mess of things," Byron said with a laugh. "That's quite unlike you, Marius. I wonder what set you so off your game?"

A good question, and one I could not answer.

"Well, as I've always held," Byron went on, "in for a penny, in for a pound. There's no way to undo what's done, so you might as well take what good there is in it."

"What do you mean?" My mind was too hazed from regret and rum to understand him.

"If you can't watch from afar, then watch from nearby. Use your acquaintance with your subject to your advantage. Get close to this person, become a friend, a confidant. What better way can you discover what you've been sent to learn?"

"But what of the Desiderata?"

"What of them?" Byron said with a shrug. "From what you've told me, your quarry addressed you first. You simply played along so as not to call attention to yourself. That's hardly what I'd call interference. In fact, it seems you behaved in quite a sensible manner."

Leave it to Byron to transform foolery into heroism, but perhaps he was onto something. After all, I had made an acquaintance with the bookseller Sarsin quite by accident, and the Philosophers had rewarded me for my work on that case. Why should this be any different? Alis Faraday had chosen to approach me, and as I was bound not to interfere with her actions, what choice did I have but to play along? And if she was to catch sight of me again, I would have to continue the charade. Of course, my manner must remain neutral, never leading her one way or another. But I could not imagine a better way to determine her thoughts, her perceptions, her feelings—to see if she had any developing cognizance at all of her unusual nature.

I clapped Byron on the shoulder. "Bless you, Byron. You've saved me."

"Then the least you can do is buy me an ale," he said, and I did.

I rode to Westminster Abbey on the next foggy day and found her, again in a gray dress, sitting in the Cloisters.

"There you are," she said, looking up from a lapful of papers. "I confess, I doubted the veracity of her admonitions. However, Lady Ackroyd warranted you'd be back."

"Proving herself a most wise old dame," I said with a bow, and to my delight she laughed, a sound as high and pure as church bells on a winter's night.

"Would you like to make a rubbing?" she asked, holding up a piece of paper and a lump of charcoal.

"You'll have to show me how." I took her hand—so tiny it was all but lost inside my own—as she rose from the bench.

We spent the afternoon in the abbey's nave, choosing the most interesting and obscure crypts. I would press the paper over the crypt stone, and Alis would scrub the charcoal over the paper, and carved words and drawings that had been too time-worn to make out appeared on the paper as if by magic. Alis laughed often, and each time the sound was every bit as enchanting as the first time I heard it. Passing clergymen would stare at us, kneeling together on the floor, but I would clasp my hands as they went by, mimicking a prayerful pose. How could they argue with piousness?

"Who's next?" I would say once they had passed, and Alis would lead us to another crypt stone.

Soon enough, however, even that simple activity fatigued her. Her skin seemed to grow translucent, and her hand shook as she made the last rubbing. When she was done, I carefully folded the paper, helped her to her feet, and led her to a bench near Chaucer's tomb.

"I am fine," she said when I inquired after her well-being. "Truly. I've laughed so much today, I simply need to catch my breath, that's all."

I nodded, and could not help notice that the shadows beneath her blue eyes only accentuated their brightness.

"I was weaker as a girl," she said, "before my family moved out to the country beyond Whitehall."

"Perhaps it's the city air that troubles you," I said. "To be certain, it's thick with soot and other foul humors."

"Perhaps," she said, though she shook her head. "The city is very great, and very loud, and filled with new contraptions. Wheels and gears and pulleys, all grinding away. I feel as if they're all pressing in on me sometimes. Were it not for the abbey, I doubt I would come to London at all." She smiled at me. "But I am glad I did so today."

"There," I said. "You look better already."

"The rest has restored me greatly. And no doubt Sadie will brew me one of her teas this evening."

I inquired politely and soon ascertained this Sadie was a servant, and one with the old woman I had met at the gates of the Faraday estate. She seemed to be something of an herbalist, and had given Alis teas to ease her discomfort and lend her strength since she was a child.

The bells tolled again, and it was time for her to go. I was pleased when she leaned on my arm instead of the iron railing as we descended the steps before the abbey. Below, her family's carriage waited. She started toward it, then paused to look at me.

"What are you, Mr. Albrecht?"

The directness of her words, and of her blue eyes, startled me. Had she suspected something of my true nature? "As I've said, Miss Faraday, I am visiting from Scotland, and—"

"Yes, Mr. Albrecht, you've told me your story." She smiled. "And I daresay you know all about me already, for there's little worth investigating there—one more silly nobleman's daughter in a country full of them. In our meetings I have divined that you are kind and generous, that your wit, for all its gentle courtesy, has teeth, and that you have a goodly face. But I still have no idea *what* you are."

Her expression was beguiled, not accusing; she did not suspect. With a deep bow I said, "I am, my lady, your servant."

That response won me a bright laugh, and I stood on the steps, gazing at the street, long after the carriage had disappeared.

We met often after that, and not always at the abbey. Despite her delicate constitution, her spirit was strong, and she was always ready for an adventure. We went boating on the river, and strolled around the Tower of London as she told tales of kings and queens who had met ill ends within, and sat for hours watching as the builders worked on Christopher Wren's new cathedral.

"It shall be finer than Westminster when it is done," I said.

She shook her head. "The crypts will not be old. There will be nothing to make rubbings of. How shall we bother the priests?"

"I've heard Wren's made a gallery, high inside the new

dome, where one's whispers run along the curve of the wall to a listener's ear clear on the other side, over a hundred feet away."

She clapped her hands. "I should like to see that very much."

"Then you shall."

"But only if I—" She turned away. "How long do you think it will be before the cathedral is completed?"

I could see the blue lines of veins tracing down her slender neck, toward a shadow at the hollow of her throat. "You shall see the Whispering Gallery, Miss Faraday. I promise you."

She turned back, smiling now. "Well, if Lord Albrecht promises it, then it will be so." She laid her hand over mine, and I smiled as well, and all thoughts of shadows were forgotten.

Our affection was limited to such innocent physical gestures as this. Always when we met it was in a public place, and one of her father's men was nearby, so no impropriety could be claimed on any part. Apparently the reports that reached the Faraday estate were favorable, for I was soon invited to dine with the family.

"My agents tell me Madstone Hall is a fine manor in the county of Midlothian," Lord Faraday said as we gathered in the hall after dinner. He was a handsome, white-haired man, hale throughout most of his life, but lately troubled by gout. He sat with his bandaged foot propped up on a stool. "The estate is not overly large, I am told, but well situated, and yielding a good income."

So he had made some inquiries. I could hardly blame him. From her chair across the hall, Alis gave me a pained look, obviously embarrassed by her father's scrutiny, but I smiled.

"It is a good estate," I said.

"And why have you come to London?" Lady Faraday said, looking up from her embroidery.

"I can tell you that," Lord Faraday interjected. "These days, what young northern lord would not wish to better his connections in the south by a visit to London? Am I right, Mr. Albrecht?"

In a way, he was—I had indeed come seeking connections, though not any he could imagine—so I simply nodded.

"Miss Faraday has two brothers, one studying to be a barrister, and the other at sea. The eldest shall inherit everything. I fear there will be nothing for her after I am gone, excepting a small dowry. She will have little to offer save her good name."

"I would say she has much more to offer than that." I gazed across the hall, and my smile vanished. Alis sagged in her chair, her hand to her brow. I hurried over to her.

"It is nothing," she said in protest. "A headache, that's all."

"Go fetch Sadie at once," Lady Faraday said to one of the servants. "Tell her Miss Faraday needs her tea."

I took my leave of the family, and despite her pain Alis managed a smile, while Lord Faraday shook my hand firmly and insisted upon my swift return to dine with them again.

Thus began my fall in earnest. I need not go into great length over my descent. Know only that as snow blanketed the countryside and Christmas neared, I loved her. I loved her truly, with all my being. While sometimes at night, alone in my bed, I would lie awake, thinking of the Desiderata and dreading the wrath of the Seekers, when I was with her such thoughts were driven from my mind. I could think only of her finespun beauty, her angelic voice, and her peculiar variety of humor and liveliness, which never failed to brighten my spirits on the darkest winter days.

"So who is she?" Rebecca said on one of the rare occasions when we dined together. Of late I had seen her little, for she had been absorbed in her own investigations for the Seekers.

"I beg your pardon?" I said, looking up from my wine.

"Who is she?" Rebecca repeated. "The woman you're in love with."

I stared, and she laughed.

"Come, now, Marius, don't deny that you're in love. I know what it looks like on you. I saw it once myself, though not so dewy-eyed as this, I must say. She's absolutely turned your head. Who is she?"

"No one," I said. "It's a passing thing. I have no time for such fancies."

Rebecca coiled a hand beneath her chin. "If you say so, Marius," though she appeared anything but convinced. "Now tell me, how is your current research going?"

I spoke briefly, in a detached manner, and I offered no particulars. Everything would be in my reports, and if the Philosophers wished Rebecca to know the details, then she would have read them. Despite being madly in love, I had managed to write regular missives to the Philosophers, describing how Alis suspected nothing of her heritage, how she was usually intelligent and sensitive, as well as bold and inquisitive, though of a fragile constitution, which prevented her from engaging in travel and other activities that might have helped reveal her nature.

As for replies and further directives from the Philosophers, I received none. I was on my own. Thus there was no one to catch me as I fell.

I saw her most days, and if a day did pass when I failed to walk with her in Westminster Abbey, or ride out to the Faraday estate, then my mood was bleak and oppressive, and so it would remain until next I saw her.

For her part, Alis seemed to enjoy all my attentions, which only encouraged me further, as did the apparent approval of Lord Faraday, who found my position and respectable manner more than acceptable. And Lady Faraday—propelled, perhaps, by a bit too much wine—proclaimed at dinner one night that surely I was the most handsome and agreeable young man she had ever met.

Alis, of course, was duly embarrassed by her mother's outburst, though the blush that touched her cheeks made her all the more lovely—like a rose so near to white that the palest tincture of its petals, once detected, rendered it more striking than the most vivid flower.

"What's the matter?" I murmured, when we were gathered in the hall after supper, bending over the back of her chair where she sat with a book. "Do you not agree with your mother that I am the most handsome and agreeable young man she ever met?"

"Without doubt," Alis said crisply. "But Lady Faraday is already spoken for, so I'm afraid you're quite out of luck in that regard."

"Then I'll just have to make do with her fair daughter."

Alis bent back over her book, but not before she could conceal the smile on her lips.

As weeks passed, the Seekers seemed content to leave me to

my own devices, even as the length and frequency of my reports to the Philosophers dwindled. Every day I become further ensconced in the Faraday household. My life on the streets of Edinburgh seemed more than a lifetime away, and I felt a deep certainty that Master Albrecht would be pleased for me—that this was what he had meant when he said he wished for me to live my life.

There was only one thing that marred my happiness: As my feelings for Alis grew stronger, she herself was growing weaker.

One day in February, when the unusually balmy weather emboldened us to stroll in the little wilderness outside the Faraday manor, Alis suddenly slumped against me, and when I lifted her into my arms she was as light and trembling as a bird.

"It's nothing," she protested. "All I need is to rest for a moment. You may put me down, Lord Albrecht."

"I will not," I said, and carried her into the house.

By the time we reached the hall, her protests had ceased, and her trembling had become a violent spasm. She was cold, and her eyes hazed with pain. I set her on a couch and duly retreated to the far end of the hall as Lady Faraday and a swarm of servants descended upon her. It was best for me to stay out of the way, though I wanted nothing more than to be at her side, to hold her hand, and to take away her pain—as if I actually had some power to do so.

She let out a moan, and I clenched my hands into fists. Words escaped me. "I cannot bear this."

" 'Tis she who cannot bear it," a soft voice said.

I turned and found I was not alone in the shadows at the end of the hall. An old woman dressed all in gray stood in a doorway, a weary look on her face. It was Sadie, Alis's beloved servant.

"You're right, of course," I said, cheeks afire with shame. "I should be stronger, for her sake."

The old woman laughed. "You help her more than you know."

"Not as you do. They tell me you brew teas that ease her pain."

"And love eases pain that teas help not."

I sighed. "Would that I knew what afflicted her. If I did, then I would take it away. I would make her as strong in body as she is in spirit."

The old woman's gaze moved across the hall. "It runs more truly in some. 'Tis their blessing, and their curse, for they feel all things more keenly." Her green eyes turned to me. "Yet in the end, all such folk will feel the same burden."

These words sent a chill through me, though I did not understand them. Or did I?

"You know something," I said, moving closer to her. "That's how you can help her as you do. Tell me, please, what's wrong with her?"

"Nothing is wrong with her. 'Tis the world that's wrong. This Earth. 'Tis harming her as it harms all like her. In the end it shall be too great. It cannot be defeated."

I staggered. These words were a knife to my heart. At last I managed to speak. "That day I first came to the gates, you said she favored sun. But I found her in fog."

"Favors it, yes. But bears it? Not well, I fear. Not well at all. It burns her, the sun of this world. She is like a figment born of the night mists, one that can only vanish in the light of dawn."

A sickness filled me. I had taken her outside because the day was fine. What a fool I was! What a miserable fool. Yet despite my agitation I felt a spark of curiosity, and for the first time in many days I remembered I was a Seeker. Who was this old woman? How did she know such things?

"I must go make Miss Faraday's tea," Sadie said, and before I could speak she turned and vanished through the doorway.

Alis was soon resting comfortably, and I made my farewell, which she was too weary to protest. When I returned the next morning she was sitting up in bed, and the day after that I found her wrapped in a blanket in a chair in the hall. She continued to grow stronger, even as outside the weather turned chill and gloomy, wet with the rains of March.

All the while, I could not forget the words spoken by Sadie. Did she know something of Alis's true nature? I had not gained another opportunity to speak to the old servingwoman, but all the same I was sure of it.

This world. It's harming her, as it harms all like her. . . .

Were there others in London like Alis? If so, perhaps they would know a way to help her.

A scheme came to me. I knew it was an utter violation of the Desiderata to do what I intended, but I hardly cared. Damn the Seekers to hell, and damn the Philosophers with them. Alis was not a thing to be watched: an insect to be caught in a jar and observed as it perished. I would find others like her, and I would make them help her.

Except, even as I began my search, I said nothing of it to Alis; I gave no hint that might reveal her true nature to her. Was this some concession to the Seekers still? Or perhaps I only wished to protect her from knowledge that would trouble her already frail health.

Even I did not know the reason, for by then a madness had begun to come over me. I could not eat, I could not sleep. I could do nothing but think of Alis and search for those like her, those who could help her.

I passed my days with Alis as before, but now by night I descended into the vaults beneath the Seeker Charterhouse, as though I were a ghoul again—just like in Edinburgh as a boy, when I slept in the family crypt of the Gilroys. Only I did not come to these vaults to rest, but instead to work, and I did so feverishly, poring over old books, sifting through stacks of crackling parchments whose faded words I strained to read even in the light of a dozen candles. As a master, nothing in the library of the Seekers was forbidden to me; surely I would find some answers there. After all, the Philosophers had to know something about those of fairy heritage, else they would never have given me the assignment to observe Alis.

I was right. After many nights of searching I came upon a missive. It was addressed to the Philosophers, though it was unsigned. But no doubt they had known who it came from, and the information in it fascinated me even as it chilled my blood.

The missive spoke of a tavern—though it gave neither name nor location for this establishment—describing it as a place where those with "most peculiar and unearthly heritage" often gathered in secret. How the author of the missive came to know of this place, he did not write, but it became plain as I read that the patrons of this tavern were like Alis: people with the blood of fairies in their veins.

The missive was maddening in its brevity, but after many nights of searching I discovered a box lost in a corner, and in it found many more letters, all unsigned, but written in the same slanted hand as the first. I read them all, and by the time the candles were burned to stumps I knew not everything I wished to, but much all the same.

To be a fairy on this mundane Earth was an agony that could not long be borne; such an ethereal creature would soon perish here. Those who possessed some measure of fairy heritage also inherited this affliction, though to a lesser degree. To dwell on this world for such a person was often painful, though not always fatal, and the folk of the tavern had created various remedies that eased their suffering.

That was it—that was the knowledge I needed—though I was still frustrated by the anonymous author's lack of detail as to the name and location of this tavern. The final missive began to glow in my hands as a shaft of gold light fell upon it. I looked up at a window, high in the wall of the vault; it was bright with the dawn. A new day had come, and hope with it. I spirited the letters back into their hiding place, then ascended the stone steps that led from the vaults, back to the world of the living.

"Hello there, Marius," Byron said. He was sitting in the hall of the Charterhouse, a book and a cup of tea on the table before him. "So was it a long night at the pub, then? Forgive my saying so, but you look absolutely wretched."

I lifted a hand to my temple, only realizing then how it throbbed. Lately, I had begun having frequent headaches. But it was only from the long nights of research, and what did I care anyway? This pain was nothing next to what Alis suffered.

"I must away," I said.

"Nonsense, Marius." Byron pushed aside his book. "Come, sit with me and have a cup. It'll do you good."

I shook my head. "I have things . . . I must away." And before Byron could protest further, I was out the door of the Charterhouse.

I believed I would tell Alis everything that night—about myself and the Seekers, and about her own true nature. Only I didn't. She was too weary, and I was weary as well from so many sleepless nights spent in the Seekers' vaults. Nor did I tell her the next morning, or the morning after that. I remained silent, and each day her face grew paler, though if possible more lovely.

She was stronger some days than others, and on the Ides of March, on a fine spring afternoon, we at last ventured together to London's new cathedral, St. Paul's.

The old St. Paul's, after much abuse and several attempts at restoration, had perished in the great London fire of 1666, and Christopher Wren had been commissioned to erect a replacement. By the look of things, Wren had much work left to do, for the cathedral was far from completed. The earth was open and raw all around, and much of the structure was no more than a stone skeleton cocooned by scaffolding. However, the dome, while not completely faced, soared toward the sky.

"I imagine you can see the whole world from up there," Alis said, eyes shining, as I helped her down from the carriage.

I laughed. "Perhaps not the whole world, but certainly much of London at least."

"No, it cannot be so. It is far too lofty to afford such a mundane view. It would show one the whole world." She gazed up at the dome. "Though I suppose I shall never know."

A solemnity came over me, and I took her hand in mine. "Yes you will, Miss Faraday. You shall see it with your own eyes."

We found the man who was directing the construction that day, and after a small amount of persuasion and a sizable private donation we were allowed in for a tour of the cathedral. Even in its incomplete state, it impressed us with its grace and grandeur. It was as light and airy inside as Westminster was heavy and dim.

"I cannot imagine I shall ever get all the way up there," Alis said, craning her slender neck to gaze at the dome high above.

"There is no need to imagine it," I said, "for we are going now." And I whisked her toward a side door before she had any chance to protest.

The steps up to the dome numbered in the hundreds, and she walked only a dozen or two on her own. I carried her the rest of the way, and though my arms soon ached, as did my head, my burden was not so great, for she seemed to weigh even less than the last time I had carried her. We soon reached the first way station, the Stone Gallery, where we were able to exit onto a narrow balcony and gaze out over the city.

"You're right," she said, laughing, cheeks flushed with excitement. "It's only London I see, though it's a marvelous sight."

I clucked my tongue. "Nonsense, my lady. It is you who were correct. For there, to the north, just beside that foggy patch, I can see my manor in Scotland. And there to the west, if you squint just so, you can make out a glint of light. That's the glass isle where King Arthur is buried. And beyond that, you can look all the way to the colonies in America. It's the whole world, just as you said, right there before you."

"The whole world," she murmured, clutching my arm. "I do see it, Marius, I do."

We stayed there until the cool spring wind chilled her, then went back in through a little door and resumed our climb. After one last effort, we came to an inner balcony, ringed by a stone balustrade, nestled within the base of the dome itself. There we could look down at the workmen far below, moving about like ants.

"Forgive me, but I must rest," Alis said, though she had walked but a few steps herself from the Stone Gallery.

I sat her on a bench, then moved around the gallery to the far side. If what I had heard was true, this was the gallery where, if one murmured against the wall, a listener a hundred feet across the gallery would hear even the softest words.

I sat on the bench and turned my face to the wall, so she could not see my lips. "I love you, Lady Alis Faraday," I whispered against the curved stones. "Be with me. Always."

Across the gallery, she leaned against the wall. I moved my ear close to the stones. Had it worked? I waited for her reply, but I heard nothing save a whirring of air. So it was only a story, then. She had not heard me after all. And perhaps it was just as well. Perhaps it was best if—

Soft but clear, as if she were whispering right into my ear, I heard her voice. "Marius . . . help me."

I pulled my ear from the wall and stood. She gazed at me

from across the gallery, her blue eyes wide. The front of her white gown was dotted with crimson.

I careened around the gallery to her. Blood gushed from her nose, and she had been unable to staunch it with her handkerchief, which was soaked red. I pulled a cloth from my coat—the silvery one I had taken from my mother, and which I had carried with me all these years—and it seemed to draw the blood into itself, while somehow remaining unstained. She held it to her nose, and the flow of blood soon ceased. However, she had lost much, and her cheeks where white as marble.

"Forgive me, Marius."

"Hush," I said, and took her into my arms.

I felt no ache, no weariness despite the hundreds of steps I carried her down. I had to get her to the Faraday estate as quickly as possible. When we reached the coach, I was startled to see one of Lord Faraday's men, Albert, standing there and talking to the driver, who pointed in our direction. Had he heard what had happened? Except that was impossible. It was well over an hour by carriage to the Faraday estate.

"Miss Faraday," Albert said, astonishment on his face, "are you well?"

She waved a hand. "It is nothing, Albert. I'm very well." Indeed, she was standing on her own now, and did seem a bit stronger.

"Why have you come?" I asked the servant.

His face was grim. "I bear ill news, I fear. Lord Faraday would have spared your learning of it until you arrived home, Miss Faraday, but Lady Faraday insisted you must know at once, seeing as how you loved her so dearly."

Alis's expression was hazed with pain and confusion. "What do you mean, Albert? What should I know?"

"It's Sadie, Miss Faraday," the man said. "I'm sorry to tell you, but she passed away this morning."

"Oh," Alis said softly, and fainted.

That night I continued my search for those like Alis with redoubled urgency, for Sadie's death had struck her both in body and spirit.

It had been sudden. The old servingwoman had collapsed in the garden while gathering herbs; by the time others reached her she was already gone. Alis was in great distress. Her nose began to bleed again. The doctor was sent for, and she was confined to her bed.

I doubted the doctor could do anything for her, save to leech her of more blood, so I spoke to the servants, seeing if one of them could brew a tea for Alis as Sadie always had. Only none of them knew what Sadie had put in her teas. Fear struck me, but I willed myself to think clearly. Were there not others who knew how to fashion restoratives for those of otherworldly nature? And indeed, how had Sadie known to make such brews herself? Surely she had been familiar with the folk of the tavern I had read about in the letters.

Taking my leave of the Faradays, I rode hard back to London, to the Seeker Charterhouse. I went directly to the door to the vaults, and though the headache came upon me again as soon as I fit the iron key in the lock, I ignored the pain and dashed down the stairs. I had to read the letters again, to see if they held any clues I had overlooked. Burning as if with fever, I went to the corner where I had found them and had hidden them again.

The letters were gone.

I searched for a frantic hour, overturning boxes and shelves, but it was no use. I had tucked the box of letters into a niche in the wall, behind the shelf where I had first come upon them. The corner was dim; there was no way another could have known the letters were there.

Unless, of course, they had been watching me.

But why would someone remove the letters? Without them, how was I to find the tavern they described, and the folk who could help Alis? A despair came over me, black and depthless, and I staggered up the stairs. I had to go back to her. It was all I could think to do.

"Where are you off to so late, Marius?"

I reeled around. The front hall of the Charterhouse was dim, lit only by a few candles; I had not seen her there, sitting in a chair near the door.

"Rebecca," I said, and could think of nothing more to add.

She coiled a hand beneath her chin. "You look all in a hurry. Is it *her* you're off to see, then? This woman you so adore?"

I could only stare at her.

"Are you well, Marius?" A light shone in her eyes; it wasn't quite concern. "I say, you look positively ill. You haven't had a lover's quarrel, now have you?"

I staggered, a hand to my brow, and she rose swiftly, catching my arm, steadying me.

"I'm sorry, Rebecca," I gasped. "I must go to her."

She did not let go of my arm. "So it is indeed the one you love whom you go to. But you have yet to tell me who she is. Come—give me her name. We shared a bed once, Marius. Surely you owe me that at least."

Her eyes were hard, her fingers dug into my flesh, and a low sound of suffering escaped me. "No," I whispered. "Please. I must not . . ."

"By the gods, it's her, isn't it?" Rebecca's face drew close to mine, white and cold as a moon. Her mouth twisted in disgust, and in triumph. "I had suspected it, only I didn't wish to believe it was true, but it is. You love her, Marius, don't you? The woman you were sent to watch and observe—Lady Alis Faraday."

Now it was I who clutched at her. "Please, Rebecca. Do not tell them, I beg you. Do not tell the Philosophers."

She disengaged herself from me. "You pitiable fool."

I staggered back, gaping at her.

"It is over, Marius," she said, her voice cool with detachment. "Do not return to the vaults. You will not find what you seek there."

"You," I gasped, but horror constricted my throat, and I could say no more. I pushed past her, running out the door and into the night, weaving the darkness around me with my old, familiar skill.

Only it did not matter. I could not hide from *them*. Their golden eyes pierced any gloom. Rebecca would tell them what I had done, if she had not already. She had been watching me; she had taken the letters. But she had not taken my will to help Alis I would find a way, with or without the Seekers.

However, that proved harder than even I imagined. They

would not allow me near the Faraday estate. I went the next morning, just after dawn, and a trio of Seekers accosted me before I could approach the gate. Richard Mayburn was among them, and Byron.

"Go back, Marius," he said, his voice uncharacteristically stern. "You are not to try coming here again." Then, in a lower voice, he said, "Please, Marius, listen to me. I know you cannot see it now, but this is for the best. Truly it is."

"What do you know of what's best?" I spat, breaking free of their grip and vanishing into the morning fog.

That evening I attempted stealth, thinking I could easily creep past them. I had performed similar feats countless times as a boy in Edinburgh. However, either my powers of concealment had fled me, or the Seekers possessed some uncanny ability to see through the shadows I wove about myself. I could not get past them.

Defeated, I returned to my house in the city, reasoning that the Faradays would soon come looking for me. However, days passed without any sign of them, and in time I learned that Byron had gone to Lord Faraday, posing as my representative and saying that I had been recalled to Scotland on sudden business, and would not be returning in the foreseeable future. I cursed the Seekers; they thought of everything.

However, I could be resourceful as well, and though I was being kept from Alis, I could help her yet. I began to make inquiries, venturing into the darkest neighborhoods of the city, asking about taverns that folk frequented, and if there were any that were unusual in some way. This line of investigation revealed nothing, save the locations of some of the most sordid drinking houses in all of London.

Just when hope began to fail, chance renewed my quest. One morning, after another night of fruitless searching, as I walked through one of the city's poorer neighborhoods, I was recognized by a plain-faced young woman who dared to approach me. Although I did not recognize her, she knew me from the Faraday estate, where she had labored as a servant until a month ago, when she had returned home to care for her ailing mother.

An idea came to me, and I asked the young woman if she knew the families of any of the other servants who worked at the Faraday estate, specifically of the old woman Sadie. She did not, but she knew someone who might—an old aunt who lived a few streets over.

I thanked her and hurried to the house of this aunt. The old woman was suspicious, but a few coins loosened her toothless jaw well enough, and I soon learned the name and dwelling place of a certain niece of the old woman, Sadie, whose last name was Greenfellow.

A visit was paid that afternoon to the niece, who spun wool in a cottage on the fringes of the city. Jenny Greenfellow was pretty despite her middling years and the burdens of a hard life, and after a long look she invited me in. Introducing myself as an acquaintance of the Faradays, I gave her my condolences regarding Sadie's passing.

"It is kind of you to think of my aunt," Jenny said, pouring me a cup of tea.

I took a sip. It was fragrant, and tasted like nothing I had drunk before. My pain and weariness receded a fraction.

"You have her look," I said without really thinking. But it was true. Her eyes were green and bright, as the old woman's had been.

"Nay," she said, smiling, " 'Tis my brother who takes after her. Everyone says he has her spirit."

"Your brother?"

"Aye. His name is John. He works at our uncle's tavern."

My cup clattered to the table, spilling tea. She stared at me.

"Your uncle's tavern?" I fought to keep my words controlled. "You mean to say the proprietor of this establishment was Sadie's husband?"

"Nay, sir. He is her brother. Neither of them ever married. Only their youngest brother, my father, ever did. But he passed away some years ago. Now Sadie has followed, and Uncle is getting on himself. I believe he means to leave the place to John when he's gone."

I hardly heard these words. It seemed impossible, yet it could only be so. According to the letters, the folk of the tavern knew how to brew elixirs to restore those of fairy blood, and so had Sadie Greenfellow. Feigning no more than polite interest, I inquired after the location of the tavern, then took my leave of

Jenny, though not before giving her several coins for her trouble, which were not refused.

I walked fast through the streets of the city, back toward the river, and for the first time in days, hope—real hope—welled up in my heart.

"Be strong, Alis," I murmured under my breath. "Endure it only a little while more, dearest. I am coming."

As dusk drifted like soot from the sky, I turned onto the street Jenny had described and craned my neck, peering at the signs hanging over the various establishments, looking for one painted green.

There was none. The street was dirty and empty, save for a stray dog that slunk away into the shadows. No laughter spilled out of doorways, no cheerful clinking of cups. Night fell.

Perhaps I had passed the tavern in my haste. I turned to go back the way I had come, and that was when I saw him. He tried to leap into the shadows, but he had not my skill. I raced after him, catching his arm, and dragged him into the light of a torch.

"Marius," Byron said. There was fear in his eyes. What must I have looked like at that moment? Fey and perilous, I can only imagine now, my eyes blazing green as my mother's had years ago.

"Rebecca sent you, didn't she?" I said through clenched teeth. "Are you her lapdog then, that you'll do whatever she bids you? Gods, man, have you no pride at all?"

Anger registered on his usually jovial face, then he shook his head. "I don't know what you're doing here, Marius, but you must stop now. Go back to the Seekers. Beg forgiveness. They'll take you back if they know you're sincere. It's not too late."

"No." I turned away from him.

He caught my shoulder. "Please, Marius, listen to me. I know you love her, but you have to let her go. It's for your own good."

Rage boiled within me, and I whirled around. "My own good? What can any of you possibly know of my own good, Byron?"

I had thought he would lash back at me, but instead he only sighed. "Marius, my friend, would that I was not the one to give you this news. But there is something you must know. I have just come from—"

"Do not trouble yourself," I said, "for there is nothing you can say that I would wish to hear." And before he could protest, I wrapped the shadows around myself and was gone.

As I moved down the street I saw it immediately, and I wondered how I could have missed it before. At the far end of the lane, above a red door, hung a sign painted vivid green. The sign seemed to shine in the gloom, and as I drew closer I read the word inscribed on it: GREENFELLOW'S. Gold light seeped through the crack beneath the door. I reached out, but before I could touch the door it swung open.

"What do you think you're doing here?" said a growling voice.

It wasn't until I looked down that I saw him. He was a dwarf, standing no higher than my waist, but well formed. His youthful face was handsome, and he peered up at me with keen blue eyes.

"I'm Marius," I said, too startled to speak anything but the truth.

"And what's your business here?" the doorman—for clearly he was such—demanded, hands on his hips. "Don't think I can't see through your little shadow trick."

Despite his diminutive size, there was something perilous about the doorman. I let the shadows slip away from me. "I've come seeking help. Not for myself, but for Alis Faraday."

The doorman's eyes went wide. "Blood and stone! Why didn't you say so?" He grabbed my hand and tugged me forward. "This way. Come along, now, no time to waste. She said you would come, and as usual she was right. I don't know why I didn't recognize you right off. It was your pesky shadows, I suppose. A pretty little glamour that is! Pretty indeed, though it would fool few enough here for long, mind you, so don't get any ideas. . . ."

So the doorman went on, his words making little sense to me, as he dragged me down a hallway, through an archway of grimy stone, and into the heart of Greenfellow's Tavern.

I will not describe the tavern at length, for you have seen it with your own eyes and know it is—that it was—a place beyond words. It was different in that time, of course. Smoke coiled among the sooty beams, straw covered the floor, and the music that filled the air was that of harp and lute, drone and tambour. Yet you would not have found it so very changed. It was, after all, a place outside of time.

I felt much attention upon me as the doorman led me through the tavern. There were many patrons, though it was difficult to get a proper look at them, for they sat in dusky corners, and all I saw were their eyes, glinting like jewels in the dark. At last the small man brought me to an alcove, its floor strewn with cushions, and he indicated I should sit. I did, and only then did I see her.

"Thank you, Arion," the woman said to the doorman. "You should return to your post now."

The doorman frowned. Clearly he would rather have stayed, but he bowed and retreated into the gloom.

"You came for this, Marius, did you not?" the woman said. She held out a clay vessel, stopped with a cork.

It was difficult to gaze upon her. She was bright amid the dimness, and I had to raise a hand to shield my eyes. At first glance she was young, her skin as lustrous as a pearl, her lips coral, her lovely face framed by raven-dark hair. But as my eyes adjusted, and I lowered my hand, I saw the wisdom of long years in her gray eyes. Shadows gathered in the hollows of her cheeks, and I knew even in sunlight they would remain, for I had seen such shadows in Alis's own visage.

"You're dying," I said, too filled with sadness not to speak the words.

"We all must die, Marius. And I have endured longer than many do. I shall not protest when it is my time. Besides, it is another that must concern you now." She placed the jar in my hands.

"Alis," I said. "You know her."

The woman nodded. "Her parents, at least. When she was born, they sensed the Light was strong in her."

"The Light," I murmured. "Like the light in you. It hurts you, doesn't it, to live on this world?"

Her green eyes seemed to pierce me. "It hurts all like us, Marius—though some more than others. Alis's parents believed that dwelling in the outside world might force her to become strong, to gain resistance to its ill effects. Most of us disagreed with them. We felt it was best for the child to stay here, protected. But there were . . . others, from outside, who convinced them to try. When the infant of a noble lord and lady was stillborn, the midwife—who was one of our own—spirited Alis into the cradle instead, unbeknownst to the mundane parents."

"A changeling," I murmured. "You mean Alis is a changeling."

The woman nodded, and understanding glimmered in me. Alis's parents had sent her out into the mortal world in the hope that confronting the source of her pain and suffering would give her some mastery over it. Only that hope had been in vain.

"It didn't work," I said. "Living out there didn't make her strong. It's killing her. Who were these people who convinced Alis's parents to send her out there?" I clenched my hands into fists. "Who were they?"

The fairy-woman shook her head. "Time grows short," she said, and I did not know if she meant for Alis or for herself. "Take this as well." She handed me a small book, bound in frayed leather.

"What is it?"

"It was his." Her gaze moved past me, to the arch of stone through which I had passed. "Go to her, Marius. You are her only hope."

Yes, I had to go. I rose and hurried back toward the door. As I neared the stone arch, I saw a shape on the floor.

It was Byron. He lay with his hands clasped around a sprig of holly, his head on a pillow. His eyes were closed, and he seemed asleep, a look of peace on his face, only I knew he was dead.

"His kind cannot enter here without great peril." Arion said. The small man stood in the archway, his blue eyes sad.

I stared at him. "But how . . . ?"

"Your skill with shadow is not so great as you thought. He must have followed you here, slipping in while I was away from the door." Arion sighed. "I fear he was lost before I could return and protect him."

I staggered back. What was this place? Why had Byron perished while I had survived?.

Arion urged me forward. "Go, Marius. There is nothing you

can do for him now, and dawn comes. You cannot leave here while it is day out."

These words made no sense. It was only just dusk when I found the tavern. I had been there but a few minutes. However, before I could protest, Arion pushed me through the door, and I stumbled out into the street.

Rose-colored light welled up from the eastern horizon. I heard a door slam behind me, but when I turned I saw a blank brick wall. There was no red door, no green sign. However, the jar and the book were hard and real in my hands. I started to turn away, and that was when I saw him. Byron's corpse slumped against the wall, his face white, drained of life. He still clutched the holly sprig.

I felt I should do something, but I knew the Seekers would find him, that they would take care of their own. I slipped the book and the jar inside my coat and lurched down the street.

By the time I reached the Faraday estate it was midmorning. I feared I would be accosted at the gate again, and I was ready to strike down any who stood in my way, no matter their number. However, as I approached the gate, I saw only Rebecca. She wore a black gown.

"Marius," she said, reaching for me, and for a moment it seemed sorrow shone in her eyes, only when I looked again they were hard as stones, and she had pulled her hand back.

"Do not try to stop me," I said.

She stepped aside. "I will not stand in your way. There is no need. Did not Byron find you last night? Did he not tell you?"

"Byron," I said, choking on the word.

She drew close to me, her face hard. "What has happened? Where is Byron?"

I shook my head, then moved past her, through the gate, and ran down the long avenue of trees toward the manor. I had to go to her. I had to see Alis. I reached inside my coat, gripping the clay jar, knowing the fluid within would restore her. She would not live forever; none of us did. She would fade, like the beautiful, nameless woman at the tavern. But not before she and I shared many glorious years together, not before—

I halted at the top of the steps. A black ribbon had been tied to the handle of the door. It fluttered in the breeze, and at last I understood why Byron had come looking for me, why Rebecca had let me pass.

The clay jar slipped from my fingers and shattered against the steps. Green fluid oozed over the stones, and a soft sigh escaped me, like the last breath of a dying man.

I believe I went mad for a time after that, for there is little of the days and weeks that followed that I can now recall.

I drank much, that I do know. Returning to my habits of old, I would drain a flask of whiskey, fall into a stupor, and when I woke, head throbbing, I would slink out in search of another bottle. On more than one occasion I was found drunk on the grounds of the new St. Paul's, calling out for Alis, and the king's soldiers would haul me back to my house, or once—failing to recognize me as a nobleman—to a pauper's jail, where I spent five days and nights shivering in a filthy cell, and did not bother to beat back the rats when they crept forth to gnaw at my legs.

Rebecca retrieved me from the jail, that much I do recall through the haze, and she took me back to my house. I remember her asking questions about Byron as well. The Seekers had found him dead in the village of Brixistane, south of the river. He had been sent to follow me, she said; surely I was the last to see him alive, and she wanted to know the reason he had died when there wasn't a mark on his body. Only I couldn't have answered her if I had wanted to. Nothing that had happened that night in the tavern dwelled in the realm of reason, and the only words I spoke to Rebecca were to ask her for more whiskey. She left in rage and disgust.

March gave way to green April. In rare, lucid moments it occurred to me that I should pay a visit to Lord and Lady Faraday, only I would take a drink first to steel my nerves, then another, then I would wake on the floor, my head feeling as if someone had taken a hammer to my temples. I considered returning to Scotland as well. Letters had begun to arrive again from Madstone Hall, piling up on my table. I determined to read them, but always the drink required to clear my mind led to many more that fogged it, and the letters remained unopened. Richard Mayburn came to speak to me, and Rebecca again, and though I did not turn them away I had nothing to say to them. Finally they ceased coming altogether.

I believe, left to myself, I would have drunk myself to death; it was what I wished for. Only there was something that kept me from surrendering altogether—something I had to do. Then, on the first day of May, I happened to pick up a crumpled broadsheet lying in the gutter as I stumbled out in search of more grog. My eyes fell upon a small printed notice, and I knew at last what I had been waiting for: to say good-bye.

I reached Westminster Abbey at midday. The sun was bright, and its rays pierced my skull, stabbing at my brain. A drink would have succored me, but I had not stopped on the way to buy any whiskey, and I had not had a drink since the night before, which was longer than I had gone in many weeks. However, as I entered the cathedral, the quiet and dimness were like a balm to my mind. The pain grew more bearable, if not diminished.

It took me an hour to find her tomb. The little article in the broadsheet had not said in which part of the abbey she had been laid, only that she had been buried there as an act of kindness to Lord Faraday, who had served the kingdom so well in Parliament. I wandered through the nave and sanctuary, and the two transepts, peering in every corner, looking for a stone that was newer than those around it.

At last I found it, in the place where I should have looked first: on the edge of the Cloisters, not far from Sir Talbot and Lady Ackroyd. The stone was small and plain, with only her name and the dates of her birth and passing upon it. I knelt, but I had no paper and charcoal to make a rubbing with, and so I pressed my hands against the stone, as if to etch the words into my flesh instead.

"Hello, my love," I murmured, and I wondered if by some strange workings, like those in the Whispering Gallery, she might hear my words. "It's your Marius. Please, dearest—you must not forgive me for what I have done. Only bid me good-bye. For surely you and I will never meet, as I belong in no heaven that might house the likes of you."

I meant to go then. My head, though in pain, was clear of the haze of whiskey for the first time in weeks, and at last I apprehended in full the knowledge I had been masking with drink all this time.

It was my fault Alis had died.

"Is that so?" spoke a soft voice behind me. "Is it truly your fault?"

Had I spoken my anguish aloud? I turned and saw a woman standing above me. She was clad in the flowing black gown of a mourner. Though her lithe figure lent her an air of youth, she leaned upon a cane, and a veil concealed her face.

"Did you know her?" I said, though it was hard to speak.

"Not as you knew her, Marius."

She lifted her veil. Her face was as pale and luminous as it had been that night at the tavern, though the shadows that gathered in her cheeks were darker than before.

"Why do you blame yourself, Marius?" the fairy-woman said.

I turned away. "I did not tell her." Grief tore the words out of me in hoarse sobs. "I did not tell her who she really was. My mission was to watch her, to see if she learned of her true nature on her own. Only she didn't, and now she's gone."

A rustling of cloth behind me. "We all must pass in time, Marius. Her kind, our kind. You could not have changed that."

"But it did not need to be so soon! I might have taken her to the tavern. You could have helped her. She could have endured for many years."

The woman sighed. "Perhaps she could have endured. Endured in suffering, and in sorrow. For she had thought herself a child of Lord and Lady Faraday, not something other—a changeling, a thing of legend. Perhaps knowing what she truly was would have given her woe rather than comfort. And even if not, why do you place all this blame upon yourself. Did not those you serve know of her true nature before you did?"

A sliver of ice seemed to pierce my heart. Yes, they had known all along what she was, but they had only wanted to watch her as she failed, not to help her. The Philosophers. And how was it they had known Alis was a changeling in the first place?

But there were others, *from outside, who convinced them to try. . . .*

I hardly saw as something soft was pressed into my hands. "Dry your tears, Marius." The woman's voice was hard and clear as glass now. "It will do Alis no honor to cast away your life. If you would serve her now, then do not forget the gift we gave you. . . ."

Her gown fluttered. Like a passing shadow she was gone, and I knew that I would never see her again. I looked down. In my hands was the silver cloth I had taken from my mother, and which I had given to Alis at St. Paul's. As always, it was unmarked with stain or rent. With it, I brushed the dust from her tomb. Then I stood and ran through the cathedral.

I reached my house an hour later, breathless, and it took me some time to find it amid the chaos and squalor, for the servants had abandoned me weeks ago for want of their wages. At last I found it beneath a table: a small book, bound in frayed leather. In my grief I had forgotten it. I took it now and sat at the table. My hands trembled, and a strong temptation for a drink came upon me—it would have steadied me—but I dismissed it and opened the book.

It was a journal.

The author's name was one Thomas Atwater, according to the title page, and the journal was begun in the year 1619.

I begin this record even as I begin a new life, the author wrote. *For on this day I have joined a newly established order of men and women who call themselves Seekers. Clever, they are, and curious and bold. They were alchemists once, but have since put such frivolous pursuits behind them, and instead search out the source of deeper and truer magicks. I am of great cheer as I write this, for at last I have found a hope of helping myself and those who are like me. . . .*

A thrill came over me as I read these words, for the slanted hand in which they were written was entirely familiar to me. There could be no doubt: The author of this journal was one and the same with the writer of the letters I had found in the vaults beneath the Charterhouse. Thomas Atwater had been one of the tavern folk.

And he had been a Seeker as well.

I read on, page after page, eschewing drink or food, only stopping to light several candles as night stole over the city outside. The journal seemed to contain more pages than possible given its size, recording the events of several years, and it was only as the light of dawn touched the windows that I finally reached the end. I set down the book, staring out the window at the new day beginning, and I knew that, once again in my life, I was just beginning as well. For what I had read in the journal had changed me completely and forever.

Atwater's writings had contained many revelations, but one above all others burned in my brain. And it was simply this: Everything which the Seekers stood for was a lie.

I thumbed again through the journal, trying to absorb all the knowledge contained within its pages. The author of those first happy lines had been utterly different than the sober and vengeful man who wrote the last pages. Atwater had joined the Seekers, as he had said, out of hope—a hope that their investigation into otherworldly magicks might reveal a way to help his kindred at the tavern, the folk of fairy descent, to ease their suffering at dwelling on this world.

It did not end that way.

Thomas was born to a maid who worked at the tavern, a woman who was badly used by a mortal man—a young lord who promised to give her a new life, then cast her into the gutter once he successfully deflowered her. She died, crushed by the weight of this world as the tavern folk often were, and Atwater was raised by the tavern's owner, Quincy Greenfellow, father to Sadie and her brothers.

Quincy Greenfellow's father had founded the tavern, in the village of Brixistane, south of London, as a haven and refuge for those who were like him—those who found the burden of this world heavy to bear. Over time, through whisper and rumor, folk similar to Greenfellow heard of the tavern, and as they came together there, they began to piece together just why it was they were different. They did not know their full history, but they knew they were descended from beings who were something other than human—beings other people called fairies.

In its early days, there were others who were attracted to the tavern besides those of more than mortal extraction. It became a favored haunt for would-be wizards as well, for those who trod down the dark, secret, and smoky paths of alchemy.

Chief among these alchemists who frequented the tavern was John Dee. At the time, Dee was widely known as Queen Elizabeth's astrologer, though he had long researched in secret the art of alchemy. In time, Dee's work led him into disfavor, poverty, and madness. But before the end, he made a discovery that greatly animated him, and which he brought to the tavern to show Greenfellow. It was an ancient scroll that Dee claimed was written by the legendary alchemist Hermes Trismegistus himself, and which he said contained writings about a tomb lost beneath the ruined palace of Knossos on the Greek island of Crete—a tomb that held the answer to the greatest mystery of magic the alchemists sought to unlock: the mystery of transmutation.

Dee never journeyed to Crete, for he fell ill and perished soon after this. But the scroll fell into the hands of some of the other alchemists who frequented the tavern, lesser magicians who had hoped to learn secrets of the craft from Dee. They vanished from the tavern and were not seen again for some years.

Then, one day, several of these alchemists did return to the tavern, and they were much changed. They were clad all in black, and their eyes were gold, and an aura of power cloaked them, as tangible to the folk of the tavern as the dark garments they wore. They called themselves Philosophers now, for they claimed to have learned the ultimate secret of the alchemists: the magic of transmutation and perfection.

These Philosophers, as they styled themselves, did not speak of what they had found on Crete, or what had changed them, but they brought several artifacts with them. Chief among these was a keystone taken from a doorway. They claimed there was a magic in the keystone, one that if they could fathom how to work it would open a door to another world—a world in which the folk of the tavern, those with the blood of fairykind in their veins, would know no pain, no suffering.

Greenfellow gave the Philosophers his blessing to erect a stone arch inside the tavern, and the keystone was set into it. The Philosophers worked many experiments on the stone, and often these involved blood taken from the folk of the tavern.

More blood the Philosophers asked for, and more, and always it was given freely, for the folk would do anything if it might mean opening a doorway to a place they could belong, if it meant the end of their pain. For as the world grew more crowded with people and buildings and things wrought of iron, their suffering grew as well.

However, no matter how much blood they received, the Philosophers could not make the stone work. "The worlds must draw closer together first," they said. And finally they withdrew from the tavern, and did not come back, and for all their help the folk of the tavern were rewarded with nothing.

Years passed, and the tavern folk waited. Surely the worlds would draw closer soon, and the Philosophers would return. Only they did not. Some heard whispers that the Philosophers had begun a new organization, and finally one young man of the tavern grew bold enough to seek out this new order in hopes of finding a way to convince the Philosophers to return to Greenfellow's and help its denizens.

And that was how Thomas Atwater joined the Seekers.

The Seekers were reluctant to let him join the order at first. They weren't certain he had the proper background, and they intended to research his origins more fully, only before they could do so word came down from the Philosophers themselves, and so he was admitted to the order—but on one condition. While he was a Seeker, he must never return to Greenfellow's Tavern. Such was his desire to help his kindred that Atwater readily acquiesced to this request, and he thought nothing of it.

Atwater's first two years in the Seekers were ones of wonder and constant discovery. He learned quickly, and seemed to have an uncanny knack for finding meanings and connections where others could not. Soon he was promoted from apprentice to journeyman, and his future in the Seekers looked bright.

However, Atwater never forgot his true purpose in joining the order. Always he sought to learn more about Knossos, and the archway, and why the Philosophers believed it might open a doorway to another world. He kept his research in this regard to himself, doing it in secret at night, apart from his other work, for the Philosophers had commanded him not to speak of his true origins to the other Seekers, and he feared if the others knew what he was doing, he would be forced to tell them of the tavern.

His secrecy proved both boon and bane. Such was his skill and cleverness that he was soon left to his own devices, and was allowed access to all the same vaults of books that the masters themselves used. And in his night work, he finally learned the truth—or at least something of the truth—about the Philosophers.

He found it in a box of papers—records set down by the Philosophers themselves, and which surely had been meant for their private library, but which had, by some mistake, been forgotten in a corner of the vaults. A corner in which Atwater would one day hide some of his own writings.

The papers were fragmentary; they did not tell Atwater everything, but they told him enough.

The Philosophers had indeed sought to open a doorway using the keystone in the tavern. However, the keystone was not the only discovery they made beneath the ruined palace at Knossos. They had found other things as well—things that changed them, and convinced them there was another world they might journey to, a world other than this Earth, where the true secret of transmutation would be revealed.

The Sleeping Ones have shown us that a state of true perfection is possible. But their blood, while a powerful catalyst for transmutation itself, is not by itself enough. It provides life, but not immortality, and must be drunk again and again for the effects to be maintained. Surely the Sleeping Ones knew of this true catalyst, what we would call the Philosopher's Stone, for their golden bodies do not age. And if the gate could be made to open, we might travel to their world and find it there. . . .

Their words had been lies. The Philosophers had not found the true secret of perfection, of transmutation, on Crete. They sought it still, and they had used those with fairy blood to try to gain it. Only when they failed, they had abandoned the tavern folk to poverty and suffering.

Rage filled Atwater at this betrayal, and despair. The last hastily written pages of the journal told how Atwater had hidden some of his papers in the vaults, hoping to retrieve them later. Then he intended to defy the order of the Philosophers and return to Greenfellow's, to take the journal to his people, that they might know the truth.

They did not wish for their own Seekers to know about us, Atwater wrote on the final page. *They feared the Seekers might learn too much about their true nature. That was why the Philosophers forbade me to return to the tavern. They did not want me to lead the Seekers there.*

That they will destroy me for what I intend to do, I have no doubt. It will not come at once—they will not wish to call attention to my defiance of their order, for fear it will lead the Seekers to the tavern—but it will come. And one day it will be my blood that will stain the keystone. That is why I leave this journal, as a record of the truth, of the cruelty and lies of the Philosophers. May it one day come into the hands of one who can seek vengeance for all of us.

There the journal ended. I closed the book, gripping it to keep my hands from trembling.

It was not my fault alone that Alis had perished. The Philosophers had known of the tavern all along. They had caused Alis to be sent out into the world, and had made me watch her—one more experiment just like those they had performed on the tavern folk.

"I am the one, Thomas," I murmured. "I am the one who can seek vengeance for you."

And thus began my plot to destroy the Philosophers.

My thirst for whiskey was forgotten; my mind was as clear and sharp as a knife made of glass. To ruin the founders of the Seekers, my first task would be to become, once again, the perfect Seeker myself. There was no other way to remain close to the Philosophers, to gain the knowledge I would need. With this in mind, I took my love for Alis, as well as my sorrow and pain, and put them away like precious things in a box, hiding them for a future when my revenge would be complete. That very day, I set out to become what I had once before resolved to be: the greatest Seeker the order had ever known.

The events of those next years are beyond the bounds of this tale. You can read of them easily enough—indeed, I'm sure you have done so already—in the annals of the Seekers.

It took several months and many acts of contrition to convince Rebecca and the rest of the Seekers that I was over my madness, that I had understood the error of my ways, that I had learned well from my mistakes. As a boy in Edinburgh, I had deceived many fair ladies into thinking me a pitiable waif in need of aid, and those skills served me now. Such was the apparent sincerity of my claims that in time the Seekers could not resist them, and I was readmitted to the order—under Rebecca's supervision, of course, and as a journeyman again.

However, these limitations were temporary. By the end of that first year I had achieved several major breakthroughs, and it seemed even the Philosophers had forgotten my past transgressions, for I was elevated again to the rank of master, and given free rein in conducting my investigations. And if I was grimmer than before, more likely to spend late nights poring over manuscripts and records than drinking with the younger Seekers at pub, then it was seen simply as an indication of my maturity and the important lessons I had learned so hard.

By the end of four years I was the Seeker you heard legends about upon first joining the order. I devised the Encounter Class system still used today, and I had achieved numerous otherworldly encounters myself, including several Class One Encounters. James Sarsin was only the first otherworldly traveler I met, but none of those events are important now. All that matters is that by the summer of 1684, I had achieved my goals. All regarded me as the finest specimen of Seekerhood ever to exist.

All that is, perhaps, save Rebecca. Her manner was ever cool and courteous to me. Indeed, we had worked on several cases together. Yet I knew she remained suspicious. She had never learned the truth of Byron's death, and it gnawed at her. I did not care; she would not stop me. And that summer I knew it was time at last to set my plan in motion.

Never, since that day they came to Madstone Hall, had I seen the Philosophers. Yet I knew they were ever present, observing what the Seekers were doing, and issuing their orders by written missives that mysteriously appeared inside a locked chest in a room in the Charterhouse.

By order of the Philosophers, no Seeker was to enter the room that contained the chest between sunset and dawn. It was during that time the missives were delivered, and I was determined to find out how it was done. If I could see who delivered the letters from the Philosophers, then I could follow him back to their hiding place. And once there, I believed I could learn what I needed to make my plan complete.

After leaving the Charterhouse for the day—making certain several Seekers saw me depart—I waited until dusk, then employed one of my oldest tricks, gathering the night shadows around myself, and slipped back into the Charterhouse. I crept into the room with the locked chest. Moments later I heard footsteps, and the door opened.

It was Rebecca. I froze as she scanned the chamber, but her eyes passed over the corner where I hid. She nodded, then shut the door, and I heard a key turning. I was locked inside the room; there were no windows by which I might escape.

I waited long hours, until I was certain midnight had passed. A headache came over me, as they still often did, and I began to drift. Then I heard a noise that at once made me alert: a scraping sound. In the gloom, I watched as one of the stone slabs that paved the floor lifted up. Gold light spilled through the opening.

A figure draped in black climbed through the trapdoor, then approached the chest, unlocked it, and placed a sealed parchment inside. The figure locked the chest again and retreated through the trapdoor, shutting it behind.

I forced myself to count a hundred heartbeats, though these were rapid enough, then crept forward, groping the floor with my hands. The trapdoor was so skillfully made that no trace of it could be detected even as I ran my fingers over it. Yet I had other senses, honed in my years in the dark labyrinth beneath Edinburgh. Now that I knew to seek it, I could detect the hollowness beneath one piece of slate. However, I could find no way to lift it. I tried to wedge my knife into the crack, but the blade broke. It was useless; the trapdoor could only be opened from within. I laid my head down on the floor in despair.

And heard voices.

"I've delivered the missive," said a man's voice I did not recognize.

A woman answered. "Very good. I believe it is past time he had new orders."

The stone beneath my ear hummed, bringing their voices to me, as if by some trick of echoes and angles like that in the Whispering Gallery. There must have been a passage below where the two stood. I pressed my ear closer to the floor, straining to hear their words.

". . . and he has redeemed himself," the woman was saying. "It seems Adalbrecht's ill influence has not ruined him after all, for we have made a fine Seeker of him at last."

I tensed, and not only because I knew they were speaking of me, as well as of my former master, but because I recognized her voice. Years ago I had crouched in the shadows outside my master's study and had listened to this very same voice tell him, *We have come.*

I had been a fool. The Philosophers employed no messengers who might lead me to them; they would never risk their secrecy in that way. They delivered the missives themselves. Only they believed no one was in the room above, and my hearing, always sharp, had been made preternaturally keen by my excitement and dread.

"Adalbrecht," the man said, his voice thick with disgust. "We must go to Knossos next month, else we shall end up as he did."

"You need not tell me." The woman's voice was sharp; I could imagine her gold eyes flashing.

"I still wonder why he chose as he did," the man said. His voice was beginning to fade; they were moving away. "Why he chose death."

"Adalbrecht was always the weakest of us. Remember, he was the last to drink of the Sleeping Ones and be . . ." I lost her voice, and I thought them gone. Then the stone whispered once more in my ear. ". . . and he always had strange notions. Yet we never discovered anything of his writings. I suppose we shall never know what his thoughts were, and nor does it matter. He is dead now."

"Something we shall never be."

The man's laughter was the last thing I heard. Then the stone ceased its humming.

I rose to me knees, and I knew what I had to do.

Crete. I had to go to Crete, to the ruins of Knossos. They would be traveling there soon, they had said so; I could get close to them there. But I needed to know more. I needed to find the secret way beneath the ruins, to the tomb of those they called the Sleeping Ones, so I could lay in wait for them. But how could I discover it?

We shall never know what his thoughts were. . . .

Yes, that was it. I wished to get close to the Philosophers, that I might learn how to destroy them. But had I not lived for years with a Philosopher? Master Albrecht had been one of their kind. After his death, I had searched his library and had found his old journal, from the years when he was still mortal. But surely he had left other records behind—records that would help me find the tomb beneath Knossos.

I waited until the room was unlocked and, concealing myself in shadows once again, slipped outside. I appeared at the Charterhouse later that morning, feigning surprise when Rebecca informed me I had new orders from the Philosophers themselves. I opened the missive and could not help but smile.

"Is it an assignment you favor, then?" Rebecca said, arching an eyebrow.

"Very much so," I said, tucking the missive inside my coat. The Philosophers wished me to go to Scotland, to investigate legends of a magical portal in a cave in the Highlands. It would be just the excuse I needed; no one would question my leaving London and going north.

I departed that very morning, and after several days of jostling in carriages down muddy roads, I reached Madstone Hall. As I stepped out of the carriage, I laid eyes on my manor for the first time in nearly ten years. Despite all that had happened to me, I smiled at the familiar sight. I was received in the front hall with great deference—and equal trepidation—by several servants I vaguely recognized. I looked around, then asked them where I could find Pietro.

An older man blinked watery eyes. "But did you not receive the letters, sir?"

"Letters?" It had been long since I had received a missive from Madstone. I could not remember the last.

"It was some years ago, sir. It was a fever that took him. Your solicitors mind the affairs of the manor now, and we keep the house in good order." He swallowed. "For your return, of course, sir."

His words were like a blow to me. The letters must have come four years ago, in the months of my madness after Alis died. I suppose I had thrown them in the fire without ever opening them. Thus I had never heard the news of Pietro's death, and it struck me now as if it had just occurred. There was nothing left to connect me to him, to Master Albrecht.

Only that wasn't true. There had to be something there, something more.

"Unpack my things," I told the servants. "I shall be staying at Madstone Hall for a time."

They stared at me with wide eyes, then did as I bid them.

I began my search that day, beginning with the library. The silver key was in the desk drawer where I had left it, and I used it to unlock the cabinet of arcane books. Inside was the small wooden box with the diary and the vial of dark fluid. I had no doubt that the reason Rebecca and Byron came to Madstone after Master Albrecht died was to search for these things by order of the Philosophers. Only I had found them first. Then, before we departed for London, I had spirited them back into the cabinet. And here they were, just as I had left them.

While the objects had not changed, I had, and I knew better what they were. The diary was written by my master before he became a Philosopher, when he was simply Martin Adalbrecht, one of the young alchemists who had frequented Greenfellow's Tavern with John Dee. Then, with his cronies, he had gone to Knossos, and there they had been . . . transformed. However, the journal had been written before that time; it could not help me.

I lifted the vial, and I thought I knew what it was as well. It was blood, taken from those they called the Sleeping Ones. Who these beings were—whence they came and why they slumbered—I did not know. All I knew was that drinking their blood had changed the Philosophers, giving them eyes of gold. And it continued to give them life.

The vial seemed hot in my hand. I shut it back in the box with the journal and locked them back in the cabinet.

I continued my search of the manor, looking for anything that might help me—any letters he wrote, any records he kept, any notes he might have scribbled in the margins of books. Soon I had the servants frantic, for they would no sooner clean a room than I would tear it apart, looking for some clue that could help me. Only there was nothing.

Days became a week, then a fortnight. I did not sleep, did not eat, and I began to crave whiskey again. The servants fled at the mere sight of my coming. The manor had become a ruin. I had punched holes in the walls and torn up floorboards in my search, but still had found nothing of my master's. The only writing of his in the house was his old journal. . . .

The journal. Midnight found me sitting in his library, staring at the journal. I read through it again, but it was the same as before: the foolish hopes and dreams of a man who believed magic was real.

Yet he had been right, hadn't he? It *was* real.

I picked up the vial. The gold spider on the stopper shone in the candlelight, the ruby set into its abdomen winking at me. Then, before I could reconsider, I unstopped the vial, held it to my lips, and tilted my head back. The fluid coursed down my throat, hot and thick. I knew fiery pain, then only blackness.

It was morning when one of the servingwomen found me, sprawled on the floor of the library. She shook my shoulder, begging me to wake, but when I finally opened my eyes she clasped her hand to her mouth, stifling a scream, and fled.

I pulled myself up and caught my reflection in the glass doors of a cabinet. Startled eyes stared back at me, gold as coins. By all that was holy, what had I done?

A strange sensation came over me. I felt, not stronger, but horribly weak, as if for the first time in my life I sensed the encroaching decrepitude, the constant rotting of my body, that was a correlate of mortality. And I also sensed that, for the moment, that mortal progress had ceased.

I called for the servants to help me, but no one answered my call. Shaking, I pulled myself up to the desk and sat. My eyes fell upon the open journal, and a breath of wonder escaped me, for I saw words upon the pages I had not seen before.

A palimpsest—I had heard of such things. They were twice-written books, created when a monk or scribe took an old book, rubbed its pages clean with sand, and cut and sewed them anew to make a fresh book to write in. However, sometimes, in the right light, the old words might yet be seen, bleeding through behind the new.

The journal was like a palimpsest. Only it was the old words that had been easily read, and the newer words that could only be seen in the right conditions. However, it was not light that showed these other words, but rather new, golden eyes. The writing seemed to dance upon the page, bright and shining, as if written with molten metal.

As I have begun a new life, so I begin this journal anew. We are different now. The Philosophers, we call ourselves, as though all mysteries are ours to understand. But I know, as perhaps the others do not, that there is far more for us yet to learn, that this is only the beginning. . . .

I clutched the journal and read. The house was silent; no servants disturbed me. At last the light outside the windows failed. I shut the little book and buried my face in my hands. What a fool I was. I had been wrong about everything.

"It wasn't you, Alis," I murmured. Anguish burned in me, hotter than the blood I had consumed. "It wasn't you at all. It was I."

"What are you talking about, Marius?"

I looked up. In my despair, I had not heard her footsteps on the carpet. She stood in the door of library, dressed in red, a smirk on her lips.

"Rebecca," I croaked. "What are you doing here?"

She sauntered in. "I might ask the same of you. This is hardly a cave in the Highlands. I had a feeling you might be up to something, Marius. You had a secretive air about you when you left, so I decided I would follow you and see what you were up to. I hope you don't mind that I let myself in, but there's no sign of your servants anywhere, so I—"

A gasp escaped her. She had moved farther into the room and was staring at me.

"Gods, Marius, your eyes. What's happened to you?"

Despite my fear, I smiled. "I think you know now why the servants fled."

She only shook her head, taking a step back. I rose.

"I'm like them now, Rebecca."

"Like who?" she said, shaking her head, only then a moment later she said, "The Philosophers."

"Yes."

Her eyes went wide. "Oh, Marius," she breathed, reaching a hand toward me. I thought perhaps it was a gesture of supplication, of forgiveness. There was a softness on her face I had not seen since we were lovers.

Rebecca's eyes rolled up, her arm went limp, and she slumped to the floor. The hilt of a dagger jutted from her back. Even as I stared, trying to comprehend, three figures clad in black drifted into the room.

"Why?" I choked on the word.

The two men pushed back the hoods of their cloaks, and the woman lifted the veil from her face. They gazed at me with serene gold eyes.

"Our kind must never be seen," the woman said.

I knelt beside Rebecca, feeling for the beat of her heart, but there was none. I looked up at them. "But she didn't see you."

"No," the woman said. "She saw you, Marius." She glanced at the men. "Leave me, Gabriel, Arthur—I would do this, if I may."

The men nodded and left. She approached the desk, brushing the journal with a gloved hand.

"Ah," she said. "Albrecht's journal."

I stood and turned away from Rebecca's body. I wanted to weep for her but could not. "You sent them here to fetch it all those years ago, didn't you? Rebecca and Byron. Only I hid it from them."

"No, we sent them here to fetch you." She laughed at my shocked expression. "Do not be so surprised, Marius. There is nothing you have read in this journal that we do not already know. As he grew weak, Adalbrecht confided everything to us. Much as he wished to betray us in the end he could not. We are bound to one another by the blood we have drunk. It sees itself in each of us, and knows its kind, and prevents us from doing harm to any other in whose veins it flows. So you see, much as I've been tempted to throttle one of the others from time to time, I cannot."

Her words horrified me, for I sensed they were true. "But what are you really?"

Her eyes fixed on me. "Do you not know what we are? And what you are, Marius?" She tapped the journal. "I believe you do."

I thought of the headaches that had afflicted me with growing frequency over the years. From my coat I pulled out the silver cloth I had carried with me for so many years. It glimmered softly in the gray light. "I'm like them. The folk of the tavern. I'm like Thomas Atwater. Like Alis."

"You were." She picked up the empty vial. "You are like us now."

I shut my eyes, thinking of all I had read in my master's journal, trying to understand. He had described his journey to Crete with the others, how they had found the forgotten passage leading beneath the ruins of Knossos, and there had stumbled upon a tomb containing seven stone sarcophagi. They opened the sarcophagi and found within seven figures masked in gold, jewels of lapis and jade adorning their burnished skin.

Impossibly, the beings seemed alive, for they were warm to the touch, and their bodies were not corrupt. However, if they were alive, then they slept, for nothing could cause them to stir, not even when one of the alchemists cut them.

It was she who had done it—the one woman among them. Her name was Phoebe. What instinct had caused her to bend her head, to drink the blood that flowed forth, my master did not know, but they had watched the transformation come upon her. Then they had all drunk of the blood of the Sleeping Ones.

All but one, that was. Eight alchemists had gone to Crete, but when one of them tried to flee, afraid to drink the blood, Phoebe had murdered him with a knife to the heart. For no one who was not one of their own must ever be allowed to know their secret.

With one dead, the alchemists were seven in number just like the sarcophagi, and so each drank from a different being—

though Adalbrecht was the last. And all of them were transformed.

The Philosophers had found other things in the tomb besides the Sleeping Ones. They had found tablets with writing they could not fathom, and the remains of a stone doorway, now fallen to ruin. Some of these things they brought with them back to London, though the Sleeping Ones they left beneath Knossos, and they concealed the passage so that no one else might ever find it.

After that, the journal told of my master's years as a Philosopher. He had not taken part in the attempts to restore the doorway, to open it. Instead he had sought to decipher the writings from the tomb. After many years he had made little progress, but he had learned enough to know that the Sleeping Ones came from another world, that they had come to escape some great conflagration, and that they were waiting for something—some ultimate act of transmutation. As always, transformation required the proper catalyst. Only what that catalyst might be, he did not know, though he had suspicions. Nor did he know the nature of the transformation the Sleeping Ones sought—only that it would come when their world drew closer to this one.

In time, Adalbrecht grew weary—weary of enduring, weary of making the trek to Knossos once every decade to drink another sip of their blood. He had begun to fade. The other Philosophers had known it, and they did not protest when he retired to Scotland. Then, one night in Edinburgh, he saw a boy on the street. He had known the folk of the tavern, and in an instant he knew this boy was like them. The silver cloth could only have been made by one of their kind. And it shone in the boy's eyes.

The boy was me. Why he took me in, the journal did not say. Perhaps it was pity, or perhaps it was some desire to make amends for what had been done to the folk of the tavern. No matter, the result was the same.

"It wasn't her," I said. "You gave me the mission of watching Alis Faraday to see if she would discover her true heritage. But she wasn't the real subject of the study. It was me. You wanted to see if I would discover what I really was."

The woman—Phoebe—nodded. "And so you have, Marius. I confess, we began to grow a trifle impatient toward the end.

Hence our words spoken beneath the Charterhouse, and our giving you an assignment in Scotland, close to your home."

I hung my head. So they had known I was there in the locked room, listening.

"No, Marius, it matters not. These were only nudges. You have learned everything on your own. This experiment is over."

Experiment? So that was all this was to her. We were simply things to be used to satisfy their curiosity. Myself. Alis. They had made me watch her die for their little *experiment*.

I glared at her now, rage filling me. "Why didn't you simply tell me these things?"

"Because you loved Adalbrecht too much. You would have done as he asked out of loyalty to him. You would have lived a quiet life here in the north. We could not allow that. And so you had to find out on your own."

My rage subsided. I was too weary, too full of sorrow. They had used Alis just like the folk in the tavern. Just as they had used me.

"I know you are angry, Marius," she said. "But it will soon pass, you shall see. Your old life is behind you now. The pain you had started to feel—the headaches, the weariness—I think you will feel no more. You have been remade." She held out her hand. "It is time for you to join us."

Astonishment replaced anger. "Join you? You mean become a Philosopher?"

"Yes. A Philosopher."

I struggled to comprehend. "But what do you need me for?"

"Adalbrecht is gone. Our number is diminished. We would be seven again." She studied me with her golden eyes. "And it is too late for you to undo what has been done. You are like us, Marius, whether you will it or not. It is better for you to be with your own kind."

"And if I refuse to join you?"

She smiled. "You will join us. You are too curious not to. After all, how can you hope to continue Adalbrecht's work in translating the writings from the tomb?"

I cursed her, even as I knew she was right, and we left that night in a carriage bound for London.

* * *

That is how I was the first and only Seeker ever to become a Philosopher. In the centuries that followed, I did just as Phoebe had said I would—I continued the work begun by my master, seeking to translate the writings from the tomb of the Sleeping Ones, trying to understand what it was they were waiting for.

However, as the carriage rolled away from Madstone Hall that night, I knew there was one thing Phoebe and the others did not know—a secret they would never uncover. I thought of Queen Dido, and how she had thrown herself on the pyre when she had lost all that she loved. In a way, I had done the same. For the Marius I had been was dead.

Yet like a ghost that lingered on, I remained, and always I craved revenge. Only I was bound to them by my transformation. As the centuries passed, Phoebe's words were proven true. The blood of the Sleeping Ones connected us. I could not harm them—at least not directly. But I schemed, I waited, and I knew the day would come when the time would be right, and when another would help me achieve what I sought.

That time is now. And that other is you.

Now you know what no other besides our own kind has ever known. Now you know the truth of the origin of the Philosophers.

And now, I beg of you, help me bring about their end.

PART FOUR

CATALYST

33.

Aryn stood at the window of her bedchamber, watching distant fires burn in the night.

Teravian lay in the bed behind her, asleep by the slow rhythm of his breathing. There was no point in waking him; she always saw the fires now. In the morning, Teravian would send his men—those that remained, at any rate—out beyond the castle, and they would find more houses burned, or perhaps even an entire village.

A week ago, Aryn herself had ridden to a village not a league from Calavere, and she had spoken to a man who had burned his family alive in their cottage.

"There was no hope for them," he had said when she asked him why he had done it, eyes blank in his sooty face. "No hope at all."

"What do you mean?" she had said, trying to comprehend. "Were they ill with plague?"

But the man hadn't answered. He had sat on the ground, drawing empty circles in the dirt with a stick, until the king's men came to haul him away to the castle's dungeon. Later, from another villager, Aryn had learned that the man's wife and children had been healthy and happy, and that he had been the proudest farmer in the village.

Aryn lifted her gaze from the fires to the heavens. She didn't need to look to the north to see it anymore; the rift had grown rapidly over these last days, spreading out across half the sky like a blight, blotting out the stars. It was visible even by day now as a shadow against the blue of the sky, and it made the sunlight feel pale and wan.

The night breeze wafted in through the window, and her nose wrinkled at the foul odor rising from the bailey. The whole castle smelled putrid. Most of the servants had left, and those that remained did so little work they might as well have departed with the others. Aryn had taken to emptying chamber pots herself, and she was forced to scrounge in the kitchens with everyone else for what foodstuffs had not spoiled. No goods had come to the castle in days, and carts stood abandoned on the road that led up to the gates. She had gotten a little milk two days before by convincing a boy to milk a cow that had been bellowing in the lower bailey, neglected, its udder swollen.

On her way back into the castle, she had passed an old woman lying dead in the mud of the courtyard. People had shuffled past her without so much as looking. Aryn had to call for guards three times before someone came to take the body away.

That same day, Teravian had ventured out for a ride. When he returned to the castle, his face had been grim. He had seen entire villages abandoned, and crops—ready for harvesting—left to rot in the fields.

"Where have all the people gone?" Aryn had asked.

"I'm not sure, but more than once I heard stories of people in white robes. They gather on hilltops where they stand and raise their arms to the sky, waiting. Waiting for something. I saw some of them, walking along the road. At first they made me think of Raven Cultists. But they were dressed in white, not black, and they were silent. I called to them, but they only stared, mouths open. I looked into the eyes of a woman who marched with them, and I saw nothing, Aryn. Nothing at all."

He had trembled as she held him, and she had wished she could brew something to calm him. However, she seemed to have forgotten how to concoct the simplest potion. Her mind was addled; she could not think. Flustered, Aryn had tried to contact Lirith over the Weirding, to ask the other witch how to make a soothing draught. However, she had managed to touch Lirith's thread only for a moment.

The stars go out, Lirith had said. *She is not coming back.*

That was all. Aryn had called out again and again with her mind, and even with her voice, but she could not reach Lirith. All the same, she had understood whom Lirith had meant, who was not coming back.

Grace. It was Grace whom Lirith had pictured in her mind.

Aryn rested a hand on her belly, but she could not feel the child move within. She tried to use the Touch to sense the little life, but the threads were too fragile, too tangled. Or maybe there was no life there to sense. Maybe the man who had burned his home, his family was right. Maybe there was no hope after all.

Behind her, Teravian let out a soft moan in his sleep. The nightmares again. Aryn knew she should go to bed. Instead she stayed at the window, gazing into the night, and watched the fires burn.

34.

The sun sank toward the horizon, its light spilling across the desert like blood. Grace knelt on the edge of the patch of slipsand, staring at the place where Travis had vanished. This couldn't be happening; he couldn't be gone.

Farr bound a rag around his right arm. "The bloodspell that created the sand creatures must have been keyed to Travis. I think he knew that. I think he knew, if he perished, the sand creatures would as well."

Larad's shadow fell upon Grace. "He saved us, Your Majesty."

"Then let us save him!" Vani said, pushing Larad aside. She knelt beside Grace. "You sensed him, didn't you? Where is he?"

Grace shook her head. It didn't matter. She had felt his thread go dark. Travis was dead. Truly dead.

Vani gripped her shoulder. The *T'gol*'s fingers dug into her flesh. "I said where is he, Grace?"

The pain cut through the dullness in Grace's mind. "There." She pointed in front of her. "Down there. Six feet. Maybe more. I'm not sure. He could have been drawn farther down after he . . . after his thread . . ." She couldn't speak the words.

Farr moved forward. "Six feet of slipsand is not enough to have crushed him. I will call the *morndari*. If I can summon enough of the spirits, they will be able to pull him out." He started to undo the bandage on his arm, then staggered.

Vani leaped up, keeping him from falling. "No. You have lost too much blood already. You will perish as well."

"I have to try." He tried to pull away from her, but he was too weak to break her grip. He gazed at her, dark eyes imploring. "Please, Vani. You know what he is fated to do. Let me go!"

Vani clenched her jaw, then released Farr. However, before he could remove the bandage Larad spoke.

"Wait—there is another way." The Runelord held the iron box that contained the Imsari. He opened it and took out the three Stones. "I am not so skilled with the Imsari as Master Wilder, but I may be able to use them."

"If you're going to use them, do it now!" Farr said, his voice edging into a snarl. "He's been down there over a minute already."

Vani's gold eyes locked on the Runelord. "You said you did not know the rune for sand."

"Then I will speak the rune of opening." Larad gripped all three Stones in one hand. "*Urath*," he intoned, and with his free hand he made a cutting motion.

It was as if the ground had been struck by a gigantic hand. A golden wave rose up, spilling outward in either direction as the sand parted.

"*Urath!*" Larad shouted, sweat pouring down his brow, and again he thrust with his hand. More sand flew up and out, and a trough formed in the sand, deeper and deeper.

"Cease!" Vani cried.

Larad lowered his hand and staggered back, clutching the Stones to his chest. The Runelord's spell had formed a trench in the sand a dozen feet deep. At the bottom of it lay a crumpled figure.

Avhir had been standing a short distance away, observing everything with bronze eyes. Now the *T'gol* stalked forward. "The walls of the trench are not stable. The sand is going to collapse back in."

"I will get him," Vani said, and before anyone could move she jumped down into the trough. The *T'gol* landed lightly, but the vibrations from the impact were enough to cause sand to begin sheeting down the walls, pouring into the trough. She crouched and lifted Travis. His body was limp in her arms.

"Take him!"

Vani was even stronger than Grace had imagined, for with a grunt she stood and lifted Travis's body above her head, though her face was lined with effort. Braced by Farr, Avhir reached down a long arm and grabbed Travis's wrist. He pulled back, heaving Travis's body out of the trough.

The edges of the trench gave way with a groan, and sand flooded in just as a dark streak shot upward in a cloud of dust. The air shimmered, then Vani was there. The *T'gol* drew close as Avhir laid Travis's body on stable ground.

"Is he . . . ?"

"Yes," Avhir said. "He is dead. The slipsand suffocated him."

Vani looked at Grace, her gold eyes brilliant in the last of the daylight. "You are a witch. You can revive him."

No. Travis wasn't dying, he was dead. All the same, Grace reached out with the Touch. Two years ago, she had failed to save a dear friend—Sir Garf—by connecting his life thread to hers; she had been held back by the dark blot on her own strand. Since then, she had learned to move beyond the shadow of her past; there was nothing to hinder her magic. However, magic itself was too weak now, and even if it wasn't, it wouldn't matter. His life thread had been extinguished. She searched, but there was nothing for her to connect her own strand to.

Larad touched her shoulder. "You can do it, Your Majesty. You have the power."

"Witchcraft is the magic of life," she said, the words bitter as poison on her tongue. "It can do nothing for the dead."

"I do not mean magic, Your Majesty. Were you not a skilled healer before you became a witch? Have you not revived others who were gone? I know you have—I have heard you speak of it."

These words jolted Grace, like the electric surge from the paddles of a defibrillator, causing her own heart to begin beating rapidly. For so long she had a been a witch, a queen; she had almost forgotten what she had been far longer, what she really was. But Travis hadn't forgotten.

Don't worry, Grace. You'll save me. I know you will. . . .

He had known sacrificing himself would stop the sand creatures. Just as he had known Grace could bring him back. She was a doctor; she could do this. Except she didn't have the equipment she needed: a crash cart, epinephrine, and a staff of nurses.

What about magic, Grace?

No, the Weirding was too weak, too easily tangled. For a moment she wondered if Larad might be able to speak the rune of lightning, to give his heart a jolt. But the amps had to be precisely tuned. Too much, and all hope was lost. There was only one way to do this.

She knelt beside Travis, letting instinct and experience take over. How long had it been since he had stopped breathing? Two minutes, maybe more. They had to begin CPR immediately. She turned Travis's head, and with two fingers she removed sand from his mouth and trachea, clearing his airway.

"Vani," she said, "kneel down beside him."

The *T'gol* did not question Grace's orders.

"Place your hands here, just above the base of his breastbone. When I tell you, perform fifteen chest compressions. Like this—press firmly with the heel of your hand, but not so hard as to fracture his ribs."

Grace moved around Travis, aware of his gray skin, his blue-tinged lips. She tilted his head back, pinched his nose shut, placed her mouth over his, forming a tight seal, and breathed. His chest rose, then fell. She breathed again, then leaned back.

"Now, Vani. Fifteen compressions."

When the *T'gol* was done, Grace breathed twice into his mouth. She tasted sand and blood.

"Come on, Travis," she said, her voice strict: a doctor's command. "You're strong. Stronger than anyone. I know you can do this."

He didn't move. As Vani continued compressions, Grace raised his eyelids. His pupils were fixed and dilated.

No, she refused to accept this. He couldn't be dead, not after everything that had happened to them, not after everything they had survived together. She breathed into him two more times.

Vani performed another set of compressions, and again Grace breathed air into his lungs. Five times they repeated the pattern, ten. Grace grew dizzy; sweat streamed down Vani's face. The others gathered around in the failing light, faces intent. Still Travis remained motionless.

It's no use, Grace. He's been down too long. CPR can stave off brain death only for so long. It's time to call it . . .

"No!" she shouted, furious at the doctor's voice in her, at its dry, emotionless tone. This was not just another patient. This was Travis. Sweet, brave, foolish Travis whom she loved more than any other person on this or any world.

"Move," she said, pushing Vani out of the way.

Grace straddled Travis. She raised a fist, then slammed it down against Travis's chest. His body flopped with the force of her blow, then lay still. She checked, but there was still no pulse. She balled her fist and struck him again, in the center of the sternum. Again. And again.

Farr's hand closed around her wrist as she raised her hand one more time. "Stop, Grace. It's over. Let him go."

A coldness came over Grace, as well as a steely certainty that could be forged only from purest rage. She looked up at Farr, and she saw her eyes reflected in his. They blazed with emerald sparks.

"Let go of my hand now, or I will kill you."

Farr staggered back, his mouth open. Grace forgot him in an instant. She gazed down at Travis. It was almost as if his voice whispered again in her mind. *I believe in you. . . .*

She believed in him, too. And she would not let him go. Grace brought her fist down against his chest. Hard.

Travis's eyes snapped open.

His back arched as he drew in a rasping breath. He clutched her arms—hard, hurting her—but she didn't care. She pulled him into a sitting position, and he leaned against her, his body shaking as he coughed up sand. After a minute his breathing eased. She checked his pulse; it was rapid but steady. Then she probed with other senses. His life thread shone: a brilliant amalgam of blue silver and molten gold.

She opened her eyes and smiled at him. "Welcome back, Travis."

He cupped her cheek in a hand, and despite the pain on his face, he grinned. "I knew you'd come to get me."

"I would never leave you behind," Grace said, tears evaporating from her cheeks. "Not for anything."

She looked up, but Farr had already turned his back, walking away.

35

They returned to their campsite at the dead oasis. Vani and Avhir offered to carry Travis, but he was able to walk on his own power with some help from Grace and Larad.

They found the camels dead, but they had expected that. The beasts lay sprawled on the ground, their corpses drained of blood. Already the wind scoured at them, and soon their bones would join the others that scattered the oasis. They rested for a time, drinking and eating a little, though Travis would take only water. Night fell, and while they made no fire, it seemed to Grace that Travis's skin gleamed in the dimness.

"I believed you were dead, Travis, when you stepped into the slipsand," Vani said, her golden eyes glinting like a cat's in the darkness. "But you live. Truly it is Fate."

"I think Fate had a little help in the matter," Travis said, holding up Sinfathisar. The Stone of Twilight shimmered in the moonlight. He set it in the box with the other two Imsari and closed the lid. "Thank you, Larad."

Larad said nothing, though it seemed the corners of his mouth twitched, curving upward.

Travis took Grace's hand in his "Fate was right about one thing, Grace. I would never have gotten this far without you."

Grace squeezed his hand. The joy she felt was too powerful to express in words.

The darkness unfolded, and Avhir stepped into their circle. He crouched. "I gathered what supplies remained in the packs on each of the camels. There was little enough. This is the last of the water." He set a waterskin on the ground. It was less than half-full.

Larad eyed the skin. "That will not last us long."

"It will not have to," Avhir said. "The dervish says we will reach Morindu tomorrow." He gazed at a dark figure that stood on the other side of the dead oasis.

"Why wait for tomorrow?" Travis said, standing.

Surprise finally compelled Grace to speak "You mean go tonight? What about the slipsand?"

"It's no easier to see in daylight than moonlight," Travis said. "And the Scirathi could already be on the other side with Nim."

He was right, of course. They had to try. But Grace couldn't help wondering who would retrieve them from the slipsand once all of them went under.

"I'll get the dervish," Avhir said.

Grace followed the tall man with her gaze, and a sigh escaped her. "He hasn't so much as mentioned Kylees or Rafid."

"Our kind do not speak of *T'gol* who are no more," Vani said, the words quiet but hard.

Grace stared at her. "Why not?"

"Because a *T'gol* does not think of death, or of others who have perished. When a *T'gol* dies, it is as if he or she never was. Their name is never mentioned among our kind again. That way we can fight with abandon, without fearing our own ends."

Grace thought she had never heard such sad words spoken in her life. She touched Vani's hand. "I would still speak your name."

"You are not *T'gol*," Vani said, and looked away.

They were silent until Avhir and Farr stepped into their circle.

"It's no use," the former Seeker said. "We cannot pass through the slipsand. Not this night, not tomorrow, not ever." He swayed on his feet.

Vani leaped up, steadying him. "You are bleeding."

There was a fresh cut on his left arm. Hand shaking, he drew out a cloth and pressed it over the wound. "For the last hour, I've been trying to call the *morndari*, but they won't come. Either I don't have enough blood left to sacrifice, or magic has grown too weak."

"Your magic, maybe," Travis said. He stood. "Larad, give me Sinfathisar again."

Travis took the Stone of Twilight, and it seemed to pulse in the moonlight. Grace couldn't help letting out a sigh. Magic was failing, but the Imsari seemed to have lost none of their luster or beauty. Why were they untouched?

Travis bent his head, murmuring a word over Sinfathisar then let go of the Stone. It did not fall to the ground, but instead hovered in midair.

"*Aro*," Travis said. "Go, seek out the way."

The Stone began to drift through the air, southward, away from the camp, hovering five feet off the ground.

"Come on," Travis said, walking after the floating Stone. The others exchanged looks, then followed.

"Are you strong enough to walk?" Grace said to Farr.

His face twisted in a look of disgust. "Don't show kindness to me, not now. If I had kept you from doing your work, he would be—you would have been right to kill me."

She winced. "I wouldn't have done that."

He gazed at her with dark eyes. "Yes, you would have." He quickened his pace, moving ahead of her, and Grace could only stare after him.

He's right, Grace. You would have done it. Given a choice between Travis and Hadrian, you would have chosen Travis.

Until that moment, something had been growing inside Grace when she was with Hadrian, something strange and beautiful, like a flower whose nature she couldn't know until it unfurled. But now she realized it had been cut: a bud nipped from the stem before it could bloom.

They passed over the ridge and came to a halt at the edge of the expanse of slipsand—to the place where Travis had died. Sinfathisar held its position, hovering in midair.

"Guide us," Travis said. "*Aro.*"

And the Stone floated out over the slipsand.

"This way," Travis said, and stepped forward. The others came after him, following in his footsteps. They moved in single file, for there was no telling how narrow were the strips of solid ground between the patches of slipsand. Nor was there any way to discern with the eye where one ended and the other began.

The moon rose higher into the sky. Its brilliance made the jagged rift in the southern heavens all the darker. The rift seemed to grow even as Grace watched, blotting out more stars. She felt sick, and did her best to keep her eyes on the ground.

Their progress was slow, and many times the Stone of Twilight halted, suspended in place, until Travis spoke the rune of guiding and the Stone floated forward once more. As the moon passed its zenith, Grace and Larad began to stumble with weariness, and at one point Grace's foot strayed from the path.

Her foot sank, and instantly she felt the pull of the slipsand. However, Avhir was behind her, and was able to grab her shoulders, plucking her up and placing her back on the safe path.

"Thank you, my friend," she said, touching his cheek.

He gave her a stern look. "I am not your friend, Sai'ana Grace. Do not care for me, as I cannot care for you."

"Why?" she said, too stunned to say anything else.

"Because to do his task, a *T'gol* must have a heart of stone. To care for another is to open oneself to weakness."

He stalked away, and Grace gazed after him.

"You're wrong," she said quietly. It was caring for another, opening oneself to that pain, that vulnerability, that made one truly strong. Strength was knowing you could be wounded, that you could lose. Her gaze drifted to a figure in a black robe, walking ahead. A sigh escaped her lips, and she continued on, careful to keep to the path Travis made.

At last the moon sank toward the horizon. Farr shuffled his feet, as if unable to pick them up, and even the *T'gol* moved with heavy steps. They had gone only a half mile southwards, but they had walked many more miles as they wound their way through the patches of slipsand. Of them all, only Travis still seemed fresh. He kept murmuring the rune of guiding, and he would wait for the others to catch up if he got too far ahead. Finally, as the eastern horizon lightened from jasper to rose quartz, Travis halted. He held out his hand, and Sinfathisar settled against his palm.

"What's wrong?" Grace said, too weary to feel panic. "Are we lost?"

Travis shook his head. "We're here."

Vani and Avhir probed carefully; the ground was stable. Travis held out the Stone, and Larad took it, nestling it back in the iron box with the other Imsari.

"Your power is greater than ever, Master Wilder," Larad said, raising a fractured eyebrow. "I could never have done what you did—commanding the power of a Great Stone for so long."

Vani's eyes were locked on Travis, and so were Farr's. Had they seen what Grace had, the way he had shone in the night?

Long ago, in the city of Morindu, the god-king Orú was chained by his own people because of his terrible power. What would happen if Travis kept growing stronger?

Only he can't, Grace. Not if magic keeps weakening.

Or could he? What if Travis was like the Great Stones? What if whatever was affecting magic had no effect on him?

They ate a little as the horizon grew brighter and drank the rest of their water. It would do more good to carry it in their bodies, Avhir said, rather than in a skin. However, moments after drinking her share, Grace was thirsty again, her throat dry.

She noticed Travis standing a short distance off. Again he had drunk a little water but had taken no food. She moved to him, and he smiled as she approached.

"I was going to ask how you are," she said. "Only you look wonderful. Better than I've ever seen you."

He drew in a breath. "I feel good, Grace. I don't know why. I should be tired, and hungry, and thirsty, but I'm not."

Grace managed a grim smile. "I wish I could say the same."

They were silent for a moment, gazing toward the east, then he looked at her. "I saw things, Grace. Down there, when I died."

She nodded. "That's common. People who've been revived often report seeing various phenomena—light, a tunnel, the images of loved ones. As far as we can tell, it's simply the brain trying to make sense of what's happening to it as it's deprived of oxygen."

"I suppose you're right. Only I didn't see those things. I saw the two twins, the ones from the story Hadrian told us. One was shining, as if he was outlined in stars, and the other was dark—so dark I could only see him like a silhouette against the night. They were struggling, destroying each other."

Grace looked up at the sky. It was too light now to see it, but the rift was still there, still growing. "The end is close, isn't it, Travis? But even an end would be *something*. This will be even worse. It will be like when one of the *T'gol* dies. It will be as if none of this—Earth, Eldh, and everything on them— ever were, or ever could have been."

Travis opened his mouth, but before he could speak a shout

rose from the others. Grace and Travis ran toward the rest of the group.

"There," Farr said, pointing. "Look."

The sun had just crested the horizon, and to the south something glinted with a spark of red fire. Grace shaded her eyes. Then she saw it, jutting up from the horizon like a splinter of black ice: a stone spire.

"The sorcerer was right," Farr said.

Vani let out a hiss. "Mahonadra's Blood. Look!"

It took Grace a moment to see them, then her heart lurched. A dozen specks moved across the desert, black against the gold sand, heading toward the spire. It was hard to be certain of distances here, but she guessed the specks were less than a mile away.

"The Scirathi," Farr said. "They must have been forced to travel around the slipsand. They are not far ahead of us."

"And we're not letting them get any farther," Travis said.

He started into a run, but Vani was already moving, racing across the sand, along with Avhir.

"Come on!" Farr said, pushing Grace and Larad, and together they broke into a run.

36.

The sand pulled at Travis's feet like invisible hands. He lowered his head and pumped his arms, forcing himself to run faster. The sorcerers were just ahead. And so was Nim.

The sun parted from the horizon, lofting into the sky, and the coolness of night evaporated. Waves of heat rippled up from the desert floor. A sweat sprang out on Travis's skin and the air parched his lungs. They were deep in the Morgolthi now, in the heart of the Hungering Land. Without water or shelter, exposed to the full anger of the sun, they could not hope to survive for more than a few minutes.

But minutes were all they needed. Like insects, the dark specks of the Scirathi swarmed up the side of a dune a half mile ahead, then vanished over the crest.

"Did you see Nim?" Vani shouted. "Do they have her?" She coursed across the sand like a black gazelle, Avhir at her heels.

"I cannot be sure," Avhir called back. "I saw one carrying something on its back—a small bundle—but what it was I cannot say."

"We must go faster. They must not enter Morindu before we reach them."

The two *T'gol* quickened their pace, speeding like arrows over the sand. Travis and the others could not keep up.

"The sand," Larad hissed, his scarred face twisting in a grimace. "By Olrig, it burns right through the soles of my boots."

Farr shoved the Runelord on the back. "Keep moving. It's only going to get worse. If we don't get off the sand soon, we'll be roasted alive."

They started up the slope of the dune. The *T'gol* were already halfway to the crest.

Go, Vani, Travis thought. *Go as fast as you can. Save her.*

Next to him, Grace stumbled. She would have gone rolling down the slope, but he caught her in time, hauling her back to her feet.

"The sun . . . I don't think . . . I can't do this, Travis." Her face was pale except for two bright spots of color on her cheeks.

"Yes, you can, Grace." Speaking was too hard; his mouth was dry as leather. Instead, he spoke in his mind, knowing she would hear. *You didn't leave me underneath the slipsand, and I'm not going to leave you out here. Hold on to my thread.*

But even if I can, that would drain your . . .

Do it!

He sensed her presence draw close to his. There was a flash in his mind of green-gold light melding with gold-silver. Then he felt it: his life force draining from him, pouring into Grace. She gasped, and her eyes fluttered open. They were brilliant: emeralds flecked with gold dust.

Travis staggered, then steadied himself. It didn't matter that some of the essence of his own life was now flowing into Grace; he had more than enough to spare. Since the moment he had awakened, after dying in the slipsand, he had felt power burning in him. He was sweating, but not from the heat rising up from the sand. Instead, the heat came from inside him, as if there were a molten sun in his chest mirroring the one in the sky. No mundane heat could harm him now; he was certain of that.

However, that was not true for the others. Farr had lost too much blood, and Larad was accustomed to cool northern climes. Both slumped to their knees.

Grace, you have to connect to Larad's thread, and Farr's as well. Bridge their strands to mine, give them some of my power. They won't make it if you don't.

He sensed Grace's understanding, then a moment later he felt it rush from him: hot, gold power. Farr's back arched, and Larad clutched a hand to his chest, then both were on their feet again.

"Come on!" Travis called, and they ran with new swiftness up the side of the dune. The *T'gol* had already vanished over the crest.

"That spell," Larad said, voice hoarse, as they climbed. "I feel as if I could run for days, even in this heat. What did you do to give us strength, Your Majesty?"

Grace didn't answer, and Travis felt Farr's eyes on him.

They kept climbing, and after several more minutes they reached the crest of the dune. Travis halted, and the fire in his veins receded under a flood of cold fear. Below stretched a lifeless, wind-scoured plain. Like a beckoning finger, a spire jutted up from the plain. The spire was forged of onyx stone, polished so smooth it glistened as if wet. Perhaps thirty feet of the tower was visible, but its proportions suggested that many times that height lay beneath the sand. As for the rest of the lost city of Morindu, there was no trace.

Vani and Avhir were still running, now halfway between the foot of the dune and the spire. A dozen figures clustered like black beetles next to the tower. Travis caught several glints of gold.

Larad shaded his eyes with a hand. "What are the sorcerers doing?"

"Trying to get in," Farr said through clenched teeth.

Even as he spoke, a darker circle appeared against the dark wall of the tower: a doorway. The Scirathi streamed into the spire. The *T'gol* had moved with impossible speed; they had nearly closed the gap.

Only they were too late. The last of the sorcerers vanished inside the tower. There was a puff of black smoke, and the opening vanished. Seconds later came a low sound, like thunder that quickly faded. The *T'gol* threw themselves against the wall of the spire and bounced off like pebbles. Travis grabbed Grace's hand and went half-running, half-sliding down the lee side of the dune.

By the time they reached the spire, they found the *T'gol* already working to clear the doorway. But Travis saw it was no use. The doorway was a perfect circle as wide across as his splayed arms, its edges so sharp they looked as if they had been carved into the wall with a knife—one that passed through stone as if it were cheese. The top of the circle had collapsed, and a pile of rubble filled the doorway. The rubble was half-melted, fused into a solid mass. The *T'gol* pried at the stones, but neither Vani's fingers nor Avhir's scimitar could loosen them. Around the doorway the walls were perfectly smooth, without crack or crevice, as if the tower had not been built from individual stones, but was instead molded from a single mass.

"You cannot gain entrance to Morindu with hands or blades," Farr said. "Physical objects are useless."

Vani whirled around, stalking toward the dervish, eyes molten. "Then use your magic to open the way!"

Farr stood his ground. "Even if I had blood enough, I could not open this door. The walls of Morindu were bound with wards and spells fashioned by Orú's sorcerer-priests. Legend holds that the stones were laved with the blood of the god-king himself." His eyes narrowed as he gazed at Vani. "But you know that, Princess of Morindu." The words were soft rather than mocking; all the same, Vani turned away.

Travis drew close to the tower. Heat blazed within him, so hot that the air radiating up from the sand felt cool in comparison. The wall of the tower gleamed with a faint iridescence, like an oil slick on black water.

"So how did the Scirathi open the doorway?" Larad said, studying the edges of the portal.

Grace pushed her damp hair from her brow. "Nim. She was the key." She glanced at Vani. "But how?"

Vani shook her head, her face tight with anguish. "All I know is that my daughter's blood is powerful, and that lines of fate weave strangely around her."

"That's it," Farr said, his dark eyes going distant. "That's why the sorcerers wanted her. She's a nexus."

The others stared at him.

"A nexus?" Vani said, frowning.

Farr's gaze snapped back into focus. "I should have realized it right away from everything you told me, Vani. Only a nexus is such a rare thing, almost mythical. I never . . ." He shook his head. "But it's the only answer. That's why lines of fate are drawn to her and tangle in her presence."

"Is that why they needed Nim to open the door?" Grace asked, the words cool, curious: a scientist's inquiry. "Because she's a nexus?"

"Yes," Farr said, approaching the door. "A spell of warding, like the one cast on this doorway, is drawn in lines of fate. Passing through the portal is one possibility, one fate. The passage can be blocked by removing the chance of that fate ever coming to pass."

Travis thought he understood. "But because Nim is a nexus, she changed fate. New possibilities came into being, others vanished, and the spell unraveled."

"Then, once inside, the sorcerers blocked the doorway," Larad said. "But what did they use to bring down the door? Surely not a spell, with the way magic has weakened."

Travis could guess. In the past, the Scirathi had brought guns from Earth. Why not explosives as well?

Avhir stalked toward Farr. "Maybe you are not strong enough to open the doorway, dervish, but what about him?" He turned and pointed at Travis. "Is he not a great sorcerer?"

Travis tried to swallow, but there was no moisture in his mouth. "Larad," he croaked. "The Stones."

Larad held out the iron box, and Travis took the three Imsari. Whatever was affecting magic had not weakened the Stones; he could feel power radiating from them. He gripped them in his left hand, then pointed his right hand at the doorway.

"*Urath!*"

There was a clap of thunder and a blinding flash. When his vision cleared he saw that the doorway remained closed. He clenched the stones, his knuckles whitening. *"Urath!"* he shouted again, and a hundred voices chanted in his mind, a chorus of all the Runelords that had gone before him. Again thunder rent the air. The ground trembled.

Travis opened his eyes. The doorway was still blocked.

It was no use. He had felt the power of his runespell roll outward like a wave—then part around the tower, flowing to either side of it, repelled by the slick onyx walls.

"I can't do it," he said, giving the Stones back to Larad.

"Perhaps not with northern magic," Avhir said, his bronze gaze on Travis. "But what about sorcery? Does not the blood of Orú himself run in your veins?"

"He can try," Farr said, his face covered with sweat and sand. "But it's no use. If blood sorcery still worked as it should, the Scirathi would have left a trap for us. Only it doesn't. The *morndari* will not come. Or perhaps they cannot come. Whatever has weakened magic prevents them from responding to our calls. There is . . . there is no hope."

They all gazed at one another, faces ashen, eyes dull. The heat was punishing now, even in the shadow of the spire. Grace could not maintain her spell for long. She and Larad and Farr would perish. Nor could the *T'gol* survive in these conditions, and while the heat did not affect Travis, even he needed water. They would all die.

Grace touched his arm. "You tried, Travis. I think . . . I think in the end that counts for something. It has to."

Travis bowed his head, his brow touching hers. He wanted to weep, only he couldn't. It felt as if there was a darkness in him, a rift like that in the sky, growing, consuming him from the inside out. He had failed to save Nim from the sorcerers. What would Beltan think of him? Travis didn't know, but he did know one thing: Grace was wrong. Trying didn't count, not for anything. In the end, trying and failing was no different than doing nothing at all. The darkness ate at his heart, his spirit. In a moment all would be gone. He would feel nothing. . . .

No. That wasn't right. Travis resisted the darkness. He *would* feel something. And if not sorrow, then something else.

Grace gasped, pushing away from him. "Travis—you're hot."

He held out his arms and saw shimmering waves radiating from his skin. Fire surged through his veins, burning away the darkness inside him, fueled by a new power: rage. The Scirathi had taken Vani's daughter. Beltan's daughter. *His* daughter.

With a cry, Travis turned and flung himself against the wall of the tower, beating at it with bare fists. He felt a strange resistance each time his fist approached the stone, as if his hands were moving through some viscous fluid. However, he gritted his teeth and was able to punch through it, his blows landing against the tower. His fists glanced off without effect, but he didn't care. Again he struck the onyx wall, again, again. Distantly, he felt pain in his hands, and wetness.

"Stop, Travis!"

It was Vani, her words sharp, but Travis hardly heard her. Fury boiled in his head, burning away thought and reason. He wanted only to beat down the tower with his bare hands, or to die trying.

"He's hurting himself. Avhir, help me!"

Strong hands gripped Travis, pulling him away. He howled at them, snarled like a wild animal, trying to break free.

Travis, please.

The words were cool as bells in his mind. He went limp in the arms of the *T'gol*, the rage pouring out of him, leaving him empty, consumed. His hands hurt; they were smeared with blood. He gazed up, into Grace's green-gold eyes. *I'm sorry*, he wanted to say.

The words were drowned out by a groan from beneath their feet.

Vani and Avhir let go of Travis, whirling around, hands raised, eyes searching.

"What was that?" Larad said.

Farr pointed at the black wall of the spire. "Look."

Blood dripped down the wall where Travis had flailed against the stones. Then, with a wisp of steam, the fluid vanished, as if drunk in by the dark stones. The ground lurched. Grace stumbled against Travis, and both would have fallen if Vani had not held them upright.

Larad let out a breath "By all the gods."

It took Travis a long moment to understand what was

happening. A gap had appeared between the wall of the tower and the ground. Even as he watched, sand poured into the gap and it widened, reaching a foot from the tower. Two feet. Three. The ground shook again. Then, at the same instant as the others, he understood.

"Run!" Vani shouted. "Away from the spire. Now!"

The tower began to thrust upward from the ground, and the sand bulged beneath their feet, as if a great bubble was forming deep beneath them. Vani pulled Travis into a run. Avhir was pushing Grace and Larad, and Farr careened after them. The flat surface of the plain became a steep slope, rising behind them and falling away before them.

Travis glanced over his shoulder and saw the black spire soaring toward the sky. He caught other shapes as well—more spires, and onyx domes—then Vani jerked his arm.

"Don't look back. Keep running!"

He could hardly hear her over the rumbling. A hot, metallic odor permeated the air. They were sliding now more than running, skidding down the slope on their heels. Sand began to sheet past them in waves, carrying them along with it. If he went down, Travis knew he would be buried in a heartbeat.

Just before them and to the left was a flat expanse of gray, wind-scoured stone, like an island in the sea of sand. The slab looked natural, not man-made. Vani veered toward it, pulling him along; they were nearly there. Then Travis felt his feet go out from under him. He fell and rolled down the slope, sand pouring over him, filling his mouth so he couldn't scream. Not again. . . .

A strong hand caught him, hauling him forward, and he rolled onto something hard. He groped and felt rock beneath him.

"Look!" a voice shouted. It was Farr.

Travis struggled to his feet. He stood on the expanse of rough rock; the others were there as well. However, the surface was no longer level with the desert floor. Instead, they were on top of a pinnacle. The ground had fallen away to either side, and a torrent of sand rushed around the pinnacle. Before them loomed a dark mountain. Travis craned his neck, looking up. Sand poured like gold waterfalls between lofty spires and broad domes, tumbling down past sheer walls of onyx stone. Then he drew in a breath, and a feeling of awe came over him.

It wasn't a mountain. It was a city.

The sound of thunder rolled away across the desert. The torrent of sand flowing to either side of the rock pinnacle ebbed, then ceased. Black domes and spires no longer thrust upward, but stood still and stark against the yellow sky. A few streams of sand trickled from the walls, then even they dwindled and were gone.

Travis stared at the onyx city, unable to move or speak. Over three thousand years ago, the sorcerers of Morindu had chosen to destroy their home rather than let it be taken. With a bloodspell of terrible power, they had buried Morindu deep beneath the sands of the desert. Now, the touch of his own blood had reversed that spell, awakening the city again.

Just like Travis, Morindu had died beneath the sands of the Morgolthi. And had been resurrected.

"Your blood," Grace murmured. She took one of his hands in hers; his scraped knuckles were crusted with sand. "Your blood did this, Travis."

No, not his blood. It was the blood of Orú that flowed in his veins. The city had known the blood of its god-king. And it had answered.

Vani stepped to the edge of the pinnacle, her black leathers dusted with sand. "This is why the Scirathi feared you, Travis, why they wanted to kill you. They knew you could command the city. They knew you were fated to raise Morindu from the sands of the Morgolthi, just as the Mournish knew. And now you have." She turned to look at him, her gold eyes shining.

Travis sensed all their gazes on him; it wasn't a good feeling. "So how do the Scirathi plan to control the city?" he said, trying to deflect attention from himself. "If they intended for me to be dead when they reached it, they must have had some other plan for raising Morindu."

"Nim?" Larad said.

Farr shook his head. "Powerful blood runs in her veins, but it is not the blood of Orú. They could not use her to raise the city."

"Yet, if what you say is true, if she is a nexus," Vani said, "then fate is changed by her very presence."

"The throne room," Avhir said. The tall assassin approached Vani. "Where Orú was shackled, and where he slept. Was it not said that only the Seven Fateless could enter?"

Vani nodded. "For anyone but the *A'narai*, entering the throne room was certain death. Orú's power was so terrible that the very threads of fate were twisted in his presence."

"You mean like a nexus?" Grace said, her regal visage pale with dust.

Travis gazed at the city. "Nim."

"They mean to use her to enter the throne room," Farr said. "To find the god-king Orú. And to take his blood."

Larad stopped shaking sand from his robe. "But Orú cannot possibly still be alive after three thousand years."

"Perhaps not," Farr said, his dark eyes on the city. "But it may not matter. If even a small amount of his blood remains, in scarabs or vials . . ."

The others gazed again at Travis. He knew what they were thinking; they had all seen the transformation that a single drop of Orú's blood had wrought in him. What would the Scirathi do with such blood?

Maybe not anything, Travis. Magic is weakening. Maybe the Scirathi are too late.

Or maybe they weren't. Magic was losing its strenth, yes, but not the Imsari; they seemed as powerful as ever. And so did Travis's blood—how else could it have reversed the spell of destruction cast upon Morindu the Dark over three eons ago? Orú's blood might yet have power the Scirathi could wield.

And even if it didn't, the Scirathi still had Nim.

When the city had risen, great clouds of dust had billowed into the sky, masking the glare of the sun. Now the dust had begun to settle, and the sun broke through. Once again heat rose in a choking miasma from the desert floor.

"Come on," Travis said. "One way or another, we have to go in there."

Avhir found steps hewn into the side of the pinnacle. People from Morindu must have climbed to this place thousands of years ago, perhaps to gaze at their dark city. Or perhaps to watch for the armies of their enemies approaching. In minutes they reached the bottom.

"The gate must be there," Vani said, pointing to a pair of delicate spires set into the wall that ringed the city.

Master Larad turned his shattered face toward her. "Will we be able to open them?"

No one answered the Runelord. It was a half mile from the base of the pinnacle to the city, and there was no shade or shelter anywhere in between. A parched wind dispersed the last of the haze on the air, and the sun glared down from the sky like a furious eye.

They ran. The *T'gol* surged ahead, hardly leaving prints in the sand. The others lumbered behind. In moments they were sweating, and after a minute Grace, Larad, and Farr all began to grimace in pain.

You can't feel it, Travis, but the sand is burning them. Any hotter, and it would melt into glass. If you don't do something, they won't make it.

"Larad, the Stones."

The Runelord could not manage words, but he held out the iron box in trembling hands. This time Travis took only Gelthisar, the Stone of Ice.

"*Hadath,*" he murmured. Again he spoke the rune of frost, and again.

The sand remained cool only for moments before the sun baked it again, but each time he spoke the rune of frost Travis directed the force of the runespell just ahead of them. Grace, Farr, and Larad were no longer limping, and they were able to make rapid progress. They reached the wall of the city. Vani and Avhir were already there.

Travis looked up, awestruck again. The wall was a hundred feet high, fashioned of the same glassy black stone as the spire. No crack or crevice marred it, and there was no sign of any gate or doorway.

He glanced at Vani. "I thought you said the gate would be here."

"It is here." She reached toward the wall, but her hand seemed to spring back before she could touch it.

Travis understood. It was like the door in the tower. It was a spell woven in lines of fate. One fate was that there was no gate in the wall; that was the possibility they saw now. But there was another possibility. . . .

Travis approached the wall and reached out a hand. As it drew close to the black stone he felt resistance. He gathered his will, pushing his hand forward, as if through thick mud.

The resistance parted. His hand touched smooth stone.

The surface of the wall rippled, like dark water disturbed by a cast pebble. Then the ripples vanished, and Travis was no longer touching solid stone. He looked up. Where before there had been only blank wall, there was now an arched opening wide enough for five men to pass.

"Interesting," Larad said. "How did you do that?"

Travis lowered his arm. He was not a nexus, a center around which threads of fate spun; not like Nim. He was the opposite of that. Lines of fate were not drawn to him, but rather repulsed. Twice he had died, and twice he had been reborn.

"*A'narai*," Vani murmured.

"Fateless," Travis said, and stepped through the gate.

37.

It was like a garden.

Travis walked down a broad avenue, shaded from the sun by date palms arching overhead. *Lindara* vines, lush with yellow blooms, cascaded down walls and coiled above arched gates through which the music of falling water drifted. Beyond they glimpsed cool, dim, green spaces.

"This is impossible," Grace said, gazing around. "This place has been buried for three thousand years. How can there be trees?"

Larad reached out, brushing an orange flower that grew from a niche in a wall. "I half expect the people to start coming out of their doors. It's as if the city is just as they left it eons ago."

"Just as they left it," Farr repeated the words, casting back the hood of his robe. "You may be right, Runelord. This may indeed be how Morindu looked when it was abandoned."

As Grace had said, that was impossible. All the same, Travis was certain Farr was right. He had expected to find a desolate ruin; instead, here was Morindu at the height of its power and splendor.

Except its people are gone. They turned to dust three thousand years ago, while these walls, even these flowers, remain.

A sleek black form moved past Travis, gold eyes seeking, hands at the ready. He was wrong; Morindu's people weren't gone. They had endured over the years in exile, their blood passing from father to daughter, from mother to son. And now, after all this time, they had returned.

"I will scout ahead," Vani said to Avhir. "Watch behind us, but do not stray far. There is no telling what remains here."

Travis studied Vani's face, trying to see what she was feeling. All the Mournish were descended from the exiled people of Morindu the Dark. But she was a scion of the royal line of Morindu, heir to its ruling class of sorcerer-priests. This was her city.

He touched her shoulder, meeting her eyes. "You're home, Vani."

For a moment, it seemed her gold eyes shone with wonder. Then they narrowed. "Be on your guard," she said, and kept moving.

They came to a square where two broad avenues intersected. In the center of the square, water droplets sprayed up from a fountain, bright as jewels, and fell back into a pool green with water lilies.

"Water," Larad said, hurrying forward and dipping his hands into the fountain. He looked up, surprise on his face. "It's cool."

"Be careful," Vani said, circling around the fountain.

Grace opened her eyes. "No, this water is pure. It won't harm us."

Larad brought cupped hands to his mouth, drinking deeply, then splashed water on his face and neck. All of them followed suit. Travis had never tasted such sweet water before. It soothed his parched tongue and throat, and it seemed to cool the fire in his veins a few degrees. At last he lifted his head, pushed his dripping hair from his face.

"Where do we go now?" he said, looking at Vani.

She gazed at Farr. "If Nim truly is a nexus, they will be taking her to the throne room."

Grace turned around. "But where is it? This city is huge. It would take us days to explore it. Weeks."

Buildings rose in all directions around the square: low, rectangular dwellings, stair-stepped ziggurats, spires, and burnished domes that called to mind the sheltered sanctuary of temples. All were fashioned of the same glassy black stone as the outer walls of the city.

"There," Farr said, pointing toward a dome that soared above all others. Unlike any other building, it was gilded with intersecting lines and circles of gold filigree, shining as if molten in the sunlight. "Gold was a sign of power and royalty in ancient Morindu."

That was good enough for Travis. "Let's go."

They followed a wide avenue into the heart of the city, toward the dome traced with gold. The buildings to either side grew grander the farther they went, and each plaza they traversed contained ever more elaborate statuary: gigantic stone lions with the wings of eagles, or obelisks inscribed with angular symbols. Above them, tall spires reached toward the sky. Which of them was the one the Scirathi had entered? Had they already reached the throne room?

No, Travis. If the sorcerers had discovered the blood of Orú, you wouldn't still be here, walking, breathing. There's still time.

They reached a grand arch dripping with *lindara* vines. Beyond was a garden moister and more lush than anything they had passed so far. Water tumbled over stone, pooling in dim grottoes. Statues peered between green fronds with lapis eyes. The scent of flowers made the air thick and sweet.

"Beware," Vani said as Larad bent his face toward a large, bloodred bloom. "There are flowers here that take their color from blood."

The Runelord quickly backed away, giving any flower that was even the slightest bit red a wide berth.

"Vani," Avhir said. "Look."

The *T'gol* knelt to one side of the lane, where a smaller side path intersected. Vani moved to him, and he brushed the plants growing in a stone urn.

"These stems are bent," Avhir said. "All in the same direction. Several people came from this side path and turned onto the main way. They cut the corner tightly, which means they were moving quickly."

Vani glanced at Travis.

"We've got to hurry," he said.

They ran along the lane that led straight through the gardens, and each time the fronds parted overhead Travis saw that the black dome was closer. Although the *T'gol* were ready for an attack, they met no resistance as they went. There were no sounds save for the rasp of their breathing and the music of falling water. Not even the trilling of birds disturbed the silence of the gardens.

The path ended, and the garden gave way to a vast plaza. A row of thirteen obelisks dominated the center of the plaza, mirrored in a reflecting pool, while on the far side a massive bank of stairs swept up toward a rectangular structure that seemed proportioned for giants. Pyramids capped the wings to either side, while the center of the edifice was crowned by the great dome they had seen earlier, its black stone lined with gold.

Larad craned his neck. "Astonishing. Nothing created in the history of the north can compare to this."

"You can study the architecture later, Runelord," Farr said sharply. "Keep moving."

They raced across the plaza, passed between the obelisks, and reached the base of the steps.

"They came this way," Avhir said, kneeling and touching the lowest step. He rose and held out his hand; his fingers were stained red.

They started up the steps. Avhir went first, stretching his lean legs to take the steps three at a time. Vani swept her gaze from side to side as they ascended, hands raised before her.

However, no attack came. Breathing hard, they reached the top. A pair of columns framed doors five times as tall as Travis. The columns were decorated with bas-relief figures, their long, delicate limbs intertwined with the shapes of enormous spiders. One of the massive doors stood ajar, leaving a gap just wide enough for a person to squeeze through.

Together, Vani and Avhir pushed against the door. It opened another inch, then stopped.

"That's enough," Vani said. "We can slip through one by—"

Travis touched the door and it swung silently inward. He looked at his hand. His knuckles were bleeding again.

Keeping close to one another, they entered a hall lined with titanic statues hewn of ruddy stone. On the right were figures of men with the hooked beaks of falcons, while on the left were women who gazed with the multifaceted eyes of spiders—eyes that seemed to follow Travis as he moved deeper into the hall. White light shafted down from circular windows high above, the beams weaving a glowing web on the dim air.

Halfway across the hall they came upon the dead Scirathi. There were five of them. At least Travis thought so; it was hard to be sure. Their mutilated bodies littered the floor in many pieces. Black robes lay in shreds; gold masks were crumpled balls. There was no blood.

Larad studied the corpses, his expression at once repulsed and curious. "What could have done this?"

"Maybe it was *gorleths*," Grace said, lifting a hand to her throat.

Vani squatted beside one of the mutilated bodies. "No. There are no claw or teeth marks. These sorcerers were torn apart. I do not know what manner of beast did this."

"We may find out firsthand any moment," Farr said, gazing around. "We should be—"

A scream echoed down the hall, floating through an arch at the far end. It was high-pitched, and forlorn—the scream of a child.

"Nim," Travis said, looking at Vani.

She was already running.

Travis pounded after her, with Grace, Larad, and Farr just behind him. Out of the corners of his eyes, he saw a dark blur speed past: Avhir. Vani moved so swiftly she seemed not to run, but rather to blink out of existence one moment only to reappear the next, twenty paces ahead of where she had been.

As they ran, they passed the bodies of more sorcerers. Like the first group, all were mutilated, their bodies torn limb from limb, and there was no blood. What had done this? Whatever it was, the sorcerers had been unable to defend themselves; the power of magic had grown too weak.

"Keep your eyes open," Farr called out from behind. "Whatever killed these sorcerers is probably still here."

Travis agreed. However, at that moment another scream echoed through the high arch at the end of the hall. It was weaker than the last, quavering with terror. The sound tore at his heart. He saw Vani disappear through the archway, followed by Avhir. Travis raced after them through the arch—

—and tried to halt, skidding on the smooth floor. A strong arm struck his chest, halting him just in time to keep him from sliding over a sheer edge and falling into endless darkness.

Travis looked down. Past his toes he saw nothing except an emptiness so black it made him think of the Void between worlds. Vani gripped his *serafi*, pulling him back. He started to ask her what was happening, then he heard Grace gasp and looked up.

They stood under the palace's dome. The circular space housed by the dome was as vast as the Etherion in Tarras. And, before its destruction, that had been able to accommodate thousands of priests.

Far above, round windows pierced the ceiling, glowing like suns in a midnight sky. A narrow strip of stone ringed the cavernous space, forming a ledge. It was on this ledge that they stood. As Travis had discovered, the ledge had no railing to prevent one from falling into the depths.

Ahead, in the center of the chamber, was a golden tetrahedron. Given the lack of reference, it was hard to be certain of the tetrahedron's size, but surely it was as large as a house, or larger yet. It seemed to float in the middle of the emptiness, like an island on a dark sea. However, Travis's eyes—remade in the fires of Krondisar—pierced shadow, and he glimpsed rock beneath it; the golden structure was supported by a column of natural stone that rose from the depths.

Travis could see two bridges, one to each side of him. The spans were slender and delicate, like creations of black spun glass, no more than two feet wide and without rails. Each bridge sprang from the stone ledge and arched across the chasm to a triangular doorway in one of the gold tetrahedron's three walls.

While he could not see it, he guessed there would be a third bridge on the far side of the chasm.

"Mother!"

The cry, quickly muffled, snapped Travis's attention to the bridge to his left. There were two figures there. One was Nim. Even at a distance, Travis could see fear on the pale oval of her face. She was dressed in a robe of gold cloth. Her cheeks were smudged with something dark.

The other figure was a sorcerer. He held Nim in one arm, crushing her against his chest, his wrist clamped over her mouth. The sorcerer's gold mask was dented, sitting crookedly on his face, and his black robe was torn. He took a limping step backward along the bridge.

Vani surged toward the span, but Avhir caught her before she could step onto it.

"Stop!"

Vani gave him an anguished look but did not break free of his grasp. As Travis drew closer, he saw why. The sorcerer held a bronze dagger in his free hand. He brought it down, resting the point against Nim's cheek. Her eyes went wide, and she squirmed in his arms. Such was her strength that the sorcerer stumbled, and one of his feet slipped off the edge of the narrow span. He stumbled, then managed to recover.

"Nim, don't move!" Vani shouted. At once Nim went limp in the sorcerer's arm.

Good girl, Travis thought. *Good, brave girl, to be able to listen to her mother even now. There's still a chance.*

However, what it was, Travis wasn't certain. The sorcerer took another limping step back. He was halfway across the bridge. There was no way they could reach him before he had the time to use that dagger.

What about a runespell, Travis? Jack's voice suggested in his mind. *Blast him off the bridge with a spell! Oh, dear. Wait a moment. . . .*

That was the problem. If Travis killed the sorcerer with a spell, the Scirathi would fall from the bridge—taking Nim with him. The others must have sensed the same truth. All strained, as if wishing to move, but remained still, eyes locked on Nim and the Scirathi. The sorcerer took three more limping steps along the bridge.

Orú's throne room must be inside that tetrahedron. Nim will open the way for him. But you can't let him get in there, Travis. If he does, you're the only one who can follow him. And if he finds the blood of Orú in there, even you won't be able to stop him. Xemeth was destroyed when he drank from the scarab, but he wasn't an experienced sorcerer. If that Scirathi drinks Orú's blood, he'll kill us all.

Larad gave Grace a sharp look. "Can you break his life thread, Your Majesty?"

"No!" Vani hissed. "If the sorcerer perishes, Nim falls!"

"It doesn't matter," Grace said, face ashen. "The Weirding is too weak. I can't even see his thread from here, let alone break it."

Vani looked at Travis, her gold eyes imploring. "Please, you have to save her."

Travis opened his mouth, but he didn't know what he would say, what he could possibly do. "Vani, I—"

"Let me through," Farr said, pushing past Travis and Vani.

Vani gripped his arm. "What do you think you're doing? If you try to approach, he'll kill her."

Farr shook off her hand. He didn't look at the *T'gol*. Instead, he turned his dark gaze on Grace. Travis saw her eyes go wide, then after a moment she nodded. She moved past Larad and Avhir.

"Let's go then," Farr said, holding out one hand, the other tucked inside his robe.

What did Farr think they were going to do? Before Travis could ask, Grace drew in a deep breath, then reached out and took Farr's hand. The two of them turned around—

—then ran forward, jumping off the ledge and vanishing into the impenetrable darkness below.

Travis was so stunned that he could only stare into the void. For a moment he thought he glimpsed a flicker of silver-blue light, then all he saw was blackness.

"Your Majesty!" Larad cried, rushing forward, and he would have gone over the edge himself if Vani hadn't held him back.

This wasn't happening; Grace and Farr couldn't have just

leaped to their deaths. Only they had. Travis had seen them vanish into the endless dark below. A weakness came over him, a watery feeling, and his legs shook as if they were going to buckle. Avhir stood motionless at the place where Grace and the former Seeker had vanished. The sorcerer on the bridge had halted, his gold mask tilted at what seemed a quizzical angle, as if even he could not fathom what had just taken place. Then, before any of them could move, a strange thing happened.

Nim laughed.

The sorcerer's grip on her had weakened, but he tightened his arm around her, stifling her mirth. Vani took a step onto the bridge, but the Scirathi raised the dagger, warning her back. She let out a low moan, a sound of both anguish and fury. Holding Nim, the sorcerer took another step along the bridge.

A ball of silver light burst into being just behind him.

The ball of light collapsed into a point, vanishing, and in its place, standing on the bridge, were two figures: a man in black robes and a woman with pale hair. Their appearance was so utterly unexpected that it took Travis a moment simply to recognize who they were.

"By the Blood!" Vani said, staggering back a step.

The two figures on the bridge were Grace and Hadrian Farr. They were no more than five steps from the sorcerer, with Farr the closest. Grace was fighting to keep her balance, but Farr was already moving, lunging for the Scirathi. The sorcerer whirled around, dagger flashing . . .

Travis didn't know whom the sorcerer was trying to stab—Nim or Farr—but Farr was faster, grabbing the sorcerer's wrist and wrenching it hard. The dagger spun into the chasm, and the Scirathi lost his balance. His right foot slipped over the edge of the bridge, and he fell onto his right knee. Nim slipped halfway from his grasp and screamed. If he let go of her, she would tumble into the void.

Only when he saw a dark blur moving along the bridge did Travis realize Vani was running. However, swift as she was, there wasn't time to reach the Scirathi. Farr lunged again, reaching for Nim. The sorcerer twisted away. However, doing so caused him to lose what remained of his balance. The Scirathi tried to recover, but his foot snagged on his robe, and he tumbled off the bridge.

Farr threw himself forward, onto his belly, arms flung outward. His fingers brushed against Nim's golden robe. And latched on.

Nim screamed again, a sound that echoed throughout the dome. The sorcerer was holding on to her legs. Their combined weight dragged at Farr, his body sliding across the bridge. Grace threw herself to her knees, gripping his ankles. However, she was only able to slow his progress toward the edge of the bridge, not stop it.

"Nim!" Farr shouted. "The mask. Take his mask!"

"Mother?" came Nim's quavering voice.

The sorcerer looked up, trying to paw his way farther up Nim's legs to reach the edge of the bridge. There was a sound of cloth rending as Nim's robe tore in Farr's grip.

Vani was halfway across the bridge. "Do as he says, daughter!"

Hanging by the back of her robe, Nim reached down and pulled at the sorcerer's mask. It was loose, and came away easily in her hands, revealing the scarred ruin of the sorcerer's face.

"Let go of me!" she shouted, and hit the sorcerer in the face with the mask.

The Scirathi let out a cry of pain. His hands gave an involuntary spasm, then tried to regain their grip on Nim. Too late. Weakened, slicked with blood, the sorcerer's fingers slipped free. His robe billowed out like black wings, and with a gurgling cry the Scirathi vanished into the chasm.

"I can't hold on!" Grace cried as Farr's body started to slide over the edge. However, the dimness unfolded, and Vani was there; she pulled Farr up with one hand, hauling him to his feet.

"Mother!" Nim cried, holding out her hands.

"My daughter," Vani said, taking the girl and holding her tight. Nim's arms wrapped around her neck, and the girl, so brave a moment before, began to sob. Carefully, Vani, Grace, and Farr made their way back over the bridge to the others. A quick examination revealed that most of the blood on Nim was likely the sorcerer's. There was a small cut on the girl's arm, but it was already scabbed over.

Vani held Nim tightly, her own face—usually so stoic—

streaked with tears. "I promise no one will ever harm you again."

"I know," the girl murmured, calm now, though her cheeks were still wet. She leaned her head on Vani's shoulder and turned her gray-gold eyes toward Travis.

Travis started to reach toward Nim, then changed his motion and took Grace's hand in his. "How?" he said simply.

Grace held up her free hand. In it was a silver coin, a symbol engraved on each side. Even without looking closely, Travis knew what the two runes were; one was the rune Eldh, and the other was the rune Earth.

"How did you get that?" he said, reaching into the pocket of his *serafi*. However, his fingers found the silver coin he always carried with him.

"It's Hadrian's," Grace said in answer to Travis's confused look, handing the coin to Farr.

Then Travis understood. Brother Cy must have given the silver coin to Farr before transporting him to Eldh, just as the strange preacher once gave the two halves of the coin Travis now carried to him and Grace. The coins were bound runes—ones of unusual power. They had the ability to return the bearer to his home world, to the place envisioned. When Farr and Grace leaped into the abyss, Farr must have used the coin to transport them to Earth as they fell. Then, just as quickly, Grace had used the coin to bring them back to Eldh, only this time on the bridge just behind the sorcerer. It was brilliant.

And Farr had thought of it, not Travis. A strange, hollow feeling gnawed at his chest.

"Magic is getting weaker," Travis said, looking at Farr. "When you jumped, how did you know the coin would still work?"

"I didn't," Farr said, the words crisp. "Though I had an idea it would. The Imsari still function, and the coins seem to be forged of a magic, if not so deep, then deep all the same. It was an educated guess."

Travis squeezed Grace's hand. "That was incredibly foolish." Despite the gnawing feeling in his chest, he smiled. "And incredibly brave."

"More the first one than the second," she said. "I wasn't sure

Farr's coin would work for me. But it did. I suppose because I had been granted one once."

Where did you go, Grace? Travis leaned in close to her. *You were on Earth for a few seconds. Where were you?*

By the expression on her face she had heard his thoughts, but she looked away.

Vani moved to Farr. She laid a hand on his arm; her gold eyes shone like moons. "I can never repay you."

He shrugged. "I don't want payment. A simple thank you will suffice. For Grace as well as for me."

Vani nodded. "Will all my heart, I thank you both." However, as she spoke, her eyes were fixed only on Farr.

"So now what?" Larad said to Travis. "Do we leave, or will you enter the throne room?"

His words shocked Travis. He had been so focused on getting to Morindu to retrieve Nim that he had not considered what might happen if they succeeded. Three thousand years ago, secrets of sorcery had been buried with Morindu. Now the city had been uncovered again. What might he find if he entered the throne room? What wondrous powers might he gain?

None of that matters, Travis. You didn't come to Morindu for magic, but to find Nim. Now you have, and only one thing is important—finding the Last Rune and binding the rifts in the sky. If it's not too late.

He opened his mouth to say this, but before he could Nim let out a gasp, her eyes widening into circles of fear.

Vani gave Nim a worried look. "What is it, daughter?"

"She's here," the girl whispered.

"Who do you mean? Who's here?"

"The gold lady."

Nim pointed, and all of them turned around. On the far side of the bridge, a woman stepped from the triangular door in the side of the gilded tetrahedron. She appeared young—no more than twenty-five. A shift made of glittering beads dripped over the curves of her luscious body, and a red gem adorned her brow. Her hair and eyes were both black as onyx, and her skin was a deep, burnished gold.

Avhir breathed an oath in an ancient tongue, and a sweat

broke out on Travis's skin, as if the temperature inside the dome had suddenly shot up.

"It cannot be," Vani said, her voice thick with awe. "Yet there is only one woman who could have entered there. Ti'an."

Farr gave her a piercing look. "Who is Ti'an?"

"The wife of the god-king Orú," Vani said.

The gold-skinned woman sauntered toward them across the bridge.

38.

Thunder rattled the panes of the library's windows as Deirdre shut the journal and leaned back in the chair. What time was it? How long had she spent reading and rereading the pages covered with Albrecht's elegant handwriting? The day had seemed to grow darker as it went on, and the light of the tin lantern had receded to a flickering circle around the desk. By the cramp in her neck and the pounding between her temples, hours had passed. However, the gnawing in her gut was not from hunger.

"It's all a lie," she murmured to the gloom.

Everything she had been taught about the Seekers, everything she had believed in—the Motto, the Book and the Vow, the Nine Desiderata—all of it was an elaborate deception, perpetuated over centuries, and wrought so that the Seekers would diligently perform the work of the Philosophers without ever knowing—or even guessing at—the truth about their nature.

We're puppets, Deirdre. For four centuries they've been pulling our strings. We've been doing their work, helping them get closer to their magic elixir—a potion that will grant them true immortality. And now they've nearly got it.

Anger rose in her, but it was drowned by a wave of sickness. To be betrayed in this way—it was like discovering the world was flat after all, and the sun was a hot coal no more than five hundred miles away. The lie had made so much more sense than the reality that had been revealed to her, yet much as she craved to go back to not knowing, it was impossible. She could not go back. Knowledge was a knife that cut deeply, and whose wounds never healed. The Philosophers were charlatans, nothing more.

Except he was different than the others. Marius.

Deirdre reached out a shaking hand and brushed the cover of the journal. She had read the final few lines so many times she did not need to turn to that page to see them; they were burned into her brain.

Now you know what no other besides our own kind has ever known. Now you know the truth of the origin of the Philosophers.

And now, I beg of you, help me bring about their end. . . .

In over three centuries of existence, he had not forgiven the Philosophers for the way they had used him, had used Alis Faraday, and had used the half-fairy folk of Greenfellow's Tavern. Only, by becoming one of the Philosophers, he had unwittingly bound himself to them, and had been unable to gain vengeance against them. Until now. He had led Deirdre there because he believed she could help him. But why her? And why now?

Deirdre didn't know. All she knew was that the Philosophers were no better than Duratek. No, they were worse. They used the tavern's denizens, and when they were done with them, the Philosophers abandoned the folk of Greenfellow's, rewarding them for their help and for their blood with poverty and suffering.

She touched the silver ring on her hand, then brushed hot tears from her cheeks. There was so much in the journal to try to absorb and understand. The Philosophers were immortal—at least so long as they periodically returned to Crete and drank the blood of the Sleeping Ones. That the Sleeping Ones were one and the same with the seven sorcerer-priests of Orú, Deirdre had no doubt; it all fit too perfectly with what she had learned from Vani.

Only now Deirdre could add to that story. The Seven of Orú had not perished with Morindu the Dark. Instead they had fled through a gate, traveling across the Void to the world Earth. They had come to Crete over three thousand years ago and made contact with the civilization there. Then they had sealed themselves in their sarcophagi beneath the palace of Knossos, falling into endless slumber just like Orú had, and there they had lain, forgotten. Until the Philosophers stumbled upon them over four centuries ago.

But why had the Seven come to Earth? That was one question the journal didn't ask. Maybe because Marius didn't know the answer. And maybe that was something the writing on the arch would reveal if they were ever able to translate all of it. She had to go back to London, to talk to Paul Jacoby, to see if he had been able to decipher any more of the—

No. How could she return to the Charterhouse knowing what she did? The Seekers were a sham. The Philosophers didn't seek to discover other worlds out of scholarly interest. All this time they had been searching for the world the Sleeping Ones came from, hoping to find a way to reach it, to discover what it was that had granted the Seven true, endless, perfect immortality— their Philosopher's Stone. Now the Philosophers were terribly close. The world they sought was Eldh, and a gate had come to light. All the Philosophers had to do was use the blood of the Sleeping Ones to open the gate and . . .

Deirdre went cold. The pieces clicked together in her brain with mechanical precision. She wanted to deny the result, only she couldn't. The dying sorcerer in Beltan and Travis's flat had said the Scirathi stole the stone arch from Crete for someone else, someone they had delivered it to.

"It was the Philosophers," she said to the gray air. "They hired the Scirathi and used them to retrieve the arch."

Once the earthquake uncovered the arch, they would have done anything to get it. They had probably been searching for it for centuries, trying to find the means by which the Sleeping Ones had traveled to Earth. Only now perihelion was approaching; the two worlds, Earth and Eldh, were drawing close. One way or another, the Philosophers were going to get what they desired; they were going to reach Eldh.

Unless he gets his revenge on them first.

Before Deirdre could consider what that meant, a chiming noise drifted through the door of the library: the unmistakable sound of a teaspoon stirring in a china cup. Had Eleanor returned with another thermos? She pushed herself up from the chair, walked to the door, and stepped into the manor's front hall.

A man sat in a chair next to the fireplace, where a cheerful blaze crackled. He wore a sleek, modern black suit, and even sitting he was tall, his long legs crossed before him. His skin was pale, his features fine and aristocratic, his wide mouth framed by sharp lines. Luxurious blond hair tumbled over broad shoulders. On first glance she would have thought him no more than thirty.

"There you are Miss Falling Hawk," he said in a rich voice she knew from their few conversations over the phone. "I had begun to fear my writing was so boring it had put you to sleep. I suppose then I'll dismiss the idea of becoming a novelist. No matter—it's not nearly so glamorous a career as I first imagined. Would you like a cup of tea? Please, sit with me."

He gestured to an empty wing-backed chair near his. Between the chairs was a tea table bearing a pot, two cups, a pitcher of cream, and a plate of lemon wedges. He smiled, an act that rendered him more handsome yet. The irises of his eyes were a brilliant gold that matched the spider-shaped ring on his left hand.

Deirdre moved to the chair and sat. She was so numb she hardly felt the teacup when he placed it in her hands. The cup rattled against the saucer, and it occurred to her she should take a sip to keep it from spilling, but she could not seem to make the muscles of her arms obey. She could only stare at him. At his gold eyes.

He took a sip of his tea, a languid motion, then gazed around at the dim hall. "It's been a long time since I've returned here, to my old home. The last occasion was nearly a century ago. Often I've longed to come back, but I didn't dare. It would not do to have the others think I cared so much about the past. That I had never forgotten." He breathed a sigh. "It's a bit shabbier these days, but otherwise just as I remembered it. The docents and caretakers have done well."

Deirdre's teacup clattered against the saucer. "You," she managed to croak. "You're part of the consortium Eleanor talked about."

Marius gave a soft laugh. "I'm afraid I *am* the consortium,

Miss Falling Hawk. I set up Madstone Hall as a private museum and created the facade of a governing board so the Philosophers would believe the manor had passed out of my hands."

"And did it work?"

He shrugged. "Sometimes I believe Phoebe still watches me. Of them all, she was always the cleverest, and the last to treat me as an equal. But the Philosophers think of little more than themselves these days, and of their ultimate transformation. Nothing else concerns them. Not even the dark spots in the sky."

"No one seems concerned about them," Deirdre murmured. "No one seems to care that they keep growing. It's as if everyone has already given up."

"You haven't given up, Miss Falling Hawk." Marius sipped his tea. "I doubt even Phoebe remembers Madstone Hall exists. Still, caution is always the wisest counsel. That's why I've kept my communications with you limited and secret."

The warmth of the fire had done Deirdre good, and her trembling—as much from sitting so long in the chilly manor as from shock—had eased. She finally managed to take a sip of her tea.

"Why now?" she said, her voice stronger. "For more than three years you've kept to the shadows, never offering me so much as a glimpse of who you are. Now here you sit, offering me tea. Something has changed. What is it?"

This time his laughter was louder, richer. "That's why I chose you, Deirdre—may I call you Deirdre? *Miss Falling Hawk* seems so formal, now that we're speaking face-to-face, and you must call me Marius. That's why I selected you out of all the other journeymen whose files I examined. You're intelligent of course—the tests demonstrated that. But it's your instincts that impressed me, your ability to know what's right even when there's no logical way you *should* know."

The tea churned in her stomach. "How long have you been watching me?"

"Almost from your first day with the Seekers. I have good instincts as well, you see." He set down his cup and rested his elbows on the arms of the chair. "After I detected the first signs that perihelion between Earth and the otherworld approached, I searched in earnest for one in whom I might place my trust. After a time I began to fear the search was in vain. Then you entered the Seekers, and I knew I had found what I was looking for. You were clever, curious, and willing to bend rules in the pursuit of knowledge—all traits I required. Yet you were also honest, loyal, and possessed of a highly developed sense of rightfulness. You are not simply a good person, Deirdre. You are a *just* person. In the end, you will place the greater good above all else, above all other desires and obligations."

Here he was at last, her mysterious helper, and Deirdre had absolutely no idea what to say. Perhaps his belief in her intelligence was overrated.

"No, Deirdre," he said, as if sensing her doubts. "Your behavior these last years has only confirmed all my beliefs in you. That I had made the right choice was apparent from the moment you began working on the James Sarsin case."

She started in the chair, and tea sloshed out of her cup, onto her slacks. "It wasn't chance, was it? I always believed it was simple luck that I stumbled on that letter from James Sarsin. No one else in the Seekers could have known it referred to Castle City. But you made sure I came upon that letter."

She set down the cup, sagged back in the chair, and half-heartedly dabbed at her wet slacks with a napkin. Her discovery that the immortal London bookseller James Sarsin and Castle City antique dealer Jack Graystone were the same man had been a major breakthrough—one that had caused her to rise swiftly in the Seekers, and to be assigned as Hadrian Farr's partner. She had always believed the discovery had been her own, and somehow she felt disappointed now, as if she was far less special than she had believed.

Again he seemed to hear her thoughts, though it was more likely he had simply read her expression. "Don't be so glum, Deirdre. The fact that I put that letter in the stack of papers on your desk doesn't change the fact that you recognized it for what it was."

"But you already knew," she said, feeling hollow inside. "You already knew Jack Graystone was James Sarsin."

"Yes, I did. As you know from my journal, it was I who first identified Sarsin's otherworldly nature. After I became a Philosopher, I continued to keep an eye on him, even though he would have nothing to do with the Seekers. Once he vanished from London, I kept searching for him, and eventually I uncovered evidence that he had traveled to America, to Colorado. After I learned you had a connection to Colorado yourself, I realized it was the perfect opportunity to introduce you to the case without anyone suspecting I was involved. It looked like you made the connection yourself because you *did* make the connection yourself, Deirdre. The same was true with the Thomas Atwater case."

"So you gave me that as well," she said bitterly. Had she done anything on her own these last five years?

"I did, though it was a bit trickier. More tea?" He filled both their cups, then picked his up in a long-fingered hand. "I wanted to draw your attention to Thomas Atwater, but I couldn't do so in a direct manner, lest the others realize what I was up to. That's why, when you were reinstated in the Seekers, I dreamed up the task of researching historical violations of the Desiderata and had Nakamura give it to you. I knew your researching skills well enough to be confident you would eventually be drawn to Atwater's case. And you were, more swiftly than I had hoped."

She frowned; something was wrong with what he had just said. Then she had it. "But that wasn't my first assignment after I was reinstated. I was supposed to do a cross-cataloging project. Only Anders took the assignment before I could start."

"Just as I had suspected he would. Which is why I waited until he had done so to pass the second assignment to Nakamura."

These words thrust a cold spike into Deirdre's heart. "Anders," she said, licking her lips. "That first night you contacted me, you warned me that he was coming. What did you know about him?"

"Only what you soon knew yourself: that he was overly eager and less than truthful."

She slipped her hand into her jacket pocket, touching the crumpled photo Sasha had taken. "I think he's working for the Philosophers. At first I thought he was in league with the Sciruthi, but now I know that the Philosophers used the sorcerers to get the gate from Crete. Which means Anders is working directly for them."

Marius nodded. "I have long suspected that some among my cohort maintain special and secret contacts among the Seekers."

"Like you've maintained me?"

"Just so," he said and sipped his tea, as if he had not discerned the venom in her words. "That's why secrecy was imperative in my dealings with you, Deirdre. I could not hide from the Philosophers the fact that you were in contact with one of us. But as long as you didn't know which of us it was you were communicating with, then they couldn't know either. And since Phoebe—and no doubt most if not all of the others—have such illicit helpers within the Seekers, none would dare press too hard to learn who you were in contact with, lest their own minions be exposed."

"What a trusting bunch you are," Deirdre said, making no effort to disguise the irony in her voice.

Marius laughed. "Oh, we're a perfect family all right. We all loathe one another, and we'd each have murdered the others outright centuries ago if we were not all of us bound to one another."

"Only now you have me to do your dirty work."

He did not look at her, instead gazing out the window at the failing day. "They're close, Deirdre. For centuries they've searched for the Philosopher's Stone. They crave it above all else. And now it's within their reach."

"Immortality," Deirdre breathed. "That's what you mean, isn't it? *Philosopher's Stone* is just a name alchemists give to a substance that can bestow perfection and immortality."

"Yes, true immortality—like that possessed by the Sleeping Ones." His lip curled in disgust. "Now, if we did not drink a sip of their blood at least once a decade, we would grow decrepit and die. Nor are we truly safe from death. Illness and age cannot harm us, but we might still be slain. However, the Sleeping Ones themselves are perfect. They do not decay, but remain ever beautiful. And when they are wounded, their golden bodies heal instantly. That's what the others desire for themselves."

"And you don't?" Deirdre couldn't keep her voice from edging into a sneer.

"No," he said, meeting her eyes. "I don't."

There was no reason to believe him. He had shrouded himself in mystery for more than three years, manipulating her to suit his ends. All the same, she did believe him.

"You want to keep them from reaching it," she said. "You want to stop them from getting to Eldh and finding what it was that made the Sleeping Ones immortal. From finding Orú."

The change was sudden. The smooth demeanor, the languid motions were gone. He slammed down his cup and clenched a fist, banging it on the arm of the chair. "They do not deserve it! They are fools and devils, and they are not worthy of everlasting life. No one on this Earth is. And if anyone could possibly be worthy of such a thing, then it was—"

He didn't speak the name, but it sounded in her mind all the same. *Alis.*

After a long moment she spoke. "That was Travis's sister's name, you know. Alice. He loved her more than anything. She was only a girl when she died. He believed it was his fault. For the longest time, he didn't forgive himself. Only then . . ." She smiled, thinking of Travis. "He did."

Marius leaned back in the chair, the rage gone, those gold eyes haunted. "I know," he said, his voice soft. "I know."

Deirdre was no longer full of awe. Marius was a Philosopher; he was over three hundred years old. However, he was still a man, and after reading the journal she felt, at least in some small way, that she knew him.

"You're still not telling me the whole truth about why you've kept your identity a secret," she said, and she knew that once again it was her Wise Self speaking. "I can understand you needed to be certain none of the Philosophers knew which one of their number I was in contact with, but that wouldn't have prevented you from letting me read that journal. I think by now you know I can keep a secret, and you could have given it to me without their knowledge. So why didn't you tell me the truth about the Seekers sooner?"

His eyes were intent upon her. "But don't you see? I couldn't simply give you the answers to all these mysteries. You're clever, Deirdre, and you have deep powers of intuition. I knew, if given just a few crumbs, you would discover the answers yourself. And in so doing, I hoped you would solve the mysteries I myself have not been able to answer all these years."

Deirdre clutched the arms of her chair. "You mean just like the way you watched Alis Faraday, wondering if she would discover her otherworldly nature on her own?"

The words were sharp, and she could see how they stung him, but she did not soften her tone. "You've used me, Marius. You used me just like they used Alis—just like they used you. And it could have killed me. It nearly did, several times over. Only you still kept the truth from me. Why?" Her voice rose into a snarl. "What did you hope I'd learn?"

"The answer to everything."

All the anger rushed out of her in a soft gasp. "*What?*"

He learned forward in his chair, a fervent light in his gold eyes. "They're waiting for something, Deirdre. The Sleeping Ones. For over three thousand years they've lain there in their stone sarcophagi in peaceful repose, their eyes shut, arms folded over their breasts, their skin as smooth as polished gold."

As he spoke, it was as if she could see them reflected in his eyes. She leaned forward herself, her face drawing near his.

"Phoebe and the others, they believe the slumber of the Seven is eternal. But I don't. I believe they're simply waiting for the moment when they will awake. And I think that moment will soon come."

"Perihelion," Deirdre said, once again understanding when perhaps she shouldn't. "You think they're waiting for perihelion."

An eager light illuminated his face. "Yes. For centuries I've studied the symbols written on the walls of the tomb where we found them. It was in their tomb that we found the clay tablet, the one whose photo I gave you. The others left the task of translating the symbols to me, for it had been my master's work, and the rest of them were too bored by such a tedious chore. Through the tomb writings, I learned much of the story of the Sleeping Ones. And I rejoiced when what I learned was confirmed by your own reports, the ones in which you described the history of Morindu as told by the woman Vani. I knew my theory was correct—that the Sleeping Ones indeed came from the otherworld, and that they are waiting for a time when they can return."

Deirdre tried to absorb this. Marius's story made sense. The

Seven of Orú had been forced to flee Morindu after interring it beneath the desert sands; surely they had intended to return to their home someday. And now that day was coming. Perihelion approached; things long buried were coming to light. "But they don't have to wait for perihelion to return to Morindu," she said aloud. "They could use the arch—the gate."

Marius shook his head. "I don't think they're waiting just to return home. From what I deciphered in the tomb, I believe that when the worlds draw near enough the Sleeping Ones will awaken."

"And then what will they do?"

"My master believed they sought some sort of transmutation."

"You mean like alchemy?"

"Yes, like alchemy in a way. I believe the Sleeping Ones seek to transmute something. Only what it is, and what they wish to transform it into, the tomb writings did not tell me. Nor did the symbols indicate what catalyst the Seven will use to bring about the transformation."

Deirdre had studied alchemy in her first days as a Seeker; given the origins of the order, it was something of a prerequisite. She thought back to everything she had learned. "The catalyst—that's something that permits a base substance to be evolved into a state of perfection. Except the catalyst itself isn't changed by the transformation. It's like the—"

"Like the fabled Philosopher's Stone, yes. The catalyst is that which will grant the Philosophers true and perfect immortality. But in so doing, the catalyst itself will remain unchanged."

Deirdre considered this. Orú's blood could cause transformation; a single drop had changed Travis into a sorcerer. Only how much of it had the Seven of Orú drunk? Surely they had consumed great quantities. What transformations might be worked with it? For some reason, she found herself murmuring the final words to a song. " 'Then after fire and wonder, we end where we began.' "

Marius stood up. "What's that?"

She looked up. "It's a song that originated on the otherworld. A copy of it was found among James Sarsin's—"

"Yes, yes, I know the song. I've read it many times over." His gaze seemed to cut her like a gold knife. "But why do you sing it now?"

The back of her neck prickled. Her subconscious had made a connection, one her conscious mind had not yet grasped. What was it? She leaned back in the chair, thinking aloud. "It was the phrase *fire and wonder* that made me stumble onto that computer file. The girl in black—Child Samanda—told me to seek them as I journeyed. So once I received Echelon 7 clearance, I performed a search on those words, and a file came up, an archive from the year you died." She winced. "Or became a Philosopher, I suppose. Only the file was deleted before I could read it." She glanced up at him. "So what was in that file?"

"My final report as a Seeker," he said, waving a hand dismissively. "Everything it contained was in the journal, and more."

She nodded. No wonder the Philosophers had not wanted her to read it. "Paul Jacoby was able to translate the words *fire and wonder* on the stone arch. That reminded me of the missing file, and it was studying the name of the file that led me to you, and to this place."

Marius was pacing before the fire now, shaking his tawny hair like a lion's mane. "I know all that. By why did you sing the song now? It's those instincts of yours. You've made a connection, haven't you?" He stopped, gripped the arms of her chair, and leaned down, his face inches from her own. He smelled sharp, like lightning. "What is it? What has your clever mind put together?"

She shook her head. "I don't know. I—"

"You *do* know, Deirdre. What is it? What were you thinking?"

The words tumbled out of her. "The song—it's just that in a way it's like what you said about the catalyst. How in the end it's the same, unchanged."

He pushed away from the chair. "Sing it," he said. "All of it."

She was afraid she wouldn't remember the words. Only they came to her lips easily, and she sang in a quavering voice:

> *"We live our lives a circle,*
> *And wander where we can.*
> *Then after fire and wonder,*
> *We end where we began.*

"I have traveled southward,
And in the south I wept.
Then I journeyed northward,
And laughter there I kept.

"Then for a time I lingered,
In eastern lands of light,
Until I moved on westward,
Alone in shadowed night.

"I was born of springtime,
In summer I grew strong.
But autumn dimmed my eyes,
To sleep the winter long.

"We live our lives a circle,
And wander where we can.
Then after fire and wonder,
We end where we began."

The last verse faded into silence. Marius was pacing again, a fist clenched to his chest, murmuring the words of the song. At last he stopped, looking at her. "What does it mean?"

Understanding tickled in the back of her brain, but it fluttered out of reach every time she tried to grasp it. "I suppose it's about beginnings, and about endings. And how maybe they're the same thing."

Only they wouldn't be the same thing anymore, would they? Not if the rifts in the cosmos continued to grow. Not if scientists like Sara Voorhees were right, and the rifts signified the end of the universe—of all possible universes. Then there would be no ending or beginnings. There would be only . . . nothing. Didn't the Philosophers understand? If the rifts kept growing, there would be no world left for them to dwell in as immortals.

But Marius had said they were blinded by their quest; they could think of nothing else. Or did they believe that by going to Eldh they could escape Earth and destruction? She shuddered and reached for her teacup, taking a sip to warm her, only it had gone cold.

Marius sank back into his chair. "I had hoped we'd have more time to try to understand what it is the Sleeping Ones are waiting for, what it is they mean to do. But perihelion comes, and it has brought the gate to light. The Philosophers mean to use it to travel to the otherworld. That's why I led you here, Deirdre, why I let you read the journal. It's why I'm speaking to you now, despite the peril. There's no more use in secrecy. At this very moment, in London, the Philosophers await the delivery of seven crates that have been shipped from Crete. I think you can guess what those crates contain."

She could. "How did they get the sarcophagi out of the archaeological site? It has to be guarded, and I can't believe the authorities on Crete would simply let priceless artifacts be shipped out of the country."

He gave her a scornful look. "Honestly, Deirdre, do you think such things are difficult for us? Our wealth and resources are beyond your imagining, amassed over centuries. And the Seekers are hardly the only servants of the Philosophers. We have contacts in nearly every government in the world—contacts who can be directed to do as we wish with a single letter, phone call, or electronic message. How do you think we've so easily arranged passports and new identities in the past?"

Deirdre shuddered. In that moment she remembered that he was a Philosopher. "And do they know how to operate the gate?"

"Yes, they do. That much they learned from their experiments with the folk at Greenfellow's Tavern."

His words made Deirdre sick. "How long?" she said.

"The crates are to arrive in London tomorrow. The location is here."

He handed her a slip of paper. She stared as if he had handed her a kipper. "What do you want me to do with this?"

"You know what I want."

Slowly she folded the paper, then stood and held it out to him. "I'm not your minion. If you want revenge against the Philosophers so badly, you can get it yourself."

He drew himself up to his full height, towering over her, his face as beautiful and terrible as an angel's. It was clear he wanted to rage at her. Instead he drew in a deep breath, then spoke in controlled words.

"Yes, I want vengeance. I have wanted it for centuries, and all the while I've been unable to so much as raise a finger against them, lest the blood in my veins burn me to ashes. I waited until I finally found a Seeker I believed could help me— I waited for you, Deirdre. But there's another reason I've waited so long. You see, the more I studied the Sleeping Ones, the more I wondered at their purpose, and what would happen when perihelion came. And the more I came to believe that they must not be prevented from fulfilling that purpose, whatever it might be."

Marius gave a rueful smile. "Perhaps it's a result of my being a Seeker before a Philosopher, but the First Desideratum is ingrained in me: *A Seeker shall not interfere with the actions of those of otherworldly nature*. I still hold to that vow. And now, more than ever, I am certain that the Philosophers must not be allowed to interfere with the Sleeping Ones, or prevent them from doing what it is they seek to do when perihelion comes." He picked up a piece of paper from the table with the teapot and held it out.

She glared at it, suspicious. "What is that?"

"It is the result of Paul Jacoby's efforts at translating the writing on the stone arch. He achieved a major breakthrough yesterday when he . . . stumbled upon a lexicon of symbols from the tomb."

"You mean when you gave it to him."

He gave a dismissive wave and held the paper toward her. It was too dim in the hall, and her hand was shaking too badly, for her to read the words on the computer printout.

"What does it say?"

"Many things pertaining to the journey of the Sleeping Ones to Earth. But perhaps the most interesting are these two lines, written on the stones on either side of the keystone."

He brought a tin lantern closer to her and pointed at the top of the page. There was a line of angular, alien symbols. Below was a translation in English: *When the twins draw near, all shall come to nothing unless hope changes everything.*

She looked up, her heart pounding. "'When the twins draw near.' It means Earth and Eldh, doesn't it? Whatever the Sleeping Ones are waiting for, it's related to perihelion. And to the rifts." But what did that last part mean? How could simply hoping change anything?

He took the paper from her. "Do you see now? This is not about vengeance anymore. I still do not know what the Sleeping Ones intend to do, what transformation they seek. But I believe it is imperative they be allowed to complete it. The fate of two worlds may well depend on it. And what the Philosophers intend to do could destroy any chance of that happening. The Sleeping Ones came to this world for a purpose, Deirdre. They were never meant to be found. After all these centuries, that is the only thing I know for certain!"

His final words rose in volume, melding with a roll of thunder. Deirdre met his eyes. "How do I know I can trust you?"

He shrugged, his expression cold. "You can't know. In the end, you can only believe." He folded her fingers around the paper with the London address written on it. She gazed at her hand a long moment, then took the paper and slipped it into her pocket.

"Now what?" she said, meeting his golden eyes. "What should I do?"

Marius opened his mouth, but it was another voice that spoke: deep, gravelly, and familiar.

"I recommend you take a big step back."

Both Deirdre and Marius turned their heads. A man stood at the far end of the front hall, in the opening that led to the foyer, his bulky form clad as always in a sleek designer suit. Deirdre staggered.

"Hello there, mate," Anders said, and pointed his gun at her.

39.

Again thunder rattled the tall windows. Deirdre was so startled she took a step forward, an antelope drawn by fear toward the lion.

Anders tightened his big hand around the gun, holding it at arm's length. "I need you to move away, Deirdre."

As always, he pronounced her name *DEER-dree*. However, his voice was no longer preternaturally cheery. Instead it was sharp and grim, and his eyes had undergone their own transmutation from vivid blue to hard steel. A wave of regret crashed over Deirdre. Then the wave ebbed, draining away, leaving her cold. How long had he been there, just outside the hall, listening?

You have to assume he's heard everything.

Which meant he knew who Marius was. Knew *what* he was.

"Come on, Deirdre," he said, motioning with the gun. "You need to get out of the way. Now."

"No," she said, her own voice going hard. "Tell me what you're doing here and how you followed me."

"There isn't time for that now, mate. You've got to listen to me."

"No. You've lied to me."

He flinched, and a husky note crept into his voice. "I know I have, mate. And I'm sorry about that, I really am. But if you've ever cared one whit about me—and I think you have—then I need you to do this for me. I need you to step aside."

"Don't do it, honey," a smooth voice said behind her. "He's trying to trick you."

Fresh shock sizzled through Deirdre as lightning flickered outside the windows. She jerked her head around. Standing in a narrow opening Deirdre had not seen before was a tall, dusky-skinned woman clad in a turtleneck sweater and tweed slacks.

"Sasha," Deirdre said, her mind trying to comprehend what was happening. Sasha's presence was an incongruity, like a polar bear in a desert.

Sasha took a step forward, and a door swung shut behind her, melding with the dark wood paneling. It was a servant's entrance, designed to be invisible.

"Stop right there, Sasha," Anders growled, taking a step forward, gun before him. So it was not at Deirdre or Marius that Anders had been aiming the weapon.

Sasha did as he commanded, resting her hands on her slender hips. She kept her dark eyes on Deirdre. "Everything he's told you is a lie, Deirdre. It's just like you suspected. Since that day we chatted, I've checked out the story he gave you, and it doesn't match up with the facts I was able to uncover. Anders is not what he says he is. I went to talk to you, and that's when I saw him rummaging through your desk and snapped his picture. Since then, I've been tailing him."

"That's not true!" Anders tried to get a bead on her with the gun, but Deirdre was still in the way.

"As a matter of fact, it is," Sasha said coolly. "Go on, Deirdre. Ask him yourself. See if he can look you in the face and deny it."

Deirdre glanced at Marius, but he only gazed at her, silent. She turned, looking at Anders. "Did you tell me the truth about why you joined the Seekers? Did you tell me about the truth about your gun? Did you tell me that you had gone through my desk, my papers?"

Again he grimaced, but Deirdre didn't fool herself into thinking it was because he regretted what he had done. He was chagrined that he had been caught, that was all.

"See, Deirdre?" Sasha cooed, taking another step forward. "He can't deny it, because it's all true."

"Please, mate," Anders said, adjusting his grip on the gun. "Step aside. I don't want to hurt you."

Deirdre couldn't say the same. "Do something," she said softly to Marius. "Stop him. I know you can."

He raised a golden eyebrow. "Are you certain?"

"Yes!" she hissed.

"Very well, then." He raised a hand.

"No!" Anders shouted, stretching out his arm.

Deirdre tensed, waiting for the fatal sound of a gunshot, but it never came. Anders continued to stand rigid, teeth bared, the muscles of his jaw bulging, his fingers tight around the gun. She kept her eyes on him; he did not move, not even to blink.

It was just like Marius had described in the journal, when Adalbrecht had rescued him in Advocate's Close. She looked at Marius as he lowered his hand. For a second green sparks shone in his gold eyes, then they faded. He took a staggering step back, and his face was suddenly ashen.

"Thanks, darling," Sasha purred, sauntering forward. "I had wondered how I was going to get rid of the big lug. How nice of you to do it for me."

Deirdre shook her head. What was Sasha talking about?

"I see," Marius breathed, his expression thoughtful.

And Sasha pulled a small pistol from the pocket of her slacks, aiming it directly at Marius's heart.

Deirdre's knees went weak, and if she had not gripped the back of the chair she had been sitting in earlier, she would have fallen. A feeling beyond words came over her. It was not pain, not exactly. Nor was it horror. It was as if a hole had opened up inside her—a void in which nothing existed, like the rifts in the heavens.

Sasha clucked her tongue. "Really, Deirdre, after all you've been through, I expected you to put up more of a fight than that. You're not quite the legend you've been made out to be." Her dark gaze flicked toward Marius. "But then, I suppose legends never are."

Deirdre shuddered. Marius had lauded her, telling her that her instincts were deep and powerful. But that was laughable. Her instincts had been wrong. Dead wrong.

Only that's not true, Deirdre. You wanted to trust Anders despite everything that had happened. Deep down, you believed in him, but your stupid brain convinced you otherwise. It was Sasha he was aiming the gun at, not you or Marius. He was trying to make you get out of the way so he could shoot her.

Only Deirdre had stopped him.

Another crash of thunder shook the windows. "Oh, this is going to be fun," Sasha said, moving closer, gun resting easily in her slender hand.

Deirdre cast a glance at Marius. Couldn't he . . . ?

He shook his head. "I do not have the strength to perform another spell," he said, understanding what she had wanted him to do. "The first took far more out of me than usual. And I am not at my full power. It has been over a decade since I've journeyed to Crete."

Sasha's deep red lips parted in a grin. "She told me that was the case. Everyone else had returned to Knossos, to renew their strength in preparation for what's to come. But not you. That's one reason she's been suspicious of you, Marius."

"Phoebe," he said softly.

Sasha shrugged. "Names aren't important."

"So she hasn't revealed herself to you," Marius said. "I wonder what else she has failed to reveal."

Sasha rolled her eyes. "I'm hardly going to start doubting my benefactor now. Not after she's been so very kind to me. I know whom to trust, Marius, unlike poor Deirdre here. It seems the little shaman has lost her magic vision." Her lips curled in a sneer. "Assuming she ever had it, of course."

Those words stung, but Deirdre welcomed the pain, letting it fill the emptiness inside her. "So you've been working for the Philosophers all this time," Deirdre said. "I suppose you were the one who gave Travis's photo to the sorcerers and told them where to find him."

Sasha pantomimed a yawn. "Of course I did. Shall I confess everything, Deirdre? Isn't that what a good villain does at the end—gloats over her victory? But really, what's the point? It's not as if you'll be around for long to lament it." She sighed. "Well, I suppose I *could* throw you a morsel for old time's sake. Yes, I communicated the desires of the Philosophers to the sorcerers. I told them where to find Wilder, and even mapped out the location in the Charterhouse for them, so they could open a gate there. The Philosophers didn't want Wilder to interfere with their plans. They wanted to get him out of the way, and the sorcerers were all too easily used to that end. There—happy now?"

Deirdre's mind raced. How long would the spell Marius placed on Anders last? She had to say something to buy them more time. "What if the Scirathi turn on you?"

"Not bloody likely," Sasha said with a laugh, "seeing as they're all dead. The Philosophers gave the few of them that were left little gold vials of blood. The sorcerers gobbled it up like the greedy things they are. Too bad for them it was tainted with something nasty. The sorcerers curled up like poor dead spiders."

Deirdre tried to cast another surreptitious look at Anders. He still wasn't moving. "How did you get that photo of Anders? Did you fake it?"

"I didn't need to, Deirdre. It was a wonderful stroke of luck, catching him in the act of going through your things."

"So what you said about Anders was true," Deirdre said, her gut clenching.

Sasha gave a satisfied smirk. "Every word of it, darling. Anders has lied to you about who he is from day one. He's been keeping tabs on you, never letting you get too far out of his sight, the loyal, pathetic git. He followed you up here to protect you."

That didn't make sense. "To protect me?"

Now Sasha's expression edged into a look of disgust. "Everyone's always saying what a brilliant Seeker you are, Deirdre, but no offense, you seem a bit thick to me. Maybe they're right; maybe you're good at spotting the footprints in the dirt. Problem is, you don't notice the elephant walking by. Why do you think Nakamura assigned a former security guard to be your partner, then let him keep his gun? It's been Anders's job all along to protect Nakamura's precious star agent. Only the lovable lump has failed, hasn't he?" The gun moved from Marius to Deirdre.

Deirdre cast an anguished look at Anders's still-frozen form. He hadn't told her the truth because he was protecting her. Only that deception had caused her to mistrust him, and now . . .

Lightning flashed, and thunder crashed outside. Deirdre thought she heard a sharp sound along with the thunder, but before she could think what it was, Marius raised a hand. Had he regained enough of his strength to try another spell?

It didn't matter.

"No you don't," Sasha said, pointing the gun at him. "You may be three hundred years old, but I can still blow your head off. And in fact, that's what they sent me here to do."

"So what have they promised you?" Marius said, gazing at Sasha. "Immortality? I know them far better than you ever possibly can. Even if they find what they seek, they will not give that to you."

For the first time the smooth mask of Sasha's calm cracked, and anger twisted her face, ruining its loveliness. "You lie, Marius, just as they warned me you would. Even at this moment, they're preparing the way for those who have been faithful. We True Seekers will be rewarded. And traitors—they will die."

It happened in an instant. Sasha swung her arm to one side, pointed the gun beyond Marius and Deirdre, and fired.

Deirdre turned. Like a statue tipped on its side, Anders had fallen over, his rigid body still in the shape it had been, arm outstretched, gun in hand. As she watched, a bloom of red appeared on his white shirt, spreading outward.

"The bigger they are," Sasha said, her smirk returning. "Now it's your turn. DEER-dree."

She pointed the pistol at Deirdre and squeezed the trigger. At the same moment, Marius took a single step forward. Thunder split the air.

The thunder rolled away into silence. Smoke curled up from the barrel of Sasha's gun.

"Oh," Marius said. He stumbled back, sitting in one of the wing-backed chairs by the embers of the fire. He looked tired, and it seemed for all the world as if he had sat down to rest. Then a spasm passed through him, and blood gushed out his mouth. He reached a hand inside his suit coat, then pulled it out, staring at his reddened fingers as if in fascination.

"Great Spirit," Deirdre whispered. She knelt beside the chair and gripped his arm. "Marius!"

He did not answer her. She looked up, her voice a snarl of anguish and rage. "What have you done?"

"Nothing more than a minor mistake," Sasha said. "After I eliminated you, I was to offer him one last chance to rejoin the Philosophers. But they doubted he would accept, and once he refused I was to destroy him. So it's no great loss. And neither is this."

Sasha moved forward and leveled the gun at Deirdre's head. Deirdre shut her eyes. One more clap of thunder shattered the dusty air.

The thunder faded. There was a dull thud as something struck the floor. Not understanding how she could, Deirdre opened her eyes.

Sasha sprawled on the floor before the fireplace, staring upward, an expression of astonishment on her lovely face. There was a hole in the center of her forehead, oozing blood.

Deirdre looked up. A rangy figure stepped into view. Rain had darkened his blond hair, plastering it to his brow, and his eyes glinted like emeralds. There was a gash on his cheek, trickling blood. He held a gun in his hand.

"That is a wicked thing," Beltan said, then threw the gun to the floor next to Sasha's body.

Deirdre's mind was numb. Did he mean the gun or Sasha? And how was he here? But none of that mattered. Fear flooded her, clearing her mind. Albrecht and Anders had both been shot.

"Beltan, go see to Anders. I'll—"

A bloody hand clamped around her wrist. She gasped and found herself gazing into gold eyes. Only they were dull now, more like tarnished bronze.

Marius licked red-stained lips. "Your partner is . . . still in stasis. There is time. Call for help. Use the phone in . . . the carriage house."

She groped inside his coat; she had to stop the flow of blood. Her hands met a wet, gaping hole. Oh, by the gods. "Beltan, help me!" she cried, her voice shaking with panic.

She heard quick footsteps, then sensed Beltan standing behind her, but she could not take her eyes off Marius. Even in anguish, his face was beautiful, his golden hair like an angel's. To her astonishment, he was smiling at her.

"Do not be sad for me," he said, the words gentle. "Three and a half centuries is far too long. I've endured only so I could find someone to tell my tale to, and now I have. I found you, Deirdre. I am ready to join her now. I am ready to sleep."

"No," she said, but the word was soft: a lament rather than a command.

Another spasm passed through him. "It seems I am not meant to understand the . . . final mystery. I confess, I never believed I would. But you still can, Deirdre. Go to them for me. Go to . . . the Sleeping Ones."

She could only shake her head, beyond words now.

"Please!" Marius's eyes flickered like the flames of twin candles. His grip on her arm tightened. "Find the catalyst. Find it and . . . bring it to them. No matter what else happens, they must—"

His hand slipped away from her wrist. The twin candles flickered one last time, then went out. His head lolled back against the chair. Deirdre stared, unable to move.

"He looks at peace," Beltan said gruffly, breaking the silence. "He was the one who was helping you, wasn't he?"

Peace. The word was foreign to her. Deirdre looked up at the blond man, trying to make her brain function. "Beltan—how?"

"That little flea Eustace shot at us with his gun. He fought more fiercely than I would have thought once I cornered him." Beltan touched his wounded cheek. "But I was able to engage him so Anders could reach the manor. I followed as soon as I finished my work."

These words registered on Deirdre only for a moment. Then sudden energy crackled through her.

"Anders," she said, standing and rushing across the front hall to where her partner lay on the floor.

He was still motionless, staring blankly. Blood had seeped from the wound in his chest, making a puddle on the floor, but not nearly as much as she had feared. She touched a finger to his neck and detected, faint but steady, a pulse. He was still in stasis. But for how long?

Her mind grew clear, crystallizing around a single purpose. She leaped to her feet. "Stay with him, Beltan!"

Without waiting for an answer, she dashed across the hall, into the foyer, and out the front door. Rain pelted her as she skidded down the stone steps and ran down the gravel drive. She saw a small form crumpled on the ground. Eustace. He had brought her the photo of Anders; he had been working with Sasha. Now he was dead.

"Hold on, Anders," she said through clenched teeth as she pushed open the door of the carriage house. "Please, you've got to hold on."

She grabbed the phone from the wall, dialed, then forced herself to speak in a clear voice. Once she was finished, she hung up. For a moment she shut her eyes, gripping her bear claw necklace, murmuring a prayer for the dead as well as the living.

Then she went outside and stood in the cold rain until she heard the distant sounds of sirens.

40

Travis watched, transfixed, as the golden woman walked toward them over the slender span of the bridge. He was aware of the others speaking and moving behind him, but only dimly. To his eyes, the woman shone like a sun. Beneath his *serafi*, sweat trickled down his sides, over the flat of his stomach.

A pale moon eclipsed the sun, blocking it from sight. Hot anger surged in him. . . .

". . . to go, Travis!"

Anger melted into confusion, and the moon resolved into a familiar face. "Grace?"

She gripped his arm, her green eyes bright. "Now, Travis—come on. Farr says we can't let her get close."

Her touch seemed to break the torpor that had come over him. Travis grabbed her hand, and together they ran from the bridge, catching up with the others at the arch that led back into the hall of statues.

"She did that," Nim said, pointing to the crumpled body of a sorcerer at the top of the stone steps. "The gold lady. She'll do it to us, too." She buried her face against Vani's shoulder.

"No, daughter, no harm will come to us," Vani said, hugging the girl tight. However, her gaze was not as confident as her voice. "Never did I think Ti'an might still remain in Morindu. I always believed she died soon after her marriage to Orú. After she became his bride, the stories of my people do not speak of her."

"But the stories of the dervishes do," Farr said, wiping sweat from his brow. "From what I've learned, she was her husband's guardian. She drank of his blood, becoming immortal just like the Fateless. It was said she would destroy any besides the Seven who attempted to draw near the throne room. We must not let her draw close to us."

Travis glanced over his shoulder. Ti'an had reached the end of the bridge. Her beaded garment swayed and glittered as she moved, and the ruby in the center of her forehead gleamed like a third eye. She did not run, but rather walked slowly, her feet bare against the stone floor. Travis met her onyx gaze, and once again he felt heat rise within him. . . .

A hard jerk on his arm brought him back to himself. He turned and stumbled after Grace down the long flight of steps, past the dismembered corpses of the Scirathi. At least now they knew what—or rather *who*—had slain the Scirathi. But how? Surely, if Ti'an were close, she would not stand taller than Grace's shoulder. How had one tiny woman torn apart a small army of sorcerers?

They reached the bottom of the steps. The hall stretched before them, the gigantic statues of spider-eyed women and falcon-beaked men standing sentinel on either side. At the far end, the crack in the door through which they had slipped glowed white hot. It seemed terribly far away. Grace ran toward it, and Travis followed.

"Avhir, stop!" cried a sharp voice. It was Vani.

Travis halted, turning around. Avhir was walking up the steps they had all just descended, back toward the arch that led into the dome. The *T'gol* was more than halfway to the top, moving slowly, mechanically, without his usual sleek stealth.

Vani took a step toward the arch, Nim in her arms. "Avhir, what are you doing? Get back here now!"

However, the *T'gol* seemed not to hear her and kept climbing. A golden figure appeared at the top of the stairs. She raised a delicate hand, making a beckoning gesture. Avhir obeyed, moving toward her. Only a few steps remained. . . .

Larad fumbled in his robes as if to draw out the box with the Imsari. "We have to stop him."

"It's too late," Farr said.

Avhir reached the final step. Ti'an's onyx eyes flashed, and her arms reached up, coiling around his neck, drawing his face down as her own tilted upward. Their lips touched in a kiss.

The *T'gol*'s body went rigid, as if a spike had been driven through him, and his arms shot out to either side. He struggled, trying to pull away, but Ti'an's small hands clamped on either side of his head, holding him in place so that their mouths remained locked. Like cracks in sun-baked mud, black lines snaked up Avhir's neck, over his face and hands.

It happened in a moment. Avhir gave a single jerk, then his

skin changed from bronze to gray. His cheeks sank inward, and his hands curled into claws. He no longer struggled, but stood stiff and still as Ti'an continued her kiss. Her golden skin seemed to glow brighter, as if burnished with oil.

Then it was done. She released Avhir, stepping away. He toppled over, rolling down the steps, coming to a halt at Vani's feet. The *T'gol's* withered face gazed blindly, eyes like gray raisins in their sockets. Inside his black leathers, his body was a shriveled husk.

"I think we had best consider leaving," Larad said, his voice hoarse. "Now."

Travis managed to tear his gaze away from the mummy that moments ago had been Avhir. Ti'an was slowly, steadily descending the steps. Her skin shone so brightly it was painful to look at her, though all the same Travis now found it hard to look away. She had drawn Avhir's blood, his life into her. And now she was going to do the same to them.

Nim screamed. The sound helped Travis to tear his gaze away from Ti'an. Vani clutched the girl and started running. Travis followed along with the others. However, they had only gone a dozen steps when he heard a groaning sound.

He risked a glance over his shoulder. Ti'an stood at the base of the steps, her arms raised before her, palms outward. The ruby on her brow shone as if on fire.

"Oh," he heard Grace say as she and the others came to a halt.

Why had they stopped? Then Travis turned around, and he understood. At the far end of the hall, the two statues closest to the doorway were moving. Sand fell from their shoulders as they stepped from their pedestals; the stone floor cracked under the pressure of their feet.

Farr was closest to them. The statue of the spider-eyed woman towered over him, twenty feet tall. Red light flashed in its multifaceted eyes as it brought a fist whistling down toward his head.

The dervish dived at the last minute, rolling to one side. The statue's fist crashed into the floor with a sound like thunder, creating a gaping pit three feet across. The figure of the falcon-beaked man lumbered forward, swifter than seemed possible for such an enormous thing, and Farr was forced to roll to one side as a stone foot kicked at him. He jumped to his feet and tried to lunge toward the crack in the door, but both statues stepped in front of it, blocking the line of white light. Farr backed away.

"If anyone has any ideas how else to get out of here," Grace said, her face pale, "now would be the time to speak up."

However, the only other way out of the hall was the arch that led back to the dome. And that would mean going past Ti'an. She was walking toward them now, the ruby on her brow blazing.

"We've got to get past those statues," Farr said.

"How?" Larad said. "I doubt they will step aside from the doors if we ask them."

Farr looked at Travis. "They might, if he asked them."

Travis shook his head. How could he control the statues?

"This city rose out of the sand at the touch of your blood," Farr said, drawing close to Travis. "And these statues are part of this city. Use your blood to command them."

Travis wanted to argue, but he felt the eyes of the others on him, and he knew without looking that Ti'an was getting closer; he could feel her like a heat.

"I'll try," he said, then moved toward the statues blocking the door.

The statues' eyes glowed crimson. They reached toward him with massive stone hands, moving faster than he had expected. Travis raked his fingernails over the knuckles of his right hand, prying away the scabs, so that blood flowed.

"Get back," he shouted, thrusting his hand toward the statues.

They kept coming. The floor shook under their feet; their hands reached for him.

"I said get back!"

Again Travis thrust out with his hand, and this time red droplets flew from his bleeding knuckles, spattering the outstretched arm of the spider-eyed woman.

The statue stopped moving. The droplets of blood glittered on its arm—then vanished, as if absorbed by the stone. The light in the statue's eyes changed from crimson to gold. It had worked. . . .

"Travis, look out!"

Grace's shout propelled him into action. He ducked barely in time to avoid the crushing swing of a stone fist. He looked up to see the statue of the falcon-beaked man bearing down on him. Its eyes still shone crimson. Travis's knuckles were already scabbing over in the dry air; he clawed at them again, trying to open them up, to make the blood flow.

There was no time. The male statue brought its fist down toward Travis's head. He tensed, waiting to be crushed to a pulp. The stone fist whistled down—

—and struck the floor next to Travis with a deafening crash. The force of it threw him to one side. When he looked up, awe filled him. The statue of the spider-eyed woman was grappling with the male statue. The colossi rocked back and forth, arms entangled, one's eyes blazing crimson, the other gold. The male statue opened its beak in a silent cry. It shoved hard against the other statue, knocking it back. However, their stone limbs were still entangled. As the one statue toppled, it dragged the other with it.

They struck the doors of the palace, slamming them shut with a *boom!* Then the statues crashed against the floor, breaking apart into a heap of rubble. The head of the female statue shattered, while that of the male rolled to a halt against the door. The light in its eyes flickered, then went out.

"You did it, Master Wilder," Larad said, gazing at the fallen statues in fascination. "You stopped them."

"And us as well," Farr said, face haggard. "The doors are blocked."

Travis stared as elation gave way to new fear. Farr was right. The debris from the statues was piled in front of the doors. And the doors opened inward; they could not be opened without clearing away the rubble. Farr pushed against the falcon-beaked head, but it was no use; it had to weigh two tons.

Grace was looking at him, her green eyes overbright. "Now what do we do, Travis?"

Nothing, he wanted to say. However, before he could speak, a high, keening wail filled the hall.

The sound was like a siren, only higher, louder, threatening to split Travis's skull. He thrust his hands against his ears, but it was no use. The sound kept building. He turned to see Ti'an no more than a dozen paces away. Her mouth was open; she was making the noise. It was a scream of fury.

Just when Travis was sure the keening would drive him mad, Ti'an's mouth shut, and the sound ceased. Farr slumped to his knees with a moan, and Nim was sobbing as Vani clutched her tight. Travis knew they had to do something, but the piercing wail had addled his mind; he couldn't think.

Before he could react, Ti'an thrust her hands out before her, and the gem on her forehead blazed with renewed flame. A sound like an earthquake filled the hall.

Larad stared up, his shattered face going white.

"No," Grace murmured. "Oh, no."

All along the length of the hall, on either side, crimson light flickered to life in the eyes of the statues—not two of them this time, but all—twenty or more. Dust clouded the air as the statues stirred, swinging stone arms and legs, turning ancient faces toward the intruders. The floor shook as they stepped down from their pedestals.

Travis pushed Grace aside as one of the male statues bore down on him, falcon beak clicking. It opened its gigantic hand, grabbing for Travis. Stone fingers, each as thick as a tree trunk, began to close around him. He rubbed his hand against them, smearing them with blood. The blood vanished, and the stone fingers ceased moving. With a grunt, he pushed himself up and out of the hand, then leaped away, hitting the floor and rolling.

He lay stunned for a moment, listening to the crash of breaking stone behind him. Had the statue turned to fight the others? A high-pitched scream jolted him out of his stupor. It was Nim. He lurched to his feet, and pain sparkled in his ribs. He turned around to see what was happening.

Then he froze. Ti'an stood before him. Her golden body shone through her beaded garment, as if she were clad only in light. He could see the curve of her hips, the fullness of her breasts, and the darker bronze of her nipples. Again fire surged in him, and he could not move. The shouts and noise of breaking stone faded to a dull roar in his ears.

Ti'an tilted her head—he was by far the taller—to look at

him. Her face was expressionless, a thing of flawless beauty
forged of gold. However, in her eyes smoldered an ancient fury.
She reached for him, to draw his head down close to hers . . .

With the last shred of his will, Travis flung his hand up in a
warding gesture and stepped back. Blood flew from his
wounded knuckles, spattering her outstretched hand. Ti'an
paused, gazing at the red droplets on her finger. Then, lan-
guorously, she brought her finger to her mouth, touching the
drop of Travis's blood to her lips.

Ti'an's onyx eyes went wide. A shudder passed through her,
rippling her garment. Then a new light shone in her gaze—not
fury but something fiercer, hungrier. Her full lips parted to reveal white, pointed teeth.

"My husband," she said, and before he could move, Ti'an
reached out and pressed a hand against Travis's chest.

Her hand seemed to burn through the cloth of his *serafi*, and
through skin, muscle, and bone as well, so that it felt as if she
was touching his heart, wrapping her fingers around it, setting it
afire. The sounds of the struggle behind Travis faded, replaced
by a rhythmic drone. He was aware of shadows moving on the
edge of his vision, some large, some small. It almost seemed he
recognized one of them.

Grace? he tried to say. He started to glance toward a woman
who had stumbled to the floor while a massive shape loomed
above her.

A hot finger touched his chin, turning his head with inex-
orable strength. Ti'an's face filled his gaze, and he could see
nothing else. Her finger traced a smoldering line down his
throat, his chest, his stomach.

The heat burned in him now like a sun in his chest. A sweat
of desire slicked his skin, and a metallic taste filled his mouth.
Her beads shifted as she moved, and he caught a glimpse of the
triangle between her legs, dark with mystery. He felt his body
stir, wishing nothing else than to become one with her. All other
thoughts fled him. He moved close to her, bending his head,
wanting to join his mouth to hers.

"Not yet," she said, her voice like sharp music, pushing him
back with irresistible strength.

For a moment Travis felt an anguish such as he had never

known. How could she spurn him? He would rather die than not have her. Then his pain was forgotten as she took his hand in her own, her slender fingers closing around his in a viselike grip.

"Come," Ti'an said.

And forgetting the dim, struggling shadows behind him, Travis followed.

41.

The floor heaved as one of the gigantic statues struck with its fists, and Grace fell hard to her knees. The taste of blood filled her mouth; her teeth had clamped down on her tongue. She tried to get up, but the floor kept bucking and rolling like an angry sea.

"Travis, stop!" a voice cried out. It was Vani.

Grace managed to look up. Ti'an stood before Travis, gold skin gleaming. He was making no effort to run from her, but was instead staring with a rapt expression. As Grace watched, he took her hand, and together they began to walk toward the steps at the far end of the hall. The statues, many of them just stepping off their pedestals as they awoke, lumbered out of the pair's way as if in deference to their mistress—or was it their master—then moved to join the others in the attack.

Grace stared after them. *Why hasn't she kissed him like she did Avhir? What's she doing with him?* Then, with a jolt of dread, she realized where it was Ti'an must be leading him. *She's taking him to the throne room.*

Before she could consider what that meant, a shadow fell over Grace. She looked up, and rational thought fled her. A statue loomed above her, its multifaceted eyes glowing crimson. It bent down, reaching for her . . .

Strong hands grabbed Grace's *serafi*, dragging her to her feet, pulling her out of the way. The statue's fingers closed on thin air. It rose up, opening its mouth to let out a soundless cry of fury. Grace turned around and gazed into Farr's grim, handsome face. He opened his mouth as if to say something.

Grace's eyes grew large. "Run!" she shouted, grabbing his

hand and pulling him to one side as another statue reached for them. They sidestepped a blow from the female statue that had tried to crush Grace, then ducked between the legs of one of the falcon-beaked men. They made it to the wall and pressed their backs against it, panting.

They're big and slow, Grace. If we just keep moving, they won't be able to get us.

Certainly they could not touch Vani. Holding Nim tight, the *T'gol* moved so quickly her outline blurred, slipping in and out among the statues. She paused a moment, deliberately drawing one of the statues toward her. Then, as it bore down on her, she seemed to vanish; the statue collided with another. Stone arms broke off at the shoulder; a head toppled to the floor, cracking open like a melon. The statues collapsed in a jumble of stone, and a cloud of dust rose into the air, illuminated by shafts of sunlight from above.

"Larad!" Farr shouted. "Use the Imsari!"

The Runelord could not move as swiftly as Vani, and he had been caught between two approaching statues. He fumbled with the iron box that contained the Stones, but then his gray robe tangled around his ankles and he fell to his knees. The box tumbled to the floor.

Operating on instinct, Grace reached out with the Touch. However, there was nothing to reach out *to*. The statues were not alive; they had no threads. And the strands of the others were only the faintest wisps shining in her mind, far too delicate to grasp. Her magic was no use. She looked at Farr, but he shook his head. Blood sorcery was as weak as witchcraft; he was powerless as well. She gripped Farr's arm as the two statues bent over, reaching for Larad.

With a loud crack, the heads of the two statues collided with one another. The colossi stumbled back, away from Larad. The Runelord gaped for a moment, perhaps astonished he was still alive, then he scrambled on his hands and knees, reaching for the box. He opened it, drew out one of the Stones, and held it high.

"Sar!"

A gray-green flash. The two statues stiffened and went still. For a moment they rocked back and forth, then they toppled over, crashing against one of the spider-eyed females. All three smashed against the floor.

You did it, Master Larad! she tried to send the words across the Weirding to him.

Grace wasn't certain he had gotten the message, but he staggered to his feet and looked at her, a satisfied expression on his scarred face. However, the reprieve was brief. More statues had lumbered toward them. There were still over a dozen of them, and they were coming all at once. One seemed to notice Grace and Farr leaning against the wall. It lurched toward them, falcon beak clicking, and they were forced to run.

"We must flee back into the dome!" Vani shouted. She seemed to blink out of existence as one of the statues swiped at her, then reappeared behind it. "If we retreat over one of the bridges, they will not be able to follow. The spans are too slender."

Energy surged in Grace. Yes, that was where they had to go. That was where Ti'an had taken Travis.

"Come on," she hissed to Farr and started running.

Though not as swift as the *T'gol*, they were able to dodge past the statues that lumbered toward them. In moments, both Grace and Farr were past the statues, as was Vani.

"*Sar!*" Larad chanted again, his voice ragged, holding Sinfathisar aloft. The Stone flared with gray-green light, and another statue ceased moving. It fell with a *boom!*

Why do the Imsari still work when other magic doesn't? Grace wondered, her logical mind operating despite her fear. She didn't know, but she was glad Larad was still able to wield the Great Stones. The Weirding had faded to a wisp of what it had been, an old cobweb in a corner, and Farr was no longer able to call the *morndari* to him; blood sorcery had ceased functioning as well.

Then why was Ti'an able to animate the statues? the scientist in her asked, still pressing for answers. She didn't know, except . . .

Ti'an drank directly of Orú's blood, and Orú was the most powerful sorcerer who ever lived. The Imsari are incredibly powerful as well, and incredibly ancient.

It made sense that the oldest magics would be the last to go:

those powers that were deepest, and closest to the source of all magic. Except they would still fade, wouldn't they? The rifts in the heavens would keep growing, and soon even the eldest magics would cease functioning.

There was no time to think about it. Larad turned and ran, catching up to them. The statues reacted slowly to this change in tactics. They milled about in a tight knot, colliding with one another, knocking chips of stone off their bodies. Then, one by one, they turned around, eyes flaring crimson, and started after their prey.

Vani led the way across the hall, Grace and Farr just behind, followed by Larad. When they reached the foot of the steps that led up to the arch, Vani hesitated. Avhir's shriveled body still lay there on the floor.

Grace thought of his bronze eyes and how they would never shine again. Avhir had feared kindness, and in the end a kiss had killed him. "He's dead," she said. "Just like Ky—"

"Do not speak them!" Vani flung the words at Grace like knives. "Do not dare to speak those names!"

Grace bit down on her tongue. Vani's face was hard and ashen, but her gold eyes were dry. She started up the steps, Nim in her arms. The others followed.

Vani was right, Grace thought. *Kylees* and *Avhir* were words that no longer had meaning. But *Travis* still meant something; Grace had to believe that. Because if Travis was gone, then there would be no one to speak the Last Rune. There would be no one to stop all words, all names—and all the things they stood for—from ceasing to be.

Panting, they bounded up the last of the steps. The arch flashed by, the dome soared above them. The beams that shafted down from the high windows were red as copper, like rays from a dying sun.

Larad glanced over his shoulder. "The statues are still coming. They're right behind us."

"The bridge!" Vani shouted.

They had reached the nearest of the slender spans that arched over the void, toward the tetrahedron of gold that seemed to float in the darkness. Vani led the way, holding Nim. Larad started to pull back, to let Grace go first, but this was no time for courtly deference. She pushed him forward, then followed on his heels. The void yawned to either side; it seemed to suck at her. She forced herself to gaze at the center of Larad's back.

"Hurry!" Farr shouted behind her. "If the statues reach the bridge while we're still in the middle—"

The span trembled beneath Grace's feet, vibrating like a piano wire. She didn't look back, but she could picture what was happening: the first of the colossi setting foot on the bridge.

Vani had reached the platform on the far side. She turned around, and Nim's eyes became circles of fear. The bridge shook again, and Grace's foot skidded off one edge. She would have fallen if Farr hadn't grabbed her from behind. Larad tripped on his robe, but he had reached the end of the span and fell to his knees next to Vani. Grace clenched her teeth. Just a few more feet . . .

The bridge gave a violent jerk. Grace no longer felt stone beneath her feet. She was going to fall.

A weight struck her from behind—hard. Farr's arms wrapped around her. They flew through space, then tumbled onto the platform.

Grace rolled to a stop on her side, cheek against stone. Her jarred vision cleared in time to see the two halves of the bridge tilt downward. With a loud *crack!* they broke free. Three statues toppled like tin soldiers, arms waving stiffly as they plunged into the void. The pieces of the bridge followed. There was one last flicker of crimson, then blackness swallowed them all.

Ten statues milled about on the far edge of the abyss, eyes flickering, their stone minds too dull to determine how to follow their prey. One of them strayed too close to the edge and toppled over. The others seemed not to notice.

Grace realized that Farr was still holding her tight in his arms. She did not resist. It felt good to believe she could be held that way by him, if only for a moment. Then, slowly, she pulled away. He let her go.

"Is everyone all right?" she said, standing. It was a ridiculous question. None of them were all right, not after that. However, Farr and Larad picked themselves up, and Vani nodded.

"Statues shouldn't be able to move," Nim said, her round face solemn.

Grace couldn't disagree. She turned around. Now that they were close to it, she could see that the golden tetrahedron was indeed large, over fifty feet on a side. The triangular door seemed to be open, but she could see only darkness within. It took her fragmented thoughts a moment to re-form, then she remembered what they had to do. She started toward the door.

Farr grabbed her arm. "You can't go in there."

She did not speak. Instead, she simply looked at him. He jerked his hand back as if stung.

"All the stories say it's death for us to enter," he added weakly.

Grace took another step toward the door. "We have to. That's where she took Travis."

Nim wriggled from Vani's arms, slipping to the floor. "He is Fateless," the *T'gol* said. "His kind may enter there."

"What about her?" Larad nodded toward Nim. "Can't she enter there as well? Can't she open the way for us?"

Vani shot the Runelord a black look. "She is a child, not a tool. You cannot simply use her!"

"Like you used her to return to Earth?" Grace said, her voice scalpel-cool. She had not meant the words to cut, but by the way Vani flinched they had, and deeply.

"It's all right, Mother," Nim said. There was no longer fear in her small voice. "I want to go in. I want to find my father."

Vani seemed beyond speech. She made no effort to stop Nim as the girl moved past Grace, to the door.

Farr made a sharp motion with his hand. "Stay close to her. It's our only chance. If she is truly a nexus, then the threads of fate will untangle in her presence."

"And if she's not?" Larad said, raising an eyebrow.

"Then our own fates will be crushed, and cease to be."

Grace tried to swallow, but her mouth was dry. *Only a dead man has no fate*, Vani's al-Mama had said to her. Two times Travis had died and been reborn: once in the fires of Krondisar, and again in the desert outside Morindu. That was why he was *A'narai*.

And what about you, Grace? Will you be reborn if you die in there?

She doubted it.

Nim stepped into the triangle of darkness. The others followed in a tight knot: first Grace, then Farr and Larad, and finally Vani. For a moment Grace feared she was lost. The darkness closed around her. She could see nothing, feel nothing. A scream rose in her throat, but she had no mouth with which to give it voice. She was the flame on a candle. The darkness constricted around her, a dark hand to snuff her out.

"This way," said a small voice in the darkness. Nim.

Grace felt herself being pulled as if by a string tied around her middle. Then the darkness vanished, replaced by a golden radiance. A shuddering breath filled her lungs. She was alive.

So were the others. Larad stood next to her, looking astonished and vaguely ill. Farr was gazing around them with a look of fascination on his face, but Vani's eyes were locked on something straight ahead. Nim took a step forward, holding out her small hands.

"Father!"

It took Grace's dizzied mind a long moment to take everything in. They stood along one wall of a large, three-sided room. Triangular doors were cut into each of the other walls; the other two bridges were visible beyond them. The chamber's walls were carved with countless symbols, and they tilted in as they soared upward, meeting overhead in a single point from which the red-gold radiance emanated. The room was capped by a crystalline prism. The prism must catch some of the beams of light that spilled through the windows in the dome outside, Grace thought, focusing them and bringing them inside.

In the center of the chamber was a dais: three-sided like the room with several steps leading up to it. On the dais rested a chair made of gold, its back shaped like a gigantic spider. In the chair sat a figure. Iron shackles bound his arms and feet to the chair, but there was no point to them.

The man on the throne was dead.

The body had shriveled to a desiccated husk eons ago. The arms and legs were no more than bones held together by dried tendons like old twine. Papery skin peeled away from bare ribs. What might once have been a royal robe of crimson was reduced to a few shreds dangling from sharp shoulders. The skull leaned back against the throne, yellowed teeth bared in a flesh-less grin, empty sockets staring.

A hiss, like that of an angry cat, drew Grace's gaze down-ward. Ti'an knelt on one of the broad steps before the dais. Be-low her, lying on the dark stone, was Travis. His *serafi* lay crumpled on a lower step, and he was naked save for a short linen kilt. She had anointed him with oil, and his skin gleamed in the metallic light, taut over sculpted muscle. He was beauti-ful—far more so than when Grace had first met him years ago—as if he was a statue himself, formed of gold.

His eyes were closed, but his chest rose and fell; he was still alive. Only not for long. Ti'an bent over him, one hand cradled beneath his head, turning it to one side, the other wrapped around a curved knife. A golden bowl sat on the next lowest step, ready to catch the flow of his blood once she opened his throat.

Ti'an hissed again, a look of anger on her lovely, eternal face, glaring at the intruders. Then she bent again over Travis. She lifted the knife, ready to strike. They were too far away to stop her. Even Vani would not be able to reach the dais in time.

The knife flashed, descending.

And Nim screamed.

The girl had screamed before, but not like this. Her cry did not cease after a moment, but continued to rise in volume and pitch, careening off the walls, doubling, trebling, until the very air seemed on the verge of shattering. Nim's hands clenched into fists at her side; her spine went rigid. Still she screamed, her head thrown back and eyes clenched tight. Larad pressed his hands to his ears. Farr staggered. Grace felt as if her skull was going to explode.

Ti'an stood, her dark eyes smoldering like coals. She opened her own mouth, and a second scream sounded, rising on the air. It was not a human sound, but rather a piercing siren, as shrill as Nim's. Farr grunted, sinking to his knees. Larad staggered back against the wall. Vani's eyes were shut, and her arms were crossed before her in a warding gesture. Spikes of pain stabbed at Grace's ears, driving deep into her brain. She could feel the very structure of her being weakening, as if she was a thing made of glass, crazed with cracks. Another moment, and this would destroy her.

Nim's scream ceased. The girl collapsed to the floor in a small heap. Ti'an closed her mouth. She gazed at the motionless girl, then turned and bent back over Travis.

Vani was the first to recover. "Nim!" she cried, running toward the girl.

Farr started moving a moment later. Ti'an glared at him, thrusting a hand in his direction. The dervish ceased moving. He stood still, staring forward, and a thin line of spittle trickled from the corner of his mouth. Grace looked at Larad. Could he do something with the Great Stones? No, he was staring like Farr, motionless, a blank expression on his face.

Ti'an seemed to concentrate on the two men for a moment, then she turned her head. For a moment she gazed at Grace, but her expression was dismissive. Then she bent again over Travis, turning his head, exposing the gleaming skin of his neck. She raised the knife.

Vani had just reached Nim and was picking her up. Larad and Farr weren't moving. No one could do anything. No one but Grace. The power of the Weirding was all but gone; she had no magic. However, she had something better.

Fury.

"Get your bloody hands off of him, bitch!" spoke a hard voice, and Grace knew it for her own.

Ti'an's nose wrinkled as she bared pointed teeth. She opened her mouth to scream again. However, Grace was already running. As the first siren-like wail rose on the air, Grace gritted her teeth, ignoring the pain, and threw herself forward, up the steps of the dais.

The wail ceased as she crashed into Ti'an. The knife flew through the air, then skittered to a stop on the lowest step. Grace's momentum carried her forward, so that she landed on top of the golden woman. It was like embracing a bronze statue that had just been broken out of its mold, still glowing with forge heat. Grace tried to pull away.

Slender arms and legs coiled around her. In an easy motion Ti'an flipped her over. Air whooshed out of Grace as she landed hard, the sharp edge of a step cutting into her back. Ti'an straddled her, thighs squeezing Grace's rib cage. Her delicate hands closed around Grace's throat, crushing her windpipe. Ti'an's face was impassive, like that of a golden sculpture; her breath was hot and metallic. Stars exploded in front of Grace's eyes as Ti'an's fingers tightened around her neck. . . .

Ti'an froze, her dark eyes going wide. Her mouth opened, but this time no siren call came out. Instead, dark fluid stained her lips.

"My love . . ." she gasped.

Then she slumped to one side and rolled down the steps of the dais.

Air rushed into Grace's lungs, delicious and painful. After several ragged breaths, she managed to push herself up on one elbow. Ti'an's body lay at the foot of the dais. The knife jutted from the center of her back. Already her golden skin was beginning to go dull.

"Are you all right, Grace?" said a gentle, familiar voice.

Grace looked up. Travis stood above her, his gray eyes concerned. Pain filled her—the good kind, the ache that let her know she was still alive.

Travis, she tried to say, but the word couldn't escape her bruised throat.

"Don't speak," he said, as if she had the power to do so. He knelt, touching her cheek. "Thanks for coming after me again."

She smiled and made a gesture with her hands, one that spoke as eloquently as any the mute man Sky had ever made. *That's what I do.*

Then she wept as he held her in his arms.

42.

Travis cradled Grace gently as she pressed her face against his chest, sobbing. Strangely, he did not feel like weeping himself. Instead he felt alive, exhilarated.

By Olrig, you showed her! Jack Graystone's voice crowed in his mind. *Thought she could use your blood for her own ends. Well, she found herself on the other end of the knife!*

"Shut up, Jack," Travis growled under his breath.

"What?" Grace said, pushing back and wiping her cheeks.

Travis helped her up. "I said, 'How's Nim?'"

"She is well," Vani said, approaching the dais, holding Nim by the hand. The girl walked beside the *T'gol*, pale-faced, but apparently unharmed by whatever Ti'an's scream had done to her.

Though unable to move, even to see, when he was lying on the dais, Travis had been aware of everything that had been taking place around him. The air of this place seemed to hum, transmitting everything that happened within its walls and carrying it to him in a way light and sound could not. He had his back to the two of them; all the same he knew Farr and Larad approached, faces haggard.

"She was sad," Nim said, gazing down at Ti'an's motionless body. "She was so sad, she wanted to hurt everybody."

Grace knelt before the girl and brushed a dark curl from her face. "Why was she sad, Nim?"

The girl pointed to the shriveled mummy chained to the throne.

"Orú," Farr said, taking a step up the dais. "So he's dead after all."

"For a good long time, by the look of him," Larad said, giving Ti'an's body a wide berth.

Travis picked up his fallen *serafi* and shrugged it on. "She wanted to resurrect him."

Grace stood, her expression startled. "Could she have?"

"She believed she could," Vani said, gesturing to the golden bowl. "She would have caught your blood in that, and taken it to him."

Travis moved up the dais, toward the mummy on the throne. When Ti'an had seduced him, he had fallen not only under her power, but under her thoughts as well. He had glimpsed his mind, as well as the single purpose that had consumed it.

"She recognized his blood flowing in me. She believed it had the power to restore him. I'm not certain if she was right." He started to reach out toward one of the skeletal hands curled on the arm of the throne, then pulled back. "I'm not sure the single drop in me would have been enough. I think it would take far more to do it. But she was determined to try. She loved him. For three thousand years, ever since the fall of Morindu, she's been waiting to bring him back to life. And now . . ."

"Now they are together," Vani said, the words rueful. She knelt beside Ti'an's body. The once-golden skin was chalky now. "She was my ancestor. I am of the royal line of Morindu. I am descended of her and Orú."

"Perhaps that explains it then," Farr said. He had been examining the mummy on the throne.

Vani looked up at him. "What do you mean?"

"She was a nexus, just like Nim. That was how she could enter this place and guard Orú in his slumber. I think when she screamed, when she was angry or alarmed enough, it . . . affected the flow of events. And I think it's the same for Nim."

Grace held a hand to her throat, wincing. "When they were both screaming like that, it felt like I was falling apart."

"That's because you were," Farr said. Travis noticed he did not gaze at Grace. Instead, his dark eyes were on Vani. "We all were. We were being torn apart by the pull of infinite possibilities, of infinite fates. Each of us might have lived our lives in countless other ways. I think what we felt were those different lives intersecting, overlapping. And canceling one another out, like sound waves can cancel each other out if aligned properly."

"Is that why they were both screaming?" Grace said. "To neutralize the other?" She looked at Nim, but the girl seemed suddenly shy and hung her head, letting her hair cover her face.

Travis wasn't certain he completely understood all this, yet Farr's words *felt* right. Only when Ti'an and Nim had screamed, it hadn't affected him as it had the others. With Ti'an's attention focused on Nim, her spell of seduction had lost its hold on Travis. He had been able to stand, take the knife in his hands, and use it against her. But why hadn't he been affected by her scream like the rest of them?

"Only a dead man has no fate," Grace murmured.

Had she heard his thoughts? No, the Weirding was too weak for that now. All the same, she had understood what he was thinking. He felt Farr's eyes on him. However, before he could say anything, Larad's excited voice came from across the chamber.

"Look at these markings. They're fascinating—more like pictures than writing. I feel I should almost be able to understand them."

"Do not stray too far from Nim!" Vani called out to the Runelord.

The girl raised her head and touched Vani's arm. "It's all right, Mother. It's safe here now."

Travis shut his eyes, again feeling the hum all around him. "I think she's right. I think what she and Ti'an did together . . . I think it pulled the threads of fate, untangling them." He opened his eyes. "And now that Orú is dead, they won't tangle again. What have you found, Master Larad?"

The Runelord was running his hands over the wall. "It's a story."

"A story of what?" Farr said, approaching.

Vani, Nim, Grace, and Travis followed. Then Travis saw the markings, and in an instant he understood.

"Everything," he said softly. "It's the story of everything."

He moved past Larad, to the wall, tracing the carvings in the stone with a finger.

"They're like the pictographs we saw in the cave beneath Tarras," Grace said, turning around. "Only there are so many of them. It would take ages to try to translate them all."

She was right about the first part. These were indeed like the carvings they had found beneath Tarras: stylized symbols that were not quite art, not quite writing, but something in between. Only it wouldn't take time to translate them, because Travis understood the symbols as clearly as if they were moving before him like stick figure actors pantomiming a play. Ti'an had granted him more than he thought when she put him under her spell. Or was it something else? Was it the very air of this place that transmitted the meaning of the symbols to him, just as it transmitted the actions, even the feelings, of the others? He could sense Grace's sharp curiosity behind him, and Farr's more urgent craving for knowledge.

"Travis?" Grace said, and he sensed rather than saw her take a step toward him.

"I can read them, Grace." His hands felt hot, and the carvings seemed to shimmer when he passed his fingers over them. He touched two stick figures standing side by side. Small dots fell from the arm of one of them, while the other held a curved knife. "Somehow I can read them all."

"Maybe because he wrote them," Larad said, and though Travis's back was turned he knew the Runelord had pointed toward the throne.

No, that wasn't it. Here were more symbols. The one stick figure sat on a chair. The other stood behind, still holding the knife. "It was she," Travis said. "Ti'an. She's the one who made these."

He moved left, running his hands over the wall, going back to the beginning.

"Here he is—King Orú. Only he wasn't a king then. Morindu hadn't been built yet. It was just him and his tribe in the desert. And then . . ." A fever seemed to grip Travis. His eyes drank in the meaning of the symbols faster than seemed possible. He was racing along the wall, moving to the right now, his fingers skimming over the stones. "Then *they* came. There were thirteen of them. They answered his call, and they were powerful. More powerful than any that came before. He took them . . . took them into him, and . . ." Travis stopped, then turned and gazed at the rest of the symbols that ringed the room. "Oh," he said.

Farr's expression was eager, hungry. "What is it? What do the symbols mean? I can't read them."

On shaking legs, Travis returned to the mummy chained to the throne. "He understood. King Orú. He understood the answer."

"The answer to what?" Vani said, hands resting on Nim's shoulders.

Travis's mind buzzed. The heat surged in him. "Remember the story you told us, Farr? The one about the twins, the ones who were born out of nothing at the beginning—one light, the other dark? Well, they're coming together again, struggling with each other. That's what's causing the rifts in the sky. Only the twins aren't trying to kill each other."

Farr's gaze was fixed on him. "Then what are they trying to do?"

"They're trying to save each other."

The others stared at him. Travis turned around. Standing here, in the center of the chamber, he could see the story unfold in its entirety.

It began not long after the dawn of Amún. Angular symbols suggested towers and ziggurats rising up from the desert beside the waters of the River Emyr. The great city of Usyr stood among them, as well as other city-states—but not Morindu. In that time, Orú was neither god nor king, but instead was the leader of the nomadic tribe that had first discovered the presence of the bodiless spirits known as the *morndari*, and that had first made blood offerings to entice the spirits into doing their bidding. Over time, other tribes grew more adept at commanding the spirits; they were the ones who raised cities. In turn, the tribe that had first discovered the *morndari* seemed doomed to die out.

Then Orú was born. A seer proclaimed he was destined to be a great sorcerer, and so as an infant his mother fed him with her blood rather than her milk. The seer spoke truly, and even as a child he was skilled beyond the eldest sorcerers at the art of summoning the *morndari*. One series of symbols showed him bringing a vast herd of cattle under his command. Others suggested trees rising out of bare ground and bearing fruit while small droplets fell from his arm.

Orú was only twenty when he became the leader of his tribe, and under his rule his people prospered—so much so that the rulers of a nearby city grew jealous of their wealth in gold and cattle.

That city was Scirath.

The god-king of Scirath launched an assault on Orú's tribe, sending a great army of warriors and sorcerers. Orú's people were far outnumbered. Death was certain—unless Orú made a great gamble.

Travis shuddered as his eyes passed over the next series of symbols. Orú sat in his tent while his wife, Ti'an, made thirteen cuts in his body. Then he made a calling such as he had never done before, and thirteen of the *morndari* came to him—spirits more powerful than any that had ever been summoned before or since. Normally a sorcerer staunched the flow of blood once the spirits came, lest they drain him to death, but Orú bid the spirits enter his veins. Greedy for his blood, they did. Then, once they were within him, Ti'an poured hot lead on his wounds, sealing them.

The symbols showed a stick figure writhing in pain. Then, in the next panel, the stick figure stood tall, lines of power radiating from it. It held out a hand, and a vast army was swallowed by the desert.

There was more in the next panel—symbols that made Travis's head swim to gaze at—but he skipped them for the moment, turning so that he saw a later point in the story. Morindu loomed above the desert now, dark and powerful. Orú sat on his throne, shackled to it with chains, asleep, while seven stick figures drank from him, careful to seal the wounds again after they did.

Travis's eyes kept moving across the wall. The story was almost over. An army like a sea flowed toward Morindu. Among the army were dots that radiated circles of power. Demons. The people of Morindu fled the city, escaping into the desert.

But not the Seven. Droplets fell from their arms, and a circle appeared in the air. A gate. Beyond was sea and stone. Then the Seven drank one last time from Orú, and when they were finished he was no longer a living man, asleep on the throne. He was a mummy, dead.

A figure holding a curved knife approached the Seven, jagged bolts of fury shooting from her eyes. Ti'an. Only before she could slay them, the Seven stepped through the gate, leaving only Orú and Ti'an. The last panel showed the city sinking beneath the sands of the desert as the army was crushed under the churning sands.

There the story ended.

Grace stepped onto the dais next to Travis. "So they drained him." She gazed at the desiccated mummy. "The Scirathi thought they would find Orú's blood here, but the Seven took it all, then escaped through a gate, leaving Ti'an. All this time she's been trapped here with his corpse, made immortal by his blood."

Travis hadn't realized he had been speaking aloud as he read the story, but all the same he must have.

"If the Seven escaped, where did they go?" Larad said.

It was Farr who answered. "Earth. Look at the way the gate is drawn. It is like a tunnel through a great darkness. That must be the Void. Which means the Seven went to Earth."

"Can we go now, Mother?" Nim said.

Vani stood. She had covered Ti'an's body with a cloth. "Yes, daughter. There is nothing left for us here."

"And where will we go?" Master Larad said. "There is water in this city, but we have no camels. We need to find the Last Rune, Master Wilder. But I don't know how we'll do that now. Not before the end comes. I doubt we'll find it lying around here."

Larad was right, the end was close. But the answer *was* there, Travis was sure of it. Only he couldn't quite grasp it.

"What about the rest of the story?" Farr said, pointing to a large section of the wall. "You skipped all this. What did it say?"

Yes, that was where the answer was. Travis licked his lips. "When the thirteen *morndari* entered him, Orú understood the truth. The truth about the origin of the world. Of all the worlds."

Grace touched his shoulder. "You mean like the story of the twins?"

"Yes, the twins." Travis drew in a deep breath, then read the symbols he had skipped, speaking as he did, describing what Orú had understood as the thirteen entered him.

"It's like Farr's story. For an eternity, there was only nothing. Then, suddenly, the nothing gave birth to two things, two entities—one of being, and the other of . . ." Travis struggled for a word. ". . . of unbeing. Earth and Eldh, they were worlds of being. And there were more. Hundreds of them, millions. But there was only one world of unbeing, and that was the Void. It was like a sea between the other worlds, bridging them, binding them together."

He was no longer aware of talking now. Instead, he was seeing it, understanding it without words, even as Orú had three thousand years before when the *morndari* entered him, becoming one with him.

It was all in perfect equilibrium, the worlds of being balanced by the Void. Or at least it was *meant* to be perfect. Only it wasn't. For from the very beginning, there was something wrong.

Travis studied the symbols. A deep line was carved into the wall. On one side of the line were myriad small specks, as well as thirteen larger dots that emanated concentric lines of power. On the other side of the line were three circles.

No, not circles. Stones.

Travis could almost see it as it had happened. A mistake was made in the creation of the worlds and the Void. Somehow, in the chaos of those first moments of formation, fragments of unbeing were caught on the wrong side of the line. They found themselves drawn in and captured by the force of one of the worlds of being. The world Eldh. There, in a later age, those fragments of unbeing became known as the *morndari*, or Those Who Thirst.

Still striving for balance, for perfection, the multiverse spontaneously attempted to heal itself. Fragments of primordial being were sent to Eldh to counteract the *morndari*, to cancel them out and remove the flaw, so that the worlds of being would be perfect like the Void. These fragments of primordial matter were the Imsari.

Although they became known as the Great Stones after the dwarf Alcendifar found them and wrought into them the power of the runes Gelth, Krond, and Sinfath, the Imsari were not truly things of stone. They were something older, deeper—pieces of the very first stuff of being that sprang out of the nothingness. If they were to be called Stones, then this thing they came from was the First Stone. It was the first pebble tossed into an ocean to create a continent. It was the very beginning of everything.

The thirteen most powerful *morndari* were similar, but opposite. They were fragments of the most primordial substance of unbeing. When the Imsari came in contact with the *morndari*, they would cancel one another out, returning to the nothingness that once spawned them. Thus the balance would be restored and the instability healed.

Only it didn't happen that way.

In the south, on the continent of Moringarth, the thirteen most powerful *morndari* were dazzled by blood and were trapped within Orú, merging with him so completely they could never be released again. And in the north, on the continent of Falengarth, where the Imsari fell, the three Great Stones were changed by the craft of Alcendifar, then were seized by the forces of the Pale King, and finally were scattered across the world, and even beyond, to the world that drifted closest to Eldh in the sea of the Void. To the world Earth.

Thus history conspired to keep the Imsari and the *morndari* from uniting as intended. And so the instability grew. Slowly at first. And then, as the end drew nearer, more swiftly.

The final symbols showed gashes opening in the fabric of creation. The line grew blurred, then vanished. And after that . . . nothing at all. Or less than nothing, for this was an emptiness that could never give birth, that never had given birth, that was without possibility. Without hope.

Travis stopped reading. He was dimly aware of his own voice fading to silence.

"She wasn't trying to kill the Seven," Vani said.

He turned. The *T'gol* stood over Ti'an's covered form. She looked at him, and sorrow shone in her gold eyes.

"I think you're right. I think she helped them open the gate." Travis studied the symbols. Fury sparked in her eyes as the Seven stepped through the gate—fury for the army that approached Morindu. "I think she knew it was crucial that Orú's blood be guarded, protected, so that one day it could be used to heal the rifts in creation."

Only she was mad in the end. Eons of dwelling here alone, deep beneath the desert, with only her husband's mummy as companion, had destroyed her mind. She had wanted only to kill the intruders, to use them, to get her husband back.

I'm sorry, Travis said silently, gazing at her still form.

"What about the other *morndari*?" Grace said. She had been studying the symbols on the wall, and now she turned around, her expression sharp with curiosity. "If the thirteen that entered Orú were part of the primordial stuff of unbeing, what were the other *morndari*?"

Travis glanced again at the symbols. There was so much he could understand, but it was hard to put it into words. "The thirteen were part of the stuff that first came into being. Or into unbeing, I mean. And in turn, that substance—"

"That first substance caused all the rest of unbeing, the Void, to precipitate out of the nothingness," Grace said, nodding. "I understand now. It was like a chain reaction. The same would have been true of the worlds of being. The First Stone appeared out of nothingness, then it caused everything else to come into being."

Despite all that had happened, Travis grinned. That scientific mind of hers.

"So the lesser *morndari* on Eldh are similar to those that dwell in the Void between worlds," Farr said, touching his arm, perhaps unconsciously tracing the scars there. "They were not so powerful that their presence on Eldh caused a great instability."

"More than that, they were balanced, too," Travis said. He studied the drawing. If he looked close, around the shapes of the three Great Stones, he could see tiny flecks etched into the wall. "Smaller grains of the First Stone were sent to Eldh along with the Imsari—enough to balance out the other *morndari*. Only they . . . they were taken in by . . ." Again he struggled to describe what had happened.

It was Larad who gave the thought voice. "Runes. They became runes, didn't they?" The Runelord didn't wait for an answer. He paced, his gray robe swishing. "There was no Worldsmith, not in the very beginning, not in the first iteration of Eldh. It was the very flecks of the First Stone that brought it into being, trapping the *morndari* even as they tried to counter them. Each fleck became a thing, a rune—sea or sky or stone— and was bound into it. The same was true for the Old Gods, and the Little People, and the dragons. There are runes for all of them."

"Even Sia," Grace said, wonder on her face now. "There's a rune for Sia, isn't there?" She shook her head. "But if *morndari* brought blood sorcery into the world, and the flecks of the Great Stone brought rune magic, where did witch magic come from?"

Larad stroked his chin. "Granted, I know little about the magic of witches, even less than Master Graedin. But from what we have recently learned, I imagine the Weirding was an effect of the creation of Eldh. We know from our studies that witchcraft is related to runes. So runes created the world, and—"

"And then the world created witchcraft," Grace said, tucking her blond hair behind her ears, as if it was in the way of her thinking. "Life gave rise to the Weirding. Just as the blood of the sorcerers, once it was dispersed through the world, gave rise to the New Gods."

Larad nodded. "It would seem so."

Travis should have felt amazement at all this. It was as if a curtain had been lifted, revealing mysteries that had existed since the beginning of time. However, his mind hummed, and it was hard to concentrate on what the others were saying.

What does it matter if we know how everything began if it's all going to be snuffed out of existence? Magic is almost gone. Everything that bound the world together, and what the world itself brought to life, is fading.

Only the Imsari still functioned, and the blood of Orú—the very oldest of things. But how long did they have until even these things ceased? And when they did, any chance of healing the rifts would vanish.

"There are a few symbols here I do not believe you translated, Travis."

Farr's voice jerked Travis out of his thoughts. Farr stood close to the wall, gesturing to a group of symbols contained within an oval shape, like a cartouche. They were the only symbols carved into the wall that Travis didn't completely understand. He supposed they had not been part of Orú's own knowledge. Instead, they must have represented the thoughts of Ti'an, or perhaps the thoughts of the Seven Fateless Ones. The symbols showed the Three coming in contact with the Seven, and jagged rays of power shooting outward. Only there was something else, something between the Three and the Seven. Travis didn't understand what the symbol meant. It looked like a triangle and nothing more.

"I think those symbols show how the Imsari and the Seven *A'narai* need to be brought together," Travis said. "Only I don't understand what that third symbol means."

Or did he? The buzzing in his mind grew louder. He gripped the bone talisman—the one given to him so long ago by Grisla—that hung at his neck, thinking. It seemed he should know what the third symbol was. Could it somehow be related to the Last Rune? The dragon Sfithrisir had said it was the Last

Rune that would heal the rifts. Surely that meant bringing the
Seven in contact with the Imsari. But Travis didn't know any
rune that was denoted by a simple triangle. Maybe Larad . . .

No. When he glanced in that direction, the Runelord shook
his head. He didn't know what the symbol meant either.

Maybe it didn't matter. The Imsari were here on Eldh, and
the Seven were somewhere on Earth. There was no way to get to
them, to bring them together. . . .

By Olrig, Travis, that's not true! Jack's voice said in his
mind. *You've quite forgotten. There is a way.*

Hope surged in Travis. The answer was here after all. He
reached into his *serafi* and drew out a silver coin.

The others gazed at him, startled, but Farr nodded, drawing
out his own coin. Yes, he understood.

"You want to take the Imsari to Earth," the former Seeker
said. It was not a question. "You want to find the Seven of Orú,
to heal the rifts."

Yes, Travis tried to say. However, the word was lost in a clap
of thunder. Beneath their feet, the floor gave a violent lurch.
Larad stumbled against Grace, and both fell sprawling. Nim
clutched Vani as the *T'gol* braced her feet. Farr gripped the wall
for support, and Travis fell to his knees. Like a candle being
snuffed out, the glowing crystal high above went dark, plunging
the room into stifling shadow. Travis, with his preternatural
eyes, still possessed dim vision, but he could see the others flailing blindly.

"What's happening?" Grace called out.

Before anyone could answer, the air burst asunder as a circle
of blue fire crackled into being on the center of the dais, just behind the golden throne, a window rimmed by sapphire lightning.

It was a gate.

43.

Deirdre paced across the white floor of the hospital's waiting
area, willing herself not to glance at the clock on the wall.
How long had it been since the nurse had come to tell her he

was out of surgery? She wasn't sure, but in the meantime night had fallen outside the windows, and the waiting area had steadily cleared out until she and Beltan were alone.

At the moment, the blond man's rangy form lay sprawled across a bank of plastic chairs. He was snoring. The day's activities—a mad dash from London to Edinburgh, the struggle at the manor, the ambulance ride to the hospital—had exhausted him more than the warrior in him would willingly admit. Every time Deirdre had told him to get some rest, he had steadfastly refused. However, a short while ago she had gone to get them some coffee. When she returned, he had been out cold.

His face was peaceful in sleep; gone were the lines of worry that had creased his brow ever since Travis, Vani, and Nim fell through the gate. A butterfly bandage covered the gash on his cheek though it hardly seemed necessary. Already the wound had scabbed over; it was healing rapidly.

You should rest as well, Deirdre, a calm voice spoke within her. Her Wise Self. *Much work lies ahead. You will need strength to face it.*

Only she couldn't sleep, not now, not when she knew what was going to happen tomorrow in a warehouse south of London. As soon as she could, she would go there. But first she had to see him, to see with her own eyes that he would live.

If you had just listened to your instincts, Deirdre—if you had trusted Anders as your heart wanted to—he wouldn't have been shot, and Marius would still be alive. This is all your fault.

No. That was her Shadow Self speaking now, and she wouldn't listen to its bitter voice. It would not help her do what she had to. Besides, Anders and Beltan had made their own decisions. She had not asked them to follow her from London.

Although she should have known—perhaps, deep down, *did* know—that they would. Only she hadn't believed they would be working in tandem. She had thought Anders a traitor, and had assumed he would follow her to stop her. Instead it had been just the opposite. He had been trying to protect her. Just like he had been doing for the last three years.

Again she thought about what would have happened if Anders and Beltan hadn't shown up at the manor. Marius would still be dead, and so would she. No one would know what the

Philosophers really were, or what they really desired. And what they were going to do tomorrow. Only she *was* alive, and she did know, and she had Anders to thank for that.

Why didn't he tell me the truth about who he was?

But she knew the answer. If Nakamura had told her he was assigning her a full-time security guard, she would have rebelled. So Nakamura had tricked her, assigning Anders as her new partner. As it was, early on, Deirdre had suspected the truth, but eventually convinced herself to believe Anders. Once again, her instincts had been right, and she hadn't listened to them. But maybe it wasn't her brain that had gotten in the way. Maybe it had been her heart. She had wanted to believe Anders, and so she had. Only all this time he had been lying to her, and even though he had been doing it to protect her, that didn't change the fact that he had been dishonest.

What about you, Deirdre? You haven't exactly kept up your vow to tell him everything.

And that was why she couldn't be angry with him. Nakamura, however, was another matter. Sasha had been a traitor, but she had been right about one thing: the Seekers did keep secrets. All this time, Nakamura had been deceiving her. But why? Why was it so important to protect her that he was willing to lie to her to do it?

Maybe she knew the answer to that. Hadrian Farr was gone. She was the only Seeker left who had direct connections to Travis Wilder and Grace Beckett, one of the most important—if not *the* most important—case in the history of the Seekers. He was hardly going to put a prize like that at risk.

Or was it more than that? *Why was protecting you so important, Deirdre? What does Nakamuru really know?*

Somehow she didn't believe he had been in direct contact with Marius. Then again, Nakamura had given Deirdre the assignments that Marius had wanted her to have, so maybe there was some connection after all. Whatever Nakamura knew, it was enough to make him want to keep her safe. Even now, he was still doing it.

When the ambulance arrived at the manor, she had expected police cars to come with it. They hadn't. The ambulance had been from a private company. They did their work efficiently, stabilizing Anders and loading him into the ambulance, but made no move to call the police, even when they discovered the three dead bodies: Marius, Sasha, and Eustace. Nor did they ask Deirdre any questions.

It was the same at the hospital. Normally a gunshot wound should involve the police, but no officers were called in, and no one asked Deirdre anything except if Deirdre knew whether Anders was taking any medications or had any existing medical conditions. She and Beltan had been shown to the waiting area. A short while later, a telegram had come for her. It was from Nakamura.

> *Do not leave the hospital. Do not speak to the police.*
> *More instructions to follow.*

So the Seekers were taking care of everything. They had connections Deirdre couldn't even guess at. Somehow, at least for the moment, they had been able to keep all of this a private matter. And whether it was because they were too distracted to either know or care what Nakamura had done for her, or because they feared they would reveal themselves, the Philosophers had not interfered

So far, at least. But though Sasha and Eustace were dead, Deirdre didn't dare let herself believe the Philosophers would not soon learn what had transpired at the manor. And while she was glad for Nakamura's help, his orders meant nothing to her now. She was not going to stay here and wait for the Philosophers to come get her.

Deirdre sat back down and shut the lid of her notebook computer, which rested on a chair. An hour ago, to help pass the time, she had logged onto the Seekers' systems. She had reviewed the results of Paul Jacoby's linguistic analysis of the writing on the arch. And she had called up the toxicology report for the syringe Anders had used on the sorcerer. According to the lab results, the syringe had contained the expected drug; Anders had not caused the death of the sorcerer in Beltan and Travis's flat.

I sure wish you had known that earlier today, she told herself with a grimace as she shoved the computer into her briefcase.

She glanced at the clock, forgetting to will herself not to, and saw that it was after eleven. It was too late to catch either a train or a flight back to London tonight; they would have to wait until morning. Would that give them enough time? The seven crates were scheduled to arrive from Crete tomorrow, but she didn't know at what time. She could only hope that she would beat them to London.

Go to them for me, Marius had told her just before he died. *Go to . . . the Sleeping Ones.*

Deirdre would go. How could she not? A Philosopher himself had asked her with his dying breath. Only it was more than that. It was the discovery of the Sleeping Ones that had caused the Seekers to come into being. To see the Seven was to see the beginning of the Order. And to see beings from another world. Whatever she thought of the Seekers now, she had not lost that desire to find and encounter the otherworldly.

And what will you do once you get to London, Deirdre? Stroll past the Philosophers and whisk away the Sleeping Ones so they can do whatever they're supposed to do? What do you think you can possibly accomplish if you go to London?

She didn't know. However, Marius had believed the Seven had been waiting all these millennia for some sort of transformation. And the writing on the arch suggested it had something to do with perihelion.

When the twins draw near, all shall come to nothing unless hope changes everything. . . .

But what hope did they have? Deirdre had no idea what sort of transformation the Seven sought, or what catalyst would allow it to occur. Again and again, as she paced in the waiting area, she had hummed the song under her breath: *Fire and Wonder*. She felt so close to knowing what the song was about, but the meaning was like a butterfly fluttering around her: lovely, beckoning, and always out of reach.

All the same, she was certain the song held a clue to the nature of the catalyst. Marius had suspected that was the case, and her own intuition—which she was listening to for a change—told her the same. If she thought about it enough, it would come to her. She started to sing the song again in a low voice. . . .

"Excuse me, miss."

Deirdre gripped her bear claw necklace and stood up as a nurse approached. The nurse was middle-aged, her dark hair caught in a neat bun, a clipboard in her hand. Deirdre felt her throat go dry.

"Your friend is out of recovery," the nurse said. "They've moved him to critical care. You're allowed to go in and see him if you'd like, but only for a few minutes. He's very tired, and still groggy from the anesthesia."

Deirdre followed after the nurse, leaving Beltan asleep on the chairs. They moved through a pair of double doors and down a corridor. The nurse gestured to a stainless-steel door. Deirdre gathered her will, then stepped inside.

The soft whir of machines filled the air, along with the sharp scent of antiseptic. She took a step into the room, and a shock jolted through her. She was used to Anders's large, room-filling presence. The man crumpled on the hospital bed looked strangely small.

"Hey there, mate," croaked a weary voice.

More emotions than she could name filled Deirdre: joy, relief, anguish, sorrow, and a dozen others. They had propped him up in the bed. A sheet covered him from the waist down, and his upper body was bare save for a large bandage wrapped around his barrel chest. IV needles had been inserted in each of his arms. He looked older than she remembered; the fluorescent light made his hair gray rather than blond. However, he managed a faint smile, and a hint of the usual twinkle glinted in his blue eyes.

"Never thought I'd see you again, partner," he said, the words hoarse. "Never thought I'd see anything again, for that matter."

Deirdre tried to speak but couldn't. She gripped his hand. His fingers tightened around hers, stronger than she would have guessed.

"Now, now, Deirdre. There's no need to cry. Turns out I'm going to be just fine. Though it's got the doctors baffled, to say the least. I gather the bullet put a nick in some important artery. They keep saying I should have bled to death in the time it took the ambulance to get there. Only I didn't."

Deirdre couldn't help smiling. "You're full of surprises. Mate."

He grinned, and though a bit shaky, the expression was as impish as ever. "Sorry about that." His grin faded. "I know you'll probably never believe me, but I didn't like lying to you. I always wanted to tell you the truth, but Nakamura wouldn't let me."

Her own smile faded. "I believe you."

A grimace crossed his face. Pain from his wound? "Aw, mate," he said. "I'm sorry."

She laid her right hand on his brow while her left kept a grip on his hand. In three years, she had hardly touched him. It felt good now to be connected. "I'm the one who's sorry. I knew deep down I could trust you, and I let Sasha convince me I couldn't."

"It wasn't your fault. Turns out Sasha had a lot of help in the matter. I never did quite trust her, though I couldn't ever put my finger on just why. She always seemed to know a little too much, maybe. But Eustace—I thought the kid was true-blue."

"They fooled us both," Deirdre said.

"Yeah, they did at that. But you stopped them."

She shook her head. "No, Beltan did. And you did. But Marius . . ."

"He's gone, isn't he?"

Deirdre could only nod.

Anders's blue eyes were thoughtful. "I have to say, I would have liked to have gotten to meet him. Crikey, a real Philosopher."

"They're not what you think," Deirdre said, her voice going hard.

"I know. Not everything you do, I'm sure. But I think Nakamura had started to suspect something fishy was going on with the Philosophers, that not all of them were getting along so well. He's been a Seeker long enough to notice when things started to change, and I think he was beginning to get conflicting orders from them. He assigned me to guard you because he had a feeling you were involved, though he didn't know how exactly." Again Anders grinned. "Turns out he was right. But it was important for him to make everyone believe I was just your new partner, yourself included. He didn't want the Philosophers to know he had assigned you a bodyguard, for fear he might get their ire up."

So Deirdre wasn't the only one with good instincts. Nakamura had gotten the sense that there was some conflict among the Philosophers, and the orders Marius kept giving him had made Nakamura believe Deirdre was involved. All the while he had possessed the good sense to appear neutral and unaware of the truth, even while assigning a guard to Deirdre without the Philosophers knowing it.

Deirdre wondered what else Nakamura knew, but before she could ask Anders the nurse tapped on the window, giving Deirdre a stern look. She started to pull away.

Anders gripped her, holding her down.

"You're going after them, aren't you? The Philosophers."

She nodded. "The seven sarcophagi are being delivered to London tomorrow. They're going to open the gate."

"Take me with you." His eyes gleamed with fevered light. "I want to help with the battle."

She bent over him. "You *have* helped with the battle. Without you, there wouldn't be a chance at all. Now it's time to rest."

Deirdre's face drew close to his, and a warmth encapsulated her: nourishing, healing. Her lips nearly brushed against his, then she moved and pressed them to his forehead in a gentle kiss.

"Come back to me, mate." Tears rolled from the corner of his eyes. "Promise me you will."

Deirdre let go of his hand. "Good-bye, Anders."

She walked past the whispering machines and left the room. For a moment she stood outside the door, gripping her bear claw necklace. The warmth that had enfolded her had been replaced by a cruel chill. Then she took a deep breath and headed down the corridor, back to the waiting area. Beltan was sitting on one of the orange chairs. He stood as she drew near, a questioning look on his face.

"Let's go to London," she said.

44

Six hours later, Deirdre and Beltan caught the first train of the morning out of Edinburgh.

Traveling by plane would have gotten them to London an hour or two faster; logic dictated that they should have headed to the airport. Instead, after they left their hotel, she and Beltan had walked up Princes Street in the gray predawn light to the train station beneath the National Gallery. Maybe it was her instincts again, or maybe it was simply a desire to stay grounded, connected with the Earth, but somehow going by rail seemed *right*.

She could only hope that was true, that they would reach London before the shipment from Crete arrived.

"I think we should have gotten more coffee," Beltan said as they settled into their seats on the train. He crumpled the paper cup they had bought at a shop in the station.

Deirdre gripped her own cup. It was still full and too hot to drink. "There'll be a cart. You can buy more."

The blond man looked around expectantly, and Deirdre didn't bother to tell him the cart wouldn't come along until after the train was under way; watching for it would keep him occupied.

Beltan looked freshly awake that morning, his green eyes bright and eager. He had removed the bandage from his cheek; the wound was no more than a thin scab now, as if he had gotten it a week ago.

It's the fairy blood in him. It's what causes him to recover so quickly.

Deirdre wished she had a little fairy blood herself. She had not slept last night. Not that she hadn't craved to; she was more weary than she could ever remember being in her life. But such peace as sleep brought was for other people, other times. She had sat at the desk in her hotel room, reading through Marius's journal—which she had taken from the manor—a second time, and a third.

Just as surely as the fairy blood had changed Beltan, the journal—and the knowledge contained in its pages—had changed Deirdre. After reading it, she would never—could never—be the same person again. But who would she be, she had wondered, sitting alone in the hotel room? Instead of countless possibilities fluttering through her mind, she saw nothing. Nothing at all. The answer to that question would have to wait until what lay ahead of her was done, for good or for ill.

She had spent the last hour in her room softly singing the song *Fire and Wonder* over and over. As before, she felt close to understanding what it meant, and she found herself wishing she had her lute, for her mind always seemed to work better when the instrument was in her hands. However, at that moment her lute was in her flat in London, and as close as she was to reaching understanding, it might as well have been a thousand miles away; she didn't know what the song meant.

As the time to leave the hotel drew near, she had found herself staring at the phone. Finally she had picked it up and dialed the number of the hospital. Before it could start to ring on the other end, she hung up. Anders was going to live; that was all she needed to know.

There was a low rumbling as the train rolled into motion. Deirdre watched as the platform slipped past. A large group of people in white sheets stood on the platform, holding signs as they always did. Only the signs no longer contained words or dark spots. Instead they were completely black. Eaten.

The window next to Deirdre went dark for a moment. Then the train emerged into the drizzly morning. The world was still here—for now.

"So, do you have a plan for when we get to London?" Beltan said, his voice low.

"I'm working on it," she said, hoping she sounded more confident than she felt. Despite staying awake all night, she still had no idea what they were going to do when they got to London.

"The Philosophers can be killed, we know that now."

"I know."

"I won't try to keep from harming them if they get in our way, Deirdre." A fey light shone in Beltan's eyes. "They sent the Scirathi after Travis. They nearly killed him, and Nim as well. I don't care if they're immortal. To me, their lives are forfeit."

Gone was the cheerful blond man who liked food, beer,

woefully bad jokes, and looking at handsome young men passing by on the street. Over the last several years, Deirdre had let herself forget what Beltan really was, but at that moment she remembered. He was a man of war. And he knew who his enemy was.

"Ah," Beltan said with a pleased look. "Here's that cart."

It looked as if the attendant was heading toward the front of the train, but Beltan stuck out a big, booted foot, bringing the cart to a lurching halt. The attendant—a pasty young man—looked ready to protest, then quickly swallowed his words after one look at Beltan.

"Coffee, please," the blond man said. "And one of those sticky buns. No, better make it two."

The attendant complied, then pushed the cart up the aisle so quickly the wheels rattled.

Beltan was about to start in on the second sticky roll when he gave Deirdre a guilty look. "You didn't want one, did you?"

She shook her head. Food, like sleep, was something she couldn't conceive of just then. While he ate, she took a sip of her coffee—it had finally cooled to a subthermonuclear temperature—then pulled out a plastic bag of things she had purchased at the shop in the train station. There was gum, a candy bar she could give to Beltan later if he started getting fussy, a pack of tissues, and a paperback book she had plucked at the last minute off a rack of best sellers next to the clerk's counter.

It was a popular science book entitled *Fall From Grace: How the End of Perfection Created the Beginning of the Universe.* The book was by Sara Voorhees, the astrophysicist who, in the article in the *Times*, had suggested that the rifts in the cosmos might be a symptom of the beginning of the end of the universe. By the date inside the cover, the book had been published a few years ago. Voorhees's recent comments must have renewed its popularity enough to land it back on the best seller list.

Deirdre had grabbed the book on impulse. It wasn't chance that the gate had come to light on Crete at the same time the rifts had appeared; both were related to the approaching perihelion between Earth and Eldh. And Marius had believed that, whatever transformation it was the Seven sought, it had to do with perihelion as well. So maybe there was a connection between the rifts and what it was the Seven wanted. If so, anything she could learn about the rifts would help her.

The city slipped away outside the window, replaced by the gray-green blur of the borderlands. Deirdre sipped her coffee, opened the book, and began to read.

Nearly four hours later, Deirdre shut the book and leaned back, resting her aching head against the back of the seat. Outside the window, the rolling hills of lowland Scotland had been replaced by the row houses and industrial buildings of the outskirts of London.

She glanced to her left. Beltan was asleep. Two crumpled coffee cups were jammed into the seat pocket in front of him. Another, empty, was held in his hand. Crumbs dusted his cable-knit sweater. She decided not to wake him; it would be a few more minutes before they reached Paddington Station, and it was best to let him sleep. He was going to need his strength for what lay ahead. *She* was going to need it. Besides, she needed a few minutes to think about everything she had just read.

Although the book was well written, Voorhees's technical background in astrophysics had been apparent on every page, and Deirdre had been hard-pressed to understand a fraction of *Fall From Grace*. All the same, some of the things she had read had resonated—especially the discussion of virtual particle pairs.

As far as Deirdre was able to understand, the basic fabric of the universe was not made of some concrete substance. Instead, the universe was founded on nothing at all. Its most basic substrate was a vacuum devoid of any kind of matter. But in that very nothingness was stored the endless potential for everything else.

The vacuum contained infinite energy because it contained infinite possibility: At any one moment, anything might come of it. And, in fact, it did. As physicists had discovered, the vacuum was constantly spawning pairs of virtual particles: one of matter, one of antimatter. The particles would exist for a fraction of a moment, then they would collide, annihilate one another, and vanish.

It was like starting with a featureless plain and using a shovel to dig. The result was both a pile of dirt as well as a hole: matter and antimatter. Infinite holes could be dug in the plain, but all you had to do was put the dirt back in one of the holes and it was gone. The virtual particle pairs were the same. Every moment, at every point in space, countless pairs popped out of the nothing and were reabsorbed an instant later; the fact that they existed so briefly was what made them virtual.

Only here was the tricky part: Sometimes the virtual particles could become real particles. For example, when a virtual particle pair appeared on the edge of a black hole, one of the particles might be drawn into the black hole's gravity well while the other escaped. Thus the two particles would never collide and cancel one another out. And there were other situations in which the particles could become real.

One was the beginning of the universe. According to Voorhees, in the beginning, the universe was perfect. It was completely symmetrical, devoid of all features. Then, somehow, that symmetry was broken, and everything fell out of the vacuum like candy out of a piñata. Matter and antimatter—in the form of tiny particles, quarks and antiquarks—would have gone whizzing around in all directions.

There should have been the same number of quarks and antiquarks; they should have all collided, exactly canceling each other out and restoring the nothingness to its state of perfection. Only that didn't happen. Somehow, in our universe, the number of quarks slightly outnumbered the number of antiquarks. The result, after all the canceling and colliding was done, was a surplus amount of matter. And that was the stuff of which stars and galaxies and planets were made.

What had caused this imbalance, this asymmetry, in the number of quarks and antiquarks, no one knew for sure. But one thing was certain: If not for this fundamental flaw, the universe as we know it would not exist. It was only the breaking of perfection that caused the universe to come into being.

It was, in the beginning, a fall from grace.

After that, Voorhees described in detail the conditions in the early universe, and by then Deirdre's head was throbbing too much to make sense of it. However, there were a couple of passages, late in the book, that Deirdre read and reread despite her headache. One was a passing reference Voorhees made when touching again on the subject of virtual particle pairs.

Almost always, Voorhees wrote, *such virtual particles are tiny quarks, the smallest building blocks of matter. However, there's no rule that says the particles have to be small. Far larger particles could just as easily spring into being, say a particle pair made up of an elephant and an antielephant. It's not that these scenarios are impossible; they're just enormously unlikely. So unlikely, in fact, that we'll almost certainly never observe such an instance. That doesn't mean such cases haven't happened and won't again. However, if a pair of enormous virtual particles did spring into being, it's a fair bet we'd never know it, as in such a situation vacuum genesis would likely occur: A new universe would form in a bubble around the particles, concealing them from our view.*

At that point, Deirdre had been forced to consult the index, and to go back to the section on vacuum genesis. It was one of the most difficult topics in the book, but also one of the most fascinating. According to Voorhees, various disturbances might cause a bubble to form in the primordial vacuum. Within the bubble, the symmetry of nothingness is broken, and all sorts of stuff falls out of the vacuum, creating a universe. That's how our own universe might have formed. And countless other universes might have formed in similar fashion. They could exist as bubbles within the vacuum of our own universe, and we'd never even know they were there. And there would be no need for the laws of physics to operate the same way in different bubble universes; each one might have its own logic.

It was a wondrous notion: all these bubbles floating in the dark sea of nothing, like crystalline balls with galaxies inside. But there was a troubling side as well, Voorhees warned.

For if two of these bubbles were to collide, she wrote, *the result would be the catastrophic destruction of both.*

Deirdre had to admit, Voorhees seemed to enjoy predicting ominous outcomes. Then again, she could very well be right. Was that what perihelion meant? Were two bubbles drawing close even now? The copy of the *Times* Deirdre had picked up at the station described how the rifts continued to grow at a fantastic pace. They were enormous now, each covering over 20 per cent of the night sky.

And yet the trains were still running. When Deirdre glanced

out her window, she saw people trudging along the sidewalks and cars jamming the streets. The end of the world was coming. At least that was how it looked. So why weren't people panicking? Why weren't there looting and riots?

A throng of people in white holding black signs flashed by her window, and she understood. *They've already surrendered. That's why they aren't rioting. Why panic when there's no hope? You either keep going on, keep going through the motions. Or you give up.*

But she hadn't given up. Not yet.

Deirdre set down the paper and picked up the book. Again she had the feeling that she was close to understanding. But understanding what? What did astrophysics have to do with alchemy and catalysts? If she could just find the link between them . . .

The train rattled as it began to slow. Ash-colored buildings blurred by, then were replaced by darkness as the train entered a tunnel. They were nearing the station. She touched Beltan's shoulder, waking him, and nearly lost her arm as he grabbed her wrist in an iron-hard hand. Only after a moment did he blink, realizing who she was, and let her go.

Never wake a sleeping warrior, Deirdre thought, wincing as she rubbed her wrist.

The train rattled to a stop.

"I'm hungry," Beltan said.

Deirdre handed him the candy bar. "Come on."

They exited the train with the crowd of business travelers and wended their way across the platform, up and out of the station.

"Are we going to take the Tube?" Beltan said, tossing the empty candy wrapper into a trash bin.

Maybe the people of the world weren't panicking, but now that she was here in London, Deirdre felt her own panic rising. "No, there isn't time."

They took a cab instead, dashing in front of a businessman and climbing inside. As the taxi pulled away from the curb, Deirdre waved at the businessman, who was giving them a rude gesture.

"Where to?" the cab driver asked in a musical Punjab accent.

Deirdre pulled the scrap of paper from her pocket and gave

him the address. The cab rolled away from the station, winding through the cramped streets of London.

Beltan let out a snort. "I drive much faster than this. We should have taken my cab."

Deirdre didn't reply. She was just as glad the cab wasn't racing; this was her last chance to think, to decide what to do. However, by the time the taxi rolled to a stop in a blue-collar neighborhood south of the Thames, she still didn't have a plan. She paid the driver, then watched as the cab drove away, leaving them in front of a strip of red brick storefronts.

"This is Brixton," Beltan said, looking around at the grimy, half rundown, half newly-gentrified street. "I take fares here sometimes. Isn't this where—?"

"Where Greenfellow's Tavern was," Deirdre said, her throat dry. In her pocket, she clenched the scrap of paper Marius had given her. She had known the moment she glanced at it that the address was the same. The Philosophers must have built a new building on the site where Surrender Dorothy had burned.

Deirdre started walking; at her instructions, the cab had dropped them off a few blocks away.

"So what are we going to do?" Beltan said, easily keeping pace with his long legs.

"We're going to get in there and stop the Philosophers from doing whatever it is they're doing," Deirdre said, surprised at the steel in her voice.

Beltan bared his teeth in a grin. "Now that sounds like a plan."

Despite the dread in her stomach, Deirdre grinned back. A moment ago she had felt so tired she could have lain down in the gutter; now she felt awake, and freshly alive.

"Let's go meet the Philosophers," she said.

45.

They walked a block down the street, and Deirdre caught sight of the building. It looked like a bank or a courthouse, with a facade of imposing columns and a frieze above the cornices wrought with Greek heroes, gods in chariots, and goddesses.

Although brand-new, the building had been stained to match the more weathered architecture around it. No one was going in or out; the tall front doors were shut.

"This way," Deirdre said, ducking down an alley.

She imagined all approaches would be watched, but there was no sense in walking up to the front door and knocking. At least not until they had gotten a closer look. They picked their way down the alley, ducking behind overflowing Dumpsters and into dim alcoves for cover. Then Deirdre caught a glimpse of the back of the building, and fear jabbed at her.

Ahead, a large moving truck blocked the alley. A ramp reached from its cargo hold to the loading dock on the back of the building. The steel doors on the loading dock were shut, but the truck's rear door was still open. Its cargo hold was empty.

She opened her mouth to tell Beltan they were too late, but before she could speak he clamped a big hand over her mouth and pulled her into the shadows behind a stack of empty boxes. Deirdre stared at him with wide eyes. He shook his head, indicating she shouldn't speak, then held up two fingers and mouthed a word. *Guards.*

Deirdre nodded, and he let her go. She peered around the boxes. A moment later, two thick-shouldered men, clad in black, appeared from behind the truck. One spoke something she couldn't make out into a walkie-talkie. The other held a gun. So the Philosophers did indeed have minions other than the Seekers.

The guards walked up the steps onto the loading dock and surveyed the alley. The one with the radio held it up and spoke something— it might have been, *All's clear*—then the pair descended back to the pavement and continued on their round. They were only a few feet from the crates when they turned and started back toward the loading dock.

It happened so quickly it was almost over before Deirdre realized what was happening. Beltan shot out from behind the crates, swift and silent as a panther. A single blow to the back of the head, and the man with the radio crumpled to the pavement without a sound.

The other guard started to let out a shout as he turned around, but the sound was muffled as Beltan's fist smashed against his jaw. The guard tried to bring up his gun, but Beltan slammed his arm back down, and Deirdre heard the distinct *crunch* of bones breaking. The gun fell to the ground and skittered across the pavement.

Beltan's other hand came up, so that he gripped the man's head on either side. He made a twisting motion. Again came a loud *crunch*. The guard slumped into a heap next to the first.

The green light in Beltan's eyes dimmed. He was breathing hard, and he was grinning. Deirdre willed herself to look away. She knew the two men on the pavement weren't simply unconscious. They were dead.

And you would be, too, Deirdre, if they had seen you.

She took a deep breath, then moved forward and picked up the gun. Beltan was already heading for the loading dock.

Deirdre hurried after him, and they moved up the steps to the steel doors. She glanced over her shoulder. There was no sign yet of additional guards. But how often was the one with the radio supposed to check in? She couldn't believe the Philosophers kept just a single pair of guards.

Beltan gripped the handle on one of the doors. It wasn't locked. He opened it just far enough for them to slip through. Beltan went first, and Deirdre followed, trying to keep a firm grip on the gun. It felt hot and slick in her hand; she wished she hadn't picked it up.

Bands of fluorescent light alternated with shadow. They were in some kind of storeroom. Bare ventilation tubes ran in all directions. Scattered on the floor were packing materials, crowbars, and long wooden crates. Deirdre didn't need to count to know there were seven of them. Beltan pointed. Ahead was an open door, and beyond a dim corridor. He started toward it, and Deirdre followed, gripping the gun.

This time it was the guard who saw them first. He had been standing a short way inside the open door. When he saw them, he swore and started to raise the radio.

"Don't move," Deirdre hissed as loudly as she dared, pointing the gun at him.

The guard hesitated, then his eyes narrowed, and he punched the button on the radio, opening his mouth to speak.

Deirdre willed herself to shoot, but she couldn't do it. However, the guard's hesitation had been enough to allow Beltan to get close. He swiped at the radio, knocking it out of the guard's hand, then swung his other fist, punching the man in the throat.

The guard fell to the floor, making a gurgling sound. Beltan stepped over him, then gestured for Deirdre to follow. By the time she stepped over the guard, he was no longer moving. She tightened her grip on the gun and followed Beltan.

They halted when they heard voices.

The voices were low, chanting something Deirdre couldn't quite understand. She knew how to speak Latin; that wasn't it. She exchanged a look with Beltan. He jerked his head, and they crept as quietly as they could along the corridor. It ended in another door, open like the last. They slipped through and found themselves on a mezzanine that ringed a circular room. Both the mezzanine and the room below were constructed of polished marble. Above was a gilded dome.

The mezzanine was littered with boxes, some open, some closed. Ancient urns, still wrapped in clear packing material, stood on pedestals, next to weathered stone statues half draped in tarps. Inside the nearest open box, Deirdre saw various artifacts—clay tablets, bronze bowls, and stone jars—nestled on a bed of packing foam.

She supposed these artifacts had all come from the secret chamber beneath Knossos. The Philosophers must have ordered their servants to remove everything before the archaeologists who came to investigate the arch stumbled upon the chamber. Fascinating as they were, her gaze lingered on the objects only for a moment.

A pair of staircases descended from the mezzanine, down to the level below. Unlike the clutter on the higher level, the main floor was precisely arranged. Spaced around the perimeter of the chamber were seven long, low shapes, each one draped with a black cloth. Another object stood on a dais directly beneath the center of the dome.

It was an arch of stone.

The chanting grew louder. Now that Deirdre could hear it more clearly, the chanting sounded more like ancient Greek, only it was a form Deirdre wasn't familiar with. A soft, golden glow filtered from the dome above, and in the light she could make out the slender steel frame that held the arch upright, as well as the angular carvings that marked the stones. Unlike the other stones of the arch, the keystone in the center was worn and pitted, its surface stained a dark brown.

Standing in a circle around the arch were hooded figures in black robes. Their chanting continued, uninterrupted. Beltan and Deirdre edged forward to get a better view of what was happening below.

One of the statues moved, stepping in front of them.

"And who do we have here?" purred a woman's voice. Gold eyes glinted behind the dark web of a veil.

Shock coursed through Deirdre, short-circuiting her nervous system so that she could not move. What she had taken for a statue draped in black cloth had in truth been a woman in a robe.

You're an idiot, Deirdre. Can't you count? Gathered around the arch below were not six robed figures, but five.

Unlike Deirdre, shock had not immobilized Beltan. He sprang forward and reached out to grab the woman.

Her gold eyes flashed, and Beltan toppled to the floor, arms still outstretched. Now it was he who was a statue. Deirdre stared at him. He had sensed the presence of the guards. Why hadn't he sensed her in the shadows?

She has her own magic, Deirdre. . . .

"Phoebe," she murmured.

She caught the glint of a smile behind the veil. "So you've read Marius's little book, I see."

Deirdre could hardly feel shock anymore. "You knew about it?"

"We know everything, child. We're the Philosophers." She lifted her hand in an elegant, indulgent gesture. "Must I explain it all to you? I thought you were supposed to be so very clever."

The chanting had ceased. "What's going on up there?" a man's voice called out.

"It's our little investigator and her companion," Phoebe called back without taking her gold eyes off Deirdre. "They've arrived just as we expected them to."

It was perilous to speak, all Deirdre's instincts told her that, but she couldn't stop herself. "Maybe you need better guards."

"Nonsense. They performed their duty perfectly. Each possessed a pulse monitor that emitted a constant signal as long as their hearts continued to beat. I was alerted the moment they died."

Deirdre winced, wishing Beltan had been able to use more restraint.

Phoebe moved a step closer. "We learned long ago not to place our reliance on weak and fallible mortals. We use them, yes, but we do not depend upon them. I knew it would be best if I dealt with Marius's little tools myself."

"But if you'd read his journal, if you knew what Marius intended to do, then why—?"

"Didn't we stop him?" Phoebe's voice was a croon of pleasure. "It's simple, child. It was better to let Marius believe his little plan had a chance of succeeding. He always believed he was better than us; that was his hubris. And that made it all too easy to defeat him. As you saw yourself in Scotland. We knew eventually he would show himself to you. And once he was out in the open, our servant easily removed him."

A sudden fierceness burned away the cold grip of Deirdre's fear. The woman before her was immortal, yes, but not invulnerable. As Beltan had said, she could be killed. "You didn't defeat Marius." Deirdre pointed the gun at Phoebe. "I'm here."

Again those gold eyes flashed. Deirdre felt as if her hand had been frozen in a block of ice. The gun clattered to the floor.

Phoebe clucked her tongue. "You didn't really think you could stop us, did you, child? Marius really did fill your head with notions."

The words were scathing, but Deirdre only grinned. Her arm was numb, and she felt weak and shaky, but she wasn't completely immobilized, not like Beltan.

"You can't do it again," she said. "Your little trick. You're not as strong as Marius, are you? I bet none of you are."

Angry mutters rose from below. Deirdre could feel the eyes of the others gazing up out of their shadowy hoods.

"Be done with her, Phoebe!" the man who had spoken earlier called out.

"Silence, Arthur," Phoebe snapped over her shoulder. "I told you I would take care of this annoyance as I did the other, the one those filthy sorcerers wanted."

The desperation in these words emboldened Deirdre. "You can't stop me."

A hissing sound escaped from the veil. "In that, my precious little Seeker, you are quite wrong."

Phoebe bent, picked up the gun, and fired.

A clap of thunder sounded in Deirdre's ears, and she felt as if she had been pushed by an invisible hand. She stumbled back, against the wall, and glanced down. There was a small hole near the right shoulder of her leather jacket. There was no pain; the numbness had crept up her arm, into her chest. Then, with her left hand, she opened her jacket.

Blood spilled down her shirt.

"Oh," Deirdre said, and slumped to her knees.

"This case is closed, Seeker," Phoebe said, and pointed the gun at Deirdre's head.

Again came a rumbling sound. Only it was different this time; lower, deeper, a moan rising from below. In moments it built to a stentorian roar. The floor shook beneath Deirdre. One of the statues toppled over, smashing an urn. Phoebe stumbled back against the railing of the mezzanine. The gun flew from her hand, falling to the chamber below.

The floor continued to shake. Above, a crack snaked across the surface of the dome. The light flickered. It took Deirdre's astonished brain an instant to realize what was happening.

It's an earthquake. An earthquake in London.

But that was impossible. There was no active fault line beneath London. Unless . . .

The fault line is here, Deirdre. Her mind was strangely clear. *It's centered around them—the Seven. Perihelion is close now. Very close . . .*

"Phoebe!" another man's voice shouted from below. "Get down here now. We must open the way!"

Below, one of the men had pushed back his hood. His gold eyes shone in an ageless face.

"I have to finish with this one first, Gabriel!" Phoebe called out.

"There's no time for that," the man called back. "It comes

sooner than we believed. If we want to escape this world before it's too late, we must complete the spell now."

Phoebe gave Deirdre one last hateful glance. "You'll bleed to death soon enough. Perhaps it's fitting that you watch as we achieve perfect immortality." She descended a staircase to the chamber below, joining the others around the arch. The man, Gabriel, raised his hood.

The building no longer shook; the earthquake had ended. Deirdre still felt no pain. She crawled forward, using her left hand for support. Only dimly did she notice the blood smearing the marble beneath her. She passed Beltan's prone form. It seemed his green eyes followed her motion, but that couldn't be.

She reached the top of the stairs. Although crystalline, her gaze seemed strangely fractured, so that what she saw below were fragments only. Here, one of the hooded figures pulled back the cloth that covered one of the long shapes around the perimeter of the room. It was a sarcophagus of black stone, its lid gone. Within lay a man with lustrous gold skin and jet-black hair, clad only in a linen kilt. His eyes were shut, his arms folded over his naked chest. On his brow was a circlet of gold and a bloodred jewel shaped like a spider.

In another shard of sight, Deirdre watched as one of the black-robed figures bent over another sarcophagus, knife in hand. The blade flashed, and blood flowed from the Sleeping One's arm, spilling into a golden bowl.

More knives flashed and six figures walked toward the stone arch, each bearing a bowl of blood, and one of them—the sole woman among them—carrying two.

Deirdre tried to move down the stairs—she had to stop them—but she couldn't stand; her legs wouldn't work right. The chanting rose again on the air, echoing up into the dome. The robed figures closed in around the arch. Seven golden bowls tilted, blood spilled.

The blood vanished.

Blue fire enveloped the stones.

46

"*Lir!*" a commanding voice intoned.

Silver radiance flickered into existence, pushing back the darkness that filled the throne room. Master Larad stood at the center of the light. Sinfathisar shimmered in his hands.

Grace's eyes adjusted to the new illumination. The floor had stopped shaking beneath her, and she managed to gain her feet, though she was still trembling herself.

"Was that an earthquake?" she called out over the groan of settling stone.

"More than that, I think," Farr said, standing up and untangling his *serafi*. "Perihelion must nearly be here."

Grace looked up. The crystal that had channeled beams of sunlight from the outer chamber into the throne room had gone dark. Had the sun ceased shining? If so, then surely Farr was right.

"Look," Vani said. The *T'gol* stood nearby, holding Nim. Grace followed her gaze. On the dais, the gate still crackled like a door rimmed with sapphire lightning. Grace saw dark-robed figures moving beyond, and many glints of gold.

"Who are they?" she said, half in wonder, half in dread. "Are they Scirathi?" She couldn't see masks in the shadowed recesses of their hoods.

Travis was the closest to the dais. "I don't know who they are," he said, his voice hard, "but I'd bet the Great Stones those are the Seven of Orú."

Past the robed figures, Grace made out several long, rectangular shapes. They were stone sarcophagi. The gate seemed to be positioned slightly higher than the room on the other side, as if there—just like here—it stood on some sort of dais. Grace could just see inside one of the sarcophagi, glimpsing the gold-skinned man who lay there, eyes shut as if asleep.

A sheen of sweat sprang out on Grace's flesh. If those were the Fateless Ones, then the room on the other side of the gate was on . . .

"Earth," she said. "It's Earth on the other side."

But where on Earth? And who were the black-robed ones if they were not Scirathi?

"We've got to go through the gate," Travis said. "Larad, bring the Great Stones. I think Farr's right. Perihelion is almost here. We've got to bring the Stones in contact with the Seven."

Yes, that was it, Grace thought, her cool doctor's logic superseding the fevered chaos in her brain. She considered the knowledge they had gained from the symbols on the walls of the throne room. The universe had a fatal disease, of which the rifts were a symptom, and the only way to cure the patient was to reverse the imbalance that had caused the affliction in the first place. The Imsari had to be joined with the blood of the Seven.

Only what does that have to do with the Last Rune, Grace? Sfithrisir said only the Last Rune could heal the rifts.

Larad stared at the gate, wonder on his scarred face, then he was moving. Travis was already bounding up the steps of the dais.

"We must not allow ourselves to be separated," Vani said, springing forward with Nim in her arms.

Farr followed after the *T'gol*, but Grace hesitated. Just a short while ago, for a few moments, she had returned to Earth by means of Farr's silver coin. When they jumped into the abyss, there had been no time to consider where to direct the coin to take them; there had been only a split second to think of a place they both knew, they both could envision. One had flashed into Grace's mind; with their hands clasped together, she had managed to transmit it to Farr over the last scraps of the Weirding. And that was where they had gone.

The Beckett-Strange Home for Children.

They two of them had stood there beneath the blue Colorado sky for only a few seconds. Grace had stared at the burnt-out ruin, unable to move or speak. The wind had hissed through dry witchgrass. This was where it had all begun. This was where she had first learned what it meant to be wounded. . . .

And where she had first learned the power of healing.

With that thought, the fear, the dread, and the sorrow within her evaporated. It hadn't been a mistake to come to this place. Instead, it had reminded her of who she really was. Not a queen, not a witch, and not an heir to prophecy, but simply—finally—a healer. She had taken the silver coin from Farr, and with a thought they had returned to Eldh, to the bridge outside the throne room.

Grace left hesitation behind and raced after the others toward the dais. For a moment she had been terrified that if she stepped through the gate to Earth, she might never return to Eldh—to her fortress and her people. But it didn't matter; she knew that now.

Grace had never meant to return to them in the first place.

She willed her legs to move faster. Travis had reached the top of the dais. He drew close to the throne.

A hand reached through the gate, groping.

Travis skidded to a halt short of the gate. The hand reached toward him, slender fingers extended. A woman's hand. Several of the robed figures were clustered close to the gate, just on the other side. At their fore was the woman, a veil concealing her face rather than a hood. She was reaching through the gate. For Travis?

No. Her hand moved past him, toward the throne. The woman's fingertips just brushed the arm of the golden chair.

Travis took another step toward the gate. The woman snatched her hand back through the blue-rimmed portal, and while Grace couldn't hear it, she was sure the other had gasped in surprise. The woman had just seen Travis. But why hadn't she and the others seen him before?

This room is dim, Grace, and the room on their side is much brighter. It's like being in a brightly lit house and looking out a window into the night; you can't see anything.

The woman threw her veil back. Her face was too sharp to be lovely, but it was regal, commanding. Blond hair was pulled back in a severe knot. Her eyes were gold as coins.

Those eyes had widened, and her mouth was a silent circle of surprise. She stumbled back, away from the gate, along with the others in black robes.

"Who are those people?" Larad called out.

"I don't care," Travis called back. "Now, Larad."

And he jumped through the gate.

"Father!" Nim cried, reaching out a small hand.

But Vani was already moving, leaping through the gate a

fraction of a second after Larad. Farr went next; Grace was the last. She did not hesitate, did not look back over her shoulder as she passed into the circle of blue fire.

She braced herself for the cold of the Void, and for a fall through darkness. Instead she felt a tingling sensation, like the touch of leaves brushing past her skin, and a moment later she was through, standing beside the others on a dais beneath a golden dome, in a building that, classical as its design was, bore countless, immediately detectable signs—from the electric lights glowing around the perimeter of the room to the switches on the walls and the muted whir of a ventilation system—that it had been built by modern, Earth hands.

Grace glanced back. Behind her, supported by thin arcs of steel, was an archway of stone blocks carved with angular symbols. Strands of blue energy coiled around the stones. Beyond she could just make out the dim outlines of the throne room in Morindu. Why hadn't they fallen through the Void?

Because the worlds are close now, Grace. Very close.

She turned from the gate, facing the six figures in black robes. Their hoods were pushed back now, like the woman's veil, and the faces of the five men—all as sharp and ageless as the woman's—bore looks of mingled astonishment and fear. The woman's look of shock, however, had changed to another expression: narrow-eyed rage.

"How can this be?" She pointed a finger at Travis. "How can you be here? We made certain you would not get in our way."

Travis cocked his head, a puzzled look on his face. Then, slowly, he nodded, and Grace knew he had understood something, something the rest of them had not. She wished she could speak to him over the Weirding. Standing there, close to the gate, and the Imsari, and the Seven of Orú—who slept in their sarcophagi around the perimeter of the chamber—it almost felt as if she could sense the Weirding's glimmering strands. But they were too faint, too fragile to grasp.

"Haven't you read the reports?" Travis said. "I have a way of getting around."

Never, in all they had been through together, had Grace been afraid of Travis, but she was at that moment. He wore a grin like a jackal's, and in the golden light his skin seemed hot and metallic, like that of the beings in the sarcophagi. He stalked to the edge of the dais. The woman and the black-robed men all took a step back.

"You," Vani said, and she was almost as fearsome as Travis, her gold eyes blazing. She held Nim tight in one arm, and with her free hand pointed at the woman. "You sent the Scirathi after us. You told them where to find my daughter."

The woman's hand darted inside her robe. She said nothing. The five men exchanged uncomfortable looks.

"You aren't Scirathi," Farr said, eyes narrowing. "So why were they working for you. Who are you?"

"What?" the woman said, her voice mocking now. "The great Seeker Hadrian Farr doesn't know the answer when it's right in front of his face? Your reputation must have been overly inflated in the reports we received." She inclined her head toward Travis. "He knows who we are. Though I confess, I do not know how he can. All the same, he does. Go on, Mr. Wilder. Tell them."

Travis opened his mouth, but before he could speak, another voice answered. "They're the Philosophers, Hadrian! We can't let them go through the gate."

The voice was weak, ragged, but it echoed around the dome. Grace turned. To her right, a staircase led up to a mezzanine that ringed the chamber. A dark-haired woman stood halfway down the staircase, hunched over the rail. Behind her, a streak of red smeared the white marble steps.

The woman on the staircase was Deirdre Falling Hawk.

Everyone in the chamber stared, silenced by shock. Farr actually staggered, a hand to his chest. Joy shone on Travis's face. However, after a second the joy flickered and vanished; he had seen the trail of blood on the stairs. The Philosophers, too, appeared surprised to see Deirdre standing there.

"Why aren't you dead?" the woman snapped, her tone what a rich woman might use with a servant who had not performed some task swiftly enough.

Deirdre gave a pained smile. "I'm fine, thanks for asking." She limped down several more steps. "The woman is Phoebe. She's their leader, Hadrian. Stop her."

Farr's eyes were on the bloody stairs. "Deirdre, you're—"

The sound of booted feet against marble rang out. A trio of men in black uniforms rushed through a doorway into the room. They held guns in their hands.

The gold-eyed woman, Phoebe, smiled. "Now this distraction will be removed." She glanced at the security guards. "Dispose of these intruders. Use whatever force is required."

The guards—all of them large, thick-necked men—leveled their weapons at the interlopers. "Walk forward slowly," one of them said. "Come one at a time with your hands out in front of you."

Travis was still grinning like a jackal. "That's funny." He glanced at Master Larad. "I'm thinking the rune of iron."

"My thoughts exactly," Larad said, and held Sinfathisar before him.

"Whatever that is, put it down or we'll shoot!" The guard targeted Larad with the gun.

"No," Travis said. "You won't."

"*Dur!*" Larad shouted.

The three men cried out as the guns flew from their hands, arced across the room, and struck the far wall. The weapons fell to the floor as shapeless lumps of metal. The guards staggered back, clutching stinging hands.

Grace staggered herself. For a moment, as Larad spoke the rune and the Stone flashed in his hands, she had heard a rushing noise, and she had glimpsed silvery threads all around her. It was the Weirding. She reached out to Touch it. However, even as the Stone faded, so did the shimmering strands around her.

"Now, Vani!" Travis shouted. He was already moving toward the guards. Farr was on his heels.

"Take Nim," Vani said, pressing the girl into Grace's arms. "Protect her."

Before Grace could speak, Vani's form blurred, and she was gone. A moment later she reappeared in midair above the guard closest to the door. Her boot flew out, contacting his skull, and he toppled to the floor as she landed without sound next to him. The other guards tried to back away from her, toward the center of room, but Travis and Farr were between them and the dais, cutting off their retreat.

Two more guards appeared at the door. Again Vani's form

seemed to blur as she attacked them. Travis and Farr grappled with the other two guards. However, Grace saw this only dimly, as if through a shimmering veil.

Once again, the silvery threads of the Weirding shone around her. She reveled in the sensation of life. How she had missed the Touch! She let her consciousness follow the glittering web.

The threads ended at the edge of the chamber.

What was going on? The Weirding had returned, but only here in this room; Grace could not follow it beyond.

Think, Grace.

The silver web had momentarily reappeared when Larad had invoked the power of the Imsari. In a way that made sense; the power of the Weirding sprang ultimately from the runes that had brought Eldh and everything on it into being. But why was she seeing the Weirding again now?

"I'm afraid, Aunt Grace," Nim said, tightening her arms around Grace's neck.

The silvery threads grew brighter.

Grace clutched the girl. Contacting Nim was what allowed her to see the Weirding. Only how could that be? Her mind fought to comprehend. The Imsari were part of the First Stone. Like the thirteen *morndari* that entered Orú, they were the most primordial of magics; they were the first enchantments, and the last to remain while all other faded. It made sense that the Imsari helped her see the Weirding. But why did Nim do the same?

Grace didn't know, but she was not going to waste this chance. The Weirding could fade again in an instant.

Deirdre? she called out, sending her presence along the shimmering threads.

Across the chamber, near the door, Travis, Farr, and Vani were still struggling with the security guards. The men had learned to keep away from Vani, but Travis and Farr kept herding them back within the *T'gol's* reach. The Philosophers had retreated, standing near several of the sarcophagi where the gold-skinned beings still slept.

"Stop them!" Phoebe shouted, her voice shrill, hands clenched into fists.

Grace didn't know much about the Philosophers, other than that they were the mysterious leaders of the Seekers. One thing was certain. Whatever power they possessed, they did not like to do their own dirty work.

Deirdre, Grace called again. *Can you hear me?*

Then she saw a thread that flickered with jade and fiery crimson. Grace brought her own strand close. Astonishment streamed across the thread. On the staircase, Deirdre gripped the railing.

Is that you, Grace? How—?

I'm speaking to you over the Weirding. It seems to still work, at least as long as I hold on to Nim.

She felt amazement and wonder vibrate along the thread. And pain. Grace probed, letting her consciousness reach deep into Deirdre's body, surveying the damage, making a diagnosis.

It wasn't good. Deirdre had been shot in the right shoulder, and the bullet had nicked her subclavian artery. She had lost a lot of blood. That she wasn't already dead was a wonder. Something seemed to have slowed her metabolism. But time was running out. Deirdre was already going into shock; Grace could sense her organs shutting down. Now that she could use the Weirding, Grace might be able to stave off organ failure for a short while and keep Deirdre's heart beating. But only if she could touch Deirdre. And even magic wouldn't help if Deirdre didn't get a blood transfusion—soon.

Deirdre, we have to get you to a hospital.

That's not important right now. All that matters is the Sleeping Ones.

You mean the Seven of Orú?

Yes, the beings in the sarcophagi, came Deirdre's reply. Despite her weakened state, her voice was clear over the Weirding, as if speaking this way was utterly natural to her. *They seek some sort of transformation. I don't know what it is, but it's important. I think it has to do with the rifts in the cosmos.*

These words filled Grace with amazement; clearly Deirdre had learned much since Travis had left her and journeyed to Eldh.

You're right, Grace spoke in return. *We've learned that the Seven have to come in contact with the Imsari, to heal the imbalance that's tearing the worlds apart. Only . . .*

She thought of the drawing that showed the Stones and the

Seven coming together, and the mysterious triangle symbol between them.

Only there's something we don't know yet. There's a key—something that's needed to allow the Imsari and the morndari *to unite. I think it has to do with the Last Rune.*

The Last Rune?

Words were too slow. Grace gathered up everything she had learned, everything that had happened since Sfithrisir alighted atop Gravenfist Keep, and sent it in a single, glittering pulse along the Weirding.

She could sense Deirdre reeling. Grace knew it had been too much to assimilate all at once, that it would take Deirdre time to sort out everything that had been transmitted to her.

The Seeker was faster than Grace had thought. *It's the catalyst*, Deirdre's voice came across the Weirding. *Something that can link the Sleeping Ones and Great Stones. The transformation the Seven seek can't take place without it.*

Excitement flared in Grace's chest. Hadn't Sister Mirrim said something to Farr about a catalyst? *Do you know what this catalyst is?*

She felt frustration, confusion in return.

No, I don't, came Deirdre's reply. *Only . . .*

Only what?

I'm not sure, Grace. I'm so close to the answer, only I can't . . . I can't quite reach it, and . . .

Deirdre had descended the last few steps, and she sank to her knees. Blood spattered the white marble floor. Deirdre's face was like marble itself. Grace had to do something. She thought about it only a moment, then she connected Deirdre's thread to her own.

Grace gasped as she felt her own life force rushing out, flooding into Deirdre, sustaining the Seeker. Across the room, Deirdre's eyes fluttered, and her back arched. At the same time, thoughts, feelings, and knowledge hummed back along the thread, into Grace. In an instant, Grace understood everything.

Before too much of her own life force drained from her, Grace broke the connection. She had done all she could with magic; she had stabilized Deirdre, but the Seeker had to have more blood or she would die.

Grace . . . ?

Oh, Deirdre, Grace said inwardly. She had seen it all, had felt it all: Deirdre's quest to unravel the mystery of the arch, only to discover the truth behind everything. The Seekers were a lie. For over four centuries, the Philosophers had desired only to get to Eldh, to learn the secret of true immortality. The Philosopher Marius Lucius Albrecht had tried to stop them, and he was dead. Deirdre's partner Anders was in a hospital. And Beltan . . .

Grace searched among the threads. There—she saw one brighter than the others, tinged with emerald. It was Beltan. He was lying on the floor in the shadows of the mezzanine. He was motionless, but he was still alive, still strong. The woman, Phoebe, had placed him in some kind of stasis. However, Grace could already sense Beltan trying to break out of it. He was struggling against the hold on him, and he was winning.

Grace couldn't help a sharp smile. Drugs, poisons, magic— even Galtish ale—none of them affected Beltan as severely or for as long as they did other human beings. It wasn't just because of the fairy blood in his veins. When he was still a boy, his mother, the witch Elire, had made him drink draughts she brewed in order to increase his tolerance to such toxins. Had Elire possessed some shard of the Sight? Had she known that he would need such resistance more than once in his life? Grace didn't know, but she was grateful all the same.

Come on, Beltan. You can do it. You can break her spell.

She could not hear his voice, but she felt his will, his strength. He was breaking free. . . .

"No!" a woman shrieked.

Grace's hold on the Weirding snapped, and her eyes opened. Across the room, Vani stepped back as the last of the security guards fell to the floor. Travis and Farr stood nearby, both breathing hard. Travis's skin was glowing like that of the golden beings who slumbered in the sarcophagi. Blood trickled from Farr's lip, but he appeared otherwise unhurt.

"So much for your guards," one of the men said, giving Phoebe a sour look.

"Stop your sniveling, Arthur," she snapped. "I see, as always,

I will have to take care of this myself." She bent down and picked something up off the floor.

It was a gun. She pointed it at Travis.

"I believe your wizard is too tired to pull one of his little tricks again," she said.

Grace glanced at Larad. He gripped Sinfathisar, and he was muttering under his breath, but the Stone remained quiescent in his hand. Vani was too far away. The *T'gol* would not be able to close the distance in the moment it took Phoebe to pull the trigger. She took aim at Travis's heart.

"You don't understand," Travis said.

Phoebe's eyes flashed. A less arrogant person would have simply shot him, but it was clear she could not let such a challenge go unanswered.

"I am a Philosopher. I understand all."

Travis laughed, and her face blanched with rage. "No," he said, taking a step closer. "You understand nothing. You're ignorant thieves, that's all."

"Stop!" she said, shaking the gun at him. "I do not need to listen to your ravings. There is nothing you know we do not."

Travis shrugged. "Suit yourself. Then again, I've been to the otherworld, to Eldh, a half dozen times. And isn't that where you're trying to go? If you want, I can tell you all about the Sleeping Ones—who they are, why they're here, and what they want."

One of the black-robed men took a step toward Phoebe, a hungry look on his bearded face. "He knows something, Phoebe, and he seems inclined to tell us. Why not talk to him before we kill him? What harm can it do? Even if he's mad, as you say, he might know something useful."

Phoebe did not look as if she appreciated the opinion. Her eyes became slits, then she nodded. "Very well, Gabriel. We'll humor you, though I think it's a waste of time." She waved the gun at Travis. "Go on. Tell us what you think is so terribly important. And be swift. The gate will not stay open indefinitely, and I do not want to waste more of the blood of the Sleeping Ones to open it again."

Travis moved toward one of the sarcophagi, gazing at the figure inside. Phoebe trailed him with the gun.

"They're nothing to you," Travis said softly. He looked up at Phoebe. "They're something to be used, a means to an end, that's all. I suppose you think they can give you true immortality."

Phoebe tightened her fingers around the gun. "They can and they will. We know that what granted them eternal perfection is in that room, on the other side of that gate. And we will have it."

"That's not what they came here for." Travis bent over the Sleeping One, as if speaking to the golden man. "That's not why they came to Earth, to give their blood to the likes of you. They've been waiting. Waiting for a time when the two worlds would draw close, when they would have a chance to do what they knew they had to do."

"And what, pray tell, is that?"

"They intend to heal the world. All the worlds. The rifts in the sky are the beginning of the end. Don't you see? You can't escape them by going to Eldh. The rifts are there, too. If the Seven don't unite with those Stones my wizard friend is holding, then it's over. For Earth. For Eldh. For everything."

The black-robed men exchanged startled looks. For a moment, even Phoebe's visage seemed clouded by doubt. Then her expression grew hard once more.

"By unite, you mean consume, don't you? What you propose would destroy the Sleeping Ones, wouldn't it?"

Travis shrugged. "It might. I don't know. But if the union doesn't happen, there will be no Earth, there will be no Eldh. There will be nothing at all."

The bearded man, Gabriel, gasped, and some of the others muttered among themselves. However, they all looked to Phoebe. Her lips curled in a sneer.

"You lie. You want the blood of the Sleeping Ones for yourself, and you tell us these fantasies to trick us. But it won't work."

Before Travis could speak, she leveled the gun at him. Grace reached out with the Touch. Phoebe's thread was a brilliant gold. If Grace could take hold of it, she might be able to stop Phoebe from—

There was a deafening *crack!* of thunder. Grace staggered back. For a dazed moment she wondered if Phoebe had fired and missed, if the bullet had struck Grace instead, knocking her back.

The thunder grew into a roar. A crack snaked across the marble floor. Phoebe stumbled into the other Philosophers, the gun flying from her hands. Travis lurched against Vani and Farr, and Larad fell to his knees. Sinfathisar spilled out of his hands, rolling away from him, skittering across the heaving floor toward Grace.

Again came a *crack!*

"No!" cried a shrill voice.

Grace managed to look up. On the dais, the stone arch vibrated and twisted, a wishbone gripped by two angry hands. With a sound like a piano wire breaking, one of the supporting steel bands snapped, then another, and another. The blue fire flickered and winked out. The image of the throne room on the other side vanished.

With a groan, the arch collapsed into a heap of rubble.

47.

Deirdre felt light.

The green-gold power that had rushed into her through Grace's life strand buoyed her like the helium in a balloon. The pain in her shoulder had faded, and her breath came easily. When the floor stopped shaking, she was one of the first to regain her feet. Beneath her boots, the marble was stained red.

You're bleeding to death, Deirdre. You can't feel this good. It's impossible.

Only she did feel good. Whatever Grace had done to her, it had made her feel awake, alive. Her mind was a flawless crystal, reflecting everything around her in its facets. Across the room, Vani was helping Farr to his feet, while Travis had pulled himself up using one of the sarcophagi. When he fell, Master Larad had struck his head on one of the steps of the dais. Blood oozed from his scalp, and pain etched the scarred mosaic of his face. He clutched a small iron box in his hand.

"The Stone of Twilight!" the Runelord shouted.

Deirdre saw it. The gray-green orb had rolled across the floor and stopped a few feet from where Grace knelt, Nim clutched in her arms. Grace started to reach out a hand, then hesitated; from what Deirdre knew, it was perilous for anyone save a Runelord to touch a Stone.

"So much for your gate," Travis said, stepping over a crack in the floor, eyes on the heap of rubble on the dais.

Phoebe flicked her veil over her shoulders. "The gate can be easily reassembled. The same will not be said for you once we are finished with you. Kill them for what they've done!"

The remaining Philosophers were untangling themselves from their robes. One of them gave the gold-eyed woman a startled look. "Are you serious, Phoebe? You mean do it ourselves?"

She glared at him. "For once in four centuries, stop being a worm, Arthur. Yes, I mean do it ourselves. Use your knife!"

From her gown, she pulled out the curved dagger she had used to draw blood from the Sleeping Ones. The men took out their own daggers. Arthur fumbled his, nearly dropping it. But others—like the bearded one, Gabriel—held their weapons firmly. Vani and Farr were the closest to the Philosophers. The *T'gol* started to spring into motion.

Phoebe's gold eyes flashed. Vani ceased moving in midair and toppled to the floor, rigid as a sculpture of black stone. Hadrian remained standing, but he was motionless as well, his eyes staring blindly. Travis gave the two a startled glance, then returned his gaze to Phoebe. He took a step back.

Deirdre, Grace's voice sounded in her mind, *what has she done to them?*

It's a spell, Deirdre spun the words back, surprised how easy it was to do so. *It's the same one she cast on Beltan. I don't know how to break it.* She thought about what she had learned from Grace. *Though if all magic is gone except that closest to the source, then she must have drunk the blood of the Sleeping Ones recently. Otherwise, I don't think she would have been able to cast the spell at all. Either way, she won't be able to do it again for a while. It weakens her, and it takes time for her to recover.*

What about the other Philosophers? Can they do the same?

Deirdre glanced at the gold-eyed men. Their eyes shifted between Travis and Phoebe.

I don't think so. She directed the words toward Grace. *If they could cast the same spell, they would have done it already. I don't think they're as strong as she is.*

Or as strong as Marius had been, or his master before him. Either might have been the leader of the Philosophers. Only neither had wanted what the others craved—true, eternal immortality—and so it was Phoebe who had become their queen.

"Take him!" Phoebe said, pointing her dagger at Travis.

The men hesitated, then started forward, blades before them.

"*Dur!*" Travis shouted.

However, magic was all but gone. Without the Imsari in hand, the rune was powerless. Travis cast a look at Larad. The Runelord fumbled with the box. But he was too far away to get the Stones to Travis, and too weary to speak runes himself. Both Deirdre and Grace were on the opposite side of the room. Neither could reach him in time, even if they had the power to stop five men. Except maybe they did.

Deirdre, help me. . . .

Grace had already come to the same conclusion. Travis edged past the motionless forms of Vani and Hadrian.

"Run, Father!" Nim cried, but he couldn't. The Philosophers had him cornered against a column that supported the mezzanine above.

Deirdre shut her eyes, concentrating. *I don't know what to do, Grace.*

I'll show you how. Weave the threads, like this. . . .

Understanding flowed across the web of the Weirding. Of course—it was so simple. Deirdre grasped the silvery threads in imaginary hands, braiding them into knots.

Deirdre opened her eyes in time to see two of the Philosophers drop their knives and fall to the floor, limbs flopping against the marble like fish on dry land.

Phoebe shot Grace and Deirdre a poisonous look. Then she searched the floor with her gaze. She was looking for the gun she had dropped, Deirdre was sure of it. The remaining Philosophers closed in around Travis; his gray eyes flicked left and right, but he could not escape. The man Gabriel raised his dagger.

Again, Deirdre! Weave with me!

Deirdre reached out to grasp the shining threads—

—and her hands touched nothing. The shimmering web vanished.

"Nim!" a voice cried. "No!"

Deirdre opened her eyes. It was Grace who had shouted. She reached forward, trying to catch Nim, but she was too slow. The girl had wriggled free of her grasp and was running forward.

"Father needs the Stone," the girl said. She crouched, the hem of her gold shift brushing the floor, and closed her fingers around Sinfathisar.

Deirdre held her breath, waiting for something terrible to happen, for green-gray energy to engulf Nim.

It didn't. The girl stood, holding the stone. "Father!" She started to run across the room. Grace scrambled after her, and Deirdre followed, feeling so light that her boots hardly touched the floor.

"Now!" Phoebe said. "Do it!"

Hands reached out, gripping Travis, holding him tight. Gabriel's knife flashed, descending. Nim screamed—

—and the room changed. The air rippled like the surface of a pond disturbed by a pebble. The domed room with the mezzanine and the ruined gate vanished, replaced by a space that Deirdre—from the thoughts and memories Grace had granted her—recognized as the throne room in Morindu the Dark. Deirdre and Grace halted. The Philosophers snapped their heads up. Phoebe stared at the mummified figure on the dais.

Nim screamed again, and another series of ripples radiated through the air. The throne room was gone. They were back in the domed chamber on Earth.

A roar sounded, reverberating off the dome. Something launched itself from the edge of the mezzanine, landing like a great cat behind Gabriel. Big hands grabbed the Philosopher by the scruff of the neck, hurling him back, away from Travis.

"Get away from him!" the blond man growled, his eyes flashing green. He moved stiffly, but he was still faster and stronger than the Philosophers. He grabbed another one of them—

Arthur—and tossed him across the room. The Philosopher landed, wailing, not far from Phoebe's feet. The other retreated.

"Beltan," Travis said, his voice thick with wonder. He touched the blond man's cheek.

"What's happening, Travis?" Beltan said, confusion in his green eyes.

Before Travis could answer, Nim rushed toward them. "Father!" she called out. "And Father!"

Again the air wavered, blurred, resolved, and they were back in the throne room of Morindu. Then Deirdre blinked, and it was Earth again. The change kept recurring every few seconds. Morindu. London. Eldh. Earth. A sharp scent, like lightning, permeated the air.

"It's perihelion," Travis said, turning around in a slow circle. "It's here. . . ."

As he spoke, waves of distortion rippled through the air— suddenly they were in Morindu again—and this time Deirdre saw from where the ripples radiated. It was Nim. The girl had stopped, still clutching the Stone, and was staring all around, mouth open. She was the center of the effect.

She was the nexus.

Something shimmered in Deirdre's subconscious, some understanding that had lain too deep for her to reach. Only now her mind was so clear she could almost see it. . . .

"Great Hermes!" a man's voice shouted.

Deirdre shook her head, clearing her vision. Not far from her, Grace gasped. In each of the sarcophagi, a gold-skinned figure sat upright. Their eyes were open, and they were not gold, but rather black as onyx. In slow, perfect unison, the Seven climbed from their sarcophagi.

Nim let out a soft cry, and the air rippled again. The domed building on Earth now. The girl reached up, but her fingers could not grasp the Stone of Twilight. It had plucked itself from her hands, and it hovered in midair above her.

The iron box in Larad's hands gave a jerk. He fumbled with the lid and opened it. The other two Stones shot out, white-blue and crimson, rising into the air, and drifting toward Sinfathisar.

The knowledge that Grace had imparted to Deirdre melded with her own experiences, and the result was a new amalgam of understanding. Yes—that was why the two worlds had been drawing closer and closer over the centuries; that was why perihelion was destined to come.

It was the Imsari and the Sleeping Ones. Their purpose was to be joined together, to heal the imbalance in the universes, and for eons they had pulled at one another, bringing the two worlds they resided on closer and closer together.

Now, at last, perihelion was upon them. The Seven approached the center of the chamber, where the three Stones bobbed. Their golden faces were ageless and serene as death masks from the tomb of an Egyptian pharaoh.

"Stop them!" Phoebe called, voice rising into a shriek. "Their blood is ours!"

But the other Philosophers retreated, letting the Seven pass by. The air rippled, and they were on Morindu. More ripples, and it was London again. Still the effect was centered on Nim. The Stones hovered just above her. The girl was gazing all around. Travis started toward her, but Phoebe sprang in front of him, brandishing her knife.

"It's the child, isn't it? She's doing this. She's making everything . . . change."

Travis tried to pass her, but she thrust with the dagger, and he was forced to leap back. As he did, the talisman he wore around his neck slipped from his *serafi*. The piece of white bone caught Deirdre's eye. It was marked with three parallel lines.

Three lines . . .

A humming tone sounded in Deirdre's mind, like the vibration of a quartz crystal. She knew. She knew what the catalyst was.

I understand, Marius. I understand the song. It's about endings, and beginnings, too, and how sometimes they can be the same thing. It's about how, no matter what happens, when all is said and done, there's always still possibility. After fire and wonder, we end where we began. . . .

Again Deirdre glanced at the talisman Travis wore. The lines were etched in parallel onto the piece of bone. However, they could just have easily been connected end to end, in the shape of a triangle, like the symbol Grace and Travis had seen on the wall of the throne room. Years ago, Travis had told Deirdre the name of the rune carved on the talisman.

It was *Nim*.

Hope.

The Seven golden figures closed in on the girl. The three Stones still hovered above her.

"It's Nim!" Deirdre called out. "She's the catalyst."

She felt Beltan's and Travis's startled gazes on her. Beltan tried to swipe the dagger from Phoebe's hand, but he still moved stiffly, and she was nimbler than the other Philosophers. She darted past him, then grabbed Nim, holding the dagger above the girl.

"Stop!"

The Sleeping Ones seemed to understand her. They ceased moving a few steps from Nim, their faces still serene, expressionless. Travis and Beltan lunged forward, but Phoebe glared at them.

She did not have the power to cast her spell, not fully, but there was still some malice in her gaze. Both Travis and Beltan staggered back, and Deirdre knew a chill like that in her own arm had touched them. However, in the time it took Phoebe to work her magic, Grace had closed the distance. She reached for the dagger.

Deirdre didn't will herself to run forward. Instead, she seemed to float over the floor. She was so light, so empty, like a bauble of spun glass. The air continued to ripple, so quickly now that with each blink of the eye the world seemed to change. London. Morindu. Again, and again, until the two blurred together, becoming one. . . .

Phoebe slashed with the dagger. A line of red appeared on Grace's arm. Grace staggered back, outside the circle of the Seven. Phoebe's lips curled in a smile. Nim gazed up, her face a white oval. The dagger flashed, then sank deep into flesh.

"Oh," Deirdre said softly.

Phoebe stepped back, a look of annoyance on her face. Nim's cheeks were streaked with tears, but she made no sound. Deirdre smiled down at the girl, to tell her not to cry. Then she saw it. The hilt of the dagger jutted from Deirdre's stomach. Nim hesitated, then reached out and touched Deirdre's hand.

Deirdre saw it at once: the shimmering web of the Weirding. She could see—no, could *feel*—Travis and Beltan staring, shock on their faces. Not far away, Larad was regaining his feet. And Hadrian and Vani, though still in stasis, were unhurt.

I wish I could talk to you Hadrian. You finally did it—you had a Class Zero Encounter.

But so had she, Deirdre supposed. The room around them was still a blur, changing so quickly that it was both London and Morindu, both Earth and Eldh, at once.

Oh, Deirdre, Grace's voice sounded in her mind, trembling with sorrow.

I see, Grace. A feeling of exhilaration filled Deirdre. The Stones hovered before her. The Seven golden figures stepped forward. *I see everything.*

Grace's voice hummed over the shimmering threads. *You would have made a good witch, Deirdre.*

Thank you, Deirdre wanted to say.

Only then the Seven took another step, closing the circle. She was aware of Phoebe trying to push them back, to break the circle, but Grace stuck out a foot, tripping her, and Phoebe went down, her black veil tangling around her.

Nim tried to pull her hand free, but Deirdre held her tight. *Don't be afraid*, she tried to murmur. *The catalyst doesn't change. That's what Sister Mirrim told Hadrian.*

She didn't know if she spoke, or if she sent the words along the Weirding, but either way Nim stopped struggling and stood still. The Seven reached out gold hands, laying them against the girl. The three Stones descended, alighting on Nim's outstretched hands.

The melded vision of Earth and Eldh vanished, replaced by darkness—pure, flawless darkness, stretching into eternity. It was like the primordial vacuum, the empty space that constantly spawned pairs of virtual particles. It was the nothingness in whose very emptiness lay coiled the potential for everything. It was the silence before the word, the slumber before the dream.

It was hope.

With her last thought, Deirdre Falling Hawk sent everything she saw, everything she sensed and understood, in a pulse along the Weirding, toward the green-gold strand she knew belonged to Grace.

It's so beautiful!

Then she gazed into ancient black eyes, and the nothingness that had brought her into being claimed her once again.

48.

Travis was cold. So terribly cold.

He was a planet, spinning alone out in space. The sun he had been bound to had vanished. Its light and life-giving warmth were gone, and there was nothing to hold him down, nothing to keep him from spinning off into the dark, endless Void alone. . . .

"Travis?" a voice murmured. "Travis, can you hear me?"

The voice was warm and familiar, like the memory of the sun. In the darkness, two lights appeared. They were stars, each as green as a summer forest. He let the stars pull him in with their gravity.

"Please, Travis. I know you're still in there. Talk to me."

The stars grew brighter, closer. Only they weren't stars, he realized. They were eyes.

Grace Beckett's eyes.

A shuddering breath rushed into him, and Travis sat up.

"Grace?"

She was kneeling beside him, along with Beltan. Vani, Nim, Larad, and Hadrian Farr stood close by. Beyond them, the dim air flickered, as if lit by a lamp swinging on a chain.

Grace smiled, a look of relief on her face. "There you are, my friend."

Beltan gripped his hand. "You scared me. I thought after all this that . . . I thought you weren't going to . . ." The blond man pressed his lips together and shook his head.

Sorrow pierced Travis's heart. Why was Beltan so sad? Travis tried to think back, to remember what had happened. It was hard. He felt thin and hollow, like a candy wrapper with nothing good left inside. Only that wasn't completely true. He still felt good when he looked at Beltan, and Grace, and Nim. They all looked well and whole, though Grace did have a small cut on her arm.

"What happened?" he said. For some reason, he couldn't stop shivering.

"There's no magic," Farr said. His face was haggard, haunted, but there was a note of wonder in his voice. "It's gone. The Imsari and the *morndari* were what brought it into being in the first place. When the Stones and the Seven came in contact, when they eliminated one another, magic ceased to be. We feared you would share their fate."

Travis frowned at him. "Share whose fate?"

Farr stepped aside and gestured to something on the floor. It was a heap of black cloth—a robe. Shriveled hands jutted from the sleeves of the robe, skeletal fingers curving like claws. A black veil half concealed a skull stretched with withered skin.

It was Phoebe.

Travis started to stand. He was still shaking, and would have fallen, but Grace and Beltan helped him. Beyond Phoebe, he saw the other five on the floor. All of them were dried mummies.

"The Philosophers," Travis said, the words a croak.

Farr stood above the mummy that had been Phoebe. "It was magic that sustained their lives all these centuries. Drinking the blood of the Seven gave them the gift of immortality. Once the Seven were no more, that gift was taken away."

Travis swallowed hard. "And you thought . . . you thought the same had happened to me."

"We didn't know," Grace said. "Orú's blood hadn't extended your life, at least not yet, but it *had* changed you. You collapsed at the same moment the Philosophers did, and we feared the worst."

Beltan touched his cheek. "Only you're all right, aren't you?"

Again, Travis shivered. It felt as if there was a hole in him where something had been excised, something rich and warm and golden. And something else was missing as well—a familiar presence.

Jack? he spoke in his mind. *Jack are you there?*

There was no answer. And there never would be again. Travis

touched his right hand, but for the first time in five years he didn't feel the familiar itch beneath the skin of his palm, the faint tingle of the hidden rune.

"Travis?" Beltan's green eyes were worried.

Travis breathed. "Yes. I'm fine." He smiled, laying his hand over Beltan's, pressing it against his cheek. "I'm more than fine."

Already a new warmth was filling the hole inside Travis. And while it was not so golden and fiery as Orú's blood, or as shimmering as rune magic, it was every bit as powerful in its own way. And as long as Beltan was at his side, it would never fade.

"Now that he is awake, we must make our decisions," Vani said, hands on her hips. "Time grows short."

Travis shook his head. What was she talking about? A note of alarm cut through his confusion.

"Where's Deirdre?"

"She's gone," Farr said simply.

Travis staggered, leaning against Beltan. For a moment he felt disbelief. Then memory returned. Phoebe had chilled him with a glance, as well as Beltan. Travis had watched, unable to move, as the circle of the Seven closed in around Nim and the Imsari.

And Deirdre.

The last thing he remembered was an orb of brilliant silver-gold light encapsulating both Nim and Deirdre. The final image he could recall was of the light beginning to dim, and of a single, tiny figure standing in its midst, like a chick inside an egg lit from behind. There had been no taller figure standing beside the little one.

"Gone," Travis repeated the word, as if it was unfamiliar to him.

Grace gripped his hand. "She was happy, Travis." A tear slid down her cheek. "I felt her, right before . . . right before she was gone. She was so happy. She understood everything. She knew that—"

"Forgive me, Your Majesty," Larad said with an uncomfortable look. "But I don't think we have time for that now." He gestured behind them.

Travis turned around, and he tried to understand what he was seeing. "Where are we? On Earth or Eldh?

"Both, for the moment," Farr said. "But perihelion is drawing to a close. The worlds are beginning to drift apart."

Travis understood. It had seemed the shadows in the room were shifting. But that wasn't it at all. It was the room itself that was shifting. The chamber in London and the throne room on Eldh were no longer blurred as one. Instead they were discrete, separate. First one flickered into view, then the other.

However, even as Travis watched, the area affected in this way shrank inward. It was limited to the center of the chamber, to the area around the dais. The rest of the chamber was solidly, unwaveringly the room in London. Again the air flickered, and the area around the dais became part of the throne room in Morindu. Orú's mummy still sat shackled to his throne. A few moments later the air seemed to wrinkle, and the throne was gone, replaced by the jumbled heap of stones that had been the gate.

Farr took a step toward the dais, his black *serafi* swishing. "I don't think we have much longer. We have to decide which side to remain on before perihelion ends."

His words stunned Travis. Decide? How could he possibly decide between two worlds? Before, when he had returned to Earth, there had always been the possibility that he would return to Eldh. Only this time there would be no chance of that.

"Perihelion won't come again, will it?"

Farr shook his head. "It was the pull of the Imsari and the Seven that brought the worlds close together. They will never draw near again. And nor will gates function, now that magic is no more."

"I suppose these aren't worth anything anymore," Travis said, pulling the silver coin from his *serafi*.

Grace smiled. "It's still worth something, Travis."

True. But it couldn't take them between worlds, could it? Travis's heart ached. He didn't want to say good-bye. Not so suddenly. Not forever.

The air in the center of the room rippled. The nexus between the two worlds shuddered, then shrank until it was no larger than the dais. One moment it was Morindu, the next London.

"I've made my choice," Farr said, moving onto the dais. "I intend to stay in Morindu."

"But sorcery doesn't work anymore," Travis said.

A smile flickered across Farr's handsome face. "It was never about magic, Travis Wilder. That's not why I searched for other worlds. It was for knowledge. For wonder. All of Morindu the Dark remains to be explored. Who knows what secrets remain to be discovered? I cannot throw away the chance to learn things no other living person knows. Deirdre would have understood."

Travis sighed. Yes, she would have. But Deirdre knew more than any of them now.

Master Larad moved to the dais, standing next to Farr. "As interested as I am in learning about another world—this Earth on which you spent so much of your life, Your Majesty—Eldh is my home, and I cannot imagine not spending the rest of my years there." He gave a sardonic smile. "Though the problem of getting out of the desert and returning to Malachor may require all of those years to solve."

Farr grinned. "I imagine we'll be able to solve that one, Master Larad. Camels aren't the only way through the desert."

Like the iris of an eye contracting, the circle above the dais shrank inward another fraction. The nexus was already not much larger than a door. They were almost out of time.

"What do you think, Beltan?" Travis said. "Which world do you want to be on?" Travis tried to sound noncommittal, even though he knew, without doubt, that he wanted to stay on Earth. Eldh was a world of beauty and wonder. But it wasn't his home. It never had been.

"I want to be on planet Travis," Beltan said solemnly. "My world is wherever you are."

"Are you sure?" Travis said, wanting to laugh and cry at the same time. Could he really expect Beltan to spend the rest of his life on another world?

"I'm sure," Beltan said, taking Travis's hand.

Doubt vanished, and Travis grinned. "I guess we've done pretty well here on Earth. I think we'll stay, if that's all right."

Beltan kissed him. It was.

Reluctantly, Travis pulled away. Now came two farewells he didn't think he could bear. Only, somehow, he had to. He knelt before Nim. The girl had not said anything since he had awakened. Did she understand what was happening?

She did.

"I want to stay with you, Father!" she said, throwing her small arms around Travis's neck. "And with Father!"

Travis hugged her tight. "I know, sweetheart. I wish you could stay with us, too. But your place is with your mother."

"I do not believe that is so."

Travis looked up, too stunned to speak. Nim turned around, tears staining her cheeks, her eyes wide.

"Mother?"

Vani knelt before her. "My brave daughter." She brushed a dark curl from Nim's face. "I love you. You must never forget that."

"I won't," Nim said.

Vani bent, kissed Nim's brow, and stood.

"I took her from you once," she said, gazing at Travis, then at Beltan. "I cannot do so a second time."

"You're serious," Travis said, finally managing to speak.

Vani nodded. "*T'gol* do not customarily have children. So in Nim, I have known a joy I never believed I would know in my life. Nothing will ever change that. However, I belong in Morindu. It is my heritage, and my fate. I would . . . I would go with Hadrian Farr."

She gave the former Seeker a glance that was suddenly tentative, almost shy. Farr gave her an astonished look in return. Then the hint of a smile touched his lips.

Beltan stepped forward. "Vani, you'll never see Nim again."

"I know." The *T'gol* moved to the dais, standing next to Farr and Larad. "But it must be so. Perhaps someday Morindu will be a living city again, but that day is long off. Right now it is still dead. And a dead city, however full of wonders, is no place for a living child." A tear slid down her cheek. "Love her, Beltan. Give her every joy you possibly can."

Beltan nodded, laying his big hands on Nim's small shoulders. She turned and buried her small face against his legs.

Bittersweet joy filled Travis. He would not have to say goodbye to Nim. Only there was another farewell he dreaded, and there was no putting it off.

"Your Majesty," Larad called out. "You must hurry."

Travis moved to Grace. He opened his mouth, but how could he put into words what he was feeling? Beltan was his partner, his soul mate, but Grace was his best friend. More than that. She was part of him.

"I'm going to . . . I'm going to miss your voice," he said, and didn't even try not to weep.

Grace brushed a tear from his cheek. "Don't be silly," she said. "That's what telephones are for."

He could only stare at her.

"I'm staying on Earth," she said.

Beltan let out a great laugh. Even Nim turned around and clapped her hands together.

"But what about . . . ?" He glanced at Hadrian Farr.

"I'm not his case subject to watch anymore. And I think Fate has something else in mind for him. For both of us." She glanced at Vani, then she looked at Travis again and smiled. "By the way, you still haven't said if it's okay if I stay here."

It was too much. Joy and sorrow and love all melded into a single, shining emotion inside Travis, igniting like a new sun.

"Yeah," he said gruffly. "It's okay."

Grace turned and waved at the figures on the dais. "Give my love to Melia and Falken and everyone. And remember what I said about holding an election, Master Larad. Tell them it was my last order. And tell them I cast my vote for you!"

Larad held up his hand in a gesture of farewell. Vani's gaze was locked on Nim. Farr opened his mouth to say something.

There was one final flicker, and the three of them disappeared. As if a door had been shut, the image of the throne room in Morindu vanished. The nexus was gone.

"Good-bye," Travis whispered.

He felt Grace's hand slip inside his. He gripped it tight.

Beltan picked Nim up, holding her in his arms. "Are you going to be all right?" he said, his expression solemn.

The girl seemed to think about it, then nodded. "I'll be sad some. A lot at first. But that's okay, isn't it?"

"Yes," he said, holding her tight. "It is."

She rested her head on his shoulder.

Travis took a step forward, toward the place where Deirdre

had vanished. He would never look into her smoky jade eyes again, would never hear the soft tones of her mandolin.

"I wish I'd gotten to say good-bye to her," he said. "I wish I could have told her how much I cared about her."

"She knew," Grace said behind him. "I was with her, in that final moment. She knew everything, Travis. She sent it to me over the last strands of the Weirding. I wish . . . I wish I could describe what it was she saw."

Travis turned around. "Try."

He could see Grace struggle for words. "She sensed . . . Deirdre sensed how happy they were—the Sleeping Ones and the Imsari. They *wanted* to come together. They wanted to balance one another out. It was their whole purpose. But the Seven had known they needed the right catalyst for the union to work. The Imsari and the *morndari* had both been changed by their history on Eldh. Alcendifar the dwarf changed the Great Stones with his craft, and the thirteen *morndari* were changed by their union with Orú. Those imperfections would have kept their union from being complete without a catalyst."

Travis looked back at Beltan and Nim. "Why Nim? Why was she the catalyst?"

"Vani was descended from Orú," Grace said. "And there was fairy blood in Beltan. Northern and southern magic were melded together in Nim. I think it was that blending that helped the Seven and the Imsari to come in contact, to unite despite the way they'd been changed."

"What about Travis then?" Beltan said. "Couldn't he have been a catalyst?"

Grace rubbed her chin. "Both rune magic and sorcery are in him—*were* in him. But he wasn't born with them inside him. Nim was. I think that made her a more perfect catalyst."

Beltan tossed Nim into the air. She let out a shriek of laughter, and he caught her. "She's perfect, all right."

"The Little People must have known," Travis said, looking at Beltan and Nim.

The sound of distant sirens drifted through the door. The earthquakes brought on by perihelion would have caused some damage. Travis hoped it hadn't been severe.

Grace touched his arm. "Are you all right?"

He looked down at his hands. Again he felt the hole inside him. But it was all right. He had spent most of his life not being magic. He didn't think it would be too hard to get used to being normal again. Who knew? He might actually kind of like it.

"Nim really was the Last Rune," he said "There are no more runes. Magic's gone."

"I suppose you're right," Grace said. "Only . . ." She cocked her head, as if listening to a distant sound.

"What is it?" Beltan said, giving her a sharp look. "Do you feel something?"

Grace smiled and shook her head.

"Just hope," she said.

49.

On another world, in a castle with seven towers, Aryn rested a hand on her full stomach and felt a strong kick deep within.

Teravian turned away from the window of their bedchamber, wonder on his face. "I can see stars, Aryn. All the stars."

She tried to reach out with the Touch, to sense the small life inside her, but there was nothing to grasp, no trace of the Weirding. It was gone. Completely gone. But it didn't matter. Aryn didn't need magic to know the baby was whole and healthy; she knew it with her heart.

"Do you want to feel your daughter kick?" she asked.

Teravian grinned. "You mean my son."

And the young king knelt before his queen, laying his hands atop hers as new life stirred beneath.

EPILOGUE

CASTLE CITY

The shiny green pickup truck blew into town with the first evening gale of October.

It pulled off the highway on a bare patch of gravel, not far from a peeling billboard, just down the road from the burnt ruin of a clapboard building. Doors opened, and four people got out. There was a man with red-brown hair, and another man, tall and rangy, who walked with a lanky stride. After them came a woman who was beautiful and regal, even dressed in jeans and a baggy sweater. With her came a girl who looked to be five or six, with hair as dark as shadows dancing on the wind.

The four joined hands, and together they walked toward a flat patch of ground where, once upon a time, a parti-colored circus tent had stood. It had taken them longer than they had expected to come to this place. But then, at first, they hadn't even known this was where they were going.

London—and much of the world—had been in something of a state of chaos for a few weeks as damage from the earthquakes, hurricanes, and typhoons was repaired. However, none of the disasters had been as bad as they might have been, as bad as some experts had feared they were going to get; the tremors in London had been localized to the area in and around Brixton. And, as suddenly as they had begun, the storms and eruptions ceased. People had been so relieved that they hadn't even noticed at first that something else had gone as well: the rifts in the sky.

Astronomers and physicists were still speculating about what the rifts were. No doubt studying the data various telescopes had collected would keep the scientists occupied for years to come. However, most people forgot about the rifts soon enough, as people tended to do when something strange departed and the normalcy of everyday life resumed. The Mouthers took off their white sheets and put down their signs. People were ready to go on with their lives. They were ready to hope again.

True, there was the occasional story of someone who had claimed to have seen green forests in the desert and mountains in the middle of the ocean just before the rifts vanished, but those stories were relegated to the tabloids, and were soon replaced by the usual celebrity scandals and UFO sightings.

Once London was back to normal, and a decision to go west was reached—or rather, maybe, a call was heard—there were still arrangements to be made. The flat in Mayfair was sold. Calls were made across the sea, and new accommodations procured with the help of old friends Mitchell and Davis Burke-Favor. Then the day arrived. They flew toward the sunset, then picked up the new truck they had bought (for some reason, it had to be green) and let the mountains call them upward.

Now the wind swirled, kicking up a dust devil right where the main pole of the big top would have stood.

"What do you think happened to them?" Grace said, glad for her thick sweater. Clouds scudded past the tops of the mountains. "To Cy and Mirrim and Samanda, I mean?"

"I think they went back to Eldh when the rune of sky was broken," Travis said, his breath ghosting on the air. "I think they returned to the Twilight Realm with the other Old Gods."

Grace nodded. She believed the same. "I'm glad we stopped here. I just wanted to say thanks to Cy, and to the others. We never would have gone to Eldh without them."

Travis glanced at Beltan. "A lot of things wouldn't have happened without them."

Beltan gave him a solemn look. Then, suddenly, the blond man grinned.

"Can we head into Castle City now? I want to see the new house. And I'm getting hungry." He picked up the girl. "How about you, Nim? Are you hungry?"

"Yes!" she said, clapping her hands.

"That's my daughter. Get in the truck, then."

Beltan urged her on with a gentle push. She ran toward the pickup. Beltan gave Travis a quick kiss, then hurried after the girl. Grace sighed, watching the two run, the girl taking three strides for every one of the blond man's.

"He's a wonderful father," she said. "Nim is lucky."

"So am I," Travis said. "I love him so much sometimes I almost can't believe it's possible."

She smiled at him. "But it is."

His gray eyes were thoughtful. "What about you, Grace? Will you ever find someone to love?"

Grace breathed in the cold air. On the journey through the desert, she had discovered she didn't love Hadrian Farr. But in learning that, she had learned she *could* love. And she did. She looked at Travis, then let her gaze follow Beltan and Nim. Despite the chill, a warmth filled her.

"I already have found someone," she murmured. "Someones."

Travis watched her a moment, then he nodded. "So you have," he said. "So you have."

They walked back to the pickup, following Beltan and Nim. It was only after a moment that Grace realized Travis was singing in a low voice.

> *"We live our lives a circle,*
> *And wander where we can.*
> *Then after fire and wonder*
> *We end where we began. . . ."*

A chill gust caught the words, carrying them away. The four of them reached the truck. Grace climbed in and Nim scrambled onto her lap. Beltan slid behind the wheel, and Travis closed the passenger door. In the valley below, a collection of lights twinkled in the deepening dusk.

"All right, Beltan," Travis said. "Take us home."

The pickup pulled onto the highway, and the wind rattled through the witchgrass, blowing away across the mountains to places unknown.

ABOUT THE AUTHOR

MARK ANTHONY learned to love both books and mountains during childhood summers spent in a Colorado ghost town. Later he was trained as a paleoanthropologist but along the way grew interested in a different sort of human evolution—the symbolic progress reflected in myth and the literature of the fantastic. He undertook this project to explore the idea that reason and wonder need not exist in conflict. Fans of *The Last Rune* can visit the website at http://www.thelastrune.com.